"At this dark hour of shuttered borders and hearts, can the novel still expose a human truth that finds no footing in statistics or news reports? With incandescent lyricism and wry fury, Spencer Wolff's *The Fire in His Wake* builds to its remarkable answer: only by confronting the existential fullness of today's refugees, migrants, and so many abandoned aspirants—the picaresque comedy alongside the tragedy—can we see that it is those of us living in the shadow of fences and walls who are truly adrift."

—Greg Jackson, author of *Prodigals: Stories*

"*The Fire in His Wake* is a work of extraordinary empathetic and imaginative power. With a lot of heart, and in vivid prose, Spencer Wolff has done that brave and difficult—and ever more rare—thing we most need our novelists to do: painstakingly imagine himself into lives and circumstances starkly different than his own. It is an astonishing debut."

—Thomas Chatterton Williams, author of *Self-Portrait in Black and White*

"A dazzling first novel about a Congolese refugee... *The Fire in His Wake* addresses pressing themes of our times—migration, human rights, and the refugee crisis. Splendidly ambitious both in narrative scope and formal innovation.... Wolff has managed, with enviable dexterity and sensitivity, to tell the story of an African without reducing his humanity or pretending to comprehend or sublimate his suffering."

—Nyuol Lueth Tong, editor-in-chief of the *Bare Life Review*, a journal of immigrant and refugee literature

"A devastating and infuriating story written with compassion, style, and grace. Beyond the harrowing depictions of torture and war, this chilling tale of a heartbreaking life is, at its core, a struggle to come to terms with something much worse: the maddening hypocrisy at our borders, the violence that Western powers inflict on the stories of refugees who arrive at their doors. —Dina Nayeri, *The Ungrateful Refugee*

McSWEENEY'S
SAN FRANCISCO

McSweeney's and colophon are registered trademarks of McSweeney's, an independent publisher based in San Francisco.

ISBN 978-1-944211-89-9

10 9 8 7 6 5 4 3 2 1

www.mcsweeneys.net

Printed in Canada

THE FIRE IN HIS WAKE

A NOVEL

SPENCER WOLFF

McSWEENEY'S

SAN FRANCISCO

Dedicated to the real Arès, and to all those who still stretch out at night on the rocky ground of exile.

Les hommes sont doux dans la mesure où ils attendent quelque chose de ceux qui sont plus forts, et brutaux quand les individus plus faibles attendent quelque chose d'eux. Ceci a été jusqu'à présent la clé de la nature de l'individu en tant qu'être social.

—Theodor Adorno

PART I

CHAPTER I

<u>FIRST RESETTLEMENT INTERVIEW</u>

<u>Do you need a translator?</u>

No.

<u>What is your native tongue?</u>

Lingala.

<u>But you speak French?</u>

Yes.

<u>Good. Before we begin I would like to explain how this interview will
proceed. You are here because we have some questions about your dossier.
Everything that you say here is confidential. Nothing you say here
will be told to anyone, especially not the government. We are not a
government agency.</u>

<u>These updates are necessary from time to time in order for us to verify
facts and to successfully serve the needs of our refugee population.
We appreciate your coming today.</u>

<u>Would you like to say anything before we begin this interview?</u>

Yes.

What?

I was a child once.

THE PROTECTION OFFICER NOTED SOMETHING ON A YELLOW PAD.

Let us begin. What is your name?

Arès Sbigzenou.

What is your date of birth?

June 9, 1980.

You are 27 years old?

Yes.

Where were you born?

In the world's largest francophone city.

Where is that?

Kinshasa.

What is your ethnicity?

Banyamulenge.

What is your father's ethnicity?

My father was Congolese.

Yes, but what is his ethnicity?

I remember one time gathering water with my father, when I was still young. A man approached us and said, "You stink like a Rwandan. I can smell you from the other side of the hill." So perhaps he was not Congolese. But my mother was not Congolese. She was Banyamulenge.

The Banyamulenge are Congolese.

Yes. She came from Eastern Zaire. Near Bukavu.

What is your father's profession?

He was a locksmith. Then he died. Now I do not know what he is.

Why did you leave your country?

Because I had to.

What forced you to leave?

I have told this story before.

Please tell it again.

It is in my file. It is not a good story. Let me tell you something else.

We have some questions about your file. This is why we need you to tell it again. Why did you leave your country?

The war. The war made me leave.

Why?

They attacked my house.

Who attacked your house?

Our neighbors. Our friends.

What happened exactly?

I have told this story. It is not an easy story. You have it in my file. Why do you not read my file?

Your file is incomplete. Please tell me what happened. When was the attack?

At the end of 1998. After the radio programs. Kill the Rwandans. The Rwandans are not Congolese. Kill the traitors.

Why did they say this on the radio?

President Kabila said it. He said the Rwandans were attacking, and that the Tutsis were rebelling. He gave weapons to the Babembe and the Barega.

Who are the Babembe and the Barega?

You do not know?

Tell me.

They were government forces. The government organized them to kill Tutsis in the Congo.

CREDIBILITY ASSESSMENT: NEGATIVE. PRA IS NOT AWARE THAT BABEMBE AND

BAREGA ARE INDIGENOUS MAYI-MAYI MILITIAS ARMED BY PRESIDENT KABILA.

Were the Rwandans attacking?

I do not know. My family did nothing. We lived in the neighborhood peacefully. My father made locks.

What are the colors of the Congolese Flag?

Blue and gold.

Name some of the provinces of the DRC.

There is Katanga, and the Kasai. There is North Kivu and South Kivu.

What happened?

It was evening. My mother was cooking.

What was she cooking?

Meat, I think. I do not remember. My father had come back from Kinshasa that afternoon. He had closed his shop early. He said there were rumors that they were killing Banyamulenge in Kinshasa. We knew nothing.

I thought your family lived in Kinshasa. You said in your file that you grew up in Kinshasa.

Our village is part of Kinshasa, but it is maybe two hours from *centre-ville*. It is called Nonloso. My father's shop was in *centre-ville*. There was no work in our village for a locksmith. No one had locks. Our doors were open to Kinshasa. To everyone.

But that night when my father came home, he locked the door. He said he was going to nail it shut, but he didn't. My mother started cooking. For a long time a goat had lived in our back yard. Then that morning my brother hung it from a tree. No one knows why.

Please tell me what happened that night.

Why you would hang a goat, I cannot imagine. I hit my brother hard across the face. He was on the floor crying. I was about to hit my brother again when six men came to the door. Other Banyamulenge. They were very frightened and out of breath. They knocked for a long time before my father opened the door. When they came inside, they said we would never survive. They said they had seen men burned alive, like tinder. So I did not hit my brother and my father locked the door.

Last time you said four men came to your house. Why do you say six now?

One of them was carrying a baby, so that makes five.

But you say six now? Why six now, when you said four before?

Five, six. What is the difference? I see you know this story. Why must I tell it again when you know every detail?

Why did they come to your house?

My father's house was the only house with locks. Perhaps that is why they came to us. My father was also well respected in the community. We were not rich, but every year my father hosted a fair. They say Mobutu even attended once, before I was born.

So they came for protection?

My father was famous for a game he had created for the fair. Every year it was this game that attracted the most people.

Did your father belong to a political party?

I do not think so. He just ran the fair. Every year, on the third day of
the fair, he arrived at sunrise with three boxes on a cart. He placed
the boxes in a circle in a large meadow. One box was silver, another
was gold, and another was wood.

Let us try to concentrate on the attack.

Inside one box was a small airplane and a visa for the United States.
This meant that you would move abroad and find success.

Inside another box was a beautiful woman and a cow. This meant that you
would not only fall in love with a beautiful woman, but also that you
could pay the bride price to marry her.

How big were these boxes? He put a woman inside?

THE PROTECTION OFFICER NOTED SOMETHING ON THE YELLOW PAD.

In the third box was a lock, which meant that my father would install
locks on your house for free.

Everyone wanted the woman or the plane, and not the lock.

What happened during the attack?

But the game was the most interesting part.

We should concentrate on why you left the country.

Next to the boxes was an immense clay jug full of keys. It took four
men to carry it. There were all sorts of keys inside: small ones, big
ones, keys in the shapes of animals, keys that did not even look like

keys but like tools or ornaments.

You could purchase a key for five million zaires. Only the sons of rich men bought them. That way my father paid for all the keys he gave away. Or else you won the right to choose a key if you came first in one of the contests: wrestling, running, long jump, the best players in the soccer match... The winners of each contest had the right to take one key out of the jug and try it in the three locks.

They always tried to guess which keys would fit into the keyholes on the boxes by inspecting their teeth. But my father was clever. He disguised the locks with masks.

Masks?

Over one lock he put the head of a crocodile. You had to insert the key into its snout and turn.

Over another lock he put the head of a lion. You had to stick the key into its jaws.

Over the third lock was the head of a serpent. You had to push the key through its fangs.

Were these religious symbols? Were you attacked for religious reasons?

Those fairs were great times for the community. Even the years when no one won. Every year at least one box would not be opened, and some years they never even found the right key for a single box, there were so many keys in the jug. My father would reach into it and find the right keys and open the boxes just to show that the keys had really been there, and that the prizes were really in the boxes.

Everyone was happy anyway. It meant more luck for next year. My father left the prizes in the boxes and added one new prize for the next time. So if you opened a box the next year, you could win two women or two planes, and this meant that your chances of these things coming true were even better. If there were three prizes in a box, then it was your destiny that this thing would happen.

I remember once, there were three years when no one had found the key to one of the boxes. Then a friend of my older brother, Yann, won the wrestling contest. On the third day, he reached into the jug and pulled out a key shaped like a fish, and when he put the key into the mouth of the crocodile it opened.

What was inside?

Inside were three beautiful women and three cows. Yann was not a good-looking man and he was not rich, but afterwards he married the most beautiful girl in our village. No one understood how he did it. The cow he gave was not impressive and the parents of the girl had never shown him a particular fondness.

After that, everyone knew that the boxes' predictions worked. So even though my father was a modest locksmith, once a year he was a *grand homme*.

Until the war began. Then the fair lost its spirit. The two years before his death, my father refused to host it anymore.

Which war?

Which war? The war. The war that lasted for ten years. The war that will last my entire life.

CREDIBILITY ASSESSMENT: NEGATIVE. PRA BELIEVES THERE WAS ONLY ONE CONGOLESE WAR. INSUFFICIENT KNOWLEDGE OF THE DRC?

There are two Congolese wars. The first from 1996-1998, the second from 1998-2002.

Two wars; one war. They are the same war. Mobutu, Kabila. It is the same president. The Banyamulenge are never citizens.

The Banyamulenge were part of the forces that overthrew President Mobutu in 1998.

Maybe. I do not know. I know that when I was a child, everyone was at the fair. My father would always give a big speech at the end. He said he was glad a humble locksmith could bring so much pleasure to his community. And his closest friend Guli would yell out every year, "Stop pretending you're so small. You're not that big."

People would laugh. Then we would go into the village and drink Skol and Lotoko. We would drink so much and dance. But then the one war two war began. Everyone was quiet and stopped laughing. The fair died. No one talked with my family because of my mother, where my mother came from.

What happened during the attack?

I have told this story before. Why can I not tell another story?

It is very important for your file.

But I do not want to talk about this.

If you do not tell the story, we cannot help you anymore.

What do you want to know? Why men light other men on fire? To listen to them crackle, I think. To see what is underneath. Is this what you want to know?

I want to know what happened.

They came. All at once.

Who? Soldiers?

No. People from my neighborhood.

How long after the Banyamulenge arrived?

I do not know. Very little time. A minute. Less. My father locked the door
and someone knocked. There was a bad smell of meat burning, but my mother
did not go to the kitchen because there were shadows in the back yard.

Shadows?

They came over the back fence. Have you ever disturbed a nest of spiders? Suddenly there are spiders everywhere. They were like this in the
backyard. They crawled through the fissures in our walls.

Perhaps that is enough. I stop now?

I know this is hard for you, but we need this information for your file.
Please continue.

My file. I think my file has replaced me. My face is made of paper.

Please continue.

You have seen spiders in your life? They kill very slowly. I wonder if
things that die by spiders arrive at a place where they do not know if
they are dead or alive. Maybe they reach a place that is both of these
things, life and death, and they see that death is not so bad. Maybe
better than this world of spiders.

Please focus on what happened.

I am telling you what happened. Am I not telling you? They killed them.
All the men there. All my family. They began with words. "Traitors.
Go back to where you came from. We're going to kill you. You are all
Rwandans. Traitors." Then there were no more words.

They took my sisters. One. Two. Three.

They beat me. Look at these scars. See here. And here. Look at my back.

They took one of the men. The one with the child. And the smell was the
same. I could not believe it. There was a man hitting me with a stick.
He was shouting "Traitor!" every time he hit me. But I am thinking,
"I cannot believe it. It is the same smell."

The same smell as what? Of what?

The goat. They smell like the goat that's burning. The last thing I remember was seeing the inside of the man's arm. He was still holding the
baby, but it was glowing red bones holding fire that smelled like goat.

THE PROTECTION OFFICER TURNED ON A FAN WHILE HE TYPED.

What happened next?

One year, I was fifteen, almost sixteen, I won the race. It was the last
time my father hosted the fair. All the fastest men in the village ran.
The race always took place on the third day of the fair. It was very
difficult. You ran across an open field, then through some woods and
then back across the same field. There were more than a hundred people
that ran that day, and it was very dangerous running through the woods
with everyone pushing.

What happened when you woke up?

There was a girl I was in love with. So I knew I had to win. I never ran
so fast and I was lucky, because the two men ahead of me tripped over
a branch and one of them broke his foot and never ran again. So I won.

Everyone thought I cheated with the key, because it was my father's
contest. But I did not know. I knew only that I was in love and for two
years before, only the box with locks had been opened.

I remember looking into the jug. There were so many keys, like a sea
of metal. But I knew right away to take the one with wings. I went to
the gold box and put it in the mouth of the lion and turned. But it
did not turn. So I went to the crocodile, which was on the wooden box,
and tried to turn. Nothing. So I walked to the snake, which was on the
silver box. I was the last one to go on the third day. No one wanted
to let the son of the locksmith go before him.

And we thought maybe that was it. Another fair without a winner. But I
put the key between the fangs of the serpent and turned. And it opened.

What was inside?

My destiny was inside. Everything that came afterwards was in that box.

What happened next?

Next is in my dossier. Next is when destiny began.

What happened after the attack?

I woke up. I was not in my home. It was dark. There was a man there, eating.
He gave me water. He told me that he had found me unconscious in the
street and brought me to his village. He said I had been asleep for days.

And your family?

He told me that I was alone. I wanted to go back and look, but he said it was too dangerous. They were hunting Rwandans. He went to Kinshasa for me. He asked my neighbors what happened, but he found nothing.

How far were you from Kinshasa?

Sixty or seventy kilometers, I think.

CREDIBILITY ASSESSMENT: NEGATIVE. CLAIM THAT A STRANGER FOUND THE PRA IN THE STREET AND TRANSPORTED HIM SEVENTY KILOMETERS TO HIS HOME IS IMPLAUSIBLE.

Why in your previous declaration did you say it was a hundred kilometers when now you say sixty or seventy?

Why do you care about these things? One war, two wars, sixty kilometers, a hundred kilometers. What are these things to you?

You promised to tell the truth.

I am telling the truth. The truth is not the distance between my house and my neighbor's house. The truth is not whether you call a war one war or two wars. That is not the truth.

Please continue.

I stayed there for two weeks, or maybe three. Whatever it says in my dossier. Then the man told me that there were soldiers looking for Banyamulenge and it was too dangerous for me to stay.

What was his name?

What name?

The name of the man who helped you.

I do not know.

Please continue.

At night I took a pirogue down the Zaire River. I stayed in it for three days. Finally I came to a fishing village. I told them nothing about my past. They thought I was Congolese. I lived there for six years.

What was the name of the village?

Dongo.

How did you survive?

I fished.

For six years?

I lived like the people of the village. I was very sick. The conditions of life were hard. The people were uneducated. Their mouths opened but nothing came out. Like fish. I forgot how to talk living there.

Why didn't you leave?

I could not leave. I was not right. All the time I was sick.

But after six years you left?

There was a merchant who came to the village once a year to sell things. He was from Cameroon. He helped me very much and we became friends.

Finally he offered to take me with him. I went to Cameroon. I tried to work there, but there was nothing for me. I left. I crossed Nigeria, then Niger, then Algeria. Then I arrived in Morocco.

When did you enter Morocco?

2004. I think. In the spring.

Why did you come to Morocco?

I was looking for peace. For a place where I could begin to live again. It was no good in Cameroon. There was no work.

How is your life in Morocco?

It is hard. Very hard. We have no rights here. It is two years now I wait for my foot to be treated. I cannot work. I go everywhere on crutches. I wait every day for the HCR to call me, to tell me I will be resettled and my foot will be treated. I wait every day for this phone call that tells me I can live again.

The process does not work like that. These things take time.

I know that the bird does not make his nest in a single day, but two years is too long. It is enough time to build a castle. My bird does not need a castle to live in. Just a nest.

We do not offer resettlement. I would urge you to concentrate on local integration.

I have no foot. I cannot work. There is no treatment here. For two years they give me the same medicine. It makes me tired, but the foot does not get better. It is not even a foot anymore. It looks like dough, like someone made a foot out of dough.

Your case is being monitored by PALS. You should try to build a future here in Morocco.

They are bad people at PALS. They do not want to help the refugees.

Local integration is the only durable solution offered to you.

I cannot integrate. The Moroccans will never accept me. I am chased out of every apartment because I am African. The children call me names in the street. *Azee. Azee.*

Two times my landlord threw me out for no reason. The second time, he would not let me back in. I lost everything. Then last month I was chased out by my neighbors. The people from the HCR were there. It must be in my dossier.

Did the OMDH follow up when this happened?

What?

We offer juridical protection to refugees. Did you file a complaint against your landlord?

No. I have no *carte de séjour*. What is a court going to do for me? I have no rights.

The law applies equally whether or not you have a *carte de séjour*. If this happens again, you should talk to someone at the OMDH.

Ok.

Where do you live?

In Salé.

Do you have security issues there? Have you had problems with the people in the neighborhood?

No. It is safe during the day. You cannot walk around at night alone, but I have no problems there, except sometimes.

Were you ever attacked? Have you had trouble with the police?

No. Yes. No.

Is it yes or no? Everything you say here is confidential. It is good to say everything.

No.

Can you please look at me when you speak.

CREDIBILITY ASSESSMENT: PRA IS SUPPRESSING DETAILS ABOUT PRESENT LIVING CONDITIONS.

Do you have any questions?

When will I be resettled?

I am sorry, but that is not an option we can offer you at this time.

It is time for you to go. Unless you have further questions?

No.

CHAPTER 2

1986–1996

I was a child once, and I was born in the world's largest francophone city.
—Resettlement Interview, 2008

KINEE-KIN-KIN-CHASA, ABACHASA-KIN-KU," HE SANG as a child, beneath the large Hagenia tree in the backyard his parents shared with two other families. He was waiting for his father, who was going to take him to *centre-ville* and show him the locksmithery for the first time.

But his father was busy. One of their neighbor's children had a worm. Arès' father was holding him down while the boy's mother slowly extracted the parasite. It was a delicate process. If part of the worm broke off in the child's intestines it would regrow.

The boy was screaming every time his mother tugged, *"Ezo sala pasi! Ezo sala pasi!"* A woman was patting his forehead with a wet rag, but it did not seem to help.

Arès ran over to the watching crowd. Already he could see it: a long glucose tape which, once released, began to spin gently like a swallow at dusk.

The children had been told not to drink the stale water in the basin next to the field where they played, but not everyone had listened.

Now the boy's swollen belly wobbled on the wooden table at every jerk of his mother's arm. Cutting the thing into pieces would just mean more worms, so they cremated it in a small pyre. There was a light blue hiss and then Arès' father collected his hand. Navigating between piebald pigs, they walked down a road lined with palm fronds and aluminum-roofed shacks.

Arès' father was a locksmith in a community without locks. Windows were open or covered by tarp, doors listed off their frames, and yards bled into neighboring plots. To be a locksmith one had to work in the city center and so his father commuted two hours every morning to his little shop in Kinshasa.

Soon, they arrived at the *marché central*. Hawkers cried out their wares, and kerchiefed mamas sold *mayi* sachets and powdery beignets. Arès hopped from foot to foot in excitement. He had been looking forward to this day for months. But the vans were unpredictable. It could be a minute or an hour before one came.

An eternity passed, and then, at last, a van rumbled down the narrow dirt road. Inside was a shaking jumble of limbs. Arès' father lifted him high and wedged him into a clucking, feathery crevice near the back window.

The boy gazed intent between dusty grills at the first blurrings of land to his memory. Brown, green, and white. Cloudfalls of rushing ochre, bloomy pixels kicked up by vulcanized tires, slow-moving beige domiciles, a sharp isosceles of stone painted with an Olympic torch, mint-green bowers lassoed by vines, minute after minute till asphalt rolled over dirt, granite barriers sprouted from earth, and buildings reared gray, silver, and glass in place of trees.

They dismounted in Ngaba near the *Cité des Anciens Combattants*. The locksmithery was at the corner of rue Lobo and Avenue de l'Université, not far from the *Cité Universitaire*. Scores of well-off students lived in the area and they liked to have their keys made by someone from the country who charged reasonable prices. Of course, the zaires they paid went a long way two hours from *centre-ville* in the forgotten periphery.

Father and son twisted through a warren of boutiques, and then down a wide lively street till they reached the store. Arès' father furled up the rumbling sheet metal grate and in they went. The lights went on.

Arès loved the luminous clutter of the place. A room so small that both of them could hardly fit, with a countertop they had to duck under anytime they busied in and out. And behind them an imbricate symphony: shanks and whirls, key bits and handles, stout brass hooks and bunker-like sanders, jangling for attention.

*   *   *

Shortly after his twelfth birthday, Arès began his apprenticeship at the smithery. That same year, the first bills worth five million zaires found their way into circulation and the old money had long since been deemed worthless. A year later, the zaire was replaced with the nouveau zaire, but the new currency did not remain stable for long, and Arès' father began to accept only U.S. dollars in exchange for his services.

When he turned thirteen, Arès left school to become a full time locksmith. Twelve months of hammering out key bits, milling bolt stumps, and jousting with the lathe had convinced him that this was his calling in life. This shop, working with his father, the exciting bustle of Kinshasa during the day and in the evening, a riverside hamlet livened by the sparks of fireflies and the singing of cicadas.

Beyond this conviction nothing else mattered. The splintering of the government, Zaire's economic woes and its flares of civil unrest—all this was of as much concern to Arès as the migrations of nomads across far-off deserts. But he was unlike anyone in his family. At times, even his father found his complacency disarming.

In addition to Arès were five other children, three girls and two boys. Félix was the oldest of the brothers. At seventeen he was preparing for the state exam to enter the Business School at the University of Kinshasa, and already his head spun with ambition. The ailing of Mobutu's regime had kindled hopes of sweeping change for Zaire and, like many of his schoolmates, Félix could rattle on endlessly about a new politics and the end of one-man rule.

Over dinner, while Arès and his father calmly chewed their meals, and the younger children scrambled under the table, Félix monologued about world affairs. He passed Paris and Belgium along with the bread and salted his plate with democratic reforms. He was going to pursue a degree in finance and move to London or Brussels, places Arès could hardly locate on a map.

"Once Mobutu is gone," he said when they were nearly done eating, "Zaire will have a tremendous future. It is the largest French-speaking country in the world. It is swimming in resources. It just needs honest men in the government."

It was a speech that Félix had practiced before. Their father just laughed and shook his head. "The big fish do not keep to the small streams, my son. The government will always attract the biggest crooks."

"All this corruption is the result of Mobutu's leadership," Félix replied, his handsome features peering confidently over the table. "When he is gone, things will change. In Europe, it is different. I will go there and see how they fish out their criminals. Then I will bring back their nets and do the same here."

Arès looked admiringly at his brother's broad smart brow, his knowing nose and his dimpled cheeks. It was hard not to be swayed by those two bright eyes aglitter with conviction.

"I am not so sure European ideas will help," their father replied. "The Congo did not fare so well last time it was under European influence."

"Last time?" Félix chortled loudly. "Father, what are you saying? Who defends Mobutu but the French? Who is helping him plunder the country?"

"Then what is there to learn from them?" Their father creased his brow and began to nibble thoughtfully on a fin.

Félix leaned in conspiratorially as he spoke. "Here, the Europeans back the criminals but there..." His hand seized the main course. "There they fry them like fish!" He ripped off the backbone and bit with gusto into the white and brown folds of flesh, smacking his lips comically. Even their father smiled. Then his face grew serious again.

"But do you think European nets will be big enough to fish out the Zaire?" Their father shook his head. "This is not some puny European river. Think of its name."

Arès' oldest sibling, Yika, coughed loudly from the corner. She was nestled into a wingchair beneath a funnel of light, studying for an upcoming exam. "Zaire," she said, "means the river that swallows all other rivers."

Félix turned and looked at his sister. Her hair was pulled back in a ponytail, and a pair of bookish lenses budded rectangular off the oval of her face. She was dressed conservatively for her age, in unpleasant blacks and grays. But when she shifted her weight, the fabric slid over a generous, curving form that was a perpetual source of discussion among the village men. Sought after by a steady stream of suitors, she beat them back with thick legal tomes and a studious absorption that was often taken for disdain.

"That is it exactly," their father continued. "Politics here are dangerous, my son. Every time someone tries to divert the great river there is a flood, and many people drown."

Félix leaned back in his chair, his eyes suddenly darkening. "How can you put up with it?" he asked coldly. "Do you not understand what it is like for us? If you are young there is no opportunity, no matter how hard you work. You have to be related to Mobutu to get a job. Is this not just as dangerous? You have always told me, '*Quand un lion mange une mauvaise personne et il n'est pas tué, demain il mangera une bonne personne.*'[1] Look around. Our country is being eaten alive by big-cat Mobutu!"

He smacked his palm down hard on the wooden table. The clamor of the children's tumbling suddenly ceased, and three small heads poked inquisitively above the table like a bundle of dolls.

"This is true, this is true." Their father softened his voice with concern. "But why have you given us a traditional saying in French? Is the language of the Europeans the only way to reach you?"

"Father!" Yika cried. "You are always quoting things in French."

Their father's face crinkled with laughter and he held up two peace-seeking palms. "Maybe I do. But maybe you recall another one of our people's sayings, '*Qui veut chercher des puces sur la queue du léopard, qu'il fasse attention.*'[2] If you go out to hunt the leopard, he may eat you as well. What do you think Arès?"

"What?" Arès replied.

That afternoon, in the communal van on the way back to Nonloso, a girl had been sitting behind him. When she stood to get off, her hand grazed his shoulder, and his whole body was still tingling from her touch. All he knew was that her name was Christelle and that she reminded him of those ecstatic dawns beside the river, when its waters were smeared with

---

1   When a lion eats a bad person and he is not killed, tomorrow he will eat a good person.
2   If you look for fleas on the leopard's tail, be careful!

honeyed light. Since then he had not been able to concentrate on anything. A secret voice kept whispering, over and over, that she was the one for him.

Félix laughed. "Arès does not have a thought in his head. He is someone to fix locks, not fix a country."

Yika's wide, intelligent eyes fired with excitement. "I agree with Félix. Zaire cannot heal itself."

"Patience," their father said. "Patience. I was like you at your age." He leaned back in his chair and a shadow fell across his face. "But change comes in its own time. It demands that we wait. The tree of patience has bitter roots, but its fruits are sweet."

"This country has been patient for over thirty years, and the situation has only gotten worse," Félix said, springing to his feet. A cup clattered to the floor, startling Arès out of his ruminations. "When there is sickness in a tree, it must be razed to the ground. When the entire forest is sick, we set it on fire. The fire burns away everything. Only then can healthy plants begin to grow."

"These sound like more European ideas," their father said. He rested his strong, steady hands, curled into fists, on the table. His children could see the veins snake up and down his powerful forearms. "We have known here for a long time that the same fire that warms our hands can also destroy the entire village. This is why we use only local fires, and then only carefully."

"Local fire, foreign fire, what is the difference? Who cares?!" Félix shouted.

The crash of clattering utensils sounded from the kitchen, and a speckled dog, trailed by a girl in a grubby tunic, came charging into the dining room. Arès' mother appeared at the door and sucked her teeth loudly.

"Yo, yaka awa!" she shouted, pointing at her feet. "You have not finished soaking the beans. There is still water to fetch."

"Mamma, how can you talk to her like that?" Félix exclaimed. "She is our cousin."

"When it is your house, you can speak to the help however you want," she replied crossly. "The girl is here to earn her keep, not play on our sentiments." The dog whined, and the girl marched reluctantly back toward Arès' mother, her bare, coal-grimed feet dragging on the floor. When she came within reach, Arès' mother grabbed her arm and yanked her back through the door.

"This is the problem with Zaire," Félix said, turning to his father. "We step on each other like cockroaches, instead of working together like the termite. The Europeans know how to cooperate. This is why they have progressed so far ahead of us."

His father snorted. "Remember, Mobutu was educated in Europe and now he is the biggest crook of them all. But he began like you. He began with ideas of a new politics for Africa and look where it led him. Think of the name he took."

"Mobutu Sese Seko?"

"No. His full name. *Mobutu Sese Seko Nkuku Ngbendu Wa Za Banga*. The all-powerful warrior, who goes from conquest to conquest, leaving only fire in his wake. Is this the type of fire you would bring to Zaire?"

"Then where should I go? And what should I bring back? I will not fish any new ideas out of that idiot river." Félix shot a condescending look in the direction of the rolling Zaire.

Their father smiled again. "I think if you look around you will find more useful things here than in Europe. Especially if you wish to help the Congo. That is why we say, *'la connaissance, comme le feu, nous la cherchons chez les voisins.'* The fire that will help us is in the hands of our neighbors."

Arès' attention wandered, and the voices around him gently condensed into a well-known tune, a fugue and counter-fugue that had played in that house a thousand times. He did not need the words. He simply loved to listen to the sturdy rumble of his father's voice, as dependable as the whetstones on which they honed their tools. He turned to his father for guidance, whenever there was some secret about the world he needed to unlock.

But Félix's melody inevitably carried the day. He spoke with vibrant inflections and everything he said sounded like a string of notes plucked from some stirring national hymn. His influence on the rest of the family was manifest. Already Yika talked about continuing her law studies in Paris. Already, Arès' younger brother and sisters knew things about China and the United States that he could hardly fathom.

It was no different in their village, or in *centre-ville*, where Félix went to the Catholic lycée. He was tall, languid, and handsome. People instinctively flocked to him. Every day after school, Félix convened a small band of disciple-friends, and spoke about Zaire as if they were all marinating in a stew of promise and only had to reach out their bowls to fill them with greatness.

His friends were like him, puffed up with Zaire's future and contemptuous of the mediocrity and complacency around them. They were all going to post themselves abroad and courier back enough civilization to reforge the country.

Félix did his best to open his younger brother's eyes, but Arès was unimpressed. What better place could there be than their small village with Kinshasa nearby? What could he possibly find out by leaving? If he stayed he would be like his father, a man with all the keys.

Each brother staked out his share of the hereditary kingdom. Félix passed the state examination with one of the highest marks and joined the incoming class at the University of Kinshasa. Arès continued to work in the smithery, learning every day more secrets of the trade.

Another year passed, and for once business was inordinately good. Thefts had increased at the university, and Arès' father was hired to install new locks on several administrative buildings. It was a massive undertaking for the two men. Hard at work, Arès barely noticed as twelve more months of his life flowed briskly by and were swallowed up by the river.

Then in 1995, trouble flooded in from Rwanda in the East and the economy flagged in the West. Business faltered, picked up again, and finally collapsed. All along rue Lobo shops lay dormant, shuttered, abandoned.

Ever hopeful, Arès' father refused to shut his doors. From time to time, a customer ghosted down the deserted lane and peeked into the smithery, bashful, half-expecting to find no one inside. Father and son waited for these rare reprieves, biding their time before streets that grew hungrier with every passing week.

Then the last customers vanished and the city slept. Its hot dusty avenues gasped as they dreamt, and the months spun out like a long incubation.

Only twice a week now they commuted from Nonloso to *centre-ville*. Business had been bad before. It would get better. But more time passed, and no one came. Even Félix and Yika began to steer clear of the shop, inventing every excuse not to drop by in the breaks between their classes. The day's hours deflated like an empty gourd, begging to be filled.

If there was electricity, Arès and his father spent their time watching one of two flickering channels on a grainy three-color TV. There was usually a soccer match on. If not, there were the swaggering state programs on the RTNC, or sketches by *Théâtre de chez nous* with Kwedi Nsengo and the Group Salongo that made Arès shake with laughter.

Only the evening news was unbearable, especially how it began. Whenever the image of Mobutu Sese Seko, descending through the clouds from heaven, flared on the screen, Arès' father unplugged the machine.

If the electricity was out, which was often, Arès staved off boredom by picking locks, or watching his father cobble together queerish keys with totemic heads and long molded shanks to throw in the massive amphora when it came time for the fair.

CHAPTER 3
APRIL 1996

I returned and saw under the sun, that the race is not to the swift, nor the battle to the strong, neither yet bread to the wise, nor yet riches to men of understanding, nor yet favour to men of skill; but time and chance happeneth to them all. —Ecclesiastes

H ER BODY WAS A parade.

Arès watched her snake between the three glistening boxes and run her hand down the prepossessing vase. Her name was Christelle Abdoulay. She was a year younger than him and the daughter of a cobbler.

Every man within half a mile was watching her. Her long slender frame was folded in two colorful pagnes, canary yellows and sapphire blues, with lilting peacock eyes that undulated as she walked. She was the only creature moving through that immense meadow of wildflowers, and colorful as she was, with purple lobelias strewn in her hair, she could have paused in a floral patch and vanished.

At the edge of the clearing, beneath the broad flat crowns of silk-cotton trees, children frolicked between palm fronds and picnickers. Wooden tables were larded with cassava and chikwanga and plates of rice and plantains topped by grilled fish. Even treasured bottles of Skol and Primus were in abundance that day (the village had organized months in advance to have enough for the fair).

But the bottles would not last and Arès looked longingly at gold labels he would never touch. Then he raked his foot into the dirt, sneaking a toe underneath the long yellow rope that marked the starting line.

Barely sixteen, he was wearing only white FIFA shorts and his lucky necklace: a golden key that hung off a metal chain. He was straight of jaw with lucid eyes and a broad nose that gabled a wide mouth often busy with laughter.

A man twice his size jostled him on the right, and Arès nearly fell over. He stepped aside and stretched his back and arms. He was lean and not particularly tall, but his body seemed carved for speed. He had been training for the race for over three months, and recently formed muscles glistened on his skin like soft watery stones.

Unhurriedly, he retook his position at the starting line. All around him runners stamped the ground impatiently and cast sour looks at the fairgrounds. The winner from the previous year, a goatherder by the name of Salifou, was laughing loud beside the picnic tables. The race would wait on him and he was taking his time.

Arès watched him out of the corner of his eye, weighing his chances. Salifou's limbs were extended and knobby, and he ran with long, gulping strides that devoured the trail beneath him. He would be tough to pass. Worse, he was likely to knock Arès to the ground if he tried to edge by him in the woods.

Yika was partially to blame for this. Salifou had practically thrown himself at her feet, and in a moment of boredom or irritation, she had trod him under. Afterwards he badmouthed her to anyone who would listen. When Yika found out about it, she light-heartedly laughed and told an inward leaning group of girls, "Monsieur Salifou can say whatever he wants, but it won't change the fact that he has the head of a goat."

The girls raced home to their families and the nickname "goat-face" spread like wildfire. It stuck to Salifou, as much owing to the animals he tended as to his high cheekbones and strangely cut eyes. Two weeks later, a fistfight broke out between Salifou and Félix. Both families were called on to apologize.

Still laughing, Salifou shot Arès a mocking glance, and then quieted as Félix strolled a little too close, trailed by a jostling band of university friends. After they passed, he made some sort of crude joke and discharged a shriek of laughter that caught everyone's attention.

A golden bottle, pearled with condensation, tipped disorderedly in his hands.

Times were not good, had not been good for a while. The soldiers' riots in Kinshasa, the hyperinflation, the schismed government, the loss of the Lake Kivu region first to the Tutsi rebels and now to the Hutu paramilitaries. The authorities seemed absent. It was even rumored that Mobutu had cancer. It was impossible to know. The "Leopard of Kinshasa," the Big Man himself, had been holed up in his jungle palace for almost two years.

No one knew how long Zaire would last.

The fairgoers celebrated in their own fashion, trying not to think of unpleasant things. Some were brasher than normal, speaking arrant thoughts and making extravagant gestures. People were a bit too drunk, talking a nudge too loud. It was the last day of the fair, and the past two days had been disrupted by several brawls.

Others, like Arès' father, seemed uncharacteristically circumspect. It was impossible not to notice that certain groups that had always intermingled now kept their distance.

In a cluster beneath the spreading canopy of a Mahogany tree, some of Mobutu's more fervent supporters were dressed in leopard print toques and martial abacosts. They looked like a pride of jungle cats. Two of them even held traditional tufted spears, a symbol of the Zairianiasation folly that the president had inflicted on the country.

In former years, Arès' uncle Guli could have been found capering in front of them, hooting like a chimpanzee and yelling something about digging up his ancestral roots. But this year he kept close to his friends and talked softly.

The felines were conversing heatedly with three or four Rwandan Hutus, newcomers to the region. There were hundreds of them streaming into Kinshasa every day, but these were the first to trickle out to the village.

Arès had heard rumors of war and more in the East. But the East was impossibly far off and insubstantial to a young man about to assure his future.

On the eve of the first day of the fair, Arès had been loping along the river's edge, returning from a late afternoon run. He was about to turn toward the village when he saw a half-silhouette capped by a diaphanous green foulard.

He slowed to a halt beside her. "What are you doing here?"

"It's too hot. I wanted to go for a walk by the river where it's cool."

"These aren't safe times," he said. "You shouldn't be walking alone. I'll walk you back."

"Maybe it will be more trouble if I walk with you."

"No, because I am going to marry you," he replied.

"Oh really?" She laughed like a cascade of water. Her eyes seemed curiously immense in the waning light. Like enormous goblets that he could drink from. "You see, already I have trouble. A few minutes ago I was walking alone and I was free, and now I've started walking with someone and I am a married woman. I think it is safer if I walk alone."

He tried to take her hand but she skipped away.

"Is it not better to be married?" he asked.

"And where will we live when you marry me?"

"Here," he said, surprised. "Where else?"

"I don't want to live here."

"We can move to Kinshasa then. My family's business is there."

"But I don't want to live in Kinshasa."

"Where do you want to live then?" He screwed his eyes together, perplexed.

"Somewhere better. Somewhere not here." She gestured indistinctly toward the river.

"Brazzaville? Why would you want to go there? It's a city of beggars. They clean our toilets."

She laughed again, like light bursting through leaves.

"There are many men here who want to marry me," she said, tears of mirth drizzling down her cheeks.

"Yes, but I am going to win the race in three days, and I am going to pick the key that will open the box with the beautiful woman. And since you're the most beautiful woman in the village, I am going to marry you."

She wound the green foulard tighter about her shoulders as they walked.

"So your father told you which key it is. But why do you think you are going to win the race? There are many men faster than you in the village."

"My father would never tell me which key it is. It's been three years since anyone opened a box. Whoever finds the right key will marry you."

"I did not know my fate was already decided. And I wanted to move away. How sad."

She turned her head away from him toward the river where a bluish heron skimmed low upon the water. Galaxies of mosquitoes fogged the air. Above, in the reddening sky, an airplane plunged south toward the airport at Ndjili, its contrails burning behind it like a trail of flames.

"We can move wherever you like," Arès replied.

"And what if you pick another box? What if you open the box with the planes? Then you'll have to move away without me."

"That won't happen." He reached out for her hand again and this time he caught it. "I am going to run faster than you can believe. Faster than that bird is flying."

"We're here," she said. He looked up and before he knew it, she had unclasped her hand and sped between two adobe huts that marked the perimeter of the village.

He wanted to give chase, but something nameless held him back.

Not far from the river's edge, he squatted down beside the ghostly roots of a silk-cotton tree and watched her melt into moving shadows as if passing through a portal into another world.

He was looking at her now, while last year's winner, cocksure of himself, took his place at the center of the front line. Arès had come in twentieth the year before, and though he found himself among the vanguard runners, he was far over to the left. There were nearly two hundred men entered in the race.

A high whistle, shrill and stuttering, stabbed through the fairground bustle. Then silence. It was the signal for the race to begin. Breaths came hot and short. Muscles bunched and slid beneath taut human hides.

Arès' father took the ceremonial position on a raised flat rock off to the side of the starting line. Then he lifted the ceremonial cane, crested high with plumage, and let it fall against the stone below with an almost deferential rap.

The earth condensed, dented and bunched, beneath the instantaneous press of four hundred feet. Then the meadow shuddered and the afternoon air cleft into a thousand moving vectors.

Arès darted forward, shoving to get in front. The course narrowed quickly as it moved from the open meadow into the jungle. Getting caught behind a slow runner where it was difficult to pass would mean falling irreparably behind.

Soles pounded through the grasslands, and the air hummed with the shuttling of startled insects. Arès kept his mouth as thin as possible while he ran. Around him erupted salvos of hacks as racers inhaled the whirring things. Arès punched ahead.

Two hundred meters gone and a group of thirty men had already separated themselves from the pack. With a hundred meters to go until tree line, a total mêlée erupted at the lead. There was something acrid in the air and shoulders ground together with more force than ever in the past. Arès watched two close friends tussle their legs and rejoiced as the faster one fell to the ground.

Fifty meters to go. The pack closed ranks.

One of Arès' neighbors moved to block him, but he goaded his elbow into the man's flank and stole ahead.

Twenty meters to go. His body, sore from months of constant exertion, sent shivering complaints through his thighs. He gritted his teeth and ran.

Ten meters.

Someone else tumbled to his left, and Arès twisted around to catch one last glimpse of Christelle leaning fatidically against the massive amphora of keys.

The path darkened.

Arès was fourth as the runners entered the forest. They were advancing now in single file, hopping fallen branches and canting into the sudden turns. In about one hundred meters the path would widen again, until it struck its largest span at the river crossing a kilometer away.

Arès had tested the waters the night before and he knew they were deep if he went straight in, but that there was a rise in the riverbed if he swung a few meters upstream.

He knew every stretch of the course, every log, every ditch, every low branch, every conceivable short cut. He had run the race every day for three months, imagining the runners beside him, imagining the prize waiting for him at race's end.

The path widened and he strummed ahead of a fisherman named Moussa. Then it was just him and the two fastest runners in the village. The winner from last year, Salifou, and a friend of his brother's named Diomandé.

The two men were vying ahead of each other, angling for an advantage, while five meters behind he was struggling to keep up. His breath rasped hot against his lungs, and he began to swing his arms, trying to gain purchase on the steeply rising trail.

His footing shot awry, and bramble and pricker bushes lashed his torso like small licks of flame. He slowed a bit but felt Moussa hot on his heels. Then four others wrapped him on either side as the trail began to plane outwards.

The jungle receded and the route swung broad and down and the river rose into view. Though only a small tributary of the Zaire, it frothed with abundance.

There were twenty runners at the front, including Salifou and Diomandé, the sharp cusps of a rushing phalanx. Forty feet pounded rhythmically against dirt, rock, and snapping twigs: a symphony of heavy breaths and synchronic arms.

For a moment Arès forgot the race, forgot Christelle, forgot even himself. He glided through pure immanence; step, thrum, step, bound, pivot off rock, dodge an arm, step, step, step, the pounds and grunts of a score of others contending beside him. They floated now, and each of their buoyant steps announced that deep meaninglessness which is the essence of freedom, and everything seemed tinged with a nimbus of light. He felt jubilant, invincible, like he could reach out and crush the world.

Then Salifou and Diomandé splashed side by side into the water and flooded downstream, bawling for help. Four runners swerved left, racing along the riverbank, trying to gain on the two men spilling like trout through the torrents.

Arès cut right up the bank, seeking a way across. The river had swelled in the night, fed by April rains. He raised his eyes and picked out a minute Diomandé grafted onto an outhanging limb, with Salifou nowhere in sight.

Some of the other runners began to wade cautiously into the flood, clasping each other's hands. Arès ramped into the jungle, bursting through veils of green. He had planned for this. Fifty meters upstream there was a massive silk-cotton tree that had been struck by lightning and its corus-cated remains bridged half the river.

Arès leapt onto the blackened limb like he had practiced, picked up speed running across it, and sprung with all his might for the far shore.

Water engulfed him.

He felt himself in a coiling wetness that spewed forth as if into an abyss. A rock jarred against his chest and pinwheels of color burst upon his inner eye. His whole body was a scudding tumble of limbs.

His foot raked the silt bottom and he pushed desperately against the sliding muck. Then the world dervished and fluxed, and all was fluid again. His breath began to leave him. Water pressed hard against his mouth.

But in that liquid confusion, rough skin clasped against his palm, and he felt himself hoisted toward the drought of the sky. He coughed and spattered and heaved.

The frontrunners had yoked their arms and forded the river as a unit. The third man in that human mesh had caught Arès and tossed him toward the shore.

When all fourteen were across, Moussa gave a loud shout, "*Allons-y!*"

And the race was on to the slap and cry of several, who clacked gripless back against the mud, and the sputtering of those who heaved forward into the slashing vegetation. A second flank of racers had massed on the far riverbank and were stringing themselves across, with the vanguard loop about mid-river, and they too let fly watery shouts.

Arès fell into a long lope, third once again, but this time Moussa and a young man named Buisha were spearing the run. After the river, the trail looped downhill and rounded back to the far side of the meadow. The wet spank of their feet against slick ground, like the thrumming of drums, the brittle thwacks of bramble, the whistle of bearded insects, the impossible jungle clatter, amidst all this Arès ran.

The forest was damp, wet, and close. He felt his breath coming short and scarce, his concentration broken by minor concussions of leaves and sprigs against his face. Soon they would be at the forest's edge and already a distance yawned between the front three and the rest of the runners, the reports of their grunts and blunders receding with every lunge ahead.

A buzzing rose in Arès' head, and he leaned in and forward, concentrating on the pulse of the four legs before him, heckling his will.

A long stretch and then dry red dirt rolled over the wet slap of leaves. The path swerved invisible around a bend.

The two men disappeared. A shout shocked out ahead and Arès pitched violently aside. The frontrunners lay toppled over a decaying trunk beyond the tall spike of a branch.

Arès rolled onto the hard-packed dirt, then yanked himself to his feet and sprinted on, hastily looking back as a voice he knew belonged to Moussa gave a tremendous cry of pain. In the narrow window of his glance, he caught the lash of a diamond-patterned snake slithering into the brush.

He ran on.

Minutes later an immense light inundated the forest. He broke into the blinding glare of the meadow to lively cheers. Half a kilometer to go. He swished headlong through the powdery grassland amidst fanfares of flowers, his body crunched in a strange lope, an alchemy of exultation and pain. At last, with heaving lungs and the first twitches of a cramp, he staggered over the invisible demarcation that signaled his triumph.

His father clasped him in a proud embrace and pressed a golden bottle into his hand. "I saved this for you."

Arès kissed his father, and setting the drink aside, stalked purposefully through the festive crowds seeking Christelle. Behind him the second cohort of runners beat across the finish line to winnowing ovations.

Limning the crowd, he espied her far off, half hidden by a cove of gladioli and nestled between the massive buttress roots of a gray-speckled tree.

He set himself directly in the sun's glare. "I told you I would win."

"Where is Diomandé... and Salifou?" she asked. "They were ahead of you going into the forest."

"They will come. Do you not want to congratulate the winner?"

"It does not make sense. You were alone when you crossed the finish line. How did you get so far ahead of the other runners?"

He narrowed his eyes. "I am much faster than I was last year."

She stroked his hand and smiled at him. "Sit down next to me."

He wedged himself between a spiraling root and the soft bow of her side. He could feel the suppleness of her skin through the thin layers of cloth that separated their hips. "You pulled some trick, didn't you? You cut through the forest?"

"No. How can you say that? I won by being the best." He struggled to contain his irritation. "Diomandé and Salifou were not strong enough. They could not make it across the river."

"Oh no," she said, and he saw fear spark black in her eyes.

"They're fine. They're fine." He gave a big-man laugh. "Last I saw they were hanging onto a branch downstream crying for their mothers."

Her body pulled away from his. "But did they make it out?"

He stood up angrily. "Do not worry about them. Their friends went to save them." Without looking back, he strode toward the fairgrounds.

As he reached the first picnic table, Diomandé and Salifou emerged into a fury of light, bearing Moussa on a makeshift stretcher of deadwood. Before them Buisha ran, waving his arms, shouting for help.

That afternoon, the ceremony of the drawing of the keys began. Three boxes stood in the open clearing, one of burnished gold, one of gleaming silver, one of walnutty wood. Their keyholes were disguised with prodigious animal masks, and the jaws of a lion, the sleek head of a snake, and the long snout of a crocodile hungrily watched the fairgrounds. Above them towered a flagpole with a large green pennant, at whose center rippled a flaming torch in a yellow circle. The rest of the fairgrounds were festooned with streamers made out of kanga cloths.

A long wending line of some fifty-five men snaked between hillocks crowned with taut brooms of barnyard grass.

At the head of the line, the amphora loomed like the relic of a forgotten myth. No one knew where Arès' family had gotten a hold of it, but it had been with them, according to family lore, for countless generations. It topped the tallest man in the village by at least a meter and was elephantine in girth. Well over a thousand keys of all dimensions fit comfortably inside.

To collect their prize, the men had to climb a rickety wooden ladder lashed together with raffia fibers. From the rim it was impossible to reach beyond the top layer of keys, and so the contestants often descended into the bowels of the jar to mine out their luck.

Arès took his place at the back of the line and watched figure after figure crab into the wide maw, seeking what had not been found for years. Each time a hand shot skywards, clutching some wag of a key—its shank molded into flung wings, a crocodile's grin, or a hooked fish—he prayed inwardly that it would not fit a lock.

One by one, the amphora regurgitated the men. They gathered, gaunt silhouettes in the fading afternoon light. From each of their hands dangled an incantatory key.

The beer had run out and the spectators had turned to potent jugs of sugary masanga and bitter lotoko. Boisterous shouts of encouragement issued from the increasingly bawdy crowd. Twice, an excited chorusing broke out as the spectators dueled traditional songs.

But when Arès emerged from the mouth of the jar and took his place among that stock-still host, silence settled over the fairgrounds.

An apparition emerged from the forest wearing a gargantuan wooden mask, a meter in height, with deep slanting eyes and painted lips. Arès knew it was and was not his father. The apparition carried a traditional shield in its right hand and a tufted spear in its left. Its arms swung together and the spear shocked against the shield three times.

A voice rang out from the depths of the mask. "Now we shall see to whom fortune promises great things!"

One by one, shadows detached from that rustle of men and passed from the golden lion to the walnutty crocodile to the silvery snake. Such was the quiet that Arès could hear the wing flaps of midges swishing beside his ears. Each time a key thrust into the lock-jaws, the silence deepened and fists clenched, fearing or hoping for a click. One by one, disappointment extended its reign.

Fifty-four shadows sighed back to the picnic tables, melting into the statuesque crowd. Arès tightened his grip on his key. He had forged the bow and the shank himself and sculpted them after ocean waves. But his father had fashioned all the key bits, so Arès could not say if his choice would turn any of the locks.

Knowing his father's supernatural logic, though, he was sure that if it did work, it would only open the crocodile's mouth. Water for water.

A murmur rose in the crowd as he headed straight for the wooden box. He plunged the shank deep into the grinning jaws till only the last of the wavelets could be seen lapping beyond the tip of the snout. Then he snapped his hand to the right.

Stuck.

He jiggled the bow, and then reinserted the device into the keyway. Stuck again.

He backed up, confused. The meadow was bathed in a crimson light, and the distant river seemed one long glistening hide. The apparition clapped spear and shield together, producing a metallic boom.

"Go on!"

Arès approached the lion and, with little hope, pushed in the key. He pulled it out again, dejected. Only the serpent was left.

The fifty-fifth man approached the silver box, its surface spooled with coppery secretions in the dying light. He could hardly make out the edges of the snake and he glided his finger along its jutting tongue to find the lock. He glanced left, scanning the crowd unsuccessfully for his brothers. Dusk had swallowed every human trait, and Arès looked upon a faceless and silent multitude. His body trembled. Then a light electric surge travelled down his arm and burst upon his fingers.

The key turned like a thunderclap.

For a moment, the only sound in that sprawling glade was the whistle of birds and the drone of insects. Then the spectators exploded with bottled-up emotion. Drums pounded into rhythm, and flames spouted from dozens of torches. Three years of unluck at last undone.

Arès' brothers were clapping and dancing in large, eccentric circles, and he could see his friend Yann swinging a pretty girl in a floral dress, her toes grazing the tall tips of grass.

Christelle had twined her arms around one of the torches, and he looked at her with all the light of destiny and then pulled open the serpent's mouth. Out of that silver cave tumbled a plane. Then two more, and Arès hopped in slight pain as one plummeted directly onto his left foot.

He bent down and picked up the airfoils, holding them high to the crowd's unrestrained cheers.

She gazed at him now, an enigmatic expression on her face. He wanted to call out to her, but his father, unmasked, clapped him hard on the back.

"You have a big destiny, my son. Congratulations."

He shouted to the assembled village before him. "It seems our great country is too small for my son! Let us wish him success in his travels!"

Those who still had plum wine raised their cups, and the rest let loose a wild uproar of ululations. Arès looked around at a unanimity of smiling faces and worried where he would go.

CHAPTER 4

JUNE 1996

———————

ARÈS WAS ALONE IN the shop.

The night before, relatives of his mother from the South Kivu region had unexpectedly turned up in Nonloso, fresh from a harrowing month-long journey across the breadth of the Congo.

When his father opened the door, the house had filled with joyous, surprised shouts. But something in the hollow, exhausted stare of the visitors quieted the family. On a word from his mother, Arès hurried to the kitchen to pour glasses of Primus for their guests. One of them nearly overflowed, so he wiped the foamy head off with his fingers and sucked them dry. After making sure no one was looking, he quickly downed half a glass and refilled it, before setting everything on a tray. He walked out beaming but his smile quickly faded. His mother's cousin Grace was sobbing in her husband's arms.

Two other male relatives had traveled with Grace, her husband Patrice, and their three small children on the long journey across the belly of Africa: by foot for days with bundles on their backs, north by truck to the bend in the great river at Kisangani, and then, from Kisangani to the capital, stocked head-to-toe in a weeklong barge.

The men thanked Arès for the beers, while Grace dried her cheeks. Then she sat up straight and announced in a surprisingly fiery voice, "Men we had never seen marched down our street carrying machetes and singing loudly." Her eyes narrowed into slits, and Arès could sense the tension in the rod-like arm she hammered repeatedly into Patrice's thigh. "Whenever they reached a house, they shouted, 'Cockroaches, come out!' and began dragging people from their homes."

"They were strangers," Patrice added, wincing as Grace thumped him again, "but they knew which homes to target. Our neighbors from the Nyanga tribe were all spared, but our home was ransacked."

Arès peered curiously at Patrice. He remembered him from a family gathering when he was a child, but his recollection was of a sturdy, vigorous man. The person before him had hands that shook when he talked.

"Why does no one fight back?" Félix asked. "Will the Banyamulenge let themselves be driven from the Congo?"

"This is the worst part," Patrice replied. "There is a general named Laurent Kabila. Everyone thought he was dead, but he has risen from the grave. He is building a Tutsi army. If his men find out that you are Banyamulenge, they force you to enlist. I have been threatened several times, and two of my friends are now soldiers."

One of the other relatives, a squat man with hooded features and thick lips, grunted in assent. "I had to jump into the lake to escape them. Since then, I have slept with my eyes open like a snake." He blew his eyes wide open and peered around comically, before chuckling to himself.

"If the Hutus don't kill you, then the Rwandans enslave you," Patrice concluded. He took a big swig of beer. Arès could see from the way the glass was listing in his hand that he was already drunk. "It is impossible to stay. There will be an uprising soon. Or worse."

"These are bad tidings," Arès' father said. His voice rumbled like the first sounds of thunder from an approaching storm.

"You should join Kabila's army," Félix said. "Now is the time to strike. When our enemies are weak."

Arès' father snorted. "I think you made the right choice by leaving. Blood may disappear in water, but its poison remains."

"Father! You speak in riddles to conceal your cowardice," Félix shouted. "That is the only poison I know."

Their father's eyes flared red, and Arès involuntarily took a step back. "The Hutus are supported by Mobutu," he replied in a granite voice, "and Mobutu will not fall. He is protected by the fetish he carries—you have seen his wooden staff. The pregnant woman carries our nation in her belly. The snake that wraps the handle has fangs as long as your fingers."

Félix's lips pursed like a frog about to release its tongue, but nothing came out. Instead, he appeared to swallow something unpleasant. "I understand, father." He rose slowly from his chair. "You are trapped in old beliefs and old ways. As you always say, '*Le cadavre du serpent reste effrayant.*'"[3] Without another word, he turned on his heel and exited the room.

There was a moment of silence while the assembled eyes watched him leave. Then Grace exploded with pent-up emotion. "How could we stay? We have no more home!" she cried. "Our neighbors hiss at us in the streets: 'Go back to Rwanda!' 'Foreigners out!'" She began to cry again, and Arès' mother escorted her upstairs with her children and put them to bed. Then the electricity went out for the third time that day.

"It's getting worse," Arès' father said.

"At least you have electricity here," Patrice replied. "In the East, the SNEL only sells power to the mining companies. If you cannot afford a generator, you have electricity for maybe two or three hours a week, and then only during the day."

Arès paced around the room lighting candles. For the next hour, he and his father sat quietly, while Patrice and the other two men drank themselves into a stupor and began snoring in their chairs.

The next morning, Arès' father announced that he would spend the day helping their guests settle in. So it was up to Arès to man the shop alone.

When he arrived at rue Lobo and rolled up the rumbling sheet metal grate by himself, he felt a quiet tingling thrill. Someday this would be his. He switched on the light and leaned expectantly over the countertop, waiting for the first customer of the day.

An hour passed and no one came. The morning streets lay deserted and unpromising. Arès turned on the radio, but all the stations were discussing a new law against foreigners, so he turned it off again. Then his stomach began to rumble and he grimaced with hunger. He had bought a *mayi* sachet from one of the mamas in the marketplace and he ripped it open

---

3 Even dead, a snake is frightening.

with his teeth and sucked down the stale water. No one had been selling beignets because flour was scarce, which meant he would have no food until evening.

He laid his head on the counter. Morning bled into afternoon. The streets stayed stubbornly empty. Even the owner of the oriental goods store next door, the only other open shop open that day, had left early and never returned.

Arès could hardly contain his boredom. He began fiddling with the key around his neck, and then looked over at the display case where his father had placed the three airplanes from the fair. They mocked him now like some heavenly blunder. He had put so much effort into winning the race, but it had brought him no closer to Christelle. Instead, Yika just teased him about his glorious future abroad while Félix and their Father battled angrily over politics.

Ever since the fair, their quarrels had taken on personal tones, and tensions at home were running high. But everywhere was tense these days. You could feel it in every squinted eye in the *marché central,* in every raised voice and hard-chopping hand. Physical altercations were not uncommon. Every day food grew scarcer and accusations of *kindoki* witchcraft more common. Dozens of children had been violently chased from their homes. Then, last week, several buildings in a nearby village had mysteriously burned down.

Arès tried to tune it all out. There were better things to think about.

He switched the radio back on and this time found a station playing some popular *Ndombolo* songs. It was National Liberation Day in two weeks' time, and there would be a big celebration with live bands. He wanted to practice his dance moves, but tapping his feet alone in that little shop, he felt like the last person on the planet dancing for a party that would never come.

One of his father's favorite songs came on the radio, *Marie Louisa* by Papa Wendo. Arès began gyrating his hips to the lively rhythms and mouthing the words:

Wendo veut voir Louisa
Pour la donner à Bowane
(et calmer ses battements de cœur)

Où est Louisa?
Mais, en attendant, Bowane, pince ta guitare et ton likembe![4]

He was shaking his torso to the bouncy guitar riffs when he saw a woman bloom like a flower in the desolate street. She was dressed in simple jeans and a blouse, and she approached like a cool river's breeze blowing down that dusty thoroughfare.

He could hardly believe it when she arrived.

"Hi Arès," Christelle said, "is your father here?"

Arès stood petrified. He rubbed his eyes comically. Then he mumbled something unintelligible, forcing her to approach closely and repeat her question. "Your father? Is he here?" She enunciated every syllable as if she were talking to a slow-witted child.

Arès shut off the radio, and then turned around and slowly shook his head. Every movement felt dreamlike and unreal.

"Because I have this locket with my mother's photo," she continued, carefully articulating every word, "and the clasp is broken. I told your father that I would be in *centre-ville* today, and he said to bring it by the shop and he would fix it for free."

After his triumph at the fair, Arès was no longer just the locksmith's boy. For months on end, the men in his village greeted him with a clap on his back and a sly sip of whiskey. Some of Yika's friends, who had never given her younger brother a second thought, began pestering her for an introduction. But it had done nothing to impress Christelle. Arès sought her out at every turn and, with her bright, sun-speckled laugh, she turned away his every proposal.

Félix tried to interest him in other girls and even dragged Arès to a university party; something, he emphasized, that was a desperate measure taken as a last resort. But Arès was unmoved by all the flashy hips shaking

---

4   Wendo wants to see Louisa / To give her to Bowane / and to calm the beating of his heart / Where is Louisa? / But while we are waiting, Bowane, pluck your guitar and your likembe!

to *soukous* beats and American hip-hop. Something in Christelle called to him. The straight line of her chin, her uncommon poise, the fierce intelligence of her eyes; already, he could see their exceptional children. Over and over again, he built a life for the two of them in his head.

Now fate had dealt him another chance. He collected himself as best he could and took the locket from her hands.

"It is not necessary to invent a pretext to see me," he said, laying the locket on the countertop. "We can go for a walk or I will take you out to dance any time you want." He flashed his most winning smile.

Christelle leaned her elbow on the countertop. "You are right. I should not have tried to deceive you." She breathed in and Arès watched her chest swell and felt his chest swell in turn. "In fact, I spent two full hours in the communal van just to come here and ask you a question."

Arès felt his heart ready to explode. "Please. Ask away." His voice squeaked a little as he said "away," and he felt the back of his neck run hot.

Christelle looked earnestly into his eyes. "I came all the way here to ask you this…" She paused. "Why is it that you wear such a silly necklace?" Her eyes went bright like a cat's and sparkled with laughter.

The heat spit up from his neck and coursed over his entire face. "What? My necklace?" he asked foolishly, pulling out the metal chain from which a golden key dangled.

"Yes, I understand that you are a locksmith, but what is that silly key around your neck? My friends and I have been wondering ever since the race."

"And you came all the way here to find that out?" Arès tried to regain composure. He looked her straight in the eyes, but his heart was beating uncontrollably.

"It is the only reason I came."

"That was smart of you," he said, "because it is the key to your heart."

She gave a great pealing laugh. "I am glad then that I do not have a lock for a heart, so that any common locksmith can pick it." She danced away from the countertop, light as a bird, and pivoted about. "But really. Tell me. Why is it that you wear this key around your neck? You have had it for nearly a year now."

Arès smiled to himself. So she did pay attention to him. He motioned her closer and gave her a conspiratorial wink. "I will tell you the secret of this necklace, but you cannot let anyone know."

"Ah. I love secrets," she said, with a throaty rasp.

"Swear that this will stay just between you and me."

"On my life." She raised her eyes heavenwards and made the sign of the cross. "I won't tell a soul."

Arès looked theatrically up and down the street, although he knew that no one was around. "My father," he began, "took the metal for this key from a sacred statue that has been in our family as long as time can remember. After he finished molding it, we traveled for days, deep into the jungle, to a place I cannot tell, where a powerful marabout lives. The marabout sacrificed a wild pig and used its heart to brew a magic potion in a monkey's skull. When everything was ready, he placed a spell on the key and soaked it in the skull for three days." Arès held his necklace up into the sunlight. The key sparkled and spun as if lightning crackled along its surface.

"This key allows me to run faster than anyone else," he continued. "The marabout also said that it would make me invisible to my enemies and would cause women to fall madly in love with me. And I can see that it has worked." He leaned toward her on the countertop and felt his lungs fill with air.

"That is a very nice story, Arès," Christelle replied, the same cat's laughter playing about her eyes. "But there are many frauds who pretend to be marabouts. They make fantastic promises and steal the money of simple-minded people. It is very sad."

A slight breeze blew down the street and puffed her blouse with air. Arès caught his breath as she smoothed it tight over her long torso. She smiled at him when she was done, like light glinting on water.

"Yes, but this marabout has protected my family for generations," Arès replied. "He is very powerful. When my grandfather was a child, the marabout cured him of a terrible illness that killed many people in Nonloso. And once again I have proof of his powers, because here you are."

Christelle rested her hand on the countertop and for a hopeful moment, Arès thought she would gather his fingers in hers. Then she picked up the locket. "My mother's locket has not been blessed by a marabout but it is very precious to me. Do you think you can fix it?"

"Let me see," he replied, suddenly businesslike. Inwardly he felt deflated, but he forced himself to sit down at the workman's table and inspect the broken clasp through a magnifying glass. "This should be easy to fix. I just need to replace the pin at the bottom."

"That is wonderful to hear." Her intonation lilted upwards as she spoke, and Arès shook his head in disbelief. The colors of her voice thrilled him like the appearance of a rainbow in the sky.

He turned on a workman's lamp and then swiveled around and opened the counter flap. "Come in and sit down," he said, pointing to a stool. Christelle edged cautiously into the shop.

Arès settled back onto his stool and began to take the locket apart. He could feel Christelle's body close to his and her eyes watching his every movement. He did his best to concentrate, but the hairs began tingling up and down his spine, and his left arm went aflame when she accidentally brushed it with her elbow. There was a cinammony scent wafting from her hair, sick and sweet like that of a water hyacinth, which he found maddening.

Then his attention returned, and he felt the joy of working on something concrete. His hands took over, manipulating the metal with skill. He could still feel her beside him, but now it was a wholesome presence complimenting his own. A warmth bloomed in his chest and spread to his limbs. This is how it would be, he thought, as he clasped the locket shut and tested his work. Christelle leaned in and put a hand on his shoulder. He closed his eyes.

"Is that why you have such a funny name?" she asked out of the blue.

Arès bolted upright in his seat. Then he spun around to look at her.

"Is it a special name that was blessed by the marabout? Did he give you your name?"

A smile grazed Arès' lips. "No. My father gave me my name."

"It is not a normal name."

"I am not a normal guy," Arès said, grinning.

"Yes, but it is not a Zairian name," Christelle replied, her face etched with seriousness. Arès' grin faded away. "Are you not Zairian?"

"How can you ask that?" A hint of annoyance colored his voice. "Your family has known my family for generations. What sort of question is that?"

"Your father's family, yes. But your mother is from somewhere else, is she not?"

"Yes, but she was also born in Zaire. Her family is from South Kivu and her people are Banyamulenge."

"Ah, so she *is* Rwandan," Christelle said triumphantly. "I thought so. Is Arès a Rwandan name?"

Arès gave Christelle a sharp look and motioned for her to exit the shop. "My mother is not Rwandan. She is from Zaire…" He wanted to say more but Christelle cut him off.

"My father says that the Banyamulenge are Rwandan and not Congolese."

Arès felt a miniscule flame bud behind the window of his eyes. "Your father is misinformed," he insisted quietly. "My mother's family has been in South Kivu for generations. How could she not be from Zaire?" He guided Christelle out of the shop, but she turned on her heel and leaned on the countertop.

"Is that where you get your name? From her people?" Her voice had softened, and Arès calmed a bit.

"No. It is the name of a great warrior from Europe," he replied, with a note of pride. "My father thought it would suit me."

"And you are expected to become a great warrior?" She smiled again and Arès lit up like a candle.

"How else do you think I won the race?" He rested his hands on his hips in a way he felt was commanding.

"Ah, I thought it was because of your magic necklace," she replied with a teasing wink.

"That too."

Christelle shifted her body slightly and gazed out at the street. "I think we have enough warriors in this country already. It is one of the reasons I would like to leave."

Arès sucked in his stomach and tried to lengthen his torso. She was nearly his height and he felt unimpressive before her. "Yes, but warriors are very useful in everyday life." He pointed to the empty thoroughfare.

The faint sounds of music could be heard wafting from an apartment complex nearby, enhancing its abandoned air. Halfway down the street, two men had settled in a doorstep and were sharing a stealthy bottle of lotoko. Suddenly, one of the men gave a loud cackle and slapped the dirt with his hands.

"It is already afternoon, and Kinshasa is no longer safe these days. If you want, you can have a warrior escort you home."

Christelle shyly lowered her head and he drank in her profile. Then she turned to him with piercing, endless eyes and Arès held his breath. Her lips parted slightly. "I cannot. I am waiting for Diomandé."

"Diomandé?" Arès said, confused. "Ah, maybe he is with my brother. We can wait together."

Christelle danced away again and Arès felt like he was fumbling after a butterfly in a field of wildflowers.

"No," she replied. "He said he is coming alone. He is bringing me to a place he knows by the river."

"Why would you go there with Diomandé?" Arès asked, astonished.

"He is very nice." She reoriented her gaze toward the vacant street.

"He is always with Félix. I don't know what to make of them," Arès said a bit too forcefully. "They are both trying to leave Kinshasa as fast as they can. If Diomandé takes you to the river, don't let him put you on a boat. I'll never see you again."

"Maybe it would be better to get on a boat," she said wistfully.

"We can go for a boat ride whenever you want. I know some beautiful small rivers near Nonloso." He looked at her, his eyes full of hope.

A bright volley of laughter escaped her lips like a flock of birds exploding into flight. Arès' face darkened. She slapped a hand over her mouth, trying to contain her amusement. "Don't be mad," she pleaded.

"It is no problem," he replied sullenly.

Her laughter died, and the sounds of music drifted closer, pervading the air. They could hear the metallic thwack of a snare drum and the faint plucking of a guitar. Christelle grew silent, and a sad expression passed over her face. Arès watched her feet carry her several steps toward the source of the melody. Then she turned to look at him from a meter away.

"It is a terrible thing, what happened in Rwanda," she said, her voice solemn.

Arès leaned heavily on the countertop. "Yes. My brother won't stop talking about it. He says the little cricket has lit the fire that will burn down the entire village. It is spreading already. That is why we have been having this hot wind recently."

"I like your brother," she said, her voice trailing off.

Arès felt a rush of jealousy but choked it down. "He is ok," he replied smoothly. "I am doing my best to show him the ropes, but it's hopeless." She smiled at him, but he in turn grew serious. "He really believes that he will go to Europe and solve Zaire's problems from there. It is total nonsense."

"You prefer to stay here?"

"*Un étranger ne se bat pas en pays d'autrui.*"[5]

"Advice from a warrior," she said, smiling playfully like before.

Arès' cheeks ran hot, and he gulped down a raspy breath. Christelle quickly closed the distance between them and placed a calming hand over fingers that had unexpectedly balled into a fist. "Not everyone who leaves goes to fight," she said. "My cousin is a musician. He even played with Tabu Ley Rocherau and traveled all over the world. He tells me the most fantastic stories about the places he has visited."

"Ah," Arès said, quieting. "My father always says, '*le pays où vous n'êtes pas encore allé fait croire qu'il est celui où le ciel rejoint la terre.*'"[6]

"I am not looking for paradise." She removed her hand. "How can you stay in a place with no future?"

Arès gazed intently at her. "How can you build a future if you do not stay in one place?"

Christelle turned and walked a few steps away.

"Are you going to be like them?" he continued. "Will you go to university and then run away?"

---

5 It is not wise to risk a fight in a foreign country.

6 The country where you have never been pretends that it is the place where heaven meets the earth.

Christelle spun around laughing. "First I am going to go meet Diomandé by the river. Then maybe I will take the exam for the university." She walked back over to the countertop and grabbed the locket. "Diomandé is helping me prepare for it. And then, well, we will see." She leaned over and kissed Arès on the cheek. Then she flashed a smile that split the sky in two. "Thank you for fixing my locket. It was very nice chatting with you."

Arès felt like he was going to faint, but he steadied himself long enough to watch her disappear down the street. Beneath his shirt, he grabbed tight to his necklace.

"The key to my future," he whispered to himself.

Two months later Christelle married Diomandé.

Arès stood on the porch of his home and watched the boisterous wedding procession pass by. When Diomandé and Christelle paraded into view, laughing and smiling at the center of that dancing celebration, Félix rested a knowing hand on his younger brother's shoulder. "*Un bateau part, mais le port reste,*"[7] he said with his habitual authority. Arès nodded, but it seemed to him like the world had ended.

The next day, the vice-governor of the South Kivu Province issued an order that all Banyamulenge leave Zaire on pain of death.

War had begun.

---

7   A boat departs, but the port remains.

CHAPTER 5
AUGUST 1998

A RÈS' MOTHER WAS UPSET. She came home from the market-place, her dress streaked with mud and a stony expression on her face. Kodwa Mompenge, their longtime neighbor, had knocked the shopping bag from her hands. When she scrambled onto her knees to collect the rolling shafts of manioc, the woman spit on her and called her filthy names.

"She is a vile woman," Arès' father said, "from a vile family."

"This was not the first time," Arès' mother insisted. "Every time I go to the market something bad happens. How can I go there, when they tell me to go back to my country? This is my country, but they tell me to go back. They even refuse to sell me food. How can we live if we cannot get anything to eat?"

"This will pass," Arès' father replied. "People are still frightened from the war. We have lived through much worse than this. You remember when the rebels came?" He paused and let the thought of that time flap ugly and silent. "That was much worse. But war has left Kinshasa. Mobutu is gone. This, like all things, will pass."

"But what will we do?"

"I will talk with the people in the marketplace. They are still our neighbors despite everything."

The war was over. The war had begun. Arès' relatives had been right. In August 1996, under the command of a man raised from the dead, the *Alliance des Forces Démocratiques pour la Libération du Congo-Zaïre* was born.

Over the next year and a half, the rebel army swallowed the Congo whole. Then, in May 1997, the Big Man, the Leopard of Kinshasa, fled his jungle palace in Gbadolite. The next day the capital fell. Laurent-Desiré Kabila proclaimed himself president and rechristened Zaire "The Democratic Republic of Congo." No elections, he announced, would be held until the government restored order.

After decades of misrule and months of war, hope sparked again for the Congo. Carried by these optimistic tides, Arès' relatives said tearful goodbyes and returned with two new children to their village near Bukavu, ready to rebuild their lives. But the promise of sweeping change was short-lived.

Félix stormed home one evening in a foul mood and harangued an invisible audience over the family dinner. "Soon there will no longer be a street corner left without a ten-meter tall poster of President Kabila," he exclaimed. "'The Elder!' *'Voici l'homme dont nous avions besoin.'* He has even hired Mobutu's propaganda minister! Why have a war if nothing changes?" He slammed an open palm against the table's edge with a resounding thwack.

"Patience," Arès' father counseled. "Change comes in its own good time."

"What?" Félix sprung to his feet. He stared at his father, his mouth sputtering like that of a fish. Then, with wild, burning eyes, he stamped furiously out of the room.

Arès laughed loudly and drummed his fingers on the table. "I think that is the first time I have seen Félix without something to say." Yika and his mother smiled at the joke, but his father gazed at Félix's empty seat with uncharacteristic concern.

The next day Arès and his father went to work. When the communal van deposited them in Ngaba, the whole city was without electricity. The Rwandan-backed forces had taken the hydroelectric dam at Inga and had unplugged the capital. It changed little for the locksmithery, whose neighborhood had not seen power for over a year.

Arès' father rolled up the grate. Inside he lit a row of tall, white devotional candles and salted them throughout the shop. Arès turned on the radio. People in the van that morning were spreading rumors that the port at Matadi had fallen. This meant that food would quickly become scarce. The Congolese radio denied the reports, but the Brazzaville radio confirmed their worst fears.

"If the Rwandans win it will be better for us," Arès said. "It will be our people in control."

"No. If they come here it will be like last time. The soldiers do not care if your mother is Rwandan or Congolese. If they see you, they will take what they want."

"We survived last time. When Kabila and the Rwandans were allies."

"Your memory is very short. We lived underground for two weeks. Many of our neighbors were killed. We cannot hope that men with guns will spare us when they do not spare our neighbors. The rain does not fall on one roof alone."

"Yes, but if we survive again and Kabila is gone and a Rwandan is in control, then who will push my mother around in the marketplace?"

"Someone who hates your father."

Arès looked up at two careworn eyes beneath a deeply wrinkled brow and for the first time, his father seemed impossibly old.

"The little hand, my son, does not beat the big hand. I do not think Rwanda will break the Congo."

"They have the port and the electricity. They have most of the East. It was stupid of Kabila to exile all the Rwandans."

"We shall see. Let us listen to what the government says." Arès' father spun the dial on the radio. Someone from the Cabinet of the Chief of State was speaking:

Wherever you see a Rwandan Tutsi, regard him as your enemy. We shall do everything possible to free ourselves from the grip of the Tutsis.

It should be stressed that people must bring a machete, a spear, an arrow, a hoe, spades, rakes, nails, truncheons, electric irons, barbed wire, stones, and the like, in order, dear listeners, to kill the Rwandan Tutsis.

Dear listeners, ladies and gentlemen: Open your eyes wide. Those of you who live along the road, jump on the people with long noses, who are tall and slim and want to dominate us.

A nation in which one class is dominated by another is like a man who has a wounded leg. The sick leg prevents all use of the healthy one. We must cut off the unhealthy leg.

The war will be a lengthy, large, and vast one, because we will show the toads that never, and never ever again, will they swallow the elephant.

Arès switched off the machine. "I am tired of listening to these things. It is a week; this is all they say."

"I think today is not a day we should work late. We will go home early and buy food for dinner, and maybe other supplies."

Around one in the afternoon, they shuttered and locked the smithery and waited inordinately long for a communal taxi. After a lengthy, agitated ride, they pulled into the *marché central* a little before five in the afternoon. The usual merchants had been setting up stalls that morning, but now it seemed as if the grounds had been deserted for years.

"We should go home."

"What will we eat?" Arès asked.

"I am sure your mother has thought of something," his father replied.

They entered a house suffused with the aroma of roasting meat. The universities had been closed for weeks, and Arès' brothers and sisters were gathered in the living room talking quietly. Small bells of light flickered upon rows of wax candles.

Arès' father cinched the two deadbolts on the front door. Then he meticulously marched from window to window, barring them with solid iron grills and thick storm shutters. Finally he checked the yard, locking and relocking decorative gates too flimsy to do anything more than pen animals in.

"You found meat," he said, when he reentered the house through the kitchen door.

"It is our goat," Arès' mother replied.

"Why did you kill the goat?" Arès asked from behind his father. "That was my goat."

"Thierry killed it," Félix shouted from the living room. "He hung it from the tree."

Thierry leaned over and punched his older brother in the arm. "Shut up!"

"Why did you kill my goat?" Arès rushed into the living room. He grabbed his little brother by the arm and began to shake him roughly.

"It wasn't your goat," Thierry replied.

Arès backhanded him across the face. "Why did you kill my goat? You hung it? Why would you hang a goat?" He hit him again. "Why in the world would you hang a goat?" He lifted his brother in the air and raised his hand to hit him hard this time, teach him a lesson.

Something bashed loud and berserk against the front door and riotous cries clipped harsh into the house.

Arès' father rushed to the door. "Who is there?" he shouted. "Who is there?"

"Please!" a voice cried. The pounding of fists, hands, and feet redoubled, drumming haphazardly against the unresponsive wood.

Arès and Félix marshalled behind their father, but he waved them back. His torso bunched, his face creased with apprehension, he swung open the door and was nearly barreled over when six or seven breathless bodies scrambled inside. One of them held a child in his arms.

Arès' father quickly slid the deadbolts back in place.

"What is happening?" he asked.

"We will die here," the man holding the child said.

"What are you running from?"

No answer came. The speaker trained lidless eyes on Arès' father. His companions stood crag-still, their chests heaving, gazing at nothing. There were only men, their faces matted with sweat, their pants rent and gaping. Arès' father went up to one of them, Guli, his brother-in-law, and shook him. Guli seemed to start out of an unpleasant trance.

"Where is your family?" Arès' father asked.

"They are lighting people on fire," Guli replied. "I am sorry, my friend. It is the end. It is the *supplice du pneu.*"

"How far away are they?"

A cry shocks out from the kitchen. Arès sprints toward its source and finds his mother, her finger flung in the direction of the picture window set in the back wall. The smell of roasting goat pervades his nostrils. It is nearly ready and his mouth waters in anticipation, even as he eyes the backyard with dread.

In the intermingling darkness, spear-bearing totems lope about. Shapeless things shimmy along the ground. Apparitions climb upon the garden wall. Murky constellations form and shear apart like revelations. And shadows of shadows hover before the Hagenia tree, as if perched upon extraordinary webs. It is a turmoil of limbs and shifting menace, and Arès looks out upon this roiling shadow world until suddenly it coalesces into a tumbling brick that slides between thick iron grills and fists through the kitchen window into a maelstrom of shattered glass.

Knuckles drub the front door. "Open or you die!"

No one stirs.

"*Mort aux agresseurs!*"

"*Toko boma bino!*"

The chants perforate the walls and blades squeal along the glazed beams of the house. Machetes thrash the kitchen door, streaking slim gashes in the frame. Another rock beats through iron barriers and crumbles a window to the living room floor.

Torches set ablaze around the house and the shadows consolidate into men—men of thirst and ire and contorted faces.

A whooping rises from outside. CRACK!! The front door splinters under the blow of a club. CRACK!! The lustful tip of a nail peeks through punctured wood.

Arès' father grabs his wife and rushes her toward the stairs. The smell of charring flesh fills the house and tendrils of smoke snake along the floors.

CRACK!! The front door folds inward and a disembodied arm juts through, wagging a machete. It retracts and hard feet flog the door's last resistance until it shelves in two.

The men spurt in, pitching the strangers to the ground. Flood upon flood of them, till they jam every crack in the spacious home. They carry machetes, clubs, rakes, and truncheons. Four men seize Arès' mother and father, while another man bends Guli in half and saws through his rubbery neck with a serrated knife.

Arès pivots toward his mother, but something hard stuns him behind the ear and he lurches to the floor. When he looks up, his oldest sister's dress is wrapped high above her abdomen. For a second he eyes her deep velvety crotch before one of his neighbors covers it with his naked thighs. He watches Yika's face, pulled tight by the roots of her hair, grimace in disgust and pain.

His younger sister is fully naked, save for a shred of flower print still fastened to her arm. Two men are holding her legs and another two her wrists. Arès sees her taut pubescent breasts, and the wide apocalypse of her mouth, and the deep screaming curve of her back, as a boy he has known for a long time seeks satisfaction.

The syrupy smell of gasoline fills his nostrils and he coils back as they set the first man aflame. In a whoosh his skin crinkles apart. His legs buckle and a flaming heap collapses to the ground, leaving a soot stain on the floor. The men are dancing and jeering now, several naked and half erect.

A spade batters Arès in the leg and he clutches the ground in pain. Beside him, two men are yanking intestinal slop out of one of Guli's companions, while he gasps and agonizes.

Another man is atop his mother, gripping her jaw, so that her bulging eyes look into his father's weeping face.

Arès wants to look away. He is ashamed of his father's tears and the flesh jiggling off his mother's limbs. He rises to his feet, raising his hand to strike one of the men, but something heavy and stiff slams into his back. His breath rattles in his throat and he collapses to the floor.

An impish man, his chest smudged with blood, jerks Félix into view. Bright red intestines flop around the young man's neck, and his eyes are white with fear.

Behind him looms a lurid tribe. Their crowns are spruced with garish wigs and archaic headdress, cattle horns and heron feathers. Their eyes burn with wild, ineffable lights.

Suddenly Salifou rises into view. Even beneath the flamboyant red wig, his high cheekbones and strangely cut eyes are recognizable. He screeches an old tire down Félix's torso, cinching his arms together. Another man anoints him with gasoline. A skirt of falling droplets glimmer in the torch light.

Arès surges to his feet but a truncheon clefts him in the shoulder, and with a whelp of pain he squirms to the floor.

Sulfur strikes before Salifou's face, shining on a broad, honeyed smile. The match pinwheels through the air and lands inside the rubber hoop. There is a holocaust of fire, and within the iridescent folds of that furnace, Arès watches the skin shell off his brother's screaming face. The intimation of a skull topples awry as two flaming legs trick to the ground.

Next they ignite his father. He budges not an inch. The only sign of his suffering are his eyes, which continue to hiss out tears even as he flakes to ashes within that fulgurating ring.

At the center of that besotted inferno, Arès pushes to his feet. Around him hurrahing, naked battalions romp upon the embers of his life. He seeks out help and for a moment, his eyes implore the unmoving stranger, cradling his child within a glorious combustion.

Then an immenseness flooded his head and he knew no more.

CHAPTER 6
SEPTEMBER 1998

———————

L IGHT SNAKES ACROSS AN ochre dirt floor. The shadow of a table zigzags within sight. A blade of sunshine slices under the sill of the door. His neck feels bloated, unreal.

All was quiet, save for the clamor of his body.

His back seemed unresponsive, discontinuous. Plots of flesh acting independent of each other, as if colonized by larva. They pulsed lethargically with pain, contracted, expanded. He heaved and nearly retched. His skin stretched thin with misery.

A coarse woven blanket covered his torso and legs and he sweated uncomfortably. It was too hot. He thought about shifting his weight, but the thought expired in the heat. His fingers clawed at a thin mattress, clenching and unclenching.

Runnels of perspiration tickled his flank. He scratched his thigh and shuddered. His legs were a torment. His right one especially. It felt laden, waterlogged. He tried to move it and sucked his breath in agony.

Then he groaned.

A jangle of noise sounded from somewhere nearby, and Arès' eyes skittered nervously. A hand he could not see caressed his brow, and the blur of a cup tipped water into his mouth.

He drunk greedily, closed his eyes, and fell asleep.

It was hot. Arès could taste the salt that quivered on his tongue. Crystals had formed on his upper lip like a silver scruff. He opened his eyes and saw the same ribbons of light, the same rickety shadows.

"Ah you're awake." The voice spoke in Lingala.

His jaw felt macerated. He tried to mash out words. Nothing emerged but groans.

He heard footsteps approaching, and hysteria scrabbled up his throat. He thrashed in the bed, gulping at the pain.

With stupendous effort, he heaved himself upright in time to identify the lean silhouette of a stranger. The man moved into the light, and Arès looked upon cheeks so gaunt and black that had it not been for the two rolling balls of his eyes, the face would have seemed a deep cremation.

Then his body's ordeal overwhelmed him.

"Try not to move this time," the man said.

"Where am I?" His jaw still felt puffed, but he could finally speak.

"You are safe."

"Where is safe?"

"You are in my home. Do not worry. Would you like some tea?"

"Yes." Arès tried to sit up but his strength failed him. He felt strong thin arms, hard as truncheons, slink under his armpits and hoist him upright. He tried to lean his back against the wall but pitched forward in distress.

It felt as if barbed wire had raked down his spine.

The man went outside to search for water. When he returned he clanked a pot upon a kerosene stove and lit the flame. The penumbra receded and a meager hut materialized out of the gloom. Less than three meters separated the cot underneath Arès from the far wall where the man spilled boiling water into a battered teapot stuffed with pastel leaves.

He placed the pot and two cups on the small end table, rutching the legs into the dirt floor to prevent them from wobbling.

"How did I get here?" Arès asked.

The man handed him a brimming cup. Arès sipped cautiously. His lips were numb and small dribbles escaped onto the floor.

"I found you in front of your house. You were barely breathing, so I put you in my wagon and brought you here."

"What were you doing there?"

"I sell fish in the marketplace of your village. I knew your mother."

"My mother!" Arès' head pounded. It was hard to think.

"Drink the tea. It will help."

Arès took two scalding gulps, only half of which reached his throat. Everything throbbed.

"Did you find anyone else?"

"There was no one else."

"Did you look in the house?"

"I put you in the wagon and I left."

"We have to go see if anyone is alive." Arès tried to raise himself off the cot but it felt as if runnels of fire were coursing through his right leg.

"You need to rest, my friend." The stranger suddenly switched to French. *"On ne passe pas deux poêles à la fois sur le feu, sans quoi l'un brûle."*[8]

"You must look for me!" Arès grabbed his hand beseechingly. "My mother, my father. My sisters and brothers."

"It is too late," the man replied. "You have been here for nearly a week."

"Then I will go," Arès said. He fell onto his knees and began to crawl laboriously toward the door, tugging his unresponsive right leg with all his strength. His breath rasped hard and heavy, and he collapsed on the ground several times before he reached the threshold.

The man calmly sipped his tea, watching his guest drag himself across the floor. "You will not survive the trip. It is very dangerous in Kinshasa." Arès looked back at him. "Especially for you."

"Then you must promise me you will go to my house and see if anyone is alive."

The sun had set. The burner extinguished and the two men were submerged in darkness. A disembodied voice swam out of that nothingness. "In two days I will sell fish at the marketplace. I will go by your house before returning home."

* * *

---

8   One does not cook two pans on the fire at the same time without burning one.

"What did you find?" Arès asked. A serpent had been writhing in his chest the entire afternoon, waiting for the man's return.

The man carried a small chair into the house and lit a candle. "Here," he said, handing him some bread. Arès chewed the loaf greedily. The man scraped two fish onto a small grill and lit the camp stove under it.

"I am sorry," he said.

"No one?"

"There was nothing inside your house. I asked your neighbors what happened to the people who lived there, but no one wanted to talk. It is very dangerous. There are patrols every night looking for Rwandans. I do not know how long you can stay here."

"How far are we from Kinshasa?"

"Two, three hours."

Arès scooped some water from a pail located next to the cot.

"Where have you been sleeping?" he asked.

"Over there." The arm pointed at two thin blankets puddled in the corner of the hut.

When the fish were ready, they ate in silence.

For two more weeks, Arès lay in the chiaroscuro darkness of the hut, drinking tea and consuming whatever the man gave him, mostly fish. After their initial conversations, they rarely spoke.

The man was not given to talk and Arès had little to say in the days following the attack. He slept most of the time. When he was awake, his thoughts were incoherent.

One night, the man came home.

"Can you walk?" he asked.

"I think so," Arès said. The pain had subsided considerably in the past week.

"Good. You must leave now. Put on these clothes."

He dressed Arès in a pair of old jeans and a shirt leached of color. "Here is some money."

"Where am I going?"

"There are soldiers looking for Rwandans. They are checking every house. I have friends with a pirogue. They will take you to a place near Brazzaville where you will be safe."

He seized Arès by the arm and half carried him out of the hut. When the young man felt the breath of cool night air, panic seized him. He clutched the jambs of the door and refused to let go.

"We must leave. Now." He pulled Arès roughly by the arm and the young man winced in pain. He tugged again, and Arès released his hold and fell once more into the world.

They made uneven progress toward the river. Several times, Arès crumpled to his knees, unable to continue. The man did not have the strength to carry him, and they idled fearfully in the shadows, waiting for Arès to recover. Twice the heavy clomping of troops approached down the road and veered away at the last minute.

When they finally reached the river, they could see houses on fire. At the water's edge, two silhouettes sat athwart a pirogue like lank forest idols.

"Quickly," one said.

They laid Arès down in the hull and covered him with a blanket. Then they unmoored.

Arès tried to raise himself, to thank the man for his help, but one of the rowers booted him sharply in the spine. He shriveled into the dugout, pain ricocheting down his back.

For days they cabotaged along the banks of the Congo.

Several times Arès felt he was going to suffocate in the afternoon heat beneath the bulky blanket. But every time he turtled up for air, one of the boaters hoofed him back down and his vision swirled in pain.

He was too afraid to protest. A word from these men and his future lay broken in the dust. So for hours each day, he gasped beneath the coarse woven cover, leaden with heat.

His only distraction was the babble of the riverway's stupendous commerce: the sensuous cries of fish hawkers, the whooping of birds, the bright salutations of passing vessels. The water traffic knew no respite and from time to time, the small pirogue was thrown by the passing wake of formidable barges, carrying upon them the devastation of the Congo's rainforests.

Then for two days they rowed through an impassable fog. The river slept and the jungle fauna were preternaturally subdued. The only sounds were the regular strokes of polished oars scooping through the oily Zaire and the occasional vibrations of something huge and invisible gliding beneath the canoe.

Then the heat rose again, withering, unbearable. Muffled sounds filtered through the kiln of the blanket: fervid river life, tart bird cries, shouted greetings, grunts and complaints, the din that accompanies sweat and toil.

Every day, around two in the afternoon, the rough heat peaked, enveloping the craft in a torrid blister. "What are your names?" Arès cried aloud at one moment of unreasonable suffering.

There was no response other than the tormented slap of the oars against the river's membrane.

Twice, he collapsed in distress, waking only when it was night. At night, at least, there was reprieve.

After sunset, Arès issued like a phantom from the floating tomb and sat and ate the fish or bread he invariably found stuffed into the tackle box beside the stern. The rowers were never there when he emerged. He never heard them disembark. It was as if they were sucked into nothingness every evening along with the setting sun.

So Arès sat alone and listened to the lustrous symphony of insects beneath uncaring skies ablaze with stars.

On the sixth day they arrived, and for the next six years he gathered moss in a riverside hamlet by the name of Dongo.

CHAPTER 7

FEBRUARY 2008

S IMON SKIPPED UP THE stairs, a thick pink folder rolled hard against his thigh. His very first resettlement interview and it was a credible case for submission! What were the odds?

He paused on the landing and smoothed his hands over the rumpled sides of his blazer. He had carried himself well, he thought. He had dressed smart, exuded authority. Sure, he had scraped his chair a bit excitedly across the floor. Twice? Maybe three times? But he had been adept, in control. Had he fidgeted? He didn't think so. In any case, the PRA had no way of knowing it was his first unassisted interview. What a rush!

He reached the top of the stairs and proceeded down a glittering white hall, his tasseled brown loafers skating over the smooth tiled floors.

Odd that the refugee was his same age—down to the day! Of course, you could never really be sure with them. The birthdays they gave were often fanciful. It could be a name day, or a national holiday, or some arbitrary date plucked out of thin air, which had special meaning for them or no meaning whatsoever.

Could they really be the same age? He paused in front of a reflective brass plate mounted beside one of the office doors. His face stared back at him, polished in liquid gold. Long, thick locks of dirty blond hair tumbled over a high golden forehead, gold-blue eyes flecked with chips of flaxen brown, a gilded aquiline nose with a small golden knob on the bridge—not a mark or blemish on his baby-smooth golden skin.

Promising features, he thought. Dynamic. Commanding. Executive.

The man he had just interviewed was of a different sort: his chocolate brown skin pockmarked with fever blisters, the wide bridge of his nose puffed awry with the signs of several bashings, his eyes two liquid sinks webbed with pink veins, his cheeks hollowed by malnutrition—and that scar, like a serpent wriggling through grass. Could he really be twenty-eight years old? His forehead seemed furrowed with misery.

Perhaps that explained the subject's noncompliance during the interview. Simon had looked a tad young to his eyes. Despite the sober suit, despite the stranglehold tie that he wrenched open as he burst onto the bright white terrace on the second floor of the UNHCR. But he had presided over that stifling room, an unflinching rod of authority, while dribbles of sweat tickled his spine.

And resettlement! He had already begun drafting the RRF in his head. What were the elements of the claim? Lack of local integration. Victim of torture or violence. Urgent medical condition with no access to adequate treatment. Was there any exclusion criteria? Record of combat? Criminal activity? Special needs assessment? He would have to review the Resettlement Handbook.

Where would he apply first? Sweden? That was the low-hanging fruit. Or maybe France. The PRA was a French speaker. He would integrate better there. The French, though, were finicky. They looked for any excuse to reject an RRF. But this one was sound.

Certainly, there were inconsistencies in the account. Minor ones. It was always like that. He had sat in on nearly a dozen interviews, and the subjects were constantly tripping over themselves. Most of the time their stories defied good sense, not to mention the laws of continuity. It was exasperating. They jumped from one event to another without obvious causal connection, like in some art-house film. But the UNHCR guidelines encouraged a principle of "benefit of the doubt," so long as the applicant's claims were coherent and plausible, and "coherent" and "plausible" wore entirely different dress in Africa.

But this one was different. He had pushed back, turned aside the current of the interview. What a dramatic tale! Like something out of Shakespeare. Or older. Less plotted—more disjointed. The *Odyssey* perhaps. Africa, with its fetishes and fallen kingdoms. *Der Mentsch trakht und got lakht,* as his grandfather used to say. If he hadn't lived in Rwanda, hadn't seen those cartloads of carved talismans coming over from the Congo, those rows of twice-faced forest idols and waist-high masks, demented laughing charms and Nkisi nail totems, all bred out of that endless bush, as if the jungle were the foundry of dreams... well, it all belonged to another world.

He stopped suddenly, shielding his eyes, blinking furiously as pulses of light crashed against his retinas like waves on the shore. Slowly the second-floor terrace dimmed into view. The roar of a crowd filled his ears, and the empty whack and skid of a polyurethane ball against shorn grass.

Baptiste, a UN Officer from Yaoundé, was camped in front of an open laptop. The computer sat on a Victorian-style table of wrought iron, painted an antique white. Above it spread the twisting branches of an olive tree, bathing Baptiste in a fluctuating web of shadow and light. A handsome man, with coppery brown skin and trim, neat features, per usual he was dressed more for the nightclub than the office. Today it was a tailored three-piece suit, a white cutaway shirt, and a black pencil tie.

Baptiste held his face fanatically close to the screen, his brow creased with the heroic concentration normally reserved for a duel.

"You're watching soccer?" Simon asked, as he stepped toward the table.

Baptiste glanced up. "This isn't soccer, *mon ami*. This is poetry with a ball. This is a ballet on grass. I am watching the Africa Cup, and once again the Indomitable Lions are devouring their opponents."

His large bright eyes twinkled mischievously and an infectious Cheshire smile extended far beyond the corners of his mouth. When he leaned back in the chair, Simon noticed a surprisingly gaudy green and gold handkerchief, with the roaring snout of a lion, poking above the edge of his breast pocket.

"Who are they playing?"

"They are up against the Black Stars, but I am afraid the Ghanians have eaten too much fufu again. They are waddling around the pitch like pregnant women. And look at Essien. It's embarrassing that the Lions are *only* ahead by one goal, when Ghana's best player is a pigeon-toed gorilla who keeps tripping over the ball." Baptiste slapped the table and took a hurried sip from a can of cherry cola, one eye still on the screen.

"So much for African solidarity," Simon remarked with a grin.

"If you spent less time planning weekends in Ibiza and more time reading African history, you would know we are not a continent renowned for its abiding solidarity," Baptiste replied, and then inched even closer to the laptop screen.

Simon's jaw dropped. "That was two weeks ago," he protested. "And I spent most of the time on the beach reading *King Leopold's Ghost.*"

"A perfect place to ponder a century of enslavement, expropriation, and mass murder," Baptiste added with a half-smile. Simon felt his cheeks burn. "But if you excuse me, I am occupied with another massacre. The Ghanaians will be weeping and tearing their hair after this game. It is a national tragedy."

"I just finished my first resettlement interview," Simon announced.

Baptiste sighed and lowered the sound on the computer. "Ah so today was your baptism by fire. How did it go?" He leaned back in his chair and regarded the young JPO for the first time.

Simon smoothed back his mane of blond hair and leaned toward the Cameroonian officer. "I think we have a solid case for resettlement."

"So he bamboozled you," Baptiste responded, without missing a beat.

"What do you mean?" The color leached out of Simon's face.

"I felt that way too after my first few interviews. Then reality settled in."

A riotous shouting shocked out of the computer. "Off the post!" Baptiste howled. "That's the third time! I think the Ghanaians have cast a spell on the ball."

"I'm no novice," Simon said when the din died down. "I've already sat through several interviews with you and Hilda. Most of them are a mess, but this one was coherent, and the refugee suffers from an urgent medical condition."

"You know they swap stories in the refugee community," Baptiste replied, still shaking his head at the computer. "That's why so many of their accounts resemble one another. I'm not saying they haven't undergone terrible experiences, but when you've heard the same general biography, with a few details tweaked here or there, from dozens of applicants, you grow a bit cynical. Then you start to probe, and suddenly none of it adds up. Sit down."

Simon slapped the pink dossier onto the table, spun a chair around and sat akimbo, his arms folded over the ridge of the back. "Well, I've never heard a story like this one before." Baptiste raised his eyebrows. "Where is he from?"

"The DRC."

"Minority population? Banyamulenge?"

"Of course," Simon replied.

"Let me guess. He saw his family killed before his very eyes."

"How did you know?"

"Typical."

"You don't think it happened?"

"Well how did he escape? If everyone in his family was killed, then why is he alive? There's only two ways. One is that he took part in the killing to save his own skin. That's not uncommon—they force one of the victims to murder the others—but that means he falls into an exclusion category, or let me guess, he doesn't know how he was saved?"

"The latter," Simon answered grudgingly.

"What happened? He was knocked unconscious and was carried to safety by an unknown individual, about whom he has sparse details, if any?"

Simon nodded. He could feel the heat rise up the back of his neck.

"I've heard this one before."

"Yes, but it was the rest of what he told me," Simon insisted. "It was spontaneous, credible, and like nothing I've ever heard."

"Ah, it sounds like he filled your head with some tall tales. *Là où tu n'es pas arrivé, les nuages sont tombés.*"[9]

"What do you mean by that?"

"Did he request resettlement?"

"Yes."

"And he has some rare medical condition that needs to be treated elsewhere? That is incurable in Morocco?"

"The complications with his foot and ankle sounded acute."

"Did you inspect it yourself? Have you consulted with Dr. Djideree or PALS to see if they are monitoring his case and what the prognosis is?"

---

9   There, where you have never been, the clouds touch the ground.

Simon looked down at his shoes and didn't respond.

"Don't be glum."

Exuberant cheers filled the terrace. "*Nkong a tiré un but magnifique! Magnifique!*" Baptiste started clapping and pounding the table. "That's it!" he cried.

As if summoned by the commotion, a moon-faced woman in a dark green smock issued from a half-occluded entrance on the far side of the terrace. She wore a grass-colored kerchief wound about her head and carried a silver tray topped with steaming glasses of Moroccan mint tea and pasty white almond *ghribas*. She placed the tray down on the table before the two men and dramatically shivered in the cool, February air.

"Would you like some tea to warm you?"

"Saana," Simon said with a grateful smile, "once again you've rescued me from near death."

"It's a cold day," she replied. "I thought the tea would help."

Simon turned to Baptiste. "You see. How can I be glum when I'm constantly plied with these culinary delights?"

Baptiste waved away the steaming glass with his hand. "Thank you, but the mint turns my stomach." He sipped again from the ruby red can, and then deftly pinched two of the powdered cookies and shoved them into his mouth. "But this," he said with gusto, "the Moroccans know how to do."

"Shall I leave the pot?" Saana asked.

"Please," Simon said. She gathered up the second glass and turned to go. "Couscous for lunch?" he asked.

"It's Friday," Saana replied, as she walked back into the kitchen.

"My favorite!" he shouted after her.

Baptiste quietly inhaled three more cookies. When Simon turned around, the tray was covered in crumbs. He glared at his colleague. Then he grabbed the silver teapot and refilled the blue and gold glass, raising the pot steadily skywards so the tea aerated as it fell into the tight vessel below.

"Interviewing the refugees is like a dance," Baptiste asserted, while Simon sipped the honeyed liquid. "Do you dance, Simon?"

"Sure. I mean, not often."

"You should come out with me tomorrow after work. There's a club in Agdal called a Thousand and One Nights. The ladies there know how to dance." He smacked his lips theatrically. "You have a couple drinks. You start to shake your hips…"

"I don't see how this is relevant," Simon interrupted.

"You're on the dance floor and the first one of the night comes up to you. She seems like the real thing, but it's because you're hungry. She shows you everything you want to see." His eyes glinted and he cracked a big toothy smile. "But like so often in Morocco, you have to learn to wait. *Le bon chasseur ne tue pas la bête qu'il ne peut pas manger.*"[10]

"You need a wingman tomorrow night, don't you?" Simon surmised.

"There happens to be a certain Ghanaian waitress who will need to be consoled after her nation's loss. As a Protection Officer of the United Nations, I feel that this falls within my mandate."

"I thought you were an Eligibility Officer."

"All the more reason to console this heartbroken waitress."

Simon laughed and shook his head. Then he thought about the man he had just sent back out into the streets of Rabat. "And what if the first one who comes to dance is the real thing?"

"*Qui tend plusieurs pièges ne passe pas la nuit affamé.*[11] My friend, I'd scrutinize the details of his claim carefully and, above all, skeptically. Call Dr. Djideree to ask whether his medical condition is really incurable or if there is an active and ongoing *suivi*. And try to conduct a few more interviews before you get us in trouble by spamming the European agencies with a bunch of weak cases."

Simon nodded thoughtfully and continued to sip the sugary tea.

"Now if you excuse me, duty calls," Baptiste continued. "I expect several Ghanaian footballers will apply for asylum after this catastrophic defeat, and I want to study the details of their cases closely."

Baptiste raised the volume on the computer and leaned toward the bright pixelated box of green, with its Lilliputian players dashing after

---

10   The good hunter doesn't kill an animal he cannot eat.

11   He who sets several snares does not spend the night hungry.

an invisible ball. Simon rolled the pink folder into a tight tube and strolled distractedly off the terrace and into the glossy white building. Just before he reached his office, Fatima, from the community services division, came tearing down the hall, screaming into her cell phone in Arabic.

He watched her disappear around a bend. Then he closed the door and sat down at his desk. To his left, through the bright panes of a tall sash window, stretched the far-off plains of Salé and the blue wriggle of the Bouregreg River, a thousand feet below. It was a calming sight.

A terse call with Dr. Djideree confirmed Baptiste's suspicions. The doctor didn't have the file on hand, but he knew the dossier by heart. The refugee's prognosis was excellent and he was being attentively looked after by their local partner PALS.

Simon sighed, turned on some Chet Baker, and began writing up his report.

Protection Officer Notes

Credibility assessment: The PRA's statements are spontaneous, sufficiently detailed, and credible on his reasons for leaving the country. His claims of harassment and violence directed against the Banyamulenge in the Western DRC are further substantiated by several reliable sources.

Among these sources are:

Immigration and Refugee Board of Canada, Democratic Republic of Congo: Current treatment of the Banyamulenge people in the Democratic Republic of Congo, 11 June 2003, RDC41641.FE, available at: http://www.unhcr.org/refworld/docid/3f7d4e0838.html

"Accused of having started the war that began in August 1998, the vast majority of the Congolese Tutsis, including the Banyamulenge, were either driven out of or evacuated from Kinshasa and other areas controlled by the Congolese government, and relocated in third countries."

Immigration and Refugee Board of Canada, Democratic Republic of Congo (RDC): The Banyamulenge (Munyamulenge) ethnic group; whether members of this group are targeted by government author- ities, 1 December 2000, RDC35883.F, available at: http://www. unhcr.org/refworld/docid/3f7d4dfe1c.html

"The Banyamulenge (literally, the people of Mulenge, a small community located near Uvira at the foot of the Itombwe mountains in South Kivu) were originally Tutsi animal breeders who arrived in Zaire one or two centuries ago. For a long time, they have been considered to be fully Zairian; however, they tend to live self-sufficiently and have a sometimes-difficult relationship with certain local ethnic groups. Since the late 1960s, Tutsi refugees from Rwanda have tended to gather under the name Banyamulenge so that they can be registered as full Zairian citizens (Feb. 1997)."

"In its 30 March 2000 bulletin, Refugees International reveals that 'hate speech and communal violence have increased alarm- ingly in the provinces of North and South Kivu,' and that this violence is directed at an estimated 150,000 Banyamulenge, who are at risk of violent attack by Mayi-Mayi militia [pro-Kabila tribal militia from North and South Kivu, see RDC33309.F of 14 December 1999]. According to the same source of information, Congolese authorities have questioned the Banyamulenge's right to citizenship despite the fact that they have made the Congo their home for two hundred years (*Refugees International 30 Mar. 2000*). This was a key issue in the 1996 war that brought President Kabila to power [in May 1997] (ibid.)."

Austrian Centre for Country of Origin and Asylum Research and Documentation/United Nations High Commissioner for Refugees

(ACCORD/UNHCR), *28 November 2002*. "Democratic Republic of Congo Country Report."

Human Rights Watch (HRW). Rapport Mondial, 2003. "Congo." http://www.hrw.org/french/reports/wr2k3/congo.htm

Minorities at Risk Project. Gil Peleg. "Tutsis in the Democratic Republic of Congo." 10 November 2002. http://www.cidcm.umd.edu/inscr/mar/data/drctuts.htm

There were nonetheless credibility problems with respect to the following material elements of the claim:

1. The PRA lacked knowledge about the number of Congolese Wars and the composition of the rebel groups involved in them.
2. It is highly improbable that a stranger discovered the PRA unconscious in the street and transported him over 70 kilometers to his village.
3. The PRA cannot remember the name of the man who allegedly saved his life.
4. The PRA digressed extensively during the interview.

The above-mentioned credibility problems are sufficient to cast doubt on the applicant's claim. It is likely that any country to which we submit an RRF will reject the request for reasons of credibility.

Therefore, I cannot recommend the PRA for Resettlement.

CHAPTER 8

SEPTEMBER–DECEMBER 1998

T HE PIROGUE RAPPED LIGHTLY upon a bank. The blanket whooshed aside and Arès blinked wildly in the impromptu dazzle.

"Sit up. We are here."

The young man hoisted himself onto the gunwale and beheld the rowers for the first time in daylight. Something about them looked amiss. Their gossamer skin, stretched thin over angular features, gleamed like wax paper and their eyes, milky, unfocused, dangled in deep sockets under obtruding brows. The prominence of their heads made their bodies seem preposterously meager, almost decrepit.

They moored the vessel, cinching ropes around protruding roots. Then they lifted Arès out of the boat on fleshless arms and pushed him along like two wasteland bailiffs. Three men of indeterminate age with deeply creased faces were waiting for them on the shore.

"This is a friend," one of the rowers said. "He has left his home and is looking for a place to live." The other rower presented the men with a bundle of fish and a pair of thick woven blankets.

The men nodded.

"Welcome to Dongo," one of them said. He was slightly taller than the other two, sturdy and rotund, with a face that reminded Arès of a bulldog. His small, avid hands fluttered as he spoke. "I am Bugingo."

"Arès."

"You are injured. Your leg is not good."

"Yes... I had an accident." He wiped his brow. "The communal van."

"Ah, I see," Bugingo replied.

The three men led Arès down a narrow dirt path that wound for about half a kilometer into the forest. There, a long-abandoned adobe hut stood within a small clearing, its dirt floor buried under rotting vegetation. The hut's thatched roof was little more than a fibrous mesh on one side and a gaping cavity on the other, though the whole structure was overhung by the naked limbs of a baobab, or bottom-up tree.

Arès collapsed onto the grassy earth when they arrived. His right leg felt like it was on fire. He peered up at the overhanging swarm of coils and hoped it would deflect the water when it rained.

"You may live here," Bugingo said. "Its owner has left."

As if to solemnize his arrival, two boys coalesced out of the surrounding greenery, bearing provisions.

"A traveler is like the morning dew," Bugingo added, as he bent down and handed Arès two tarnished glasses, some dried fish, and a thin blanket.

Arès thanked the wrinkled men and then watched them wind down the narrow path and dissolve into an alley of palm fronds.

He sat in the road, alone. Eight hours later night fell, and still he had not moved.

Days passed. Arès reclined against the bottom-up tree, his muscles lax.

At night he stretched upon the rotting vegetation inside the hut. Several of the tree's gourd-like fruits were decomposing and he piled them in a fleshy mound beside the door.

Once, when he grew hungry enough, he tore off the fruit's silky green fuzz and chewed on its juicy white flesh and thick crackling seeds.

Often it rained, and streams of water gullied along the baobab branches and leapt hard and cold onto Arès' body. Yet he did not stir. Not even to relocate under the remnants of the thatched roof.

One clear evening he stared up at the cold shine of far-off galaxies draining through the limbs of the tree. He dozed off for a moment and when he awoke, he noticed the milky whirl of a gargantuan web flung across nearly a dozen branches. Stenciled against its luminous center was a glittering albino spider, nearly the size of his chest.

He watched it with detached curiosity until it began to descend toward him on an invisible reel, its eight gangly legs spinning in the air.

Arès shoved himself out of the hut and lurched halfway to the river, collapsing in the road. He woke around sunrise, his arms and legs bloated by mosquito bites. In a half daze, he hobbled to the village marketplace and bought some string, a knife, and a rickety ladder to use to thatch the rest of the roof.

The next day, he took stock. His money was nearly spent, and he was hopelessly alone. In all the days since he had arrived, no one had passed by the hut to check in on him. He felt like weeping, and he dropped his head into his hands and heaved his chest, but no tears came. After sitting dazed for several minutes, he forced himself to his feet.

A small sapling stood nearby. Arès stripped off a branch and spent the rest of the morning carving a slender fishing rod. Afterwards, he limped back to the village, intending to use the last of his money to purchase a hook, line, and bucket.

Beside the entrance to the marketplace, a squat fisherman sat cross-legged on the ground. His bulbous eyes, wide chin, and fleshy lips lent him a vaguely amphibian air, as did the surprisingly agile tongue he jutted out when Arès told him what he wanted. He took the outstretched bills, smudged with sweat and rain, and smoothed them repeatedly over the barrel of his belly before holding them up to the sunlight. To Arès' surprise, his hands were marked by dozens of evenly spaced keloid bulges, as if the flesh underneath was permanently aboil. Ringing his arms, Arès noted light ritual scarring that reminded him of the serrated teeth on a key.

Curious, he asked what sort of tribe lived in Dongo, but the fisherman replied with a hostile grunt and continued inspecting the bills. Thinking that he had misunderstood the question in Lingala, Arès asked him again in Kikongo. The fisherman grinned oddly at the young man, and then abruptly hopped to his feet and hurried away, leaving the items in the dirt.

Arès watched him vanish into the trees. His head felt terribly heavy, and he longed for the seclusion of his hut. But something wasn't right. Where had those rowers carried him in their pirogue?

Dozens of people were trading at the marketplace. Nearly all of them bore signs of scarification on their hands and arms, peeking out from the folds of loosely draped cloth. Arès approached a cobbler sitting on a small wooden stool and asked to purchase a pair of shoes. In response, the man peered resolutely at the ground. When he drew near a woman selling fruit, she quickly gathered up her skirt and fled. Arès suddenly noticed that the other villagers were actively giving him space, as if he bore the telltale signs of some loathsome disease.

His mind reeled with confusion. Quickly, he collected his purchases and returned to his forest hut.

The next morning, he awoke light-headed to his stomach's insistent growls. A small tributary of the Zaire flowed through the jungle not far from the hut. He followed it upstream until he came to a large stone outcrop. Before it lay a tranquil blue-green pool that looked like it might shelter fish. So he made a seat for himself on the great granite slab and fed his line into the water.

Soon his eyes grew glassy and smooth, and his mind dipped and rose with the rolling skin of the river. For hours he sat there in a trance, forgetting his hunger. It was almost dusk when a sharp crunch of leaves startled him alert. He assumed it was a passing animal and did not turn around. Then he heard a human voice clear its throat.

Slowly, he spun his head. Bugingo's rotund frame filled the space between the massive roots of a red mahogany tree. He was dressed normally, in a blue jacket and gray slacks, but he held a massive walking stick carved with elaborate animal motifs, and over his jacket hung a marabout's necklace of cowrie shells, animal bones, and monkey skulls.

Arès rubbed his eyes and looked again, uncertain if what he was seeing was real. Bugingo stood there impassively, waiting to be acknowledged. Finally, Arès nodded at the vision.

"Greetings," Bugingo said.

Arès tried to reply but the words died on his lips. He cleared his throat loudly and tried again. "Greetings," he replied.

"You are comfortable here, I take it?" Bugingo asked.

The young man's eyes glittered devilishly for a moment. Then they calmed. "It is cool here by the river."

"Yes, it is a very beautiful place." Bugingo paused and surveyed the area. "It is a pity that the water is no longer good."

Arès regarded the apparition confusedly. The creases in Bugingo's face folded deeply as he spoke, and it reminded Arès of the discarded skin of a snake. So too, did the sinuous veins that bulged off his thick hands where he gripped the knob of the walking stick, and the curling scars that puckered off his right arm.

"I have been drinking the water all day. It tastes fine," he said guardedly. "Also, I have caught several fish today." He pointed to the bucket where small splashes of the dying animals could be seen.

"Sometimes you admire a piece of fruit," Bugingo replied, "only to find that it is rotten when you bite into it."

Arès looked at the tranquil pool again. The surface lay calm as a mirror, and he could see the dark green canopy of trees and a sky with reddening wisps of clouds reflected in the water.

"The water is no good," Bugingo insisted. "We have seen bodies floating downstream in the river. Many of them. Have you not seen the bodies? Sometimes the river slows there are so many of them. The water is thick with blood and has trouble flowing."

Arès stared at the water again and grimaced in disgust. For a moment he thought he might retch. He clutched his head to keep it from spinning.

Bugingo regarded the stranger silently. Monkeys screamed in the trees and branches rattled and shook. Arès looked up to see a shower of leaves cascade through fiery light and land in the blue-green pool. Slowly, they melted into the river. Still Bugingo did not speak.

"I am sorry, but I feel sick," Arès said. "What can I do but drink the water?"

"You can leave," Bugingo firmly replied.

"Leave?" Arès' heart started beating fast in his chest, and he felt the bile rise in his gut.

"The bodies appeared shortly after your arrival. It is a bad omen. Do you not hear the dogs crying through the night? Have you not noticed how dark the evenings are? The roosters wake late in the morning and do not crow."

"I have not seen any bodies," Arès said. "I have not heard anything."

Bugingo's eyes gazed past the young man to the river. "Yes. They say that the water in which a dog drowns is drunk by strangers."

Nauseated, Arès eyed the darkening pool. He felt as if he were drowning, and simultaneously, as if the river's waters were rising up in his chest and swelling his limbs unbearably.

"Perhaps you have not seen the bodies," Bugingo continued. "The water runs backwards here. Near the village, there is a place where the river penetrates the jungle and divides in two. One branch continues south, but the other branch reverses its flow and travels north to this pool. It is very good for catching fish, but the villagers do not come here. They say that it is out of step with the rest of the world. Some say that this is where Mokélé Mbembé sleeps."

Arès shivered at the name of the legendary monster and edged back from the water. Bugingo stared hard at the young man, while a gust of wind cried through the trees. "The bodies do not come to this pool, but I believe that you have seen them. Before you came to Dongo. I do not think you should visit the village anymore. I do not think that you should stay here. We do not want any trouble."

"Have I caused any problems?"

"No. But the spider spins its web slowly. And when you fall in it is too late."

For a moment, Arès inspected the lavishly wrinkled topography of Bugingo's face. These were not the kindly, permissive creases of old age. They looked instead as if they had been excavated with a knife. The young man shook his head.

"There are many people fleeing this violence. Are there not? Maybe I am one of them," he said.

"We have seen no survivors," Bugingo replied.

Arès squeezed his eyes tight and covered his ears. He could feel tears spit down his cheeks. He rocked back and forth on his hips and then opened his eyes and wiped the tears away.

"None?" he asked.

"None."

Arès hung his head. The water spun inkily before him. He thought of slithering in to join his family. His hand slid along the stone.

Bugingo's voice snapped him back to life. "If you are fleeing, why do you not continue? Why do you linger here?"

Arès looked at the man, baffled. He sought for words to explain that he had nowhere to go. He could barely even walk. But he knew Bugingo would not care to understand. The man stood in a defensive position with his staff held in front of him as if prepared to attack, or like some forest marabout warding off a plague.

"Do you see that fish over there," Arès said, pointing to a light blue cichlid swimming upstream, slightly before the entrance to the pool.

Bugingo nodded.

"The fish is swimming hard, but he is not going anywhere. Perhaps he is fleeing something too. But the forces opposing him are strong. So he swims as fast as he can in order to stay in place." Arès looked intently at the old man with suffering eyes. "Perhaps that is all he can do."

Bugingo relaxed his grip on the walking stick. "And you are like this fish?"

"I am fleeing as fast as I can."

Bugingo dropped his chin into his chest, thinking hard. His right hand thumbed an alligator snout carved into the walking stick. After a minute he raised his head. "I will tell this to my people, but they are not happy with your presence. When there is a great violence and someone escapes, death trails him. It is joined to him like his shadow. Wherever he goes, it follows."

"Then that person is cursed for life?" Arès asked. The horror of his situation dawned on him.

"It is not my concern. I have to protect my village. If a snake comes into your house, you do not leave it there. You kill it before it bites someone."

"But what if you mistake the fish for a snake?"

"I will speak with the villagers. We will give you some time, but the fish will have to learn to swim harder. I cannot be responsible for their actions. When people are frightened, they sometimes do harmful things."

"Thank you," Arès said. "I promise you I am a friend."

"I hope so." Bugingo looked back at the river. "The water, it is said, does not move without a reason." Then he turned and hammered Arès with his stare. "When the rainy season ends you should be gone."

Arès nodded in thanks and when he looked up again, the apparition was gone.

He knew now that he was an exile from the world. Not just from everything he had ever known, but even from the community of man itself.

It was a condition unthinkable to the brash boy he had been only a few months before. But his head was full of disordered thoughts, and he accepted the solitude of his new existence. Every morning, he hiked to the peaceful blue-green pool, and spooled his fishing line into the water. Then he sat quietly on the stone outcrop, like a spider at the edge of its web.

Through quiet days, when flakes of light drizzled through the dense foliage and the forest floor birthed and chittered, and through days of watery cannonades, when rains detonated against the jungle canopy and made all the world one vast heaving lung, Arès sat imperturbable, his eyes little more than two polished saucers daubed on a wooden mask.

Nights were different. At dusk a violetness crept over the jungle, and Arès' stirless frame slowly immersed in a noisework of nighttime stridulations: the cicadas singing to the eve, small electrified elephant fish rustling on the water's rim, snakes slithering through the tall grass, the guttural cricketing of herons that reminded him of the slap of paper against the spokes of a bicycle wheel.

Only a few nights after Bugingo's appearance, Arès suffered the first of his waking visions. The jungle sounds suddenly died away, and silvery shadows spilled across the water to where he sat. Frightened, he turned his head. Dozens of squat, half-naked villagers massed behind him, armed with machetes and metal rakes. Fiery torches lit their scarred torsos and faces. Sometimes, he recognized Salifou standing tall among them, flames flickering about his strangely cut eyes. Slowly, they advanced.

Each time, Arès' chest cracked with fear and he spurted to his feet as fast as his wounded leg allowed. Gripped by hysteria, he bashed uncontrollably through the jungle, pursued by shadowy assailants. Sometimes, he made it back to the adobe hut, but most times he collapsed in anguish, his leg on fire, his foot twisted over some careless root. The next morning, he awoke covered with scratches and bruises. No memory of the hallucinations remained, only a lingering sense of dread.

The visions exacerbated Arès' injuries, especially to his right leg. Soon he could barely manage the hike to the pool. Often, it was impossible to make the journey back. On such occasions, he prayed for a quiet night. Then he settled his back against a mossy tree and did his best to fade into the splay of the jungle around him. Still as some ancient jungle totem, the last vestige of a long defunct tribe, he kept vigil over Mokélé Mbembé's pool.

CHAPTER 9

DECEMBER 1998

S OME THREE MONTHS AFTER his arrival, a stranger drove past Arès' hut in a small motorized tuk-tuk. Behind it rolled a lumbering wagon nearly the size of a stagecoach. It was the first time a vehicle of any sort had passed down that rut of a road on the way to the village. Having never ventured down it, Arès was surprised to discover that it in fact led anywhere.

The vehicle traced a wide bow around the hut on the way in. Seeing Arès sprawled before the door, a certain vacant tipsiness in his stare, the stranger pulled to a halt.

"*Quand le coq est ivre, il oublie la hache,*" he said in French, looking down at Arès.[12]

Arès regarded the outlandish apparition before him. Wild tufts of feathers sprouted off the driver's head, and a glistening python coiled around his neck. His torso was shelled in dried animal skins. He had large glittering eyes, a squab nose, and a well-built jaw.

"Young man, the day is getting old. You live beneath the tree of life and you pass your time in a drunken stupor. *La paresse engendre la misère. Nous ne grandissons qu'une fois.*"[13]

"I am not drunk," Arès said. "I am sitting."

"So this is the young man that stays at home while the monks go out to dance?" The stranger's voice was melodious and gay and full of eccentric timbres like rare baubles from far-off places.

---

12 When the rooster is drunk, he forgets the axe.
13 Laziness breeds misery. We only live once.

"Are you a marabout?" Arès asked. "I have a problem walking." He extended his legs. The right one tricked off at an odd angle and bucked slightly in the middle.

"Turn around. Let me see the other side."

The shirtless young man labored to his feet and then spun on his left leg. The bright sunlight revealed a tapestry of raised welts and scar tissue plunging from his shoulders down to his lumbar region and then winding in smaller striations down his right leg.

"Can you help me?" Arès asked.

The man was silent for a moment. "The scars on your body are not ceremonial. You are not from this village, are you?"

"No. I came here some time ago. Maybe a few months. I do not know. Do you have a cure for my leg?"

"My father was a marabout, but I am just a trader, my friend."

"But maybe you know something?"

"Perhaps I do. What is your name?"

"Arès."

"That is not a lucky name."

Arès settled back on the ground. "You have a luckier name, perhaps?"

"My name is Paul."

"Paul?" Arès stared at the wilderness vision before him.

"Yes," he said, and with one swift motion uncoiled the python from his neck and looped it onto the steering handles of the tuk-tuk. "So Arès, who has come from somewhere else, you were a soldier perhaps?"

"No. I was a locksmith."

"A locksmith?"

"Yes."

"This village is not a place for locks, or locksmiths."

"I know."

The trader flipped open a hidden door on the side of the wagon. A small blue-crested cock hopped out on a delicate chain-link leash and began poking at the earth. The trader's bracelets clinked musically as he reached deep within the wagon, and a low growl from some large animal accompanied the appearance of a bottle of whiskey. The wagon trembled a little as Paul broke the seal. "Do you have any glasses?"

"I have two," Arès said, and he went inside to fetch them.

The trader walked to the hut and sprinkled the sill with several amber drops. Then he filled the glasses to the brim. The men sat down in the shade of the baobab tree and sipped contentedly.

"Ah, it is good that you live here beneath the tree of life. Do you know the story of this tree?"

Arès shook his head.

"It is said that after creation, each animal was given a tree to plant. The hyena found the tree given to him ugly, and up to his old tricks he planted the baobab upside down to show his spite. This is why its roots are in the air."

"So, the tree was ruined by the hyena?"

"We cannot say ruined, just upside down. Perhaps it was an improvement. The baobab is the oldest of all the trees. It can live thousands of years, and its trunk holds enough water to nourish a village. Sometimes the tragedies that happen to us in our youth are the source of strength in our old age."

Arès continued to sip. The whiskey burned his throat pleasantly and gathered like liquid honey in the well of his stomach.

"The fruit is very salubrious," the trader continued. "You should eat it. In East Africa they make a candy out of the flesh called *ubuyu*." Paul smacked his lips. "Only never pluck one of the flowers or you will be eaten by a lion."

"It is too late," Arès said. He hobbled into the hut and ferried out a bundle of immense, crinkled white buds that had bloomed the night before.

"These flowers last only a single day. Yet you picked so many?"

"They fell into my house."

"All of these?"

"Most of them."

"Ah, then you will be eaten by several lions someday. I am sorry, my friend."

Arès spun the sinuous crown of one of the flowers and watched the whirl of its declinations.

"Maybe I should stay away from lions," he replied after a moment.

"Yes. Let us drink to that." They sipped dry their golden cups.

"What you should do my friend is soak the seeds of the baobab gourd in your water. It will protect you from crocodile attacks."

"That is quite useful."

"Yes, and I think it works even better with whiskey." The trader winked at Arès as he reached out and cracked open one of the rotten gourds laying nearby. After removing the juicy junk, he plopped two seeds in each of their glasses and refilled them to the rim.

"Arès from somewhere else," he asked, "why did you come here from somewhere else?"

"There was trouble where I am from. I had to leave."

"Trouble with your family?"

Arès revolved the albino flower thrice. "Yes."

"And you will spend the rest of your life here, sitting beneath an upside down tree, toying with wilting buds?"

"I do not know."

"Ah, *tantôt triste, tantôt gai*. That is how life goes. But perhaps you must walk again to be able to leave."

"Yes."

"I have a cure. It is the cure of the marabout, " he said. "We must kill a goat."

"I do not have money," Arès replied.

"Do not worry my friend. *Personne ne peut percer l'abcès qu'il a au dos.*[14] I would not like to come back here next year and find yet again that the occupant of this hut has died. I will take care of it. But give me time."

Three days later, he returned from Brazzaville trailing a billy goat with a black splotch of a star on its muzzle.

"This animal will give you its force," he said. Arès smoothed his hand along the animal's coarse beard and stared intensely into its two frosted eyes cut by grim rectangular slits.

---

14   No one can pierce the abscess he has on his back.

The trader anointed it with strange perfumes and oil and dressed it with feathers plucked off his blue-plumed cock. Then he hamstrung the goat and slit its throat with a rapid crisscross motion that made Arès blanch. While they chewed on its meat, the son of the marabout boiled the animal's bones.

"Undress yourself and lie down," he said.

Arès did as he was told. The trader dipped the bones in a pail of cold water glutted with baobab seeds. Then he used the bones to massage Arès along his wounds, chanting quietly: femur for femur, tibia for tibia, ribs for ribs. After a few minutes of this, Arès fell into a deep sleep.

When he woke the next day, he was cured.

That evening, Paul drove his unwieldy freightage up to the hut. He was wearing aviator goggles in addition to his python and feather tufts. The wagon bulged with merchandise like an overfull belly, and pots and pans clanked off its sides. Arès jumped down from a branch of the baobab tree, where he had been sitting, swinging his legs and whistling.

"My friend, you feel better, perhaps?"

"It is incredible. I went for a run today. I went running down that road that sent you here, and you know what I found?"

"What?"

"More jungle! There is only jungle here." He smiled an oversized smile and clapped his arms around the trader. Then he began to dance on his rejuvenated leg.

"Since you have already started running that way, maybe you will continue your journey with me?"

Arès arrested his gyrations. The color seeped out of his face. "No. I cannot. I am sorry."

"You know my friend, *la grosse grume reste un siècle dans l'eau, elle ne devient jamais crocodile.*"[15]

Arès sat down against the coiling roots of the baobab. His youthful

---

15   A big log can wallow in the water for a hundred years, but it will never become a crocodile.

face seemed lined with care. The strength that had lived there before was departed. "It is safe here," he said.

"Ah I see," Paul replied, almost as if talking to himself. *"Blessure de cœur n'est pas blessure de jambe: elle ne peut pas être recousue."*[16]

His father had been full of sayings like that, Arès remembered. He clawed back into the swamp of memory and tried to fish out a proverb or two, but all was fog, tar, and pitch.

"Ok my friend. I shall let you rest, and I will come to fetch you this time next year."

"You are leaving now?" Fear gripped his throat.

"You can come, my friend, but I have finished my business here. As you can see, my wagon is full." The wooden box trembled as he spoke, and snarls sounded from within.

"How can you travel down that road with so much weight?" Arès asked, concerned. "It is in very poor condition. You should take the main route from the center of the village."

Paul's laughter was nearly drowned out by the braying of monkeys from the trees. "My friend, *le sentier s'élargît à force d'y passer.*"[17] He clasped Arès warmly on the back.

"*A dieu,*" Arès said, "and thank you."

"*Au revoir, mon ami. À la prochaine.*"

The ungainly caravan wobbled forward over the rutted path. Near the first bend, Paul throttled the straining engine, startling a bright passel of yellow-capped weavers into flight.

---

16 A wound to the heart is not a wound to the leg. It cannot be stitched up.
17 The path widens by traveling down it.

CHAPTER 10

DECEMBER 1998–FEBRUARY 1999

I T WAS MID-FEBRUARY AND the rainy season was nearly over. Arès woke one morning to find a small travelling sack carefully placed before the entrance to the adobe hut. Inside, he found dried fish, fruit, and other provisions for the road. He remembered Bugingo's threat and, for a moment, wished he had accepted Paul's invitation all those weeks before.

Then he smiled ruefully. He had lost everything. What could they possibly do to him when the rainy season ended? This life was hardly even a life.

That night, the waking visions returned. As he careened wildly through the jungle, fleeing imaginary pursuers, he cut himself badly on a splintered log. The following night, it happened again. He woke the next morning smarting with pain and plagued by a panicked memory of Bugingo slashing at him with a knife. He knew it was no longer possible to return to the blue-green pool, so he spent the early hours of the day canvassing the river for a new place to fish.

About a kilometer closer to the village, he located a deep pool with a long sandy bottom. There, a half-submerged log, pelted with green moss, rose out of water of a deep navy blue. The river's banks were choked with lavender-colored water hyacinths that sheltered an ample population of catfish and little blue cichlids. Arès settled himself on the downed trunk and cast out a line.

The new location was backdropped by a large clearing. Sometime in the early afternoon, a group of village children arrived and began playing a makeshift game of soccer with a ball woven out of dried palm fronds. Their ecstatic shouts ricocheted off the river and brought an involuntary smile to Arès' lips. Hadn't he once played with friends in a clearing like that? It must have been not so long ago, but he could hardly remember anything.

A dozen scrambling feet kicked up clods of dirt behind him, and then a boy yelled "Here! Here!" followed by two hard whacks and a burst of elated cheers. The same boy shouted, "Sign me up with the *Leopards*! I'm going to play for Kinshasa!" and a memory came scudding out of the past with all the speed of a penalty kick.

Arès and his friends were facing off against a squad from a nearby village in a field not far from the river. All afternoon they had run out their hearts and then, just before sundown, Arès scored the winning goal to a fanfare of shouts. Félix lifted him triumphantly on his shoulders and loudly announced that he was taking his brother to Kamanyola Stadium the next day to sign him up for the national team.

He could feel his heart beat with the excitement of that day and his face flushed with pride at his older brother's praise. He was savoring the memory when something snapped on his line. Hand over hand, he slowly reeled in the catch, all sunflicks of silver. Then a shuddering cry rose from the clearing. He wedged the pole between two forked branches and raced to its source.

One of the children held a snake by its tail, and with a resounding blow, cleft its red and brown head with a machete. A young boy, in dusty green shorts, had floundered to the ground and was writhing in pain. Arès crouched beside him.

He could see the fang marks slightly above the ankle and he sent a child sprinting to the town to search for a *pierre noir*. Then he lay down beside the boy and began to suck, trying to extract the poison.

It was no use. The boy's leg tremored, and his eyes filmed over. Soon, his breath grated loudly in his chest. Quickly, Arès tourniquetted his shirt above the wound. "Look at me," he said. "Look at me." No response. He slapped the boy's cheeks and shook him vigorously, but he seemed to have fallen into a trance.

Arès began to recite a prayer under his breath. An old prayer that his mother used to utter before family meals: "*Tata na biso ya likolo…*" It had been a long time since he had mouthed the words, and he halted midway, searching for the rest. Nothing came. He looked hopelessly up at a sun that had swelled in the sky like a sore muscle.

Suddenly a shouting erupted and a dark blur carved through the barnyard grass. A gray pouch, tied with long white string, swung into Arès' outstretched hand, beside falling droplets of sweat. Arès loosened the knot and the pouch folded open like a flower. Inside, several pebbles, black as ebony, lay on white tissue paper.

He extracted two and touched them briefly to his tongue. Both of them hung there as if magnetically bound. He removed the pebbles, and when he pressed them against the fang holes, they appeared to suck onto the boy's skin.

The swelling slowed and then stopped. After a few minutes, the milkiness receded from the boy's eyes, and he surfaced as if from a nightmare. His calf slowly diminished in size. The boy sat up with a dazed look in his eyes. After about half an hour, the pebbles plopped to the ground.

A child reached out to pick them up, but Arès knocked away his hands. "Be careful!" He wrapped the *pierre noir* carefully in the white tissue and closed the pouch.

"Boil the stones in water for at least ten minutes," he told the boy who brought them. "Then place them in a cup of milk for at least an hour. Otherwise you cannot use them again. Do not touch them with your bare hands!"

The boy nodded and bounded across the meadow, trailed by a gaggle of friends. Arès lifted the wounded child. His forehead still felt feverish to the touch, and he lay limply in the crook of Arès' arms while he carried him back to the village.

The parents of the child were waiting at the outer perimeter of huts when he arrived. Wordless, the father took the child from him, and together the couple gratefully nodded their heads in Arès' direction.

Bugingo was there and he greeted Arès by shaking his hand. Arès could feel the rows of scarred protrusions rub against his fingers.

"Thank you," he said, "on behalf of the village."

"I could not let the child die."

"Of course," Bugingo said. "But we lost two children to snakes last year.

They are very dangerous animals." He looked carefully at Arès as he spoke. After a pause, he pointed at the villagers. "The people are very grateful for your actions."

Arès nodded. Then he left.

The next morning, Bugingo visited the adobe hut with the two men who had greeted Arès on the day of his arrival. One of them was carrying a plate covered with a yellow and brown cloth.

"The village council held a meeting last night, and we decided that you can stay," Bugingo announced.

"Thank you," Arès said. "Please wait." He entered the hut and fetched the travelling sack, still laden with provisions. When he walked back out, he offered it to the three men.

"Please keep it as a gift," Bugingo said. Then he motioned to the man carrying the plate. "The boy's mother prepared this for you. It is smoked fish with saka saka. She hopes that you enjoy it. She also asked that you keep the dish."

The man handed the plate to Arès. He could smell the food steaming beneath the porous cloth and his mouth watered uncontrollably. It had been months since he had tasted home-cooked food.

"This is all very kind," Arès replied.

Bugingo stepped forward and warmly shook the young man's hand. "Please accept our thanks, and please visit the village more often."

Arès nodded in assent.

The three men turned and disappeared back down the forest trail. The young man quickly squatted on the ground, and tearing the cloth off with his teeth, he scooped a delicious hand into the warm dish.

Months passed. The upside down tree shed its leaves. There was no more fruit and the tree appeared barren to the eye.

Every morning for Arès was indistinguishable from the last. The small nudge into being that was his weak morning tea. The crackle of the newspaper in which he had wrapped the leftovers of the previous day's catch. The slicing of bait with a serrated knife that the trader had gifted him.

More and more, he had trouble recalling where he was from, or how he had come to this place. His memory seemed like some bleary and fragile gauze stretched over the pit of his being. Whenever he tried to tear into the past, to cast a line of meaning into that hot abyss, his mind reeled with vertigo and he blacked out. After each of these spells he awoke, his head a vast desolation, and for days he was incapable of meaningful thought.

So he lived day by day, without future or past, tending only to the immediate needs of hunger and discomfort. After a year of bunking in the dirt, he built a cot and purchased blankets on which to sleep. Now that he had been given permission to stay, he began adventuring into the village to trade fish or his labor for supplies and household items. The villagers slowly accustomed to his presence, and Bugingo always had a spare job for him, but he grew close to no one.

Afterwards he retired to his hut or to the riverside. He had begun to inhabit his loneliness, to appreciate the solitary evenings. The sunset baked the Zaire gold and it seeped past like burnished lava or one of those honeyed rivers of legend. Slowly, he forgot what it was like to share such things with others.

Then one morning, without warning or reason, his muddied thoughts gave way to an unpleasant lucidity. He began to take note of his surroundings, to diagnose his hunger, to assess the poverty of his existence.

In the exacting sunlight, he could see how much he had regressed, as if the demons of the past had chased him into the past, and he was living out some ancestral curse. This was not what his father had wanted: his child reclining in a jungle boudoir, immersed in a cloud of swollen green flies, plucking fish out of some primordial basin.

His condition embittered him, and it added to his sense of loss. So much gone: his family, his vocation, his thousand bright assurances about life; in sum, everything he had ever known.

He wanted to weep, but it was as if someone had smoked his tear ducts dry. So instead, he began to shout. Alone in that cage of vines, he shrieked his throat hoarse, and above him the leafy trees thrashed, and the water's cool surface rippled in distress. He vented the full bellows of his lungs, and as he gasped for breath, a pair of firefinches exploded out of the reeds beside him like two sparks escaping an immense conflagration.

He wheezed, and slowly, slowly, regained his breath. The glade quieted. The river purled sedately before him.

And now what? He peered into the swirling water searching for an answer. Nothing came. Instead it dawned on him how impossibly lost he was. He mumbled a hopeless jumbled prayer and pounded the slab of stone beneath him with a fist coiled like a snake. When he looked up again, Félix was there.

He shot his back straight and rubbed his eyes. Then he thumbed them open again. Félix stood fifty meters back, urging him down a miniscule path at the edge of the clearing. Arès hesitated, but he wanted to please his brother. So he rose and paced a few meters toward the path before he seized up with fear.

Félix shook his hands vigorously, shouting at him, waving him on. But Arès was not his brother. Going down the uncharted path, seizing the future: this had been Félix's destiny, not his own. He could not even picture what lay beyond it. The very idea terrified him, and the unknown world pressed about his small domain like a sea of blindness in which he could easily drown.

So he sat back down beside the river, trembling with loss and fear.

CHAPTER 11

MARCH 2009

S IMON FOLDED UP HIS files for the day and inserted them brusquely into the wire rack holder on his desk. Then he grabbed an ornate silver pot and filled a glass with leaf-green mint tea. Without missing a beat, he extended it toward the other side of the room, where his officemate Georg peered intently at his computer.

"May Africa's elections remain as irreproachable in the future as they have been in the past!" he toasted loudly.

Georg harrumphed. "You have a strange sense of humor, even for an American."

A tall, attractive man with a statistician's charm, Georg had just returned from a three-week, German-funded mission to the Republic of Congo. Everything about him was careful and methodical, from his carefully combed brown hair, to his vigilant, unsmiling eyes and cautiously symmetrical jaw.

"There's just something about ninety-percent-plus wins and ten-term presidents that tickles my funny bone," Simon replied. "Nguesso's been head of state since what? 1980?"

"We plan on having hundreds of observers in place to ensure the integrity of the elections," Georg stated. "I am not worried."

"Yes, I'm sure this one will be a model of fairness." Simon raised the glass to his lips and drank the hot viscous tea, feeling an addict's pleasure at the saccharine rush.

"I don't know how you can drink that stuff all day long," Georg commented disapprovingly. "It's pure sugar."

"It is," Simon confirmed, sipping again. "Still working on your scheme to strap voting booths to crocodiles so you can get them into the deep bush?"

Georg shook his head. "That would be impractical, not to mention inefficient. No, I am trying to map out the polling stations in Pointe-Noire so the different ethnicities are proportionally represented, but it is rather tasking given recent demographic shifts." He bent close to the monitor, and his rectangular eyeglasses shone a watery blue in the artificial light. Behind them, two sand-colored eyes glimmered like stones on the ocean floor.

"Well don't help them too much," Simon warned. "If they finally get their act together, there won't be any more refugees, and we'll be out of a job."

Georg mis-hit his keyboard and the computer gave a loud squawk. "*Scheisse!*" he said under his breath. Then he looked up at Simon. "Our mission is to put ourselves out of a job."

"I don't know how it works in Vienna," Simon said, "but where I come from, we call that bad business."

Georg seemed poised to respond, but instead shook his head and turned up the dial on a small stereo. Congolese rumba, mixed with eccentric makeshift sounds and jaunty lyrics, flooded the room.

Simon groaned and put his hands over his ears.

At one point during his mission, Georg had boarded the ferry from Brazzaville to Kinshasa, a ten-minute boat trip that famously takes an entire day. Shortly before nightfall, a colleague rescued him from a multi-hour shakedown by the customs officials and brought him to a concert by an oddball group of handicapped street musicians. Georg had purchased their debut album, and ever since his return, the junkyard songs had been bouncing off the walls of the small office.

Simon exited the room but turned on his heel and leaned back through the open doorframe. "One thing, could we vary the music selection a bit tomorrow?"

"Listening to the same song helps me concentrate," Georg replied. He started drumming his fingers on the table to Staff Benda Bilili's "*Allons Voter.*" "Also, the theme is relevant."

Simon stuck his fingers in his ears and stepped definitively out the door. After winding through several white, airy corridors and down two flights of stairs, he left the HCR.

The ambassadorial neighborhood of Rabat, with its broad quiet bou-levards, sentineled gates, and pink profusions of bougainvillea opened up before him. Even after nearly six months in the capital, he still marveled at these perfumed streets, and reveled in the forty-minute stroll home that carried him through the monarchical splendor of the city center and into the labyrinthine ancient medina, with its sugared walls and flagstones bruised by history's passing.

But that evening he was in a rush. There was a party in one of the bohe-mian riads in *les Oudayas*, and word had gotten around that the Alliance Française had hired a fresh crop of cultural attachés. The expat community in Rabat was small to the point of being incestuous, and the prospect of new blood tickled Simon's fancy.

He flagged down one of the sprightly blue taxis that always roamed that part of town and hopped in.

"*Labes?*" he asked the driver.

"*Labes. L'hamdullilah,*" the driver replied.

"*Quartier de l'Océan. El Kanissa. Shokran,*" he instructed.

The car glided smoothly ahead. The driver was listening to Sufi devo-tional music and the twinkling sounds of sitars and the thrum of a pair of bendir drums put Simon into a quiet trance.

Soon, the taxi left the administrative sector behind and coasted down the imperial boulevard of Mohammed V toward the distant sparkle of the sea. Lined with towering palm trees that tilted toward the sky like balle-rinas en pointe, the wide four-lane boulevard was divided by a landscaped pedestrian park with dozens of neatly trimmed grass beds. Simon rolled down the window as the taxi rolled ever downwards, past the imposing red box of the Moroccan Parliament, ribbed with white Roman columns, and the tree-lined terrace of Hotel Balima, with its prosperous clientele in expensive designer clothes.

A few minutes later, they reached a roundabout beneath the tower of Hassan, circled the pale red walls of the medina, and entered the Quartier de l'Océan. The cab began to stutter across proliferating potholes, and shabby cafes with cheap laminate tables and secondhand stools crowded the sidewalks. Kiosks of nutmongers, fronted by big burlap sacks full of fresh mint leaves, alternated with the blind eyes of long-shuttered storefronts or ATMs with handwritten "Out of Service" signs.

The streets were livelier there, but the dress was either non-European, colorful djellabas over dusty babouches, or had the castoff character of workmen's clothes. The buildings were functional blocks with worn facades painted in light yellows or dirtied whites, marred by brown amoebic blotches wherever the paint had peeled. An indecent number of auto repair shops floated by the open taxi windows.

At a roundabout presided over by a layered cake of a church with a conical white dome and a peaked green roof, Simon said, *"Sufi Sufi. Shokran."*

He hopped out of the cab and began striding purposefully ahead. Soon, he turned up a road that rose like an immense ramp toward the sky. At its apex stood a six-story building with a facade of faded sunflower yellow. The building's lower windows were armored by thick wrought-iron grills. Directly across the street, a man in a gray burnouse leaned into the open hood of a three-wheeled Toyota Camry and tapped a hammer against some inscrutable part of the car's engine.

Simon sprinted inside and up the six flights of stairs. He frowned slightly as loud shouting issued from the fifth-floor apartment. On the sixth floor, he thrust open his front door and stopped in his tracks.

Beneath a small cloud of lazily drifting flies, a half-eaten watermelon spilled its bright red juices across the dining room table. Nearby, a serving dish brimming with butchered meat sat on the sideboard of a smoking grill. A blue chair lay felled on the floor beside an unrolled sleeping bag, several beaten suitcases, and a collection of soccer jerseys with United Emirates and Paris-St. Germain logos. A cigarette burned unattended on the barman's counter, and the suction of air from the opening front door caused a detonation of white ash to explode over the couch.

"Lise!" he cried. "Nathalie?"

It had been barely a month since the two interns from the HCR had moved in, but each day provided new evidence that Simon's once comfortable living quarters were gradually transforming into a squat. Social work students from the Universities of Grenoble and Lyon, they came from backwater villages in forgotten corners of France. Mornings, they dressed for work as if they were heading to a folk music festival instead of a regional bureau of the United Nations. Evenings, he often passed them mingling with the Moroccan Rastas, those medusa-headed fixtures at the *Place Bab el Had*, who fogged the sunsets with fat clouds of hashish, foot-rocked to reggae, and conversed madly in an affected, Jamaican-inflected English.

In a rational world, he would never have offered them housing, but he wasn't officially permitted to be in that neighborhood of Rabat. The Quartier de l'Océan was considered a *zone tendue*. Terrorist threats had increased in recent years, and rules had gone into effect restricting cadre employees of the HCR to the business district of Agdal, the lifeless condos of Hal Ryad, or the gated beachside communities half an hour out of town where most of the HCR's executives resided. Simon's lease pre-dated the new security measures, but his decision to stay had resulted in unwelcome controversy.

For some reason, the rules did not apply to interns; apparently their kidnapping and ransom wasn't a cause for alarm. He was under official orders to move out, but he liked the proximity to the medina and the beach. He hoped that by taking the two girls in, the orders would be harder to enforce. He often regretted this decision.

Nathalie burst into the room. "You summoned, mi-lord."

"Har har," he replied. The two of them made a striking contrast. He in his wool blazer, oxford shirt, ironed chinos, and derbies; Nathalie in polka-dot fisherman pants with flared bottoms, a loud green top, and thin-soled Birkenstocks. Short and squat, she had a pretty face with lively eyes, a big brash mouth, and wild waves of sun-tinted brown hair, from which a single dreadlock wriggled like a snake.

"It looks like a war zone in here," he continued.

"Yes, the rebels stormed the living room earlier today, but we managed to fight them off."

"I see we had some serious losses." He swept his arm before him. As he did, he heard a guitar strumming from the recesses of the apartment. "And it sounds like there's still some fighters camped out here."

"Yes. It's our new flatmate, Kinani. Doesn't he play well?"

Simon screwed his eyes together and stared at Nathalie. "What do you mean 'new flatmate?'"

"Kinani got kicked out of his place, so we're putting him in Lise's room and the two of us will share my room from now on."

"What?" Simon was momentarily speechless. "Did you ever consider asking the person who let you live here?"

"What does it change for you?" Nathalie flexed her knees and placed her hands on her hips—a poise which, Simon had come to understand, indicated gross disapproval of his actions. "You have your own private bathroom."

"We're not running a hostel here," he said through clenched teeth. "Can I remind you that this is UN housing?" The sound of the guitar increased in strength, and Simon made out the notes from a Beatles song that tickled his memory.

"Can I remind you that we're permitted to be here and you aren't, Mr. Junior Professional Officer?"

Simon felt his hackles rise. "So you're kicking me out of my own place?"

"If you have a problem living with a real African, instead of just giving them handouts and sermons, then maybe it's time to go join the official UN Staff."

Simon clenched his jaw.

It was just one more reminder that he should have kept with his own. His parents had warned about this, about what they called his "little heresies"—his preference for the colorful over the practical, his irrational short-lived mutinies against the rules of the game.

All his life, he had heeded the itinerary handed to him at birth. From boarding school, to Princeton, to a Master's in International Security at Sciences Po Paris, France's factory for its gilded elite, the promised land was always Geneva. Geneva, with its glittering glass offices and glittering blue lake. "I see frosty swans in your future," his father liked to joke.

Then he had responded to an open call for a position at a microfinance organization in Rwanda.

"If you want to go peer around with a lamp in the wilderness," his mother had tartly remarked, "that's your prerogative, but my friend Joanne at the State Department is looking to fill a few positions."

Simon politely demurred. Over the years, he had felt a growing resistance to his prefab life. It was too predictable, too back-office. He preferred to be in the field. He wanted to be linked with the big movements of things, the drama of disaster. His parents might picture him at cocktail parties in D.C., but he wanted to bounce down dirt roads on the back of moto taxis and interview *genocidaires*. The long-term goal was still Geneva. He had just opted for a slightly more scenic route. Still, it was not without its inconveniences.

"Anyway, it's the law of the desert," Nathalie said, taking a more mollifying tone.

"The law of the desert?"

"He has nowhere to go. If you come across someone in the desert and that person asks you for help, even if it's your worst enemy, you have to offer them three days and three nights of shelter in your tent."

Simon harrumphed. It was the usual half-mystical, faux-indigenous fluff that he expected from his flatmates. The two girls ingested heavy doses of left-wing ska, paid close attention to the phases of the moon, and left books around like Raoni's *Memoir of an Indian Chief*. The HCR needed people like these, who saw this work as a calling instead of a career. But their dedication interfered with the efficient administration of the refugees' files. So they caused their little scenes but never rose high in the ranks.

"He can stay until he finds another place."

"I think you're going to like him," she asserted brightly. Simon followed Nathalie through a white mullioned archway and down a spacious corridor painted in creamy lemon yellows. For the first time, he noticed a small peace sign etched onto her left shoulder in *encre de Chine*.

The door to her room was open. Inside, two single beds crammed into a tight corner beneath a colorful web of prayer flags. A funnel of light poured through a narrow window and illuminated a young man with a shaved head, in a white soccer jersey and jeans, leaning over a cedarwood guitar.

The young man looked up with a broad smile and dimpled cheeks. His eyes were remarkable. They sparkled like two precious stones buried in the coffee-colored earth of his complexion. Below a high regal forehead descended a fine, straight nose and a clean jaw. When he stood up to stretch out his hand, he revealed a lanky, cat-like frame that moved with surprising speed and precision.

"Ah, you must be l'Américain," he declared in a deep, resonant voice.

Simon smiled. "Guilty as charged. Nice to meet you..."

"Kinani," the young man replied. "Are you coming from a funeral? You're dressed to kill."

"We work in an office." Simon stared disapprovingly at Nathalie. "I try to maintain a professional appearance."

"Of course," Kinani replied. "Thank you for welcoming me into your fine home." He smiled ingratiatingly as he spoke, but his eyes sparkled with mirth, and his voice had the tone of a prince acquiescing to bed down in the stables for a night.

"*Marhaba*," Simon said.

"Ah you speak Arabic?"

"*Shwiya Shwiya*." He smiled. "When in Rome..."

Kinani chuckled, still grinning an outsized grin. "Render unto Caesar what is Caesar's due."

Simon shot his new flatmate a second glance. The religiosity of Africans continually amazed him. One would think that they would have cast out the Church along with the colonizers. Instead, even fashionable young men like Kinani still clung to the cross, like a life raft tossed from the sinking ship of the past. "A man of the bible, I see," Simon remarked with a raised eyebrow.

Kinani replied with a hearty, rolling laugh. "Not at all. It's a phrase we often used in Zaire. We had our own Caesar, you know."

"You're Congolese? From Kinshasa?"

"No. Gbadolite in the north." Simon gave him a quizzical look. "Don't worry, l'Américain. You wouldn't know it unless you like catching diseases in jungles."

"Rings a bell," Simon said unconvincingly. But the name *did* ring a bell. Where had he heard it before? He must have studied Kinani a bit too intensely, because the young man's smile suddenly lapsed, and Simon caught a glimpse of something else—a haughtiness that seemed the vestige of another life, like a fire seen from a great distance. Then the sprawling smile reasserted itself.

"And you, l'Américain. Where are you from? East Coast? West Coast?" Kinani asked, a bit of rhythm in his voice.

"East Coast."

Kinani smiled even wider and strummed the guitar: "I got love for New York City, and they got love for me and B-I-G…"

He continued singing the lyrics while Simon inspected Nathalie's room. The posters of reggae stars thumbtacked into cheap gypsum walls, and the narrow beds, buried under mounds of crumpled clothes, mala bead bracelets, and flea market jewelry, filled him with unaccountable dismay. Finally, he cut Kinani off with an unenthusiastic, "Thanks."

"Let's go sit in the living room," he added, and strode out into the hall. As he walked past the girls' bathroom, he looked in. It was already a forlorn affair, with a soapy blouse hanging off a tall brass washboard and a plastic pail brimming with dirty suds. Now it was to be shared by three people. The whole arrangement spelled trouble.

"Speaking of jungle diseases, I see you're building a habitat here," Simon observed as they entered the living room.

"We have guests coming," Nathalie replied in a surly tone. "Lise is at the market buying vegetables. We want to welcome Kinani to his new home."

"If you hang around, l'Américain, you may even enjoy yourself," Kinani added, his wide smile undiminished. Simon wondered if he ever stopped smiling, or if his mouth had frozen like that as a way of placating white people. "The rest of my hip-hop group is coming over and we're going to rehearse some songs."

"Hip-hop group!" Simon nearly sputtered. "You have a hip-hop group? Is that what you do?"

"Does that bother you?" Nathalie asked, her face glowing with satisfaction.

Kinani walked over to the charcoal grill and stoked the fire. When the flames began to dart their orange tongues through the cooking grid, he went to the fridge and removed several beers. "Actually, I'm finishing a

Master's in applied physics at the Université Internationale de Rabat. But a little fun is food for the soul. You should try it sometime."

"Oh," Simon said, relieved. "My father warned me against fun when I was a boy. Apparently it leads to regrets."

"Good fun does," Kinani replied. Simon had trouble reading him. His white teeth lined up in his mouth like an impregnable wall. They were surprisingly orderly and sparkled unnaturally, like a dental advertisement. There was no way to know if Kinani spoke in jest, or if there was some barb to his comments.

"So what are you doing here, l'Américain?" Kinani asked, as he opened a silver can with a small pop and handed it to Simon.

"This is my apartment," Simon replied. "Actually, I don't know what everyone else is doing here."

Kinani let loose a rollercoaster of a laugh. "I mean, what brought you to Rabat from the East Coast? Why did you decide to come live with the king?"

"The king?" Simon blinked confusedly for a moment. "Oh, you mean why did I leave a peaceful democratic country for a moderately corrupt monarchy?" This time he grinned as well. "I applied for a position in Geneva, but headquarters thought I needed some more field experience first, so I ended up here."

Kinani involuntarily spat out half his beer. "Field experience?" he exclaimed, wiping his arm on a rag.

"Yeah, they insist on a certain familiarity with the terrain before you can advance to the supervisory roles at headquarters."

"So we're field experience for you?" Kinani asked, his smile waning.

Simon looked at Nathalie, who had crossed her arms disapprovingly. "Your friend is a little touchy," he remarked.

"What the hell is field experience?" Kinani continued. "Is this the jungle? Are you here to hunt monkeys with rifles?"

"Honestly this living room is beginning to feel like a jungle," Simon grumbled. Then he leaned a hand on the dining room table and immediately yanked it back. "Is this *amlou* on the table?" He held up the brown mess of his hand toward Nathalie. "What do you do? Do you just pour the *amlou* on the table now and wipe the bread on it as a snack?"

"I'll clean it up," Nathalie said tersely and headed into the open kitchen.

Simon wiped his hands on a paper towel, but it only smeared the oily gunk over his fingers. Then he looked up at Kinani. "Don't take it so personally."

"Said the fisherman to the fish."

"Sorry, I don't follow."

"Don't worry, I'm just one of the animals in the field," Kinani said. This time, Simon could sense a cold register to his voice. "It's fine. It reminds me of a joke about Americans."

"Oh yeah?" Simon replied, while Nathalie exited the kitchen bearing a massive yellow sponge lathered in white froth.

"What's the difference between an American and a pot of yogurt?"

"You got me."

"Unlike an American, if you leave the yogurt alone for a few years, it will eventually develop a culture."

"Funny," Simon said, scrunching his hands between a wad of paper towels. "Maybe culture is what you find in the field."

"If the animals don't eat you first," Kinani retorted, his features perceptibly hardening. Simon quietly sized him up. Although Kinani barely came up to his shoulders, there was a military rigidity to his posture and a litheness to his movements that suggested an athletic or otherwise physical past.

"What is the matter with you two?" Nathalie snapped. She attacked the table with the sponge, swirling the honey-brown *amlou* into the soapy lather in a way that reminded Simon of a late-period Rothko.

"Oh the refugees don't bite," he replied, ignoring Nathalie.

"What do they do, then?" Kinani asked, sipping his beer with a funny expression on his face. The haughty, piercing look had returned to his eyes and Simon wondered if his affable exterior was merely a mask.

"Mainly they hold out their hands and we put things in it," Simon continued. "Loans, medical help, microfinancing."

"The refugees must have it easy, then," Kinani said, his smile rushing back in resplendently, like clouds parting to let in the sun. "They just sit back and wait for the riches to rain down from heaven." He lifted up his arms in a fake hallelujah.

The doorbell rang.

"If you'll excuse me," Simon said. He strode to the front door and opened it. His flatmate Lise stood there, market bags sagging off her arms like hanging gourds. Simon lifted several and swung them into the living room, staggering under their weight.

"*Merci*," she said, and arched her spine contentedly. She had a slim, balletic build that she expertly concealed under a billowing peasant blouse. Like Nathalie, she wore tan fisherman pants and leather sandals, but she was self-contained where Nathalie was expansive. Her light-brown hair was pulled back into a tight bun and a dainty nose ring glittered in her left nostril, suggesting a wayward side to her character that Simon had never seen.

They set the bags on the kitchen table. When Simon turned to shut the door, he heard boisterous shouting. A group of stylish young men in Yankees hats and track pants bounded up the stairs, laughing and jostling each other. Some had diamond studs in their ears. Others sported silver rings on their hands and flashy gold chain necklaces. All wore name-brand sunglasses, which Simon assumed were fake.

As the young men entered the apartment, he tried to absorb a series of increasingly exotic names—Thierry, Désiré, Soli, Senam—that reminded him of the ones he came across daily in the HCR dossiers.

The living room filled with congratulatory shouts of "Nice digs, my man," convoluted hand clasps, multi-stage fist pounds, and raucous laughter.

Simon turned to Nathalie and said, "I'll be right back."

He fled down the lemon-yellow corridor and opened a large wooden door at its end. Shutting the door, he stepped into a high-ceilinged room almost twice the size of the living room. A window looked out onto a small private balcony and framed a postcard-perfect expanse of a sparkling blue sea, the gray backs of seagulls, and a turquoise fishing boat puffing contently along the horizon. On the far side of the room was a small bathroom covered in hand-painted Spanish tiles.

The room's centerpiece was a massive king-size bed with a large wooden headboard. The headboard was engraved with the motif of an African fisherman perched on a boulder before an onrushing stream. The scene was rendered in naïve woodcut style, the water's force conveyed by angled gashes in the wood. The features of the fisherman were exaggeratedly tribal, his long oval face endowed with a great hooded brow and a heavy shelf of a jaw, similar to a Congolese war mask. The fishing rod and line were two elegant arcs, the leaping fish ovals hatched at the tails.

Simon found the woodcut tacky, but sometimes, after a stressful day at the office, he liked to imagine himself as the placid fisherman, spending his contemplative hours perched over a pole. It was a fantasy of a simple, satiated life, and it helped lull him to sleep on troubled nights.

He showered quickly and swapped out his button-down for a T-shirt, evening blazer, and light scarf. When he walked back into the living room, Thierry, Soli, Kinani, and a tall newcomer in a canary-yellow wax print shirt were performing before a crowd of strangers:

On est parti de rien
On fait tout de rien
On rêve en group de rien
Slam coute pour rien

Ils auront le sud
Ils auront le nord...[18]

Simon walked straight up to Nathalie. "I don't like that guy," he said.
"Well, we do, and he's here to stay."
"Until he finds another place," Simon reminded her.
The rappers broke off to a tumult of whistles, shouts, and clapping.
"So what did you think, l'Américain?" Kinani asked, striding purposefully toward Simon and clapping him on the shoulder. "You come from the land of hip-hop."
"You guys are good," Simon said grudgingly. They had been good.
Kinani smiled wide. "Maybe we'll get you on the mic later on."

---

18 We began with nothing / We've done everything with nothing / Together we dream of nothing / Slam costs nothing / They will own the south / They will own the north

"I wouldn't do that," Nathalie cautioned. "They don't freestyle much at his country club."

Simon waved his hands sheepishly. "I have another engagement tonight." He looked over at Lise and Nathalie. "You're not coming to the party in les Oudayas?"

"Maybe later," Lise replied with a friendly glance. Nathalie just shook her head.

Kinani grabbed the tall newcomer by the arm and pulled him toward Simon. "This is my man, Aristide."

Aristide raised his fist and pumped it with Simon's. "Peace and love for Africa," he said.

"Right," Simon replied. He could see now that Aristide's shirt was covered with miniscule black and white adobe huts floating amidst a wash of canary yellow. It looked vaguely political. "Are you all Congolese?" he asked, turning back to Kinani.

"No. My man Aristide here is from Cameroon, Thierry is from Gabon, Soli is from Senegal, and our vocalist, who isn't here yet, is Moroccan. Together we are AMER," Kinani replied.

"Bitterness?" Simon asked confused.

Aristide gave a laugh that shot up from his stomach and rattled around in his chest before bursting into the room. "No my man, not the French word 'amer.' We are African Musical Entertainment Records."

"Ha. Good one," Simon said. "Well make yourself at home. I'm sure we'll all see each other when I get back."

"*Meshi mushkil*," Kinani said.

"What does that mean?"

"It means 'no problem,' l'Américain. You should learn that phrase. The more you say it, the easier life gets. *Meshi mushkil*. No problem, man!"

"Thanks for the Afrocentric advice." Simon turned to leave.

He was about to open the door when the bell rang again. Two Moroccan girls with the burnt features of the desert were standing in the hallway. One was dressed conservatively in an olive-green tunic with a dark blue hijab cowled over her head. She had a pursed face with a pretty, hooked nose, and dark olive-green eyes. The other girl had broad smiling features and a profusion of wavy black tresses that cascaded over her shoulders. Fine freckles speckled the wide wings of her nose and trail-blazed along her high cheekbones. Her jade green eyes were almond-shaped, and profligately colored. She was wearing a bright red tunic that cascaded in a daring cleft down the center of her chest and ran off with Simon's breath.

"*Coucou!*" Nathalie shouted.

Kinani approached from behind and placed an authoritative hand on Simon's shoulder.

"This is Nadia," he announced, "the singer in our group. And she," he said, pointing to the girl in the olive-green tunic, "is her sister Ouled."

"*Enchanté,*" Simon said, and meant it for once. Ouled held out her hand, and then Nadia leaned in for a *bise*. A collection of silvery bracelets jangled on her arms as their bodies seesawed back and forward. Then they switched places, the two girls entering the apartment and Simon heading out into the hallway. He turned around one last time, his foot on the stairs, and his eyes caught Nadia's like a fish snapping on a lure. Then the door shut behind him.

Moments later, he was ambling down Avenue Abdelkrim lost in thought. His feet carried him past the *Centre de droits de l'homme*, with its perennial entourage of sleek black Mercedes; past the arched gateway to the medina, whose crenellated contours made him think of a fairy-tale castle; past shoemakers bent beneath dangling bulbs, who twisted soles in their hands looking for cracks; past blood-stained butchers waiting beside flayed carcasses that buzzed with fat green flies; past juicemongers half-hidden behind tall citrus pyramids, till thirsty with thinking, he paused.

"*Wahed asir limun,*" he said, and watched the man harvest three oranges and deftly halve and press them. He accepted the sloshing, sticky glass, and sipped contently, occasionally spitting out a seed. His eyes were turned toward the bustle of the street but registered little of what was going on. In his head, he kept turning over the same scene: the door had opened to his apartment and Africa, with all its contradictions, had tumbled in— its track-suited hip-hop crews and wax print revolutionaries, its bohemian expats, the hijabed sister beside the starlet singer. And there, at its center, was Kinani—ringmaster to that circus, with his showman's smile.

Something about him troubled Simon, some menace lying behind those constantly bared teeth.

The sudden glug-glug and subsequent roar of several firing generators reminded him that night was approaching. Then the muezzin's voice began to throb in the evening air. The words *"Hayya 'ala-s-Salah,"* but elongated, distorted, unfurled across the sky, and he instinctively lifted his head toward the heavens. The call to prayers had begun.

He hurried toward les Oudayas. To the left stretched whitewashed walls and a weedy collection of graves called the Cemetery of Martyrs. Far below it, rising on stilts out of a metallic blue sea, stood the king's Surf Club, where Simon had twice taken longboard lessons. Then the pavement ramped toward the red fortress on the hill, and he sped up splayed imperial steps and passed through the massive ochre gate that led into les Oudayas.

It was the calmest part of the city, and Simon often spent afternoons ambling through its winsome blue and white lanes. Now, as the day cooled into evening, beachgoers strolled back from the nearby *plage de Rabat*. Simon passed swim-suited Rastas carrying slick surfboards under their arms and plump parents steering candy-faced children over the cobblestones.

He turned into the side streets, heading toward the riad where the party was to be held. The passage there was narrow and labyrinthine, but of uncommon beauty, the buildings shelled in soft lime, their decorative front doors made of forged iron and wrapped in vividly colored moldings. The lanes rose and fell, with playful little steps, and Simon navigated between massive blue amphoras crowned with red azaleas. As he neared the perimeter of the fortress, he heard Gnawa music rising from an esplanade that overlooked the city beach. Wanting another moment with his thoughts, he tracked the lilting desert tune to its source.

A group of musicians, with heavy copper castanets and three-stringed wooden lutes, played trancelike songs before a group of hand-clapping young men in baseball caps. They were bathed in a hazy reflective light that announced the nearness of the sea. Simon walked to the edge of the esplanade and looked out over the vermilion wash and the wheeling parade of hundreds of evening swallows. To his left, couples with chastely clasped hands spread along the ramparts, while muffled shouts rose from the golden sands below. The sun had begun to set, and a papier-mâché moon hung in a plum-colored sky with an expression of surprise on its face.

Simon listened to the melodic desert music and watched all this pleasant peace and thought how lucky he was to have been spared Morocco's blacker sides. He knew they were there. He read the reports. He dutifully cata-logued the daily affronts to life and dignity recounted to him by refugees in the HCR's spartan interview rooms, to the refreshing hum of a whirring fan.

But his duties rarely carried him beyond the well-sentineled walls of the bureau, and the same, in sum, could be said of his company. His free time was spent with the Gallic-heavy expat community, partying in bohemian riads or attending cultural events at the Alliance Française. It had been that way in Rwanda too: riding around all day with American aid workers in SUVs, "discussing genocide and the weather" as they liked to put it. Evenings spent at the Hotel Milles Collines, trading rounds with an assort-ment of UN personnel, South African mercenaries, and the occasional BBC reporter. For the most part, it had felt like a curated adventure.

His few years of humanitarian work had shown him that this sort of par-titioning was common. There was a tacit understanding. Despite officially being in the field, they did whatever they could to keep the field at bay.

But now his home had been raided by all the mayhem of that continent, by people from countries where they consulted with shamans and lynched neighbors with burning tires. And worse, they made no allowance for this difference. He could see Kinani bridling at the mention of "field experi-ence," and felt that he would have to raise defenses as strong as the fortress of les Oudayas to survive the coming months. He wondered what troubles these people would bring.

A cold wind kicked up off the water and murmurs of dissatisfaction rose from the lovers to his left. Simon shivered and contracted his body, but he did not leave. The first pinpoints of light appeared in the crepuscular sky and he stared at them, and at the small sea that lay between him and Europe, and at the vast ocean that lay between him and home. The muezzin droned on, hypnotically, cyclically, suffusing the evening with the hymns of the twice-told prayer. The spell of his voice stole over Simon, and slowly, slowly, the chant of the muezzin became the wail of ancient voices rising from the sea, and the sea which had glowed with soft violets and purples became a bloodshed of crimson, and all this seemed the song of some unnamable catastrophe that would never end.

Then the muezzin launched into the closing refrains of the *Adhan,* suffusing the world with its holy sounds. Three times, the phrase *"Allāhu akbar,"* with ever-increasing operatics, pushed toward the heavens. The divine voice faded and the wind hushed. Gray seagulls wheeled and squawked overhead. Simon took a deep salty breath and listened to the hollow boom that reported the nearby violence of the sea. All of a sudden, his body tensed. The surrounding air seemed to gather unto itself and condense. After a moment of pregnant silence, the last refrain of *God is Great* exploded into the sky and the flaming orb of the sun burned into the sea.

Nighttime had arrived.

CHAPTER 12

MARCH 2000–MAY 2004

A T THE END OF the rainy season, the trader returned. He rumbled up to the hut, trailing his discombobulate wagon, piled high with all of life's paraphernalia. The engine cut, he released the blue plumed cock, and with grand flourishes spirited out an unopened bottle of whiskey.

Arès was in the same position as last time, recumbent against the trunk of the baobab, a listless gaze in his eyes. Only this time he held the day-long flower in his hands, twirling it slowly. He seemed not to notice the trader until Paul sat down beside him, still wearing his headdress and aviator goggles.

"You are back?" Arès said surprised.

"If you pass by a tree and it gives you fruit, you will pass by again," the trader replied with a resplendent smile. "How have you been, my friend?"

"I am alive."

"That, *mon ami*, is not certain. But congratulations anyhow. *Avoir beaucoup de mil est bon, mais se trouver en vie l'année prochaine vaut beaucoup mieux*," he added in French.[19] "Do you still have your glasses?"

"They are inside," Arès replied, smiling at the trader's insistent good cheer.

Paul entered the hut and came out carrying the two tarnished cups.

"Your snake is gone," Arès remarked.

"Yes. There was a drought, so I gave him to some farmers north of Bangui to help them call the rain."

---

19   To be rich is good, but to still be alive the next year is worth even more.

"You have been to Central African Republic?"

"I have been everywhere, my friend. I have been to Cameroon, to Togo, to Gabon, to Mali, to Burkina Faso, to Nigeria, and even a little into Niger, but it is too hot there. The sun bites your feet when you walk. And you, my friend? Perhaps you have been busy in my absence?"

"I have been here."

"Always before your tree?"

"No, I go to the river to fish, and I have begun to go to the village sometimes to work."

"As far away even as the village? Let us drink then to travel."

"*Santé.*"

"*Santé.*"

Arès felt flushed after the first sips. It had been over a year since he had tasted alcohol.

"I am here and in Brazzaville for a week. If fortune smiles, I will return afterwards to Yaoundé. Maybe you would like to come with me this time and see my country?"

"Why should I move away?" Arès asked. "What has moving ever brought me?"

"Maybe you will find something that will change your mind. If not, you can always come back. Or perhaps you will keep going. A serpent, it is said, eats by moving."

Arès drew his finger through the red soil beside his hut. Then he shook his head.

"My friend," Paul continued, "when you travel it is best to be like the gold diggers in Venezuela. In the beginning, they found false rocks and sold them to survive. But they journeyed on and in the end they finally struck gold."

"As my father used to say," Arès replied, "*la première richesse est la paix.*"[20]

Paul removed his headdress and sat down beside the young man, placing a comforting hand on his shoulder. "Peace is a fine thing, but a man without friends is truly poor. You remind me of a wilderness hermit seeking spiritual enlightenment. Did you know that in the deserts of Niger there

---

20   The greatest wealth is peace.

are men who live on the tops of tall pillars and meditate in the high sun and who eat only locusts? Would that sort of life appeal to you?"

Arès looked over at the trader. "No," he said. "I am not trying to come closer to God."

"But I do not think that in my absence your family has come to join you?"

"No."

"Then perhaps there is a young woman in the village who has caught your eye. *Le sacrifice est le premier signe de l'amour.*"[21]

"I am more interested in the fish."

Paul laughed out loud, and even Arès cracked a smile. "Well, my friend, I could use your humor on the road with me. And maybe you could use mine." He gave a waggish, gap-toothed grin and clinked his glass against Arès'.

"I think you should leave me in peace." Arès put down the glass.

"*Qui se perd dans la forêt se fâche contre ceux qui le ramènent sur le bon chemin.*"[22]

Arès sighed. The trader was relentless.

He looked down at the flower. It reminded him of a white egret. He wished that he had been born a bird. Or some sort of forest animal. Animals knew how to behave from the start. The hardest thing about being human was being asked to make something of one's life.

He looked up again. "And what if I die abroad?"

"If you're afraid to die, maybe you should not have been born."

"You have an answer for everything."

"My friend, I do not know what happened to you, but it is also part of this world. You cannot hide from it in the forest. It will find you here too, just as the fire that warms our homes also burns our hands. This is why they say, *c'est le feu qui cuit notre nourriture, mais quand le feu détruit le village, tout le monde s'en plaint.*"[23]

"I think if you knew what happened to me, you would not say such things."

---

21 Sacrifice is the first sign of love.
22 A person lost in the forest gets angry at those who lead him back onto the right path.
23 Fire cooks our food, but when the same fire destroys the village, everyone complains.

"Then you should tell me on the road to Yaoundé. I think that you are still too close to what happened. Some distance might help. *C'est en gardant une certaine distance qu'on s'échauffe à un feu violent.*"[24]

"I cannot," the young man said. He stared up at the canopy of green, his eyes glazed and distant.

The trader finished his glass of whiskey and set the blue-crested bird back in the wagon. "I will come by again before I leave for Yaoundé, and we will drink another glass of whisky. But I will not importune you. I think maybe you will know when it is time to go. The ripe fruit falls by itself."

Arès' sides quaked with the unabashed hearty laugh of his youth.

"What is it?" Paul asked.

"You see, my father always used to say, *si tu manges le fruit d'un grand arbre, n'oublie pas de remercier le vent.*"[25]

The trader laughed in turn. "This is true as well."

For four more years, Arès sat beside the sunset sunrise river and watched the currents of his life and the mottled terrors of the past flood downstream. He sat golem-still, entranced by the river's endless eddying: its water-riddles, pregnant with jungle morass, whose meanings he would never unlock. Only the occasional flicker of irritation, when the snout of a mosquito bore deep into his skin, or a fog of gnats drifted too near, or a red parade of ants trooped over his legs, distinguished him from his surroundings.

For the most part his mind was quiet, empty. Only sometimes things rose out of the waters, husks of once life wading close from other shores, whirlpools of memory that drew him in—trances broken by the sharp call of predators at dusk or the hundredth tug of a killifish on his line.

In his sixth year in Dongo—years that he had long since ceased to count—Arès stood upriver from his former post. The creeping moss had devoured his half-submerged log, and he had begun using nets to sieve fish from the fast-moving rapids upstream.

---

24 It's by keeping your distance that you warm yourself on a violent fire.
25 If you eat the fruit of a tall tree, do not forget to thank the wind.

Near to where he stood was a crossing of slick boulders and the trapped remnants of toppled trees. Arès was swooping a long-handled net through the morning torrents, when he heard a loud splash and cries for help. Out of carelessness, ineptitude, or something else, a man had tumbled into the white water. He was glugging in and out of the river, his hands deliriously snatching at the gripless stuff, like a butterfly struggling to free itself from a spider's web.

Two villagers careened along the banks, shouting their lungs hoarse, trying to outpace the river's rush and rescue their friend, but they were blocked at every turn by lush jungle growth.

Arès' landing gear was too frail to catch a man, so he grabbed a nylon casting net and waded out into the water, holding tight to the low-hanging branch of a sapele tree. The rapids swirled around his thighs, stuttering him downstream, stunning him with their might.

He did not know how to swim, and his body instinctively recoiled toward the banks. He steeled himself and held his ground.

He could see the man somersaulting through the water, submerging for longer and longer periods of time. He was well out of reach, so when his floundering body seemed about ten meters upstream, Arès whistled loudly and cast his net as far as he could, hoping the man would snag against it.

Two seconds later he was swept off his feet, head engulfed in rushing water, his right hand clutching desperately to the rapidly diminishing length of a leafy branch. The man had grabbed onto the net and the pro-pulsion of his body had flipped Arès like a deck of cards.

The man began crawling upstream along the net, while the tendons in Arès' arms burned. He could feel the skin slowly peel off his hand as it scraped across the rough knurls of bark. Hysteria stormed through his eyes.

The man dragged himself ever nearer, torturously slow. Soon Arès knew they would never make it. He could feel the circumference of the wood diminish to a vanishing point and he could not hold on. He took a deep breath and prepared to shoot into the bath of white.

A hand grabbed his wrist. Salvation! Arès craned his neck backwards. A mid-sized man, his right foot braced against a mossy boulder, his face contorted with effort, struggled to hold them all in place.

Then, like some cosmic joke, all three men catapulted into the rapids. As the sun submerged and the sky flipped on its back, a martial din thundered through Arès' head, a detonation of ire against all of eternity.

Three corkscrewing bodies drilled downstream, heading for a waterfall some fifty meters below.

Arès clawed through the water with his one free hand, holding tight to the net with the other. For a second his mouth frogged above the river's lip and he sucked a breath of swampy air.

Then the streaming aqueous world again, all dim blues and muddy browns, and soon world's end as space and time bucketed out into the abyss, and all three men flung headlong over the falls.

For an instant, Arès awoke. Six years of dreaming sped from his eyes, and a roar of affirmation burst from his soul, a deep world-quaking cry for life. And with an incredible jolt, his drop came to an end.

Arès rocked gently in the air on a nylon swing. A couple seconds later, he swung past the man he had rescued, hanging from the other end of the net.

They noticed each other and began to smile and shake with laughter, uncontrollable, exuberant laughter. Looking up, they could see the jutting rock on which the net had snagged. Harmonizing their movements, they climbed up the nylon web toward the outcrop.

It was a tricky operation pulling themselves over the ledge, but once there, they sidled along a water-dashed ridge and, grappling from stone to stone, arrived at the summit of the falls. In minutes, they pulled themselves over to the safety of the riverbank.

Arès gasped, and smiled, and basked in the warmth of the sun. Again he laughed, tears springing out of his eyes.

What would his father think of him now? A clown hanging by a fishnet above a waterfall. Félix and Yika would have been rolling on the floor with laughter. He wished he could tell them. Tell them about their fisherman brother, who had begun fishing men. Instead, he stood up in the glorious sunlight and strode purposefully back toward the village.

One hundred meters downstream, the battered frame of the third man washed gently along the banks. Then the river swallowed it whole and soon all that was left was the popping of bubbles and a swirl of olive-green water.

A month later the trader arrived. As he had for the previous four years, Paul asked Arès if at last the fruit was ripe.

The young man smiled broadly. "Let us go, my friend."

CHAPTER 13

MAY 2004

A RÈS CLIMBED ONTO THE pillion seat on the rear of the tuk-tuk. It shifted unsteadily beneath his weight and he inspected it nervously. Paul looked at him and laughed and then throttled the engine to life. The machine juddered forward over the uneven forest path into palisades of green.

As they neared the forest's edge, Arès looked back at the sunny glade. The adobe hut sat beneath the bright bloom of the baobab tree. It had sheltered him for so many years and he wondered if he would ever see it again. He nearly jumped off the moving vehicle, so strong was his momentary longing to stay. Then they veered around a bend and a canopy of jade hid it from view.

The rutted path twisted for hours through dense vegetation, seeming at times to vanish completely. The top of the wagon, which Arès now noticed was reinforced with stout iron braces, drummed hard against the overhanging bows with a regularity that at times seemed rhythmic. Birds screamed. Monkeys shrieked, and the endless buzz of crackling vegetation and whirring insects hummed a counterfugue to the noisy prattle of the motor.

After a few hours the narrow trail suddenly widened. Immense expanses of blue spread above jungles that stretched without horizon. At the far end of a winnowing road, the land bulged skyward into the monumental central plateau. To either side plumes of smoke helixed calmly above the trees, wherever invisible hands manufactured coal.

"There's only jungle," Arès exclaimed.

"That or desert," Paul laughed. "Big mountains, bottomless lakes, and endless plains. And we haven't even left the Congo. Did you really want to spend your life sitting on a log, my friend?"

Arès gripped the saddle tighter and marveled at the vastness around him. He felt skittish in so much space. With his free hand he clutched the key that hung off his neck and muttered a silent invocation.

For over an hour, they rose gently above the jungles on a lightly trafficked road and soon they were skidding across the boundless verdure of the central plateau: a sea of lush blazing greens and fluorescent chartreuses.

For hours more they journeyed on to the ceaseless patter of the tuk-tuk. From time to time, the trader whistled out a merry little tune that sounded to Arès like a sprinkle of sunlight through the clouds.

Arès was overwhelmed by all that he saw, by so much distance crossed. At last, the sun began its plummet, as it does near the equator. Shortly before dusk, they stopped at a small village beside a blue mountain lake.

They unrolled thin bedding over the stiff ground and drank a celebratory glass of whiskey.

"You have been quiet for a while, *mon ami*," Paul said, as he poured out the spirits.

Arès grunted in reply.

"Ah, *le poisson pleure dans l'eau, mais nous ne voyons pas ses larmes.*"[26]

"What does that mean?" the young man asked.

"You are like the fish who finds himself out of water for the first time and is afraid. He hopes that if he keeps quiet no one will notice him."

"I've never left home before." Arès inhaled a deep gulp of whiskey. His throat tingled pleasurably, and he felt his nerves calm.

"Dongo did not seem like much of a home," the trader observed.

"It was not home, but it was beside the river that ran beside my home." Arès gazed off into the distance, searching the horizon for his past.

"To learn to walk, the fish must leave the water. At first he stumbles." Paul leaned close and tapped their glasses together. He had yet to remove his aviator goggles, and his bug-eyed appearance made Arès grin.

"Ah, that made sense." Paul downed his whiskey in a single shot and

---

26　The fish weeps in the water, but we do not see his tears.

then opened a hatch on his vehicle. The small blue-crested bird hopped out on its leash.

"I was thinking of my brother," Arès replied. "He was a great wrestler and he would often pin me to the ground. Then he would order me to do a chore instead of him, something I hated, like carrying water from the river. I'd beg to do something else, but he'd tell me, 'it's not up to the fish to choose if he will be grilled or fried!'"

Paul laughed out loud. "But you are not a little fish anymore. You have left the small waters behind."

"Yes, but did I make the right choice?"

"*Si le chimpanzé accepte de se battre, c'est parce qu'il compte sur l'aide du gorille.*"[27] Paul smacked his chest dramatically and poured another glass.

"You are saying I am a monkey now?" Arès grinned, his teeth bucked wide, but there was little humor there.

"No. You are a fish. You have swum in the river all your life, and now you must learn how to walk. It will be hard, but you have no other choice." The laughter drained from the trader's face, and he looked concernedly at the young man. "But I must leave you now. There is someone I need to see about some merchandise. I trust you will be safe with my bird."

He lifted the blue bird and flicked it onto Arès' shoulder, where it gave a tiny squawk. Then he strode off into the small warren of houses that made up the unremarkable town.

Arès toyed with the creature for a while and then tied it to the wagon. He wandered aimlessly down the street. He felt unsettled, confused. For the first time in years, images of Nonloso rose before his mind's eye: A group of neighbors chatting in the street, the knob of Christelle's knee as she bent down to adjust her shoe, the slam of a gate, a red cloud of dust billowing in the road, the tap of his sister's pen while she studied, cries of "*Mayi! Mayi!*" in the marketplace, the blue and white uniforms of the school children, the metallic scrape of a knife against a whetstone, the braying of a goat in the backyard.

There was no rhyme or reason to the impressions, and while he struggled

---

27 If the chimpanzee agrees to fight, it is because he counts on the help of the gorilla.

to make sense of them, his legs carried him mechanically down the gradient toward the lake. To his surprise, he found himself suddenly perched at the water's edge without the slightest recollection of how he had come there.

To the west, the sun bloodied the meridian and evening mists gathered above the water's oily surface. He calmed, mesmerized by the skittles of light on the lake and the scudding of sun-bellied insects.

His thoughts of the past subsided. The sun touched the horizon and the sky draped itself in purple. All was silence. Arès rested there in hushed appreciation, unmoving, content.

Sunrise found him stretched out on the moist bed beside the lake. It was a morning like every morning Arès had known for the last six years. He roused to the gabble of insect wings and the rantings of invisible birds. Wisps of fog wrapped their tongues about the trees and he could hear the distant click-clack of machete crews setting off through the forest in search of wood.

His face was misted with dew and he wiped it dry on the hem of his shirt. Instinctively, he clutched at his neck, and fiddled for a moment with the golden key that hung slightly above his chest. Then he walked back up the hill to where the massive wagon stood on its crest.

The trader woke late. His breath smelled of dibondo and he complained of a headache that he attributed to the mountain chill. They brewed coffee with a rusted kettle on a kerosene stove and ate leftover saka saka from Paul's dinner the night before. Afterwards, they set off in a sparse drizzle. An hour later it began to pour and though the wagon had large vulcanized tires, they swiveled uselessly through the slop that gradually engulfed the road.

Wherever the rains were fiercest, the wagon joined long queues of vehicles being grunted over rust-colored bogs by crews of local men. To pass the time, Paul palavered with the other drivers, while Arès stared out at the tremendous, pulsing green of the jungle and at the streaming red rivulets that everywhere bled from the earth as though the rain were slicing into it. When their turn came, Arès lent his shoulder to the centipede-like rows of pushing men, all of whom Paul invariably hailed by name.

They all seemed to know Paul and Paul seemed to know everyone, from the soldiers in their dark green fatigues and floppy black berets, to the laborers hauling rock or wood, to the countless other merchants they encountered. On the rare occasions he was not already on greeting terms with passing wayfarers, his outlandish attire attracted shouts and salutations, and almost inevitably he pulled over to chat with strangers and managed innumerous small sales that way.

During one of these impromptu exchanges, the rains finally let up. The lumbering wagon forged ahead and day's end brought them to the town of Makoua.

"Quickly," Paul said when they arrived. The two men dismounted and hurried onto a small grassy vista, marked by a large stone cairn that looked like an angry finger jutting toward the sky. Behind a film of gray mist, Paul tried to estimate the precise time of the setting of the sun.

"Three, two, one," he counted down. "Six p.m. on the dot." Paul snapped his fingers and held up a stopwatch he had synchronized off an official clock. "You see, I was right. We are at the Equator." Below the two men, the land caved into a large lagoon spotted with metal barges and long chestnut canoes.

"So this is the center of the planet? It doesn't look like much." Arès peered around, unimpressed.

"What were you expecting, my friend? *Quand un arbre tombe, on l'entend; mais quand la forêt pousse, pas un bruit.*[28] You will always hear reports of disasters, but where life flourishes, there is little noise."

"Disasters can be silent," Arès began to say, but his voice wrestled out of control. "Disasters..." He couldn't finish. The mist caught in his throat and he felt like he was drowning. He clawed for air. Paul swatted him hard on the back and Arès coughed loudly, his breath flooding back in. For a moment he staggered around dizzily. Then he straightened his back and stared bewildered at the trader. What was he doing here with this eccentric man, so far from home?

Without saying another word, he turned and strode down a grassy slope.

---

28 When a tree falls, we hear it, but when a forest grows, there's not a sound.

His head was whirling with emotions and he barely heard Paul call out to him several times.

He needed to reach the water's edge. It looked safe there, calm and cool. His feet hurried downwards. He was only a few meters away when he was startled by the whiplash motion of a crocodile shimmying after something on the shore. Reluctantly, he retreated uphill. Soon he was squatting on a small promontory that overlooked the wine-dark lagoon, and behind it, the uncharted forest swamps of Likouala.

For nearly an hour he sat quietly, watching darkness smoke across the sky. His breath calmed and not a thought troubled his mind. The first bright stars revealed themselves. Arès closed his eyes. Then he felt a hand on his shoulder.

"No more nights by the water," Paul said. "Come with me."

Arès shook his head.

"It is not good for you here. If you keep going to the water, eventually you will drown."

Arès shook his head again stubbornly.

"My son. You are like the spider that runs out of webs to spin, so it waits in the one it has spun."

Arès shifted uncomfortably and looked up at the trader. "I am no spider," he said softly. "I am just a person and I feel better here."

"Then act like a person and accept an invitation when it comes. A spider sits alone in its web. But a person prefers to be with family and friends. That is the beauty of our time here on earth. You will have other opportunities to be a spider. There will be days in the future with no invitations. At least you will have this one to look back on when you feel too much like a spider."

Arès felt his resistance slipping away. He thought of the albino spider above his hut with its long spinning legs. Of the terrible spiders that hunted in the garden behind his parents' home in Nonloso. His chest constricted, and his breath began to rasp hot in his throat. He tried to rise but his body felt glued to the earth, as if stuck to a web.

Paul towed him to his feet. With an arm around Arès' shoulder, the trader guided him back to the wagon. Together they rolled mats onto the hard earth and before Arès fell asleep, Paul lay a fraternal arm on his side. The two men slept beneath the lethargic spin of the stars.

Day three was dry and the ungainly wagon rumbled comfortably down a long sepia strip of a road. At times, the road appeared to be a mere part in chin-high savanna grass. Other times it briefly parodied a well-kept asphalt highway.

Arès gazed out at his passing continent: the gaunt figures somnambulating along the roadsides, the slums radiating out from the exuberant towns, the swollen-bellied children amidst so much verdure.

Everywhere he looked he was astonished. Dongo seemed to him a feverish dream from which he was finally awakening. Every time a procession of twice tall women strolled by, with wood-crammed reed baskets adding meters to their height, he felt an overpowering lust to plant his seed in the muck of the world.

He shouted out to one of them, and she turned her head and smiled, but there was something of his sister Yika in her chin and he looked away. His father's voice came back to him suddenly: *"Produire beaucoup d'enfants destine à multiplier les tombes."*[29] At the time his father spoke, rebel soldiers swept like breaking thunder through their living room while the family slowly smothered in a camouflaged vault.

Over the shocks and skids of the tumbledown roads, Arès began to talk of these things to Paul. Per usual the trader had a maxim for every situation. When Arès reflected on the adversities around them, Paul snapped the rolled cigarette from his mouth. "As you can see, my friend, the rain does not fall on one roof alone."

"Yes, but in the Congo, it seems to fall on everyone."

"There is not much shelter here, that is true."

Arès glanced at a mud-colored hornet's nest, sagging like a mottled tumor on the trunk of an African teak. "Why bring people into such a world? It does not seem right."

---

29   Begetting many children only serves to multiply the tombs.

"Celui qui laisse un fils, vit toujours."[30]

"So you have children?"

"For the moment a short life is enough for me." The trader gave off a melodious laugh. Then he turned back and grinned at Arès. "But we shall see. *Les enfants que vous avez engendrés dans votre jeunesse, les voyages que vous avez entrepris tôt le matin, vous donneront de la joie quand tombera la nuit."*[31]

"I am not sure about that, but it feels like I am seeing women for the first time."

Paul wagged a finger at the young man. "Then you have truly forgotten your past living in Dongo."

Arès shook his head. "My older brother Félix was always lucky with women, not me. He used to tell the girls at his university that Zaire's future depended on their sleeping with him."

"And this worked?"

Arès smiled. "My brother could inspire patriotism in nearly anyone."

The trader let fly another volley of laughter. "I think I would like to meet your brother. He is still in Kinshasa?"

"Yes," Arès said. Then he leaned forward on the trader's shoulder, his eyes puffed like two balls of smoke.

"You'll have to give me his address," Paul replied, "and next time I am there, I will pass by to greet him."

With a tremendous thwap! the wagon jolted into a deep puddle and swept the motorcycle with a frondlike spray. Arès shook the muddy beads of water from his hair and removed his shirt, lifting it high in the flapping wind.

When it was dry, he looked down at it. The red soil kicked up by the wheels had clotted onto the fabric, so that it appeared to be streaked with blood. He tried to brush it off, but the rust-colored stains clung stubbornly to the shirt.

---

30 To leave behind a son is to live forever.

31 The children you beget in your youth, the voyages you undertake early in the morning, will give you joy when night has fallen.

He slipped it back over his torso and leaned close to the trader's ear. "My father used to ask me a question when I was young that I could never answer."

"Yes?"

"When he wanted me to be quiet, he would ask me if it were possible for God to make a rock so heavy that he could not pick it up."

Paul laughed. "That is a good question."

"I thought about this question for the last six years, and I decided that the Congo may be this rock."

Arès began to recount his life story: his youth in Kinshasa, the fair, his love for Christelle, the race, the slaughter of his family, his gaunt years by the river, right up to his defiant shout as he tumbled over the waterfall to certain death.

"God at last heard my prayers," he finished.

"I hope so, my friend." Paul scrutinized Arès from behind his protruding goggles. "The gods play tricks sometimes. Especially in Africa. Sometimes, I think, when the gods wish to punish us, they give us what we want."

"I do not think getting what I want is a problem I have."

"We shall see," the trader responded, his crest of feathers fluttering in the wind.

Somewhere north of Cabosse, they reached the border with Cameroon. Paul pulled to a halt a few meters before a chalk line in the ground. On the north side of the line, a blue-rimmed sign read "Cameroon." On the south side, in bold red letters, "The Republic of the Congo."

"You are ready, my friend, to leave the Congo?"

The young man looked at the trader with an elated grin. Then he dismounted and began to run. There was a slight down gradient and he picked up speed as he advanced, his long loping stride bursting into bounds. In full sprint he slid off his shirt, casting it like a leaf to the wind. His necklace whipped over his shoulder, and the golden key dangled behind him as he leapt across the invisible boundary.

"How was that?" he yelled at Paul, who replied with a fanfare of musical honks. "How was that!" He felt incredibly light, as if he had let fall a jacket of lead.

The wagon rolled forward, and without waiting for the vehicle to stop, Arès sprung onto the passenger pegs of the tuk-tuk. Paul had scooped up his shirt, and the young man began spinning it like a sling as they launched precipitously toward the north of Africa.

Half an hour later, they ran into the first blockade. Three men in army fatigues minded a lazy pike laid across rack barriers. One of them waved Paul aside and gave him a hearty embrace. They settled on a large stump to sip whiskey and shoot the breeze.

Arès sidled over to watch two other soldiers harangue a group of European tourists, who seemed dauntingly out of place. The officers were demanding a fine of 400,000 CFA, and the four women were protesting violently.

"It is the law in Cameroon. It is illegal to travel without permission from your husbands." The soldier was tall and thin and he paced around the women with a theatrical, prowling gait.

"This is unheard of!" one of the women shouted. She looked about fifty, her face squared behind thick-lensed glasses with heavy tortoiseshell rims. Like her companions she was dressed in a matching khaki Safari jacket and hat, with leather hiking books strapped over her pants. All four of them had sleek backpacks with Nalgene bottles riveted to the side.

"I'm not even married," a tall, blond woman about twenty years younger said.

"Then your father or your brother should have given you written permission," the other soldier replied. He rested his hands on the handles of his sizable paunch and displayed a toothy grin.

The women stamped their feet in outrage, while the soldiers continued to leisurely palaver in the metallic morning light.

"Look at the Mzungus," Paul said. He had slunk up behind Arès without his noticing.

"What did you say?"

"Mzungus are always running into trouble in Africa. They drive around in their expensive jeeps and think they are on a big safari. They forget that people live here, and that these people also have rules. It is true the Mzungus are rich and powerful, *mais la sagesse du lion n'est pas la sagesse de la panthère.*"[32]

"It's funny that you use that word," Arès half-replied, a distant look in his eyes.

"What word?"

"My mother also used to call them Mzungus. My father always teased her about that." All of a sudden, Paul watched a smile sculpt a sunny valley across his young friend's face.

The whole family was gathered in the house—Arès must have been about twelve years old—and his father was listening to a Jacques Brel album. Outside it had been pouring for hours, and the children were collapsed in a bored stupor on the living room floor.

The Belgian singer's stuffy crooning was the last thing Arès wanted to hear, and he nearly jumped with joy when his mother bustled in from the kitchen and sternly scolded his father: "Stop playing this depressing Mzungu music and put something on that doesn't dry out our limbs. I want children who move their feet, not these rag dolls on the floor."

His father looked up unhurriedly from behind a newspaper. "I imagine you want to break my ears with some album by Papa Wemba. One of these days, you'll trip over yourself dancing to that noise."

It was a long-running debate between Arès' parents who was the greater musician: Papa Wendo, "the father of rumba," or Papa Wemba, "the king of soukous." The children had all chosen sides, and Félix and Yika started shouting for Papa Wemba's jaunty rhythms, while Arès and his younger sister Marie-Louise banged the table and demanded Papa Wendo.

Arès' mother dashed to the record player and triumphantly grabbed a disc by Papa Wemba. "You see!" she shouted. "First-class music always comes first."

---

32 The wisdom of the lion is not the wisdom of the panther.

Then she and Félix moved to the center of the living room and ener-getically shook their bottoms and flashed their feet to Wemba's *"Mété la Verité."* While the song played, Arès' father covered his ears and contorted his face in exaggerated expressions of pain, occasionally winking at Arès and Marie-Louise. When it was over, he gave a satisfied grunt, and put on *"Youyou aleli Veka"* by Papa Wendo. Soon he was spinning Arès' mother around the room to the children's claps and cheers.

When Papa Wendo launched into the refrain, "uu-yayi—uuuu—yaaayyiiii," Arès' father sang along while wagging his hips, and Arès caught a glimpse of the carefree young man that he had once been.

It was a nice memory. He would have to try to hold onto memories like those, he thought.

Without saying a word, he began slinking toward the soldiers. He had decided to help the Mzungus, to add some small good to the world's scant reservoir. But he hadn't taken more than five steps before the tall soldier pursed his lips and began hissing, "sshhhhhhh," while flapping his left hand at Arès.

The message was unmistakable; even more so when his right hand unlatched the safety on the Kalashnikov by his side.

Arès casually redirected his feet and went to inspect Paul's wagon, as if that had been his intention all along.

The tall soldier carefully minded the young man for another minute. Then he relatched the safety and began once again to stalk pantherlike around his prey. The four women huddled together sullenly, with their eyes downcast. Then the big-bellied soldier slapped his gut, and one of them palmed over a small sheaf of bills.

For hours, the road continued westerly through dense jungle. They crossed cloudy streams on flattened slabs of wood barely wider than the wagon's wheels, and mudslides frequently obstructed the way ahead. Then the forests thinned, giving way to chiaroscuro clearings populated by lonely adobe huts and small villages that bustled like formicaries.

In Cameroon, they hardly made thirty kilometers a day. Everywhere Paul had business. Everywhere he had friends. They bounced from town to town, and the evenings were alive with musicians and dancing to bend-skin hits, and oversized bottles of 33 and Tuborg that passed in circles from hand to hand.

More than a week elapsed before they reached the department of Mfoundi, whose capital, as well as Cameroon's, was Yaoundé. As they pushed closer to their destination, diesel trucks and rusted yellow taxis began to crowd the roads, and the berms thronged with carts and plodding mules and women in superwax wrappers. The poverty around the towns became more graphic, but so too did the vitality in the streets. It was as if by living in large concentrations, the city dwellers could ward off the vegetative torpor of the jungles around them.

At last, Yaoundé! They pulled into the city shortly after sunset to martial booms and cannonades of color. Arès clutched the saddle tight every time white tracers lit up the starry sky, or balls of yellow, green, and red crumbled like titanic spores of pollen. Crowds danced and sang and street artists leapt like locusts beside the main entrance to the city.

"Ah, it must be *la fête nationale*," Paul said. "Welcome to my home."

Paul's residence was in Mimboman Chateau on the outskirts of Yaoundé. His house loomed high on the mountainside, facing the rugged forests that spread out from the central city. They walked through a large swinging gate and entered a capacious courtyard encircled by wooden ranch houses with galvanized iron roofing. Men in blue and avocado boubous were milling about and women in simple buff-colored wrappers stirred something aromatic by an open fire. None of them gave any sign that they noticed Paul's entrance or that he was in any way a denizen of that place.

As they proceeded through the courtyard, they crossed paths with a woman dressed in a sapphire blue pagne and a diaphanous green foulard. Her smooth, winding gait and the pursed bud of her lips reminded Arès of Christelle and his cheeks sagged with memory.

Paul clapped him on the back. "Remember, my friend, a woman is like the flesh of an elephant. Everyone takes a cut."

"Not everyone," Arès replied truculently.

"Do not be bitter, mon ami. *Un arbre en fleur reçoit toujours les visites des insectes.*[33] Not every insect can land at once, but every year the flowers bloom anew."

"Then I will have to stay here for many springs."

"No," Paul said. "This is not your destination. You have much further to go. But we will stay here for a short time. Perhaps it will be good for you."

They entered a large ramshackle residence that had no center, but sprawled outwards in a confusion of rooms and corridors. Arès could not tell how many inhabitants the building held, but as they penetrated deeper, it seemed that every conceivable nook had been padded with bedding or converted into makeshift sleeping arrangements.

"You live here?" Arès asked.

"It is my house," Paul replied. "But many people share it. I just pass through from time to time. Follow me."

They continued to twist through a dizzying span of interchangeable rooms and meandering corridors, climbing and descending small risers. After ten minutes of near uninterrupted advance, they arrived at a large backyard at whose far end stood a hut wrought out of lava rocks.

Paul put down his bags and removed his headdress, aviator goggles, and even the wild ripple of his animal skins. He motioned at Arès to follow him. Together they entered a caramel-colored sauna lined with resinous planks of ayous wood. Paul lit a fire, and both men stripped down and bathed for an hour in a soft white heat. Then they crept outside and on the soft grass fell into a deep and untroubled sleep.

---

33 A flowering tree always receives the visits of insects.

CHAPTER 14

APRIL 2009

S IMON WOKE LATE, DISORIENTED from a dream.
He stood on the *plage de Rabat* next to the woodcut fisherman
from the headboard engraving on his bed. Over and over again,
the fisherman cast a silver line into the sea and yanked out stiff wooden
figurines that he tossed onto the beach. Slowly, the figurines came to life.
They began to totter toward Simon, giving out great wailing cries. He
wanted to run away, but his feet were mired in the sand. Wave after wave
of the figurines massed onto his limbs. Panicked, he lurched about, trying
to shake them loose, but they were too many. Eventually, they crushed him
under their weight.

He awoke in a cold sweat, gasping for breath. It took him several minutes to realize where he was and that he was safe. His flatmates had already
left for work and he hurried to dress, get to the bureau, and banish the last
dregs of terror from the dream.

He was still rubbing his eyes when he opened the door to his office. To
his surprise, Federika, a Community Services Officer from down the hall,
was standing beside his desk, tapping her foot impatiently.

"You're late," she said.

"*Der spate Wurm entgeht dem Vögel*," he joked.[34]

"That's not funny," she replied in English. "We have rounds to do." She
inspected him with two unblinking, blue eyes. "Let's go. I've been waiting
all morning."

"I'm only fifteen minutes late," Simon protested.

---

34   The late worm evades the bird.

"They hang you for less in Germany," she said, and pushed out the door.

Simon stood slack-jawed. He was often caught off guard by Federika's casual severity. Her strawberry blond hair, innocent retroussé nose, and broad freckled face suggested a sympathetic person with a possible relation to the Von Trapps, not the brusque Brunhilda who was constantly upbraiding him. He pulled himself together and rushed after her. "Where are you going?" he shouted.

"You mean where are *we* going," she replied curtly.

"We?"

"Fatima is busy today, so you'll have to do the rounds with me."

"The rounds?"

"Yes, we have several visits to make. You're about to see the nicest parts of Rabat."

"You know *rounds* aren't really in my job description."

Federika sighed. "I'm sure you'd prefer to nurse your hangover in an air-conditioned office, but I'd advise you to take some slight interest in how our refugee population actually lives, if you intend to stay on for another year."

She turned her back and marched resolutely toward the stairwell. Simon briefly dawdled in the hallway, affecting nonchalance for an unseen audience. Then, cursing under his breath, he sped after her.

The sun was ferocious that morning and he gritted his teeth as he traversed the walled courtyard that fronted the building. By the time he ducked out of the security entrance, he was drenched in sweat. To his right, a thirty-meter long queue of asylum demanders snaked up the street. Several of them held limp pieces of cardboard over their heads or fanned themselves with crumpled copies of *le Matin* or *Aujourd'hui*. The rest stood still as loaves of bread, baking in the sun.

"They look miserable," Simon thought. Then he heard Federika call his name. He glanced over to see her next to a small blue taxi, vigorously gesturing at him to get in. He stole a last jealous look at the gleaming white facade of the HCR, imagining its fresh interiors and the comforting drone of the air conditioning beside his desk.

"*Chateau d'eau Takadoum*," Federika instructed the driver, as Simon grudgingly climbed onto the back seat.

"*Le quartier des Africains?*" the driver replied. "I will have to charge extra."

Federika shrugged. "Please set the meter and we can add twenty dirhams."

"*Waha*," the driver said.

Fifteen minutes later, they pulled up before a conical white water tower that sat high above the neighborhood of Takadoum. It reminded Simon of an abandoned spaceship. But why it would ever fly here... ? he thought. Below it stretched an open-air market thronging with shoppers. Federika paid the fare and they headed toward the busy stalls.

The market was loud with the trilling tones of the Moroccan language, full of its high-pitched warbles and guttural explosions. Customers haggled over prices and vendors promised miracles along with their wares. The scents of idle donkeys and overripe fruit tickled Simon's nose and mingled with the fetor of boiled sweat exuded by the men they passed. The market was almost entirely populated by men, robed in sober earth-tone gandouras with gold trimming, shuffling around in dusty babouches, choking the thoroughfares with their unhurried palaver.

Simon rode in Federika's wake, following the bounce of her strawberry blond ponytail and the weaving path of her light blue blouse. She was at least a head taller than most of the crowd, and she casually boxed aside several idlers, as if moving around chess pieces on a board. Their astonished expressions, when they saw who had manhandled them, were oddly gratifying to Simon. But soon his fun came to an end. Federika's light blue blouse skirted down a narrow cleft of an alleyway and into a warren of streets.

"This is Takadoum, where many of our refugees live," Federika explained, as if leading Simon on a sightseeing tour.

After the cacophony of the market, the coiling lanes seemed preternaturally silent. For nearly a quarter of an hour they wound ahead, encountering only infrequent pedestrians. Still, Simon could sense dozens of eyes marking their passage. There was an uncommon promiscuity of life there. The buildings hugged each other like passengers on a sinking ship, and windows hung brazenly open on all sides, exposing ample torsos in creamy camisoles and naked faces that hungrily surveilled the streets.

Soon they arrived in front of an abandoned apartment complex—its windows shattered as if blown out by mortar blasts. Through its gaping cavities, Simon could see that the roof had run off with the northern wall, leaving the structure hatless and three-sided.

"This is where Dominique said he was," Federika announced doubtfully.

The concrete stairs were damaged but intact. They climbed to the fourth floor, where scores of migrants had gathered. It was apparent that there had once been a fifth, and possibly even a sixth floor, but both had collapsed. Despite being some forty feet above street level, Simon had the impression of entering a deep pit.

"Would you call this a roof or a floor?" he asked Federika when they stepped off the stairs.

She shrugged and moved decidedly toward a raft-like arrangement of soiled mattresses, where over a dozen Africans appeared to be holding a symposium beneath an overhanging blue tarpaulin. Nearby, a man with a nappy mohawk, clad only in basketball shorts, lifted a makeshift dumbbell over his head, doing reps. Several other men were washing laundry in pink buckets, and long clotheslines, hung with tattered towels and fluttering bedsheets, divided the space like curtains in a theater.

Behind the missing northern wall appeared the cresting hills of Takadoum. The vertiginous jumble of white and pastel-colored buildings, rising off several tiered escarpments, reminded Simon of one of Cézanne's early landscapes, with the addition of satellite dishes.

A young man covered in bandages waved at Federika when they neared the blue tarpaulin.

"Issiaka!" she cried, rushing over to him. "What happened?"

"Hello Federika. How are you doing today?" he asked.

"I am fine. But how are you? What happened?"

"Oh. I am not so bad."

"What happened?" she demanded for a third time, impatience creeping into her voice.

"Ah yes." He inspected his bandages as if noticing them for the first time. "You see, I left my place early in the morning to go to the water tower. That is where we meet the trucks for the construction sites. I have found a job recently, God bless. The work has been steady and my employer has paid me regularly."

"Yes," Federika said, tapping her arm, "but you are injured now."

"Yes," he replied. "I was passing by the cybercafé, not far from the pharmacy, when a young Moroccan approached me with a knife. He requested my phone and all my money. I refused, so he cut me on the left arm with his knife, here." He pointed at the bulge of compresses jutting off his arm. "I cried for help. Very loud. I was so loud, I think I even woke some people up. At least I saw some lights go on."

"So the neighbors helped you?"

"No. No one opened their windows. But two other Moroccans heard my shouting and they came running over."

"Ah that's good," Federika said relieved.

"Yes. I thought, thanks be to God, I am saved. But one grabbed me by my hair while the other one stabbed me here on the arm and here on my side." He pointed to his other bandages. "With the help of God, I finished at the Hospital Souissi, but I lost my phone and nearly all of my savings. Luckily, I always keep money stashed between my buttocks, where the attackers were not clever enough to search." He chuckled at his ruse.

"I am sorry to hear that," Federika said. "Did they take care of you at the hospital?"

"They asked for identification before they would let me see a doctor, but after I showed them my card from the HCR, God bless, they agreed to treat me."

"Good," Federika said.

"Yes, but my friend Mbata was with me. He tried to save me, but he ended up worst of all. He threw one of the men to the ground, and the other two jumped on him with their knives and stabbed him many times. He does not have a card from the HCR, so when they brought him to the Hospital Souissi, the nurse told him that they could not treat him. She told him to call his family for money, but the thieves had taken his phone with all his numbers. He was bleeding very badly. By the grace of God, a soldier from Mali arrived and he saw that Mbata was dying, so he forced the doctor to treat him. But the doctor only put bandages on his wounds without an x-ray or even an examination. Mbata is there now," he pointed to the group of men under the tarpaulin, "and he has asked for a priest before he dies."

"Did you fill out a police report?" Federika asked.

"A police officer was there, but he told me that without a residency permit he could not take a report."

"That is not true!" she exclaimed fiercely. "You must not let them tell you that, Issiaka! You have the right to file a police report, whether or not you have a residency permit."

"I am sorry," Issiaka replied, hanging his head.

"It is not your fault," she added in a calmer tone. "But you must insist!"

"I will insist next time. I promise."

"Good. I am going to call Dr. Djideree now to make an appointment. You must have these injuries inspected."

"Thank you," Issiaka said. "God bless."

"Does this happen often?" Simon asked.

Federika shot him an annoyed glance. "This is my colleague, Simon. You may tell him anything that you would say to me."

"It is very nice to meet you," Issiaka said. He held out a limp wrist, which Simon awkwardly clasped in his hand.

"Nice to meet you too." The two men stared at each other. Issiaka had a glazed look in his eyes, and Simon wondered if he was ill. "Has this happened to you before?" he asked again.

"I have been spared injury so far, God bless. But this country is not safe. Every day someone is hurt. Many of us here have been beaten up by the *Alits*. My friend Tabo, who is sitting there beside Mbata, has been pissing blood for weeks since they beat him."

"The *Alits*?" Simon asked.

"The Moroccan auxiliary forces," Federika explained. Then she turned to Issiaka. "Will you be able to work? If not, we need to make an appointment for you at the F-O as well."

"I think I can work," he replied. "By the grace of God, in maybe one or two weeks. Maybe more."

"Ok. Please wait here while I make some calls."

Federika moved off to the side and began shouting loudly into her phone. Simon tugged uncomfortably at his collar. Rabat was generally temperate, but on days like these, feverish winds blew in from the desert and every gust felt like stiff gauze being drawn tight over his mouth. He longingly eyed the blue-tinted shade where the migrants sheltered under the tarpaulin. Then he began to inch toward them.

As he approached, he espied Issiaka's friend Mbata stretched at the center of a ring of men. His limbs and chest were wrapped in soiled bandages and a simple loincloth covered his sex. The compresses on his body were caked with amoebic-like stains, rust-colored at the center with aureoles of whitish-yellow that faded to pus-green at the edges. His mouth hung open, and his eyes had rolled back in his head. With his knobby frame, protruding ribs, and sunken stomach, the scene resembled a painting of the lamentation of Christ that Simon had seen with his parents on a trip to Italy. The almost dozen men circled around him, conversing gravely in low tones, did little to dispel the impression.

Simon felt an uncharacteristic surge of pity. He was about to say something, to offer some word of comfort or compassion, when a plump African woman plopped down authoritatively beside the injured man. Despite the heat, she was wearing a velvet green jacket with a dashiki pattern over a blouse and jeans, and had a small baby strapped to her back with a pink sling. She began to swap out the old bandages for new ones, cleaning the wounds with succinct, skillful movements.

The wind shifted direction and almost immediately Simon detected a muffled stench, and he saw the Africans nearest to Mbata crinkle their noses. Then the odor of rotten flesh engulfed him—rank, tart, and syrupy at once. Simon nearly gagged. He staggered back into the sun, waving his hands before his face.

A white bedsheet hung parallel to the tarpaulin, high above the sitting men. Simon focused his gaze on that unmoving rectangle and tried to steady himself. He felt lightheaded and strange, as if remnants of the morning's dream still clung to him. Then a breeze kicked up and the bedsheet began to slowly undulate against the blue wash of the sky. Simon had the sudden impression that the men on the mattresses were sailing off into the distance, leaving him behind.

Federika gave him a sharp pat on the shoulder. "You look a little green. Are you alright?"

Simon smiled weakly. "Real raft of the Medusa we've got over there." He pointed at the men under the tarpaulin.

"What are you talking about? Those are just mattresses." She examined him again. "Are you sure you're not sick?"

Simon shook his head. It wasn't worth explaining. "Did you ask Dr. Djideree to come down here?"

"Why would I do that? Issiaka is perfectly capable of meeting him at PALS tomorrow."

"Yes, but that man over there is dying." Simon pointed at Mbata. "He needs to see a doctor fast."

Federika glanced over at the tarpaulin, where the woman in the green jacket was gathering up the used bandages and Mbata was moaning weakly. "Yes. He looks pretty bad. He should go to a hospital."

"Can't we just ask the doctor to come here? I'm not sure he can be moved."

"Dr. Djideree is for the refugees."

"You mean you're not going to ask him to come?" Simon exclaimed, aghast. "Aren't we here to help people?"

Federika regarded him sternly. "We're here to help refugees and asylum demanders. The doctor won't even see that man if he's an economic migrant."

"But he tried to save a refugee's life!"

"Yes. It was very brave of him," she said admiringly.

Simon began to pace back and forth. Then he arrested his step and looked at Federika with a sliver of hope. "Let's just tell the doctor that he's an asylum demander, and later on we'll say we made a mistake."

Federika stared at Simon with a shocked expression. "You're asking me to lie?"

"I'm asking you to save that man's life."

"If you're really concerned," she replied, "you can help him as a private individual. You can come back this evening on your free time and bring him to a doctor, but you *cannot* as a representative of the UNHCR."

"Doesn't that seem a bit cruel?"

"If we helped everyone, then what would be the point of refugee status? What would be the difference between a protected individual and an economic migrant?"

"I thought we were human rights workers."

Federika snorted with exasperation. "No. We are refugee rights workers. Weren't you in Rwanda before this? What did you do there with injured people?"

"There weren't any," Simon protested. "My job was to produce spreadsheets for development agencies. I wasn't responsible for anyone's life, and even if I had been, I wouldn't have had any way to help."

"Well we are," Federika replied, "and that's why we have to defend our refugee population. If we help that man, then we have to help all the others. There are thousands of migrants who come through Morocco every year and who desperately need assistance. They would all contact the HCR, and to be perfectly honest, we don't have the resources to service even a tenth of them."

"So we tend to our flock."

"Put it any way you want, but we're wasting time. We need to find Dominique."

Federika began to explore the rooftop, leading Simon through a maze of clotheslines and half-collapsed walls. After several twists and turns, they came to a sort of workspace on the far side of the roof. Two bent men were carving oars out of waste wood, and beside them, a second group of men were busy patching a rubber dinghy.

The mohawked man was there too, surveying the labor and pumping the makeshift dumbbell over his head. Standing beside him was a neat-looking adolescent in a yellow sports jersey. He had a high forehead topped by short crinkly hair, dark brown eyes, and a sensual curve to his thick lips.

"Dominique!" Federika shouted with relief. She pulled him aside and they began to converse in low tones. Simon moved toward her, but she waved him away with the back of her hand.

He pirouetted lightly on his heel and approached the bodybuilder.

"Looking good, my friend," he said with a big smile. "Working out for fun?"

"I know I am," the man replied, grunting with effort. "But this is not for fun. We have to stay in shape so we will be ready to burn."

"To burn?" Simon inquired.

"To go by water to Europe. If the motor on our boat fails, then we have to cross the sea with the strength of our arms." He lifted the crude dumbbell high over his head, then suddenly dropped it and flexed his biceps.

"Looks like you could row to America," Simon said with a smile. "How many people are you going to put in that little thing?" He pointed at the inflatable dinghy.

"It is made to hold ten," the man replied, clearly pleased by Simon's response. "But we think it can fit twelve or maybe even thirteen."

"Twelve or thirteen!" Simon exclaimed, looking at the miniscule craft. He wouldn't cram more than six people inside. They were out of their minds. "Are you sure you'll make it? That seems a bit dangerous."

"Takadoum means 'progress' in Arabic," the man said, "and it is from here that we will progress to Europe and to our new lives!"

"And them?" Simon asked, pointing to a third group. The men were stitching black canvas together and appeared to be fabricating odd-looking hook ladders. "Are they going with you?"

"No. They are preparing to *choquer*."

"What does *choquer* mean?"

"It is when you try to enter Europe via the barriers in Melilla or Ceuta. They are part of Spain, even though they are in Morocco."

"Yes. I know."

"But I cannot do that. That is war. I prefer to fight the ocean than face men with guns. I have had enough of that where I am from." He seemed to look at something far away. Then his eyes lit up and his lips rounded into a broad smile. "At least if I die in the ocean, I will feed a fish!"

"What is your name?"

"Michaux."

"Good luck, Michaux." Simon shook the man's hand, feeling his fingers crushed in a vice-like grip.

"Every journey is a school of wisdom. It makes us grow," Michaux said. Then he raised the dumbbell above his head, breathing heavy with exertion.

A few minutes later, Federika approached with Dominique and introduced him to Simon.

"They're going to put twelve men in that thing," Simon announced, gesturing toward the poorly-patched rubber dinghy.

"What?" She stormed over to the men. "Are you going to try to cross to Europe in that?" She pointed at the offending object.

"With the help of God, Insha'Allah," one of the men replied. He was wearing a bright orange Maroc Telecom T-shirt and had a surprisingly large head.

"You must not do that," she asserted.

"Why?" another man asked, concerned.

"It is against the law," she exclaimed, and crossed her arms in disapproval.

There was a moment of silence and then the migrants burst out laughing, slapping their knees and whooping uproariously.

"She is very funny, your friend," one of them said to Simon.

Federika glared at the men, her eyes aflame.

"You're not worried about being caught with all that?" Simon asked.

"Not at all," said the man in the Maroc Telecom T-shirt. "We will split into two teams to go north. Tomorrow, one group will leave with the oars and the life vests to Tangier. Another group will go later with the Zodiac. There, we will meet up with the *passeur*, who will take us to the launching point. Afterward is in God's hands."

"Let's go," Federika said tersely.

"Safe travels," Simon wished them.

"Insha'Allah," the man replied, his hands clasped in prayer.

Dominique led them to a forlorn building in a narrow alleyway. Three stories of filthy windows sat below a crooked roof, whose unfinished edge sported a large crack like a cleft lip. The front door tilted dangerously off its hinges and led them into a vertiginous staircase that coiled upwards like a snake poised to strike. Each floor housed a single small room, seven to nine square meters in size. The rooms were covered wall to wall with bedding, save for tight blackened corners that held small braziers half filled with burnt coal and paltry bags of lentils or rice.

Dominique resided on the top floor. A pregnant woman in a somber

THE FIRE IN HIS WAKE

brown pagne sat on the bedding, fanning herself with a piece of cardboard. She introduced herself as Antoinette. The room was visibly insalubrious. There was a smell of rot coming from somewhere, and a prehistoric-sized cockroach hung off the wall like a misplaced doorknob. When Dominique picked up a stool to offer it to Federika, Simon remarked a pearling of smooth black insect eggs along the legs.

"This is where you live?" Federika asked.

"Yes," Dominique replied, motioning at Federika to sit down. "I sleep here with Antoinette, her son, and three other men, two of whom are also from the Congo."

Simon cast an assessing look over the miniscule space. They might as well sleep in a rubber dinghy, he thought.

"Have you been eating?" Federika asked.

"As much as twice a day. There is rice with vegetables and sometimes sardines. There is a *ganda* nearby, where they make *bouillie de farine* and even donuts. When I am out of money, I know a butcher who gives me spare chicken feet and heads. These are very nice." He smacked his sensual lips together. Simon couldn't help staring at them. They seemed utterly out of place, as if the mouth of a sybarite had been surgically grafted onto an adolescent's face.

Federika took out her notepad and handed it to Simon. "Please take notes," she instructed.

"Sure," he replied. She motioned toward the stool, but he gave it a queasy look and sat on the floor after scuffing it first with his shoes.

"How much do you pay in rent for the room?" she asked.

"The five of us pay 1750 dirhams a month."

Simon inhaled sharply, and then coughed several times. It was almost two-thirds the rent he paid for his massive flat in the Quartier de l'Océan.

"It is very hard to find the money," Dominique continued. "The butcher I know gives me jobs from time to time, but sometimes we are late on the rent, and then I have to do work I do not like."

When he said this last phrase, Dominique cast his eyes down at the floor, and something in the imperceptible tremble that ran through his body caused Federika to rush over and pull him aside. She began whispering animatedly with him. Simon strained to hear, but they were wedged into the corner, not far from the unmoving cockroach, which more and more resembled a permanent fixture of the room. After a minute, she grabbed the notebook from Simon, sat down on the stool, and began frantically scribbling.

A door slammed on a floor below. Simon could hear feet treading up and down the stairs, and then a ruckus that sounded like elephants dancing on the roof. Antoinette rose and shouted several musical sounding phrases into the stairwell and an entire chorus of voices gave a ringing reply, followed by loud laughter and more noise. The joints of the building began to creak and snap and Simon could sense the claustrophobic press of bodies all around. He felt as if he were slowly asphyxiating and his breath came short and shallow. He was about to rush out of the building when Federika clapped him on the shoulder.

"We can go." She turned toward Dominique. "Thank you for showing us your home."

Simon greedily sucked the air the moment they stepped outside. Then he whistled theatrically. "Man, and I thought I was *slumming* it in Rabat!"

"This is actually some of the better housing," Federika replied matter-of-factly. "As an unaccompanied minor, Dominique receives extra funding from one of our local partners and so can afford a larger room."

"What? How bad can it get?"

Federika was about to reply when a man in a stained white kaftan, brown slacks, and yellow babouches staggered up to them. His eyes were bleary and unfocused. "Are you looking for something?" he hissed. "I can find you whatever you want. Hashish? Girls?" He looked at Federika. "Boys?" His breath reeked, and Simon forcefully shook his head.

"*La,*" Federika replied.

They continued walking, but the man stumbled after them. Federika tried to wave him off, but he was persistent and bumped into her several times with his unsteady, syncopated step. It became clear that he was more interested in the client than the sale, and Federika's voice went from annoyance to rage.

"*Baalek! Baalek!*" she shouted and raised an open palm menacingly.

The man scampered down a side street, but not before letting fly a volley of unprintable oaths.

"I'm glad I don't understand much Darija," Simon remarked.

"Yes," Federika agreed. "A few words are more than enough. *Baalek* comes in handy far too often."

"Dominique's a nice kid," Simon said, changing the subject. "How did he end up a refugee?"

"Him?" Federika replied, distracted. "Oh. He was a child soldier. He claims to have murdered dozens of people and I think he burned a family alive in their home at some point. It's all in his file. You'll be writing a summary of it when we get back to the HCR."

"Can't wait." Simon grimaced. It felt as if something had curdled in his stomach.

They walked in silence through the twisting lanes. The turning of a corner brought them in sight of the white water tower. Only now, it reminded Simon of the hull of a shipwrecked vessel, bleached from centuries under the sea.

"How do you think they stand it?" he asked suddenly.

"Stand what?"

"Living in these miserable conditions. Being assaulted in the streets. Dealing with the memories of what they did or what was done to them. Preparing for the dangers they have to face?"

Federika walked thoughtfully ahead while the buzz of the approaching souk grew in intensity. "I think that when you have no choice you become very resilient." She fell silent again, as if she were brooding over something. "You might notice that people who have to live with the weight of the past are very broad-shouldered. They can carry a lot. We Germans know something of this."

She opened her mouth, as if to say more, when a chattering avalanche of pear-shaped kaftans in full chromatic spread, from coral pink to apple-green to Indian blue, squeezed them tight against the wall. Then the lane freed up again and their feet carried them back into the commercial bustle of the bazaar. After elbowing their way through the busy throng, they managed to hail a cab.

Federika began making phone calls as soon as they climbed in. Simon sat back and gladly watched the carnivorous streets of Takadoum fade from view. He breathed a sigh of relief when the necropolis Chellah appeared on its craggy bluff, high above the plains of Salé. A well-regarded international jazz festival took place there every summer, and Simon was looking forward to it. It was comforting to know that civilization sometimes left its calling card in Rabat.

Shortly before they pulled up at the HCR, Federika hung up the phone. "Anna-Heintz wants to see you. Afterwards, I'll need your help with the summary for Dominique's dossier. There may also be a few others."

CHAPTER 15
JUNE 2004

THE NEXT MORNING, THEY picked sunrise papayas from one of the trees in the courtyard and headed to the *marché Mokolo* at Mfoundi. Amidst the busy clatter of daybreak, the whistle of kettles, and the pounding of manioc, they laid out Paul's pan-African wares.

By eight in the morning, the market was cacophonous. Hawkers cried, pots clanked, beasts brayed, blades clacked and thumped, radios blared, dust swirled, and all humanity chattered with inconsequent discord.

It was too much for Arès. The press of people, the tussling voices, the sickly pungencies of sizzling meat and frying fish. He left the trader's stall and staggered about as if on a spinning carousel. As he hurried toward the exit, he came across a basin of frittering caterpillars, exoskeletons glistening, dozens still alive and thrashing in the stew. The sight was too much and he bent upon a swiddle of dirt and emptied his belly.

Afterwards he purchased a small sachet of pure water and cleansed his pallet. Clutching his brow, he stumbled on. The crowded streets outside the market were no better. The adamant honking of the cars, the strident cries, the air poisoned with dust and exhaust; he crouched down on the ground and tossed his head in his hands.

Time ached ahead and a soft hand enveloped his shoulder. "Perhaps it is not yet time," Paul said. He handed Arès a Fanice ice cream bar. "Try these, they're from Ghana."

Arès bit into the creamy paste. He had not tasted ice cream since he was a child. The flavor was good, and the patina of chill sliding over his tongue soothed him.

"I'll show you the way home."

The next day was better, as were the following ones. Arès gradually read-justed to close-packed humanity, with all its boisterous unrest. He slowly shed his yearning for the calm of the riverside.

But he missed his family dearly. He missed his father's steady presence, and the quiet safety of their home. He missed his mother's touch. For six years he had barely wept, and now his nights were storms of grieving. Paul brought him warm tea or sat up beside him, drinking whisky while he sobbed.

After a few weeks, he could stand it no more.

"I cannot stay here."

"I know," Paul said.

"Where will I go?"

"When you do not know where to go, look at where you are from."

"I am from Kinshasa," he said.

"Whose Kinshasa?"

"The Big Man's. Mobutu's."

"Well then maybe you should follow your father, the Papa Maréchal."

"The Big Man is not my father."

"On est plus le fils de son époque que le fils de son père."[35]

Arès sighed. Sometimes it was impossible to talk with the trader. "I cannot go back to Kinshasa," he replied firmly.

"Ah, but the Big Man is no longer there. He resides in Rabat, where he is buried. You shall go to Morocco, my friend."

Arès nearly laughed out loud. "Morocco?" It was like telling him to go to the moon. "And what will I do in *Morocco*?"

"There is work there," Paul said confidently. "I have many friends who have gone. Also, you should not stop there. *Si tu marches avec un éléphant, la rosée ne vous embêtera pas.*[36] Follow the Maréchal all the way. Go to Europe. Find his palaces in Switzerland or Belgium. And when you get there, write to me and tell me that your father was right when he said you had a great destiny before you."

---

35 One is more the son of his age than of his father.
36 If you walk with an elephant, the dew will not trouble you.

Arès looked down at his hands while he thought. It struck him how much they had hardened during his years in the forest. His fingers had become thick and gnarled with patches of skin that almost resembled bark.

"And in Europe what will I do?" he asked the trader.

"Why you will find a wife."

"So I am going to go all the way to Europe just to find a wife?" He cracked a big grin.

"You cannot stay here my friend, and you cannot go home."

Arès paused. The trader was peculiar, but he was right. "I will go to Morocco," he said, and felt a sudden rush of excitement tinged with fear.

"Good, my friend. Good. I think this is the next stage in your journey. It is at the end of the old rope that you tie the new."

"I hope you are right. Sometimes the old rope breaks if you pull on it too hard."

"Sometimes this is true, but either you tie the old rope to the new or you throw it away."

Arès looked at him silently.

"I will bring you to a *Nganga* I know. He will tell us whether this is the right decision for you."

"He is a good sorcerer?"

"*Il est si intelligent qu'il voit passer les fourmis enceintes.*"[37]

"That is a good sorcerer."

"Remember, though, if you ask questions, be prepared to hear the answers."

"I think I am ready."

They walked to a metal shanty not far from Paul's home. A thick white steam, scented with peppery spices, issued from under the sill of the shack's corrugated metal door. Arès breathed it in and his mouth watered instantly.

Inside, a man squatted in slacks and a blue boubou and stirred a wooden ladle around a small gray cauldron. He looked up at them with luminous, wide-set eyes.

"Welcome," he said. "Would you like some soup?"

---

37   He's so smart he can see if a pregnant ant walks by.

Without waiting for a reply, he raised a bowl to the rim and tipped the cauldron. The long loops of a blackened snake splashed neatly in, followed by a mudslide of thick, puce-colored soup.

"Be careful when you chew. It is full of bones, but it is good for you." He spoke in even, measured tones, but there was something incantatory and insistent in his voice and Arès took the bowl mechanically and began to eat. It had a lovely taste, but the bones poked everywhere and sliced his gums when he was not careful.

"This young man is about to set off on an important journey," Paul said. "We would like an auspication."

"There is a Beti ceremony tonight. Let him finish the meal I prepared. Then bring him there."

Arès had nearly emptied the bowl when he saw the *Nganga* pour out the rest of the soup. "You are not going to have any?" he asked, surprised.

"The soup was for you, my friend," the *Nganga* replied.

They heard the voices and clapping from nearly a kilometer away. While they climbed the steep mountainside, Arès rubbed his tongue tenderly over the scrapes in his cheeks. The pain chafed him, yet he felt fortified by the soup, and his legs pumped to the rhythm of the music and the stamping that sounded from above.

They crested a ridge. Opening before them was a natural amphitheater and within it, a parade of silhouettes with flinging arms and flashing feet. Fast roulades sounded from a pair of skeletal balafons over the sonorous pounding of djembes.

Next to a bonfire, a man strummed a double-sided harp with a tortoise-shell-shaped calabash grafted onto its side. He sung a bright lilting melody that resonated in the air. Whenever he fell silent, the flanks of dancing women responded with rambunctious choruses.

As the two men drew near, the pace of the music increased, and the dancers' steps blurred beyond recognition. Their rapid shimmying reminded Arès of fish flicking themselves upstream against the white spill of cataracts.

Abruptly a woman broke free from the rippling mass. She shook her body in an ecstasy of bottoms, backs, and shoulders, her hands stuttering out quadruple claps. Arès recognized her. It was the woman from the courtyard who resembled Christelle. He watched with eager fascination as the other women began to whistle and hoot, and their dance fractured into berserk leaps like an explosion of cicadas.

"What are they saying?" Arès asked the trader.

"They are praying for their men to make better love to them. They are singing of all the lovers they take at night when their husbands pass out from drink."

The woman who resembled Christelle began to flip and fold her body with stunning violence, like a net being flittered back and forth. Her form became a fluttering blur, faster than the padded sticks cascading along the balafons, until the music abruptly stopped and she let loose a metallic cry, like the crack of a hammer against an anvil, and collapsed into a puddle of dust and flesh.

"It is your turn," Paul said.

In the local dialect, he shouted something harsh and unexpected that reminded Arès of the squawk of a bird caught by a crocodile. Then he pushed the young man into the middle of the clearing, beside the slowly stirring body. The circle of women closed upon him, swallowed him whole, while a glacial theme issued from the double-sided harp. The musician playing the balafons began to sing an elegiac tune in a language Arès did not understand.

The feminine ring spun languorously around him, and in the small vents of firelight afforded by their motion, he could see that there were tears in their eyes. Paul began to sing the hymn as well and the women joined in. However, it sounded not like a chorus of the thirty or forty individuals on that hill, but like that of thousands strong: as if all the forests of Africa were chanting the same melancholic song and had drowned the world in its flood.

An indefinable sorrow took hold of Arès and tears washed hot from his eyes. The women rustled ever closer, still weeping out their song, and the young man began to feel a snake braid within his chest. His breath gasped hot and fast and he flattened his palm against his sternum, trying to pin the creature in place. But the convolutions continued, and the snake whipped through his body, runnelling up his arms and legs and writhing inside his spine. He closed his eyes, concentrating on the hideous sensations, willing the thing to stop. Instead it crept ever upwards until it lodged in his head.

A heaviness settled on his brain and he fell to his knees as visions flashed before his eyes: *The ochre tongue of a long route unrolled and then twisted before him. Men passed by in painted leather shoes and flowing Muslim dress. Stones flurried against an alabaster building. A dark form washed onto a mountainous coast ridged with monstrous fans. A man stroked alone amidst silvery ripples beneath a wash of stars.*

CHAPTER 16

JULY 2004

———

W HEN HE AWOKE AT dawn, his travelling sack was
perched beside him, puffed with unfamiliar possessions. He
un-noosed the top and pulled out new shirts and jeans and
a small roll of banknotes. At his feet stood a pair of brown leather shoes.

As he did every morning upon waking, Arès reached up toward his
neck, seeking the golden key. This time, his hand scrabbled over naked
collarbone and breast. He shot upright, raking his fingers through the dirt,
his eyes wheeling. It was gone. He called Paul's name, but there was no
answer. He sprung to his feet and darted into the house.

The corridors were eerily empty, as if the house's many occupants had
fled during the night. The depleted rooms jutted awkwardly and turned
in on themselves. All was as silent as a suspended thought.

Arès made one wrong turn, then another. He found himself over and
over in the same hollow, indistinguishable spaces. Every shout of Paul's
name splintered into receding echoes. Finally, he rounded a bend and came
before a rectangle of light. When he passed through it, he stepped not into
the front courtyard as he had expected, but rather into the backyard where
he had awoken.

Paul was there in full regalia, the curving crest of feathers, the bulging
gray goggles, the ponderous drapes of animal skins. Below his left hand, in
a gyrating sparkle, hung the golden key. The sky was light blue, leaf-thin
and luminous.

"You have my key," Arès said.

"I brought it to the *Nganga* while you slept. He put a spell on it. It will
protect you while you travel."

Arès slid the key back over his neck. It felt cold and delicious against his skin.

"Thank you," he said. "What are all these gifts?" He pointed to the bursting sack.

"They are for your journey. But we must hurry. You slept too long and they are waiting for us."

"Where am I going?"

"Why to visit Mobutu's grave. I have arranged transport. Let's go."

Arès moved to reenter the house, but Paul stopped him. "This way," he said, and unfastened the latch on a gate hidden behind an acacia tree. They walked out into the street.

"Do you really think this is the right path to take?" Arès asked.

"You will tell me when you get there." He motioned the young man onto the back of his tuk-tuk.

The jeep was parked at the *Gare des voyageurs* not far from Avenue Monseigneur Vogt. Beside it, the driver and several other men smoked hand rolled cigarettes and stared vacantly into space. Two of the men had billowy blue *cheches* wrapped tightly around their heads and down under their chins. Nearby, a pair of women in lime green polka-dot dresses played with three small children.

"This jeep will take you to the border between Morocco and Algeria. I have given the driver money to pay the *passeur*. He will bring you across. Afterwards, destiny is yours. Remember, *dieu n'a fait qu'ébaucher l'homme, c'est sur terre que chacun se crée.*[38] Good luck my friend."

Arès clasped the trader hard against his breast. Something of the sadness of the previous evening welled up within him. "You have been so good to me. How can I repay you for all you have done?"

"It is easy," Paul grinned as he spoke. "Someday you will help someone else. That is how you will thank me."

"I hope I have the opportunity."

---

38   God only sketched man; it is on earth that each person makes himself.

"Be patient, my friend. At patience's end heaven lies."

Arès smiled. "My father used to say that."

The two men embraced. Then Arès squeezed onto a narrow jump seat in the trunk of the jeep and waved farewell to his friend.

The northwest of Cameroon fled before them in a constant climb toward the Adamawa Plateau.

At first, fog lay thick about the rainforests like bunched balls of cotton. Then, as the morning sun burnt into the day, mountains etched veridian and brown out of the mist. Signposts heralded a progression of interchangeable, alliterative names—Bafia, Bafoussam, Bamenda, Bachuo, Besongaban—but the land altered dramatically as the jeep pushed indefatigably against gravity.

Dense broadleaf canopies thinned and raveled rivers flung first into cataracts and then waterfalls. The jeep rose further, and puny cattle wandered through moist savannas. High above, granite ridges sawed the sky, and below, blue crater lakes were rimmed by reddish-brown banks. The young man spun his head every time a chimpanzee hooted from the branches of yellowwoods, or lime flashes of red-crested Turacos hopscotched upon heaped leaves.

Three other men crowded beside Arès on the four jump seats bolted into the rear of the jeep. He considered them the lucky ones. Three women and a man were crammed across the middle seat with three small children wriggling between their legs. Though the bench seat in the front held only a married couple and their daughter—in addition to the driver—the man's legs spread over the clutch and he squirmed every time the driver shifted gears.

To Arès' right sat a sturdy fellow with earthy, sunbaked features, who looked as if he could out-plough a pair of oxen. Every time he shifted his weight, he inadvertently crushed the young man against the hard plastic backing to his side. The passenger across from him was headwrapped in a blue *cheche*, and Arès could only make out a lightly freckled forehead and two ink-black eyes.

Directly in front of Arès beamed a handsome, svelte fellow with a crinkly aura of hair, delicate features, and glittering eyes. He was smartly dressed in a blue button-down shirt, a linen blazer, beige trousers, and alligator shoes that were fashionably inappropriate for the trip. Arès took him for some sort of *sapeur*, one of those Kinshasan dandies who used to provoke so much laughter in Félix and his friends. He was unlike anyone else in the jeep, with their bedraggled, lived-in clothes and hardy features.

The passengers kept uncommonly quiet for the first few hours of the journey, their sparse chatter muffled by the dense fog of the rainforests and weighed down by the enormity of the choice they had made. But as the sky slowly brightened, the sapeur first began to whistle, and then to sing in a language that Arès did not understand, but which sounded like Tshiluba. He had a remarkably clear and beautiful voice, and even the children in the middle of the jeep stopped their scrambling and poked up their heads to listen.

Then the sun broke through the clouds, and the sapeur burst into an upbeat song by Tabu Ley Rochereau called "Mokolo Nakokufa." It was a famous tune, and Arès could see a smile creep across the rough features of the fellow to his right. When the sapeur began singing the lines about sending his children to Europe, the man joined in, provoking a radiant smile from the well-dressed stranger.

Arès knew the words as well and the call of the song grew irresistible. When the chorus arrived, he added his voice to the two others.

Ntángo namelaka ngáí na baninga
Ah Mamá uh
Mokolo Nakokufa[39]

Soon the three men were alternating lines and laughing as they did.

"Ah, I see I am in a jeep with two other Zairians," the sapeur said when they had finished. "My name is Kiwaka." He took Arès by the hand.

"I am Michaux," said the man to Arès' right.

---

39   When I drink with friends / Ah Mama uh / The day that I will die.

"Arès." He smiled broadly and tried to meet the eyes of the fourth man wrapped in the blue *cheche*, but the stranger stared resolutely out the window and didn't say a word.

"That is a very interesting name, Arès," Kiwaka said. "Are you sure you are from the Congo?"

Arès put on his best smile. "My parents are Zairian, but I come from nearby Brazzaville."

Kiwaka gave a shout of dismay. "That is not the Congo! Ah, the privations you must have suffered there. What was it like living among people who climb naked with the chimpanzees in the trees?"

Arès looked dumbfounded at the stranger. Then he felt an incredible release of tension and broke into solid laughter. "It was very difficult," he replied, tears of mirth coating his cheeks. "I went years without having a normal conversation."

"Well I am glad that you have escaped Brazzaville and rejoined us in civilization," Kiwaka said with a wink.

"This does not look like civilization," Michaux interjected, pointing at the passing wilderness outside the jeep.

"One must always pass through a valley on the way to the mountaintop," Kiwaka replied. "Soon we will be at civilization's highest peak."

"Ah, so you think Morocco is a greater country than Zaire?" Arès grinned. "Some patriot you are."

"Morocco?" He looked at Arès in disbelief. "I'm not headed to Morocco. I am going to Europe, *chef*, where they hand out Prada suits in the street, and everyone is on TV."

Michaux laughed heartily and grabbed Kiwaka by the hand. "So you have decided to make a big name for yourself. But why not do so in Kinshasa?" He rubbed the lapel of Kiwaka's satin collar between his thumb and forefinger. "It looks like you are not wanting for fancy clothes like they have in Europe."

Kiwaka's face grew sad and serious. "My story, my friends, is a very sad tale of lost love. Are you sure you want to hear it?" He began to sing a soft, melancholic tune in the language that sounded like Tshiluba. Arès thought mournfully of Christelle, but Michaux laughed again and wagged a finger at the sapeur. "This sounds like a very good story for this journey. Please tell it."

"If you insist, *chef,*" Kiwaka replied, and then whistled out a short trilling scale of notes. "As you can both see, I am a very good-looking man." He paused and waited for the two men to nod in affirmation. "This has caused me no end of trouble. I am from a village that lies not far from Mbuji Mayai in Eastern Kasaï. The chief in my village had a very ugly daughter. Very ugly." He blew out his cheeks and made a grotesque face. "And she was very much in love with me."

"This sounds very bad," Michaux said. "I think I already know why you fled the Congo."

"Ah," Kiwaka cautioned, raising his hand. "This would not be a love story if I had simply run away."

"You are right," Michaux replied. "Please continue."

"As I mentioned, the chief had a very ugly daughter, but he also had a very beautiful and charming young wife."

"Ah, now I see," Michaux said, laughing.

"As a musician, even a very talented one like myself, it is not easy to make a living. The chief was very wealthy, so I thought to myself, why not marry his daughter, and that way I will be at ease." He clapped his hands together four times in rapid succession and smiled at the two men. "Even better," he continued, "in my tribe, after marriage, the husband moves in with the wife's family. So, I said to myself, by marrying the chief's daughter, I could also grow very close to his young wife."

Michaux hooted loudly, and even Arès cracked a grin. Instead of continuing, Kiwaka broke into lyrics from yet another famous Tabu Ley Rocherau song:

Pitié toi mon amour, pitié toi mon cœur
Je travaille nuit et jour pour ton seul bonheur
Pitié toi mon amour, pitié toi mon cœur

Je travaille nuit et jour pour ton seul bonheur...[40]

While Kiwaka sang, the jeep climbed ever skyward. Evergreens ceded to bamboo and a mosaic of gallery forests and grassy savannas ridged the black rocks of extinct volcanoes. Soon they rode past sylphish stinkwoods, pluvial ferns, and clumps of stubby yellowwoods. Then the jeep breached the treeline and they rollicked upon the rooftops of the world.

Kiwaka came to the last refrain of the song, and the fine warble of his voice died away. There was a moment of silence, and the whine of the motor and the noise of the rushing tires filled the jeep. Then he resumed his story. "There was a large ceremony where I performed masterfully and filled the entire village with happiness. As you can well imagine, I was also a very dutiful son-in-law. Despite my reservations about my wife's attractiveness, I gave her a child very quickly so the chief would be pleased."

Michaux slapped his knee and laughed loudly.

"The village was happy. The chief was delighted. And I could play music all day, which was all I desired. Even better, guess who began coming to the river quite often to listen to me practice?"

Kiwaka regarded the two men with smiling, guileless eyes and Arès shook his head. "I know you will both be surprised, but it was none other than the chief's youngest wife, Yika." Kiwaka winked at his listeners. Then he looked concernedly at Arès, who had nearly jumped out of his seat when he heard the name. "All good, pappy?"

"Yes," Arès said and tried to smile.

"Do not worry," Kiwaka replied. "This story is like a jug of masanga, it gets stronger and better while you wait." His grin was infectious, and it spread across the jeep, even though Arès was sure that many of the other passengers did not understand Lingala.

"Soon I was giving Yika private music lessons almost every night, and without asking for anything in return. Unfortunately, beginners have much to learn, and sometimes the lessons would go quite late. The chief became

---

40 Pity you my love, pity you my heart / I work night and day for your happiness / Pity you my love, pity you my heart / I work night and day for your happiness...

suspicious. Also, one night my wife woke up and I was missing, so they both became suspicious together."

"It is very sad," Michaux remarked. "The family was once a sacred thing, but now married couples no longer have faith in one another."

"Yes, *chef*," Kiwaka exclaimed and shook Michaux's shoulder heartily. "And even worse, the chief began sleeping in the same hut with his young wife instead of in a separate hut, like husband and wife are meant to, so it became very difficult to continue offering music lessons to her at night."

"This is a terrible family tragedy," Michaux commented, and then hooted with laughter.

"Yes, but luckily I have always enjoyed playing guitar after dark by the river, and I began to institute this as a practice. I like to prepare for all eventualities, so I built a hut with a very comfortable bed in case I grew tired and wanted to sleep there. It was not only a very scenic location, but it was also very well-positioned." He winked at the two men and Michaux snorted and hopped in his seat, knocking Arès against the plastic backing with surprising force. Outside the jeep, the sun glittered across the peaks of passing mountain ridges.

"On a clear night you could hear my guitar all the way to the chief's home," Kiwaka continued. "When the beauty of the stars or the moon inspired me, I would go to the river and begin playing the guitar, and if the chief was snoring soundly, then Yika would come for her free lessons."

"And the chief never noticed?" Arès asked.

"I made sure the lessons were very quick and to the point. I am a very effective teacher when I want to be."

"But something went wrong," Michaux said.

"Yes. And it again comes from this breakdown of the family we discussed before. One night my wife awoke with pains in her stomach. Instead of waiting patiently for her husband to return, like the elders would have counseled, she instead went to consult with her father, who was snoring loudly alone in his bed."

"Tssk. Tssk," Michaux said, shaking his head.

While Kiwaka recounted his tale, the panoply of Africa, with all its browns, greens, and golds opened itself to Arès. The jeep descended and rose on the foothills of Nigeria's Gotel Mountains, and Arès peered through dirt-streaked windows as chartreuse fields gradually gave way to brush and bumbling elephants. To the left the Chappal Waddi tapped the clouds and ahead more jungle, and then even more as they trailed the river Benue past Makurdi and raced up the spine of Nigeria.

Their unflagging driver spoke as rarely as he stopped, their unceasing advance punctuated only by dozens of police roadblocks manned, at first, by Cameroonian soldiers in olive-green fatigues with standard-issue red berets; and then, as they penetrated into Nigeria, by a motley parade of stern police officers in black-on-black uniforms, muscular men in army fatigues and bulletproof vests, and finally, keyed-up teenagers in backwards baseball caps, mirrored sunglasses, and ripped-sleeve T-shirts, aggressively flaunting their AK-47s. The driver appeared to have perfected the art of slowing the vehicle to a crawl, plucking a *dash* of light blue CAF notes, or later, lime-green Nigerian naira, and tossing them toward the armed men to an aggressive volley of shouts and retorts in several languages. Then the wheels spun out the dirt and the jeep forged relentlessly north once again.

"It was a beautiful night," Kiwaka continued, "and Yika and I had decided to interrupt our music lessons to go for a refreshing swim in the river. It was therefore very inconvenient when the chief showed up with four of his brothers, all carrying torches and machetes."

Michaux guffawed loudly, and Arès covered his eyes with his fingers. It sounded like something his brother Félix might have gotten into.

"Luckily, I am not only a very talented musician, but I am also an excellent swimmer. So I swam to the other side of the river and then I ran naked through the forest for two days before the chief and his brothers gave up chasing me."

Michaux slapped his knee again, and Kiwaka began singing a famous song, "Mario," about a gigolo and his jealous lover.

Oh Mario, je t'ai déjà interdit
d'aimer des femmes qui ont beaucoup d'argent.

Écoute comment elle te dénigre auprès des femmes et des hommes
Toi qui a cinq diplômes, Mario.[41]

"After another few days of walking, I found a village where a kind young woman offered me clothes and a place to sleep, but there was nothing for me to do there. I had no guitar, and really, Zaire is no place for a serious person. After wandering from town to town for several months, I decided I'd go to Europe. Europe, *mes frères!* Where they need good-looking men like me. I'll start by playing music in the streets, but I'll probably end up a movie star."

The three men laughed loudly and heartily clapped each other on the shoulders. "This sounds like an excellent plan," Michaux proclaimed confidently.

"What happened to Yika?" Arès asked anxiously.

"I see you are a ladies' man like myself!" Kiwaka replied with a sparkling smile and rubbed Arès' knee affectionately. "Do not worry about her, *chef*. She is fine. I spoke with one of my brothers before departing for Cameroon. All the chief did was beat her and cut off her hair. When I get to Europe and earn my first million, I will arrange for her to come so we can continue her music lessons."

"Ah," Arès said. He fell silent, lost in thought. Michaux pattered on, asking Kiwaka whether he planned to go to France or Belgium, and what style of music he would play for the Europeans.

While the passengers conversed, yellows and tans began to trespass upon the elixir of greens, and deserts and savannas took crocodile bites out of the rainforests. Somewhere between Kaduna and Zaria, Africa's two extremes met at a green-yellow border, and the desert swallowed the jungle whole.

Above them the sky lustered a cobalt blue, and below everything browned and yellowed. Hours later, almost ten hours after they had begun, the jeep stopped for a few minutes so the passengers could load up on water and purchase fried kosai cakes and peppery stew.

Through half-cracked windows streaked with afternoon light, Arès

---

41   Oh Mario, I've already forbidden you / to love women who have a lot of money. / Listen to how they belittle you to other men and women / you with your five diplomas, Mario.

gazed at the desert dwellers. They wore rounded kufi caps and flowing agbadas, barely differentiable from the Cameroonian boubous. He leaned out the window and longed after the hippy women skirted with checkered wrappers and crowned with colorful head ties. Kiwaka caught him staring at a pair walking arm-in-arm and gave a low teasing whistle. Arès pulled his head back in.

The jeep beat steadily north. The buildings fell away into smoldering turf and were supplanted by dense patches of tuman grass and a horizon that pedestaled only emptiness. After the brief respite, the passengers fidgeted uncomfortably in their seats.

"But what is your story, my friend?" Kiwaka asked, reaching a hand across Arès' chest and onto Michaux's shoulder. "Are you also fleeing a jealous lover? You look like a man with a guilty secret." He smiled and elbowed Arès lightly in the ribs.

Michaux's face soured. "My story is not so colorful, unfortunately. I am afraid that it will make no one laugh."

"Tell it anyway," Kiwaka said. "The road is long, and telling about our past, especially when it is heavy, lightens the heart."

Arès said nothing, afraid that he in turn would have to tell his tale.

"My story is very simple," Michaux began. "I am the son of farmers, who have always farmed the lands near Rubaya in North Kivu. I do not know what you know about our region, but there is much mining there as well."

"For my entire life, we lived and farmed alongside the miners without any problems. But when Mobutu fled, the Rwandans invaded the region and the mining fell into the hands of foreigners. Soon Mzungus were canvassing the lands around our farms in large white jeeps filled with soldiers. One of them discovered a large deposit of valuable metal near my father's farm. The metal is called coltan and it is very deadly. They began to dig, and the runoff from the mine poisoned the water and all of our crops died."

"Everything?" Kiwaka asked.

Michaux nodded. "Not just ours, but also the crops of the farms nearby. People in my village could no longer drink from the town well, and they began to get sick and many of the children died."

Arès gritted his teeth in anger. "What did you do? Did you fight back?"

"Yes, my friend. The community organized a protest to force the mine to provide clean water and to stop polluting the land. My father was one of the organizers, and everyone from the surrounding villages came. There were hundreds of protesters. But when they marched up to the entrance of the mine, the soldiers opened fire. They shot many people. I was there. I saw them murder my father and one of my brothers. I barely escaped with my life." Michaux hung his head.

"I am sorry," Kiwaka said. "This is not a happy story."

Michaux stared out the window at the arid landscape rolling by. "Afterwards, many of the farmers began to work for the mines. Everywhere, the farms died. But I refused to work for the people who killed my father and my brother. So I left. This is why I am headed to Europe."

Arès could see tears rolling down the farmer's cheeks, and his heart went out to the man. "And you say the Rwandans did this?" he asked.

"Yes. After the war in their country, they decided to bring war to the Kivu region. The fighting raged for years. Eventually, we drove them out. But they came back with the help of foreigners. They hide behind the Europeans, but we know who is running the show. The Rwandans are toads who do not care about the people who live in Kivu. They spread everywhere like insects and destroy everything with their greed. If I ever meet a Rwandan, I will stomp his face into the dirt."

Arès looked down and saw that Michaux's powerful hands were balled into fists. His face blanched with fear.

Kiwaka began to whistle an elegiac tune. The tune slowly brightened as it went, and he finished by singing Kabasele's "Independence Cha-cha," the song of the Congo's liberation.

Indépendance cha-cha tozuwi e!
O Kimpwanza cha-cha tubakidi!
O Table ronde cha-cha, ba gagné o!
O Lipanda cha-cha, tozuwi e![42]

---

42   We won independence! / Look at us finally free! / We won at the Table Ronde! / Long live the independence that we have won!

When he was done, he looked at Arès. "This was a sad story. There is much violence in our country, but I hope it has not found you as well, my friend."

Arès smiled carefully. "I am a simple fisherman," he said. "I am headed to Europe for the same reason as you. To become a movie star. Also I have heard there are many pretty girls there." Kiwaka laughed out loud and even Michaux cracked a grin.

"That is the right story for travelling," Kiwaka affirmed.

Michaux's grin quickly evaporated and he looked at Arès suspiciously. "You speak French very well for a fisherman. I heard you talking with your interesting-looking friend when we were waiting for the jeep."

"Yes," Arès said, a cold ball of fear gathering in his stomach. "There was a missionary, a priest, in my village. He took a liking to me and he taught me French."

"A missionary... ?" Michaux began.

"Religion is a very good thing," Kiwaka interrupted. "I am very, very religious." The two men looked at the musician in disbelief, and he gave a devilish grin. "You see, I am always praying to God to help me find a beautiful young woman, and God is good and always helps me when I am in need."

Arès felt his fear ebb away as he and Michaux laughed.

Then Michaux gave a sudden grunt. "It is getting quite hot." The farmer began pulling at his collar and Arès realized that he too was itchy around the neck. The three men looked out the window and for the first time noticed that the landscape had radically changed.

They had entered the Sahel Belt, with its burred plains of cram-cram grass, lone acacia trees, and camel herds. Feverish desert air whipped into the jeep and blew out again, as if the windows had been rigged with elastic membranes that inflated with breath-stealing quickness. Arès struggled to inhale and watched the arid and alien lands with unguarded agitation.

Faintly at first, then like a sudden tirade against solidity, the granite universe crumbled into sand. Soon the jeep sailed between endless scalloped dunes, each one a saucer into which light elements had been poured, a ceaseless flux of creamy ochres, honeyed coppers, bright lemons and burnt sienna.

In the vital yellowness of that afternoon, Arès wondered—as he often did those days—if his Kinshasan youth had been but the curious invention of a lonely Dongo fisherman. The faces of his family had fused into a shifting cloud of tender gestures and soft voices and the townships of his memory were as lonely and spectral as the abandoned wastes around him. The only proof of his boyhood lodged in the golden key around his neck and he touched it to reassure himself that he was not some condemned phantom erring through the deserts of eternity.

Far off, rising out of that undifferentiated dust, was Nigeria's second largest city, Kano, with its great pits of indigo and imposing city gates. On its outskirts, men mongered groundnuts beside yellow fields, and horsemen in purple regalia stampeded through the streets. The jeep paused to refuel, and Arès bought a large bag of piebald nuts, which he distributed to Kiwaka and Michaux.

Then desertwards they fled, shepherded by the hexagonal pillars of the Great Mosque, rising lofty and alabaster into visionary skies. The first signs appeared for the Trans-Sahara Highway, that forever fragmentary road linking Lagos with Algiers, half asphalt and half sand sheet. It would carry them through Niger, into Algeria and eventually to Laghouat, where they would branch off toward Oujda and the Moroccan frontier.

Beneath a crescent moon, they crossed the border into Niger. The city of Magaria stabbed out of the sand and children pounded yellow millet with double-winged wooden clubs before obscure mud structures. Farther on in Zinder, they stopped for bowls of *kuka* soup made from the leaves of the baobab tree.

"I feel like we have driven to the moon," Kiwaka said.

Michaux grunted his assent and slowly shook his head at the devastation around them.

For hours more, the jeep throbbed over irregular paving toward Agadez, where they were to spend the night. To the right swept a billowing sea of sands known as the Erg of Ténéré. Arès peered at long, winding dune slopes, a multitude of crests and troughs that cascaded for thousands of miles, and mumbled a silent prayer for his salvation.

Kiwaka began to sing again, lonely, sad melodies that carried the jeep through the indistinguishable ashen plateaus that had swallowed the road whole.

At last, Agadez!

They arrived far too late for the *Isha* prayers, but as they bedded down in the bus station, several of the passengers announced their intention to worship the next morning at Agadez's famous mosque. Even at night, the sacred structure was uncanny to behold: a sloping parallelogram, skewered by fourteen courses of protruding timbers and built entirely out of orange *banco* sometime in the sixteenth century. The tallest mud-brick minaret in Africa, it rose well over thirty meters, with a bulging entasis at its midpoint as if pregnant with distinction.

In the iridescence of first dawn, the muezzin's voice summoned the faithful to the *Fajr* prayers. Four stylized calls of *"Allahū-Akbar"* wheeled heavenwards and drew Arès out of a troubled slumber. He sat up and rubbed his eyes. It was the first time he had ever heard the *adhan* and he shivered at the sounds of the lilting desert song.

Chants of *"Aŝ-ŝalātu khaĩru min an-naūm"* were greeted by matudinal groans from the drowsy heretics around him.[43]

Arès rose to his feet and clambered onto an adobe wall. Before him, droves of purple-clad worshippers streamed like phantoms toward the listing mosque, russet in the roseate morn.

They were strange, these Africans, with skin like burnt copper or hued a light violet by the dyes they used. Their faces exhibited slanting or bowed features and large convex brows of smooth skin, as if sanded down by the winds. They urged white donkeys and dromedaries through a lucid auroral light that seemed to issue from another planet.

After the *Fajr* prayers, the travelers gathered for a breakfast of leftover *kuka* soup. The familiar taste of the baobab reminded Arès of how far he was from his quiet hut beside the river. He shivered again and felt alien and terribly alone.

Kiwaka came up from behind him and clapped his hand soundly on

---

43   Prayer is better than sleep.

Arès' shoulder. "I see the fisherman is worried that he will not find anything to fish in the desert."

Arès smiled and put his hand on Kiwaka's elbow. "And you? Who will you sing to in this strange place?"

Kiwaka laughed confidently. "Musicians are welcome everywhere they go. Anyway, these people are not so different from you and me. If they did not dress so badly, I would even think of staying." Arès grinned at the sapeur's unflappable good humor. It reminded him of Paul.

Kiwaka pulled Arès to his feet. "Don't worry. Soon we will be at the ocean, and you will have all the fish that your heart desires."

Arès nodded and still smiling, climbed back into the jeep.

The engine burned and tires crunched ahead. North of Agadez, gravel plains interspersed with alkali flats and small water pools called *gueltas*. For a brief moment they coasted alongside naked children climbing through salt pits and villagers shooting arrows at puny vultures from rickety bows. Further on, men in white kaftans and headscarves led caravans of drome-daries through murmuring deserts tossed by Aeolian winds.

They traveled north toward Arlit. For hours, the road was populated by nothingness, then small standing monitor lizards, and then more noth-ingness. To either side, in the vanishing distance, white vortexes whirled erratically upon stone plateaus, furling and unfurling.

The only vehicle they encountered heading south was a massive tank truck, painted with atomic symbols and bookended by French military vehicles. Headscarved soldiers in camouflaged battledress swiveled the ball-mounted machine guns in their direction as they drove by.

Then between Arlit and Assamakka the road vanished. The only traces of the Trans-Sahara were sinuous depressions carved into the sands by recent passings. The scenery flaunted an almost existential desolation. A wasteland of rocks seared white beneath the unrelenting hammerstrokes of the sun.

After hours riding roughshod through indistinguishable wastes, they arrived at the border with Algeria slightly south of In-Guezzam. Their crossing into the Maghreb was commemorated only by the death of a horned viper, whose wide serrated snout collapsed under the weight of the jeep's barreling left wheel. Arès looked back at the invisible demarcation that marked the endpoint of black Africa and shed not a tear.

"Here we go," Michaux said, and Kiwaka burst into a surprisingly accurate imitation of a muezzin's call to prayers. Arès applauded the parody, but the headscarfed man in the middle seat swung around and stared stonily at Kiwaka until he quieted down.

The highway scrolled onwards alongside polygonal tables of cracked earth. The husk of an ashen car cooked in the sands. A gray donkey idled alone beneath the umbrellaed canopy of a leafy acacia tree.

They stopped for a rest at a marker that read 338km to Tamanghasset. The passengers descended in a placid sea of undifferentiated yellow. Kiwaka pointed up at the piercing blue of the sky, and Arès saw that wheeling raptors yet managed to eke a living out of the fallow land.

Then, once again, they hurled and hatcheted across impenetrable wastes. The jeep skidded occasionally, buffeted by relentless winds and reeling djinns. Arès felt like an anonymous bullet, shot at random, gouging through space.

Clock hands spun, geography hastened, and before them stretched the crimson homes of Tamanghasset, nestled between the incurving slopes of a desert wadi. On either side reared the rocky Ahaggar mountains, bathed in ardent light, and ahead the road rushed through desert tundra.

They did not sleep that night but drove maddened besides mountainous dunes and anamorphic rocks to reach blue Ghardaia by sunrise. They slept that morning in the white city mosque, and before it came time for the *Dhuhr* prayers, they were once again seeking the north.

Soon they reached Laghouat and bid farewell to the Trans-Sahara Highway. Now they cruised amid orchards of date palms, savanna esparto grass, and thin oases that mirrored cloud-puffed skies.

A gladness infused the jeep at this floral return, and the passengers whispered small hymns of relief. They had crossed a wilderness so hopeless and remote that they felt nothing could follow, not even the past.

Excited chatter filled the jeep. Michaux and Kiwaka eagerly exchanged plans for stealing into Europe. Kiwaka knew of a boat that was leaving from Tangier in a few weeks' time. Michaux had heard that it would be easiest to sneak into Spain through the town of Ceuta, which lay at the northern tip of Africa. All three men discovered that they were bound first for Rabat. They decided that they would take a communal van together from Oujda and split the costs.

While they talked, Algeria sped under vulcanized tires in a blaze of greens, blues, and browns. As they passed through various towns, Michaux began to point exuberantly at the pale faces of the people. "Look at all the Mzungus."

Kiwaka whistled. "Forget the Mzungus. Look at those threads." He gestured toward a crowd of triangular women, sweeping by in matching white burkas. "The clothing here leaves much to the imagination."

The jeep devoured the road with greedy, unchewed bites. The town of Degiene skimmed past in a drab blur and half an hour later, the driver arrested his unceasing sprint at the *gare routière* in Maghnia.

Parapets of white buildings backdropped the balloon balls of smoke that wafted from the jeep's overheated engine. Their hadj was over and only just begun.

"*Nous sommes arrivés,*" the driver announced. They were the first words he had spoken to the passengers since the start of the trip.

CHAPTER 17

JULY 2004

———————

BESIDE THE EMPTY LASSO of a road, Michaux, Kiwaka, and Arès huddled for warmth. Nearby, a group of adults insistently hushed several small children. Farther off, on the road's berm, two women crouched, their faces screened behind opaque laceries.

The night was hollow and vast and sown with stars. A horned moon grinned halfway above the horizon.

Arès crumpled and smoothed the banknotes in his hand. *Trois cent balles* for the passeur, plus six hundred dinars for the driver to taxi them to the crossing. He looked at the elaborate images so neatly etched onto the paper and wished that the whole world had been put together with such care. Then he consulted the pools of blackness on either side of him.

Tires mulched the road, and a pickup truck dusted to a stop. A dozen adults and four children packed onto the cargo bed, securing themselves as best they could.

"I hope you will change your shoes," Michaux whispered to Kiwaka.

The musician shook his head. "Tssk. Tssk. A man must always look his finest, no matter what the occasion."

The truck glided off through a silvery scrubland, bringing them to a town called Sidi Embarek. There, the passeur, a man by the name of Hassan, waited to shepherd them across the border.

When they arrived, Hassan ghosted among them, plucking bankrolls from outstretched hands and bundling them into a small burlap bag, which he fastened under his robe.

"Silence!" he commanded harshly. Then he set off.

Behind him a bedraggled line spurted like a centipede through penumbral spinneys and scrubs. The night was calm and the group moved quickly over the gently rolling terrain. Soon they passed into a sparse woodland full of Aleppo pines, Holm oaks, and junipers.

The stars sparked overhead and the silhouetted trees seemed but a geometric parade of spheres, rhomboids, and cones. In the angular moonlight, their shadows resembled long, crooked fingers combing the ground.

The travelers treaded noiselessly forward, all scrapes and shuffles, alert to invisible dangers. Soon Kiwaka slipped on a stone and he bumped his forehead against a low-hanging branch. When he gave a quiet grunt, Hassan replied with a piercing look and put a finger to his lips.

A few minutes later, a three-year-old tripped over some roots and began to cry, but her mother hushed her immediately. Then two of the women disturbed a nest of rodents. The humped things burst about the landscape in dark vectors, accompanied by muffled shouts.

Hassan spun toward them with a sharp hiss. "Keep quiet! Do you want us to be caught?"

The party skulked on in silence. Soon they had crossed the border and were in Morocco. Nothing had changed. Hassan squired them on through indistinguishable coppices and dense tangles of chaparral. Arès had no sense of how long it would take to reach Oujda and the passeur gave them no indication.

Abruptly, the front of the line axed to a halt. Arès stumbled into Kiwaka. In front of them, Michaux coughed loudly and scraped wildly at his face. Then, laughing sheepishly, the farmer peeled thick cobwebs off his hair. Behind him dangled the relief of a lank spider, and behind it a shadow's blur. Arès froze.

"What are you looking at?" Michaux asked.

A shadow bounded toward the men, the fog of its fist raised high to strike. Arès shoved Michaux out of the way and stretched out his hand to meet the falling blow. For a thin second he felt hard flesh slap against his palm. Then his mind reeled into nothingness.

"Why did you push me?" Michaux asked, surprised.

Arès' chest heaved with fright. He bent over, wheezing, and laid a hand on Michaux's shoulder to steady himself. With his other hand he clutched the key that dangled off his neck.

"What is it?" Michaux asked again.

"*Taisez-vous!*" Hassan hissed. He slithered up beside them. "*Taisez-vous!*"

One of the women screamed, a loud pealing keen that whistled like a rocket through the empty forest.

From out behind a thicket of desiccated junipers, a band of men loped like hounds. Whooping orders in a pidgin tongue, they waved pistols and light machine guns. The party scattered in all directions. Kiwaka grabbed Arès' hand and they scrambled together toward the first breach of dawn's light.

Within seconds, they overtook a pair of women doubling back on their flight. Five more assailants had fanned out, guns drawn, cutting off their retreat. Arès spun about and caught sight of Hassan strolling placidly back through the woodlands. The passeur saluted one of the bandits and then faded into a shadowy copse.

"*Argent! Documents!*"

The attackers' eyes bounced wildly in their sockets. Several walked on unsteady legs and wore nonsensical dress. They circled tightly around their prey and the rising light redoubled their advance with armgaunt and cricketing shadows.

The travelers handed over their bags and reluctantly produced small wads of banknotes, snapped tight with rubber bands. An armed man with a soft, squashed face walked around collecting them. He arrived in front of a petite woman, curved tightly against the torso of her husband. Arès had admired her large eyes and flush lips in the jeep, and he tensed when the bandit pushed her roughly. "*Argent,*" he said.

Her husband drew her close and thrust out the bills before him.

"*Argent!*" The bandit yanked the woman away her husband, while another assailant cradled a gun against the man's temple.

"*Pas d'argent. Pas d'argent,*" she protested, but the bandit was not listening. His hands scrounged all over her body, investigating her embarrassments for hidden bills. "*S'il vous plait,*" she said weakly, but his fingers only multiplied their obscenities. She gave a cry of humiliation as he jerked open her dress, and in the sudden silence that followed, her buttons clicked and spun against the hard earth.

Her husband bucked forward, gnashing his teeth, but a small brute with spiked hair and crazed features stampeded toward him, gun drawn. *"Tuer! Tuer!"* he shouted, and the husband recoiled, fists still clenched, veins popping off his neck.

The other bandit rubbed his torso against the full, bared breasts of the woman, his moist tongue lolling on her chin. After a moment, she thrust him back, and her spouse stabbed uncontrollably forward, his fist hatcheting against the attacker's chest.

"You crazy!" The smaller bandit raced up and pistol-whipped him above his cheek. As he staggered back, holding bunched fingers against his bloody eye, the assailant leveled his gun and released a chamber into the man's missing head.

The horde was upon them.

One of the men from the jeep collapsed onto his knees, hands clasped to his crown. He was booted in the chest and spirited backwards into the dust. Michaux and Kiwaka cracked to the dirt and groaned as kicks burst the length of their bodies.

One of the women began to run, her knees clawing against her colorful wrapper like the skewed spokes of a broken wheel. Within seconds she was pinned to the ground, and she shrieked and moaned as a bandit raked apart her attire.

Her face sodden with tears, the woman of plush lips was frantically disrobed. The palace of her body gleamed briefly in the auroral light before her drugged assailant flattened her to the earth.

The other two women bowled over their children, shielding them with their bodies.

Arès blurred among the boxwoods. A thunderclap sounded from behind him and the air whistled above his head. He ducked, and when he leveled his chest again, the butt of a machine gun swished out of nothingness and into his jaw. His teeth crunched in his mouth and his body flagged in half. He tried to rise, but a boot battered his stomach and he retched. Two men dragged him back to the group, bashing him occasionally in the nose as they walked.

There were over fifteen attackers, berserking about, pummeling the men, copulating with the women, and gleefully torturing all who resisted.

Dawn fanned red across the horizon and the woodland theater reverberated with screams, laughter, and laments.

Arès curled in the dust, spitting up blood. He heard Kiwaka grunt and moan in pain. Spinning right, he watched a bandit wearing only a woman's skirt grip onto the musician's wiry curls while their conjoined hips incested in the soil.

Arès twisted onto his knees. He was about to stand when he heard a high-pitched hoot and a compact mass squashed him to the ground. A heavy stick rammed repeatedly into his back while he gasped for air, choking on topsoil. Then something hard and plastic cracked against his head, and he went limp. The attacker rolled off him, giggling, and crabbed once more into the fray.

Seconds, minutes later, Arès spun his head, sputtering out dirt. His vision swam with amoebic sploshes of light and tears dripped from his eyes.

With great effort, he smeared his hand across his sweat-drenched brow. To the east, planes of sunglow breached the horizon and the morning trills of woodland birds surged from all sides, mixing their melodies with the wails and sniggers of men. A small spotted fowl with a crimson neck that Arès had never seen before alighted beside his head and began to peck at the soil. Without knowing why, he bent out his contused right arm and stretched it toward the bird.

Then a foot stamped out the light, and Arès lay broken and half blind in the Moroccan dust.

CHAPTER 18

JULY 2004

H E WAS HIDING IN the forest again.
This time, though, it was far removed from the leafy canopies and purple hyacinths of the Congo. Around him stunted
oaks interspersed with spiny tamarisks, boxwoods, and corkscrewing mas-
tics with their springy leaves. At night, he slept against a graceful poplar
on a borrowed blanket.

A week earlier, Michaux and Kiwaka had revived him to a scene of
awful depredation. His two friends helped him to his feet, and he swayed
unsteadily beside four corpses ravaged against red-brown soil. His nose
felt grisly and sore, and his back shivered with pain. All his money and
documents were gone, as were theirs.

The other survivors had fled, fearing the arrival of the border police.
Only two women remained, weeping and inconsolable beside three puny
bodies and the headless trunk of a man. A little way off, the petite woman
with plush lips lay dead. Her nether regions were pink and distended, as
if she had been impaled.

"Please come with us," Kiwaka said to the two women in French, but
neither responded. When he reached out and touched one of them on the
shoulder, she began to shriek madly. The three men raced off, worried
about being discovered.

For hours they marched in silence, unsure where they were headed,
consumed by thoughts of what had occurred. Their clothes were torn and
soiled, and Michaux stumbled repeatedly over the tattered remnants of his
pants. Kiwaka mumbled irritably to himself as he walked. With concern
in his eyes, Arès watched the carefree musician obsessively fold and refold

his rent linen jacket, and slap madly at the streaks of dirt on his trousers.

Then, after they had crested the hundredth indistinguishable tan hill, Kiwaka suddenly began to sing "Mokolo Nakokufa" again. He sang the song wildly, a bit out of key, and with a grieving tone very different from the original.

Michaux tried to shush him, and Arès scanned around nervously for the border police, but Kiwaka only redoubled the intensity of his voice. Both men could see that he was crying as he sung:

Liwa ya zamba soki mpe liwa ya mboka
Liwa ya mpasi soki mpe liwa ya mayi
Oh mama uh
Mokolo nakokufa[44]

There was nothing to do, so the two of them joined in as well. Together, the three men walked through the lethal Moroccan hills in the high morning heat, and bellowed out the lyrics of "Mokolo Nakokufa," until they collapsed in exhaustion and cried out their eyes.

Then, without so much as a word, they stood up again and marched onward. After several more hours, they reached a promontory overlooking an immense vista. The far-off city of Oujda greeted them, no more than a collection of cuneiform specks, dotting sandy plains, bordered by mountains.

They arrived in the evening. Skirting the city center, they chanced across another group of clandestines creeping through the shadows. The strangers directed them to a tent city that had recently been erected on the Oujda University campus. Kiwaka had recovered his composure, and he swung a friendly arm around Arès' shoulder when they entered the haphazard camp.

"You see. I told you we would soon be living at the height of luxury," he teased. Then he patted Arès on the arm until he smiled.

The three men navigated between the improvised shelters until they

---

44   Will I die in the forest or in the city? / Painful death or will I be drowned? / Oh mama oh / The day that I will die.

found a small clearing where a number of migrants had gathered. Kiwaka shouted for attention and began loudly singing popular Congolese hits, while Michaux played percussion with a pair of dead branches. Eventually, some of the listeners invited them to their tents and offered them dinner.

For the next few days, the three men roamed the Oujda University campus, seeking a path forward without money or documents. Many of the other migrants were in similar straits and could offer little guidance. Arès felt as if he were falling into a pit of despair, and whenever he looked over at Michaux's sullen face, it soured him even more. Only Kiwaka seemed halfway content. He had befriended a Congolese tailor, who was willing to mend his jacket and pants in return for a private concert.

"The clothes make the monk," he exclaimed, strutting back to their small encampment with a sparkling smile.

"I thought the expression went the other way," Arès said.

"That is something a simple fisherman would believe," Kiwaka replied, and gave a rich musical laugh. "With these threads, we will earn our passage to Europe in no time." Arès smiled. With Kiwaka around there would always be hope.

Then on the fifth night, at around four in the morning, hundreds of police officers stormed the tent city.

Again, it was time to run. Again, Arès witnessed men and women pulped with clubs and rubber batons. He sprinted alongside Michaux into the forest, while Kiwaka, only a few steps behind, still wearing his ridiculous alligator shoes, was knocked to the ground.

The police had brought hounds, and for the next few hours, Arès and Michaux dodged through the wildwoods, starting at every shadow and heckled on by ferocious barks and howls. At daybreak, they collapsed in a camouflaged grove beside two panting strangers.

When they crept back to the campus the next afternoon, all that was left were cinders puffing in the wind and dredge marks where the bulldozers had passed.

The next week was spent in the forests near Oujda. Arès and Michaux emerged only at night, to beg for food and to search for Kiwaka. There were dozens of other clandestines skulking through the sparse woodlands, but none of them had encountered a charismatic musician wearing a soiled linen jacket and alligator shoes.

Still they could not abandon their friend. So they lingered in that purgatorial place, afraid that the police might return at any moment.

Every morning upon waking, Arès massaged his face. The swelling around his lips and forehead was gradually diminishing, but he could feel a nasty scar stitching along his cheekbone. And whenever he rubbed his tongue along his gums, it invariably flossed into a gap where one of his canines had sprung loose.

So much violence, he thought. He could never have imagined such horrors in his youth. He was deeply afraid of becoming used to it, or even, some day, participating in it. He tried to recall his father's steady demeanor, and their calm, satisfying work in the locksmithery. He could hear Yika admonishing him, "Stop dreaming, Arès. Concentrate on your studies." He remembered his brother Félix placing warm fingers on his shoulder as he joked, "You'll never do anything brave, little brother. That's why you'll always be happy."

No, I am not some monster, he told himself. Not yet. But the violence seemed to have been etched into his face with a knife.

At the end of the week, Michaux took him by the elbow.

"Kiwaka is not coming back. Let us go to Rabat. I have spoken with some of the men here. There is a place there called the HCR that can help."

"What is it?" Arès asked.

"You tell them the story of why you came to Morocco and sometimes they give you a card. Then you can stay in the country without a problem. Once you have the card, you can work and save money for the passage to Europe."

Arès hesitated. It felt terrible to give up on Kiwaka, to forego the promise of his bright presence on the long journey ahead.

"I know what you are thinking," Michaux said. "But we will end up like Kiwaka if we stay here. He would not have wanted that either."

Arès nodded in agreement. Rabat was his destination. He had the Big Man to see. "How will we get there?" he asked.

"We will walk," Michaux said. "We will walk and we will beg."

CHAPTER 19

APRIL 2009

S IMON TRAMPED UP THE stairs to the second floor of the HCR and threaded down a narrow white corridor. Soon he reached a wooden door on which stood an imposing bronze nameplate without a name. He knocked tentatively.

"*Entrez*," someone replied in a flat voice.

Sitting inside a windowless office was a straight-backed woman in a charcoal blouse and gray pants, with a hand-knitted shawl draped over her shoulders. She had raven-black hair, pale sharp features, and blue-veined arms. Her eyes were intensely alive.

On her desk stood the framed photo of an overweight cat, and next to it a brochure entitled, "Refugees: Everyday People in Extraordinary Situations." She was typing something on the computer when Simon entered the room.

"You wanted to see me, Anna-Heintz?" he asked.

"Why yes," she replied without looking up. "Have you finished the summaries of the judicial trainings yet?" As she spoke, her fingers stabbed away at the keyboard, underscoring her words with a rhythmic clickety-clack.

"They're nearly done," he dissembled. "I'll get them to you by this afternoon at the latest."

"Please do... clickety-clack... I need to include them in a progress report for our donors. How is your mission here going otherwise?" She lifted her head for the first time. "You look a bit pale."

"Well, yes." Simon tugged at his collar. "I spent the morning visiting some of the refugees in Takadoum with Federika. It's quite awful how they live. Don't you think?"

"I've never made any site visits. That's not in my job profile."

"Of course," Simon assented with a dutiful nod. "But it must be tough for them."

"They seem to manage... clickety-clack."

"On the outside, sure, but I can't imagine what's going on in their heads."

Anna-Heintz hit the keyboard with a resounding thwap! and swiveled her chair toward him. Her eyes sparkled a frosty blue, like the tip of an iceberg catching the sun.

"I wouldn't worry too much about that," she said authoritatively. "A famous philosopher named Wittgenstein once wrote, 'Even if a lion knew how to speak, we could not understand him.'"

"Right."

"Do you know what that means?"

"Sure." He briefly inspected the photo of the rotund cat on the desk. Its egg-shaped eyes stared at him confrontationally, framed by an august crown of flaming-orange fur. "Well, no actually. What do you mean by that?"

Anna-Heintz smacked her lips in apparent satisfaction. "You see, Wittgenstein considered language to be a referential system that relies on shared cultural knowledge. So even if a lion could speak perfect English, or in this case, German, its world is so alien to our own that any thoughts it could express would be gibberish to us."

"That makes sense."

"The general idea," she continued with a pedantic precision that made Simon grit his teeth, "is that when two speakers come from backgrounds that are radically alien to one other, even if they speak the same language, they will be unable to make sense of what the other person is saying."

"But these are people, not animals."

"Yes," she said, her smile widening, "but philosophically speaking, we cannot understand them. Our references are too far off." She folded her hands and laid them across her lap. "Have you ever fled a massacre, or visited a shaman for a cure, or traversed a desert on foot thinking you were going to perish?"

"No."

"Precisely," she insisted with a triumphant lilt to her voice. "Experiences like those can never be comprehended by someone with a Western background, and vice versa. Just *try* to explain Shakespeare to an African herdsman! What I found working in Indonesia these past ten years is that we can cater to the refugees' obvious biological needs, but we can never pretend to imagine their inner lives."

Anna-Heintz's voice had keyed up a pitch, and she peered now at Simon with immense conviction, like a missionary about a conversion in some hostile jungle.

"In that case, how do we know that our work even helps them?" Simon demanded. "Maybe we're just making their lives worse. What grounds do we have to continue?"

"It's in our mandate," she said, slapping her hand down on the refugee brochure with an authoritative smack. "As the French say, '*un animal blessé, tu ne marches pas dessus.*'[45] They have the most evocative expressions in French."

"Yes. It's the language of poets," Simon replied distractedly.

"And I think that's the problem, really!" she exclaimed, her ice-blue eyes lighting up with the bright feather of a new idea. "I've been hosting these judicial trainings for several months now, but I have the impression that the judges here never absorb a thing. And I think it's the language! If only they spoke sensible clear German, or even English, this would all be so much easier. Can you believe it? Two of the judges who attended our trainings, just this week, deported three of our refugees! They sat there for over two hours, taking notes on international asylum law, and then, only a *few* days later, they illegally refouled individuals under the official protection of the United Nations. I can't help but think that the French language has something to do with it."

Maybe they couldn't understand you, Simon nearly responded. Then he looked at those two burning eyes in that pallid face and held his tongue.

"Where did they send them?" he asked instead.

"Ach! It's always the same." She slapped the desk again. "They bus them to the desert somewhere past Oujda and drop them in that no-man's land on the militarized border between Algeria and Morocco. I think half of our

---

45   One should never step on a wounded animal.

refugee population has done a tour there by now."

"Really?" He hadn't realized that the refoulements were so frequent. "How do they get back?"

"When we find out in time, like in this instance, we send Fatima and Ibrahim to go fetch them. So now they're driving three hours across the country to play detectives in the desert and hope they can locate them. We would call the refugees, but *of course* the Moroccan police steal their cell phones, though you didn't hear that from me."

"And when you don't find out in time?"

"Usually, they walk back on their own. It's not even an efficient deportation." Anna-Heintz adjusted the black shawl on her shoulders and glanced quickly at the computer monitor. "There's nowhere to go in Algeria, so they have to re-enter the country in any case."

"And the other times?" he asked, regretting it almost immediately.

"We've lost several refugees there." She snorted and then peered intently at Simon. "Didn't you receive the circular last week about the attack?" Simon shook his head. "The desert there is a wasteland controlled by glue-sniffing Nigerian gangs. They murdered a whole party of migrants two weeks ago and they raped a three-year-old. A three-year-old! I can't even imagine what sort of state of mind you have to be in to do that. But of course, that goes back to our earlier discussion." She rested her hands on the desk as if to say I told you so.

Simon gulped. "Right."

"And that's not the worst of it..." she added, her eyes aglimmer. Simon hastily interjected, "I should go finish those summaries." Then he opened the door and sped out of that airless chamber, before she could add another Conradian turn to her enumeration of horrors.

He needed somewhere to think. His feet started toward the outdoor terrace, but after only a few steps, he slumped dizzily against the wall as if physically drained. For nearly a minute, he massaged his temples. Then he exhaled.

He had wanted to challenge himself in hardship environments, but they were often exhausting. He thought of his friends at cushy posts in Brussels or D.C., with their holiday ski weekends and gold-ticket galas. At times he longed for the pleasant affirmations of frilly cocktail dresses and aperitifs on fancy rooftops.

When he finally stepped onto the terrace, the sun was shining brightly through the tapered leaves of the olive tree onto the antique white table. The Country Director, Maarten, and the Vice-Director, Hilda, sat in a fluctuating nimbus of light, eating strawberries and conversing loudly in Dutch.

Maarten sprang to his feet when he saw Simon, and vigorously shook him by the hand. He had executive blue eyes, a heroic chin, and the slim athletic shoulders of a seasoned sailor. "I heard Federika took you on a tour of the city this morning," he said in a commanding voice. "How did you find our little community here?"

Simon smiled wanly. "It was great. She showed me all the sights."

"Tip-top," he replied.

"Please Simon. Sit down. Have some strawberries!" Hilda exclaimed with a vivacious laugh, as if she had told a joke. Her radiant face beamed the sort of imperturbable contentment found in orderly, prosperous nations with lots of spare tulips. "There's clotted cream there on the table." She pointed to a blue porcelain bowl brimming with frozen white wavelets.

"Thank you," Simon replied. When he leaned over to pluck out a strawberry, he noticed a glass jar topped with a bright yellow plastic cap. The jar was filled halfway with a clear, syrupy substance that resembled molasses, and the yellow cap had funnel-shaped portholes fitted onto either side.

"What's that?" he asked, curious.

"It's a trap for the bees. We have quite the infestation here. Haven't you noticed?" Hilda clasped her hands together and sighed.

As if summoned by her affirmation, a pair of missile-shaped yellow jackets landed on the apparatus and shimmied into the right porthole. They crawled down to the viscous lagoon and began hungrily sipping, cheerfully wagging their long cylindrical bottoms with curved black stingers. Simon absentmindedly munched on the tip of a strawberry and watched one of the bees, his belly presumably full, crawl out of the porthole and buzz back to the hive.

"Hardly a perfect system," Simon observed.

"Take another look," Maarten suggested.

Simon peered closer. Dozens of black and yellow bodies lay drowned at the bottom of the jar, cocooned in a waxy, glutinous substance. Their limbs were curled inward as if they had died in a fetal position.

"A few escape," Maarten continued, "but the system is designed that way. The survivor will bring word to the nest and encourage others to come, most of whom will fall into the trap. Eventually there will be so few workers left that the nest will die off on its own."

"Why don't we just destroy the nest instead of luring them here to drown?" Simon asked, reaching for another strawberry.

"One, we don't quite know where it is," the Director replied, pacing around the table now with a martial, Napoleonic stride. "And even if we did locate it, it's quite risky to destroy. Have you ever attacked a nest of African wasps? Few live to tell the tale." He clasped his hands behind his back and shook his head dramatically. "Even when you're successful, it's a messy business. This way we just set the trap and they drown on their own. Problem solved."

"Except for the ones who get away," Simon remarked.

"Yes. Except for those. But we don't want to totally eliminate the bees, otherwise who would pollinate the plants? The goal is to effectively manage the population, so they don't become too numerous, but can continue to do the work we need."

"We have one at our house as well," Hilda volunteered. "You should come by some time, Simon. It's right on the beach in a lovely gated community. We could have dinner there later this week? The sunsets are glorious."

Before he could reply, a door slammed and a sharp drumming of clogs sounded against the tiled terrace. Simon's face crumpled when he saw Anna-Heintz swoop in, her feathery, dark shawl flapping behind her.

"My spies informed me that there were strawberries on the terrace," she announced gaily.

"Please, help yourself!" Hilda gave off another vivacious laugh. Then she reached up and lightly adjusted the navy blue hair tie that held back her blond bob of hair.

Anna-Heintz pounced toward the bowl of strawberries but abruptly reared back, masking her eyes with her hands. "Oh. Take it away! I can't bear to look."

"What?" Maarten asked, alarmed.

"That thing," she said, peeking through spread fingers and pointing at the yellow-capped jar.

"You mean the bee-trap?" the Director asked doubtfully.

"They're only bees," Simon exclaimed, laughing.

"Yes, but I can't stand it." Her face took on a pained expression. "It's horrible watching them struggle for hours until they drown."

"Ok," Maarten replied, a wry look on his face. He picked up the contraption and placed it on a ledge away from the table. "But it's not going to change anything. They're going to drown all the same."

"Well let them drown out of sight," she insisted. Then she turned her penetrating gaze on the young JPO. "Simon, shouldn't you be working on those judicial summaries?"

"I was just getting some tea to pep up," he apologized.

"I've found it's best to pep up in front of a computer when I have work to do."

"Actually, Anna-Heintz," Maarten cut in, winking at the young man. "I was just about to steal Simon for a meeting, if you don't mind?" He turned to face the JPO. "Tip-top secret, confidential stuff. If you could please pass by my office first, then you can finish the report for Anna-Heintz."

"Yes, of course," she replied stonily. Her hand clawed several strawberries out of the bowl. Then she stormed off, her clogs snapping like crocodiles against the tiled floor.

Maarten leaned over to Simon and whispered with a grin, "Some people produce happiness *wherever* they go, and others *whenever* they go."

Simon gave a puppyish nod, delighted to be taken into the Director's confidence. "Why don't you go grab that tea and meet me in my office in about ten minutes," he instructed.

"Will do," Simon said.

CHAPTER 20

JULY–AUGUST 2004

I T WAS NOT THE first time that Arès had lost everything. This time, at least, he had a companion in distress.

It took them nearly a month to reach Rabat, even though a communal taxi would have carried them from Oujda in under six hours. For the most part they traveled at night. They were too frightened to walk along the highways, so they forged across deserts and silvery scrublands, scaled starlit fields and forded streams that purled dreamily in the lunar light.

Time and again, Arès silently thanked the trader for the new pair of leather shoes. Michaux's boots were old and worn, and they slowly perforated on the asperous rocks. There was no material to resole them, and after two weeks of walking, he discarded them in a fit of anger. Afterwards, he hiked in flip-flops, forcing them to rest for longer and longer periods as the days passed.

Every morning, they crawled under culverts, or, failing that, found shelter beneath scrawny canopies of leaves. For bedding there was dirt or grass, and always the murmur of slithering things.

Twice while dreaming, Arès felt a soft hand caress his brow. He spoke his mother's name and reached up toward her face. When he opened his eyes, the pre-dawn sky glimmered soft and sear above a mesh of leaves, but there was no one there. Once, he could not help but weep.

Days passed without food. The two men barely exchanged words. There was nothing to say and it was too tiring to talk.

At one point Michaux killed a rat, and they roasted it over a fire that took hours to coax into being.

"This is the best tasting rat I have ever eaten," Michaux said with a feeble grin.

Arès laughed, but it hurt his sides. "Yes. Maybe we can open a restaurant when we get to Rabat."

"Who will buy food from starving men?" Michaux asked, suddenly serious.

Arès dropped his head and then looked out at the bleak shrubland. Something had been bothering him ever since their arrival in the Maghreb. "Have you noticed how long the sun hangs near the horizon before it sets? It is unnatural."

"It is the God of the Moroccans watching us," Michaux replied.

Arès trembled at the thought and both men crossed themselves. Then, with sore eyes, they endured a protracted sunset whose gushing red light reminded Arès of a savage bleeding out, as if the sun were a colossal heart that had been pierced. It was so different from home where night snuck up on one like a thief, so that you could be joking with your friends and suddenly realize that someone had stolen all the light.

After an interminable delay, the sun began to shimmer like a hallucination on the horizon and, finally, it vanished, leaving the sky stained with murderous streaks of red. The first cold winds blew in from the desert and the two men shivered and huddled over the fire.

Arès heard a loud crack and he saw that Michaux had snapped one of the rat's legs in half and was sucking the marrow from the bone. When he noticed Arès hungrily staring at him, the farmer split another leg and handed it to the young man. Wincing, he stuck it in his mouth and began greedily sucking.

"This is really a very good rat," Arès remarked, and Michaux gave a fitful laugh in response. "Did you prepare this dish often at home?"

"Only on special occasions." Michaux tried to smile, but the flesh was thin and drawn over his cheeks and the friendly expression came out as a grimace.

The light drained out of the sky, and the sparse shrubs and dusty hills silvered before a rising moon. Under the cover of night, the flickering of the fire accentuated their gauntness. Arès noticed that Michaux's lean frame had begun to ebb away, articulating the skeleton within. Before lying down, he ran his fingers over his own cadaverous cheeks and probed the waste around his ribs.

After a week of walking, they arrived in Fes. They celebrated by rummaging through a pit of refuse dug into a hillside below featureless tenements. Crabbing among discarded appliances, shredded plastic bags, and human refuse, they sucked dry the rotting yellow rinds of Moroccan melons and warded off the prowling mutts with small, sharp stones.

Below them spanned an immense cemetery, and below it, the pale medina with its obscure winding lanes and honeycombed tanneries. They crouched and felt primordial and dark in the face of that ancient civilization.

The next morning, a Moroccan by the name of Karim contracted them to make concrete and mix cement at a construction site. For two weeks, they ground clinker into powder and blended it with gypsum, or hauled bags of gravel, sand, and cement, added water and poured out the grayish meal.

At night, they slept on the second floor of the unfinished building, alongside dozens of Moroccan laborers. They had been promised fifty dirhams a day, but when the time came to collect their wages, Karim threatened to denounce them to the police. He brandished a wrecking bar and chased them off the site while the other laborers laughed.

A rod of metal piping found its way into Arès' hands, and in a paroxysm of fury he rushed back onto the *chantier* looking for blood. When he reentered the building, he found ten of his coworkers waiting, heavy tools in hand.

It took them three days to walk the fifty-five kilometers to Meknes. There, after questioning several black Africans in the streets, they were steered toward work harvesting dates for twenty dirhams a day. This time they were paid regularly, and two weeks later, they had saved enough money for a communal taxi ride to Rabat.

After all that walking, Arès felt like royalty riding in a vehicle again. He stared triumphantly out the window as the white Mercedes rolled through the sinuous green countryside. Orchards of wiry argan trees interspersed with olive groves, and orderly vineyards braided between saffron fields of grain. For the first time in days, Michaux cracked a smile.

"Kiwaka was right," Arès said, looking at the stocky farmer. "Here we are, riding toward Europe like kings."

Michaux smiled and nodded. "I almost feel like a human being again."

The other passengers in the taxi were all Moroccan. They babbled contentedly for the duration of the trip, unperturbed by the loud, synthetic beats of Algerian Raï that blasted unceasingly from the car speakers.

Two hours later, a large sign read الرباط and underneath it "Rabat."

The vehicle passed beneath a lofty red tower and rolled alongside burnt sandstone walls broken by gates etched with Arabic script. Then one of the Moroccans said "*Sufi*" to the driver and the taxi stopped.

A few minutes later, Arès tried out the word. "*Sufi*," he said, and the taxi stopped.

At first Arès and Michaux lived in Takadoum.

Their room measured six square meters, barely enough space to squeeze a thin mattress over a tattered Moroccan rug. A small wooden table brooded in a corner beneath sacks of rice and flour, and next to it, a rusted brazier trestled a kerosene stove.

The walls were uneven and minutely fissured. A grilled aperture opened into a small boutique that fronted the building. The boutique traded in natural gas, and whenever the owner wrenched open a canister for a client, the fumes puffed into the room like a poison cloud. For this reason, the insubstantial door, which let into the front hall a mere meter from the busy street, was invariably open.

Arès and Michaux shared the room with another Congolese man named Toti, and their evenings were a scramble of flesh.

Every morning, Arès and Michaux massaged flour and water into a thick dough that they carried to a communal bakery three and a half twists and turns away. They moved warily at first, alert for the olive-clad policemen, fearful of being refouled at Oujda, of having to retraverse those yellow plains of violence. After a week they grew more daring, and with every subsequent day they expanded the compass of their wanderings.

It was in strolling the streets of Takadoum that Arès first intuited his blackness, both from the black looks he attracted and from the pale swarms of people sweeping by. Blackness was a thing he had never reflected on before. It was a considered imaginary, like the radical dryness of deserts or the barrenness of lunar seas. It was unknowable until he experienced it.

And in Morocco, as he soon found out, attention was not good. When he was young, the raucous cries of *"mundele!"* he had catapulted at the rare white people he saw—inevitably lost on the fringes of the University of Kinshasa—had been friendly and astonished. In Takadoum, he and Michaux were stalked by bunched bands of youths who hissed at them, or shouted *"azee!"* with smoke in their eyes, or worse, showered them with stones.

Whenever he ventured into those streets, Arès thought of Kiwaka and the dead men at Oujda and wondered if the next few steps would carry him into a policeman's heavy hand, the blasts of a whistle or the swish of white batons. Every bend in the road seemed an incalculable risk.

Travelling in groups lessoned the likelihood that he would be detained. Arès knew he was fast, much faster than anyone around him. Even after six years hunched by a river, he could feel the explosive strength in his legs.

He looked older though. Michaux had salvaged a long, crescent-shaped shard from a broken mirror and mounted it on the wall. Even in the pasty tungsten light, Arès could see that exile had not been kind.

He recognized himself, but marred, as if there were imperfections in the glass. His right cheek was pockmarked from a blistering fever he had contracted by the river, his left cheek gullied with a sinuous scar. His nose appeared puffed and crooked and his once strong features had softened.

He searched for the nobility that it is said suffering brings, but saw none of that. Rather the gleam had faded from his eyes and the once-healthy contours of his boyish face were angular and drawn. All the traits he knew had been buried beneath a wooden mask of singular devising.

He still hoped he could take off the mask. He drew hope from the fact that Paul had occasionally been startled by the presence of someone else, a waggish and sturdy youth, swimming below the surface of the shipwreck before him.

A couple weeks into their stay, Michaux came home with news. He had heard of a foreman hiring *sans papiers* at a construction site. It was a job for steel fixers and involved positioning and nipping steel mesh and installing rebar onsite.

"I hardly even know how to thatch the roof on a hut," Arès protested.

"Don't worry," Michaux said. "We put up all the buildings on my father's farm. If you do not know how to do something, I will show you."

"Remember," Toti advised, "if the wall is about to fall on you... jump!"

The two men laughed, while Arès stared sheepishly at the ground. Later that afternoon, they hurried to the site and were hired as day laborers.

For the next two months, they took a *grand taxi* every morning from the *Chateau d'eau Takadoum* to the Quartier de l'Océan. Arès stuck close to Michaux and gradually mastered the tricks of filling corner voids with rebar and embedding steel rods into mortar joints before they hardened. It was painstaking work, and his stomach knitted with anxiety every time the foreman circled too close.

After a particularly grueling afternoon, Michaux grunted, and slapped the young man on his back. "For a lazy fisherman, you work well."

"Where I am from in Brazzaville, fishing is a very active sport," Arès replied with a glint in his eye. "We sit by the river and we wait for a crocodile to catch a fish. Then we wrestle the crocodile until he gives up the fish."

Yes," Michaux said, stroking his cheek, "this sounds like the sort of stupidity someone from Brazzaville might invent."

Arès laughed and playfully jostled the farmer. A sharp hiss sounded out behind them and the two men spun on their heels. One of the Moroccan laborers stood there. "I know you Africans like to dance, but we are paid to work here. Pick up those spacers." He pointed to the metal stacks lying on the concrete. "And bring them up to the fourth floor."

Without another word, the two men bent down and loaded their arms with as many spacers as they could carry.

"I think we may need your crocodile wrestling skills if we keep working here," Michaux said as they sweated up the stairs with bowed backs.

"Are you sure Europe is worth all this effort?" Arès asked, grunting beneath the weight.

"What? You are giving up?" Michaux clucked his tongue in disapproval. "What happened to becoming a movie star?"

Arès grinned. "I am more interested in the designer suits that Kiwaka promised us." The two men laughed loudly. Then they tossed down the spacers with a resounding, clattering crash.

On most days, the foreman halted work shortly before the *Asr* prayers, and the two men hastened home before sundown. Occasionally, though, they labored well past nightfall beneath the ragged glare of dozens of high-wattage bulbs. No one, however, was permitted to work past the start of the *Isha* prayers. When the muezzin's first orisons sounded from the nearby minaret, the workers dropped their tools where they stood.

On those nights, the Moroccans laid out bedding and griddled meat, while Arès and Michaux threaded among them, gathering and shelving the fallen tools. They were never invited to partake in the meals and the aromatic gusts fretted their hunger until they were finally dismissed.

When they at last arrived at the *Chateau d'eau Takadoum*, they fussed impatiently until a sizable group of black Africans had assembled—similarly tardy in their arrival, similarly rankled by appetite—before hazarding the hostile streets. It was too risky by themselves. Toti had warned them on the day of their arrival: "The nail that sticks up gets hammered down."

For a full week, they borrowed eight dirhams a day from their roommate to pay for the *grand taxi* rides to work. At the end of the week, they settled up and celebrated their fortune with two sextuplets of Flag beer.

Toti snapped the cans free of the plastic web and slapped them firmly into their hands. He was a man whose muscles always seemed bunched, and his eyes, under a jagged scar that wriggled transverse across his temple, were restless and seeking.

Arès often felt uncomfortable around him, but that evening he thought of Paul's unflappable good cheer and tossed a brotherly arm over Toti's shoulder. They clanked their cans. Then Arès ceremonialized the moment by pouring a few pale driblets of beer on the doorsill in veneration of his freewheeling friend.

"It is a shame Kiwaka is not here," Arès said. "He would have been singing songs all night, and this room would be full of pretty young women now instead of the ugly faces I see around me." He grinned and Michaux poked him amicably.

"Don't you know that there are no women in Morocco?" Toti asserted in a disgruntled voice.

"What are you saying?" Michaux asked. "I see women every day in the streets."

"For the Moroccans, yes," Toti replied. He sucked his teeth loudly and spit out the door. "But for us, no. For black Africans this is a country of lonely young men."

"You are exaggerating," Arès protested.

"Women want men with a future," Toti insisted, shaking his head. "In Morocco, we only have our present, and barely that. Some of us have even lost our pasts." He looked challengingly at the two men. Michaux met his stare, but Arès looked away.

"You two are new here, so let me make things clear. To live in Morocco is to live in a port. Nothing stays in place. Your job today will be gone tomorrow. Your closest friend will be on the next boat out. We sleep in bunks no bigger than coffins." He stretched out his arms, easily grazing both walls with his fingers. "Sometimes a woman arrives, but she is a ship you cannot board. And you will not admire her for long. No woman worth anything stays in a port."

"You are a master of celebration," Michaux said, tapping his can against Toti's. "I am glad that we could share our small triumph with you." He regarded the two men with an ugly crocodile's grin.

Toti shrugged. "I do not want to ruin this evening. Let us celebrate." He took a big swig of beer. "But do not let yourselves become too comfortable here. It will only lead to disappointment." He fell silent and his eyes clouded with some inner distress. The long scar puckered along his temple and began to twitch like a worm on a hook.

"I have been in Rabat for three years now, but I also thought it would only be a few months," he continued. "Life is rough here. There is nothing lonelier and more desperate than a man trapped in a port. And there are only two ways out. On a ship or burial at sea." He slid his finger across his neck as he finished his speech.

"Kiwaka would have found some ladies," Arès asserted in a tense, over-bright voice.

Michaux shook his head and smiled. "No. I do not think Kiwaka would have enjoyed this life. Can you imagine him pouring cement in his white linen jacket and alligator shoes?" He laughed ruefully and began lightly singing the words to "Mario." Arès joined in and the two of them duetted in memory of their lost friend.

"Did you fellows inhale too much of the natural gas today?" Toti asked, and gave a braying laugh.

Michaux smiled guardedly and sipped his beer. Suddenly, he tilted forward with a gleam in his eyes. "I was talking to the foreman during lunch, and he told me the secret to hiring the best carpenters."

"A traditional Moroccan secret, no doubt?" Toti said, grinning. Even his smile bothered Arès. His lips curved up like a sickle and his cheeks puckered as if crammed with hard pebbles.

"He makes the applicants hold up their hands," Michaux continued, "and if they still have all their fingers, he won't hire them." He thumped his can against the table for emphasis.

"This sounds like the usual Moroccan stupidity," Arès remarked, glad for a change of topic. Toti was ruining the night. He was the sort of man who preferred to trip you in a race and fall down himself, rather than let you get ahead.

"No," Michaux replied, "he's right. Any carpenter who's worked here long enough to be any good has lost at least a couple fingers." The three men laughed.

Then a hard-stamping screaming broke out upstairs. Something shattered, and several children began to wail.

"Sounds like they are praying again," Arès said.

Michaux smirked and raised his beer. "To living and working in Rabat, and to Moroccan hospitality." None of them clanked their cans.

The toast shushed them and they sipped on in silence. Soon the first round was gone. They started into their second beers and then their third. After a while, things began to seem a bit glad and hopeful again, and for a moment, Arès thought that maybe they would survive.

The next afternoon, when Michaux treaded home to the lift and lilt of the muezzin's song, Arès loitered at the entrance to the construction site. There was no work the next day and he felt a vague abhorrence at the idea of returning to the congested flat and the spiteful streets of Takadoum.

"What to do?" he wondered, as he basked in the diffuse afternoon light. Before he knew it, he was loafing ahead. His feet carried him through several anonymous streets that eventually spit him out onto Avenue Abdelkrim. He kept up a steady pace and soon he arrived at a vaulted sandstone arch that led into the old medina.

Inside stretched a long commercial street filled with bespectacled tailors and soft-knocking cobblers, grocers peddling succulent fruits, and grim butchers fanning flies off their bloody wares. It was Arès' first visit to that ancient city, and he was surprised to find the shopkeepers slotted into dozens of small alcoves that honeycombed the medina's incurving walls.

He pressed on and came across a squat building surrounded by fancy cars and bearing the words, *le Centre des droits de l'homme*. Then, on his left, he passed whitewashed cemetery walls and another arched entrance. Curious to see how the Moroccans tended to their dead, Arès stepped inside and paused before a sloping panorama of weed-tufted tombs. Far below, backdropped by a hammered sea, a white, two-story building rose off stilts. Above it blurred an opaqueness of swallows, a mottled beach, and the sparkling crests of waves.

A gruff voice called to him, and he retreated quickly out of the cemetery. There was a saying in Takadoum: "If a Moroccan shouts at you, walk away. If he chases you, run. If he catches you, pray." Arès had trouble believing that the Moroccans were all such brutes, but he did not want to find out the hard way.

The fortress of les Oudayas loomed ahead, its crenellated battlements daubed with copper trims by the evening light. He passed awestruck beneath its massive ochre gate and wandered through its twisting blue and white lanes.

Blue and white for what? So much in Morocco seemed a puzzle to which he lacked the key.

Swimsuited teenagers rambled by with curious planks of wood under their arms. Dreadlocked musicians strummed guitars that emitted enigmatic desert tunes. Arès reached the end of les Oudayas and gazed out over silvering seas, while the spinning light of the lighthouse flashed its warnings at him.

He felt confused but elated. It was his first touristic jaunt, and he marveled at all that he saw. He had to admit it, the Moroccans had built a beguiling city. For the first time in weeks he relaxed. Lost in thought, he began to retrace his steps back toward the medina. Then, a sibilant hiss burst out of a doorway, and Arès nearly jumped out of his skin.

He spun left and saw a trio of adolescents laughing at their prank. He smiled at them to show there were no hard feelings, but they hissed again, so he turned his back and moved on. Tonight, he realized, was special, and he did not want to dwell on the stupidity of boys. He merged into the crowds streaming back from the beach and noticed for the first time that he was hungry.

From a stall fronted with colorful candies, plastic bottles of Sidi Ali, and small crates of fresh mint, Arès bought fifty grams of cashew nuts. *"Cinquante grams acajou,"* he said, and the vendor peeled off a small sheet of cornflower blue paper, scribbled with children's writing, and with a deft motion twirled it conical and shoveled in the salty nuts.

Munching on the cashews, unutterably content, Arès wandered toward the Place Bab el Had. There he watched hooded men in white djellabas and colorful babouches scrape over ancient cobblestones on their way toward the mosque. On the far side of the square, the female faithful streamed by in nearly identical dress. Toti may be right, he thought. The women here are not for me. Then he chuckled.

Dusk gave way to twilight, and pods of luminescence blossomed on the cityscape. He ambled ahead, enchanted by the night, by how it suppressed all the idle details. The mosque began its starlit warble and Arès passed down long-laned Mohammed V, past the police with their whistles and white batons, past Hotel Balima's tree-lined terrace bar, the red-ribbed parliament, and here and there, a prone worshipper, his rump raised toward the heavens.

On a whim, he meandered into the side streets, wondering what he would find. So much to take in and no one to guide him! What he would give for his father's steady hand and confident ways; for Paul's canny advice.

It was then he remembered his pledge to Paul and he turned back on his tracks. Before the ramparts of the Place Bab el Had, a small crowd of Rastas bobbed about like medusas caught in a tidal flux. A short, tubby one, with coils of hair piled half his height, waved him over.

"Feeling eerie, man?"

Arès shook his head. "No English," he replied.

"I am Bob Marley," the Rasta said in stuttering French. "Where you from?"

"Zaire."

"Ah, Rumble in the Jungle! Good to meet you man!" The diminutive figure danced about in a trance haze, an ember cone tracing curlicues of smoke with every dip and bend. Then, without another word, Bob Marley drifted back to the other Rastas, jamming and puffing before the brown battlements.

Arès peered after him. He had trouble telling whether the Rastas were Moroccans, or black Africans like himself, or some hybrid of the two. They treated the Place Bab el Had like it was their personal playground, but no one seemed to bother them. It defied all understanding.

Nothing makes sense in this city, he thought as he re-crossed the Quartier de l'Océan, and trailed down Avenue Sidi Mohammed. Soon he passed the local *gare routière*, with its rows of chrome buses slumbering beneath the shine of cobra-headed street lamps. A few minutes later, he came to the Christian Cemetery.

Without bothering to look around, he spidered onto a low-hanging branch and slid over the wall. For the next half hour, he strode through the granite darkness until he came across the Big Man's grave.

On the door hung a stylized gothic M, and an immaculate cross bottony with trefoil lobes, crowned the gabled roof. The tomb's perimeter was choked with extravagant bouquets and potted plants. Arching above and shading it beneath its perennial foliage were the thorned and twisted limbs of an acacia tree.

Inside, slept the monster who had broken the Congo with his legendary appetites. An arrogant, insatiable man, *Mobutu Sese Seko Nkuku Ngbendu Wa Za Banga*: the all-powerful warrior, who goes from conquest to conquest, leaving only fire in his wake.

"I did it," he said. It had been little over a month since he had promised to Paul that he would visit the Maréchal's grave, but experientially, it felt like a century.

What now? What had the trader wanted? He knew what Félix would have told him to do. He would have seized his younger brother by the arm and looked at him with those commanding eyes. "Spit on his grave, Arès. Dig up his corpse. Desecrate his resting place. Leave his spirit no rest."

How could he argue with Félix? It was wrong that the Big Man should enjoy peace in death. Not when so many still wandered through the ashlands he had left behind. Not when so many were forced to stretch out at night on the rocky ground of exile.

Still, Arès made no move. He tried to stir his anger. He thought of his father aflame, his eyes steaming out tears. He thought of his mother's embrace, and his youngest sister's luminous laugh. For what seemed like hours, he bided before an unapologetic silence; waiting for some thought, some sign, some surge of emotion, hate or satisfaction or even a spark of sadness.

But all he felt was a deep emptiness when he looked at that bombastic mess of stone, a white and black mausoleum, walled with veined marble.

Suddenly, he laughed. So loudly and abruptly that he startled himself. It had just occurred to him. The Big Man's tomb was significantly larger than the room he shared with Michaux and Toti. For a few seconds, he listened to the echoes of his laugh ricochet off the stones around him, and then he understood why the trader had sent him there. He circumferenced the tomb, measuring it with his hands, more than confirming his suspicions.

"It's five times the size of our room. The bastard!" He started laughing again. He couldn't help it. He shook to the ground, tears pouring out of his eyes. His laughter bounded through the cemetery and came back to him, and in that lonely place, he heard a melodious laugh full of eccentric timbres and he knew it was Paul's.

He leaned against an anonymous tomb and closed his eyes, still chuckling.

Gradually, the evening cooled and the still-humid air shed its saltiness. And then, for a moment, the weather was right, and the soft nighttime breezes carried whispers of home to Arès. It was that same wet, sweet air, edged with a crispness, that he had known his entire life. Within every draft he could make out the comforting rumble of his father's voice, and hear the creaking of trees in his parents' garden, and sense the wonderful freshness of opening the back door late at night.

A few minutes later, a gust of salt-drenched air blew in from the sea and Arès awoke from his idyll, wonderfully restored. One of his father's favorite sayings came unbidden to his lips. He stood up and addressed it aloud to Mobutu's tomb: *"La justice est comme un feu, si vous l'enveloppez, elle brûle."*[46] He thought the words sounded grand, but then he started chuckling again and he knew what he would do.

Beside the mausoleum stood a wooden effigy of the Big Man, dressed in his habitual abacost, bearing a wooden staff, and capped by an oversized leopard-skin toque. Arès perched off the statue's left foot, reached up, and deftly plucked off the toque. Striking a royal poise, he settled it onto his head. Then he located a fallen stick and scratched the soft loam beside the acacia tree: "When an old man dies, a country burns."

The cemetery entrance was easy to find. He scaled the front gate and stood in a funnel of light in the deserted street, looking foolish in his stained workmen's clothes and leopard-skin toque. It was too dangerous to return home at this hour, so Arès slid seawards and wandered amidst grottos and hard cracked earth, his nose puckering at the gouts of sewage that spilled every hundred meters into the gray and frothing waters.

In half an hour's time, he re-passed the instable beam of the lighthouse and grappled down the sand wall onto the *plage de Rabat*. He walked across a bed of sand as fine as soot and, overcome by an irresistible fatigue, settled against one of the white pilings beside the shore.

On the sea fringe of the beach, among tide pools shaped like cauldrons, rubbery snails slunk through watery obscurities. Beyond was the seamless slick of the sea, and to the right, tumbles of dark rocks and a long, curving

---

46   Justice is like fire. If you try to smother it, it burns.

escarpment that sheltered the mouth of the Bouregreg River and the nearby beaches of Salé. The night was clear, and above a capsized moon, the Pleiades wept and novas blazed.

Arès looked up at the illegible skies, and then stretched out among plastic rinds and rusted tins.

"The bastard," he said again. Still smiling, he fell asleep.

The next morning, he awoke half-submerged in the onrushing tide. Spurting up into splashes of sunlight, he reached toward his head, but the leopard-skin toque was gone.

CHAPTER 21

APRIL 2009

S IMON WHISTLED AS HE traversed the bright white terrace and ducked under the low doorway into the HCR kitchen. Inside, two squat women in matching green smocks tended several boiling pots on a medieval cooking range. "Double double, toil and trouble..." he chanted under his breath, before greeting them with a hearty "*Salaam!*"

Two matching chestnut-brown faces twisted toward him. Behind them, a porthole window offered a view onto a miniscule wriggle of blue amidst a far-off shock of green.

"*Salaam*," they replied in unison.

"Would you like some mint tea?" Saana asked.

"You are a light in the wilderness," Simon replied, as she poured him a steaming glass of tea.

"*Shokran bzef!*" he added, placing a forefinger on the glass's fragile rim and a thumb on its thickened bottom. He sipped contentedly, watching the fire snake around the gas rings on the cooking range and wondering what was for lunch.

When he was done, he re-crossed the now empty terrace and accessed the main building. Soon, he arrived at an imposing wooden door with *Maarten Van Wassenaer, Country Director* written in gothic letters on a massive brass plate.

He rapped lightly on the frame and opened the door. Inside was a commodious corner office, with gaping bay windows that let in the rumble of the traffic below.

The walls were crammed with framed diplomas, letters of recognition, gold-leaf certificates, and numerous awards. An executive L-shaped desk dominated the room, and above it rose a tall hutch stocked with clothbound legal tomes. On one wing of the desk, a detailed to-scale replica of a sailboat rested on a mahogany stand. The Country Director stood over the model, fiddling with one of the three jibs on the bowsprit.

"That's a very impressive ship," Simon remarked.

"Yes, it is," Maarten replied. "It's a nineteenth-century racing ship called a Flying Fish. When I retire, I'm going to buy something similar and sail it around the Mediterranean."

"Sounds like a great way to spend your retirement."

"We all have to dream of something," the Director said with a wink. He backed up a few steps to better admire the model. Then he trained his executive blue eyes on the JPO. "For the moment, though, we have to keep our ship here on course. I need a native English speaker to draft some funding proposals for the Spanish government. I want to make sure they're watertight."

"Funding?" Simon asked, surprised. "The UN doesn't finance the HCR?"

"Not quite," he answered, with a slight twist to his lips. He glided back to his desk and laid a possessive hand on a pile of brown folders. "Regional bureaus are expected to contribute as well. We receive backing from several actors, the European Commission, the Netherlands, co-financing through joint-programs with the Office of International Migration, and, well, Spain."

"Since we fit into Spain's security portfolio," Maarten continued, "they provide most of our ammunition. We intend to request another three years of funding. I hope you won't mind hopping onboard for this project."

Simon was tempted to say, "Ay ay, Captain."

"Of course," he replied. "Are there any political sensitivities I should keep in mind? Since we're primarily funded by Spain does that mean their migration policy takes precedence in the proposal?"

Maarten strode to the window and gazed out at the jagged brown bluff of the Chellah, suspended high above the Bouregreg Valley like a wave about to break.

"Well, we certainly do our best to align our proposals with the priorities of our donors," he said, keeling about, "but we never want to stray too far from the protection needs of our refugee population." The Director bestowed a reassuring smile on the young JPO.

"I'll keep that in mind," Simon said. He speedily scrawled some notes on a blue notepad.

Maarten glanced at his model ship and then abruptly circled some sixty degrees around the room. Placed now before the high hutch of clothbound tomes, he regarded the JPO, his arms spread akimbo with martial flair.

"Do you know who Tariq Ibn Ziad was?" he inquired.

"No." Simon looked at him expectantly.

"Tariq Ibn Ziad was the Muslim commander who led the Moroccans in their conquest of Andalusia around 700 A.D. The Rock of Gibraltar is named after him—in Arabic it's actually *Jabal Tariq,* or the Mountain of Tariq. Ibn Ziad landed his fleet on that rock and the Moroccans went on to rule Spain for over six hundred years. By coincidence, or not," he gave an outsized grin and drifted a few degrees to the right, "the HCR is situated at the summit of Avenue Tariq Ibn Ziad. I hope, with your help, we'll sail our fleet here for a similar triumph."

"All hands on deck," Simon said.

"I like your spirit. Just keep this between us. These projects are highly confidential. Remember: loose lips sink ships."

The JPO nodded energetically. "When would you like me to get started?"

"This afternoon would be great."

Simon tugged his collar. "It's just... I have to finish those judicial summaries for Anna-Heintz."

"Well those shouldn't take too long," Maarten said affably. "Here are the initial project reports that you should review before moving onto the draft proposal." He pointed to several thick brown folders piled on his desk. "This is a rather urgent matter, so it would be best to push out an initial draft soon. It's Tuesday, so how does Friday morning sound to you? We can discuss the draft over Friday couscous; that way we'll have several things to chew on at once." He beamed down at the young man with an encouraging smile.

Simon gulped. "I'll do my best." He picked up the folders, feeling the heavy ballast in his arms.

"I'm confident your best will exceed my expectations. Americans are such go-getters." The Director clapped a firm hand on the JPO's back, escorting him out of the room.

"Go get 'em," he said, and shut the door.

Clutching the thick folders, Simon headed down the hall. A few seconds later, he stopped at an open office door and leaned in. Federika glanced up at him, her pen still scribbling furiously across a document.

"*Salut*," Simon said, speaking in French. "I've just finished my meeting with Maarten and thought I'd pop in to see about the summary for Dominique."

"Great," she replied in English. "We're having some issues with one of our local partners and I have to intervene, so you're just in time."

Splendid, Simon thought.

"Here's a list of the protected individuals whose dossiers we are summarizing. You should start with Dominique, since you met him this morning. If you go to the dossier room and pull a few files at random, you'll come across other summaries that you can use as templates."

"Sounds straightforward."

"It's not," she said with an exasperated sigh. "Please begin in my absence. You'll find the dossiers downstairs. I need Dominique's summary by tomorrow morning."

"No problem."

Simon bounded down the two flights of stairs and quickly traversed the wide, open-air courtyard that fronted the building. A small side entrance led into a narrow office outfitted with three rectangular desks arranged in rows. Each desk abutted the wall to its right, leaving only a narrow passage on the left side. Lise and Nathalie were sitting at the second desk, noses deep in pink dossiers, flipping pages with nearly synchronized arm movements.

Behind the third desk stood Ibrahim, a heavily jowled man with scruffy cheeks and amoebic bags under his eyes. When Simon entered the office, he was breathlessly barking into the phone.

"Mr. Mustapha, you missed your meeting yesterday. You must come today or else you will lose your protection as a refugee.... No. I've told you this many times, we cannot reimburse you for the trip.... Yes, I know it is expensive, but you have to come or else we can no longer help you. *D'accord?* I am putting you down for Wednesday, but this is your *final* warning. No more chances," he growled.

"Using your gentle voice today, Ibrahim?" Simon remarked.

Ibrahim slammed the phone onto the receiver. His face, which a moment before had been disfigured by an almost Old Testament fury, softened and took on a kindly, hangdog look.

"Would you like to speak with the refugees instead of me?"

"God forbid," Simon said.

Ibrahim grunted and then slid his right forefinger down a list of some twenty names. His hands were fleshy and well groomed, and a silver wedding band glinted off his ring finger.

Simon was about to ask him how he was doing, when the phone gave off a shrill clang, and Ibrahim's face contorted angrily. "*Allô?*" he shouted in a hoarse voice. "No!" he bellowed. "You cannot reschedule your interview!"

A heavy, studded door at the back of the office swung open and a young woman in a black leotard and a green canvas skirt emerged with a dozen, tattered pink folders. She plunked down at the first desk and began plucking out papers like she was de-feathering a chicken. Lise leaned over and grabbed several folders. Then she looked up at Simon with friendly brown eyes.

"Do you need something?"

"Just the pleasure of your company," he replied.

"Do you ever work?" Nathalie demanded.

"Ah yes, it must have slipped my mind." Simon whistled out a short allegro tune. "I did have something or other to do here."

He sidled down the tight passage to the back of the office and wrenched open the sturdy door. An exhalation of frigid air enveloped him and he shivered reflexively.

Within the dossier room, a single fluorescent bulb emitted a wan, yellow light. Simon had never been inside before, and he had the spooky sensation of entering a mausoleum. The feeling was exacerbated by the room's winding architecture, which concealed most of the filing cabinets around a perpendicular bend. He shivered again and was glad that even through the reinforced door, he could still hear Ibrahim roaring into the phone, muffled, distorted, and strangely comforting.

Simon soon discovered that the cabinet classifications bore no relation to the reference numbers on his list. For some reason, the files weren't coded either by year or order of reception. Instead, the numbers jumped around unpredictably according to a logic that was impenetrable to him.

He began pulling out files at random and sat down on the cool, tiled floor to inspect them. Each pink dossier contained a photograph of the refugee in question and transcripts of interviews, some of which lasted for dozens of pages. Many of the refugees had been interviewed on five or six separate occasions and their folders bulged with the recordations.

Several overstuffed dossiers had burst at the seams and been sloppily taped back together. They swelled obscenely with all the varied flora of bureaucracy—medical reports, psychological evaluations, BIDs, resettlement requests, x-rays, doctors' prescriptions, microfinance loan applications, questionnaires—the paper results of lives lived.

Simon leafed through the folders, extracting short summaries wherever he could, reading through dozens of them. Described in laconic detail, pithy to the point of poetry, the summaries were biblical in bent: violence, kidnappings, daring escapes, rape, murder, enslavement. They were as far removed from the tidy, ordered world in which Simon lived as Shakespeare's tragedies. He would hardly have been surprised if the stiff folders had yielded up accounts of admonitory ghosts, magic potions brewed by witches, or supernatural interventions.

He had had inklings of this other, disorienting world, from the asylum interviews he had conducted. But seeing those thousands of dossiers filling those hundreds of cabinets gave him a sudden, unexpected thrill, not unlike the shameful voyeuristic excitement he'd once procured from reading pulp novels in his youth. He felt as if he had been admitted into an exclusive sect, privy to deep, blasphemous secrets about the world that good, honest citizens were never meant to know.

He thought of the desperate migrants he had met that morning in Takadoum, and of their lunatic good cheer while they plotted their suicidal crossings. He understood something now of the madness they had fled. He realized as well that they still carried embers of that madness with them, like a burning talisman, and that this accounted for much of their strength.

"God bless!" he exclaimed, and chortled loudly to himself. The laughter reverberated in the hollow chamber and chilled him with its empty, cackling sound.

He looked up at those impassive cabinets in that sepulchral light and felt, suddenly, like he had defiled a sacred space. A fear stirred in some obscure cavity of his soul; ancient, Mosaic, profane. The refugees' stories now seemed to him an unheeded warning, and the world a much wilder place than he had ever supposed.

At that moment, out of the corner of his eye, he detected a flicker of movement, like the phantom lash of a tail.

"Woah!" Simon shouted, lurching out of the room and banging his hip against the steel door.

"What's the matter?" Lise asked.

"It sounds nuts, but I swear I saw just a snake in there."

"In the dossier room?" He heard Nathalie snort loudly.

"I'm not kidding," he said, his cheeks reddening. "Maybe it was some other animal."

"Ibrahim?" Lise swiveled in her chair. "Did you let any snakes into the dossier room?" Ibrahim took a deep breath, shook his head, and then continued thundering into the phone in Arabic.

"No snakes, Simon," Lise concluded.

Simon lit the flashlight on his phone and cracked open the door, sweeping the beam into the cobwebbed corners. When he was satisfied with his inspection, he crept gingerly back into the room. After reshelving the unneeded dossiers, he looked at his watch. There was work to do.

He poked his head back out into the front office. "Nathalie!" he shouted. "Would you mind lending me a hand?"

"Are you having trouble with another snake?" she shouted back.

"Yes," he said. "It's wrapped around my leg and I can't get it off." No response. "It's getting quite tight. Would you mind?"

Nathalie tossed down a pile of pink folders and bustled into the dossier room. "If I had a machete," she muttered, "I'd just whack it off with the leg." He stared at her humorlessly. "What do you need?" she asked.

He handed her the list. She looked over it for a minute and then zipped around, pulling out the dossiers. Thirty seconds later he held a pink stack in his hands. "Americans!" she exclaimed and returned to her desk.

Simon hurried back to the third floor and sat down in his office. There were several emails from Anna-Heintz, demanding the judicial summaries in increasingly strident tones. He spent the next hour polishing them off and then turned to Dominique.

Dominique Mutombo
Single, Male, 16 years old, Congo (République Démocratique)

```
Arrival Date in Morocco ........................12 June 2005

Registration Date with the HCR Rabat ...........20 April 2006

Recognition Date of refugee status ............9 October 2006

Birth Date ................................. 21 February 1993

Birthplace ................ Goma, Congo (Democratic Republic)

Religion ......................................... Christian

Ethnicity .......................................... Swahili

Education ......................... 4 years (primary school)

Address in Morocco ........ Rabat, Takadoum, Tel: 013 55 77 27

Last Home Visit by the HCR .................... 11 April 2009
```

Flight from Home Country

In 2002, when Dominique was coming home from school, he was kidnapped along with several other children by Rwandan soldiers who pretended that their vehicle had broken down. Brought to a camp in Mwenga, he was given rudimentary military training before being forced into combat. During the conflict, the young man claims to have burned down houses and committed massacres.

232

He insists that he was drugged the entire time and claims memory problems since then. As a simple soldier, he lived in extremely rough conditions, sleeping on the ground and rarely eating.

In 2003, following an extremely bloody battle during which two of his friends were killed, he decided to escape. He took advantage of a torrential downpour to hide in the jungle. For two months, he walked north toward Central African Republic, aided by the inhabitants of small villages along the way. From there, he crossed Chad, Niger, and Algeria before arriving in Morocco in June 2005.

He has had no news of his parents since his kidnapping in 2002.

Situation in Morocco

Upon his arrival, Dominique was lodged in a church in Rabat. After being registered with the HCR, and the recognition of his status as a refugee, he began to receive modest financial support and moved into a room with three other young Congolese men and women in Takadoum.

However, he was made increasingly uncomfortable by the continuing harassment of the Congolese residents of the neighborhood. A month after he moved in, a crowd of Moroccans attacked him and five other Congolese men. They all suffered serious injuries from the stones and bottles thrown at them, followed by knife attacks. All six were hospitalized. The local police refused to intervene and Dominique was forced to give up his apartment and move to new lodging. As a result, he reports great difficulty with local integration.

In addition, he continues to suffer from nightmares due to his experiences as a child soldier. He also feels a deep sense of guilt for his actions, which is impacting his social and affective life.

Despite these challenges, Dominique is fighting to build a future for himself. He recently finished three months of intensive Arabic lessons. He also completed a six-month course in computer science. He is passionate about computer science but has agreed to receive training as a mechanic in order to ensure his financial stability. However, without a work or residency permit, it will not be easy for him to find employment as a mechanic or continue his studies in computer science.

Mental and Physical Health

Dominiqué suffers from Post-Traumatic Stress Disorder (PTSD). This disorder is caused by an event during which a person feels intense fear, distress, or horror. Dominique has not managed to sleep through the night even once in the past several years. He often has headaches and he is undergoing medical treatment in order to fight against his insomnia and recurrent nightmares.

PART II

A RÈS WANDERED THROUGH THE market at Takadoum, grazing his fingers over the unaffordable junk: old paperbacks in English, a stuffed baby camel with alabaster eyes, a lone Wellington (who would ever need a single boot?), a pair of jeans that he coveted, a Congolese war mask.

Eventually, he stopped and sat before the northern entrance to the market and prayed business would come. Around his neck hung a sign, *"Serrurier."*

Moroccan girls passed by. Beautiful girls, some in tight jeans and T-shirts, with strong bones and almond-shaped eyes. Others in roomy kaftans, their hair covered, their faces floating amidst a swishing nothingness, like studied perfections.

He longed for these women. For the hundred dirhams that could buy him *"une tour"* on the streets of Rabat.

He had thirty dirhams left from some construction work the week before, this time making bricks. He had to be careful. For a brief moment, he glared at all these people with their charmed, unfettered lives. Here he sat in the dust, surrounded by cripples and beggars.

He scanned the crowd, inclining his tradesman's sign ever so slightly toward the heavens. When his eyes gravitated down to earth, he leaned back with loathing.

A man sat on the far side of the market, a denatured limb on luxurious display. Two armpit crutches, neatly folded, flanked his normal leg. The other leg—it was a hardly a leg—stretched forth, an improbable mass ribbed with white scars. Several twiggish bones appeared to have been slotted roughly under the skin and the flesh petrified and seared. Only a few last meaty bits still budded off that black rock, halfway above a cauliflowered knee.

Old women in cowled robes paraded by, dropping small silver coins into the beggar's outstretched palm. No one in the neighborhood could compete. Not even the old Chinese man who hobbled impossibly about, one mangled foot dangling tenuously off a foreshortened leg and the other foot carelessly inverted.

Arès hitched his tool bag onto his shoulder and began to circle the marketplace, holding up his "*Serrurier*" sign. He kissed the golden key around his neck for luck.

A few minutes later he saw a gesture. He walked over to a woman in a black burnous. She sat atop a soft brown donkey with a bright yellow muzzle and two pink, plastic containers balanced on either side.

"At your service," he said.

"Any luck?" Michaux asked, when he saw Arès unlatch the door.

"A little. A hairdresser had me fix the lock on her shop."

"The one over by the marketplace?"

"How can you ask such a question? There are over ten hairdressers within five minutes of the market. I have never lived in a place with so many hairdressers."

"There are many salons in Kinshasa," Michaux responded.

"Yes, but not like here. Here there is one on every street corner and sometimes two. And they are open till three in the morning. You'd think the Moroccans would be very well coiffed with all these hairdressers, but they do not have particularly nice hair."

Michaux grinned. "So you made some money?"

"Yes, fifty dirhams." Arès threw a clatter of coins and bills onto their low wooden table. "But I was stopped by a policeman and he tried to confiscate my tools, which are worth far more than fifty dirhams."

"What did you do?"

"I ran like I always do. It was very close this time. He had friends, and many of the Moroccans tried to block me, but I went over a fence that the fat pig couldn't jump."

Michaux laughed earnestly. "Well at least we can pay the rent now."

"You should really go to the HCR," Toti said. "If you have a refugee card and the police catch you, sometimes you are not expelled, and if they are in a good mood that day"—he lifted a fake joint to his lip and sucked in deeply—"they let you keep your money."

Arès and Michaux both laughed. Then Arès' face took on a serious expression. "But I do not want to stay here. Why would I bother to register in Morocco?"

"It's a good scam either way," Toti replied. "How long do you think it will take to save the money to pay a *passeur* to go to Europe? You should register at the HCR, so you do not get deported to Algeria in the meantime." While he spoke, Toti crouched down in the corner and lit the propane stove. Then he placed a pot filled with black beans on the burner.

"Why do you not have a refugee card?" Arès asked.

"I did not know what to say," Toti replied. "I tried, but they rejected me. You have to tell them that you saw your family killed in front of you. Or that you were tortured or raped. Or that you come from some oppressed minority. If you lie and tell them that you are Rwandan but from the Congo," he spat out the door, "they will give you a card."

"This is not why you left the Congo?" Arès asked.

"I left the Congo because of the war," Toti replied. "I did not see my family killed in front of me, but I know that they are dead. The Rwandans came and when they left, my house was a hole. I hid in the forest for over two months eating insects. But the HCR refused me because I did not see my mother raped in front of me!"

"You have to see the violence to be a refugee?"

"Yes. Or you have to be persecuted." The beans began to sizzle and pop and Toti stirred them with a spoon. "They told me that if I was Banyamulenge, if I was one of the Rwandans who had caused the war, and the Congolese had killed my family, instead of being Congolese and having the Rwandans kill my family, then I would be a refugee. This is what they told me. Is this right? I have to be one of the people who started the war to be a refugee?" He slammed his fist down on the table and Arès nearly jumped.

"No. It is not right," Michaux affirmed. He spat out the door as well.

"Or because I was not tortured by the Rwandans or raped at Oujda by the Nigerians. Because of this I am not a refugee."

"Then what are you?" Arès asked.

"I am undesirable. They told me that I should go back to the Congo. They said they would help me through some travel agency called the IOM. They told me it was safe to go back. How is it safe for me? My family is all dead, and the Rwandans are in power. Is this justice?"

"No, it is not," Michaux affirmed. The beans sizzled violently and several exploded with loud pops. Toti cursed under his breath. Grabbing a soiled towel, he wiped the splattered sauce off the wall. Then he turned back to the two men.

"So, I have to lie," Arès said.

"Yes. I do not know what happened to you, but say you are Banyamulenge and get a card from the HCR. This is what Michaux is going to do."

"I will never say that I am Banyamulenge," Michaux said. Arès looked down and saw that the farmer's heavy fist was clenched. He felt a brief tremor of fear.

"Or say then that you were tortured by the rebels," Toti continued, "or that you belonged to Mobutu's political party. This is how it works."

"Where do I go?" Arès asked.

"The building is next to the American Embassy on Avenue Tariq Ibn Ziad. You must go on a Monday or Tuesday. They will give you a *carte de demandeur d'asile* at first, and that will last at least a year, because even if they reject you, you can appeal."

"Can you work with it?"

"No, but if you fall sick, sometimes they will help. And if you become a refugee, then they offer courses and even give you money to help you start a business."

"It sounds like a good scam," Arès said. "I will go."

"Good," Toti replied. He dashed some spices on the beans and ladled them into three colored bowls. Arès' mouth was watering by the time they sat down to eat.

On the following Tuesday, Arès took a *grand taxi* to the medina. For almost an hour, he walked in an unaccustomed direction across the city until he reached its administrative district.

He asked a passerby for directions, but quickly lost his way. Soon he found himself wandering among broad, peaceful avenues lined with stately mansions, fronted by flower-strewn gates. He could hardly believe his eyes. What a contrast to the crowded streets of Takadoum, where they crawled over each other like caterpillars! He strolled ahead, smelling the fresh hibiscus and honeysuckle and peering at leafy shadows that shimmied beneath the trees like the silhouettes of deep-sea fish.

Eventually, a gardener redirected him and he arrived at a noisy turn-about called the *Place Abraham Lincoln*. A small garrison of traffic cops, dressed in cornflower blue uniforms with conical white wrist cuffs, strutted martially about blowing whistles. Around them, an unbroken stream of vehicles angled up and down the road's banked circumference like roulette balls along the edge of a spinning wheel.

Arès looped halfway around the traffic ring to where Avenue Tariq Ibn Ziad began. Then he turned up its long, up-sloping sidewalk. On the far side of the street, he could see the American Embassy, with its concrete bunkers and armed retinues, baking in the sun. Far off, on a sandy bluff rising high above the surrounding landscape, the necropolis Chellah brooded beneath a wheeling parade of birds. And there, at the apex, stood the HCR, a bright white beacon on a hill.

The light blue flag of the United Nations—with its whitened world stamped on a white grid wreathed with olive branches—tilted obliquely off the beige roof. The building was bleached, three stories high, its stucco walls hatted by a spiked fence, its sidewalk studded with thick, white bollards noosed with chalky metal chains.

Before the HCR hurried a honking abundance of cars and trucks, then a slim rim of grass, a precipice, and far below, the backs of black and white birds gliding over the river Bouregreg and the verdant plains of Salé.

At 8:30 a.m., a sizable group of sub-Saharans queued beneath a grilled awning that fractured the sun into ribs of heat. There was no shade anywhere and the early September morning was uncomfortably hot. The line advanced and arrested in mercurial spurts, and it was not till 11:00 a.m. that Arès found himself anywhere close to the applicants' entrance on the southern wing of the building.

By then, the sun smoldered white-hot in the sky. Most of the asylum demanders had long since curdled onto patches of sidewalk, and if they moved now at all, it was to fan themselves with loose sheaves of paper. Arès had not thought to bring water, and his tongue lagged uncomfortably in his mouth like a dry sponge.

He wiped his brow. Then he slipped off his shirt and used it to tent his scalding head. On his back, long plaits of sweat glistened like diaphanous webs. The line inched forward.

For another quarter hour no one entered the building. The golden key burned irritably against his chest and Arès could feel his back char in the heat. So he squirmed back into his shirt and canopied his hands above his head. He missed the purling calm of the riverside. He missed dusk and watching flakes of light fall like pollen through the trees.

Why did I come here? he thought for the thousandth time.

Thank you for coming today.

This is a preliminary interview to gather some details about your person. It will later be used in order to determine whether or not you are a refugee.

At the end of this interview, we will give you a date for your refugee status determination interview.

Please talk about your life story in a manner that is open and above all honest. Everything you say here is entirely confidential.

We will not share your information with anyone, especially not the government. We are not a government agency.

Please give us as much detail as possible, because it is only by knowing your full story that we can determine whether or not you should be qualified as a refugee.

What is your name?

Arès Sbigzneou.

What is your phone number?

I do not have a phone.

Do you have a friend who has a phone, where we can call you?

Yes.

What is his number and his name?

06 16 24 08 23. His name is Toti.

Where are you from?

Kinshasa.

What is your date of birth?

I was born about twenty-four years ago.

Yes, but what is the exact date? What year were you born?

1980.

What day and what month?

I think it was in June. On the ninth or tenth day.

Thank you. What is your father's name?

Christian Sbigzneou.

What is your mother's name?

Léontine.

Do you have any brothers or sisters?

No. Yes. I had brothers and sisters.

How many?

I had two brothers and three sisters.

They are no longer alive?

I do not think so.

Are your parents alive?

No.

Do you have any family or relatives in Morocco?

No.

Please tell me about why you left the Congo.

My house was attacked. Everyone was killed except for me.

In what year was this?

I was eighteen.

So… 1998?

Yes.

Why did they attack your house?

Because my mother was Rwandan.

Were you there at the time of the attack?

Would you like to see the scars?

Thank you. I believe you.

THE INTERN WROTE SOMETHING IN HER NOTEBOOK.

Were you or was any person in your family a member of a political party
or association either affiliated with or persecuted by the government?

I do not think so.

Are you sure?

I do not know.

When did you enter Morocco?

In August.

1999?

No, this August.

2004.

Yes.

What did you do in the intervening years?

I fished.

Where?

In a river.

In what country?

South of Brazzaville.

You fished for six years?

I like to fish.

During this time did you look for your family?

By fishing?

No, by looking for them.

They are dead.

How do you know?

I saw them die.

I am sorry. How did you escape?

I do not know.

How do you not know?

There are many things I do not know.

Yes, but why do you not know this?

I was hit on the head and I lost consciousness. When I woke up, I was two hours from Kinshasa in the house of the man who had saved me.

Do you know why he saved you?

No.

Was this man of Rwandan origin as well?

I do not know.

Where do you live in Morocco?

Rabat.

What is your address?

I live in Takadoum.

By yourself?

No. With two other Congolese men.

Are you afraid that you might suffer prejudice or harm if you return to your home country?

Return?

Yes. Would you like to return to Kinshasa, or are you afraid that you would suffer prejudice if you return?

You want to send me back?

No. I am asking if you are afraid to go back. Do you fear persecution if you return?

It is impossible to go back there.

The DRC is safe now. There are no more attacks against people of Rwandan origin.

THE ASYLUM DEMANDER DID NOT RESPOND.

Thank you for the interview. Please hold still while I take a photo.

Thank you. Please wait here. I'll be back in a few minutes.

THE INTERN HANDED THE ASYLUM DEMANDER A CARD ON WHICH WAS WRITTEN *DEMANDEUR D'ASILE* FROM LEFT TO RIGHT, AND THEN FROM RIGHT TO LEFT طالب اللجوء

That is your *carte de demandeur d'asile*.

If you are stopped by the police, please show it to them. There is the number of the HCR on it, and you should give us a call if you are threatened with refoulement.

You have not been recognized as a refugee, and so we cannot offer you legal or health services, but we can normally intervene if you are at risk of expulsion.

Thank you.

And here is your date for your refugee status determination interview

This says February 7, 2005.

Yes. That is the date.

That is in five months.

Yes. I am sorry. This is how long it takes.

Is it not possible to come back sooner?

No. I am sorry.

Thank you for coming today.

Good luck with your refugee status determination interview.

CHAPTER 24
DECEMBER 2004

T HREE MONTHS LATER, ARÈS walked disconsolately through the twisted alleys of Takadoum. He had argued with Rafik again that morning. The man owed him over two hundred dirhams for the locks he had fixed, but getting him to pay was like wringing water from a stone.

When he rounded the bend, Arès could see that his roommates were home.

Michaux met him at the front door. "We must pay the REDAL for the electricity, but Toti and I do not have enough money. We need fifty dirhams. I know you cannot pay rent anymore, but can you help us with this?"

"Yes, of course. I do not have the money yet, but there is a Moroccan who owes me two hundred dirhams. I wasted all morning arguing with him and could not look for other work."

"How long have you tried to get the money?"

Arès furrowed his brow and made a show of counting on his fingers. "It has been almost two weeks. I have talked with him three times, but he never budges. One time he said he would pay the next day; then the next day he said the lock broke again, so I hadn't fixed it correctly and he wouldn't pay me. A few days later he let me look at the lock, and it worked, but he claimed that he paid someone else to fix it because he could not trust me."

"You will never get the money," Toti said. "You know how the Moroccans are."

"How are they?"

"The Moroccans are slippery like the catfish. They can never be caught."

"No, the Moroccan is like the lizard," Michaux said grinning. "He lies

in the sun with one eye open, and when you get near him, *zppht*, he's gone."
Toti and Michaux laughed uproariously.

"So what should I do?"

"When I was young," Michaux said, "my brother used to catch lizards.
He would lay a noose in the dirt, and when the lizard came by he would
pull, and the body would stay but the head would go."

"How did he get them to walk over the noose?'

"That I never figured out."

"You put a stick on their back, or you clamp down on them with your
foot. Then you attach the noose," Toti said.

"Perhaps this is what we should do with the Moroccans?" Arès suggested.
They all laughed.

"Yeah, but there are those lizards, the bright blue ones," Toti continued,
looking for a description.

"With the red heads?"

"Yeah those. With the skin, you would say, like a crocodile. You do not
want to get near them."

"You know what we used to do as children," Arès said. "We would
catch grasshoppers, the big long ones, and we would tie their legs to
something and scare them. They would take off, and if they were lucky
they bounced back, but if they jumped too quickly, their legs came right
off. Maybe I should frighten Rafik and see if he loses the leg with his
wallet."

Toti laughed again. "The jumper jumps too often, so he breaks his leg.
Then the jumps cease."

"Yes, but we cannot give the REDAL grasshopper legs," Michaux
grumbled.

"I have twenty dirhams. That is all. I can give it to you now, and I will
go back to the market today and see if I can find more work."

When Michaux took the money, he held onto Arès' wrist. "I've been
meaning to talk to you. Some people are saying you are not Congolese, but
that you are Banyamulenge."

Arès turned toward him, his eyes flashing. "Who says this? And what
if I were Banyamulenge? What difference would that make?"

"It is the fault of the Banyamulenge that we are here," Michaux replied, his teeth clenched. A vein on his forehead began to throb. It looked to Arès like a worm pushing through soil. "They caused the war. I would never live with a Banyamulenge. My family is dead because of them."

"Who are you speaking to?" Arès replied, balling his fists. "Did we not flee in the same jeep together? Who caused who to flee?"

"I fled with someone who claimed to be a fisherman from Brazzaville, but then I discovered that he was a locksmith," Michaux said coldly.

Arès' eyes blazed red with anger. "Are you calling me a liar?"

The two men squared off, their spines arched slightly like bent springs.

"Stop this talk," Toti said. He moved his solid mass between them. "I know a way for us to make money. There is a private party this evening where they need two idiots to guard the door. Since you are both available, you can come."

"Why would they hire blacks?" Arès asked. He turned to inspect something in the corner, but kept one eye at all times on the men behind him.

"It is an African party. I know the older brother of one of the organizers. He offered me the job and told me to find two more guards, but if you kill each other, I will have to ask some other friends."

"Since you could not possibly find anyone else who can stand you," Michaux replied, clasping Toti by the elbow, "we will put aside our differences to help." He turned to smile at Arès, but it looked to the young man like he was baring his teeth.

"I will come," Arès said.

They padlocked the worm-eaten door and headed out into the twisting streets of Takadoum. Within minutes, a posse of local children had latched onto them. They hooted out monkey calls and clambered on all fours.

The Congolese men quickened their stride. A pebble sailed over their heads, clattering against the cobblestones ahead. Arès swiveled to see where it came from and the beak of a whirling stone sliced open his cheek.

He could see the child who had launched the rock, and he could see three of his friends arming themselves with projectiles. He felt blood rushing to his head and clotting along his upper lip. He turned to chase the boy when Toti grabbed his arm.

"Don't. They'll kill us."

"What? They're just children." He tried to wrench his arm free, but Toti held him like a vise.

"Not the children." Arès peered around. At the edge of the bend he could see some of the neighborhood youths, their vacant eyes glued to the Congolese, full of idle menace. A stone whistled by his ear and he ducked involuntarily and heard the children laugh.

"Walk quickly, but do not run," Toti said. The three men skitter-stepped beneath a rain of chucked missiles, their eyes smoldering hotter with every cry of "*azee!*" and simian hoot. Arès heard Michaux huff as a pear-shaped stone punched him in the back, and Toti shielded his head amidst an uneven trot.

Eventually they lost control and dashed toward the sheltering throngs that jammed the entrance to the outdoor market. Several Moroccans jeered at the sprinting Africans and egged the children on. To a last clatter of stones against hard-packed earth, they melted into the crowd.

A few minutes later, they panted raggedly before the *Chateau d'eau Takadoum*, like three convicts fresh from a prison break. Arès burned at their helplessness.

"You run fast," Toti said.

"Yes," Arès replied. Then he smiled. "They give us many opportunities to practice here."

Michaux laughed and jumped a little to stretch his legs. "In a year, we will be ready to try out for the Olympics."

A *grand taxi* brought them to the *gare routière* in Rabat Ville. After getting out, Arès and Michaux retreated beneath the russet shadow of the medina walls, while Toti attempted to flag down a *petit taxi*. Almost two dozen scooted by without stopping. Arès could not tell if it was because they were black, or because of the frightening dagger of a cut on Toti's forehead. Finally, one screeched to a halt.

"How are we going to pay for this?" Michaux asked anxiously.

"They promised to cover our transportation," Toti replied.

The *petit taxi* shuttled up Avenue Mohammed V, turned right at the Gare de Rabat, and proceeded into the commercial district of Agdal. Arès had never been to that side of town, and he was astonished by all the cheerful shoppers and upscale boutiques. It struck him once again that he lived only a short ride away from carefree people, who thought only of what they would eat for dinner or what clothes they would wear when they left the house. I used to be like that, he thought, and his exile pained him worse than the ragged cut on his cheek. Then he swore under his breath for caring about such petty things.

The taxi left Agdal behind and entered a broad boulevard lined with posh restaurants behind impressive stone walls. Arès rolled down the window. He could hear the tinkle of glasses and rich laughter sounding beneath bowers of green. He leaned into the cold rushing air and strained his eyes to hold onto the sight as the taxi swept around another bend. When he plopped back into the seat, his right hand mechanically sought the golden key dangling above his chest.

"Where are we going?" he asked.

Toti shrugged in response.

The last squibs of daylight turned violet and then a deep purple, and the boulevard reduced to imprints of shapes and asterixes of light. The temperature dipped suddenly, unexpectedly, and Arès snapped the window shut. They rolled by the radiance of a large shopping mall and popped left into a leafy neighborhood of high metal gates and armed guards in fatigues. Some minutes later, they pulled to a halt in front of a large wrought-iron entrance.

A sturdy young man, wearing an oversized fur-lined jacket and a large medallion necklace, was loafing beside the door. When Toti waved at him, he paid the taxi driver and told them to wait outside.

It was New Year's Eve and they shivered in their skimpy dress. A young man in a slick white suit, with a flashy gold necklace and designer sunglasses, came outside.

"Whenever someone comes to the door, you collect their tickets. If they don't have one, they can buy a ticket for one hundred dirhams. Otherwise they can't come in. My name is Kinani. This is Thierry." He pointed at the fellow who had greeted them. "We're part of AMER, African Musical Entertainment Records." He shook their hands warmly.

Something about Kinani stoked a familiar feeling in Arès, but he could not say why. It fluttered close, tickling his memory, and then glided out of reach.

"You are musicians?" Michaux asked.

"We are a hip-hop collective. We will be playing inside. If there is trouble, come and get us. At the end of the night, we'll pay you two hundred dirhams each. Do you want any whiskey?"

The three men nodded.

Kinani went inside and came back out carrying three plastic cups. "This is Black Label, so drink it slow," he said, smiling. "Only the best for AMER." He gave them all fist pounds and then bounded back inside.

Arès greedily sipped the spirits. A flush of warmth began to spread through his chest and limbs. When his shivering finally subsided, he turned to inspect the house. The ground floor was arcaded with spade-like apertures that opened into a small outdoor verandah with canvas chairs and stone-potted plants. Inside was an immense glittering salon, where hundreds of balloons floated about. Gold divans lined the walls and two marble lions pawed blue and white tiled floors.

The second story was strewn with festive lights. Arès stared transfixed at glittering ceilings handsomely enameled with colorful Zellige tiles. His eyes traced along the octagonal mosaics at whose centers cabochons glimmered like polished eggs.

Despite the opulence of the residence, something in the stamp of its contours, or the indistinct profile of the winter flora and spreading trees, reminded Arès of his parents' modest home in Kinshasa. He felt a dull and uninspired sadness at the resemblance and drank his whiskey and brooded by the door.

Soon the partygoers arrived in bunches. As they collected tickets, the three men overheard conversations in Lingala, Wolof, Diola, Kinyarwanda, and French, tainted with several national inflections.

"What is this?" Arès asked, taken aback.

"The musicians are from five different countries," Toti replied. "I have been at these parties before, and it is like a meeting of all of Africa. There are people here like us. People who have fled their homes. But Morocco also offers scholarships to wealthy students from many African countries."

Arès shook his head, confused. "Why would they do that?"

"The sons of powerful men come here for an education. They study in Morocco and receive a Moroccan diploma, and when they finish and go back to their countries, they have a connection to Morocco. Afterwards, if they want to do business with another country, they think of Morocco first. It is very clever," Toti said admiringly.

"Is this how they have this house? Do they rent it?"

"No. They have bribed the caretaker."

"What?" Michaux exclaimed.

"I don't know how they find out, but they wait until the owner of a large house goes on vacation. Then they offer the caretaker three thousand dirhams to look the other way while they throw a party."

"And they accept?"

"The caretakers barely make a hundred dirhams a week. How can they refuse?"

"But what if the owner comes back?"

"I have worked the door five times, and it has never happened."

It began to rain, a cold, splattering shower that sprayed across the garden and plunked like spittle onto the three men. They huddled together and peered through the ceiling-high windows at the attractive glow inside.

Arès could see people his age, people that resembled him, dancing and drinking. He looked at young women like Christelle, with bangles and necklaces shaking to the music, and at the warmth exuded by those affluent quarters.

A makeshift stage had been assembled out of several divans, and it floated in the center of the salon like a puffy, silk raft upon a sparkling sea. The five musicians bounced about, shouting into microphones. The young men outside could feel the heavy throbs of bass, the thrumming of guitars, and a sort of muggy vibrato that could have been lyrics. Then a window thrust open and the text came through loud and clear.

On est parti de rien
On fait tout de rien

On rêve en group de rien
Slam coûte pour rien

Ils auront le sud
Ils auront le nord... [47]

Arès leaned against Toti, trying to conserve warmth. Listening to the lyrics, he felt incredibly marginal, amputated not only from his comfortable upbringing, not only from the alien and pernicious people with whom he was forced to live, but even from his contemporaries in exile. For the first time since Dongo, he felt the full flush of his youthful ambitions, his desire for a wife and a home, and accompanying that ictus of desire was a rancor and a deep desolation.

The rain pattered on and the flow of guests diminished to a trickle. There were well over a hundred revelers inside, hastening together toward 2005.

The caretaker, a man by the name of Akram, had been kind enough to lend them a tarp, and they lofted it over their heads in the darkness. He was an old man with a grizzled face that looked like it had missed its share of happiness in life. They offered him some whiskey and watched him shamble back to his compact, rectangular shed.

"Seems like a good party," Arès said bitterly and shivered again.

"I'm wet to the bone," Michaux griped. "They could invite us in. What are we, invisible?"

"This is the job," Toti replied. "Did you think the rain would stop for us because we are poor?"

"I would rather some girls came out here to warm us up," Arès said with a smirk. He began to shimmy his hips to the music, moving in step with the dancers inside.

---

47   We began with nothing / We've done everything with nothing / Together we dream of nothing / Slam costs nothing / They will own the south / They will own the north

Toti grinned. "It is said that a man is naked without a wife, but that is something you only begin to understand when you are very, *very* cold."

The three men laughed. Then they began to dance together under the tarp, holding it high above their heads like a great flapping wing. Soon the rain let up and a few sly stars snuck out from under the clouds.

Midnight had to be near, because Kinani arrived with three cups of champagne. "I'm glad to see the sky has cleared," he said, looking up at the stars like he owned them. Again, something about him tugged at Arès' memory.

"Thank you," Toti replied.

"Drink up," Kinani added with an irresistible smile. "I'll be back later." He was about to rejoin the party when they heard an insistent pounding against the front gate.

Toti opened the metal door.

A hunkering man in a wide-brimmed hat and a trench coat stood in a soft nimbus of light, his face obscured by shadows.

"*Hal el bab!*" he shouted.

"Where's your ticket?" Toti replied in French.

"My ticket? My ticket! This is my house. Let me in!" He pushed past Toti and then froze in the middle of the lawn. Inside, a hundred cups were raised and open bottles of champagne frothed onto the floor and coated the kissing couples in a light, bubbly foam.

Watching the homeowner with a mocking grin, Arès drank the full draught of his cup.

Shouts of "Akram! Akram!" cut across the waterlogged garden. The caretaker slunk out of his shed. Within seconds, he was no more than a flattened blot against the grass being thrashed with a belt. He covered his face and shouted in Arabic. The belt froze in the air and Akram pointed at Kinani and the other members of AMER. Then the man in the trench coat beat and kicked him till he ran out of breath. When he was done, he turned toward the members of AMER.

Arès sidled near.

"You bribed my guard and invaded my house," the man shouted. "I'm going to call the police. You are all going to jail. Get out! Get out now!"

"What?" Kinani said. "This is your house? You live here?"

"Yes, this is my house!"

"And you did not know we were having this party?"

"What?"

"We were looking for somewhere to throw our New Year's Eve party, and this man here," he pointed at Akram, "told us that he could rent us this house on behalf of the owner. We paid him 3000 dirhams, but we thought that you knew. Sir, we are only college students. We did not want to do anything illegal."

"What!" the owner shouted. He spun toward the quivering mass of his caretaker and began to kick and abuse him with such fury that Arès grabbed him from behind. The homeowner's arms twisted in the air, and his elbow shocked into Arès' jaw, weakening his grip. In a second he was free, and he clouted the guard toward the shed, screaming in Arabic.

When the caretaker exited again, he was holding a bundle of money in his hands.

The owner slapped him on the back of the head when they arrived in front of the group. "Akram will reimburse your money." He hit the man again, and the guard held out the banknotes with shaking hands.

"This is really not necessary," Kinani said. "Please. You keep the money. We are going to end the party and clean up your house right away."

Arès' feet rooted into the grass. He had it now! Kinani spoke with the same lively inflections, the same rolling, implacable conviction as Félix. He nearly wept as his brother's persuasive voice leapt the hot chasm of so many years to issue from a stranger's mouth.

"No. You rented the house," the owner replied. "You can finish your party. Just please leave in an hour and tidy up. My staff will clean the house in the morning. Also, I want you to have the money. This man lied to you, and you should not have to pay for a lie." He grabbed the money out of the caretaker's hands and gave it to Kinani.

"*Shokran*," Kinani said, his eyes sparkling like a pair of stolen jewels.

"I will go to my neighbors' now. They called to tell me about the party. I will come back in the morning. Please be careful and clean up." Then he switched back to Arabic, yelling and flaying Akram.

With curious emotion, Arès watched the old man drag a duffel bag full of his belongings out of the shed and be ejected from the premises.

Kinani turned to the three Congolese men. "Here are 300 dirhams each. You can go now. Thank you for your help."

Still carrying the tarp above their heads, the three men headed out into the dripping night. Arès was lost in thought, and he hardly noticed the wet and wandering hour they spent before finding a *petit taxi* to take them home.

FEBRUARY 7, 2005

Thank you for coming today.

This is an interview to determine whether you are a refugee. If you can, please talk about your life story in a manner that is open and above all honest. Everything you say here is entirely confidential.

We will not share your information with anyone, especially not the government. We are not a government agency.

Please give us as much detail as possible, because it is only by knowing your full story that we can determine whether or not you should be qualified as a refugee.

Do you understand what I am saying?

Yes.

You have understood everything that I have just said?

Yes.

At the end of this interview we will give you a notification date. You will come back to the UNCHR on that date, and we will render your decision.

The decision will be either positive or negative.

If the decision is negative, we will explain to you the reasons why we do not consider you a refugee. If you disagree with the decision, you have the right to appeal.

You will then have another chance to tell your story, and a different Eligibility Officer will decide your case.

If the decision is positive this time, you will be accorded the status of refugee.

If the second decision is negative, it will be final. There is no appeal. We will consider your dossier closed. If you then wish to return to your country of origin, we can facilitate your repatriation through the International Organization of Migration.

Do you understand everything?

Yes.

What is your name?

Arès Sbigzenou

When were you born?

In 1980.

You are 24 or 25 years old?

24.

What month were you born in and what day?

The ninth of June.

Thank you. What is your country of origin?

The Congo.

Congo Brazzaville or the DRC?

From Kinshasa. Do I look like I come from Brazzaville?

I cannot tell the difference.

Where are you from?

From Cameroon.

Then maybe you know. Maybe you do not know. The people from Brazzaville are dishonest. They lie. They steal. They have no education. They are only good enough to clean our toilets. I am not from Brazzaville.

That's what the Congolese from Brazzaville say about people from Kinshasa.

You see. I told you they are liars.

THE ASYLUM DEMANDER AND THE ELIGIBILITY OFFICER LAUGHED.

Do you have a passport or a national identity document from the DRC?

No.

Do you have a birth certificate?

No. I did not bring anything with me when I left.

THE ELIGIBILITY OFFICER TYPED SOMETHING INTO HIS COMPUTER.

<u>Describe the Congolese flag.</u>

It is a green flag with a man holding a flaming torch in a yellow circle.

<u>When did you leave the Congo?</u>

It was in 1998.

<u>The flag is blue now with a gold star in the corner and a red diagonal stripe.</u>

They have changed the flag?

<u>They have changed many things. What was the national anthem?</u>

I do not remember.

<u>What was the currency in Zaire?</u>

The nouveaux zaire.

<u>Now it is the franc congolais. What are some typical Congolese dishes?</u>

There is kwanga that we eat with soup. There is Moambe chicken, which my mother used to make, hmmm…

<u>What else?</u>

There is chikwangue, which is made out of cooked manioc. There is also fumbwa, which is made with spinach. Fufu, too, we prepare with fish or meat.

Ok. Thank you. You are from Kinshasa?

Yes.

What is the neighborhood next to the University of Kinshasa?

La Cité des Anciens Combattants.

What is your favorite football club?

Bayern-München.

Ah, you should have said Cameroon. Who is your favorite player?

It is Roger Milla of course.

Ah, good answer. Now you are beginning to make sense.

What is your father's name?

Buisha Sbigzneou.

What is your mother's name?

Christelle Mompenge.

THE ELIGIBILITY OFFICER TYPED THE ANSWER INTO THE COMPUTER.

Do you have any brothers or sisters?

I think you know the answer to this.

No. But I think you know the answer.

I think it is written on that machine in front of you.

Please just answer the questions.

I had seven sisters and four brothers.

How many?

Seven sisters and four brothers.

Why last time did you say three sisters and two brothers?

Because that was the truth.

Then why did you tell me just now that you had seven sisters and four
brothers?

Because I am afraid that I will have to repeat the same story as last
time in exactly the same way.

This interview is meant to determine whether you are a refugee. It is
very important.

I think maybe it is more important for me than for you. Why must I tell
the same story again?

Some people give us one set of information at pre-registration, and
then they tell us something else when they come for the registration
interview.

Yes, but sometimes stories change.

Only if they are made up. In evaluating a refugee status claim, we
look at whether the information provided by the applicant is credible.

Whether the material elements are consistent and plausible.

What if last time I forgot about one of my sisters? Last time I was very tired and hungry. I am sure I forgot many things. Maybe I found out I have another sister. Does this mean I am not a refugee?

If there are any inconsistencies, you will have the opportunity to explain them.

What if my story is unlikely? Sometimes I do not believe it myself. It seems like I dreamt it.

Please just answer the questions truthfully so that we can determine whether you should be recognized as a refugee.

But I do not even know what a refugee is.

Just answer the questions, and I will tell you if you fulfill the criteria of the 1951 refugee convention.

I do not understand what you have just said. Can you not tell me what a refugee is? How can I know if I am one if you do not tell me what it is?

You are here because you think you are a refugee.

My friends told me to come here and tell my story and that the HCR would help me. But they do not know my story. I do not like to tell it. It is not a good story.

Everything you say here is confidential.

So is everything I tell my friends, but still I do not tell them this story.

For us to determine whether you are a refugee, you will have to tell me your story.

Yes, but I would first like to know what a refugee is. Because maybe I am not one, and I can go home with my story.

A refugee is an individual who has suffered persecution due to his race, religion, nationality, belonging to a certain social group, or political views, who has fled his country of origin or habitual residence, and who manifests a well-founded fear of harm or continued persecution if he returns to his country of origin or habitual residence.

Please. More simple.

THE ELIGIBILITY OFFICER BEGAN TO TAP A PEN AGAINST THE METAL EDGE OF THE TABLE.

A refugee is someone who has fled his country as a result of persecution and who cannot return because he is afraid.

I will answer your questions.

What is your father's profession?

He was a locksmith.

Your mother?

She took care of the house.

What do your brothers and sisters do?

I do not know.

What were their professions when you left the DRC?

My older brother was at the University of Kinshasa studying Business. My older sister was studying law at the Free University of Kinshasa. My younger brother was in *secondaire* and my two younger sisters were in *secondaire* and *collège*.

Do you still have any contact with members of your family in Kinshasa?

No.

Have you tried to contact them since you left? If you like we can perform a tracing to put you back in touch with missing family members.

I think it would be very difficult to contact them.

They are no longer alive?

I do not think so.

Are your parents alive?

No.

Are you aware of any surviving family members?

No.

Were you or was any person in your family a member of a political party or association either affiliated with or persecuted by the government?

No.

Were you ever enrolled in the military or did you ever participate in a military or paramilitary group?

No.

Please tell me the reasons why you left your country of origin.

My home was attacked. Everyone was killed.

Were you there at the time?

Yes.

So not everyone was killed.

THE ASYLUM DEMANDER STAYED SILENT.

When was this?

In 1998. During the war. Kabila told them to attack us.

Whom did Kabila tell them to attack?

The Rwandans. The Rwandans in the Congo.

You are Rwandan?

My mother was. She was Banyamulenge. This was enough.

What happened?

I told you. They came and killed everyone in the house. They did things…

I know this is difficult, but I cannot offer you refugee status if you do not tell me what happened.

Perhaps I do not want refugee status.

I think you do. I know Morocco does not have a very good soccer team, but it is better to stay here than be refouled to Algeria or back to the Congo.

THE ELIGIBILITY OFFICER WROTE SOMETHING ON THE COMPUTER.

We can help you. We can give you medical care if you are sick and job training so you can begin to make a life here for yourself.

However, I have to make sure that you fit the criteria. This is why I am asking you for details. Who came to your house and when was it?

My neighbors came. People I knew. Even someone who used to be my friend when I was young.

What month?

I do not remember. I remember that the rebels had taken the port and the electricity plant. Toward the end of the year.

Why did they come to your house?

They killed all the Rwandans in our town. Not just my family.

Did they call you names when they were attacking? Did they tell you why?

Yes. Traitors. They called us traitors.

But you survived?

Someone saved me. He found me when I was unconscious and dying and brought me to his home.

What was his name?

Paul.

Are you sure that everyone in your family is dead?

Yes.

How? Did you look for them afterwards?

I am sure. I saw them die.

I am sorry. Do not worry. Take your time. We can take a break.

Do you want some water? I will get you some.

THE ELIGIBILITY OFFICER LEFT THE ROOM AND CAME BACK WITH A CUP OF WATER.

What did you do next?

I escaped to a fishing village near Brazzaville.

How long did you stay there?

Six years.

Six years?

Yes.

Why so long?

I did not feel right. I was very confused. It was a very bad time.

Why did you come to Morocco?

Life was too hard there. I was looking for something better. I was always sick.

When did you arrive?

Maybe a year ago. In June.

Did you come with anyone?

No.

What countries did you pass through on the way to Morocco?

Cameroon, Nigeria, Niger, and Algeria.

Thank you. Where have you lived since you first came to Morocco?

I was living in Takadoum with two friends. Then I had to leave and I slept in the streets for almost two weeks.

Why did you stop living with your friends if you had nowhere to go?

A guest is like a fish. When it arrives, it is fresh and shiny, but after a while it begins to stink.

Your friends did not want to live with you anymore?

One of them did not want to live with a Banyamulenge and forced me to leave. He blamed me for the war. As if I could cause a war.

Do you have any family or relatives in Morocco?

No.

What is your phone number?

I do not have a phone.

Do you have a friend who has a phone, where we can reach you?

Yes. My roommate.

What is his name and his number?

His name is Buisha. His number is 06 16 00 61 60.

Ok. Wait a minute.

THE ELIGIBILITY OFFICER BRIEFLY LEFT THE ROOM.

Here is a rendezvous for Friday, February 18. At that time we will give you your decision.

As I said at the beginning of the interview, the decision will be either positive or negative. If it is positive, we will provide you with a refugee card.

If it is negative, we will list the reasons why it is negative and you will have the right to appeal.

Then I will have to tell my story again?

Yes.

Ok.

We will call your friend Buisha if there is any change to the date. Is there anything else you would like to tell me before you go?

Yes.

Tell me.

It is very difficult to live here, to survive.

I know.

Yes, but here there is no hope. If you want to start a business, they ask for a *carte de séjour*. If you try to sell things in the market, the Moroccan police come and take everything. They do not want to see black.

You have to put everything on your back and work as a *marchand ambulant*. There is no rest. You can never stop walking.

Sometimes you have to run.

I hope things change for you soon.

My father used to say, the serpent does not have hands for his defense, so he counts on God.

CHAPTER 26

MAY 2009

———————

"Y OU'RE PLAYING GUITAR AGAIN," Simon remarked, when he walked into the apartment late one Saturday morning. Kinani sat on one of the living room chairs, nimbly plucking the notes on a waltzy flamenco piece, his face set in studied concentration.

"Simon," he said, looking up but still strumming the strings, "a guitar is like a woman who knows that she is attractive."

"How so?" Simon asked.

"It requires continual effort."

Simon laughed cheerfully and tossed his beach bag, and then himself, onto the couch.

"That's a nice melody," he remarked, after Kinani flourished out a final arpeggio of notes. "Sounds familiar."

"It's the 'Gran Vals' by Francisco Tárrega," Kinani said with a slight bow, "but you probably know it from the ringtone on your phone." He pointed at Simon's stubby blue Nokia.

Simon chuckled sheepishly. "That must be it. I'll say, I'm occasionally glad I didn't kick you out of the apartment."

"Don't worry," Kinani replied, his eyes alive and glittering, "I'm sure some Moroccan will do it instead."

"Why? Has there been trouble?" Simon sat up, alarmed.

"Only the usual everyday trouble."

"Ah, ok." Simon sank back into the couch. "Then what are you worried about?"

Kinani's fingers began strumming out another flamenco tune, but he stopped abruptly and peered at Simon with penetrating eyes. "You may not have noticed, but for most Moroccans, a black person is like a camel. He can carry your things, but best keep him outdoors."

"And yet strangely enough, here you are, housed with us," Simon retorted.

"Only because two European girls snuck me in." He gave a cold smile. "Just wait till the landlord catches wind."

"Wonderful," Simon said and stood up. He moved toward the kitchen but abruptly pivoted about. "And how about all of our refugees living in palaces in Takadoum? How did they manage to find housing?"

"That's true," Kinani replied. "Every now and then they give us some stables to live in. Otherwise they know we'll shit all over the street." He gave a loud, pealing laugh.

"Well please don't shit on the floor," Simon pleaded. "I'm not cleaning up after you."

"Unfortunately, you don't have much of a choice. My shit is your shit now."

"That's precisely what I'm worried about."

"*Meshi mushkil*," Kinani quipped. He began to play an Enrico Morricone tune from some old Western. Suddenly, his features sobered.

"You'll never be able to understand," he muttered. He fell silent and his mouth twisted unpleasantly as if he were chewing on a bitter root. "It's infuriating," he began again. "The Moroccans claim to be afraid of us, but they prey on us every chance they get. It's like the lion pretending to fear the gazelle."

"Well my friend, you chose to come to the lion's den."

"I didn't exactly *choose* Morocco."

Simon looked at Kinani, surprised. "I thought you came here on a student scholarship. Why did you leave the DRC then?"

"I do have a scholarship," Kinani replied, placing his guitar on a wooden stand, "but that's not why I came. There is a saying in the Congo that an unjust ruler is like a river without water." His lips thinned, leaving only a trace of his habitual smile. "Let's just say I got thirsty."

"So do you want a drink?" Simon asked, hoping to lighten the mood. He walked into the open kitchenette. "I think we have some soda and maybe even a beer if you're lucky."

Kinani gave a full-bellied laugh. "I am sometimes grateful for your deeply American lack of curiosity."

"Hey, I listen to stories of exile every day." Simon squatted down and rummaged around in the fridge.

"Yes, I've noticed that you've improved somewhat recently."

"Have I?" Simon opened a bottle of Sidi Ali and took a quick sip.

"Yes, you've grown slightly less..." Kinani searched briefly for the word, "... contemptuous."

Simon nearly choked on the stale water. "What?" he said, sputtering. "Is that how I seem? Contemptuous?"

"Mixed in with a bit of neocolonialist arrogance," Kinani added, grinning furiously.

"Well, that comes with the job description," Simon replied. "And sure, I'll admit it. The migrants here may have a harder lot than I first supposed."

"At last. Sympathy from the devil!" Kinani drumrolled his fingers against the guitar.

Simon groaned. "Come get your beer."

Kinani treaded into the kitchen and propped open the door to the small balcony. There was a sudden drop in air pressure and a wet mist suffused the room, salting it with seaside smells. Outside, a rolling white fog camouflaged the world and reduced the surrounding buildings to mere sketches. Far off, they could hear the resounding boom of waves bashing against rocky shores.

Kinani leaned against the kitchenette column and looked down at his flatmate. "Ah l'Américain, if you stop batting your eyelashes at our singer, maybe someday I'll tell you my tale of woe."

"Your singer? Who? Nadia? What are you talking about?" Simon protested. "I just like her voice."

"We all do. Which is why I hope you'll be careful with her. It's hard to sing when you've been crying all night."

"I've only been chatting with her." Simon carelessly dislodged a can of beer, and several crashed to the ground. He cursed under his breath and began grabbing at the rolling cylinders.

"Yes, but it's the first drop of water that begins to break the stone."

"Ok. Sure." Simon stood up with two silver cans in hand. "But we're talking about the Rock of Gibraltar here. Haven't you noticed? All of her sisters wear the veil." He held out a beer to Kinani, who took it with a slight incline of the head.

"Ah, they are just like everyone else."

"Except I can see other peoples' faces."

"So you think," Kinani replied, his smile curving illegibly.

"I'm not sure I follow." Simon took a sip of beer.

Kinani gave another musical chuckle. "I'll tell you a story. A few years ago, I was in a chemistry class with a girl who wore a full burqa. Head to foot. All you could see were her eyes and barely even that. We were assigned a week-long project together. One afternoon, we decided to work on it at my place. She asked to use the bathroom, and when she came out, she had taken off the burqa."

"Just like that?"

"Just like that."

"Was she wearing anything else?"

"Very little and not for long." Kinani raised his can in a toast, his eyes gleaming like gemstones. "They may be forced to wear burqas, but underneath they are just girls. They have the same desires and the same fantasies as anyone else."

"Yes, but according to Nadia, her sisters *choose* to wear the veil."

"Well this is why you are not seducing her sisters!" Kinani laughed his oversized laugh and Simon laughed with him. Then Kinani grew serious again. "But do not think you can make love to her, and then run off like every other Mzungu."

"Excuse me?"

The doorbell rang.

Kinani held up an admonitory finger and walked to the front entrance. "What are you doing here?" The surprise in his voice carried all the way to the kitchen.

Simon turned to see Nadia glide into the apartment as if propelled on a draft of air. Her hair was tied back in a bun, and she was wearing a white summer dress that billowed about her legs and collected a skirt of creamy mist. Her wrists, as always, jangled with silver bracelets.

"What do you mean?" she asked, her eyes opening expressively. "It's 3 p.m. I'm here to rehearse."

Kinani threw up his hands. "*Les femmes*! When they're not late, they're an entire day early. Rehearsal is tomorrow."

"*Les hommes*! *Sditiha ntouma rejala*!" Nadia replied, mocking his tone. "You said it was today."

"Then why are you the only one here?"

"Because everyone else in our group is male," she retorted, crossing her arms. Kinani shook his head hopelessly. "Let's rehearse my part now anyway. I can't tomorrow. And look," she said, pointing at Simon, "we even have an audience. Although..." she clucked her tongue and appraised him with clinical eyes, "he appears to be regrettably male as well."

"I'm leaving to tutor a student in twenty minutes," Kinani replied. "Are you sure you can't come tomorrow?"

"I'd love to hear your new song," Simon ventured, earning a reproving glare from Kinani.

Nadia shook her head. "I have an exam on Monday. We're cutting up cadavers and I need to spend all Sunday looking for a victim."

"I could volunteer," Simon proposed.

She gave a loud, sparkling laugh. "Thank you, but the school requires someone with his head on straight."

"Children," Kinani interrupted, clapping his hands. "Let's get to work. You sit over there." He guided Simon back toward the couch. "And try to pay attention for once. And you," he said, pointing at Nadia, "come stand next to me."

Simon sat down, while Nadia swung a light blue shawl off her shoulders and positioned herself next to the guitar stand. There was a clipped briskness to her movements, as if there were urgent things about and she was short on time. Simon wondered how she moved in concert and then his thoughts drifted elsewhere.

Kinani lifted the guitar off the stand and strummed out some chords. After a moment, he began mixing a percussive, rhythmic slap into his playing to create a modified hip-hop beat.

"I'll sing Thierry's part," Kinani said:

Mec, qu'est-ce qu'on dit
On était jeune et optimiste
Mais la vie ne se révèle pas comme on l'a prédit

Tu te rappelles de tous nos rêves d'enfant?
C'était bien excitant
Aujourd'hui chacun de nos projets
Traînent dans le temps

Ici tout est aléatoire
Un jour c'est bon
Le prochain, ils te disent
Rentre chez toi![48]

The music was bright, but bittersweet, with a pulsing tempo that carried the lyrics forward. At first Nadia swayed kittenishly behind Kinani, but soon her voice took center stage. She sung in a husky contralto, alternating lines with him, adding unexpected shades of meaning to the words. At certain points, her voice ranged to soprano highs, carrying the melody skyward, and then drifted down to earth like a cool breeze.

Qu'est-ce qu'on dit?
On nous prend aujourd'hui pour des bandits

Mais mec, qu'est-ce qu'on dit
J'espère que tu traînes pas
Dans n'importe quelle combine

---

48   My man, what is it they say? / We were young and optimistic / but life didn't turn out as we expected. / Do you remember your childhood dreams? / They were exciting then / but now all of our projects / are going nowhere. / Here, everything is based on luck / One day, everything's good / the next day, they tell you / Go home!

Enfants, nous rêvions de grande victoire
A présent, nous célébrons la simple vie

Mec, qu'est-ce qu'on dit
On était jeunes et optimistes
Mais la vie ne se révèle pas comme on l'a prédit
Mec, qu'est-ce qu'on dit?[49]

Toward the end of the song, Kinani dropped his comedic smile, and a certain nobility touched his countenance that seemed at odds with his habitually pleasing looks. Once again, Simon had the impression of peering briefly behind a mask, but the moment was so fleeting that he wondered afterwards if he had seen anything at all.

"What did you think?" Nadia asked, bringing her gaze to bear on the young man. Her eyes were the piercing green of a fresh leaf, the young green of the star of Islam that waved on every red Moroccan flag.

"I thought it was great," Simon said, blinking rapidly, overwhelmed by all that green.

"It's a shame you can't choose your audience." Kinani lightly sucked his teeth and turned toward Nadia. "It was far too clever for him."

"I take offense at that," Simon said, smoothing back his mane of blond hair. "But I'm impressed. We should celebrate with a drink."

"I have to go tutor that student," Kinani demurred, placing his guitar back on the stand.

"*Les gens pressés sont déjà morts,*" Nadia exclaimed.[50] "Why don't you stay for a drink?"

"You should try to take it easy," Simon added.

Kinani raced around, gathering up his affairs. He was halfway to his bedroom when he spun on his toes and bared his teeth at them. "You two

---

49   What do they say? / These days they think we're bandits / but my man, what is it they say? / I hope you're not involved in some scam / When we were young, we dreamed of the greatest victory / now we celebrate just being alive / But my man, what is it they say? / We were young and optimistic / but life didn't turn out as we expected. / My man, what is it they say?
50   People in a rush are already dead.

really belong together."

"And why is that?" Nadia crossed her arms over her chest and glared defiantly at him.

"You're the two most insufferable people I know."

"*Qui aime bien châtie bien*," she retorted.[51]

"I'm leaving now," Kinani announced, "but *please*, make yourselves at home."

"This is my place!" Simon protested.

"*Meshi mushkil*," Kinani said. On his way out, he whispered in Simon's ear. "Be careful with Moroccan girls, l'Américain. If you leave her, it won't just be a question of broken hearts."

Then he waved at Nadia and shut the door behind him.

---

51   He who loves well, teases well.

CHAPTER 27

APRIL–SEPTEMBER 2005

T HEY SAT IN A café in Agdal dressed as elegantly as their means permited. Arès had tailored his jacket from a triple-XL suit he had found at a CARITAS giveaway. Buisha and Sekou both wore sleek black waistcoats, their shoes shined to a pitch.

Arès' two companions radiated prosperity: Buisha, with his brass-knobbed mahogany cane, pinched features, and measuring mercantile eyes; Sekou, telegraphing Buddhic ease with his padded belly, bonhomie, and booming voice.

The scam was easy. They waited for someone to sit down nearby. Then Sekou claimed he had a chemical that allowed him to perfectly counterfeit Moroccan currency.

On the table before them stood three pots of gunpowder tea and three stubby glasses, painted with blue and gold calligraphy and stuffed with mint leaves. Several pricey packs of Marlboro Reds were conspicuously arrayed, but none of the men smoked while they chatted.

A month earlier, Arès had been cornered by the police, thrust to the ground, and booted several times in the ribs. His brand-new refugee card, along with his locksmith tools, were confiscated, and he was refouled near Oujda. He spent a night cursing God and man, while he marched miles through dead chaparral beneath cold, uncaring stars.

Shortly before dawn, he crept through the murderous groves that lined the border in such a state of panic that he thought his lungs were going to burst. He was less unlucky that time, and crossed to Oujda unscathed, but it took him nearly two weeks to make it back to Rabat. When he arrived, he found his flat rented to a Moroccan and all of his possessions gone.

For the next eight days, he wandered the streets in a state of desperation, living off handouts that sifted his way and small discs of bread and oranges that he nicked on the run. Eventually he met Buisha, who agreed to take him in so long as he could find a way to pay half the rent.

He applied as an apprentice to several locksmiths, but no one would hire him. The construction jobs had dried up as well. There were too many migrants flowing into Morocco. Thousands of people trying to get by until they could *burn* to Europe or *shock* their way into one of the two Spanish enclaves, Melilla and Ceuta, that were situated on Moroccan soil.

So much time had passed, almost a year, and still he was in Rabat. Slowly, he was figuring out how to survive.

He scheduled his activities now to the rhythm of the five prayers. He had learned that the Islamic day begins and ends at sunset and not sunrise. He had mastered small squibs of Arabic: ordered his orange juice with *asir limun*, his banana shakes with *asyr banane*. He knew that bread was *khoubs*, left *lessr*, right *leemen*, and straight *neeshan*.

Gradually he had hardened to the hostility in the streets, had accepted it as another expression of the universal hostility of the strong toward the weak. He had come to terms with Rabat, city of maimed feet and hairdressers.

Now he sat in a café, waiting for a middle-class Moroccan to take a chair beside him. Too rich and the man would not care. Too poor and he would not have enough money to lose. He swirled the mint tea in his mouth and swallowed. It was unbearably sweet and he rubbed his tongue against the roof of his mouth, trying to scrape off the saccharine glaze.

"*Khouya, khouya!*" Sekou waived at a man two tables down, immersed in the daily *Al Bayan*. "*Salaam aleikhoum.*"

"*Wa aleikhoum salaam,*" the man replied. He was dressed in a gray flannel suit that was more or less presentable, but his shoes were a battered brown, and his tie an unflattering olive color cut in an unfashionable shape. His midriff was one long extended bulge over his thighs. Below a balding pate dangled heavy chops and a stiff walrus mustache.

"*Khouya*," Sekou said, "perhaps you can help me. My friend here," he pointed at Arès, "does not believe that I have a chemical that allows me to perfectly copy banknotes." He gestured toward two silver canisters sitting on the floor next to him. "You see, I have bought him a suit, I have paid his rent, but he thinks I am so foolish as to earn this money with a job."

The man grunted and ruffled his paper noisily. He had an officious air about him. Whenever he turned a page, he did so with an industrious snap. But he seemed one of those men who would spend their productive years trying to scramble out of the rank and file and would fail, not for lack of vigor, but due to some genetic unsuitability for any higher post in life.

"*Khouya*, what is your name?"

The man scrupulously folded the paper and set it on the table, creasing the margins with the back of his hand. "Mohammed," he replied.

"I am Michaux, and this is Blanchard and Guli," Sekou said, pointing at Buisha and Arès. "If you can indulge me for a minute. I have copied money in front of my friend several times, but he does not believe me. He thinks I am using fake bills. I need an outside observer and, most importantly, someone's else's money."

"I am not going to give you any money," Mohammed replied scornfully.

"Not give, *khouya*. Make! Here is a hundred dirhams." Sekou placed a mud-colored banknote on the table in front of the man. "This way you know that you will not lose anything. Now, if you will give me a hundred dirham bill of yours, I will copy it perfectly with these chemicals and give you two hundred dirhams back. Of course, if the idea bothers you, I can ask someone else."

The man turned over Sekou's bill in the light. Then he grunted again and after reaching into his pocket, unpeeled a hundred dirham banknote from a bulging, multi-colored wad of bills. "*Waha*," he said as he handed it over.

Sekou took the bill and unscrewed the top of the first container, a silver cylinder about half a meter in height and twenty centimeters in diameter.

He removed a platinum set of tweezers from his right breast pocket and, holding them gingerly, dipped the bill into a clear liquid.

"You have to be very careful," he said. "These chemicals are quite toxic."

He unscrewed the second container, which was riddled with air holes, and put the bill inside. Then he produced a blank piece of paper, cut the same size as the hundred dirham banknote, and dipped it in the clear liquid. Afterwards, he sealed it in the second container with the first bill.

"It will take a moment for the bills to dry. Let us have some tea while we wait, or whatever else you would like, *khouya*. It is my treat." Mohammed ordered an orange juice, and Sekou posed a few questions about his life.

He was a low-level manager at Maroc Telecom, where he had been employed for almost ten years.

"Communications is a very important business," Sekou said, rubbing his hands together. "Very lucrative. I am sure you have a prosperous future ahead of you."

"Only if I am promoted," Mohammed replied. "My salary is decent, but not enough. Especially with my family. I would like to send my children to private school, but I cannot afford it."

"Well, I hope then that you are promoted soon, Insha'Allah."

"Insha'Allah."

"Ah, I think the bills are ready." Sekou shook the silver canister next to his ear. "Yes. It sounds ready." He unscrewed the top and pulled two one hundred dirham notes out of the container. Both were slightly humid.

"See," he said to Arès. "Do you believe me now?"

Arès turned the bills over in the light. "It is incredible," he exclaimed. "These bills look exactly the same."

"I told you so," Sekou gloated. Then he turned to Mohammed. "Here *khouya,* keep them both." He handed him the two banknotes.

"Are you sure?" His mustache twitched in disbelief.

"Keep the other hundred dirhams as well. What do I care?" Sekou said with a magnanimous wave of the hand. "I can make new money whenever I want."

"Thank you," Mohammed said. He smoothed the bills on his thigh. Then he quickly stuffed them into his wallet as if afraid they might puff into smoke. "Where did you get these chemicals?" he asked.

"Ah, African secret," Sekou said, wagging a finger. "Just do not tell anyone where you got the two hundred dirhams. If they found out, we would both be in trouble. But you will have to excuse us. I believe it is time for our massages."

The three men rose, shook hands with Mohammed, and walked away.

Four days later, they returned to the café. As Sekou had predicted, Mohammed was there.

He rushed up and shook Sekou vigorously by the hand and then kissed him on both cheeks. "You have come back. I have been at this café every day waiting for you to return!"

"Ah, it is good to see you my friend. Do you have good news that you want to tell me? Have you been promoted?"

"No, no. In fact, it is the opposite. I have a favor to ask of you."

"Well you have done me a favor, so I am at your service," Sekou said with a good-natured Buddhic laugh.

"I was hoping you could copy some more money for me."

"Would you like another hundred dirhams? Here, you can have it." Sekou took a hundred dirhams out of his pocket and gave it to Mohammed. He pushed the money back into Sekou's hands.

"No. It would be something slightly more. My friend, I have fifty thousand dirhams. I would like you to copy them for me."

"Ah, I was afraid it might be something like that." Sekou's brow stitched together, and a look of hesitation came over his face.

"You cannot do it?" Mohammed demanded anxiously.

"It is not that, *khouya*. It is only, I do not want to spend my life copying bills. If I do this for you, then I will have to do it next for your friend, and then that man will have a friend."

Mohammed took Sekou by the elbow and escorted him to the back of the café. "My friend, it is only this once, and only one time. I promise."

Sekou hummed sonorously. "Yes, but you saw. Each banknote takes five to ten minutes to copy. It will take a long time to make all these new bills. Fifty thousand dirhams will take me at least a week. Also, I will want to copy fifty thousand dirhams for myself. These chemicals are not free. I will have to send to Cameroon for more afterwards."

"My friend, you can take all the time you want. One week, two weeks. I will give you the money tomorrow, and you can call me when everything is ready. Do you have a phone?" Sekou produced a slim, silver phone, which Mohammed snatched to punch in his number.

"Now call me," he said. Sekou rang him and hung up.

"Ok," he said, jabbing the keys on his mobile. "Michaux was your name, if I am correct?"

"Yes," Sekou said.

"Let us set a rendezvous here at noon tomorrow and I will give you the briefcase." He half-turned to go, but Sekou rested a hand lightly on his shoulder.

"*Khouya*, let us make it on Saturday."

"But that is in four days!"

"Yes, but I am not going to copy anything before the weekend. I am waiting on a new shipment of chemicals and I was going to copy about one hundred thousand dirhams for myself over the next two weeks, so I will just include your fifty."

"My friend," Mohammed edged closer to Sekou so that the oblongs of their bellies carved an opaque butterfly in space. "I will give you the money tomorrow at noon, and you can call me when it is all finished. That way I will know it is safely in your hands and I can begin to prepare my future."

"Ok," Sekou relented. "But you cannot tell anyone about this. I do not think it is legal. If someone found out, we could both go to prison."

"*Sahbee*, it is our secret."

"Then we will see each other here tomorrow at noon."

"Yes."

"Goodbye my friend. *Bslama*."

"*Bslama*."

That night, Arès woke up somewhere near morning.

"*Yes, yes, yes! Yes!*" sung out from above the rattle of creaking boards.

Buisha rolled over next to him. "Ah, you are up as well."

"They are having sex again?" Arès asked groggily.

"She is extremely positive this evening," Buisha said.

Smiles curved in the dark.

Then night engulfed thought.

The next afternoon, they tossed the chip from Sekou's phone in a dumpster and skipped town.

For hours they bused eastwards beneath a sky of perfect blue. Arès watched the landscape roll by with a mixture of boredom and elation. He knew the topography by heart. Twice already he had taken the same road from Oujda to Rabat. But both times he had been half-broken and spitting up dust. Now, with everything running in reverse, he felt blessed in a myriad of ways.

He did not think his father would approve of what he had become, or how he had won his newfound prosperity. He could hear his father's measured, admonishing voice in his head, "*Le mensonge donne des fleurs, mais pas de fruits.*"[52]

Then his anger flared. How dare you, Papa, he silently remonstrated. How dare you teach me so little of the ways of the world. His father, Félix, Yika, himself—they had worked virtuously toward the future. They had built their lives on so many rocks that had crumbled into sand: prudence, honesty, trust in their fellow man. All lies themselves. All flowers without seeds.

"*Quand on se noie, on s'accroche à tout, même au serpent,*" Paul had repeated to him again and again.[53] He had wasted so much breath objecting to the trader's cynical wit. But the trader had been right. Paul was so much fuller in wisdom than Arès' father had ever been.

He suddenly felt himself as much the trader's son as his father's. He

---

52   Lies produce flowers, but never fruits.
53   When you are drowning, you will grab onto anything, even a snake.

had left his family behind, had become an outlaw and a child of the world. He clutched the prophetic key on his chest and swelled with pride. Then a terrible shame came over him. "Forgive me, Papa," he pleaded.

"What did you say?" Sekou asked, looking over with a condescending smile.

"Nothing. I was just dreaming. I must have spoken out loud."

"*Qui a soif, rêve qu'il boit*," Sekou replied, chortling with his eternal bonhomie.[54]

Arès smiled. "A friend of mine used to say, 'even fish, who live in water, are always thirsty.'"

"That is also true." Sekou gave a belly-shaking laugh. "I think that very soon you will find out how true it actually is."

Shortly before sunset, they disembarked at a whistle-stop by the name of Tiflet. Sekou led them to a ramshackle flophouse at the edge of town, where they let a three-person room.

"Why don't we get something nicer?" Arès asked. "We are rich now."

"Save your money," Sekou said. "We will have lots to spend it on here." He and Buisha laughed and tussled familiarly.

They wandered out into the streets. After a short meander, they came to a broad thoroughfare split down the middle by creeping, afternoon shadows. On the sunbathed side of the street, a hive-like concentration of shoppers swarmed around dozens of boutiques and makeshift stalls, buying and selling goods. On the other side, shadowy buildings sat between several down-sloping lanes.

To Arès' surprise, he saw two men slyly detach themselves from the bustling throngs, slink halfway across the thoroughfare, and suddenly fox into those murky, back alleys. Sekou gave a loud hoot and led his companions in the same direction.

"Where are we going?" Arès asked, anxiety playing about his face.

Sekou's eyes puckered with laughter and he put a finger to his lips. "African secret, my friend." He took Arès by the arm and ushered him forward.

---

54 When a man is thirsty, he dreams that he drinks.

While they advanced, several more men slid gingerly across the road and spirited away. It was as if the middle of the thoroughfare marked an event horizon beyond which the magnetic pull of those lanes knew no resistance.

Buisha took Arès by his other arm. "You can knock on the door of any house in this neighborhood and the father will bring down his daughters, and you can pick one, two, three, whatever you like, and pay to use a room upstairs."

"Moroccan girls?" Arès asked.

"Yes," Sekou replied. "When you have money, color does not matter in this country. It is the great equalizer."

Arès looked at the wraparound lanes, paved with mud or occasionally wood-planked. Two- to three-story buildings listed obliquely beneath a purple sky meshed with electric wires and telephone lines. Shadowy figures skulked in and out of entrances and led swishing hips into intermittent obscurities. From time to time, Arès' muscles tautened nervously and he sensed an approaching onslaught of insults or perhaps even stones.

"It looks like Takadoum," he said.

"Yes, except here we screw their daughters, instead of their sons screwing us." Buisha laughed loudly and slapped Arès on the back.

"Did you know that there are forty-three words for love in Arabic?" Sekou asked, his heavy jowls rippling in and out of a smirk.

"Yes, and fifty words for throwing rocks at blacks," Arès replied.

"Do not be bitter, my friend. Tonight, we will use a Moroccan's money to enjoy one of his cousins. This is the nature of life. Those who are on top one moment are on the bottom the next." He laughed heartily, enjoying his joke.

They stopped before a three-story residence. The ground floor was painted a cheery Mediterranean blue that murked into patinas of navy and royal blue as the residence stretched toward the sky. The building seemed better kept, almost flourishing, in contrast to the hulking tene-ments around it. As if to emphasize the singular fortune of its inhabitants, two massive satellite dishes perked off its roof like the erect ears of some fairytale giant.

"This man has a most fecund and profitable wife," Sekou said. "She only gives birth to females, and often to twins, and she does so almost every year."

He knocked on the door, while Buisha put his arm around Arès. "This will be your first time to a Moroccan prostitute, yes?"

"Yes."

"Just remember, before you sleep with her, make sure she washes herself."

"Ok."

"And inspect her. If she has any spots, warts, infections, or anything, send her back downstairs and get another."

Arès nodded nervously. All of a sudden, he felt feather-light before this man barely his senior.

The door opened, flooding the street with a bright gleam.

"*Salaam aleikhoum*," Sekou said.

"*Wa aleikhoum salaam*." The words issued from a creased mouth of indeterminate age. Above it glimmered fatherly eyes, fine placid wrinkles, and neatly smoothed silver hair. The man was dressed in a burgundy cardigan that exuded familial warmth.

"Mr. Sekou, what a pleasure to see you again. Come in. You are my first customer this evening. This is very good luck. I will give you a special price. Please, please come in. The girls are already in the salon."

"Thank you," Sekou said with a slight bow.

Arès and Buisha followed the two men through a narrow corridor that opened into a Moroccan salon. Crimson divans, festooned with puffy cushions in shades of pink and carmine, skirted around damask walls. The floor was padded with thick Berber rugs, and the ornate, cedar-screened windows were hung with curtains of velour. Baroque lanterns cast intricate shadows on a ceiling bedecked with mosaics of red and turquoise stars and curling white arabesques.

The man clapped his hands as they entered the salon and his daughters dioramaed themselves on the divans. Ranging from twelve to twenty-six in age, the fourteen girls were dressed in blue or scarlet kaftans, somewhat more revealing than the laws of *hadith* would ordinarily allow.

Several of the girls clung together, their shiny black tresses mingling in an incest of glistening locks, their large mascaraed eyes, like fantastic eggs, gazing provocatively at the men. Only one girl, her immature body cut short by a blue tunic, played on the carpet with some elaborate toy.

Sekou and the proprietor stepped close together and began haggling over prices. Whispers of *"bshkhal... juge... khti"* caressed Arès' ears.

"How about her?" Sekou said loudly, pointing at the twelve-year-old.

The proprietor wrinkled his brow with paternal concern. "No. It is impossible. She is too young." He shook his head. "It will be her first time. You would have to pay a very special price."

"I will know if it's her first time," Sekou said. "Are you sure she requires a special price?"

"Ok, ok. Perhaps not her *first* time, but certainly one of her first times. She is but a spring sapling. I cannot let her go for the same price as the others."

"Where is Fatima?" Sekou asked.

"Ah, my sincerest apologies," the paterfamilias replied with a florid gesture. "She is already busy with someone else."

Sekou turned to Arès and Buisha. "It is 300 dirhams for one girl and the room all night, or 400 for two girls."

"All night?" Arès asked.

"On reste longtemps où l'on a trouvé du plaisir," Buisha replied laughing.[55]

"Yes. Do not tire yourself out too quickly," Sekou counseled, an irreverent smile playing about his lips.

Then he strutted up and down the row of daughters, fondling their chins and appraising them with his derisive, glittering eyes. Sekou had a fondness for youth and he selected two who looked to be around fourteen and sixteen years in age. He bustled them upstairs, fluttering them on their rears, *"Allez! Allez! Au travail!"* With every step, his belly bounced agreeably up and down like a nodding head.

Buisha slid alongside the oldest girl. Resting his hand on her prepossessing seat, he steered her up the stairs in a totter of elliptic reds and plumb line blacks.

A carousel of eyes whirled toward Arès, causing him to blush. Their attention bothered him, especially the stereoscopic gaze of the identical

---

55   One tarries a long time where one has found pleasure.

twins, twined upon each other like serpents on a rod. Their lacquered, expressionless faces reminded him of the eerie Russian dolls that he had once disassembled as a child in a curiosity shop in Kinshasa.

"*C'est à vous, monsieur*," their father said.

Arès' eyes fluttered around the bordello, a moth seeking the light. Something about each of the girls left him wanting, and for once in his life, he craved satisfaction. A friend had told him long ago that right before drowning, a dying man has the sensation of a deep thirst at last being quenched. That night he felt like drowning.

While he paced back and forth, two of the girls rearranged themselves becomingly on a bolster. Behind them, a previously hidden sister sat aslant on a pyramid of cushions. Arès arrested his gaze. She almost perfectly resembled a girl from Takadoum who hissed "*azee!*" at him every time he walked by. She had the same heavy, almost convex lids, and the same doltish bearing and slovenly, exciting body.

"I will take her," Arès said.

With a smile, she flashed speckled, malachite eyes.

She sat on the edge of the bed, her legs spandreled, the hem of her dress hitched high on her thighs. Arès ran his finger up the gradient of her arm, across her shoulder, and then along her fleshy lips, lightly pursed in the shape of a fresh-cut fig.

He did not ask her to wash, nor did he pry the musky darkness between her legs. Rather, with a suddenness that startled even himself, he was ravenous upon her.

She whipped beneath him on the spring-worn bed, everything thrown loose in a riddle of limbs. The paisley pattern on the quilt spun against the mosaics on the walls in a kaleidoscopic ferment. His head and abdomen jerked. Her back craned against the neckrolls. His eyes closed.

In the post-communion of arched spines, between small apoplexies of sensation and amidst the moans, groans, and tramples of the surrounding sluttery, Arès huffed out heavy breaths. The girl curled upon him like an open parenthesis. He watched her toy with the golden key around his neck and lick small sweat beads off his chest. He ran his hand down the soft lash of her body, marveling that there was so much bounty in such a niggardly universe.

Two months later, the three men strolled bleary-eyed through the central market in Rabat. The sky was dim, and the medina lights flared like diamonds.

The bacchanalias in Tiflet had consumed nearly half of their savings, and they were deliberating how to replenish them. Sekou had an idea for another "theater piece," as he termed it, but he needed to see a friend about acquiring some Euros and locate two suitcases and some fake currency for the show.

When they turned onto rue Souika, a pea-colored uniform blocked their way.

"*Papiers.*"

"*Bien sûr,*" Sekou said. He slid a sealskin billfold out of his breast pocket and removed diplomatic papers from *la République de Cameroun.* "These two men are my associates. We are here on official business."

The gendarme licked his thumb and began rifling through the documents. "These papers are not in order. You will have to come to the prefecture and explain this to my supervisor."

"Of course, of course," Sekou replied. "But my associates and I are in a bit of a hurry. Perhaps we can overlook this minor irregularity just this once." As he spoke, he palmed a bright blue two hundred dirham banknote into the officer's empty hand.

Arès took a hesitant step back, devising an escape route through the crowded lanes. Someone gripped his shoulder. He jumped forward and spun around.

It was the devil's own luck.

The man they had defrauded was there with an entire van load of gendarmes. Arès scanned the olive-colored noose for even a small fissure. Then he slowly raised his hands. Sekou and Buisha thrust out theirs and the police snapped metal cuffs onto their wrists. They were escorted in all their finery across the Place Bab el Had and settled onto splintered benches in the back of a small fourgon.

They sat in a holding cell, somewhere on the outskirts of Rabat, tooling their shoe-tips against the grim concrete.

"We should pray for release," Buisha said. He knelt on the floor, hands clasped in devotion.

"I am very careful with my prayers," Sekou said. "I do not want to bother God too often, so when I call on his grace, I make sure only to pray for a woman." His booming laugh shocked through the paltry space. Arès admired him. Even in the stark crumminess around them, the man's belly bubbled with mirth.

"I've had my fill of women for now," Arès responded sullenly.

"Ah, a stoic," Sekou teased, wagging a reproving finger. "After Tiflet you have decided to give up pleasure to better torture yourself? What the Moroccans do to us is not enough?"

"No," Arès replied, rapping his knuckles against the thick concrete, "but I am not sure the pleasure is worth the price."

"We all have to pay for our pleasures, *mon ami*," Sekou replied. His face crinkled into an intricate web of creases, and his Buddhic smile spread radiant in the dim light. "You are still inexperienced, so you dream of pleasure without any inconvenience, but that is a mistake. If we could stay forever in Tiflet, you would come to regard even that paradise as a sort of prison. But because we are in a *real* prison, Tiflet will be all the sweeter when we visit it again."

"I am not interested in going back to Tiflet," Arès muttered. His admiration for Sekou had quickly turned to disgust. Who knew what would happen to them now? He was furious at the two men and enraged with himself. He had been starving in the streets, and they had reeled him in with their schemes. Now he was caught like a common criminal, when all he had ever desired in life was an honest day's work.

"Next time I earn some money," he told Sekou, "it will be to pay a *passeur* to take me to Europe. I want a simple life, a family. There was a girl I was in love with at home. I want to find someone like her and marry her."

"If you are speaking of happiness, then that is another matter," Sekou conceded, nudging his large belly over his legs as he slid down the wall. "In that case, money will only get you so far."

"It will get me to Europe," Arès insisted.

"Yes. Well, when we are free men again, I will help arrange your travels. But don't think that happiness will seek you out, because you have a few Euros in your pocket. Everything bought comes with a price."

Arès walked to the other end of the cell and splayed his fingertips against the scabrous walls. They were impossibly thick and cold to the touch. From where he stood, Sekou was reduced to mere contours, the petite circle of his head perched above the long oval of his abdomen, the form of a fat spider digesting its prey.

"None of this matters unless we escape." Arès loked over at Buisha, still prostrate on the cell floor. "And I do not think that God will turn that bucket of shit into a way out." He pointed to the corner, where a soiled pail, brimming with feces, awaited their desperate arrival.

"This is why I am not praying, my friend." Sekou smiled again and smacked his soft stomach, unleashing a jelly-like roll. "Anyway, I do not think it will be too bad. The man gave us money for an illegal purpose. At least in Cameroon, that means you forfeit it. I do not see how they can punish us for not counterfeiting money and for not giving money back to a criminal."

Buisha rose off the floor, his mumblings drawing to an end. "Well I have prayed, and I hope God hears me."

"I think we will have to rely on ourselves," Arès asserted. He had to break out. First out of this prison, then out of this country.

"How, my friend?" Buisha asked. "We are helpless in here, and when you are helpless, you must count on God. That is why it is said, *le serpent n'a pas de mains pour sa défense, mais il compte sur Dieu*." Buisha gazed up at the cracked ceiling. Then he crossed himself.

"Ah, I think God outfitted the serpent quite well," Sekou said with a spreading grin, his hands splayed across his still rippling paunch. "I think the serpent is defenseless, much like a woman. You do not see their weapons until it is too late." His chortle reverberated within his chest, like the rumble of pressure before a volcanic blast.

"Anyway," he continued, arching his back against the concrete wall, "I am always happy in jail. It is the only place where I am sure to get some sleep." He put his arms behind his head and closed his eyes.

In only a few minutes time, Sekou began snoring. Try as he might, Arès could not repress a rueful smile. Then he slumped down against the wall and shut his eyes.

Half an hour later, one of the guards marched over to their cell and rapped his white baton against the bars. He pointed at Arès. "You. Come with me."

The young man rose languidly to his feet. The door swung open and he felt himself grabbed roughly by the wrist and yanked into the hall. The guard pressed the nub of the baton into the small of his back and shoved him forward. He could feel the hard wood worrying his web of scars, and he moved docilely ahead, afraid to look back.

Another guard joined them at the far door. Arès was herded out of the building and into a large courtyard. To one side, stood a structure that resembled an outhouse with bars. The guard pushed him into it and turned the bolt.

The brisk evening air drained freely in and Arès hopped up and down to stay warm.

"It is cold here," he said. "Is it possible to have a blanket?" He rubbed his arms vigorously against his chest.

"You won't be here for long," the guard replied. "They are going to interrogate you, and then you won't be cold." He cackled as he finished his sentence.

Then he rolled and lit a cigarette and ambled off. Arès could smell the sweet scents of Moroccan hashish wafting within the curls of smoke.

He leaned between the bars and surveyed the grounds: only one guard, smoking and half-slumbering in the thick grass. Carefully, he slipped a pin and a tension wrench from under his sleeve. He had seen the guard's key and from the look of it, the cell door had a standard tumbler lock. It would be easy to pick, but he had to work fast.

He inserted the wrench into the plug and jiggled it side to side until he found which way it turned. Then he raked the pick pin across the lock pins while applying pressure. Two of the five pins misaligned, and he could feel the missing weight when he tapped the loose heads. He looked up again.

The police headquarters glowed fifty meters away. Its windows were partially shrouded by the fanlike bowers of two massive ficus trees, and they reminded Arès of a row of sleepy, half-lidded eyes. Far off, the solitary guard squatted against the stone wall, puffing contentedly and watching something in the street.

Arès began to apply modulating bits of pressure to the other three pins. Two more of them clicked up. There was only one left and it was the easiest. He thought of his father and wondered if he would be proud of his son's handiwork. Then he scanned the area one last time.

The door was rusty. It would squeal when he opened it. His best bet was to nudge it lightly, squeeze out and then bolt to the left, where there were no lights. The wall looked to be about two meters high, and he was sure he could scramble over it on his first try, though it might leave him open to a shot.

He took a deep breath and pushed up the last pin. The cylinder spun to the left. The door creaked, and a foot padded out. He looked up and saw the back entrance to the police headquarters dissolve into a rectangle of light that was quickly filled by two chatting guards.

Arès exploded out of his cell. He heard shouts behind him and the whistle of his elbows carving vortices in the air. His legs burst through soft grass. As he skirted a small bush, there was a whiplike crack, and a cloud of dust mushroomed off the wall.

But already he was there, and astonished at his own speed, he nearly smashed into the brick wall. He sprung at the last moment and flattened against its surface to the thunder of cries, and again a bomb-burst crack, and then he was up, a crouched spider silhouetted against a low gibbous moon, and a blur among trees, and a thing of speed and ragged breath.

He punched through a family of thickets and found himself on a suburban street. As he pivoted down it, a white police car with a blue stripe peeled around the corner.

He hurtled across a front lawn and then vanished into the dense foliage beside the house.

The police car, its blue lights wheeling, flashed on by.

CHAPTER 28

MAY 2009

─────────

F OR THE FIRST TIME, Nadia and Simon found themselves alone. There was a bashful silence.

"*Un ange passe*," Nadia said after nearly a minute had gone by.

"What do you mean by that?" he asked.

"It's what people say when a silence goes on for too long. An angel passes by."

"That sounds a bit lavish." Simon relocated to a living room chair and motioned at her to do the same.

"What?"

"Keeping an angel on hand for when you have nothing to say."

Smiling at him, Nadia sat down well out of reach. "Oh, we have lots of angels in this country."

"That's nice." He slid his chair close to her. "I've heard they're good luck."

She gave him an amused glance. Then she began lightly humming a tune, a cat's laughter playing about her emerald eyes. A sea breeze streamed into the apartment, swelling her gossamer white dress so that it billowed about her legs. Breathless, Simon watched the fabric tease him with glimpses of her thighs.

After a moment, she smoothed down her dress and floated to her feet. "I'm going to need more than luck to pass my exam on Monday." She glided toward the front door. "I think I'll go prepare for it."

"Wait!" Simon said, popping out of the chair. "Have you ever played three-card monte?"

"No. Never heard of it," she replied, still skimming across the floor.

"It's also called catch the queen. You hide a ball under some playing cards and shuffle them around. Then you have to guess which card it's under."

"I'm not sure I have the time." She placed a fugitive hand on the door-knob. Simon could see the bones flex on her delicate wrist beneath several looping, silver bracelets.

"*Les gens pressés sont déjà morts!*" he cried.

Nadia released a sunburst of a laugh. "*D'accord*," she said, and turned back around.

Simon went to the cupboard and extracted three Moroccan tea glasses from the shelves. Then he rolled a small piece of paper into a ball and placed it on the dining room table. "Please sit down."

They positioned themselves across from each other, like opponents on a chess board. "First, I hide the ball under one of the glasses, and then I spin them around like this." He began rapidly shuffling the glasses. His hands were surprisingly dexterous, and the vessels whirred across the table.

Nadia cupped her face in her hands as if feeling its lovely shape. Then she stared at him with luminous, disbelieving eyes. "But I can see the ball!" she exclaimed.

"Well that's why I need all the luck," he replied with a showman's grin.

"What do I win if I guess right?" she asked, still balancing the jewel of her face in her hands.

"If you guess right, you win a kiss," Simon announced grandly, and with a flourish brought the moving glasses to a halt. The ball sat on the table beneath the center glass.

"And what if I don't want a kiss?" she demanded archly.

"Then you better hope you don't guess right."

She gave a smile that made the freckles on her face spread out like stars in the sky. Then she briefly inspected the glasses.

"Ooohhh..." she said, "I just don't know."

Her finger lingered briefly over the center glass, moved to the one on the right, then to the far left, then back to the middle. It flexed at its second joint and suddenly pulled away. "Well I just don't know," she repeated.

"Guess at random, then." His eyes twinkled mischievously. "You have a one-in-three chance if you're blind."

"Did I mention I was blind?"

"I inferred it. Let me help you out." He placed his hand over her bangled wrist, but she drew it away immediately.

"Simon, we have to stop," she said sharply.

"You don't want to try your luck?"

"Not the game." She reached up and tightened the elastic band around her voluminous black hair. "We have to stop *this*."

"But we haven't even begun," he protested. "Let's first begin, and later on we'll decide if we want to stop. How does that sound?" He gave her his most innocent blue-eyed stare.

Nadia shook her head. "Even if I felt emotions for you, it doesn't matter. There's no future for us."

"But that's the beautiful thing about emotions," he said cheerfully. "They lead us into all sorts of interesting situations."

He grabbed her wrist again and this time she didn't pull away, but he could see she wasn't pleased.

"I think our emotions should lead us outside," she coolly replied. "Let's take them for a walk down by the beach so they can air out a little."

"What if our emotions don't want to go for a walk?" He rubbed her wrist lightly.

"All the more reason to take them outside." She stood up and grabbed her bag. "Are you coming? *Yalla*!"

The shore that day was veiled by a fluctuating mist. Simon and Nadia picked their way over an uneven coastline, almost entirely made up of lithified sandstone. Everywhere, shallow pool apertures scalloped the ground, so that Simon had the disconcerting impression of walking over hundreds of small, hungry mouths.

Half-chewed fish heads and melon rinds lay strewn about, and the tangy, salt-infused breeze and the stench of the nearby sewers needled his senses. There was something else too, an indolent smell of decay—not recent decay, but of something that had been rotting for thousands of years, which at times caused his nostrils to snort and burn.

Nadia seemed immune to the putrefaction, and she pointed out the colorful mollusks clipped onto the rocks, and the tubular sea slugs slinking through the shallow pools. Then she stopped, with a melodious "oooh," and called Simon's attention to a half-decayed starfish that seemed to have recently fallen from the sky.

From time to time, at the edges of the rolling mist, they could see the jumping crests of wavelets on the sea.

"What a fog," Simon exclaimed. "I wonder if this is what it feels like to be a ghost."

Nadia gazed at the ashen haze. "In Morocco, it's said that the dead govern the living." Her voice sounded airy and light, as if it were about to float off somewhere.

Simon was about to respond when the mist clotted up and they stopped in their tracks. The world vanished before their eyes. Alone, they stood on a yellow rock in a pale cloud. He tried to slip his arm around her waist, but she shrugged him off and stepped away.

"And now Rabat has totally disappeared," he said in a quiet voice.

"I wouldn't mind that," Nadia replied dreamily. She pirouetted her arm through the thick fog, birthing curlicues of mist that wreathed about her like wispy, white snakes.

"You and Kinani both."

"He likes the mist?" she asked with a distracted lilt.

Simon shook his head. "I think Kinani doesn't quite feel at home here."

"Neither do I," she said, her voice suddenly present.

"But you're from here." He turned toward her, surprised.

"I'm Berber."

"You don't call yourself 'Moroccan?'"

"Morocco doesn't call me 'Moroccan.' This is a Berber country, but Tamazight isn't even an official language." She looked at him, her eyes flashing.

"I'm guessing that's what you people speak?"

She ignored him and began to pace back and forth, fluttering her hands as she spoke. "Did you know that in the past, when they arrested Berbers, for *whatever* reason, they would keep them in prison until they learned Arabic well enough to go before a judge."

"Really?" he exclaimed. "How long did that take?" Far off the sun began to burn into the mist, a hazy smudge of yellow in the sky.

"Months in some cases. Years in others." She was revved up now with the story of her people, and her voice intensified accordingly. "We're the oppressed majority, if that's even possible."

"And there's never been an uprising? Why isn't there a Berber state?"

"There have been several uprisings. But the Berbers reject borders and national identities. We would never found a state." Her voice lifted and fell. It wafted about like a desert sirocco, capricious and commanding. "Humanity may be imperfect, but we belong to it."

"You sound like a dangerously idealistic people." He smiled at her again.

"The Berber poet Terence said it best. *Homo sum, humani nihil a me alienum puto,*" she concluded with a sharp intake of breath, as if ready to burst into song.

"You speak Latin?"

"Berber comes from Latin. The root is *barbarus,* or those who speak a foreign tongue." She gave him a condescending bat of her eyelashes.

"I think it's originally Greek," he gingerly corrected, "but *touché*. Still... Latin?"

"We learn it for medical school." Her voice had returned to its normal register.

"What does it mean?"

"I am human, and I believe that nothing human is foreign to me."

He reached out and caught her wrist, and this time she let him pull her close. They stood there, shelled together, bathed in an oblivious white fog, on an island without longitude. Then he pressed his hungry lips against hers and they closed like a parenthesis. He lingered there in the balcony of her arms until a brilliant rectangle of blue materialized in the sky and she pushed him away.

"Don't!"

"I thought we got over all that from different places stuff," he grumbled. "What happened to nothing is foreign to me?"

"No. It's not that," she whispered, peering anxiously around.

"Then why not?"

"I could be arrested."

"What?" he exclaimed.

"You're not Moroccan and we're not married. If the police catch us kissing in public, I'll go to jail for prostitution." She pivoted hastily about, sharpening her eyes, as if hoping to cut through the fog.

"That sounds like a particularly barbaric law."

"To the police here, you're the barbarian."

"Which goes to show how backwards things are in this country," Simon said. Then he tossed up his hands. "Why am I kissing a barbarian anyway? You'll probably cook me in a stew if I'm not careful."

"Don't forget," she said, jabbing him between the ribs with a deftly placed finger, "I'm still looking for a cadaver for my exam on Monday."

He laughed and pulled her close, but her eyes lit up with fury and she yanked away. "It's not a joke," she said harshly, and looked around, panicked. "I do *not* want to go to jail!"

"I'm sorry, I'm sorry," he said, the full weight of the situation beginning to dawn on him.

"It's ok," she murmured softly. Then she turned her face up at the sky and stuck out her tongue. "I think it's raining."

Simon stretched out his hand. "Either it's raining or I'm dreaming."

"Maybe it's both." She began skipping about in the rain and laughing. "The sun's out too."

Above them, prismatic blobs of color burst into being wherever raindrops crossed planes of sunlight, and a golden nimbus wrapped the clouds. Simon hurried after her, but suddenly cried out in pain.

"What the hell."

They looked down at his leg. A sinuous trickle of blood seeped out of a shallow gash, and next to it, the rusted bar of metal on which he had scraped himself.

"That's going to need cleaning," she sighed.

They headed back to the apartment. Simon was limping and Nadia tried to support him with an arm, but every time a car approached, she distanced herself demurely.

* * *

There's no Betadine!" she shouted from the bathroom. "Do you have onions?"

"Onions?" he replied, confused. "Yes. Of course. What are you going to do with them?"

"Sit tight!"

She dashed into the kitchen, turned on the stove, and heated several slices in a pan. Then she washed and cleaned Simon's wound, and began laying onion strips over the exposed cut.

"Are you kidding me? What is this? Oww. Those are hot!"

"Stop blubbering like a baby," she said. "Onion has allicin, an antiseptic."

"You people truly merit the name Berber. This is some savage desert stuff," he griped.

She gave a strange, bugling hiss and cuffed him playfully. "You should be glad I don't amputate your leg from the knee down."

"Again, I repeat. You deserve to be called Berbers."

"You know," she said, walking away from the couch and opening a window. "We disapprove of the name Berber. We call ourselves the *Amazighs*, which translates as 'the free people.'"

"Free to do what? Torture patients with scalding vegetables?"

"To go where we like. To live and work wherever we please. To flout borders."

"Oh great," he commented from the couch. "You're beginning to sound like one of the refugees." He wagged a finger at her. "Are you sure you're not one of them?"

"Do you kiss the refugees often?" she replied spiritedly.

"It's part of our standard procedure."

"Oh really? Are there any other benefits to being a refugee?"

He sprung up from the couch, lifted her, and carried her into the bedroom.

An hour later, Simon opened his eyes and began nuzzling her ear. Her body slid against his with electric warmth. "Thank you, doctor," he said. "You provided excellent care."

"We try to do our best for our patients." She ran her hand along his taut belly and then twirled a curlicue of hair in her finger. "And that was customary service for the refugees?"

"They have it pretty tough. We are obliged to provide extraordinary levels of protection." He nestled against her and began kissing up her neck till he reached her generous mouth. They breathed together for a time, until she laid back on the bed.

"They must go through such troubles," she said.

"Who?" he asked.

"The refugees."

"Oh, yes, them." He ran several amazed fingers through her astonishing abundance of hair. "They do. I've been summarizing several of their cases recently and it's pretty grim stuff."

"What are they?"

"A girl from Mali, who leapt from a burning house in Timbuktu and landed in a prostitution ring in Casablanca. A teenager caught up in the Kinshasa attacks in '98, who fished all the way to Morocco. A rebel from the Ivory Coast, knifed by masked Moroccans and saved by a dead man."

She pushed away from him and gave him a dubious glance. "These sound more like stories than real cases."

"I'm poeticizing a bit." He smiled and pulled her back toward him. "But the refugees do the opposite. They go through these dramatic experiences and reduce them to dry recitations of fact. I never thought I'd be bored listening to accounts of daring escapes and dangerous crossings."

"You don't think it's because they're trying to please you? You're part of a bureaucracy after all. We have the same issue at the hospital. We don't really want the details, just the diagnosis."

"Could be." He shrugged.

"Well I'm glad I'm not a refugee." She burrowed into his arms. "We don't even have a country to flee."

He snorted loudly. "Maybe if the Berbers picked a place to settle down, then they'd have the luxury of exile." He gave a disappointed shake of the head. "Honestly, I don't even believe you people are nomads."

"What?" she cried.

"All this talk about a being a free people is just to cover up the fact that you're indecisive."

"Don't forget that we're also barbarians." She leapt onto him and began play-fighting. They wrestled in bed until she looked at her watch and exclaimed, "Oh no!"

"What?" he asked, alarmed.

"I have to leave before Kinani gets back!"

"I don't think he'll mind."

"Yes, but I will." She clasped her hands together like a saint and gave him a kiss. Then she pulled her dress smooth over her body like snakeskin.

"*Un ange passe*," Simon said as she disappeared out the door. After, he fell back into bed and fell asleep.

CHAPTER 29
OCTOBER 2005

A CHARCOAL RING OF swallows swung above superannuated walls and landed beside sugared ruins half buried in yellow sands. A blue waterspout budded out of frothing seas, shattered upon gravity's fist, and sizzled downwards through the golden prism of a setting sun. Canons detonated above the beaches of Salé, heralding the end of another day of Ramadan.

Arès wandered through unpeopled streets lined by shuttered windows. Moments later, he crested a rise and looked across the river to where the hills of Rabat rolled in sinuous smiles.

For him, Ramadan was a divine dispensation. From sunup till sundown an inviolate truce pacified the streets, and for once the city was his. No stones to dodge; no interpellations; no sibilant hisses trailing his steps; no Moroccans on the beach, muscular from beating blacks. Nothing till the evening, when the sun dipped before the deserted city like the final burndown of a nuclear holocaust.

"If only it could stay like this," he half prayed to the abandoned streets. He had conceded so much, and his demands had become so hushed. He almost felt as if he could accept this life, if only it would afford him a little peace. He would gladly sell all his dreams for some quiet lanes and a day without worries.

And it was beautiful, he had to admit. The turnabout walls of the ancient medina. The soft, smooth paving stones. The tan fortress burning resplendent at dusk. The singing of the muezzin at the call to prayers. If only the people could be as beautiful as the place, he thought and smiled at his tired joke.

Then the last canon pounded out its breath, heralding day's end. Around him, the neighborhood spurred into being, and Arès hastened his steps, hoping to etch just one more tranquil lane into his scrapbook of memories.

As he strode, he could smell the tantalizing aroma of vast pots of *harira*, brewing in anticipation of the breaking of the fast, *el Fat'r*. Inside the quiet homes, spoonfuls of the saffron soup, turgid with cheese and lentil pods, were splashing into ravenous bowls, and small porcelain plates, pyramided with honeyed *chebbakia*, were delicately being set on tables.

He paused before an open window redolent with the smells of cooking. He was tempted to lean into the window and sniff like a hound. He could just imagine the family's horrified reaction at his big black face poking in, licking his chops and saying "Hmmmm..."

It would mean another sprinting escape, but the prank was delicious. He stepped a little closer, a lopsided grin on his face. One more step. He was about to grab the windowsill, when he doubled over in pain at a sharp crackling in his stomach.

Despite a reed-thin diet of bread and rice, he had been incontinent for several weeks. He could never be certain, but he suspected that his shower was the cause. The recent battering rains had overwhelmed the neighborhood sewers and plugged the toilets on the ground floor full of wastewater. Since then, an olive-colored stew had gurgled about his ankles while he bathed and worried him awake at night with its stench.

He felt the wave of nausea pass, and he moved on, forgetting his prank. He couldn't hazard it in his condition.

But the day was not yet done. He had a destination in mind. Pursing his lips, he began to whistle out a light, chirping tune that the trader had taught him on the road. Then his feet tapped around a corner, and the melody trailed only seconds behind.

A week earlier, Arès had come home from a restocking job to find his neighbor's wife sitting on a puddle of cushions on his living room floor. Beneath the twisted canopy of her hair, she shot him a glance as delirious as it was supercilious. He could see the frilled white hem of her slip and a bulbous nipple sloshing out of her bright yellow tunic.

One of his roommates, a short frantic man from the Ivory Coast named Yaya, was begging her to leave. The woman splayed forward on her knees and began to shout, *"Clandestins! Clandestins!"* capping the slur each time with a sharp, bugling hiss.

She reminded Arès of the plump canaries caged in the central market in Salé, and he could not banish the image from his mind as he crossed the hall to rap on her husband's door.

A ferret-faced man poked out his head. He was a tense character, unable to conceal his disrelish at living in a building full of Africans. Arès saw himself reduced, multiplied, and warped in the Moroccan man's pitch-dark eyes.

"Yes?"

"Salaam aleikhoum."

"Yes?"

"Sir, your wife is in our living room and she refuses to leave."

"What? What have you done to my wife?"

"Could you please take her back to your apartment?"

The man shoved his small frame against Arès, and then bungled around him when he did not budge. The young man watched his neighbor fly into his apartment like some wizened vulture and flap his hands against his wife, and finally drive her bawling and disordered across the landing and behind their shut door.

"What happened?" he asked his flatmate. He tried not to grin, but Yaya's nose twitched comically whenever he was distressed, and it spasmed now like a rabbit caught in a snare.

"I don't know. I came home and the woman was sitting there. She told me that thieves had broken in and she was looking around to see if anything was missing."

"The downstairs door was unlocked?"

"No. I used my key to get in."

"So she is lying." Arès furrowed his brow, and clouds of worry smoked across his eyes.

"She refused to leave and then you came home."

"We should check to see if she stole anything."

They failed to locate a cell phone and a watch. The two men walked back down the landing, one man long, limber, sinews rippling; the other, his nose atwitch, all his weight bundled in a low-hanging chest. They pounded on the door, respectfully at first, then with rising indignation, but it remained shut, silent, unperturbed.

Two mornings later, Arès and Yaya carried pans and a batch of loaves back from the communal bakery. When they reentered their flat, she was there.

The second they unlatched the door, she flew into a fit of hysterical screeching. The two men stood stupefied while she ripped her dress halfway over her head and thrashed to the floor in a fracas of thumping legs, worming breasts, and paisley-patterned undies.

Confused, they backed out into the hallway. The woman's shrill cries had roused half the neighborhood, and Arès leaned over the railing as a dozen women in a creamy spectrum of kaftans poured into the building. From above, their glossy hoods and pear-shaped contours called to mind a flock of painted penguins and Arès worked hard to stifle his laughter as they bumbled ungainly up the uneven, buckling stairs.

Then it was no longer funny. Upon seeing the two Africans lurking in the hallway, and hearing the high-pitched squealing from inside, the neighborhood women clawed and pecked the men out of the building.

Back in the street, Arès caught his bearings. Another apartment lost! He threw down the bread in disgust. *"Elle nous a foutus!"* he exclaimed, infuriated.

"What do you mean?" Yaya asked, confused.

"We have to move now."

"No. She will leave again in a few hours, or her husband will come home and take her back."

Yaya put his hand on Arès' elbow, but he shook it off and squatted in the dust. "It does not matter. She is deranged. She will say we raped her, or attacked her, and we will go to jail."

"You are exaggerating," Yaya protested, but his nose twitched worriedly.

"No. You are new here. I have seen this before. The same thing happened in Takadoum, where I used to lived. You must understand. We are guilty. Of whatever she says. No matter how crazy she is. I know someone who is in jail now, if he is still alive. It began just like this."

"You can move. I am going to stay here with Desiré."

Arès sucked his teeth. "You can do what you want. You will see. My life since I have arrived has been this. Move, move, move. The Moroccans never leave you in peace."

"But what can we do?"

"Leave. We must leave. Let me tell you something. Living in Morocco is like living in a port. Nothing is permanent; not work, not housing, not even friendship. And there are only two ways out. On a boat or burial at sea." He gave Yaya a wild look and stormed off down the street.

He could hardly believe himself, repeating Toti's words. When he had first heard them, Arès had taken it for the exaggerated cynicism of a tense, bitter man. But Toti had been right.

He wondered for a moment what had become of Toti. Of him and Michaux. He hadn't run across either of them in months. They had been friends and they had abandoned him. He was hardly even angry about it anymore. The reasons men murdered each other in this place were so minor as to be laughable. At least they had just tossed him out.

He shrugged his shoulders. Either Toti and Michaux were in Europe, or they were dead. There were only two exits from a port.

In a grimed side street of Salé, Arès paused before an aquamarine door, its jambs sunk into crooked foundations. Knife blades had defaced the wood in several places, and he rapped his hands lightly against the spidery nicks. A bolt shuddered, then a latch unclasped. He crouched as he entered.

The sudden dimness blinded him. "You were sleeping?" he asked. In the corner, he could barely make out the hulking shadow of his friend, slowly coaxing a flame from a ball of wax.

"Just resting." Guli's voice rumbled as he spoke. It sounded like a mountain shifting place.

"You are recovering from last week?"

The wax ball caught, and a thin flame shucked light onto the room. The behemoth turned toward him and lifted up his shirt. Arès leaned forward. In the scant illumination, he could make out a starfish-shaped welt radiating out from where a rubber bullet had punched into his friend's back.

Guli turned and held up an arm covered with bruised and swollen sacs, wherever truncheons had laid blows on his skin

In his slow, monolithic voice, he began to recount the assault on Ceuta.

Arès tried to picture it. Thousands of sub-Saharans, a teeming sea of blacks, flooding into those barbed fences like an oncoming tide. He could hear the cracks of rifles, see the ash wafting over watchtowers, and he was excited. Excited by the idea of an African uprising. The rich, white tourists that he saw waddle fat through the streets; the pale Moroccans who spat on him and stole his goods; trod underfoot like a worm, but there were thousands of him, millions of him, an entire continent surging north.

He looked at the older man with admiration. Guli was a pillar to the community of exiles. His physique radiated permanence and determination. Ten years in the Maghreb had not touched him in the least and his face still resembled a figure carved into limestone cliffs millennia ago.

"We are going to try again at Melilla in a week. We have to move quickly. They have plans to reinforce the barriers."

"I will go with you," Arès said. Getting to Morocco had just been the beginning. Now, he had to get out.

"It is very dangerous my friend. Many people died at Ceuta."

"How many were there?"

"At least three thousand, maybe four."

"That died?"

"No. I think maybe three or four dozen. They arrested perhaps three hundred and expelled them at Oujda."

Arès shuddered.

"They shot them?"

"We were pinned." His forefinger thudded against the table and drew a circle. "They waited for us to come over the first fence, then they launched tear gas and opened fire. I turned to run, but the Moroccan police were advancing from behind. I was lucky. A Spanish bullet hit me in the back. The Spanish were shooting rubber bullets, but the Moroccans were firing real ones. I saw someone take a Moroccan bullet in the neck. It was terrible. It was like being at war again."

"But this is why I must go with you. I want to live in a place where they shoot rubber bullets, not real ones."

"Yes. This is why I will try again."

Guli repositioned his bulk and everything trembled in the cramped space, as if touched by a light earthquake.

"How many made it through?" Arès asked.

"At least four hundred, maybe five hundred."

"They're all in Europe?" The triumph amazed him. "What do they do once they get in?"

"It is Europe, my friend. Things are easy there. You can find work. If you have nothing to eat, there are places you can go for food and shelter. If the police catch you, you apply for asylum. Sometimes they give you a piece of paper, which says that you must quit the territory, but then you do not leave. If they do not catch you, you can take a boat to Spain. It is only three hours away and there are no border controls. You are already in Europe."

"I will take the risk," Arès said.

"Do you have money?"

"How much is a ticket to Spain?"

"Maybe five hundred dirhams."

"Tell me when you are leaving. I will go with you."

Guli smiled and clasped Arès' hand. "I am glad to hear that. *Le ver de terre, à force de se traîner, arrive au marigot.*"[56]

Arès wanted to rejoice with him, but there was something off in Guli's smile. It looked wrong on his immense features, like one of those gaping grins cut into the wooden masks that Arès' father used to wear at the fair. He shivered at the memory, at all it implied. But he knew he could do this.

"They've mistaken the snake for a worm," Arès replied.

"Let us hope so."

---

56 By crawling steadily, the earthworm makes it at last to the water.

They left early in the morning by *grand taxi* from the *gare routière*. The driver forced Guli to purchase two seats for his enormous bulk, but he did not waste time protesting. They both figured that they would not be coming back.

The white Mercedes sped for six hours along the same road that lead to Oujda. Once again, Arès saw the countless hills and valleys, the lush farmlands and olive groves, the fortifications of Meknes and the labyrinthine medina of Fes. The taxi dropped the travelers at a nondescript town called Iaallatan. Three other men, acquaintances of Guli, awaited them there. Together, they took another *grand taxi* north for an hour. Soon, it began to wind its way into the heavily wooded Massif of Gourougou. At a certain place known to him, Guli tapped the driver on the shoulder and they all got out. The five men walked down a leafy, wooded trail for half an hour until it opened into an immense clearing.

Arès gasped. This was not an encampment. It was a city. There were hundreds and hundreds of Africans there. Maybe thousands. Tents sprouted off the hillsides like troops of wild mushrooms.

On one particularly flat plateau, the migrants had built semi-permanent structures out of wood. Hundreds of them, he found out, had been camping there for months, preparing for the assault. He could not imagine how they all survived.

"Do not get comfortable," Guli said. "We are leaving at one in the morning. It is a two-hour walk. There are many of us, and we have much to do."

Arès nodded. Then he lay down on a bed of pine needles and tried to rest. Soon he fell asleep.

In his dream, he was alone in a house on fire. Everything around him burned. The front door was veiled by a black shroud of smoke and fast-moving flames flowed up and down the walls, consuming everything in sight. Eventually, Arès' clothes caught fire as well. He was startled, but he felt no pain. The flames curled about him like bright, orange cats and he stood there, watching himself incinerate, until the roof collapsed on his head.

"It is time to go," Guli gently said.

*   *   *

On October 9, 2005, over a thousand men assembled in a starry field close to the border with Melilla. Slightly before dawn they began making final preparations for the assault.

One in every ten men carried a makeshift ladder—deadwood twined together with loose string or rope, ranging from four to five meters in height. Others had rudimentary hooks, coarse woven mats to throw over the barbed wire, and work gloves if they were fortunate. The strategy was the same as Ceuta: overpower the border guards with sheer numbers in a disorderly, desperate rush.

Guli peered around and then hushed the crowd, "Sssshhhhhh!" His breath rumbled like thunder from an oncoming storm and the men quieted. He turned and smiled at the young man standing next to him, miniscule beside his colossal bulk. "When the river is full, it is strong, but it is silent."

Arès nodded. He flexed his muscles and waited for the race to begin.

The world held its breath as the horizon slowly brightened and vermilion fingers crept up the metal arch of the sky. In the distance, they could hear the muted wails of the *Fajr* prayers welcoming the dawn. Two of the men next to Arès began to chant under their breadth, *"Allahū akbar. Allahū akbar."*

Then it began, gradually, hesitantly, more like a slow drift than the great rush Arès had envisioned.

"Be careful," Guli said to him as they began to march ahead. "Remember, the Spanish shoot rubber bullets, but the Moroccans shoot real ones."

"I will be careful," he said. His friend's heart boomed beside him, large as a boulder. "We will see each other in Spain." They clasped hands.

Then Arès kissed the talisman that hung around his neck and began to lope ahead, merging into an encroaching line a hundred meters long and forty men deep.

The land sloped down and swept up again. Cresting a small hummock, they could make out the indistinct pattern of double-barbed fences and slender watchtowers jutting above the lingering darkness. They picked up speed, readying themselves for impact.

All of a sudden, four men pitched forward, and Guli and Arès barely leapt the vibrating wire, strung some ten centimeters off the ground.

Spotlights flashed upon two of the watchtowers and arc lamps blazed amidst *fil de fer* on the inner fence. The high keen of an alert siren competed with the devotional arias of the muezzin.

The triggering of the trip wire sparked a panic among the Africans, and the controlled storm exploded into a desperate blitz. Small *ptooms!* sounded from the Spanish side of the fence. Half mesmerized, Arès slowed his pace to watch the graceful topple of the canisters as they breached the first yellow planes of light leaking over the horizon.

Dozens of ladders banged rudely against the metal fences. The men behind Arès began to cough and gag, and he was swept along in an unstoppable flood of humanity. The fences jangled under the weight of scrambling limbs, men flinging themselves up and over the first barriers, tumbling dangerously against the concrete slabs ten feet below.

The air reverberated with whiplike cracks and men careened off ladders, clutching the purpling flesh wherever they had been hit.

As the first men dropped over the barbed wire, soldiers in gas masks leaned into them with heavy truncheons. Arès could hear the sickening crunch of bone and he saw men pitch to the ground vomiting from concussions. Then two more canisters cracked down in a gaseous belch that engulfed the scene.

Drumfire crackled on the Moroccan side, and Arès swiveled left. On the small hillock to the west, a detachment of Moroccan gendarmerie leaned into shoulder stocks and popped off salvos at the migrants. The fence began to ping with fusillade and men gave cries of disbelief as their bodies shocked apart.

Those still standing ducked and swerved erratically and hastened up the ladders. Guli had gripped the top rail of the first fence and was lifting his enormous bulk over the rim when the air zinged above Arès' head, and his friend slumped onto a stew of metal and blood. Arès froze on the third-to-last rung of the rickety ladder and listened to what sounded like storm winds heaving through a seaside grotto. He placed a hand on the immense granite back before him and leaned out to see if Guli was still breathing.

From afar there came a quiver in the air and an onrush of something great and barreling. A sledgehammer thwacked against his chest, and his torso caved forward even as the force of the projectile lifted him off the ladder and flung him to the ground some two meters behind the fence.

He lay on the concrete writhing in agony. In the corner of his vision, men fell helter-skelter upon the pavement, pelleted and gouged by bullets from two directions.

All around him, panicked migrants trampled their wounded companions, shattering heads against concrete and crushing necks like cardboard flutes. Rifles crackled. Video cameras whirled, and the howls of men and the keening of bullets throbbed in the air. Near the horizon, the sun hung like a malevolent eye, swollen and incarnadine.

Feet clattered close to Arès and he shielded his head. Then the heel of a man popped off his shoulder, wheeling him about. Staying low, he dragged himself across the brutal terrain, trying to ignore the rawness in his chest.

When he reached safety, he looked back. Hundreds were still skirmishing, and the armored shadows of Spanish soldiers bedlamed through the mist. For a moment, he regarded the savage scene. Then, head bowed, he treaded once more into the Kingdom of Morocco.

As he walked, he could hear the muezzin singing adorations above the noise of the fray, and it seemed to him a prayer that they should never escape. His left breast ached horribly and he could not lift his left arm. He grazed a finger over the wound and retracted it at once. It was at that moment he realized he had lost another friend.

For several more minutes, he made his way through yellow hills under a caramel sky. Then a detachment of Moroccan gendarmes crested a rise beside him. They leveled their rifles at his chest and he sank deflated to his knees.

As one of the officers bound his hands, the muezzin's voice fell silent. The *Fajr* prayers were done.

CHAPTER 30

MAY 2009

SIMON WAS SITTING ON the kitchen balcony when he heard the front door slam. Lise and Nathalie stormed into the apartment in matching red and yellow dashiki shirts. Nathalie marched straight up to him and smacked a pink dossier down on his lap.

Simon kicked back in the chair and nearly fell over.

"What the hell is that?"

"*That,*" Nathalie said, "is an HCR dossier."

"What the hell is it doing here? You know we're not allowed to remove those from the building." He shook his head in disbelief. "What are we going to do if you lose something? Do you want me to report you?"

"That won't be a problem," Nathalie replied icily. "If we lose anything, we can just ask our flatmate to replace it."

"What is that supposed to mean?"

"Look at this," Lise said.

She flipped the folder open to a page marked by a red piece of tape. A black and white photo of Kinani, several years younger, stared out at his flatmates. In the stark light of the grayscale portrait, his face looked dignified, almost regal.

"Kinani di Gisuma," Nathalie read out loud, her lone dreadlock hanging down like an exclamation mark.

"Gisuma?"

"It's his family's ancestral village," Lise explained.

"I figured," Simon said. "I'm just surprised. It's right across from Bukavu in South Kivu, where a number of the Congolese refugees come from. But hold on, he's Rwandan? I thought he was Congolese."

"Wait till you hear his story!" Nathalie exclaimed. "You're not going to believe it."

"I won't need to, because you're not going to tell me," Simon snapped. He shut the dossier and stood up.

"What do you mean?" Lise asked.

"I don't want to know." He looked at them reprovingly and stepped back into the living room. "I can't believe you read it yourself."

Nathalie followed hot on his heels. "Don't you want to find out who you're really living with?" She snatched the dossier from Simon's hands and held it before her like a shield. "He's been sharing our apartment for over two months and he never mentioned that he was a refugee. All three of us work at the UNHCR!"

"That's his right," Simon retorted, surprising even himself. "Why does he have to tell us he's a refugee? Did I ask you if you were a refugee before you moved in? How the hell did you even locate his file?"

"I found it," Lise confessed in a subdued voice. "His mother came in for her annual status update, and I pulled her dossier to review it before the appointment."

"And all the family files are stapled together," Nathalie added, her cheeks flushed. "How could we not read it?"

"Ok," Simon said. "I understand why Lise read it, but Nathalie, you never should have gone near the file."

"Simon, there are things you need to know about him!" She waved the dossier now like a matador's cape, while the bright red patterns on her dashiki shirt flashed warning signs.

Simon took an involuntary step back. "Is he dangerous?"

"Hard to tell," Nathalie asserted at the same time that Lise cried, "No!" Nathalie stared down at the floor. "I don't know."

"Any evidence of military or paramilitary service?"

"There's mention of weapons use," Nathalie replied.

"What a mess," Simon muttered. His head ached and he could feel a vein begin to throb above his right temple. Without another word, he left the room and began to pace back and forth on the balcony, staring out at the sea.

The afternoon sun had burnt off the mist and the infinite blue expanse of the Atlantic stretched before him—a placid, watery plane that masked the dangers below. Every now and then, the shadow of some great finned form glided beneath the surface, dwarfing the tiny fishing boats that sailed obliviously above.

There was no good solution. His initial fears about Kinani revived and took on monstrous proportions. He was furious with Lise and Nathalie for bringing him into the apartment. Instinct told him to toss them all out into the street.

Yet how could he? Now that there was Nadia. Now that a sentiment he could hardly fathom resisted exposing his flatmate.

"In any case, I don't want to know," Simon said as he re-entered the living room. "Pack that thing away. We'll bring it back tomorrow and I'll pretend this never happened."

"You don't want to confront Kinani?"

"With *what* right?" Simon demanded. "With *what* right?"

Nathalie gave Lise a beseeching glance. Then she opened and closed her mouth soundlessly, like a fish gasping for air.

Simon sighed. "Maybe he's embarrassed that he's a refugee. Did you ever think of that?"

"So we should pretend we don't know? Carry on like nothing happened?"

"What do you have to reproach him with?"

"I like honesty in my flatmates," Nathalie insisted hotly, and Lise nodded in agreement.

"Honesty doesn't mean telling you everything," Simon shot back. "Are you going to reveal your traumatic experiences from growing up? Should we discuss the skeletons in *your* family closet? If so, then fine. We can all strip down naked in the apartment and bare everything to each other, if that's your idea of honesty."

"You'd like that, wouldn't you?" Nathalie swept her gaze from Simon to Lise and gave an audible snort.

"Excuse me!"

Nathalie threw up her hands. "Fine. We'll do this your way. But now we're the ones pretending to be something we're not. We'll have to lie and say we don't know something that we *know*."

"I'm sure he'll tell us when he's ready," Simon replied in his most placating tone of voice. "And if he never tells us, then that's his right too."

"You're taking a big risk," Nathalie said sourly. "You don't know what's in that file."

"Hopefully, I'll never find out."

F OR HOURS ON END, he wandered the streets.
He kept up a deliberate pace, walking out his anger. Steady,
unflagging, save for short interludes when he rested an arm against
a lamppost or a wall and waited for the squirms in his gut to subside. His
stomach ailments continued to torment him, and his days scored themselves according to the tempo of his pain.

When they arrested him at Melilla, the border patrol took nearly everything. Only a few hundred dirhams remained, stashed in his buttocks, and
his necklace, which somehow they overlooked. He was refouled again, and
again he crept through the thornlands along the border.

He found no work upon returning to Rabat, and he even wasted precious
funds foraging for jobs in Casablanca. For almost a month now, his landlord
had shadowed him, haranguing him about the rent.

Then the HCR intervened, secured him a stay of execution, but it was
all no good. He had nowhere to turn, no idea what to do. Since Melilla,
nothing seemed worth it anymore.

He constantly dreamt of home and woke in the middle of the night
crying. He longed for his father's patient words and his brothers' lively
banter. He wanted to make his little sister a present for her birthday. What
he would give to dash out of the kitchen and be scolded by his mother for
pinching food. What a terrible thing it was to be all alone with no way
home.

He never should have survived. He was stubbornly convinced that he
had cheated death, and that in doing so, he had unleashed some nameless,
implacable curse: Guli murdered, Kiwaka missing, Sekou and Buisha in

jail, betrayed by Michaux and Toti; crumb by crumb, the curse would gobble up what little he had till it returned him to his family where he belonged. It was his punishment for abandoning them.

That morning, he awoke with his brain on fire. His head felt heavy and molten, and whenever he tilted it, he could feel hot lava swish around and cook the insides of his skull.

He sat up dizzily and brewed his morning tea. The headache lessened after he drank it and he even managed to shove down a half-petrified roll of bread. Gradually, his forehead cooled to the touch. But his relief gave way to a sluggish pounding, as if the blood vessels in his temple were slowly being pumped full of sludge.

He pulled on his clothes and headed out into the streets of Salé. Several times before he had been like this, and the only remedy was to keep moving. He knew it would pass, but knowing did not lighten his mood.

For hours, he treaded the winding medina lanes. The streets were dusty and full of noise, but they drowned out the pounding in his head. He did his best to keep his mind clear. Whenever he failed, whenever he thought about his situation, a sour flame lit inside and hollowed him out. Then the pounding resumed and he felt like he would go mad.

It was best not to think. He circled the ancient, weathered walls that enclosed the old medina. His feet marched mechanically ahead, carrying him to the beach.

Twilight smoked over the sky and Arès began to breathe a bit easier. The sea was calm, and the water scraped its thin blade back and forth over the sands. A foghorn sounded, long and lugubrious, and blinking lights sparked an elliptic path across the heavens. Arès looked up to see a puff of cumulous clouds engulf a silver jetliner.

He curled his toes into the sand and waited for the plane to shoot out the far side. In the past two years, the air traffic around Casablanca had nearly doubled, and Arès often spent hours watching these silver flocks, pregnant with passengers, glide placidly along the coast. He drew a special pleasure from those valedictory moments when a northbound plane touched the edge of his vision and he roped his dreams to its vanishing trajectory.

But that evening the plane did not reappear and Arès moved on.

Near a mound of sand and sea stones, the Rastas had lit a bonfire. They danced and waved burning spliffs that floated like fireflies at dusk. Beside the bed of flames, Arès saw plump little Bob Marley fluff his dreadlocks in the dark.

He parked himself on a slim dunecrest slightly beyond the perimeter of firelight. Five months had elapsed since he had participated in the raid on Melilla, but its wounds remained. He rubbed a swollen sac, in the shape of a spider, lodged slightly above his heart. Then he watched the Rastas revel and chant and felt locked out of the world.

Soon, he realized it was getting dangerously dark. He hurried back to the muddy streets of Salé, being careful not to run. He did not want to attract attention.

When he found himself in his neighborhood, he slowed his pace again. He was reluctant to return home, sick of the curfew of violence that had scheduled his life for so many years. He was walking, his head low, a couple blocks from home, when an arm shot out of an alley and grabbed his wrist.

Arès looked up, preparing to run.

"I have been looking for you," a quiet voice said.

Arès stared into the shadows. Then he gave an audible sigh of relief. It was his former roommate, Desiré.

"You know, it is not nice hiding in alleys to scare old friends," he joked, his mood lightening.

"Buisha is out of prison," Desiré announced. "We have organized a little party for him, and it would be good if you could come."

"Of course."

Desiré took him by the hand, and they walked westerly through the streets.

Finally, something to celebrate, he thought, and a bit of pressure alleviated in his skull.

After nearly an hour's walk, they arrived at an unfinished building on the outskirts of Rabat. Glassless windows faced the city like blind eyes. A few rooms on the fourth floor, however, were strung with lights. The scene reminded Arès of some of the construction sites he had worked on during his early days in Rabat and he almost smiled at the memory.

Desiré led him up several flights of stairs, piled with bags of clinker and spare planks of wood. When they reached the fourth floor, Arès found a couple dozen black Africans milling around a table laden with steaming cassava, some sort of meat stew, six-packs of Moroccan beer, and a few cheap bottles of whiskey. Most of the attendees were men, but there were three or four women tending to the food.

Arès knew many of them, had known them for what felt like a lifetime. So many years they had spent in Morocco, and this was all they had amassed. A little stewed meat in a tenement and two beers a piece. If only they could get ahead, he thought bitterly.

But then he saw Buisha sitting there, surrounded by friends, and his face lit up with joy.

Buisha caught sight of his old co-conspirator and waved him over, smiling broadly. "My friend. You are alright!"

Arès embraced him warmly. He was surprised by how glad he was to see him. "I see you grew tired of the free room and board and have come back to struggle with the rest of us," he teased.

"Life in prison was too easy, my friend," Buisha said, holding onto Arès' wrist. "If I were a loafer, I might have stayed. After some time, though, it becomes a question of dignity." He thumped his chest proudly. "A real man works for his living."

"Ah, then you intend to convince the Moroccans to finally give us jobs?"

"I did not say I was a prophet come back to work miracles," Buisha replied with a roguish wink. The two men exploded with laughter. Arès clapped his friend on the back and noticed how lean it had become.

The wife of one of the refugees, a gregarious woman by the name of Merveille, handed Buisha a steaming plate of meat and rice. "Finish this quickly so I can bring you seconds and thirds. I've never seen anyone so scrawny. Did they only give you crickets to eat in prison?"

"On Fridays, it was couscous with crickets," Buisha said smiling and waving her away.

She gave a spirited laugh. "I'm getting you seconds now."

Arès beamed. "My friend, it seems like you have just traded one prison for another. Here you sit, doing nothing, while others fetch you food."

"Yes, but unlike in prison, no one has yet brought me a beer." The group around him laughed, and Arès walked over to the table to retrieve a couple of cans.

Desiré was there, flashing his eyes at a young woman named Divine. A dark blue pagne, decorated with lilting peacock eyes, twined around her fleshy, attractive body. Ostensibly, she was stirring one of the pans, but Arès could see her giggling at Desiré's antics. Everyone knew she was married, but her husband was perennially absent, which meant fair game in an exiled community that was seventy-percent male.

Arès felt a surge of jealousy that he struggled to suppress. "Where is Yaya?" he asked, tapping his old roommate a bit sharply on the shoulder.

Desiré gave a small jump and spun toward the young man. "What?"

"Yaya. I don't see him."

"Ah," Desiré replied sadly, "our former roommate has taken Buisha's place in prison."

Arès felt his heart sink. "The crazy woman who broke into our flat?"

Desiré nodded. "One man in. One man out."

Arès sucked his teeth. "I tried to warn him."

"I did too. He said he felt safe in the apartment. As if there was such a thing as safe in this country."

"*Le poisson a confiance en l'eau et c'est dans l'eau qu'il est cuisiné*,"[57] Arès said gloomily. He felt terrible about Yaya, but the experience of madness could not be taught. It was impossible to believe the things that happened in Rabat. They had to be lived to be learned.

Desiré turned back to his friend's wife, and Arès began retracing his steps, two beers in hand. Just before he arrived, Buisha stood up and loudly declared, "If you want to make God laugh, tell him your plans." Without another word, he marched over to a lonely corner of the building. No one followed.

Arès stood confusedly for a moment. Then he padded toward his friend.

---

57   The fish feels safe in water, but it is in water that he is cooked.

Buisha was standing with his back to him, staring out of a missing window.

Arès laid a gentle hand on Buisha's right elbow, but the arm convulsed beneath his touch and Buisha sprang half a meter away. He spun around, staring at Arès with wild, blazing eyes.

"I did not mean to scare you," Arès apologized. He examined Buisha with concern. His friend looked haggard, and his breath came in deep, ragged gasps. Arès stayed motionless and waited for Buisha's breathing to calm. Gradually, his eyes came back to the present.

"I am sorry," Buisha said. "There was a guard who used to touch me like that when he entered my cell at night." There was a long pause. "He wouldn't leave me alone." Buisha fell silent again.

Arès shifted uncomfortably. He too had had an experience like this. One night, his old habits had caught up with him, and he had sought the water's edge at the Bouregreg River. It had been imprudent. Four police officers had discovered him there. They were drunk after a soccer match, and they weren't interested in arresting him.

He shuddered at the memory. Many of them had stories like these that they shared with no one.

"You are no longer in prison, Buisha."

"I know." He leaned on the windowsill. "Now I am looking at this beautiful view over the slums of Rabat. Remember our trip to Tiflet?" Arès nodded. "I came to Rabat hoping to build a new life. Now I just want to see the city burn to the ground."

"Many of us do," Arès admitted. "But the leopard does not bring down the lion. None of us can accomplish this feat."

"Then I want to see that guard lit on fire. I want to remind him that when you bite someone, he too has teeth."

Arès frowned. "Give up this fantasy. It will eat you alive. How would you even find him again?"

"It is very simple. I will buy a knife and I will wait outside of the prison until he goes home at night."

"This is a plan full of madness. They expect this sort of reprisal. And if they catch you, you will lose not only your freedom or your teeth. You will lose your life. And even worse. There are things much worse than that."

Arès put the beers down on the windowsill. He had no interest in drinking them anymore.

Buisha glared at him, his face screwed up with anger. "What else is there to live for?" He prodded Arès in the chest with his finger. "After what I have been through? You tell me."

"You are living for vengeance?" Arès was angry now too. Buisha had touched a nerve. "What good is it to you? Will it clothe you when you are cold? Will it feed you when you are hungry? Is it not better to leave for Europe? To live a long life and forget this place?"

The fire dimmed in Buisha's eyes and he regained his composure. "I remember you used to talk differently, *mon frère*," he said in a baiting voice. "What would you do if you saw the people who murdered your family here? What would you do? Would you just let them be?"

Arès began to say something, but his eyes smoked black at the thought and he felt the fever rise up again in his brain.

Buisha looked out of the window and kept speaking. "Because you know it could easily happen. There are many refugees here who have run across their family's murderers. You have nothing to say?" He turned around to find Arès biting his lip, fists clenched, choking on a rage he did not even know existed.

"Ah, I see. That is the response I expected."

He opened one of the beers and began sipping greedily.

Arès stared at his friend with narrowed eyes. "There is a difference."

"Tell me," Buisha sneered.

"The people who killed my family were my neighbors. They set my parents on fire. They raped my sisters. They condemned me to exile." He spat out the window onto the broad expanse of Rabat. "The Moroccans who do these things know nothing about us. They are merely the fire that consumes the trees around them. The fire does not consider the trees." He put his hand firmly on Buisha's shoulder this time. "We are the ones standing in a burning forest. We cannot put out this fire. But we can leave."

"How?"

"We will burn the water. We will leave by the sea."

"It is too dangerous."

"Is it not more dangerous to stay here?"

"Do you know how many have died? I have lost two friends who tried to cross." Buisha gestured toward the far-off ocean, laying infinite and cold beyond the fortress city.

"Are we not dying here ourselves?" Arès cupped his hand over Buisha's elbow and began to lead him back to the party, back to the warm festivities and the carefree chatter of the guests.

"It is winter now," Buisha said.

"I know. But in the spring the boats will leave and we should be on one."

"Do you know how to swim?"

Arès laughed. "I am scared, too. But if we have to choose whether to die by fire or by water, I choose water."

"How much do you think we need?"

"It is five thousand dirhams."

"How much?"

"Five thousand per person."

"Do you have the money?"

"No. You?"

"No." Buisha paused for a moment, looking out the window. Then his face lit up with an idea. "But I think we have a friend who does."

CHAPTER 32

MAY 2006

T HEIR TRANSPORT WAS A patera, a flat-bottomed fishing boat rigged with a battered outboard motor. When Arès and Buisha arrived, forty-five people were already aboard, and the gunwale dipped precariously close to the lip of the sea. Over fifteen more bided by the shore.

Arès did not know boats, but he knew this was madness. Then again, so was everything he had ever lived.

He climbed aboard with Buisha, and they settled their bags next to the small turquoise cabin that doubled as a wheelhouse. A slender mast with a patched sail lofted against an azure sky.

The day before their departure, Sekou advanced them the ten thousand dirhams without the least hesitation.

"I do not know how to thank you," Arès said, as his friend rubbed one hundred cinnamon-colored banknotes onto the mahogany table.

Sekou's eyes glittered, and his Buddhic belly, which had swelled significantly in the past year, shook with contentment. "Do not worry my friend. You know I can copy new money whenever I want to."

The two men chuckled loudly and Buisha leaned over and slapped Sekou on the back. Then every sound in the neighborhood was swamped under as Sekou's mouth split open like an overripe fruit and a seismic roar of a laugh burst out of his massive carriage.

"You should come with us," Buisha said when the room had quieted again.

"Why should I?" Sekou asked. He swept a surprisingly supple arm before him. "I am doing better in Morocco than I ever did at home."

Arès' eyes followed the arc of Sekou's hand as it flaunted the commodious triplex he now inhabited. Sekou was right. The apartment was dressed in riches, and at its center he sat, a minor deity radiating ease. Arès felt a surge of admiration and envy for this man whom nothing seemed to touch.

"How do you pay for all of this?" he asked.

"African secret," Sekou replied, and another quake of laughter shook the room. Then he hoisted himself out of his chair and unlocked a cabinet. When he turned around, he was holding two diamond-patterned snake skins. He handed one to each of the men. They were oily to the touch, and Arès' greased out of his palm and onto a patterned Berber rug, where it briefly appeared to vanish.

"What are these for?" Buisha asked.

"One of my Moroccan partners told me that before doing anything particularly risky, I should sacrifice at least one snake skin for good luck. I have done so in the past and, as you can see, it has worked."

Arès groped blindly about the floor. When he located the skin, he folded it into his knapsack. "You are working with the Moroccans now?"

"Moroccans, Nigerians, Americans, I work with anyone who pays. There are limitless opportunities here. The trick is to have a nose for it." Sekou tapped the tip of his snout and smiled broadly. Then, as if to underscore the present glut of his days, he smacked his belly with a resounding clap and not an ounce of flesh wobbled.

Arès' eyes popped wide with disbelief. Sekou's soft, padded stomach seemed to have hardened into a shell. He looked again at his old friend, this time closely.

The man had changed since he had last seen him. He still dressed in the same sleek black waistcoat, still carried the same dandy of a cane, but there was something undeniably tough about him now. Something outrageous as well, as if he were related to one of those clawed animals that live at the bottom of whirlpools and prey on the disorder around them.

"But my friends," Sekou continued, "I will have to wish you both a *bon voyage.* I have a business appointment and I am sure you have preparations to make."

The three men shook hands. Buisha tried to embrace Sekou, but could not reach his arms around him, so he patted him on the back instead.

"Ah, but wait. Here are another two hundred dirhams. Go to this address in the medina and ask for this man." Sekou handed Arès a small piece of paper. "He will teach you how to properly sacrifice the snakes."

"Thank you again," Arès said.

"It is my pleasure, my friends. I wish you all the happiness money can buy." Sekou paused for a moment and regarded the two men with his knowing, Buddhic smile. Then he ushered them out the door.

That night, Arès and Buisha sacrificed the snake skins on a small pyre. They sat in Buisha's room, naked and cross-legged, and recited the chants they had been taught. Entranced, they watched the firelight puddle in coppers and crimsons upon the diamond-patterned scales. Then they opened their hands and the skins fell into the flames.

Seconds later, the world submerged beneath an ashen bath. Arès groped blindly to his feet and cracked open the window. Buisha pushed close beside him and the two of them leaned out, coughing and gasping for air. Blinking wildly, they peered up at the sky. There, in the interstices between tidal drifts of smoke, glittered the bright coasts of wintry stars.

Now Arès stood on the ship's deck and listened to the swish-shwack of the sea against littoral rocks and the endless thunder of its shorecrashing. Slowly, the sun bled above the horizon.

On the nearby beach, opaline sheaths of water glided over the sands. Dozens of translucent jellyfish lay about, their purple sacs of poison quivering inside like human hearts. Farther up, the silhouette of a gull flew above the dunes and was strobed white for a second by the sweeping beam of the lighthouse.

And everywhere, pebbles lay about like indecipherable runes and all these beauties, vast and inexpressible, flared upon Arès' mind.

* * *

Their captain was a tall Nigerian in a Yankees cap who reminded Arès of the bandits near Oujda. He spidered onto the cusp of the ship and blasted a loud, shrill whistle.

"I am Jonah, your captain. You will do what I say at all times. If you do not listen, you can swim."

A low muttering arose from the topside, where tight groups of travelers crouched in defensive rings around their belongings. A dozen or so parents tended to scrambling, saucer-eyed children, and a lone, elderly passenger was bent in prayer near the bow. The dominant emotion was fear, not anticipation.

Arès marched aftwards, barely able to distinguish the rags from their owners. He sequestered a patch of deck by the stern and caved himself onto the floor. Buisha followed close behind him.

"We are on a floating coffin," he remarked as he sat down.

"Would you prefer to stay?" Arès looked intently at his friend. Buisha shook his head.

"When you live in a port," Arès said, "there is only one way out."

"Yes, on a boat." Buisha slapped the deck with the back of his hand. "But this is a piece of wood with a sail. I think it would have been safer to swim."

Arès looked at the cheap resin patching several cracks in the boards. "We may have that opportunity." Then he pulled the golden key out from under his shirt and, holding it tight, said a silent prayer.

The captain cast off the lines and the passengers felt a slight tug in their guts as the ship unmoored.

They cabotaged north. To their right, faint wisps of morning smoke rose over Rabat.

"*Garru?*" Arès asked Buisha. He held out his hand and received a rolled cigarette damp with sea mist. He had to flick the lighter several times to sprout a flame.

"*Yalla!*" he said with a voice full of bravado, followed by a light slap to his friend's shoulder.

"*Yalla, yalla,*" Buisha replied with a big smile.

The ship rode all day on the waves.

From time to time, silver 737's screamed low across the sky and beguiled every eye toward the heavens. In their wakes, billowing white contrails hung for breathless minutes before dissolving into space. When nothing remained, the migrants reset their fervent gazes on the hypnotic blue shimmer of the horizon.

At night, the captain used a wooden sextant to chart the stars and keep them on course. Arès and Buisha hermitted together near the stern. To the other passengers, they were but two silhouettes before the immense crescent of a capsized moon.

From time to time, men and women bent over the gunwale with their pants drawn or dresses hitched and deposited plops into the sea. Children crawled through the jumbled bags and bodies, and whenever a small form drilled too close, Buisha growled low and mean, and the two of them chuckled at the ensuing shrieks and tumbles.

Later, all was silent save for the flutter of the sail and the shallow slap of the keel against the waves. Bright novas punctured the sky, the blazing firepits of the universe.

Arès rose and bent over the gunwale to splash water on his face. For hours he had felt light-headed and unstable, besieged by alternating runs of emotion. For minutes on end, he gripped the splintered planks in fits of panic. Then, suddenly, he felt like dancing to his feet, giddy with joy at his abduction from the penurious continent.

He looked over at his friend, wondering what he was thinking. Buisha sat on the deck, his noble face, with its high brow and deep, sad eyes, as impassive as a mask. Arès settled down beside him.

Silently, the two men watched the oily waters, their eyes glittering like flintstones at the dawn of the universe.

The second morning found the patera aglide on an undifferentiated plane of blue. They had been told that the crossing would take about two days, and the passengers clung to the sides of the boat and pried the horizon for a formless brown that might indicate land.

Arès gnawed on a hardening disc of bread, his eyes vacant. Then he smiled to himself. What would his family think if they could see him now, splashing his way to Europe across a tidy, blue sea? It was a gem of a thought and he held it up in the light and let it sparkle there prettily.

He was sure his siblings would have liked the sea, especially Yika with her fondness for blue. He liked it too. The crispness of the air, its saline tang, the immenseness of its light.

He tried to imagine them with him on the boat. He raked through the muddle in his mind, straining to recall their faces. Nothing came. He clutched the golden key around his neck and tried again. Its hard, metal contours forked into his flesh and his brow stitched together with effort. Then, like a miracle, they were there.

Their features were blurred, and a bit unrecognizable, but he knew it was them. There were his brothers, jostling loudly beside the wheelhouse, and his father pacing back and forth on the deck, steady as a metronome. He smiled and waved at them and they waved back. To his right, two of his sisters sat on a bundle of sleeping migrants, studying for upcoming exams. One of them said something and his mother looked up from her sewing. When she saw Arès, she chided him to sit up straight and he did. Then his little sister pinched his arm and they all disappeared.

For a minute he blinked wildly, unable to believe they had gone. He reached out to Buisha, but his friend was plunged in his own thoughts and did not register Arès' hand on his shoulder. When Arès shook him lightly, Buisha grunted and turned away. It was obvious he was in no mood to talk.

Arès shut his eyes and stuck his head between his knees. For a long time, he drifted in loneliness. Then he looked up. Nothing had changed. The deck was inert and half asleep and beyond it lay the imperturbable sweep of the sea.

Time plodded into the wash. The sun wheeled over the horizon. Wriggles of light snaked along the waves. The patera ghosted ahead in the omnivorous glare.

All of a sudden shouts of excitement erupted from the bow. Arès lifted his eyes from the wooden planks. A sleek white vessel, with a stripe of blue, bobbed like a mirage on the distorting prism of the horizon.

"It is the *Marine Royale Marocaine*," the captain shouted. "Get down! Get down!" He thumped along the deck, shoving bodies against the slick boards, as if they could hide what they were.

Then he wheeled the boom and the sail billowed and wrenched. The sudden portside tack jolted the boat into a light ocean swell. Arès slid and clung to the deck, at all times keeping an eye cocked on the far-off geometry of their pursuers.

Out they rode, seawards on the sea. The sun compassed halfway around the vessel as it jibed off course, diminishing itself in the perilous distance.

Gingerly, over time, dozens of heads peeked out of cover and gazed over the gunwale. The alabaster ship glinted, unmoving, in their ken. It neither retreated nor gained on their flight, but seemed roped to them by some invisible cord.

Buisha crawled onto his knees and stared out over the wash. "We are nearly in Europe, and still they do not let us go," he muttered angrily. Then he steadied a hand on Arès' shoulder and, hoisting himself to his feet, spat in the direction of the distant vessel.

"Yes." Arès clucked his tongue. "If they had wanted us to stay, they could have been a bit friendlier while we were there."

Buisha chuckled as he sat down. Then his fine features clouded over and he sucked his teeth. "They chase us out, and now that we are leaving, they try to pull us back in. I feel like we are trapped in a story from my childhood."

"Which one?"

"In my village, we often recount the story of how the little Turtle tricked the mighty Elephant and the powerful Hippopotamus."

Arès smiled and nodded enthusiastically. He knew the story well. "Please tell it."

Buisha took his friend by the elbow and swept his eyes over the deck. Then he began to speak. "When the Lion was first named king of the jungle, he decided to hold a large celebration. As the main attraction, he announced a tug-of-war to determine who was the strongest of all the animals. The mighty

Elephant and the powerful Hippopotamus immediately presented themselves, and afterwards, no other animal dared to take part." Arès settled his back against the slick bulwarks. His grandmother had told him this story when he was only a child, and he shut his eyes and thought back to that innocent time.

"No animal, that is, except for the clever, little Turtle," Buisha continued. "On the day of the contest, the Turtle approached the mighty Elephant. 'Mr. Elephant,' he said, 'you are mighty on the land, but if I take this rope into the water, I am sure I can out-pull you.' The Elephant looked down at the little creature and laughed. 'Do whatever you want,' he said."

Arès opened his eyes and saw that two young boys had crept close to Buisha and were listening intently. He smiled at them and they smiled back.

"So the Turtle took his end of the rope and swam to the powerful Hippopotamus. 'Mr. Hippo,' he said, 'you are powerful in the water, but if I take this rope onto the land, I am sure I can out-pull you.' The Hippopotamus laughed at the little Turtle and told him to do as he wished. Soon, the Lion announced the start of the contest. The mighty Elephant dug his massive feet into the dirt and the powerful Hippopotamus gritted the rope in his teeth and swam with all his might. To their great surprise, no matter how hard each of them pulled, neither of them could overpower the little Turtle." The children giggled brightly when they heard this and Buisha noticed them for the first time. His high forehead creased and he gave them a thin, vanishing smile. Then he continued speaking.

"The two indomitable animals strained for hours and hours, until they collapsed in exhaustion. One after the other, the mighty Elephant and the powerful Hippopotamus admitted defeat. The clever, little Turtle was proclaimed the victor and was known thereafter as the strongest animal in the jungle." Arès grinned and slapped the deck with his hands, and the two boys rolled around laughing with delight. But Buisha's face remained stubbornly grave.

"Like in the story, I feel we are being pulled between two colossal forces," he said, turning his head and glancing distractedly at the sea. "Europe is the mighty Elephant and Africa is the powerful Hippopotamus."

"And you think that we are the clever, little Turtle?" Arès asked, still smiling.

Buisha stood up again and stared mournfully at the glittering, white vessel on the horizon. "No. I think that we are the rope."

Arès' smile vanished. He stood up next to his friend and put an arm around his shoulder. "Let us hope, then, that the rope does not break." With their free hands, the two men held tight to the grab rails and glared at their pursuers.

Beneath them, the patera rocked on gently rolling seas.

The second night was starless and the ocean an arrant blackness of swishing oil. The only light came from the faint, indigo gleam of the ship of the Royal Marines.

Arès swallowed his last piece of bread as arsenic-colored clouds huffed low across the sky. The sea began to shake and heave and the winds careened through watery valleys. On the boat, the passengers shielded their faces from the wet, whipping air. Cradled near the stern, Arès remarked a far-off keening, like the laments of women about a bier.

For hours, the vessel pitched through an omnipresent and discombobulating darkness. Rain clouted the balled passengers. The ship shuddered. Beams cracked. The furled sail slapped against countercurrents of air.

On the deck, the passengers slid about in a rolling penury of fear and retching. Three hours in, a woman cascaded toward the prow and catapulted into the abyss without a voice of complaint. A child clawed and shrieked after her. Arès watched a dark hand reach out. In a crack of lightning, he observed silvery runnels of water stream between thick wrinkles like veins of quicksilver in fissures of stone. Then the child disappeared into the frothing wake and the doleful hand retracted.

The waves dished about, rising and sinking like the backs of ancient sea beasts. A titanic waterspout whirled past the boat, siphoning the granite-hued seas toward the heavens. Arès held his breath as the spout passed. He knew they were lost, and he fell to his knees and prayed, and awaited only the tail of the leviathan that would smite their vessel into the drink.

* * *

By midmorning, every passenger aboard was depleted and ill. The waves had mostly subsided, but the indefatigable rocking offered no respite. Hunger too had begun to prick at their nerves. Their supplies were nearly exhausted and the boat seemed hopelessly adrift.

With tired eyes, Arès watched Jonah desperately yank the starter cord on the outboard motor. Each time, it sputtered and died. A few hopeful passengers scoured the horizon for the Royal Marines, but the sleek white vessel was nowhere to be seen. The fishing boat swayed helplessly, pushed about by powerful winds.

Then the seas calmed and sunlight fanned through a part in the clouds. Jonah unfurled the sail and the small, blue patera scudded ahead.

Another day they sailed. Hunger crawled inside of Arès, scratching and gnawing. He saw others clawing at their guts, trying to dig the animal out.

The winds livened and faded and roused again. An armada of clouds materialized on the horizon. Slowly they massed and flexed and blackened. Eventually they advanced in the shape of a maw that threatened to swallow the ship whole. But beneath their approaching menace, the migrants could make out a formlessness rising from the sea.

"*L'Espagne! L'Espagne!*" cried out from all sides.

Arès sprung to his feet, unable to believe it. He grabbed Buisha and pointed at an impression of coastal hills that blended into crowns of thunder.

"We are saved!" Buisha shouted, and Arès squeezed his friend's shoulder tight. The patera creaked as it hurtled toward the promised land.

All at once, a flurry of convecting winds spun the vessel round. Jonah sprung atop the see-sawing cabin and lashed the sail about the mast. The passengers' cries were whipped away by tempestuous gusts as the shallow hull listed on madcap waves. Then the flat keel burrowed into a hillock of water. Arès lurched forward against the jambs of the small cabin as several passengers were flung overboard. Those who could snatched onto the grab rails, while the boat thrashed about.

In minutes, the waves trebled in size and great watery curls gobbled at the deck. Arès looked around for Buisha, and saw his friend braced against the stern of the boat, holding on for dear life. The captain unhitched a ratty tube from a small hook and, without a word, flung himself with it into the frothing sea.

Arès pushed into the cabin seeking the wheel, but a mountainous wave squalled him across the deck. The winds bansheed and the boat pitched on improbable angles.

When he pulled himself upright again, Arès locked eyes with Buisha, still clutching to the stern. His friend opened his mouth to say something and then flew off the up-jutting deck and disappeared into the wake. A head-splitting crack drowned out all the cries. The patera rent in pieces and Arès felt himself swing obliquely out on a titanic blue splinter toward the uprushing sea.

The cool water swallowed him whole. He floated, stunned, enveloped by a ubiquitous rumble, like the breathing of a sleeping giant. Then his arms scrambled to the surface, thwacking against the turquoise plank. He hugged himself up into that mindless din. Within seconds, the tides had carried him far from the sinking wreck.

For hours, he clung to the trembling flotsam, flung about upon rampaging waters. A hundred times he nearly slipped into the wash, a hundred times he glugged to the surface and spat out lungfuls of salty brine.

But whenever he crested another architecture of water, he could make out the gloomy outline of a shore tending ever nearer. Was it Spain, or Morocco, or even Portugal? He gripped his necklace and prayed for landfall, wherever it was. The plank scudded ahead and Arès curled his body tight over the wood, anxious about the things swimming beneath him in the vortexes of the deep.

Slowly the gale diminished. Slowly the currents reeled him shorewards. A wave lifted his dark form, a body laid across a plank like a cross, and spilled it onto the shore. The next wave pushed him a bit further up the beach. Mantled in foam, Arès crawled onto dry sands, where he wept as only as a nighttime shadow can weep. Then he stretched out and fell asleep.

CHAPTER 33

MAY 2009

———————

I T WAS EARLY MORNING. The sunrise lit up the bay window like a
cinema projector with the promise of something to see. And beside
him stretched a bounty of black tresses and a soft undulating form. He
traced a finger along the curved lines of her hips where they raised toward
the shelf of her belly, like a welcoming island upon a deep-flowing stream.

"You're up already?" she groaned, and pulled the pillow over her head.

"Dawn does not come twice to wake the man," Simon said.

Then he reached his hand down along her tingling stomach and deep
into that warm rift between her legs. He left it there until he heard a sharp
intake of breath and then a heavy exhalation, and she turned toward him
with the sensuous weight of her body. Just as he entered her, the sun's rays
tipped over the windowsill and everything lit up with a fulguration of
feeling and light.

Afterwards she sat on the bed with her hands over her eyes.

"What are you doing?" he asked.

"In Arabic we say 'Taiwarti fih' or 'I blinded myself in him,' to say 'I am
falling in love.'"

"Ah," he said. "And in English we say 'love is blind.'" He kissed her on
her closed eyelids, one at a time, feeling the wingtip flutter of her lashes,
and the small, electric tremor every time they touched.

"Are you going to stay over again tonight?" Simon asked, laying back
on the bed.

"I can't." She shook her head, still holding her hands over her eyes.

"Why? Because you're blind now and won't be able to find your way
back?"

"No." She gave a melodious laugh. "My parents are beginning to suspect something."

"Let them suspect." He pulled her tight against his body.

She pushed away from him. "Do you want my father to hunt us down, gut you like a fish, and marry me off to some old goat in the desert? I'll spend the rest of my days making tagines over a stone pit. Is that what you want?"

"Ok, ok." Simon raised his hands helplessly. He stood up and began rummaging around beside the bed. "Have you seen my contacts anywhere? I swear I left them on the nightstand."

"You wear contacts? So you're the one who's blind!"

"I'm short-sighted," he said defensively. "It's a prerequisite for working at the United Nations." He beamed at her blindly beneath a mop of blond hair.

"Lise and Nathalie don't wear glasses."

"That's why they're interns, who will never get promoted," he stated matter-of-factly. "So where are you hiding them?"

Then he pounced on her, and they rolled around on the bed.

For once, he was early to work.

It was not yet 8:00 a.m., but there were already half a dozen asylum demanders queuing before the official entrance to the HCR. Most were men in dusty, day-laborer clothes, but one young woman caught his eye. She was attired in a vibrant yellow pagne, with an almond-colored sash draped over her shoulder like a contestant in a beauty pageant. A small, brown head, with cartoonishly large eyes, poked above her chest.

A few of the applicants watched Simon exit the taxi and briskly traverse the intervening space, as if dodging sniper fire. About ten meters down from the main entrance, he rang at a half-camouflaged door, and quickly stepped inside. The uniformed guards led him through a small shed whose upper half was paneled with live security feeds.

He took his time greeting them. Then, with a chipper springing gait, he climbed the shallow steps that rose in a swinging crescent across the front courtyard. Midway up, he stopped to waive at Andreas, a new intern recently arrived from Zurich. Assigned to the outdoor desk for the hot summer months, Andreas wiped the sweat from his eyes and bravely waved back at Simon with that sort of cheerful stoicism particular to the Swiss.

Simon sped through the empty front office and into the large entrance hall. Inside, the cool air clung to him with a heavy marble quality that reminded him of a church. To his surprise, the HCR's habitually bare walls had been decorated—like stained-glass windows in a cathedral—with posters sent from Geneva in anticipation of World Refugee Day.

In one poster, a dewy-eyed Semitic child crouched beneath a discarded blue and white jacket with the UNHCR logo emblazoned on the back. In a second, a Caucasian doctor with snowy white hair held a stethoscope up to a bronze-skinned woman, dressed in the purple and indigo costume of a Thai hill-tribe. In a third, three turbaned Sudanese girls, with creamy complexions and luminous eyes, posed before a high volleyball net. The center girl extended a bright yellow ball forward, as if challenging the viewer. At the bottom of each poster, the slogan REFUGEES: REAL PEOPLE, REAL NEEDS was printed in a bold, cinematic typeface.

"Maybe I should take a photo of Kinani grilling hamburgers for one of these," Simon said to himself and chuckled. Then he bounded up to the second floor and headed down the hallway.

The door to Federika's office was open, but she hadn't yet arrived. Fatima sat at her desk, looking like she had been there for hours. An attractive Moroccan woman, with tasseled black hair and strained eyes, she was scrambling a number of documents into an oversized purse, while talking nervously into the phone. She waved briefly at Simon as she bolted into the hallway.

Simon shrugged and continued up to his third floor office. Georg was back in Brazzaville, ensuring the future of African democracy, so he put his feet up on the desk and switched on his computer. He had finished reading the news and was answering a number of personal emails when an internal message pinged in from Baptiste.

"*Mes amis*, we are only two weeks away from World Refugee Day. Because it can happen to everybody in this life, please don't turn away!! Please read Angelina Jolie's message for World Refugee Day."

Simon raised an eyebrow and opened the attachment. In it, Goodwill Ambassador Jolie recounted her adventures sharing tea in a tent with two Afghan women and chatting with a paralyzed boy in Tanzania. She related the inspiring story of three orphans in Sudan and extolled the extraordinary resilience and courage of refugees.

The message was linked to videos of her visiting displaced persons camps around the globe. With growing fascination, Simon watched the slim, pale celebrity inspect primitive latrines, squat among Somali villagers, and hold emaciated children in her arms beside their starving mothers.

He pinged Baptiste. "Another superstar patronizing the refugees?"

Almost immediately, Baptiste replied. "A person in danger is the ambassador of all humanity. Anyone who comes to their aid is welcome."

"If you say so."

"Why don't you join me for a refugee status determination in a few minutes? It's with a Nigerian applicant so it will be in English."

"*D'accord.*"

Simon stopped by the kitchen for a pot of mint tea and then spun down the HCR's helical, center staircase to the multilevel hall on the ground floor. Tall picture windows looked out onto the glittering tiled courtyard, and to his right, a short staircase ended at a frosted door.

Inside was a roomy, windowed office with six desks spaced evenly about, each topped by a bulky desktop computer, swing-arm lamps, and letter racks stuffed with dossiers. Several posters hung on the walls, recounting stories of flight and peril with the tagline: "It Takes Courage to be a Refugee."

When Simon opened the door, "Billie Jean" was playing on a small speaker and Baptiste was moon-walking across the floor. He mouthed the lines "be careful what you do 'cause the lie becomes the truth…," while two other employees clapped their hands and shouted encouragement. A heavyset woman with thick glasses sat at her desk, sipping from a white mug with the phrase "*Je m'en fish!*" written beneath the picture of a dopey-looking cartoon trout.

Baptiste was dapper as usual, attired in a white cutaway shirt, stylish herringbone pants, and a maroon tie. He splayed his hips and set his arms akimbo when he saw Simon enter the room.

"You see, I am so good I'm attracting an audience!"

"Billie Jean is not my lover!" repeated loudly in the background until someone dialed down the sound.

"Is this how you prepare for an RSD interview?" Simon asked laughing.

"Before a match, any player who's worth anything does a warm-up," Baptiste replied with a gleaming smile. Then he glided backwards in his stylish brogue shoes.

Simon shook hands with Pacifique, a tall, monkish-looking fellow in an earth-toned abacost, and then high-fived Khadija, a short girl from Senegal. She had chubby, round features and large, prominent eyes that lent a childish air to her face. For this reason, she often dressed in sober gray blazers and cigarette pants, that day with a white, piped shirt. A thick shower of beaded braids streamed over her shoulders, adding a dash of colour to her outfit.

Without bothering to get out of her chair, Solène, the only French Protection Officer in the bureau, lifted her coffee mug above her desk and gave a terse, *"Salut."*

"Should we get this show on the road?" Simon asked Baptiste.

"The show is here, *mon ami.* But if you prefer a story to a dance, then yes, let's get on our way."

"I'm a sucker for a well-told tale."

"That's good because you never know what you're going to hear." Baptiste opened the frosted door and the two men re-entered the multilevel hall. "I've interviewed some real loonies in my time." He gave a long, melodic whistle and shook his head. "I keep a collection of the most outlandish claims. I want to publish it someday, but I'm not sure whether to sell it as fiction or nonfiction."

Simon laughed. "And what's the nonfiction you tend to get from Nigeria?"

"The real cases are serious." Baptiste paused in front of a reinforced metal door. He held up a cautionary finger while he gazed through the rectangular vision panel. "The north is Muslim and the south Christian, so you get persons displaced by religious clashes in central Nigeria. Then, in the Niger Delta, there are the oil conflicts. We have some asylum demanders targeted by native armed groups, and, on the other side, there are Ogoni leaders fleeing targeted assassinations by paramilitaries, who, you didn't hear it from me, are likely funded by Royal Dutch Shell. After that, there are the usual political prisoners, trafficking cases, and of course, if you're homosexual in certain regions and someone finds out, you'd better pack your bags."

"And the crazies?"

"Oh there are all sorts of things. I particularly like people fleeing *mmuo* spirits or curses placed on them by local marabouts. Those tend to be the most colourful."

"How do you know they're not telling the truth?" Simon asked, deadpan.

Baptiste blinked his lively eyes, and then an infectious Cheshire grin crept over his face. "You're right," he agreed. "But it doesn't matter. They're still not refugees." He gave a curt wave at an invisible guard, and Simon heard the bolt snap back in the door.

The three interview rooms were located in a tight hallway on a bridge between the administrative half of the UNHCR and the applicants' waiting room. Each box was lightly soundproofed and boasted a large observation panel carefully surveyed by a uniformed guard, who was permanently stationed in that airless corridor.

Simon looked in at a young man in a sleeveless jean jacket, black jeans, and a red Yankees hat, who sat slumped in his chair. Baptiste opened the door and Simon involuntarily recoiled at the oven-hot blast of air.

"Boss!" the young man shouted, jumping to his feet and stretching out his hand. He had a chocolate complexion, a slim athletic body, and finely chiseled features.

"Sit down," Baptiste said. "This is my colleague, Simon." The two men shook hands while Baptiste booted up the computer. Afterwards, he reached over and turned on a small desk fan. Simon felt a spurt of air and then nothing. He rolled up his sleeves and placed a yellow office pad and pen on the table.

Thank you for coming today.

This is an interview to determine whether you are a refugee. If you can, please talk about your life story in a manner that is open and above all honest. Everything you say here is entirely confidential.

We will not share your information with anyone, especially not the government. We are not a government agency.

Please give us as much detail as possible because it is only by knowing your full story that we can determine whether or not you should be qualified as a refugee.

Do you understand what I am saying?

Yes.

Have you understood everything that I have just said?

Yes.

While Baptiste spoke, Simon watched the shadow of the fan's blades spin over the table like a saw. Something in the Nigerian's poise reminded him of Kinani, and he thought of his smiling flatmate. He too must have sat in that chair and answered those same questions and stared at his distorted shadow stretching along the floor like some grotesque mask. He wondered if Kinani's smile had held.

For the next hour and a half, the asylum demander recounted how a student fraternity, called the Eiye Confraternity, had terrorized his campus at Kwara State Polytechnic. As part of their initiation rituals, they had robbed and murdered several students and raped a close friend of his. When they tried to recruit him, he refused. So they accused him of being a member of the rival Aiye Confraternity. After he returned home to find a decapitated bird in his bed, its entrails tied around his pillow, he fled.

Baptiste finished typing up the account to the whir of the fan and the tap of Simon's pen against his knee. The asylum demander waited expectantly. After a moment, Baptiste looked up from the computer.

Do you believe that you face persecution or the possibility of violence if you return to your home country?

In the Yoruba language, *Eiye* means bird. The Eiye confraternity is a falcon that flies everywhere. It sees all. Nowhere in Nigeria is safe.

I will mark that as a "yes".

What reasons do you have to believe that you may have difficulties if you are sent back to your country?

I can never go back. It is impossible.

Do you fear death?

I fear worse. Those who hold others down in the mud must stay in the mud to keep them down. That is worse than death. That is life in the mud. I leave that to them.

Thank you.

Here is a rendezvous for Friday, June 12. At that time, we will give you the decision in your case.

As I said at the beginning of the interview, the decision will be either positive or negative. If it is positive, we will provide you with a refugee card.

If it is negative, we will tell you the reasons why it is negative and you will have the right to appeal.

Thank you for coming today.

"Man. I thought my fraternity hazing was harsh," Simon said after they had stepped out of the room.

"Do you feel up to drafting the report on our friend..." Baptiste looked down at his pad, "Chinua?"

"With a little guidance, sure." Simon took the dossier from his colleague's hands.

"First, you should review his country of origin information. Log onto Refworld and go over any recent reports about Nigeria. Feel free to visit the dossier room if you want to look at some RSD's for other asylum demanders."

"Sounds straightforward."

"It's not," Baptiste cautioned. "You have to cross-check the applicant's claims against the current sources on Refworld, especially if you have questions about any of the external conditions that led to his displacement. I'd recommend you consult the country-specific information about the various conflicts, ethnicities, and political movements in Nigeria, so that you can make a substantive analysis of the case and decide whether there is a well-founded fear of persecution."

"Ok. I'll check it out."

Baptiste peered at Simon for a moment. "Did you notice the discrepancy in his account?"

"What?" Simon shook his head. "No, I didn't."

"After he found the dead bird, he claimed that he hid at a friend's house until he left the country. Then later in the interview, he mentioned that he kept working at his uncle's restaurant up to the day he departed."

"Maybe he needed the money."

"Maybe," Baptiste said, pushing open the frosted door. "It doesn't sound very credible, if he was scared for his life."

A cocoon of cool air enveloped Simon when they entered the office. Baptiste sat down at his desk. "Do you have any other questions?"

"Yes. What's the web address for Refworld?"

"You haven't used Refworld yet?" Baptiste looked at him askance. "What do you actually do with Georg in that office? Do you just drink tea all day?"

"We shoot hoops sometimes too," Simon replied with a grin.

"Come here." Baptiste typed in a web address and "Refworld: The Leader in Refugee Decision Support" appeared in blue letters, the same shade as the UNHCR flag.

"Nice branding," Simon said dryly.

"I think so too. I find the blue very calming. I can get easily stressed out by all these colleagues of mine who don't take their jobs seriously. Thankfully, there are these relaxing blue and white motifs everywhere."

"If I didn't know better, I'd think you were questioning my professionalism." Simon furrowed his brow.

"I would have to see some evidence of it in order to ask questions about it."

"I'll send you some later today." Simon picked up the dossier.

Baptiste gazed up at the JPO with gleaming eyes. "As the king of pop once said, 'if you want to make the world a better place, take a look at yourself and then make that change.'" He sung the lyrics on key, followed by a small drum roll with his fingers on the edge of his desk.

Simon opened his mouth to reply, but smiled instead and retreated out the door. He re-crossed the multilevel hall, took a lap around the courtyard, and entered the building on the far side. Lise and Nathalie were out, but Ibrahim was barking into the phone with the gnashing fury of a cornered bulldog. After rummaging around in the dossier room, he popped briefly into the kitchen and then retired to the terrace.

Alone at the antique white table, he sipped sugary mint tea, and decided a man's fate on his laptop. The breeze was spirited that day, and the olive branches fluttered above him, camouflaging his face with moving shadows.

He spent nearly an hour on Refworld, reading baroque reports about Nigeria's student gangs. Afterwards he scanned several RSD's, reviewed the factors for assessing an applicant's credibility, and began filling out the Assessment Form.

The form began with a stock list of questions that required "yes" or "no" responses. Yes, the applicant's statements were internally consistent and sufficiently detailed. Yes, the statements were consistent with country of origin information. Yes, the applicant has a subjective fear of return to his country of nationality. Yes, he has an objective basis for that fear.

When he arrived at the Persecution Section, Simon paused.

"Does the harm feared by the applicant relate to one or more of the grounds of the 1951 Convention or the 1967 protocol: race, religion, nationality, political opinion or membership in a particular social group?"

He refilled his glass of tea and swirled the honeyed liquid around in his mouth. The leaves rustled overhead and the sun sprinkled him with light. He could hear the constant rumble of traffic straining up Avenue Tariq Ibn Ziad, and then a phalanx of winged forms floated overhead, weightless, unreal. He circled "No."

Only one question remained:

"If the applicant does not fulfill the inclusion criteria of the 1951 Convention, is he/she outside his/her country of nationality or habitual residence and unable to return there owing to serious and indiscriminate threats to life, physical integrity, or freedom, resulting from generalized violence or events seriously disturbing the public order?"

Simon scratched his head and inspected the tips of his hair. They were getting a bit long. He would have to have them trimmed. He briefly wondered where he would find a competent hairdresser in Rabat. Then he turned back to the form. Did this count as generalized violence? He poured another glass of tea.

The wind gusted up, and moments later, the Country Director came wafting by. He caught sight of Simon, lost in thought, his right hand suspended over the pile of papers as if held in place by an invisible force.

"Good work on the funding submission, sailor!" He clipped his heels together and gave a short salute. His heroic smile centered on the young JPO with a luster of approval.

"My pleasure," Simon replied, laughing. "How has the response been?"

"Very favorable. It looks like we'll be able to keep this ship afloat for a while longer."

"That's tip-top!" Simon felt a puppyish rush of excitement at his modest success. "I'm surprised they fund such forward-looking projects," he added a bit rashly.

Maarten's valiant smile briefly waned and then fired up once again. "I find it very sensible of them. You don't build a ship for fair weather but for the storms that are to come."

"Storms?"

"Do you think the current wave of migration is just going to taper off?" Maarten thrust out his chest and fearlessly scanned the horizon. "No. These are just the first gusts from a far-off tempest. The typhoon is still brewing."

Simon tracked his gaze toward a placid blue sky puffed with clouds. "Certainly," he agreed. "But what if the storm never comes?"

The Country Director winked at the young man. "In that case, there is a phrase I picked up here that I quite enjoy: '*Il faut vendre tes poissons dans la mer*,' or in English, 'sell your fish before they're caught.'"

"Ay ay, sir," Simon said, with a seaman's salute.

Maarten moved to leave, but turned sharply on his heel and looked at the young JPO with a mark of appreciation. "I nearly forgot!"

"Yes?"

"I spoke to your father recently at a conference in Geneva. Very impressive fellow. He's quite the old lion in the diplomatic world."

"Yes he is."

"And I see the apple doesn't fall far from the tree. Keep up the good work."

"Thank you sir," Simon mumbled with a mixture of embarrassment and pride.

CHAPTER 34

MAY 2006

A RÈS OPENED HIS EYES to the bright nimbus of a flashlight and
the gum-curled growl of a Rottweiler on a chain-metal leash.
Before he could move, he was spun around and handcuffed.

Questions were posed to him in Spanish. *"Como te llamas? De donde vienes?
De cual país?"* He felt elated even as he shook his head. *"Vous parlez français?"*

"Attendez," one of them said. The agents of the *Guardia Civil* led him
to a nearby command post and into a holding cell. A long shank slid into
the lock and the barred door clanked shut.

There were nearly a dozen men in the cell, all of them black. Arès
recognized one of the other passengers from the shipwreck. He huddled
silently in the corner, his head buried like a charcoal globe in the saucer
of his arms. Arès sat down next to him, seeking human comfort. The man
looked up at him.

"You survived too," Arès said.

The man nodded.

"Do you know where we are?"

"No."

The two men crouched in silence, till suddenly, words spilled from the
stranger's half-buried lips, words still chattering with cold from the sea.

"When my father died," the stranger said, "we built a cement tomb in
his bedroom and the entire family slept on it for nine days so that his spirit
would not return."

Arès was unsure how to respond. "It was a large tomb?" he asked.

"Two meters by two meters, with four people on top and the rest of us
taking turns sleeping beside it or exchanging places with those on it."

"Why nine days?"

"After nine days the body is desiccated and the spirit cannot feed on its juices. After nine days the soul cannot return to haunt the relatives of the deceased. Then it can leave this world behind. But who will sit on the tombs of our friends we lost at sea? Who will build them tombs here in this cell?"

"Many men die at sea," Arès said. "Think of how many of us have died trying to burn to Europe."

"Yes, and their spirits wander the ocean, waiting for burial. I am certain this is why our ship went under."

For a moment, Arès did not respond. He thought again of the insatiable misfortune that ghosted in his wake. It had claimed Buisha now as well. Could he really be cursed? The idea was as chilling as the cold, gray floor on which he sat.

Yet he was alive. What's more, he had made it to Europe against all odds. No, if some marabout had laid a hex on him, it had failed.

The warm glow of a smile curved deliciously up his lips. Europe. It seemed impossible, unreal. The locksmith in Europe! It should have been Félix or Yika, or even Thierry, but not him. He would have to experience Europe for them. They were part of him after all. Maybe he could carry something of them with him.

"Those are just legends," he said to the stranger. "We must forget them if we are to progress. We are in Europe now."

These were Félix's words, not his, but they came to him with ease, even across the gulf of so many years.

"You can forget them. I cannot." The stranger sucked his teeth and spat out the swishing saliva in one great gob. "If the spirits come back, we are lost. It is our responsibility to take care of them. If not, disaster will follow. I am praying for forgiveness, and for them."

"You can pray for the dead," Arès replied, "but do not forget that we are still living."

From out of a small pocket inside his breast, he slipped a sliver of metal with a pointed hook and the glint of a needle.

"The guards have left?" Arès asked.

"Yes, but what good is it? The doors are locked."

"Not for ghosts. You are afraid that ghosts will get through these bars. I will show you how the living can do it too."

"You can open them?"

"*Si ton père a cultivé les aubergines, toi aussi t'en connais les graines.*"[58]

"I do not think we should," the stranger said. "We are in Spain now. I do not think they can deport us."

"I do not trust them," Arès said. "I met many men in Morocco who were sent back from Spain. They were all caught at sea, like us."

"It is too dangerous. A tree, even if it is cut down, can return to life. But men do not. Men fall apart completely."

Arès looked at the stranger. His ribs smiled through his tattered shirt, and his limbs were meager and sere, like sheaves of bark.

"If you want to taste honey, first you must brave the wasps," Arès retorted with unaccustomed bravado.

A lively, melodious laugh rippled through the cell and Arès spun about. The dozen detainees drooped like rag dolls. It could not have been one of them. He crept to the bars and peered up and down the stony corridor, but no one was there. Suddenly he knew it had been Paul and that he alone had heard it. A small, affectionate star lit in his chest. The trader would have approved of him in this moment. He wished that he could speak with him now, show him what he had become.

As the last bright notes of laughter died away, Arès surveyed the area. No guards were in sight and the building was bathed in gloom. He inserted his tools into the hourglass plug and began to manufacture small metal clicks.

One of the other prisoners sidled up to him. "What are you doing?"

"I am escaping," Arès said.

He twisted the tension wrench and the door greased open. Arès slunk down the corridor. There was another locked door and then the front office. The lights were off. The building seemed deserted.

Arès repeated the operation and spirited into the office. He felt invisible.

---

58   If your father cultivated eggplants, then you as well know its seeds.

Two of the other prisoners hubbubed behind him, and he shushed them with a hiss. There was a small transom window above the front door. Balancing on a chair, Arès peered through it.

A large enclosed yard, canopied with cork trees, extended through a silvery darkness. A hundred meters away, before a wide gate barred with an orange pike, a guard smoked a cigarette in a small booth house.

Arès waited for the guard to leave on a break. The man puffed cigarette after cigarette, his eyes riveted to the police station. For over an hour, the prisoner stared into that glowing cube of light. At last, the guard sat down.

"When I open the door," Arès said, "we have to run for it."

The other two prisoners nodded. Arès shunted his weight against the frame and whirled the handle.

Alone, the refugee sprinted across open plains.

There had been more guards than expected. Hidden on the other side of the wall, a uniformed foursome were playing cards in a shed.

When the three prisoners first burst across the yard, the sentry in the booth house sprang to his feet, but the strap of his rifle snagged on his chair and he collapsed back to the ground. For a few seconds, he slapped wildly against the glass to alert the other guards. Then he untangled himself and leapt upright.

They had nearly covered the full hundred meters by the time the sentry wrenched open the door and stepped in their path. Arès was the first to arrive, and he jammed his shoulder into the man, flinging him back into the booth.

Behind the stone wall, the four guards knocked over their glasses and sent a flush of cards gusting to the wind. When the prisoners hurtled past the gate, a firearm discharged in the air, and Arès' cellmates froze in their tracks.

Arès tacked left and increased his stride. Another shot rang out and this time there was a keening in the air. One of the guards threw himself in the refugee's path, but Arès blurred before him and the man pitched onto his knee, grasping at air.

In an instant, Arès was winging up rugged slopes. Behind him three men accelerated over familiar terrain, their flashlights bouncing. The refugee vaulted ahead.

Soon the guards had dwindled into wavering pinpricks of light that flickered like far-off fireflies. Even the most athletic-looking one was no match for Arès. The night was eerily hushed and despite the growing distance between them, he could hear their belabored breaths.

His legs pumped beneath him like greased pistons, and he sensed each sure, unwavering impact of his muscular feet against the uneven lands. He began laughing as he ran, suddenly, uncontrollably. He laughed at his inconceivable life, at being chased across alien lands by fat Spaniards with guns. He laughed at their feebleness and his god-given prowess, at his deft rushing forth, at the wind streaming behind him, and at the speeding darkness of the ground below.

On high mountain crests above, enormous white wind turbines with airfoil blades twirled in rhythm to his spinning limbs, and he laughed too at these, and then laughed as he nearly slammed against something dark humping off the dirt.

Was it a rock or a log? He could hardly see, so he leapt and dodged and laughed his heart out. It felt wonderful to stretch his legs after all that time on the boat. He bounded across the earth, floating so high with every leap that he was amazed each time he touched back down. He laughed and ran and whooped his joy, loping across Spanish foothills, in Europe at last! Destiny at last! And he was still laughing as he fell with insane acceleration into a ditch.

Something struck against his foot, but he was up almost immediately, scrambling out of the hole. He stopped only for a second, against the husk of a long-dead tree, to assess the damage. Then, he felt something he could never have imagined. It was as if the levees in his lower leg had opened, and wet cataracts of blood cascaded inside.

His foot was growing heavy, impregnating with fluid. He pushed it charily against the ground and winced. Oh no, he thought. No. No. No. It's not possible. He tried again to press his foot down and was nearly blinded by pain. He could feel a trickle of blood or sweat dribble along his cheek, but he ignored it.

He began to hop and then to lunge forward but he could no longer bear the throbbing. He fell down onto his knees and tears squirted from his eyes. He began to crawl across the ground. The border guards were vying closer. He could hear their heavy-set grunts, and worse, he could make out the charging advance of the athletic-looking one, shouting, "*¡Lo veo! ¡Lo veo!*"

"*¡Para!*" the man cried. Arès continued to clump forward. "*¡Para! ¡Para!*"

And abruptly, irrevocably, the guard was upon him, a foot hoofing into his spine, clapping him into the dirt. Arès' jaw crunched against stone, and his jolting teeth mashed the tip of his tongue. He gave a bloody moan and then furious grunts and a harsh howl of pain, as the guard drove his knee into Arès' swollen foot.

The rotund twosome arrived, and even the sweat dripping from their flabby chops was greased and foul-smelling. Each of them grabbed one of his wrists and began to laboriously drag him across the rocky turf while he brayed in pain. They stopped, and one of the guards enveloped Arès' jaw in four blubbery fingers, shouting "*¡Cállate! ¡Cállate!*" slapping him on the cheeks for emphasis.

But he continued to shriek until the athletic-looking guard drove his thick leather boot straight into Arès' stomach, knocking the wind out of him. His head cocked back and his mouth opened in a fervent gasp. The fourth guard arrived, limping and cursing loudly. Together they hauled the refugee's sagging body across the mountainous terrain.

Arès was returned at night on a sleek maritime craft that jostled with shackled Africans. As Tangier throbbed with the call to the *Fajr* prayers and dawn flared like brushfire in the east, two members of the Spanish Coast Guard heaved Arès into a crowded cell.

An hour later, a pair of Moroccan gendarmes arrived and informed the detainees that they would all be refouled at Oujda the next morning. Arès' foot was a tumescent mass, nearly the size of a ripe melon. The constant shivering pain brought hot tears to his eyes. He banged on the bars until a guard arrived.

"Hospital." He pointed at his foot. "*Khouya, l-sbitar.*"

"*La*," the guard replied. "You can look for a hospital in Algeria."

Arès took out his refugee card, its plastic sheath smeared with sweat and sea-water, and pressed it against the bars. The guard backed away.

"*Prenez-la.*" The guard ignored him. "*Khoudha!*" he gasped.

Reluctantly, with comic slowness, the guard pinned the card between the tips of his index and middle finger. He rotated it in the light, his eyes glazing over. Then he lit a cigarette.

"You call HCR?" Arès asked.

The guard stared lazily at the caged refugee, his cigarette lolling in the corner of his mouth like a lizard's tongue. Without removing it, he gave a hoarse cry.

Far off a bolt clanked, and a heavy door screeched open. Minutes later, a plump uniform, spangled with clinking bronze medals and topped by a drooping black mustache, swaggered down the hall. It rested a hand on the shoulder of the first guard, and confiscated the laminated card.

The two guards conversed in Arabic. Neither of them looked at the injured prisoner. Arès tried to glean a word or two, but their voices seemed to recede further with every pulse of pain through his body. The light stung his eyes. Whenever the new guard shifted his stance, small coruscations flashed along the rounded knobs of his brass buttons and shattered against Arès' retinas.

"You call the HCR?" he cried between gasping breaths. He pointed at his foot. "Please! *Mouayet. Ana mouayet! l-sbitar?*"

The new guard stared at the refugee. His face had a rubbery quality to it, as if it had long ago solidified into a single, imperturbable expression. Thick, swollen fingers kneaded paper and tobacco along a silver wedding band. Then a cigarette met puffy lips astonishing in their redness, even against the lighter's flame.

Shoulder to shoulder and ribbed by stocky steel bars, the two guards breathed smoke upon the injured man.

For a moment, Arès forgot the pain, mesmerized by the vision before him. The eyes that watched him were leaden and inert. Only the periodic flicker of the cigarettes and the regular contraction of their lungs showed that these were not wax figures. Time creaked along, unhurried.

The new guard's cigarette died. Two swollen hands held up a small tulip flame. The tip of the butt flared and puffed and flared. Curled as well within those hands was the refugee card. Arès watched the only proof of his existence veer imprudently toward the fire. A small blue and green blaze sprouted from its hissing tip as the lamination blackened and curled.

With an incurious eye, the guard inspected the damage he had wrought. Then without so much as a twitch of emotion, he spun the red flame once more into being and unhurriedly set it at the center of the refugee card. Small, violet flashes shimmied up and down the plastic sheath. The core vulcanized and spewed out a long gout of flame.

Calmly, almost solicitously, the guard held the burning effigy up to Arès' eyes. The refugee watched his image melt and peel. As his face perverted beyond recognition, something inside him snapped.

He collapsed against the concrete floor and began to convulse. His body paroxysmed, battering his already battered foot. His mouth foamed. His eyes rolled white.

The first guard fumbled at the iron key ring on his belt. The other guard stood stock still, watching the refugee's body flop on the cell floor like a dying fish.

The door wrenched open to cries for help. Other prisoners began to shout, and the guards ran along the cells, rapping their white batons against the iron bars.

After a few minutes, the spasms abated, and the refugee's body lay still. His swollen tongue sagged in the corner of his mouth.

They called the HCR.

That afternoon, Dr. Djideree arrived in a gray, three-piece suit with a florid handkerchief folded into his breast pocket. His face, a cheery bubble of enthusiasm on arrival, sagged at the sight of Arès.

"This is not good." He examined the refugee's foot. "Very worrisome."

A cherry-red ambulance dispatched Arès to the Military Hospital in Tangier. The roads were full of potholes and every time one of the little maws swallowed a wheel, the jolt yanked Arès back into consciousness.

He thought he was still on the boat and he began calling for Buisha and profaning the sea. Then he drowned in pain.

The ambulance arrived at the hospital and, after a two-hour wait, they x-rayed his foot.

Hours later, a doctor cruised by and, lifting the ice bag off Arès' appendage, gave a low whistle. He held the x-ray up to the light. "Nothing is broken." He touched the foot and Arès moaned and tried to retract his leg, and then groaned again at the pain of moving.

The doctor held a brown clipboard with a pad. He mumbled to himself as he wrote:

"*Traumatisme de la cheville gauche. Existence probable d'une rupture du ligament calcanéo-fibulaire. Contusions importantes des malléoles internes et externes, épanchement intra-articulaire avec épaississement très important des parties molles du pied.*"

Then he walked away.

Four days later, Arès was released with a plaster cast on his leg and a wonky, plastic cane that one of the doctors had lent him out of pity. No one would cover the cost for a full pair of crutches.

The bus trip back to Rabat lasted almost five hours. Overcome by exhaustion, Arès dozed most of the way. A representative from the HCR, a Moroccan woman with a motherly bearing and a face creased with worry, was waiting for him at the *gare routière* when he arrived. The bureau had accorded him a stipend of five hundred dirhams per month until he could work again. Two hours later, he had spent more than half of it to recover his old room in Salé.

CHAPTER 35

JUNE 2006–JULY 2007

A RÈS HOBBLED BETWEEN TWO beige walls toward the entrance to PALS, the HCR's local health partner.

The trip from Salé to Youssoufia-Est, where PALS was located, lasted nearly three hours, and the pain was so excruciating that Arès stopped every few meters to gasp for breath. It was nearly impossible to keep his foot from percussing the ground with only a flimsy cane to lean on, and every brush with the pavement sent a shiver of pain racing up his spine. Several times, he collapsed in the street, his sight wrecked by tears.

In the months following the accident, Arès twice heaved his broken body to the distant health clinic, seeking treatment for his foot. At the end of each of these ordeals, he arrived around 10 a.m. to be told that the doctors were finished seeing patients for the day, even though the sessions were supposed to last until noon.

Eventually, he called the HCR to complain. They made an appointment for him at PALS two weeks later and promised to send someone with him when the date arrived.

With the exception of these two trips, Arès' movements during those months were restricted to a purgatorial ring, whose outer limit was a city block away. Twice a week, he sloughed out of bed and into the communal shower cum toilets, and then, if he had the strength, to the general store to stock up on food for the coming days.

The rest of the time he lay in the gloom of his cement lair, upon a coverless mattress that abutted three of the four walls of the room. Above him, an unsheathed bulb hung tenuously off a single aluminum wire.

His left leg was ramped off a small pyramid of pillows, and he had propped a plastic bucket at an angle so he could satisfy most of his needs without having to stand up. He lay perfectly still, moving only when the cramps in his limbs forced him to adjust the tonnage of his cast.

Standing was a crucifixion. Whenever his body tipped across an invisible axis, somewhere between forty-five and sixty degrees, the floodgates in his left leg opened and unseen fluids torrented into the mashed receptacle of his foot.

Though he was aware that his ankle was in fact swelling, it felt to Arès as if someone were slowly crushing it in a vise. Sometimes he could not keep from screaming. Sometimes he gripped the key around his neck so tight that its serrated edges engraved his palm with an intaglio of blood.

It was only when his foot had bloated to its limit—and he imagined his skin stretched like gauzy vellum beneath the hard shell of his cast—that the torments at last abated.

Once upright, he mentally braced himself for the unpleasantness ahead. The communal water closet in Salé was a pollution. Its drainage was poor and a nauseating slop forever greased the plastic basin. After gritting his way down the hall, Arès ran the faucet for as long as possible over the dreck, but he could no longer bend down and scrub the bottom before entering, and he could not bear the pain of staying erect for very long.

Eventually misery overwhelmed him. Shedding his clothes, he placed his naked buttocks between the two jaundiced plastic feet. Then he leaned back and buttressed his traumatized leg high against one of the slick walls. He washed and tried not to sink into the belching hole beneath him, but the cast was heavy, and his ungainly body slid about every time gravity pulled his foot to the ground.

During the first six weeks after the accident, he only once managed to steel through the combined torture of a shower and a trip to the general store on the corner of his street. The rest of the time, he fasted in an unbroken murk in his windowless chamber and sobbed and willed his ankle to bind anew.

He recalled now Paul's warning that there would be days when he would live like a spider, and his only companion would be memories of the past.

The trader had been right. Nearly all of Arès' friends were dead or departed, and if any remained, none came to visit.

Even more than the pain, the solitude threatened to overwhelm him. Sometimes he would panic and wildly call out his father's name. The only thing that kept him from delirium was the sobering, metallic chill of the key around his neck.

Almost sixteen hours a day he slept. Occasionally, he dreamt of Kinshasa, of running beside the Zaire, of his father's fair, and of the beautiful women in his village. The rest of the time he had nightmares.

In one recurrent nightmare, he sat in an unlit, empty auditorium, while someone, presumably his brother Félix, gave a series of dream lectures on the future of Africa from behind a writhing wall of flames. In another, faceless men shoveled dirt on him, burying him alive in his bed. In yet another, he sprinted through a wasteland of scrubs, chased by unseen pursuers.

In the worst of these terrors, Arès awoke in his room, his limbs gummed to a glittering web. The silky threads were so thick and round that they resembled strands of white taffy. Above him, an immense, albino spider spun slowly down from the ceiling, the spindles of its legs eerily lucent. Arès yanked deliriously at the web, his eyes berserk with fear. When the globe of the spider's abdomen drooped over him, the thing pivoted two of its pincers and fastidiously set about eviscerating his belly while he twitched and screamed.

At the end of three and a half months, he was seen by a doctor at PALS. The clinician ushered him in, and without examining him, dashed off a prescription to have his cast removed at a clinic on the other side of Rabat.

The same representative from the HCR, whose name he now learned was Fatima, taxied him to the clinic and then whisked off in a flurry of apologies to handle some other crisis.

When the doctor removed the cast, Arès' foot appeared no less swollen than it had been on the day of his release from detainment. A winding abrasion—perhaps from the rubbing of the plaster against the distended flesh—snaked along the appendage, and between its thick crimson lips his foot was matted with a suppurating puss, yellowish in hue.

"You must take antibiotics for this. Your foot is infected and it is not healing because of that. This is the cause of your chronic pain."

"Can you give me the antibiotics here?"

"I am sorry. You must have a prescription for me to give you antibiotics."

"Can you not just write me the prescription?"

"No. You must go back to PALS to get the prescription."

"PALS?" Arès stared at the doctor in disbelief. "It took three months before they gave me a prescription to remove the cast. They will never give me a prescription for antibiotics."

"I am sorry. I cannot help you."

"You must give me something. I am sick. Look at my foot."

"I am very sorry for you."

"If you are sorry, then do something!" Arès snapped.

The doctor removed his glasses and slowly wiped them against a white handkerchief with blue trim. "I will have one of my attendants escort you out of the hospital. Try to keep your foot raised at all times and make sure you take antibiotics."

Another two weeks of biding in the prison of his room, and another intervention by the Moroccan woman from the HCR. When at last Arès took his seat again in the antechamber of PALS, an immense blistering sore had spread over his foot like a wild bloom of algae. This time, with Fatima standing furious guard, the doctor issued him a prescription for three months of generic antibiotics.

Then he returned to his room. The days crept by like spiders. After an interminable week on the drugs, the soreness in his foot at last began to subside.

Slowly Arès regained mobility. It no longer hurt so much to grapple upright, and he could hold himself erect for longer and longer periods of time. After a month, he could take a shower standing.

Two months later, seven months from the date of his accident, he tossed a bit of weight onto his leg, and gingerly at first, and then with increasing boldness, began to clump along on his rotten foot. As lopsided and piteous a figure he drew, walking again was a jubilation.

For the first time in seven months, he smiled. He was outside in the streets, walking in the open air, tears of relief spattering his cheeks. He felt like a condemned man whose sentence had been suddenly and inexplicably commuted. Leaning on his plastic cane, its shaft slightly bowed, he staggered forward, giddy with excitement.

Only one thing worried him. As the pain receded, his foot did not diminish in size. Rather it seemed to be hardening, taking on a rock-like solidity. It was as if the excesses of blood that had pumped down his leg were now caking inside of him. Day by day, his foot grew heavier.

He was weak these days too. His landlord had raised the rent, and he was left with only one hundred and fifty dirhams a month, or about five dirhams per day: just enough to purchase two modest discs of bread and a few pieces of fruit. He needed to start working again, but it was impossible like this. He scrounged together what little he had saved, added seventy-five dirhams from the money the HCR had given him at the start of the month, and bought a pair of used crutches in the medina of Salé. He hoped that by keeping his foot off the ground, he could somehow reverse its outrageous metamorphosis.

For a full week he ate nothing but a single disc of bread. He thought of selling the golden key around his neck, but he could not bring himself to relinquish this last piece of the past. Instead, he conserved his strength, never leaving his cryptlike room. For seven days, he sat and waited and watched minute beasts clutter the cracks in the walls.

Then he called Fatima.

This time when he arrived at PALS, his body was light as a bird. It was as if the famine of the past week had rooted through his marrow and hollowed out his bones. Only his foot clumped to the earth, an irritated mass sending anxious jabs up the empty rod of his leg. He pushed through the glass entrance, down a short corridor and into an overly bright waiting room.

A man built out of reeds, with a cavern for a face, beckoned to him. Arès had no mirror and he did not know that he resembled one of the seropositives, who clustered like rows of spindles in an ill-lit corner of the waiting room. He shied away from them and headed toward the reception, his stride a half hobble, half glide.

The receptionist was rumped onto a padded office chair behind a large, curving desk. A slight dais on her side of the divide, or an imperceptible depression on his, caused their leveled eyes to meet.

If Arès' body was wrought of angles and inkscales, hers was a heavy bubble of pink, with sausaged arms and a blond bud of hair ribboned with fuchsia bows. Her pudgy fingers gripped an omelet and kefta sandwich that caused Arès' ravenous hands to twitch.

"I have an appointment today for a consultation," he announced.

The receptionist bit into the sandwich and began to slop it around in her mouth. A small dollop of grease plopped onto the countertop. Arès could hardly resist scooping it off with his finger. He waited expectantly as she swallowed.

She took another bite.

"I have an appointment for 11:30 a.m." He tried to think of the words in Darija. "*Nadaj wu nous.* Appointment."

The receptionist continued to chew, the blond buds of her hair rising and descending slowly with her jaw. He waved his hand in front of her face. Nothing. He wanted to rip the sandwich out of her hands. Hunger and shame stormed through him.

The reed-like man crept over to him and clutched his wrist. "It is lunchtime. She does not speak until she is done."

"What, so I do not exist?"

"Only during lunchtime."

"Does she not see me here? Is this how they treat refugees?"

Arès waved his arms vigorously in her face. She did not even move to brush them away.

"Do not bother her. Last time they made us wait outside in the sun when we were too bothersome. There is no shade there."

"Get away from me." He only meant to nudge the man aside, but his hand swept through him as if through air. The seropositive folded sound-lessly to the ground. A twittering noise rose from the corner of shadows. As the cackles grew to howls and curses rained down on Arès, the receptionist unscrewed a bottle of Coca-Cola to a resounding fizz.

He felt a flood of revulsion for this acrid and unpardonable world.

Reluctantly, he retreated toward the cleanly-lit benches that held the refugees. The majority of them had been there since early morning, wait-ing to be seen. Two of them scooched apart to make room for him. They had watched his interaction with the seropositives and began to speak heatedly.

"Why do they put us in with these sick people?" The man on Arès' left jabbed his arms angrily toward the poorly-lit corner.

"We come in here and people think we are depraved. That we have slept with chimpanzees, and now we have AIDS like them. It is not right, not right." At the end of each sentence, the man on Arès' right slapped his palms against his knees.

He could tell from their accents that they were from the Ivory Coast. Their voices sounded like gunfire. Ratatatat. Several of them sucked their teeth noisily to show their disgust.

"It is very dangerous." He pointed at Arès. "You let that man touch you. You may be infected now. Those people should not be allowed to walk around free." As he spoke, one of the seropositives bent over and in a flash vomited an oblong retch of brown onto the battered tiles. The mess loosely resembled their continent, with frothy saliva swirling across its northern reaches in lieu of the sprawling Sahara.

"And look at how she treats us. There." Another one gestured emphati-cally at the receptionist. "Like we are worms." He spat on the floor. "Why do you take it?" He prodded Arès' with his forefinger. His hair sprouted off his head in a hundred thin naps, like a crown of black grubs. "Why did you let the secretary ignore you, like you were nothing?"

"*On n'enlève pas une épine avec une autre épine,*"[59] Arès replied.

"Do you know," the first one began, "we must wait here all day, but they

---

59   You do not remove a thorn with another thorn.

do not let us use their toilet. They tell us it is broken and that we should go in the garden outside. Like animals. But then they use it themselves."

"I went to pee outside in the garden," a fourth man chimed in. He seemed incredibly old, his face ravined with age. Sparse, irregular tufts of hair sprouted off an otherwise clean dome, and below that archipelago of fuzz dangled the darkest face Arès had ever seen. The very light around its edges seemed diminished. "And the gardener yelled at me. He told me this is not the jungle. That we are not zebras. We cannot just drop our shit everywhere."

"What is this country? I was a good man back home. Here I begin to have violent thoughts. These people should be cursed for how they treat us," the man on Arès' right exclaimed. The sucking sounds started anew, rolling up and down the rows of refugees.

The old man put his hand on the black bristle of naps beside him. "My friend, purity is in the man, not the place."

Arès did not speak. He glanced sidelong at the charnel house in the corner and felt a sudden heaviness. He cradled his head in his arms. His deepest longing was for the purling quiet of the riverside. He pictured the idylls of his youth. He wished he could set all the intervening years aflame and watch them woosh away like clouds of ash wafting from a pyre.

The front door creaked open and slammed shut. Footsteps approached the refugees and Arès lifted his head. A monstrosity of sweat trickled down his spine.

Salifou sat down on the bench directly across from him.

His thick bush of hair had thinned and the skin sagged unhealthily about his jowls. But even after so many years and so much distance, his high cheekbones and strangely cut eyes were instantly familiar. He glanced directly at Arès without a spark of recognition.

Arès looked away and back again and away. His stomach growled. He was so weak. It felt almost as if he were floating. He clutched the golden key that dangled over his breast. Then he peered at the other refugees, trying to make out if they too had noticed Salifou's presence.

No one spoke to the new arrival. He sat placidly, his empty unfinished gaze bobbing in Arès' direction.

Visions of his final night in Kinshasa, of Salifou in his crimson headdress machete-ing men apart, of hot sulfur flaming in his hands and engulfing Arès' brother, of his high hammering laugh as he savaged Arès' sister... Arès lurched to his feet and wobbled toward the toilet.

He turned the knob, but it was locked.

Two nurses were sitting at a small table, watching a soap opera on a bulky TV.

"Out!" one of them yelled. "In the garden. Outside."

Arès pounded on the door and gave off retching noises. The other nurse grabbed a broom and bustled toward him.

"Outside," she hissed and whisked the broom at his feet. "It is broken here. Go outside. Out!" He felt the broom handle slap his ribs, and though his legs were impossibly weak, he let himself be prodded along the wall until he felt a hot gush of sunlight and staggered into the garden.

He crouched at the roots of a laurel tree and tried to retch, but his stomach was empty and all that came out was a lather of gastric juices and foul pockets of air.

When he re-entered the building, his place on the bench was still free. He sat down and tapped one of the Ivorians on the shoulder. "Do you know the man who just arrived? The one sitting across from us?"

"Yes."

"Who is he?"

"He is from the DRC. I met him at the Fondation Oriental. He has been here for maybe a year. He told me that he fled persecution. He did not say much else. I think his name is Salifou."

"Can you introduce me?" Arès asked. The room seemed to seesaw as if they were riding on a ship.

The Ivorian waved, "*Chef, ca va?* Have you stopped by the clinic to see your friends?"

Salifou gave a pained smile, revealing neat rows of teeth. "My head hurts. I have come for a prescription."

"Ah. So you would not like to meet anyone new?"

He smiled again, a web of thick wrinkles radiating out from each of his eyes. "Where I am from, it is said that good company is even better than a good meal. Of course, I will meet someone new." He leaned forward and held out his hand.

"I am Salifou."

"Arès." They clasped hands.

"You have hurt your foot, I see." Arès nodded. "You are new to Morocco?"

"No. I have been here for many years," Arès replied. "After living in Cameroon, I came here. Where are you from?"

"I am from Kinshasa."

"I am from Kinshasa as well." He looked at Salifou with hard eyes.

"I am sorry?"

"Kinshasa. I come from Kine-Kinshasa."

"It is hard to hear you. Why don't you come sit over here?" Salifou said. "Next to me." He motioned to an empty spot on the bench beside him.

As if in a dream, Arès floated off the bench and settled down next to Salifou. He clasped his left hand around Salifou's right wrist. "I said, 'I am from Kinshasa too.' Perhaps we know each other."

"I doubt it. Kinshasa is very large."

"Yes, but perhaps you do not come quite from Kinshasa, but from a village somewhat outside the center. Perhaps an hour and a half north up the Zaire."

Salifou looked carefully at the attenuate man beside him. "I once knew someone named Arès. This is true." He spoke with astonishing lentor. His mouth screwed shut after every word, as if he were biting off the last syllable before exhaling it into the air. "But he died the night they attacked the Rwandans in Kinshasa. He was Banyamulenge like myself."

Arès' eyes narrowed to hot, thin slits. "But perhaps you are only pretending to be Banyamulenge. Perhaps you were one of the perpetrators, now pretending to be a victim."

Salifou sucked in a heavy, hissing breath. Then he exhaled loudly. "I think that would be a very dangerous thing to say. I am a refugee. Here is my card." He reached into his jean jacket and took out a blue and white laminated card with writing in both French and Arabic. He flipped it over and began to read. *"Le porteur de cette carte est refugié sous le mandat du Haut Commissariat des Nations Unies pour les Réfugiés. Toute assistance qui lui serait accordée sera hautement appréciée."*

Arès' stomach knotted up with rage. Salifou a refugee like himself! His right hand tightened on the key around his neck. He could feel its sharp bits prod the calluses on his palm, and he clenched hard, letting them dig in. He looked over at Salifou, half blind, smoke swirling in his eyes.

"I have the same card," he said a bit too loudly. Flames were licking at his words and he needed to control himself. He sought back to the tranquil blue-green pool where he used to fish. He could almost hear the dim rustle of leaves and the sighing of mist on the water's edge. He doused himself in the memory of that place until he felt damp and cool.

"Then you are a refugee too," Salifou said.

"Yes, but all you need to get this card is to tell a story." Arès leaned close and in a half-whisper spoke again. "Perhaps you are good at telling stories?"

"It is not that easy." A yellow light flickered in Salifou's eyes. "They ask you many questions. They try to trick you."

"Yes, but perhaps you told someone else's story. The story of someone you knew, who deserved this card." Arès took a deep, liquid breath. "Perhaps you even told my story?"

He could feel Salifou's body tense beside him.

"I would have to know you to tell your story." He squeezed close to Arès, and his breath fanned hot on his neck. "And even if I did know you," he murmured, "even if I told someone else's story, am I not a refugee too? Did I not flee my country? Was I not driven off by poverty and violence? The Congo is no good. I could not stay there. I want a better life than that." He spat on the floor.

One of the nurses shouted from the corner, *"Vous pensez que vous êtes chez vous?* This is not the forest. If you want to spit, go outside." She glared at their row of benches and then turned up the volume on the TV.

"I am going to expose you," Arès whispered back.

"Expose what?" Salifou cried, and a few other refugees glanced in their direction. He hugged himself close and hissed into Arès' ear. "Go ahead. I will go to the HCR tomorrow and tell them that you are not Banyamulenge at all and that you killed my family. That you are the one telling other people's stories."

"I will get there first," Arès said.

"Go first." Salifou kicked Arès softly in the swollen foot. "But I believe that like when we were young, I am still faster than you."

Arès clapped his head in his hands. A syrupy smell pervaded his nostrils, making it difficult to breathe.

"But I will not go there today or tomorrow," Salifou said, holding fiercely to Arès' wrist. "You can go, but if they call me in, I will tell them that when you saw me and I wanted to expose you, you threatened me. I will tell them that I was afraid to say anything because I thought your friends might kill me. They will not know whom to believe. There is no proof of anything. Just my word against yours, and I think by now, I know your story better even than you do."

Arès' back convexed and his body hollowed beneath some tonnage of invisible pressure.

He had to kill Salifou.

He owed it to his family. He owed it to whatever tired sense of justice was left in this world.

He looked up with new determination in his eyes. Then he pitched back in his seat. Across from him, in the spot he had just occupied, sat his brother Félix; gaunt, exsanguinate, his lidless eyes a jellied white, like spider eggs. He was shirtless, and the skin on his torso crackled from some inner combustion, curls of smoke wafting off his smoldering limbs. Patches of his chest and arms had collapsed inwards and underneath, molten webs pulsed yellow and red as if lit by a dying star.

The nappy-headed refugee from the Ivory Coast leaned toward Arès and axed his arms back and forth. "*Chef*, everything ok? Do you feel sick?"

Arès waited for his brother to say something, anything, but Félix's lips remained sealed like a winter bud. If only he had a knife, even a nail, he could it use to stab the goatherder in the eye. Or something heavy or solid, a spade or an iron, to bludgeon him, to crack that smug, murderous grin into a thousand howls of pain.

He snatched feverishly at the key around his neck, but feeling the dullness of its edges, dropped his hand. The entire right cheek flaked off his brother's face, revealing a tight seam of muscles and the red-hot bones of his jaw.

It was impossible. There was no way he could overpower Salifou in his state. His eyes swelled with helplessness, swelled and swelled until it became unbearable. They bulged off his face like two overripe berries, like they might mash open any second and pour forth the rot inside. He tried to cry to relieve the pressure, but instead of cleansing salty drops, some syrupy slag, like burning lava, cracked out of his tear ducts and singed his cheeks as it slowly wormed floorwards.

Salifou rested the tips of his fingers on Arès' shoulder. "Are you ok?"

He shook himself free of Salifou's grasp. "I am fine."

For the next few minutes, he kept up a busy, noiseless crying. Then, slowly, an idea hatched in him. He wiped his eyes clear and peered over at his family's killer. This time he studied him carefully, observing all the years that had burrowed into the goatherder's skin. Eight of them in sum. They had clawed thin gashes into his forehead and made dim nests under his eyes. Eight long, intervening years had greedily sucked on his juices, and now his face, much like Arès', appeared thin and drawn.

When he looked back toward the other bench, Félix was no longer there.

"You are not even sorry for what you did?" Arès asked. His voice strained with the effort.

Salifou looked surprised. "Sorry? I do not know." He paused for a moment and scratched at his thin head of hair. "I was with many others. It was part of the madness of that place, part of why I had to leave. Sorry? I do not think I would do those things again. Is that an apology? I do not know."

Arès stared numbly ahead, while some internal cogwork hissed tears from his eyes.

"But perhaps I can help you now," Salifou said with sudden inspiration. "You look like you need help."

Arès shut his lids and laid his head in his hands. Across an incredible distance, Paul's mocking face ferried back to him. *"Un diable que vous connaissez vaut mieux qu'un ange inconnu.*[60] What he would give to have the trader with him now!

"I can do fine by myself," Arès said into the clenched bowl of his palms.

But Salifou was swept up in the glittering net of this new idea. "No," he said with conviction. "We are from the same small village and we are very far from home." Then he grinned and something diabolic crept back into his voice. "One should never refuse an old friend. I have some food." He reached into his backpack and removed a kefta and omelette sandwich. "Here. Take this."

Arès' mouth watered at the warm, buttery smell of the cooked eggs. A silent war, between largely unequal forces, waged within him. Then his hands trembled as they retrieved the half-pulped bread. He felt his senses kaleidoscope with the first bite and he scrambled the rest of the sandwich into his mouth. He was gasping for breath when he finished.

"This is my number. If you are in trouble, contact me." Salifou crumpled a piece of paper into Arès' breast pocket. "I will do what I can to help. There is no reason to starve. I have a job here selling mobile phones. I can bring you food. Remember, old friend. Fire leaves only ashes behind." Then he rose and left.

In the wake of his departure, Arès bent his torso over his knees and quietly wept.

Around 1 p.m., the door swung open with devilish gaiety and in strutted Dr. Djideree, always in a three-piece suit with a flamboyant handkerchief folded neatly in his breast pocket. Arès clumped toward him.

"Not now," he said and disappeared into the recesses of PALS.

Two hours later, Fatima arrived from the HCR. One of the refugees had called to complain that they were not being seen, and she flurried in, trailed by a tall, white girl. Several of the patients clustered by the office to listen to her squabble with the doctor on call.

"But we have been seeing the refugees! We tell them to come at 8:30 a.m.,

---

60   A devil whom you know is better than an angel you don't.

but they all arrive at 11 a.m. and then complain that they are not being seen right away... No, the other doctor is not here... I know we are supposed to have two doctors but it was an emergency... of course the refugees can use the bathroom facilities. The toilets are open. Try the doors... No, I really think they like to complain. They believe they should have the same quality service as rich Moroccans. You should make them aware of their situation. As you know, even Moroccans have to wait a long time to see a doctor."

Arès saw one of the Ivorians pull aside the white girl. She looked young, around his age, with a broad freckled face, prominent cheekbones, and sympathetic blue eyes. "They are only letting us use the toilet now because you are here." The girl nodded, but she looked uncertain and confused. Her bearing was so simple, friendly, and straightforward that it aroused Arès' suspicions.

Within the next hour, the doctor on call examined the forty refugees who had milled outside of his office since early that morning.

He gave Arès some Voltarene and told him to rub it on his wound. Then he wrote him a prescription for blood-thinners and another round of x-rays at a hospital an hour's ride from Salé.

"And how am I supposed to get there?" Arès asked. "I have no money left. It is eight dirhams for the two *grand taxis* to get there and then eight dirhams to go home. That is sixteen dirhams. I have not eaten in nearly a week, and I spent my last eight dirhams to come here."

"You should try to find work," the doctor said.

Instead, he began to beg. He paraded out into the dusty streets of Salé, his crutches and the petrified bolus of his foot on aggressive display, hoping to fetch attention in the oversaturated market for pity. But competition was tough.

In the grand theater of the medina, there was every day staged a full bazaar of human afflictions and immiserations—men shorn of limbs and cleft of lip, appendages inverted, heads swelled and denatured, and even an orphan with noma, the yellow kernels of his remaining teeth sprouting through the disintegrated walls of his cheek.

To survive and save money by begging was not easy, but Arès managed somehow. When at last he squirreled together enough to pay for a round-trip ride to the hospital, he was told on arrival that the x-ray machine was broken and would not be fixed for at least two months.

CHAPTER 36
JUNE 2009

L ATER THAT DAY, SIMON pushed open the frosted door to the
HCR's main office. Khadija and Pacifique were typing industri-
ously at their desks and Baptiste was leaning back in his chair,
quietly singing along to Otis Redding. "Sitting on the dock of the bay…"

"Ah!" he said, kicking down his heels when he saw Simon. "You need
some more help?"

"Actually, I finished the write-up," Simon announced. Before he could
say another word, Baptiste leapt to his feet and snatched the RSD Assessment Form from his hands. Simon stood by while the EO perused his work.
After a few minutes, he narrowed his eyes and peered suspiciously at the
blond JPO. "This is actually quite good. You did this yourself?"

"Yes."

"Well, I'll be," he muttered. "So why do you always seem to be mon-
keying around?"

Simon grinned. "As my grandfather used to say, 'If they find out you're
competent, you'll never have a moment's peace.'"

Baptiste gave an appreciative laugh. "I'm glad to hear that laziness runs
in the family."

"Sure," Simon said distractedly. The gleam faded from his eyes and he
stepped decisively toward the collection of refugee posters hanging on the
wall. Baptiste padded behind him and placed an apologetic hand on his
shoulder. "*Mon ami*, don't take my jokes so seriously. It's only office humor."

"No. It's not that," Simon said, his voice unusually strained. Faint fretful
creases radiated out from the corners of his eyes.

"What is it then? You look like you've seen a ghost."

"That's just it." He gazed solemnly at one of the posters. It showed an attractive East African woman wrapped in a diaphanous green shawl. Two bright, determined eyes stared defiantly over a long thin nose toward an uncertain future. Behind her hung a pleated brown curtain with the word COURAGE stamped in khaki letters across the top. And unfurling in mock-newsprint typeface across her torso was the following text: "*Attacked with machetes. Escaped barefoot across the stony desert. Surviving on roots and insects. Now home is a tent. A daily handful of maize. And unquenchable hope.*" At the bottom of the poster stood the UNHCR logo and the tagline, "It takes courage to be a refugee."

Simon turned back toward the EO. "It appears our asylum demander doesn't quite meet the acceptance criteria."

"That was my estimation as well," Baptiste confirmed.

"So he will be sent back."

"That is normally the consequence of a refusal. He will have a chance to appeal, but eventually he will be offered a free ticket home, courtesy of the IOM."

A vein began to throb along Simon's right temple. "Doesn't that bother you?"

Baptiste shrugged. "The law is like a cobweb. The weak get caught, but the strong break through."

"You say that even as we reject him."

"What else am I supposed to do?"

Simon massaged his forehead with his fingertips. He could feel a migraine brewing. Then he looked up at the EO. "He's a college student who needs our help," he insisted. "He could be murdered if we send him back."

"How can you be so sure?" Baptiste grabbed Simon tightly by the arm and steered him out into the multilevel hall. "For all we know he could be a swindler, or even a member of the rival gang, like he was accused of."

"You're implying that he's a criminal?"

"I'm implying nothing of the sort." Baptiste increased his lock on Simon's elbow. "The greatest harm you can do is to divide the world into the good and the bad, the truthful and the liars."

Simon freed his arm with a brusque movement. "How about the murderers and the victims?"

"In our line of work, they're often the same people," the EO said grimly. He began leading the JPO up the stairs. "The way I see it, there are only the privileged and the desperate. Maybe he's just some poor kid from Nigeria. Wouldn't you tell a tale or two to get help if you were in his situation?"

"I'd tell a dozen," Simon affirmed. "So why don't we make an exception in this case?"

Baptiste's face hardened and his voice took on pontifical tones. "It's not up to us. I have a mandate that is given to me. If I do not fulfill that mandate, then I will be removed, and someone else, who will carry out that mandate, will take my place."

"So you're worried about your next paycheck?"

Baptiste halted on the stairs. "We are not angels of mercy," he stated in an authoritative voice, looking down at Simon from several feet above. "We are bureaucrats carrying out a mission on behalf of the United Nations. We have to defend the idea of a refugee. Otherwise why do this job?" Baptiste's hands were clasped together now, as if in prayer.

"And our friend Chinua?"

"You mean the asylum demander we just met for the first time?" Baptise exclaimed. "We cannot make exceptions for individuals. If we started doing that, the entire system would fall apart."

"Yes, but he has a credible and objective basis for fear. This is not just some loon running from a curse." Simon suddenly thought of Kinani. He wondered what sort of violence his flatmate had fled.

"Everyone in danger is not a refugee." Baptiste thrust open the door to the terrace, and the two men emerged from the somber hallway into a blinding deluge of sunlight. "There is no such thing as a refugee from violence or poverty or even death threats," he continued. "You know the history. No nation wanted to open the floodgates."

Simon shielded his eyes. He could feel sweat bead on his forehead under the assault of the afternoon heat. "How about for reasons of generalized violence? It sounds like these student fraternities are widespread and homicidal."

"So is the mafia in Italy!" Baptiste cried, exasperated. He motioned toward the antique table and the two men sat down beneath the shady, coiling branches of the olive tree. Baptiste leaned close to Simon and whispered in a low, urgent voice. "You may not be aware, but our relationship with the Moroccan government is tense. If we don't keep our criteria rigorous, they'll ship us out of here on the next boat, along with all the refugees."

"I'm sure the refugees would be quite pleased," Simon replied in an aggravated voice. He wondered if he even cared about the Nigerian asylum demander. The argument, he realized, was larger. He felt morally unqualified for the sacerdotal business of the HCR.

Baptiste laughed and wagged a finger. "Yes, *mon ami*, if it went to Europe. But we receive weekly protests from the Ministry of the Interior about our 'lax' standards. They're keeping close tabs on how many refugees we recognize."

"So we just dance to their tune?" He bent close to the EO. "What happened to 'a person in danger is the ambassador of all humanity?'"

Baptiste rose out of his chair and strode to the middle of the terrace, his hands clasped behind his back. "You know Simon," he said, turning around, "refugee status is hardly God's gift to sub-Saharan applicants."

"You mean black Africans," Simon corrected.

Baptiste nodded. "That is *precisely* what I mean. If he were Algerian or Middle-Eastern, I might have second thoughts, but a Nigerian applicant won't receive a residency permit or working rights. Even with refugee status, Morocco is just a slow death for someone like him."

"Better than ending up like that bird," Simon half-heartedly objected. It was useless picking a fight with the EO. He might as well try to pull honey from a wasp's nest with his bare hands.

"Depends on the sort of death," Baptiste asserted, drawing his finger dramatically across his throat. "Our Nigerian friend has to return home. But he will have time before he departs, and hopefully the falcons will begin to hunt other mice. And maybe, seeing the situation of the migrants here, he will realize what he has gained."

"What do you mean?"

"*Une personne malade remercie Dieu si elle voit une personne morte; un borgne remercie Dieu s'il voit un aveugle,*" he intoned in a modulating voice.[61]

"You're speaking in African riddles again." Simon stood and leaned against the tree. "I'm beginning to see why the Moroccans want to keep sub-Saharans out of the country."

"And I am beginning to see what a diet of fraternity parties and American television has done to your understanding. Do you not have wise sayings in your country?"

"No. Only pop stars and celebrities." Striations of light rippled across Simon's blond features as he smiled at the EO.

Baptiste shook his head and sat down again. "Our friend believes that it is bad in Nigeria, but I think after a few months in Rabat he will be happy to go home."

"Or head to Europe."

"Perhaps," Baptiste said thoughtfully. "Many of my African brothers and sisters believe Europe to be a paradise, whereas their lives would actually be far better at home. Sure, there is less economic opportunity, but there are all the joys of family and community. This is true of our refugees here as well. There are dozens who could be repatriated, but convincing them to go back is like trying to turn a river aside."

"Of course, Anna-Heintz thinks we can never understand what the refugees really think and feel."

Baptiste snorted. "Yes, well, have you noticed that the higher-ups here are a bit disconnected from the day-to-day struggles of our refugee population?" He reached into his jacket and extracted a ruby-red can of cherry cola, cracking it open to a loud hiss.

"They're busy people," Simon asserted.

"There's a difference between busy and irresponsible," Baptiste replied between sips of soda.

"You're talking about the executive officers of the HCR."

Baptiste peered around carefully. "There is an old saying I like: 'It is only when you draw close to someone that you smell his breath.'"

---

61   A sick person thanks god if he sees a dead person. A one-eyed person thanks god if he sees a blind person.

"More African riddles," Simon said dismissively.

"It is only a riddle if you do not wish to understand it."

Simon settled onto a chair across from the EO. "I didn't know you had this side to you, Baptiste."

"Well I cannot only discuss soccer all the time," the EO replied with a wave of his hand. "It brings me too much suffering." Then his face lit up with its usual Cheshire grin.

Simon laughed and smoothed back his lion's mane of hair. Baptiste took several more sips from the ruby-red can. Then his features grew sour and pensive again. "I do admit, though, it troubles me from time to time, this great river of sorrow flowing from south to north. I often wonder if it will ever dry up."

"I feel like we're doing a lot here at the HCR to stem the flow," Simon replied.

Baptiste gave a knowing smile. "Of course you do. You're privileged, and privilege is a great adversary of the imagination. It is like a rose-colored cocoon you spin around your head."

Simon gaped at him. "Are you questioning my dedication to the refugees?" He couldn't believe it. Now he was on the defensive.

"No, you fit your dedication in admirably well between vacations."

The vein above Simon's right eye began to twitch again. "I thought we were going out drinking in Agdal after this. Is that part of your moral commitment to the exiled?"

"Ah *mon frère,* do not confuse merriment with morality," Baptiste said with a toothy smile. "I am bringing you to an African bar. How am I supposed to carry out my functions if I lose touch with my people? Bars are dens of disguise and misdirection. They are the perfect place to practice telling half-truths from lies."

"Especially if your subjects are disguised as eligible young women." Simon shook his head. The EO was incorrigible.

"I do admit that those are the most interesting half-truths," Baptiste answered with a ribald wink. "But like all saints, I am only going there to convert the sinners. This does not work when you are also a sinner. Then you are just going there to drink."

"I would never pretend otherwise."

There was a loud droning sound and a wasp landed on the table.

"More of these," Simon said, swatting away the small beast. "Where the heck are they coming from?"

"Welcome to Africa," Baptiste said with a honeyed smile. "You're not worried about being stung?"

"Their buzz is worse than their bite," Simon quipped. He quickly scanned the area, hands primed for action. "They seem to be everywhere these days."

"They come in waves but they die out pretty quickly. The habitat here isn't suitable for them."

"Of course, there are always more where they came from."

"Yes," the EO replied, lost in thought. "The trick, though, is to see your own destiny in that of the wasp. Then you feel sorrow for it."

"Why would I ever want to do that?"

Baptiste glanced toward the sky. "The light is falling. Let's go get that drink."

They headed back down to the main office. Baptiste signed and stamped the RSD Assessment Form and stuffed it into the outbox on his wire rack. Then they exited the white building and strolled out into the ambassadorial quarter, rife with the sweet fragrances of hibiscus and honeysuckle.

Upon cresting a hill, Simon could see the sun swelling on the horizon beneath a coppery sky. The city glowed a delicate pink in the waning light, but the pavement beneath their feet still throbbed with the day's fierce heat. Simon felt like he was walking across a vast, dying ember, slowly cooling through a hundred molten shades of red until it faded to black.

By the time they reached the bustling streets of Agdal and stood before the tacky entrance to the VIPER BAR, with its cheap neon green cobra in place of an "I," the day had rolled over into darkness, and the call to prayers had begun.

Shortly before 1 a.m., Simon cracked open the door to his apartment and crept down the unlit hallway to his room. He was halfway there when he heard a low moaning come from behind Kinani's door. He toed to a halt and listened quietly. The moaning grew in cadence and frequency until it crescendoed in a sort of thrilling, joyful wail.

He wondered who Kinani was with and felt a sudden burning rush of jealousy that it might be Lise, and then an unexpected, primordial rage, which he quickly and shamefully suppressed.

He slept fitfully and awoke sometime before dawn. The light drumming of rain sounded against the roof above. His door lay open to the hallway, even though he always kept it shut. He looked around, confused.

Wan moonlight poured through the windowpanes, bathing everything with a spectral glow. A gust of wind lifted the thin curtains and the flimsy door creaked on its hinges. Simon thought he saw a blur of movement. He blinked with tiredness and when he opened his eyes, Kinani was standing motionless in the doorway staring at him.

Simon held his breath.

Silvery light pooled on the shaved crown of Kinani's head. Below, his features hung woodenly as if etched with a knife. His eyes were two dim gashes beside the narrow cut of his nose. His body was one long shadowy spear. The smile was gone. His long mouth was set tight like that of a predatory fish.

There was a thunderclap outside and Simon swung his head. When he looked back, Kinani was gone.

T HEY CAME THAT DAY.
      One from the Fondation Oriental, where Arès received his
      financial assistance. The other two were from the HCR.
After so much time, they came.

Attired in a dull gray shirt, cotton pants, and worn, leather sandals, Arès
perched off a low wall in the small public square not far from his apartment.
He felt stiff that morning and it had taken him nearly half an hour to cross
the two hundred meters to the square. But he did not want to stay at home.
His landlord was prowling around the building again.

He stared vacantly ahead and toyed with the golden key around his neck.
Slightly after 10 a.m., Abdellah bounded up. He greeted Arès from five
meters out, his hand stretched forth emphatically. "Looking good today,
my friend. You'll be dancing again soon, won't you?"

A spry man of medium build, Abdellah had a permanently scruffy face
that was often atwitch with a smile. The receding remnants of his hair were
gelled into two curly clumps that sat off his head like squat horns. He had
a mixed reputation among the refugee community: some liked him greatly;
others said he lacked respect. Arès was wary, but he had met Abdellah a
few times and he seemed well-intentioned.

The refugee shuffled forward on his cane and shook the outstretched hand.
"This is Camille from the HCR," Abdellah said, gesturing behind him.

Moving toward them was a young woman with a gamine bearing. Man-
dala hoop earrings bookended a wavy bob of chestnut hair and outsized
brown eyes. She skipped up to Arès and held out her hand, palm tilted
down, like a lady to a courtier waiting to be kissed.

Arès nodded hello. Something about Camille's colorful waxprint dress and the lithe curve of her frame plucked at his memory, and he felt an urge to take her by the arm and pull her close.

"Pleasure to meet you, " she said.

"Yes," Arès replied with some difficulty.

"Camille will be taking notes," Abdellah informed him cheerfully. "That way we can make sure our local partners are meeting your needs. So don't say anything you'd prefer to forget." He gave a hearty laugh and squeezed Arès' shoulder hard enough to make him wince. "We're just waiting for... well, here she comes!"

A woman whom Arès knew came running up in a powder-blue blouse, jeans, and a bead necklace that dangled pendulously above her breasts. She had strawberry blond hair, a broad forehead, and extraordinarily clean features with large, friendly eyes. "I'm sorry I'm late. I was held up by traffic. Hello Arès."

Her name fatiguedly settled on his tongue, as if arriving after a long journey. "Hello, Federika."

"You look good." She tapped him on the upper arm.

"Thank you," he replied, craning his neck up as he spoke. It was disconcerting to have a woman loom so tall above him.

"Would you like to invite us to your apartment?" Abdellah asked.

"I do not think it is a good idea," Arès said. "I can answer your questions here."

"I would really like to see your new place," he insisted. "I heard you moved. You know how passionate I am about real estate."

"I am having trouble with my landlord. I do not think we should."

"It is this way, no?" Abdellah said, steering him by the shoulder.

Arès was too tired to resist. He shuffled between Abdellah and Federika, his iambic stride giving him the air of a shackled prisoner led off by two jailers. Camille glided behind them, inking a small blue notebook with dainty strokes of the pen.

They crossed a busy thoroughfare and then a small plaza. A narrow alley between two high rises brought them to an open courtyard surrounded by arcaded buildings and partitioned by shared gardens and communal spaces.

"This is quite nice," Abdellah said with a flourish of his arms.

"Yes. It was public housing, but the government opened it up to migrants," Arès replied. He looked around at the orderly span of the gardens with a proprietary air and was freshly pleased with his new location. "But some of the neighbors are not happy that we are here," he added as an afterthought.

"Where do you live?" Federika asked. Her voice was eccentrically pitched, and it startled Arès almost every time that she spoke.

He stopped to lean on his cane. His foot was aching and he needed to rest. "I am up there." He pointed to a window on the sixth floor of one of the buildings.

Abdellah whistled. "I bet you have a nice view up there."

"Can you make it up with your foot?" Federika asked.

"It is very hard," Arès said. "Many days it hurts too much to go up and down the stairs, so I stay in the living room and watch TV."

"You have a TV!" she exclaimed with an astonished intake of breath.

"Yes. My other landlord did not like television because of the high *consommation,* but here it is ok."

"I don't even have a TV," she said.

"It is easy. You economize a little and at the end of every month, you pay fifty dirhams until you are done with the TV."

"I like to read. Do you read at all?"

"No," Arès replied. *"La lecture me bouffe la tête."*

"Sorry, I didn't catch that." Camille glanced up from the small, blue pad with expectant eyes.

"Reading tires his head," Abdellah paraphrased.

"You should read," Federika insisted. "Reading's good for you." Her voice skipped up the high notes of a musical scale, reminding Arès of several advertising jingles he had heard on TV.

"You know with TV or with music, I relax. I am tranquil," he answered quietly. "Sometimes I begin to read. I read something. But then I put it down again."

"I think reading is very important," she persevered.

"I will try," he promised.

They moved into the building together. The landing was cool and dim, a relief after the shrill blasts of the sun.

Arès paused in a mesh of shadows beside the base of the stairs. Then he slowly began to mount the spiraling steps, leading with his cane.

"How do you make money?" Abdellah asked, while they rested on the second-floor landing.

"I cannot." He pointed at his foot. "Or only sometimes. I have friends who are shoemakers and they offer me little jobs. They say do this or do that. I have another friend, a Moroccan, who owns a telephone boutique. He gives me small errands to run."

"To walk you mean." Abdellah clapped him hard on the back, eliciting a small "oof." Behind him, on the steps, Arès heard a half-stifled giggle.

They continued to converse as he onerously climbed to the sixth floor. "There was one time that my neighbors were locked out of their apartment and I picked the lock for them, but it is all I can do as a locksmith ever since the police confiscated my tools. I cannot afford to buy new tools and so I cannot exercise my profession."

"Maybe you should sell your TV," Federika suggested.

"It is not mine." He paused on the fourth-floor landing and gazed challengingly at his visitors. "Three years in a row I have applied to AMPAM for financing to buy the tools for a locksmithery, but they never want to help me."

"Did you call them to follow up?" Federika asked.

"Yes, but it is always an excuse: 'You are on a waiting list, and there are many others ahead of you.' But then I see projects awarded to refugees who arrived a year or more after me." He could not understand why they were always lying. These people were supposed to help him, but trying to get them to actually do anything felt like battling a jungle. Every way he turned the path was blocked, and everything was as crooked and tangled as vines.

They reached the sixth floor and Arès opened the door to his apartment. A narrow entranceway bellied into a cozy living room. Several individuals were chatting inside an open kitchenette, and a wrinkled infant with large owl eyes stared at them from a bright blue pagne sashed across a woman's back.

Arès ushered his flatmates off the premises while his visitors settled on the couches. In the corner, a black cart held a boxy TV. A low wooden table, stained with cup rings, crouched at the visitors' feet.

"I am a professional locksmith," he said as he sat down. "I do not see why they cannot help me open a shop. Now that I know many people, I could make a living, instead of just scraping by."

"We should call the AMPAM," Camille suggested.

Arès glanced over to see her rapidly pirouette a pen across the pages of the blue notebook. On its front, he could make out the white emblem of the UNHCR: a bald, besmocked refugee, standing between two elongated hands whose forefingers arched above to form an imperfect shelter. It was meant to be a symbol of safety, but it seemed to Arès that the two hands could just as easily crush that frail figure imprisoned within their grasp.

"I'll follow up with them," Federika replied. "But Arès, are you sure that your project is self-sustainable? The AMPAM analyzes every proposal to see if it is feasible. Maybe you should try another project. They may have some suggestions about other options."

"I am a locksmith..." Arès began to say, but the front door opened and several men bustled in. They spoke in a fast rat-a-tat French scented with Ivory Coast accents. They were in heated conversation and did not even nod at the strangers as they disappeared into the back rooms.

"How many people live here?" Abdellah asked.

"There are three bedrooms in the back. I share one with two friends, and there are five men in another, and the woman you saw when you came in has the third one with her three children."

"Is there a bathroom?"

"Yes. There." Arès gestured toward the rear of the apartment. Then he lifted a small mason jar off the table and used it to pour several drops of water onto an odd-looking plant. Bathed in a latticework of light, it rose out of a clay basin beside a window and resembled a cloven hoof crowned by radiating green shoots.

Camille looked up from her notebook. "What is that?"

Arès edged forward, trying to make out what the young woman was writing. Pages and pages were filled with a schoolgirl's looping cursive script, perfectly blocked within the lines. He squinted but the letters danced unsteadily, leaving him with an impression of ruled sheets that seemed torn from his years of schooling.

"A baby baobab," he replied. "One day it will be a magnificent tree."

"Not if it stays here," Abdellah said, giving the cramped space an assessing glance.

"You should plant it outside," Federika suggested.

Abdellah took a sip of water from the mason jar. "Not even a cactus can flourish in the sand," he murmured.

The letters came into focus and Arès saw the young woman write, "Baby baobab tree."

"I would like to open a boutique," he continued, "but it is impossible here. You'll never see an African who has his own boutique. The police come and say, 'where are your papers?' Then they take everything. Unless you put your products on your back, they won't leave you alone. They make the Africans walk. As if I have not walked enough. I walked here from the Congo and they want me to walk even more. You can never stop walking."

"You are sitting now," Abdellah remarked.

"I am sitting because I am injured. If my foot worked, I would be out there walking."

He shook his head wearily. When he was healthy, he never had to plead with anyone. Now it was all he ever did. This was the worst part of his injury: to be dependent on others, when you could only count on yourself. He remembered the day he had won the race. No one had been faster than him then.

"How is your foot?" Abdellah asked.

"How is it? Look at it. I still cannot put on shoes after two years. I must wear sandals all the time and buy special socks."

"What do the tests say?"

"Every day I take this pill and this pill and this pill..." He arranged several apricot-hued vials on the table. "And for months I have been injecting myself with these blood-thinners." He pulled a hard-plastic shell from under the couch and snapped it open. Inside, lay a dozen hypodermic needles, half of them used. "They helped for a while, but my foot is beginning to petrify again. And they make me feel sick all the time."

"Arès, have they sent you for tests?" Federika interrupted.

"All they do is send me for tests, but when I arrive at the hospital, I never get my tests. The hospital they send the refugees to does not work. I went there three times, and every time the x-ray machine was broken. It took four months just to get one x-ray. But I knew the x-ray was useless. I went to PALS with it and the doctor tried to give me more Voltarene. Do you know that when you go to PALS, they do not even examine you? They do not take your pulse or listen to your breathing. This is not normal."

He was stirred up now. Two years of this mess. Two years of injury and insult and injustice. Being a refugee was all he had ever been given in return for his inordinate suffering. But what was it worth? The HCR, together with the nations of world, had promised him something when they recognized him as a refugee. Discovering the fragility and the rude limitations of that promise had been yet one more bitter, sickening pill to swallow.

"A normal doctor takes your pulse," he insisted. "At PALS they just look at you and write you a prescription. It is not right." He couldn't believe it. It was so hard talking to these people. Did they think the refugees were children? Or pygmies from the jungle who had never seen a doctor before? He could feel the jungle around him now, pressing in.

"So all you have is the x-ray?" Abdellah asked.

Arès sighed. "No. I called Fatima, and she talked with the doctors at PALS." While he spoke, he began to chop at Camille's knee. Each time the palm of his hand slapped against her leg, the young woman winced and her eyes shot wide. "So they sent me to another clinic where I was supposed to have an MRI. But when I arrived at the clinic, the doctor refused to administer the test without my dossier. I had to go all the way back to PALS, but they told me that Dr. Djideree had my dossier and he was not there. I tried to call him, but he never picks up his phone."

"He always picks up when I call him," Federika said.

"Yes, but when the refugees call him, he never replies. Ask the other refugees. He never picks up for us."

"So you could not get your dossier?" Abdellah demanded.

"No. He finally picked up, and I asked him if he could bring the dossier to the Fondation Oriental or to me, but he never has the time. So he told me he will only give me the dossier if I go to the Quartier de l'Océan to meet him. Do you know how far the Quartier de l'Océan is for me? I have to take three *grand taxis* to get there. Who is going to pay for that? It took hours to get there and when I called him, he told me that I took too long and that he had left. I do not understand why he could not meet me at the Fondation Oriental when I go to pick up my financial aid, or why he could not at least leave the dossier there."

Arès did not notice the young intern yank her leg back. His hand suddenly encountered no resistance and he toppled halfway onto the floor.

Abdellah leaned sideways and helped the refugee back onto the couch. "Should we call the doctor then?"

"It is not necessary," Arès said, staring suspiciously at Camille. "Dr. Djideree told me that he left it at PALS. So I went all the way back to PALS and picked up the dossier. It cost me nearly fifty dirhams to have my dossier. This is food for two weeks."

"Have you had your MRI yet?" Abdellah asked.

"Let me tell you something. When I looked at my dossier, the charts were all wrong. They showed thirty consultations with me, but I have only been to PALS maybe a dozen times. Also, there were three dates when I arrived for a consultation and they told me that they were full for the day and could not see me. But they wrote down that I had seen a doctor and received medication. Then another time, they only gave me two of the four medications prescribed for me by the doctor, but they marked down that they had paid for all four. PALS is no good. *C'est la grande arnaque!*"

"That's terrible!" Camille exclaimed.

"These are very serious charges," Federika said. "Can you really prove this?"

"Of course I can. I have my dossier right here. I can show you every time they lied about treating me."

He stuck his arm into the crack between the couch and the wall, and pulled out a crumpled envelope, packed to the brim with records of his infirmity. He handed it to Camille, who passed it to Abdellah, who flipped it onto Federika's knees, and before Arès had taken two breaths, it had sailed merrily around the room and dropped back into his lap.

He stared down at it for a moment and had to keep his hands from tearing it to shreds.

"How do you feel otherwise?" Abdellah asked.

Arès stared sullenly at his interrogators. "Things are not good." His head felt swollen, and the tendons groaned in his leg. "Look at this. Read what they wrote about my foot." He took Abdellah lightly by the wrist and slid a paper out of the cockroach-brown envelope, placing it in the Moroccan's hands.

Abdellah's eyes glittered as he read: "*Présence d'un aspect désorganisé et un hyper signal T2 du ligament calcanéo-fibulaire évoquant une rupture, associée à un épaississement des parties molles en regard de la malléole interne.*"

Arès leaned down to massage his Achilles heel. He could sense the hard calcification of the ligament that rubbed underneath.

"That is not good," Abdellah admitted, putting the file aside.

"Two years I have been like this." Arès tossed his head from side to side. He felt miserable.

"Has it really been two years?" Camille asked. "I'm sorry. I'm an intern, so I only arrived a couple months ago."

Arès grabbed her hand, pinning it in place. "Ah, I am glad that you are here then. It is good that you are visiting the refugees. Now you will see the truth. See how we live and suffer. Every day I pray for the call telling me I will be resettled."

"It's not easy," Camille replied. "It's not the HCR that decides. The resettlement countries make the decision and they don't accept many refugees."

"Yes, but see what you can do in my case. I talked with my friend Matondo, who is in Holland, and he is so good there. There he gets treatment and has a life. I want to start my life. Find a wife and a family. Here I am only sick. Here there is no future." He looked beseechingly into the intern's eyes. All he needed was one person who would help him.

"I am sorry," Camille replied.

"PALS is no good," Arès repeated. "Do you know, when I was first injured, they did not give me crutches. I had to buy the crutches myself.

Then I could not eat for two weeks. Is that how you make a man healthy? You stop him from eating for two weeks?"

"PALS is our local partner," Federika said brightly. "We know there are some issues, but we are committed to building their capacity."

"But I cannot work and I cannot live on six hundred dirhams a month. My rent is four hundred dirhams. How am I supposed to eat and live and travel back and forth to the hospital with two hundred dirhams a month? The HCR added fifty dirhams to my assistance last month, but I think it was only so I could buy a rope to hang myself."

"These things take time," Abdellah said. "We are negotiating with the Moroccan government. It looks like they may give the refugees work permits soon."

"You have been negotiating with them for twenty years!" Arès sighed audibly. It was the same shabby story every time.

"Do you think things would be better if you had a residency and work permit?" Camille asked.

"They will never give us a residency permit." He was angry again. All they ever did at the HCR was ask the same questions, and they were never the ones that mattered.

"You have to have hope," Federika said in her singsong voice.

"This is not about staying here. This is a question for resettlement." He pounded the table. He was tired of begging. "They cannot treat me here. They make me take generic drugs. For two years, I take the same drugs and they do nothing except make me sick. And I have to wait four months just for a consultation. Not a conclusion, just a consultation."

"Things take time in Morocco." Abdellah put a placating palm on the refugee's arm. "The Moroccans wait for a long time as well."

"This is a question for resettlement!"

"Have you demanded resettlement?" Abdellah asked.

Arès' heart skipped a beat. "What do you mean demand it? It is the decision of the HCR."

"You should write a letter requesting resettlement," Camille advised.

"Why did no one tell me this?" He was speechless. All these years, and no one had told him to request resettlement. He did not even know what to write. "Can you help me with it?"

Abdellah nodded. "I will. When you come by the Fondation Oriental next time, we will write the letter together."

"Let us write the letter now." Arès hobbled to the kitchen and began rummaging around for a pen and pad.

"I am sorry," Abdellah said. "We have a meeting now. We really have to go. But you will come by the foundation in two Mondays for your financial assistance, no? We will write the letter then."

The visitors rose to leave. "Goodbye my friend." Abdellah shook the refugee's hand.

"I will walk you out," Arès replied. "I cannot stay here today."

"You do not have to come with us. It is ok," Federika said.

"Let us go." Arès accompanied them out the door and they slowly drifted with him down the stairs. On every landing, Arès paused, his head caged in the thin bars of light that splintered through the latticed windows. Ten minutes later they crossed the arcaded walkway and passed through the narrow alley out into the street.

When they reached their initial meeting point, Arès placed his hand on Camille's shoulder. "I am glad you came. You know this is the first time in years that anyone has come to see how I live. I tell Abdellah all the time, 'See how I live. See that I am not telling lies.' Here I am like a fish swimming against the river. I am not advancing. I am not retreating. No matter how hard I swim, I only stay in one place. But someday, I will have to progress. Otherwise, I will die an old pappy here."

"I am sorry," Camille said. "We will do our best."

Abdellah shook Arès' hand again. "It was good to see you, but why do you never invite us for lunch? This is the fourth time I've come to your neighborhood and there's never anything to eat. How about some African food next time?" He smiled broadly and Arès smiled a little too.

"If you want, there's an African restaurant right around the corner."

"Real African food?"

"I will take you there right now." Arès took a step in that direction, but Abdellah stopped him with his hand.

"We have this meeting. I can't. But next time... You said right there?"

He pointed at a fat flock of birds on the corner. Arès lifted his finger to give a more precise indication, but Abdellah had already turned away. Camille and Federika said goodbye and left in turn.

The refugee gave a short, shuffling wave as they melted into the market's lively bustle.

A few minutes off, Arès' three visitors paused in the street. Nearby, a thick cloud of flies buzzed around a cart heaped with ripe yellow melons and brown bunches of bananas.

"Has it really been two years?" Camille asked, waving her hands to ward off the flies.

Abdellah counted on his fingers. "It has only been a year and a half, but that is too long. Even Moroccans do not have to wait this long for treatment. His is a really bad case."

"We should do something," Camille said.

"I will call Dr. Djideree tomorrow," Federika promised.

Abdellah shrugged. "Where should we get lunch?"

CHAPTER 38
JUNE 2009

S IMON AND GEORG WERE sipping coffee in their office, hunched over their computers like praying mantises. A terrorist warning had been dispatched to all the regional UN branches in the Kingdom of Morocco.

> Date: Wed, 15 June 2009 09:50:17 -0400
> Subject: Assurer Des Procédures d'Accès Strictes au Niveau des Sièges ou des Bureaux des Projets
>
> Chers collègues,
>
> For your information: Following recent arrests by the Moroccan special security forces, related to a terrorist group partially dismantled last month, we have received notice that the same group has smuggled several vehicles with Spanish license plates onto Moroccan territory. They intend to "equip" them with explosives and detonate them in several different cities in the Kingdom. The investigation is still open, and for the moment, we have no information about the group's exact targets...
>
> I would strongly remind you that the United Nations remains in the crosshairs of terrorist groups around the world. We must remain vigilant. I ask you therefore to ensure that the attached security procedures are fully implemented in order to prevent incidents which could have disastrous consequences.
>
> Avec mes meilleures salutations,
> F-------------
> UNDSS SA
> Morocco

"Always nice to wake up to a terrorist alert in the morning," Simon said, glancing over at Georg. "Really gets the blood flowing."

"I believe that is their goal," Georg replied, deadpan. "Would you like some more coffee?"

"Thanks, but I'm getting too jittery. I think I'll switch to tea."

Simon grabbed an ornate, silver pot off of a sideboard and flipped open the top, releasing a hot spout of steam.

Georg turned back to his screen, but quickly looked up again. "Did you know that Morocco has been called '*le laboratoire du pire?*'"

"Is that a tourism thing?" Simon asked, while carefully centering a short blue and gold glass on a metal tray.

Georg grunted and shook his head. "The idea is that everything bad that happens in Morocco goes on to repeat itself, but worse, somewhere else in the Arab world. If there's a small revolt in Casablanca today, it will iterate, ten years down the road, as a countrywide revolution in, say, Tunisia."

"Gotcha." Simon began pouring the mint tea from a precarious height. He watched the liquid splash into the hand-painted glass and silently swore when it overflowed. "You don't think it's somewhat arrogant making predictions about things like that?"

"Like what?" Georg asked.

Simon took a sip of tea. "The future of the Arab world."

Georg gave him a humorless stare and began typing something into his computer. After a moment, he looked up again. "Is anything ever serious to you?"

"How are those fair and free elections going in the Congo?"

Georg grimaced. "There have been some regrettable irregularities."

"You mean the exclusion of all the main opposition candidates and nearly a million phantom voters in a country of 3.5 million people?"

"3.6 million," Georg corrected.

"Yes. Sorry for the regrettable irregularity in my math." The Austrian JPO glared at him. "But see, that's ripe for humor. I hope the newspapers are cracking jokes about all those ghosts on the voting rolls."

"The subversion of a national election is nothing to laugh about."

"Do you have any way to invalidate the results?"

"We will air our concerns."

"I'll take that for a 'No.' So are you going to tear out your hair? Sit in the street and light yourself on fire?" Georg regarded Simon with impassive eyes. In the wan fluorescent light, his rectangular glasses shimmered like blank monitors. Simon could never make out what the Austrian was thinking. He seemed like someone who dreamt in statistics.

"I'm not saying you should throw a party," Simon continued, "but if you let yourself care too deeply about the mess of horrors that is our world, you'll end up like Fatima. She's been trying to schedule her third heart attack for months, but she can't find the time with all the refugee crises."

Georg removed his glasses and began wiping them with a white handkerchief. "At least she will earn it by protecting the people in her care."

"I'm sure her funeral will be very well attended."

"And you'll be there laughing."

"*Una risata vi seppilera*, as the Italians say."[62] Simon gave a small bow.

Georg shook his head hopelessly. Then he placed his hands on the table and stared earnestly at his colleague. "Have you no interest whatsoever in trying to make the world a better place?"

Simon burst out laughing. Tears dribbled down his cheeks and his stomach shook with concussive exhalations of air. He nearly lost his balance and had to steady his arm on the desk to keep from falling out of his chair.

"What's so funny?" Georg gave him a horrified look.

Simon wiped the tears from his cheeks.

"Nothing. Nothing. I can't wait to tell this to Baptiste."

He got up to leave the room. Georg sprang to his feet. "What?" he demanded with an offended look.

Simon left the room, batting his hands helplessly in the air, his torso convulsing with laughter.

He was ambling down the hallway, giggling to himself, when Federika pounced on him.

"Just the man I was looking for," she said with a predatory gleam in her eyes. "We have PROGRES updates to do."

---

62 A small laugh will bury you.

"Oh no!" Simon exclaimed. "This is worse than the terrorist threat." He began to back away.

"You're being a little dramatic, don't you think?"

"Isn't this what interns are for?"

Federika shook her head. "We need someone we can trust."

She seized Simon by the elbow and marched him back to his office. "*Sieh mal, was ich aufgefischt habe*," she bragged to Georg.[63]

"*Das ist ein fetter Fisch*," Georg replied with a shark's grin.[64]

"You know I understand German," Simon grumbled.

PROGRES was a glorified Excel spreadsheet that the UNCHR used as a searchable database to track its ever-evolving refugee population. Federika seated Simon before his computer and left the room. A few moments later, she strutted back in with a staggering pile of dossiers and thumped them down on his desk.

"This should be a good start," she said with missionary cheerfulness.

Simon refilled his tea glass and spooned in an extra shot of honey. Looking morosely at Georg, who had finally found something to laugh about, he began the process of reducing dozens of refugees' lives into monochrome code.

He was tapping a particularly long entry from an RSD interview: "WR-UW, SP-PT, LP-VO, LP-VA, VSV-COD, LP-TO, LP-DO," for "sexually assaulted in home country; abandoned by husband in Morocco; detained and tortured for five months; beaten by partner," when the chat box on his computer pinged.

Simon breathed a sigh of relief.

11:02 AM Christopher.Guillerme: Salaam Aleikam!

Me: Wa Aleikam Salaam from Rabat. How's the weather down there?

Christopher.Guillerme: 40 degrees plus man. hot as fuck. how's life in Rabat?

Me: We're hitting 32 today and I'm sweating. I assume you don't have much AC over there?

---

63 Look at what I fished up.
64 That is one fat fish.

He waited for a response and then noticed that the chat box had taken on a faded hue. His friend was in Darfur or Chad, he couldn't remember which, but he assumed the internet was irregular.

He coded for another few minutes before it pinged back to life.

11:08 AM Christopher.Guillerme: hey Simon. Sorry. network is in and out today. How's Morocco and the UNHCR mission?

Me: Good. Just another morning in the office, another report drafted, another refugee neatly filed away. And you?

Christopher.Guillerme: here we work basically as a sub-contractor for "le HCR." I'm taking a lot of brusque meetings about how we need to "better know what's going on in the field" from people who never leave their air-conditioned offices...

Me: Ha. glad to hear you're still in an office. Thought you'd be a child soldier by now.

Christopher.Guillerme: Man... that is just not funny. 30 kids came in from the front all shot up today. Rough... some like 12 years old.

Me: sorry. That many?

Christopher.Guillerme: yeah, it's been in groups of 10 to 100 about three days a week now for weeks.

Me: Are they fleeing the fighting in Darfur?

11:11 AM Christopher.Guillerme: No. They're part of JEM, a rebel group. it's been bringing its troupes to MSF to patch them up.

Me: So MSF patches them up and they go out to fight again?

Christopher.Guillerme: they go out again if they can. I don't think all the kids made it. They'd been traveling for three straight days. They can only move under cover of night, since even in Chad the sudanese airforce flies over all the time.

Me: No one goes out to help them?

Christopher.Guillerme: There's no way. JEM is doing its own aid programs, so the population shoots at the NGOs because they can't tell the difference between us and the rebels.

Me: and the NGOs stay?

Christopher.Guillerme: 32 carjackings in Chad this year and all the NGOs are still here. Only Save the Children left.

Me: You all bunking together?

Christopher.Guillerme: this isn't summer camp, Simon. We're a small town, 600–800 people with UNHCR, UNICEF, WFP, MSF and a German NGO called HELP—all about a 30min to 1h30m drive from the three IDP camps (otherwise known as rebel military bases) that we're running for "le HCR."

Me: Sounds like I should apply to HCR Chad next time.

Christopher.Guillerme: you like the desert buddy? 48 degrees today.

Me: Only if there are swimming pools.

11:13 AM Christopher.Guillerme: and there are VERY few trees around. Bring a hat and sunscreen. Also, how do you like rice and overcooked lamb? you get that 7 days a week. we have a saying around here. God made the food, but the devil made the cook.

Me: Guess that's why they call it a hardship post. Pretty tan? You're there for 4 more months? Do people ever stay longer?

Christopher.Guillerme: Tan, but thin as a rail man. Yep. 2 to 3 years. the pay is good and it's a compelling conflict.

Me: So you like it?

Christopher.Guillerme: "like" isn't the word. Chad is rough, but I've been made Program Manager for refugee programming, so I'm plenty busy.

Me: felicitations.

Christopher.Guillerme: Applied for the job full time, which would keep me here another year... not sure if I'm crazy or not...

Me: desert sun must be getting to you.

Christopher.Guillerme: could be.

Me: What does the job entail?

Christopher.Guillerme: Basically managing 165 Chadians, 7 expats and 8.5 mil USD a year of programming.

Me: Doing what?

Christopher.Guillerme: everything but wiping the refugees' asses... and medical MSF does that. .

Me: just what you need during a genocide.

Christopher.Guillerme: Yeah... that and lots of urgent supplies. We gave out seeds, hand plows, you name it to hundreds of villagers during the rainy season so they'd have crops next year.

Me: Aren't they farmers?

11:15 AM Christopher.Guillerme: Man. Their villages are razed to the ground. they stopped being farmers years ago. Now they're professional IDPs. you don't even need an attack anymore, just a rumor and they'll sell the shirt off their back for a ride out of town.

Me: Ride out of town? People are just driving around in Darfur?

Christopher.Guillerme: There are always local trucks coming through who'll take everything a villager owns in exchange for transport. Welcome to war.

Me: Shit. How do you make a dent in all that?

Christopher.Guillerme: It's hard to measure impact. as they say, human rights work, c'est une acte de foi.

Me: any resettlement for the IDPs?

Christopher.Guillerme: Resettlement in Chad? have you seen the news lately? No solution to the conflict on the horizon. it's mostly just "keeping them alive in the desert."

Me: And in Darfur?

Christopher.Guillerme: Not a chance. The ICC indicted Al-Bashir in March and in return he kicked half the NGOs out of Sudan, and the other half are on lockdown. The ICRC is the only one travelling on the ground anymore and only with heavy UN escort.

Me: so much for the unintended consequences of international justice.

11:18 AM Christopher.Guillerme: Yeah.

Me: So what are the NGOs doing since the lockdown?

Christopher.Guillerme: drinking a lot. Or at least they were until two of the blue helmets went blind a couple weeks back, and then another one died this week.

Me: What?!?

Christopher.Guillerme: yeah, man. you think we're drinking Moet? There's only black-market alcohol. People slip 50cl flasks of Johnnie Walter in with the cargo consignments, and that's what everyone sips after work.

Me: Johnnie Walker?

Christopher.Guillerme: No. Johnnie WALTER. same label as Johnnie Walker,

but it's some bootleg bathtub stuff they smuggle in from Libya. We've been
drinking it all year. then a couple weeks ago two of the blue helmets went
blind, and two days ago another one died.

Me: Wait. You kept drinking that poison after two people went blind?

Christopher.Guillerme: Hey, either you drink Johnnie Walter or you drink
sharbut, the local alcohol. It's brewed in the dirt in a tukul somewhere, and
tastes like sewage mixed with coca-cola. I'd rather risk death. Johnny Walter
at least tastes like something you're used to.

Me: That's nuts.

Christopher.Guillerme: In methanol we trust... man, hate to cut the conversation short, but the Lakers are on Canal Plus. game 3, got to catch that.

Me: you're kidding me.

Christopher.Guillerme: No Canal Plus and I'd be out of here. enjoy the rest of
your mission and let's keep in touch!

Me: send me updates sometime.

Christopher.Guillerme: will do.

Simon. I'll see if I can make it to Chad

Christopher.Guillerme: why not man. It's where all the action is.

Me: Sounds like it.

11:20 AM Christopher.Guillerme: talk to you soon. Time for hoops!

Me: a+

Simon went back to typing in the codes, but soon he was imagining
horsemen galloping through whirling dust, iron hooves pounding the sand,
grim AK-47's aimed at hundreds of blue and white UNHCR tents. They
were sitting ducks in those camps, but he couldn't think of another way.

He slipped out for a pot of tea, this time with extra pellets of gunpowder.
Then he diligently glued himself to his chair. The day passed, while an
ever-elongating string of letters centipeded across the flickering screen
before him. Eventually, he found himself staring at an imposing accumu-
lation of nonsense.

He rubbed two bleary eyes and stared vacantly out of the narrow sash
window. His mind had started to wander when an explosive bang from
Avenue Tariq Ibn Ziad caused him to vault out of his chair. His body

tensed for flight and he spun toward Georg. Imperturbable as always, the Austrian was hammering assiduously at his keyboard. After a moment, he glanced up.

"Truck backfire?" he asked.

"I'm just stretching my legs," Simon replied.

The soothing rumble of the avenue's unceasing traffic reasserted itself over the office. Simon sat back down, his pulse still racing. "Twenty more dossiers to go," he muttered under his breath.

Hours later, he rubbed his neck and rose shakily from his chair, with all the satisfaction of having expertly completed a disagreeable task. He locked the office door and began the long stroll home through the hushed ambassadorial quarter.

Outside, a purple stain was spreading across the sky, and already, there was a stir and bustle among the stars.

FIRST RESETTLEMENT INTERVIEW
FEBRUARY 2008

O
VER THREE YEARS HAD passed since Arès had first received his refugee card.

He sat on the outdoor terrace of a café with two men, Iliass and Yann, who frequented the apartment where he lived. Yann was a short, stocky fellow, who reminded Arès of his uncle Guli and had a similar clowning attitude toward life. Iliass was more reserved. Tall and rangy, he had a long face and an even longer nose, and the same explosive, cackling laugh as a stork. Arès liked them both, but he knew better than to set much store by their company in a place like Rabat.

After several minutes without a waiter, the two men headed inside to place their order, leaving Arès alone at the table.

He studied his foot while he waited, willing it to emerge from the fleshy shell that encased it. When he rubbed it with his thumb, he could feel a cushion of fluid slide beneath the skin. The Nigerians, he had been told, believe that a handicap attracts bad luck. There were many days when Arès felt this superstition confirmed.

The sound of footsteps approached and he looked up again.

"She told the doctors that it had been the devil and not her husband," Yann said, as he and Iliass sat down again.

"Who?" Arès asked.

"We are talking about the wife of the president of Gabon. The one that died recently."

The waiter arrived with three decorative glasses and a pot of mint tea. Arès took the pot and hoisted it in the air as he poured, so that an effervescent froth crackled on the tea's surface. When the first glass was full, he opened the lid of the pot and dumped the contents back in. Then he repeated the operation several times.

"What happened?" he asked once the ceremony was over.

Yann leaned conspiratorially over the table and motioned at the two men to draw near. "She came home from shopping one day and walked into a room where her husband, the president of Gabon, was sodomizing their ten-year-old son. She fainted and when the doctors revived her, she went crazy. She swore that she had seen the devil," Yann paused and chuckled, "with big curling horns and a blue goatee, raping her boy."

"The devil?" Arès poured another glass of tea, lofting the pot higher and higher until he was satisfied with the crown of suds.

"Then she disappeared. Not a word. We found out a few months later that she had been sent to a psychiatric institution in Casablanca. The president kept her locked up there for three years." Yann lowered his voice another notch, so the two men had to bend even closer to hear, "but the devil finally caught up with her last week at a hospital in Rabat." He slapped the table with a hard thwack! and began to laugh loudly.

"Why did he send her to Morocco?" Iliass asked.

"That is where every African ruler goes," Arès said with a twinkle in his eyes.

Iliass flashed his bright white teeth. "There or *la France*."

"But we were talking about her," Yann continued, still chuckling, "because the president had her buried in Morocco instead of in his tomb in Gabon, which is essentially a confession that he killed his wife to shut her up."

"Why?" Arès asked.

"We say, *chez nous*, that if you do not bury your wife next to you, it is proof that you killed her. It is not like that where you live?"

"We do not kill our wives very often in Kinshasa."

Iliass laughed, but Yann ignored the comment. "Oftentimes people, *chez nous*, when there is suspicion on them, during the funeral they will go up to the body of their dead wife in front of everyone and say, 'If I killed my wife, do not let me live six months.' But it is a very risky thing to do."

"How come?" Arès screwed his eyes together. Things sounded very strange in Gabon.

"Well often they don't survive the six months."

"God punishes them?"

"No," Yann replied with an impish grin. "But some people say to themselves, 'Well, he said six months, and so they help God out a little." He slapped his knee and chortled with laughter.

Arès took a sip of mint tea.

"But why sodomize his own child?" he asked.

"I don't know. The president of Gabon is still alive, so it must do something. Everyone wants that bastard to die!"

Yann cracked a toothy grin and Iliass cackled heartily, drowning out the sounds of the café around them.

"And he was re-elected," Iliass added with a despairing shake of his head.

"Ah, *c'est l'Afrique*," Yann snorted. "I think President Bongo won the last election with 94% of the vote. He likes to let the other parties get 6% so the French can claim they're supporting a democracy. You know he is the best friend of Sarkozy. He even funded Sarkozy's last campaign."

"Yes, it is like Biya," Iliass replied, scratching his long nose. "I think he has had over 90% of the vote since 1982."

"The big fish do not keep to the small streams," Arès said and smiled quietly to himself. Instinctively, his fingers reached for the key that hung around his neck.

Yann lightly sucked his teeth. "I agree. Africa will never change."

"No. I think we need to wait for this generation to die," Iliass objected. "That is how things change in Africa. Not with elections, but with the death of the Big Men. Then a new generation comes into power and things progress a little."

"I do not know." Arès took a deep sip of tea, while he thought. "My brother Félix used to say the same thing, but Kabila overthrew Mobutu and things only got worse. Now someone has assassinated Kabila, and his son is in power. For years he has promised democracy, but it is like asking a leopard to guard the chickens."

Iliass chuckled. "My father always said, '*le lion est mort, les léopards font la fête.*'"[65]

"Yes, but Bongo has made a deal with the devil so that he will never die," Yann said. "He even sucked all the life out of his son by sodomizing him." He caved his cheeks in as if he were sucking on a straw, and then blew them out again in a frog-eyed explosion of laughter.

"Why has no one tried to kill him?" Arès asked, when Yann had quieted down.

"The French protect him in return for Gabon's oil," Yann explained, his roguish eyes still glittering. "The opposition tried to overthrow him in 1993, but the French sent in their troops. Since then, there is nothing anyone can do. An African president is like a wasp that has landed on you. You should not move unless you're sure you'll kill it."

Arès leaned over and began massaging his foot. "Of course, sometimes death seems like a good option."

"In Islam," Iliass said, "they preach that when you die, you come to a place of four rivers: one of milk, one of wine, one of sweet water, and one of honey."

"And yet they do not drink alcohol?"

"Ah, the Muslims drink just as well as the Christians." Yann said, wagging a coy finger at Iliass. "Only they are more discrete about it." He gave another exuberant laugh.

Before Iliass could reply, his phone rang. "*Oui, allô?... Non, c'est Iliass qui parle... Oui, il est là.*" He handed the phone to Arès. "It's for you."

"Hello?" Arès said.

"This is Lise from the HCR calling. We would like you to come in to talk about the gaps in your file."

"Is this about resettlement?"

"No. We need to talk to you about your file."

"Then I will not come," he said through clenched teeth. Again! His file. They were shameless at the HCR.

"It is in your best interest to come," the woman on the phone said. "You

---

65   When the lion is dead, the leopards celebrate.

cannot be considered for resettlement with an incomplete file."

Arès put down the phone. His breath came short and quick. He swallowed a glass of mint tea in a single draught and picked up the phone again.

"I will come, but I would like to talk about resettlement. You have not answered the letter I sent."

"I am looking at your dossier, and I do not see any letters requesting resettlement. If you come in, you can make a formal request and we will treat it as soon as possible."

"I will come right away." He handed the phone back to Iliass. "I have to go to the HCR."

"You have not had your third glass," Yann said with a smirk.

"What?"

"*Le premier verre est aussi amer que la vie, le deuxième est aussi fort que l'amour, le troisième est aussi doux que la mort.*"[66]

"Ah, then maybe it is better I leave after two," Arès said laughing.

On three legs he hobbled off.

It was early afternoon by the time he arrived at the bright white building with its high spiked fence. After the long dry season, the Bouregreg River was no more than a sinuous wisp of azure almost imperceptible amidst the grasslands of burnt sienna below. No birds were to be seen.

One of the powder-blue guards passed Arès back and forth several times through the metal detector. Then he led him up a short flight of stairs to the interview room.

Arès settled onto the spongy chair while the guard gently shut the door. A few seconds later, the door swung open again with an emphatic thump.

A tall blazer and khaki pants bustled into the room. "Hi, Mr. Sbigzenou!"

Arès started halfway out of the chair and was yanked to his feet by a vigorous handshake. "I will be conducting your interview today," Simon said. "Please sit down."

The refugee gritted his teeth. Then he sat back down again.

---

66   The first glass is as bitter as life, the second is as strong as love, the third is as sweet as death.

Thank you for coming today.

Do you need a translator?

No.

What is your native tongue?

Lingala.

But you speak French?

Yes.

Good. Before we begin, I would like to explain how this interview will proceed. You are here because we have some questions about your dossier. Everything that you say here is confidential. Nothing you say here will be reported to anyone, especially not the government. We are not a government agency.

These updates are necessary from time to time in order for us to verify facts and to successfully serve the needs of our refugee population. We appreciate your coming today.

Would you like to say anything before we begin this interview?

Yes.

What?

I was a child once.

They proceeded with the interview.

CHAPTER 40

MAY 2008

T HREE MONTHS LATER, ARÈS took a *grand taxi* to the Fondation Oriental to pick up his financial assistance. When he arrived, Abdellah ushered him into the office and handed him a two-week old letter from the HCR.

UNHCR

26, Avenue Tariq Ibn Zyad
Rabat-Maroc

tél: 00 37 76 76 76
fax: 00 33 87 87 87

Le 16 Avril 2008
Monsieur Arès Sbigzenou
918-05C-8080

objet: Votre demande de réinstallation

Cher Monsieur,

Nous accusons réception de votre lettre datée du 15/01/08 par laquelle vous sollicitez la réinstallation dans un pays tiers.

Après un examen minutieux des motifs que vous évoquez à l'appui de votre demande, et de tous les éléments d'information contenus dans votre dossier, nous sommes au regret de devoir vous informer que le HCR n'est pas en mesure de répondre favorablement à votre demande. Votre situation, en effet, ne répond pas aux critères de réinstallation tels que définis par le HCR et les Etats de réinstallation.

Nous vous encourageons vivement à rechercher avec l'aide de nos partenaires opérationnels des solutions en vue de faciliter votre intégration dans votre pays d'asile, le Maroc.

Nous attirons votre attention sur le fait que cette décision est sans appel.

Veuillez agréer, Monsieur, nos salutations distinguées.

Maarten Grotius
Représentant
UNHCR Rabat

"I am sorry my friend, but hope is not lost," Abdellah said. "Negotiations are underway with the government to get you work permits."

Arès tossed the letter on the ground and limped off without saying a word.

As he cut across the grounds of the Fondation Oriental, Salifou appeared at the far entrance. He caught sight of Arès and pivoted toward him.

"*Ca va, mon ami?*" he said, waving.

Arès stopped dead in his tracks. His heart hammered against his chest, and he could feel a snake hiss gently through his guts.

"What? Am I invisible to you?" Salifou said in a teasing tone, and waved his arms theatrically.

Before Arès could choke out a reply, an energetic refugee from the Ivory Coast bounded up and clasped Salifou in his arms. "*Mon frère,* where have you been? Up to your old tricks?" The two of them laughed slyly and poked each other in the ribs. "Come with me," the Ivorian beckoned. "There are young ladies waiting." With a coaxing smile and a conspiratorial tug, he drew Salifou toward the far side of the garden where a lively group of women were laughing gaily.

Salifou waved one last time and turned his back. Arès did not move. It felt as if the ground were sinking slowly beneath his feet.

CHAPTER 41

JUNE 2009

S IMON STROLLED DOWN AVENUE Mohammed V, listening to the call to the *Maghrib* prayers. When he reached the *Place du Marché* inside the medina, he joined a long line of customers waiting to place their orders at the Bami Boulangerie.

"*Wahed bstela b'djaj*," he said at the counter some minutes later. A white-aproned server handed him a square white box covered with cursive Arabic writing in blue.

Simon exited into a side street close to the Place Bab el Had. The air was filled with the sandpaper sounds of hundreds of worn babouches scraping toward the entrance to the nearby mosque. Beside Simon stretched a wall covered in bootleg DVDs, and beyond it, rows of street vendors griddling kefta sandwiches and omelets on outdoor hotplates.

To the faint melody of the *iqama*, Simon opened the box, its bottom translucent with warm grease. He lifted out the round disc like a holy sacrament. Then he bit into its flaky brown crust, with its dusting of sugar and layered almond interior, and felt a moment of sensory bliss.

There was a juicemonger nearby, so he washed down the meal with a fresh-squeezed orange juice in a suspiciously streaked glass. As the Imam's voice faded away, Simon plunged deeper into the warren of the souk, training his feet toward les Oudayas.

The American riad on the northern end of the kasbah was hosting another one of its bohemian affairs. After a brisk walk, Simon arrived at the familiar arched doorway, with its gargantuan terracotta vase topped with spiny aloe. It was propped open, so he entered the riad and traversed the wide-open atrium. Vertiginous stairs carried him toward an insistent bass beat a few flights above. When he stepped onto the roof, "Hiya Hiya" by Khaled was playing loudly and Simon could see nearly a hundred people milling about.

Near the entrance, a long patio table sagged under the weight of wine and beer. The parties at the American riad were famously well-stocked, even though the Fulbright stipends allotted its residents were hardly princely sums. Simon suspected there was a dash of pedigree in the room. Someone with connections had invited a group of fashionable Casablancans, all splashed in designer gear like Kinani's friends, except this time Simon assumed it was real.

The Casablancans were standing by the drinks, conversing in flawless English with one of the Fulbrighters, a pretty, chestnut-haired girl wearing colorful sandals and a flouncy beach tunic.

"Did it take you long to get here from Skybar?" she asked.

"It is only half an hour between here and Casa," a tall, slender youth in a blue blazer, with a heavy silver Rolex on his wrist, replied. "Maybe twenty minutes if there is no traffic."

"Only if you drive at 215 kilometers per hour like him!" squealed a girl with glossy hair and inflatable lips. She was wearing a Balenciaga T-shirt and holding an expensive designer bag.

"I was racing Saad," the tall one replied. "He wanted to test out his new Beamer."

"You're not worried about getting a ticket?" the Fulbrighter asked.

The Casblancans gave patronizing smiles and the glossy-haired girl tried to stifle a laugh. "Not a problem," the tall one said, spinning the Rolex around his wrist. "They pull you over. You make a little joke about your house being on fire, then you slip the officer fifty dirhams and you leave."

"Wow. I wish I could do that in L.A."

Simon grabbed a Flag beer and pushed his way through the swirls and eddies of the crowd. It was a warm evening and the vividly attired partygoers flitted about like songbirds in a garden. The rooftop itself was vegetal, choked with potted plants and sinuous creeping vines that snagged on one's feet. And every few meters, colorful Chinese lanterns glowed softly like collapsing stars.

Several of the cultural attachés from the Alliance Française were sitting around a brass table near the edge of the roof, smoking cigarettes and chatting between sips of wine. Simon recognized a blond girl named Alice, who taught French and tended to sing when she spoke, and a brunette named Victoire, with whom he had briefly flirted. He waved at them and sat down, but they continued speaking as if he wasn't there.

"Did you hear that Serge Assier will be exhibiting his work at the French Institute in Rabat?" Alice hummed.

"Yes. It's the year of German-Moroccan friendship," said a man with thick geometric glasses and a goatee. He had a gravelly Spanish accent, and Simon recognized him as one of three consular officers from Madrid who often attended the riad parties.

"I love his portraits of the stars. Have you seen his photo of Serge Gainsbourg and Jane Birkin?" Victoire half whispered, forcing everyone in the group to lean inward. As they did, she grazed her hand gently against the sleeve of the consular officer.

"They're sublime," the man excitedly replied. "Though I'm really looking forward to the Jazz festival at the Chellah."

"How could it ever be better than *Mawazine*?" Victoire asked breathlessly. "Enrico Morricone played right in front of the Bouregreg River. It was magical!" Her voice rose to the level of a low moan. "I can't believe you missed it!"

"Did you see Stevie Wonder?" Alice asked, refilling her glass. "I heard the king invited him personally."

"He was fantastic, but then there was that awful stampede during the Abdelaziz Stati show," Victoire lamented, tossing up her thin, beautiful hands. "Eleven people died. Eleven! I think I'm going to keep away from crowded concerts for a while."

"Just stay away from cheesy Moroccan pop stars, and I think you'll be fine," Alice remarked with her lively crystal voice, and several of them laughed.

Simon wandered off, wondering if anyone had even noticed him. He toyed with the idea of abandoning ship, but Nadia had promised to meet him there later. Then, in a poorly-lit corner, he heard the rising crescendo of an argument. A pair of Israelis were quarrelling heatedly with two

Moroccans in black muscle shirts and camouflage pants, with checkered black and white keffiyehs looped around their necks. Simon drifted over like a moth drawn to a flame.

"If you do not want to be besieged, then do not build a fortress," the burlier of the Moroccans shouted.

"You want *us* to reform our government?" a trim, clean-shaven Israeli replied. "You're the ones living in a monarchy. Maybe you should tend to your own garden."

"Our government is not oppressing an entire people. It did not steal land," the other Moroccan replied. He had a spikey goatee and a compact, coiled body that seemed capable of exploding at any moment.

"Did not steal land? How are your Berbers doing? Why do you have a UN army parked in the Western Sahara?" The trim Israeli gave a bantering smile, but Simon watched him subtly shift his stance, planting his back foot solidly against one of the roof tiles.

"We are not letting an entire people starve to death on our watch."

"What are you talking about?" the other Israeli replied. He was shorter and rounder, with a thick beard and a jolly gleam in his dark eyes. "Have some hummus. Have a beer. We're Israelis. We love sharing. Just not territory."

The taller Moroccan spat on the ground. "I would never share a meal with an Israeli."

One of the hosts, a shaggy young man wearing a Grateful Dead T-shirt and orange fisherman pants, came rushing over. "Settle down! We're at a party. Can we keep the politics to ourselves for one night?"

"*Tfou ala tassila*!" hissed the shorter Moroccan. Then he spat on the ground for good measure, and the two of them marched off with their corner revolution.

"He has great talent for hatred, that one," the trim Israeli observed. Then he turned toward Simon and held out his hand, "Tomar."

"Simon." He shook the hand. "I'm beginning to understand why people argue with Israelis all the time."

"Because we're honest and we know history," Tomar replied. "Where are you from?"

"The States."

"*Am-e-rica?*" he said with long, mocking vowels. "Do you even have history there?"

Simon looked at him, unamused. "We try not to."

"Good answer. Makes life easy. Especially when you come to a party in les Oudayas with your American friends and *several* cute French girls, I see." Tomar's eyes scanned the group of cultural attachés and locked onto Victoire with sniper precision.

"It's the nicest part of town." Simon shrugged and glanced around. He wondered where Nadia was.

"Exactly. You have no idea about its past." Tomar said, gazing at Simon with a recondite look that irritated him.

"The only past I see are a bunch of people who can't move on from the past and have a good time," he replied stonily.

"That's what I'm talking about. You Americans have no interest in anything built before last week. You're lucky the Europeans were there to discover you. You never would have discovered yourselves."

"We'd probably be a happier people."

"Depends on who discovers you," Tomar retorted with a trace of a smile. "Which brings me back to our current home. Rabat takes its name from a *ribat* or a fortified convent. The kasbah of les Oudayas," he swept his arm before him "was called *Ribat el Fath,* the Fortified Convent of Victory. It housed and trained the Muslim warriors who conquered Spain and for hundreds of years waged holy wars against the Christian armies of Europe. And you think we have problems in Jerusalem!"

"Well we've managed to stop the fighting here," Simon said truculently.

"So you think." He held up an admonitory finger. "Rabat is the staging grounds for a new sort of invasion. Why do you think you UN people are here after all?"

"How did you know I work at the UN?" Simon demanded, suddenly alert, his eyes narrowed.

"It's written in flaming letters on your Oxford shirt and blazer," Tomar replied with a condescending look.

Simon shook his head. The man was exasperating. "So what do you mean about the UN presence here?"

"It's obvious." The Israeli's dark, prominent eyes bore into Simon unnervingly. "You are the modern Christian soldiers of today. You are fighting Europe's last holy war. In simpler terms, you are here to stop the African invasion."

Simon snorted loudly. "That's utter nonsense," he said through clenched teeth. He could feel the vein on his forehead begin to throb again. "We are here to aid individuals persecuted in their home countries for ethnic, religious, or political reasons. For that matter, we have a healthy number of Palestinian refugees in Morocco." That should shut him up, Simon thought.

"Ah, so I've met a true convert," Tomar intoned, winking at his bearded companion. Simon regarded the two of them with hostility and didn't say a word. "Well, let me ask a few questions of the faithful," Tomar continued. "If a group of Sudanese flee a famine in Sudan, are they refugees?"

Simon's eyes were mere slits now, and he could feel a tight ball of heat travel up his spine. "No," he said, trying to keep a level voice. "It's certainly a tragedy but they are not being persecuted."

"So they would be sent back home."

"Yes."

"But let's say this famine gives rise to ethnic tensions and a Muslim militia begins slaughtering the black Christian people in that part of Sudan. In that case, would these Sudanese be refugees?" Tomar spoke with a heavy, thudding intonation, so that his words had the same resonance as chess pieces being slapped onto a wooden board.

Simon stared at him warily for a moment. Then he replied, "You're talking about Darfur."

"Bingo!" the Israeli cried gleefully. "That's what you say in America, I believe?"

Simon looked at him sullenly.

"Now let's say there are reprisal attacks against Muslims civilians in the same region and those people also flee. Then they are refugees as well."

"Well, sure," Simon admitted grudgingly. "Both sides would be considered the victims of persecution on ethno-religious grounds."

"But the famine, which would kill them all the same, is not enough."

"There's no persecution in a natural disaster, so they don't fit the criteria."

"That's interesting," the Israeli replied. "Because most famines are political in genesis. Let's take the DRC for instance. A country with immense resources, but after thirty years of Mobutu's rule, food became so scarce that most of the population was down to a meal or two a week. Yet if someone fled that misery and came here, he wouldn't be considered a refugee?"

"Mismanagement is not persecution," Simon replied wearily.

A supercilious smile, not without a certain slyness, curled up Tomar's lips. "But it was only mismanaged for certain communities, *habibi*. Mobutu's tribe in the north feasted like kings. So afterwards, when there is an uprising, and the ethnic groups start massacring each other over lack of food, which is really about an ethno-political distribution of food, does a holy miracle occur and do they all become refugees?"

Simon paused to think it over. "Well, yes," he said haltingly. "As long as it's different ethnic groups killing each other."

"But this means that you are mere gatekeepers."

"To what?"

"To Europe. You parse the world into the deserving and the undeserving according to arbitrary religious tenets. And worse, you are self-righteous about it. I don't see any difference between someone fleeing a famine and someone fleeing the violence caused by the famine. The end result, if they stay, is the same."

Simon peered at Tomar for a moment. Then he turned and looked out at the dark plane of the sea. Far off, he could see the occasional flickering lights of massive oil tankers, balanced precariously on the blade of the horizon.

Reluctantly, he reoriented his head. There was a brief silence during which the two men stared at each other combatively.

Finally, Tomar spoke. "Have you never questioned these narratives?"

"Why would I?" Simon hedged. "This is what the United Nations decided. I am but a lowly bureaucrat carrying out its orders."

"I see. It's hard to make a man understand something when his job depends on him not understanding it."

Simon scanned the party. His eyes brightened when he caught sight of Baptiste chatting with Georg. "My colleagues are over there." He gestured vaguely toward the far side of the roof. "I think I'll go share your ideas with them." He started toward them, but the Israeli grabbed him by the arm and held him in place.

"Remember Simon. Sometimes it seems like God is asleep, but if there is one thing we know, he always wakes up."

"Who's the believer now?" Simon scoffed. He tried to free his arm but he couldn't break the man's grip.

Tomar gazed intensely at the JPO. "We have a saying in Israel: 'Anyone who does not believe in miracles, is *not* a realist.'"

"I don't need any miracles," Simon grumbled.

"I am not talking about for you," Tomar said, and let him go.

Simon exhaled with relief as he crossed the rooftop toward his colleagues.

"Ah, and here is our friend Simon, who doesn't believe in anything," Georg exclaimed, raising his beer in a toast.

"That's not true at all," Simon replied. "I believed I'd find you as close to the alcohol as humanly possible and here you are." He grabbed a beer and took a parched swig.

"I am talking about ethical beliefs," Georg said earnestly.

"In that case, I believe exactly what you believe," Simon answered. "Which is why we work together at the HCR."

"*Ach so*. And what is it I believe?" Georg asked with a crinkling of his eyes.

Simon regarded his colleague with a shocked expression. "Well, I'm certainly not going to tell you what *you* believe. That's really up to you."

"Sure," Georg responded shrewdly, "but I've forgotten what I believe. I was hoping you could remind me, since we believe the same thing."

Simon turned to Baptiste with a despondent look. "You see, after only a year at the HCR, Georg has already forgotten what he believes in."

Baptiste shook his head. "It is true that this work challenges all of our deepest convictions."

"Talking with the two of you is like riding a merry-go-round," Georg griped.

"Think of it as free entertainment," Simon said dryly. "You should be grateful. How anyone affords a good time on these meager UN salaries is a mystery to me."

"Ah, *mon ami*, it doesn't take much to have fun." Baptiste gave his colleagues a ribald wink. "For instance, it costs nothing to look, and if you look right now there is a charming group of ladies over there."

Simon and Georg spun their heads. Two attractive girls with smoky velvet eyes and laughing scarlet mouths were rocking back and forth in a swing chair, pumping their feet and giggling joyfully.

"I believe they're Moroccan," Simon coolly observed. "I thought you were trying to get closer to your people, Baptiste."

"In fact, I am waiting for a young Cameroonian waitress named Kaïssa," he confessed with a silvery grin. "But the Moroccans are also my people. We are all Africans here."

"The Moroccans don't think so," Simon retorted.

"Yes, their heads are full of confused European ideas," Baptiste remarked sadly. "They think they are Spanish, whereas the Spanish consider them to be Arabs, and the Arabs here forget that they are really African. Humanity for them is like a burnt pot. They all want to be on the lighter end toward the top, because they know that the flames strike the bottom. But they forget that we are all cooking on the same fire, and whether it takes a minute or an hour, the heat redistributes perfectly and no one escapes."

"To dodging the flames as long as we can," Simon said, raising his bottle.

Baptiste clinked his beer against Simon's. "Speaking of which, how is it going with your Berber romance?"

"I think you're confusing one thing for the other," Simon replied hotly.

"That, *mon ami*, is a common mistake around here."

"Hmmm…" Simon said, eyeing the EO. "To be honest, we're from pretty different backgrounds and it's been causing some problems. Right now, things are a bit touch and go."

"You mean you touch and she goes?" Baptiste laughed jovially. "I have several relationships like that."

"More or less," Simon conceded, chuckling. "She'll be by later tonight. You can ask her then… Ah Nadia!"

Simon gave an energetic wave as Nadia emerged from behind a purple umbrella of light cast by a nearby Chinese lantern. She was wearing the same eye-catching red dress as the day he first met her, and she moved toward them with a sinuous, winding gait.

"You're here!" he inadvertently roared. His voice carried embarrassingly far on the rooftop.

"I said I'd come," she replied defensively.

"Is it one of the tenets of a free people to show up extraordinarily late?"

"The Amazigh arrive when the spirit moves them," she said, tossing back her head. "I'm sorry, but we were completely underwater at the hospital. Two of the nurses didn't show up and it was total chaos."

"Well I'm glad you're here."

She gave him an affectionate squeeze. Then she combed her fingers through his tangled mane. "Your hair's all wavy today."

"Yeah it's the humidity," he said self-consciously, ruffling it with his fingers.

"It's just like a lion. Makes you very Moroccan."

"How so?"

"Like the national team. The Lions."

"I'll take that as a compliment." He leaned in for a kiss. Her lips were soft pillows and he rested there until he heard Georg cough loudly. "Do you want something to drink?" he asked, rubbing her wrist.

"I'm fine."

"I know you're fine, but what do you want to drink?"

She looked at him sternly.

"Wine or beer?" he insisted.

"*Kif-kif.*" Her face was expressionless now and with her high cheekbones and angular features, it looked statuesque. Simon wondered for a moment if this was what had first attracted him to her. The proximity of her traits to that of a wooden mask.

"Is there any wine left for the lady?" Simon asked a stranger, who was fussing with the bottles on the table.

"Just enough for a glass," he replied. Simon held out a plastic cup and the stranger poured out the bottle. Then he glanced over at Nadia. "Last drop. Looks like you're getting married! Congrats."

She laughed gaily while Simon blushed. When he handed her the cup, her smile disappeared. "Why do you drink so much?" she asked.

Simon winked at Baptiste. Then he pulled Nadia aside beneath a red Chinese lantern, bathing them in a dramatic, fiery light.

"I didn't realize that what I drank was too much."

"It seems like a lot to me."

"Well, I guess these sorts of affairs make me thirsty and, in my profession, I find myself going to a lot of these affairs." He tried to take her hand but she pulled it away.

"Is this what you want to do with your life? Is this what your parents do?"

"What? Go to parties?" He grinned at her.

"No." She shook her lovely head, and her dark tresses waved like black kelp on the bottom of the sea. "I mean, do they do this sort of work as well?"

"Well my parents are diplomats, so they basically go to parties professionally."

"I'm being serious." She gave a moue of discontent. Then she sipped her wine and gazed at him expectantly. The scarlet glow of the Chinese lantern made him feel like they were in some cheap telenovela, so he took her gently by the elbow and moved them toward the parapet that ran along the edge of the roof.

"So am I," he said.

"You're working at the UN so you can go to fancy parties? That's your big dream?"

Simon gave her a wounded look. Then he turned and gazed out over the city. Before them, the rooftops of les Oudayas rose and fell like an ocean in tumult.

"Don't get me wrong," he said. "I really care about my work with the refugees." He put an arm around her shoulder and began combing his fingers through her abundant hair, watching it part in sinuous waves. "It's just that every additional day I spend at the HCR leaves me feeling slightly more cynical."

"Maybe it's because you think of them as 'the refugees.'"

"And how should I think of them?" he asked.

"They're not a category," she said, taking his hand. "They're individuals who need your help. You've begun to look at them as a task instead of a relationship. It happens to me to at the hospital sometimes."

"Except that you get to help everyone," Simon objected. A vision of the dying man in Takadoum, with his knobby frame and soiled compresses, danced before his eyes. "We spend half our time turning people away."

She let go of his hand and suddenly relocated under an overhanging trellis. A nearby lantern imbued her with a soft carmine glow. "This is not Europe," she asserted with a jangling wave of her wrist. "We only help those who can pay."

"Really?" he said, stepping after her. "What happened to your Hippocratic oath? Aren't you required to carry a snake on a stick or something?"

"I left it at home," she replied with a mischievous grin. "But if I had it with me, I'd throw the snake at you."

"Just what I would expect from a barbarian doctor." He tried to catch her in his arms, but she coiled her body and slid aside.

"Why are you so bothered by how the HCR treats its refugees?" Her green eyes flashed at him confrontationally. "The girls told me how you tried to keep Kinani from moving in when he needed a place to stay. What about *your* Hippocratic oath?"

Simon stared at her speechless. Then he began to pace angrily back and forth before the Chinese lantern, his red face aglow as if lit by some inner combustion. After a minute, he turned back toward Nadia, his eyes puffed like two balls of smoke. "Yeah, well, I didn't want to let a snake into my home."

He expected some sort of protest, or even a sharp intake of breath, but instead her features suddenly hardened. "Snakes are funny creatures," she replied in a wooden voice. "They can kill you or cure you. That's why doctors carry them on their staffs."

"So you know," he said accusingly.

"What do you mean?" For a tense eternity, he studied her face. Then she looked away.

"Everyone's got so many secrets around here," he muttered irritably. "Why didn't you tell me he was a refugee?"

She pivoted back toward him. "He didn't want you to know. And what does it matter? Especially to you." Her traits seemed altered in the crimson light, and Simon momentarily had the impression that he was arguing with a stranger.

"I'm just tired of everyone wearing all these goddam masks."

"The masks are in your head, Simon. Kinani is just a person who needed help. They all are. In his case, it was just a place to stay. You're the one who refused."

The blood drained from Simon's face. His forehead began pounding again and his ears filled with a noise not unlike the crashing of waves. He walked back to the parapet and leaned onto the shadowy railing, his body caved in the form of a dark vault. "Maybe you're right," he admitted grudgingly.

"Who told you?" she asked, placing a soft hand on his shoulder. His body tingled at her touch and he inclined into her curving form.

"Lise stumbled onto his file at the HCR, but I refused to read it. I'm tired of processing people."

"Are you going to confront him?"

"I would have to see him first." Simon gazed at her now with placid eyes. "Ever since we discovered he's a refugee, he's become invisible. Sometimes I hear footsteps late at night, but it feels like I'm living with a ghost. Has he mentioned anything to you?"

"He's been busy," she replied nervously. Then she leaned toward the empty blue and white lane below. "I think he may have had a fight with the girls, so he's been staying away from the apartment."

Simon was about to respond when a commotion broke out nearby and they both looked over. A group of well engineers from the French oil concern ELF had surrounded a French-Moroccan architect, whom Simon had met before. He could hear her mechanically repeating "*La, mabritch shokran*," and then just, "*La mabritch, mabritch*," while one of her girlfriends yelled at the men to back off.

Simon knew their ringleader, a burly fellow by the name of Bernard. He cycled through Rabat every few months, on the way back from exploratory digs in remote African jungles, and had briefly dated Alice from the Alliance Française. Now he was leaning over the architect like a pressurized derrick about to plunge. Simon hastened their way. As he drew close, he could hear the engineer cajoling, "Stay cool baby, we just want to have some fun."

"Hey Bernard," he interrupted, "this isn't the bush. Try to act like you're back in civilization again."

"Hmmph." Bernard surveyed the millennial-old fort with disdainful, assessing, eyes. "If that's what you call it." Then he grabbed Simon by the arm, jerking him forward with drunken force. "Mate, we've ordered some fun back to our place. There's a few extra birds if you want to join."

"Why are you inviting me?" Simon asked, surprised.

"*El janneh bala ness ma btendess*," he replied in heavily accented Arabic.

"What?"

"When in heaven, the more the merrier." Bernard gave a soused wink that creased his face into dozens of small furrows, like crumbling sediments of earth.

"Thanks but no thanks," Simon said. "Have fun drilling a bunch of underage Moroccan girls."

Bernard snorted. "It's all about resource extraction mate. We're the experts." He pushed away from Simon and turned to his mud crew. "Let's move out." There were a few grumbles, but the men began backing away. Simon watched them slink off the roof and then stormed back to Nadia.

"What was that all about?" she asked, concerned.

"Just a bunch of baboons acting like baboons." He waved his hands as if shooing away a pest. "Someone needs to send those guys back down a pit. It's where they belong. They're absolute predators."

"Like white people have always been in Africa."

"Sure. But these days, we're supposed to pretend that we're not." He kissed her on the top of her head. Then he surveyed the rooftop. Small galaxies of guests were whispering in hushed tones and no one was dancing. "Man, leave it to the oil boys to ruin a perfectly mediocre party."

She clucked her tongue. "You focus on the wrong things. The stars are there in the sky. You just have to look at them."

"Is that a line from a song?"

"Could be." She smiled becomingly and took his arm. They both gazed up at the heavens. Simon could see Orion's belt, and high above it, Aries glimmering softly not far from Pisces.

Just at that moment, the song "Aux Champs Elysees" began playing on the speakers and the effect was similar to raising the dead. The entire crowd from the Alliance Française gave delighted shouts and popped up to dance. Soon the lively melody took hold of the roof, its call irresistible.

Aux Champs-Elysées, aux Champs-Elysées
Au soleil, sous la pluie, à midi ou à minuit
Il y a tout ce que vous voulez aux Champs-Elysées

Hier soir deux inconnus et ce matin sur l'avenue
Deux amoureux tout étourdis par la longue nuit
Et de l'Étoile à la Concorde, un orchestre à mille cordes
Tous les oiseaux du point du jour chantent l'amour

Aux Champs-Elysées, aux Champs-Elysées
Au soleil, sous la pluie, à midi ou à minuit
Il y a tout ce que vous voulez aux Champs-Elysées

Several women were sashaying around and kicking up their heels, while couples spun out into the night like whirling dervishes.

The first chorus arrived, and half a dozen Fulbrighters raced over and began breathlessly shouting out the lyrics, their arms thrust high in the air, and even the *jeunesse doré* of Casablanca began to sing along, rich smiles painting their lips. Soon Simon heard Nadia's lush voice join in and intensify with such purity that it soared alone.

The crowds began intermingling as the partygoers tumbled hilariously about, catching each other in their arms, and Simon even saw the fractious Israelis laughing and gyrating, elbows interlocked with the chestnut-haired girl from L.A.

He wondered how many of them knew that the song was written by a Jewish kid from Brooklyn, and then he realized it didn't matter. It was a joyous song and it was good to be joyous once in a while. He enfolded

Nadia in his arms, and the two of them began flinging their feet beneath the firmament of stars, while the earth tilted out toward the moon and the ancient kasbah slumbered around them.

CHAPTER 42

FEBRUARY 2009

R
UMORS WERE SURGING THROUGH the refugee community.
Fifty of them had been resettled.

Fifty—out of the blue!

It was a stunning number, almost five percent of all the refugees in Morocco.
Arès was enraged. All these years he had suffered and he had not been
chosen. And when he found out who was—people hardly as ill or hard up as
himself! He knew he should have toadied up to the staff at the HCR, gone
to their training sessions, or signed up for one of their useless Arabic classes.

He caned into the kitchen, foul emotions buzzing in his head like a
swarm of flies. He needed tea. He needed a moment to think.

The sink was a mauve swamp of dishwater and soiled pots. He hesitated
for a moment, and then with an amphibian hop, plunked his right hand
into the marsh and fished out a small blue kettle. Using a half-blackened
sponge, he scrubbed it to a sort of acceptable dinginess. Mechanically, his
limbs set about brewing a pot of mint tea while he mulled over the news.

Two spoons of gunpowder tea from China. Wash. Soak. Boil. Purge
water. Reboil. A fistful of mint. Three white fortresses of sugar.

He sat on the couch, sipping the saccharine stuff, trying to tease some
sense out of the world. While he thought, he absentmindedly spun the
glass in his palm and was comforted by its dependable equilibriums.

How was it possible? He knew almost all the members of the refugee
community, whether in person or through hearsay. Resettlement, he knew,
was only accorded on the basis of medical need. By the HCR's own criteria,
he was one of the worst cases around.

He sipped the tea, the gears of his mind whirring silently, letting each sugary sip flow down to his stomach, fueling his thoughts.

He sat up. Either they were lying about their selection process or... His arm violently hurled the tea glass against the kitchen counter. The metal band running along the counter's edge disemboweled the glass, sending its belly bouncing across the linoleum tiles.

A suspicion had slithered out of some subterranean crevice in his mind and bloated so large that he thought his skull might crack.

"Salifou!" It could be no one else. The room smoldered before him as if caked in fire. The goatherder had gone to the HCR and told them he had lied. This was why they hadn't resettled him. There was no proof either way, but they certainly were not going to resettle a suspected murderer.

One of his flatmates popped out of his bedroom. "What is going on?" Then he saw the shards of glass on the floor. "What is this? What are you doing?" he shouted.

Arès did not even see him, did not respond. Everything crackled and smoked around him.

Scheming behind his back to ruin his chances for resettlement! As if what he had done hadn't been enough! He should have killed Salifou at PALS. He should kill him now.

His family's murderer had resurfaced, and Arès had eaten his sandwich. And now he was paying for it.

An enormous violence seethed within him.

That evening, the more active members of the refugee community convened a meeting in the gardens abutting the Fondation Oriental. There were nearly a hundred of them, pushing about in a mêlée of grief-making. Some of them talked of picketing the HCR. Others said they should burn the building down.

Arès arrived late. His thoughts still bore the embers of the morning's violence and he looked out at the world through a veil of soot. Beneath a leaden, starless sky, he plodded toward the gathering. Every time he threw his weight onto his cane, he could feel the stubby kitchen knife slide beneath his belt.

He had spent the entire afternoon plotting the goatherder's death. He knew there was no way he could overpower Salifou in a straight fight, and that asking around for his address would only arouse suspicion. But in a large crowd, especially at night, Arès could sneak up behind him, and maybe, when Salifou was distracted and no one was looking, he could have his revenge. He had to be careful though; he would not survive years in a Moroccan jail, not in the condition he was in.

Cold gusts blew across the grounds, and Arès wrapped his meager coat tight about his frame. Only two lamp posts were lit, and before him wavered a confusing jumble of shadows and silhouettes. He scanned the crowd from afar in vain, and then gingerly advanced.

He was halfway across the garden when he caught sight of the murderer, gesturing vigorously at the center of a small commotion.

"You see!" Salifou was shouting, "They can resettle anyone they want. They have been lying to us!"

"No. They have criteria. They can only resettle certain people," a refugee named Emilie from the Congo shouted back. She was a large woman with coppery skin and a well-molded face that commanded respect.

The crowd erupted into jeers and hollering. Arès edged closer to Salifou. Thirty meters to go.

A tide of angry faces washed before him. He was devising a way through them when twenty noses suddenly tacked to the right. A few steps away, the group of Ivorians from PALS were causing a ruckus.

Over the past few months, Arès had learned some of their names. The man with the larval sprouts of hair went by Fofana, and every word he uttered shocked into the crowd. "We should protest in front of the HCR until they resettle all of us! The people they resettled do not even fit their criteria. They just resettle their friends!"

"They have criteria. They only resettle for medical emergencies," a voice yelled from behind Arès.

"No! They only resettle the *good* refugees. The rest of us are just a paycheck," Fofana blared back.

"They are making money off of us!" another man shouted.

"What do you mean?" Laurent, a refugee from the Congo, quietly asked.

The crowd hushed. Laurent was one of the earliest refugees to be recognized by the HCR, and his words carried special weight. His sad eyes and soft demeanor seemed a testament to his many years of hardship in the Maghreb.

"They need refugees to get paid," a tall man replied. "If they resettled all of us, they would no longer have a job."

Arès was standing beside Laurent and he felt an irrepressible urge to speak. "I do not know," he said. "I was told that I had to make a formal request to be resettled."

Fofana cried out again. "No. We know who was resettled. There was Rachelle. She was not even sick. There was Yendi. He was not sick either. All he was missing was a finger. They have no criteria!"

The shouting revived and Arès crept onward. Fifteen meters to Salifou.

"They resettled children too," a shadow cried from the back. "Children who can work."

"Jean-Baptiste was resettled. He was Abdellah's best friend."

"They are holding us prisoner!"

"I wrote a letter and they did not offer me an interview!"

"What about our rights?"

Five meters to go. His hand slid onto the stubby knife.

Another Ivorian named Doumba stood on a stone bench and shouted over the brouhaha. "Everyone should formally request resettlement. Then we will see if they are honest."

Voices shouted him down. "Sit-in! Sit-in!"

Two meters to go.

Doumba waived two pathetically thin arms above his head. "We must stay calm!" he pleaded. "Stay calm!"

Arès was standing behind him now. The syrupy smell of cheap cologne wafted off Salifou's neck, and he wrinkled his nose in disgust. It would have to be a clean blow, through the back, straight to the heart. His hand tightened around the blade.

Suddenly Salifou cried over the lot, "Burn the HCR down! Let's set it ablaze! Then see if they ignore us!"

Arès raised the knife as a chorus of affirmative shouts burst like plumes of ash from the mouths around him. He had heard the same ugly noises, looked at the same contorted lips, his final night in Kinshasa. More cries ignited on all sides and blasted him back to that time when even the cool riverbanks spat with fire and the water was just more fuel for the flames.

Had it started like this in Zaire? All these incendiary, sulfurous words? He had never gone to the government rallies, had never concerned himself with politics. But he imagined it had been similar. A pack of rabid animals, snarling with slights real or imagined, looking for something, someone, to unleash their madness onto.

He could not let what happened in Kinshasa replicate itself in Rabat.

His hand paused in the air like a viper ready to strike. A flood of chanting rose around him: "Burn it down! Burn it down! Burn it down!"

No one was looking at Salifou now. This was his chance. Cold sweat beaded on his brow, and he thought of his father. He thought of Félix and Yika, and all their wild promise and unrealized dreams; of his mother he would never see again; and his younger siblings who would never have a chance to grow up.

He thought of his countless years of suffering. Of his broken body and all his broken hopes.

He thought of his words to Buisha on the night he was let out of prison, and Guli's death, and all the meaningless carnage he had seen on the road to Rabat, which was the road to Europe. He thought of Kiwaka's unflappable good cheer and of Paul's boundless kindness.

Then, suddenly, he was back at the race in Nonloso, the race he had won, whose prize was the punishment of exile; and there he was, making his mighty leap off the coruscated tree, all by himself, while Salifou and Diomandé washed downstream and others went to save them. He remembered tumbling into that mighty river, and feeling the water press hard against his breath, and the sensation of being swallowed up whole until a hand hoisted him toward the drought of the sky, saved by that selfless yoke of runners—his rivals, his saviors—who brought him across that body of water to the other side.

The knife slipped out of his hand and tumbled onto the arid ground. He could not do it.

He lurched to the edge of the crowd and collapsed onto the curling roots of an acacia tree, gasping in the frigid air. It might mean betraying his family, betraying even himself, but he did not have the strength. Whatever Salifou had done to him, was still doing, he could not add another body to the count.

The chanting continued unabated. Gradually, Arès caught his breath. He took a rag out of his pocket and wiped his brow. Doumba had relocated to a bench beneath one of the functioning lamp posts and was shouting himself hoarse. "Use your heads!" he cried over and over. "Use your heads!"

Astonishingly, this time, the refugees quieted down. "Write in the letters that we know they can resettle everyone," Doumba urged with the remnants of his voice. "Tell them it is our turn to be resettled. They can no longer resettle only their friends! We do not care about their jobs."

"We have rights!" someone brayed from the back.

"Resettlement!" someone else shouted.

For a moment, it seemed that Doumba had carried the day. Then a short while later, the fracas rose again. It was the natural anarchy of an accidental community; all these anonymous souls washed up on the shores of Rabat, borne in the wake of a thousand flukes and calamities. Now they were bound together by place, by shared exile, and by collective suffering. But there was no one to lead them, no principles to guide them.

Even the dependable placeholders, the machineries of tribe and nationality, had broken down. Though an instinctive rift divided the Congolese from the Ivorians, each faction was itself riddled by the innate distrust of individuals who barely knew each other and who seldom interacted.

Even more, they were riven by jealousy, of those who received more financial assistance, of those who were accorded micro-projects, or who were close (or seen to be close) to the employees of the HCR and, most of all, of those who had managed to be resettled.

For the moment, moderation prevailed. Doumba rallied the Ivorians, while Laurent padded about, placating the Congolese, calming them with his quiet, prudent words.

Unobtrusively, Arès rejoined the crowd. He felt hollow and light-headed, and resignation had wrapped itself around his heart like a net. As far as he could tell, no one had seen a thing.

CHAPTER 43

MARCH–JUNE 2009

O VER THE NEXT FEW weeks, the refugees established working groups to draft letters to the HCR. A number of them had worked as civil servants for now-defunct governments and the petitions they produced were surprisingly eloquent. Arès reread his letter several times before mailing it, exulting in its subtle phrases and measured judicial airs.

Then he settled in to wait.

Piecemeal, over the months that followed, the refugees received negative responses. But it was not until May that even half of them had heard back, and of that fortunate fifty percent, more than two-thirds were summoned to the HCR to explain gaps or contradictions in their files, with hearings scheduled to take place between June and August.

To keep up the pressure on the U.N., Doumba and Fofana organized phone banks. Half a dozen to a dozen refugees gathered in apartments throughout Rabat and telephoned the bureau repeatedly to inquire about the status of their resettlement petitions.

The responses varied, but the message was always the same: "The HCR does not offer resettlement as a durable solution." Or, "local integration is the only durable solution." Or, "the HCR will contact you for a resettlement interview if it believes that your file has a chance of success with one of the resettlement countries."

"Liars!"

Their frustration mounted. The bureaucrats at the HCR obstinately pretended that resettlement was out of their hands; that the European governments were the sole gatekeepers to salvation. Yet there was this sudden fifty, all of them buddied up with the HCR, all of them now on permanent holiday overseas.

The refugees began to mobilize.

The phone rang.

"Yes?"

"Arès, it is Laurent. We are having a strategy session and we would like you to join us."

"When is it?"

"Tomorrow afternoon, during the *Asr* prayers."

"Ah, I am busy then."

"I think you should find a way to come."

Arès leaned over and massaged the hard shell of flesh around his foot. It had been throbbing painfully all morning, probably due to the recent humidity. After a moment, he responded. "What do you need me for? I am handicapped. I would not be of any use."

"All the better. *C'est la petite tortue qui trompe le lion.*[67] I think you could be very helpful."

Arès smiled and thought of Buisha. His friend had wanted to fight back too, but Arès had talked him out of it. Now he was dead. He could hear Buisha call to him across that uncrossable distance and urge him to join the other refugees. But he shook his head.

"If you look at me, you will see that I have not been so clever in the past."

There was a slight pause on the other end of the line.

"Arès, it is for you that we are meeting. If anyone should have been resettled, it should have been you. No one is worse off in Morocco than you."

"I do not know." Arès fingered the golden key around his neck. It was difficult to resist Laurent's coaxing. "I have had so much trouble here already. I do not want any more. My father always said, *tu marches sur une bûche et la marmite se renverse.*"[68]

---

67 It is the little turtle who tricks the lion.
68 You walk on a log and you spill the pot.

"Yes, my friend, but *les pirogues chavirent même en eau calme.*"[69]

Arès chuckled. "Yes, this I know."

"Then you will come?"

There was a long silence on the end of the line. The throbbing was fiercer now and the pain came and went like the slow build and crash of waves. "I cannot, my friend. I would like to, but it is impossible right now. I have suffered enough."

Ah, I see," Laurent said. "*Un serpent t'a mordu, tu auras peur d'un bout de corde.*"[70]

"Yes."

"Well, then I will call you next week, and the week after. Not to harass you, but perhaps your courage will find its roots again."

Arès put down the phone.

Like he had promised, Laurent tried to recruit him a week later, and the week after that.

Arès was as furious as the others, perhaps even more so, but the HCR was his last hope. He knew that he was one of the worst injured in their roster, and he suspected that the coming protests would convince them to resettle more refugees, among whom he hoped to number.

That is, if he wasn't blacklisted already.

Shortly after Laurent contacted him for the first time, Arès telephoned the HCR in a panic and tried to find out whether Salifou had denounced him. The Protection Officer on the line informed him in a slightly bored tone that without substantial and corroborated evidence, the HCR did not consider accusations by one refugee against another.

He had trouble believing her. He knew things did not work that way. But there was nothing he could do.

The refugees continued to hold their weekly meetings and write their petitions without him. Hundreds strong, they tugged against destiny with all the stubbornness of a hippopotamus, and the HCR resisted with all its elephantine might.

---

69   A canoe can capsize even in calm water.
70   If a snake has bitten you, you will be afraid of a piece of rope.

Arès watched and waited. Whenever Laurent tempted him with a phone call and a bit of flattery, he thought of Buisha's clever little turtle and kept to the sidelines.

He would let them duke it out themselves.

Life pattered mercilessly on.

Every morning, Arès made the rounds of his neighborhood, looking to pick up odd jobs. If there was no work to be done, he hermitted alone in his room or caned to the shore, hoping to tranquilize his thoughts.

The news of the fifty resettlements had reawakened his bitterness. Europe lay just over the horizon, but it could be on the far side of the moon for all that it mattered. Day after day, he sat on the yellow sands and seethed with injury, while the waves curled before him like long, mocking grins.

He was walking to the *plage de Salé* one evening, when he noticed a dog limping shyly behind him. Its mangy fur was pocketed with bald patches and sores, and its eyes were clouded with a grayish haze. The mark of death was upon it.

"What are you looking for, mutt? Why are you following me?" Arès asked and caned onward, trying to lose the animal in the tangled medina lanes. When he neared the beach, he looked back and was glad not to see it. Then he felt it rub against his healthy leg.

"I have even less than you, stupid dog." He dug into his pocket and felt a hardened clump of bread. "Take this, from one dead beggar to another."

The mutt bounded onto the bread and gnawed it apart with bonecrack snaps.

"Look at you, dog. You don't have much time left, do you? One year? Two? This is what Morocco is, a dying dog's life. You're trapped here, but I'm leaving. You'll leave too, of course. But not the way I'm going."

They walked onto the beach and he knelt down and clutched the dog by its ears. Fleas hopped onto his hands and the air reeked with the animal's breath. "I am promising you something now, *Monsieur le chien*, I will leave before you do."

The dog wrested itself from Arès' hands and scampered onto nearby ruins, where it began to yap. Arès turned away and moved toward the water, crouching just beyond its moist rim. The waves hurled themselves up the sloping sands, and every time they scraped back down, the ocean gave off a great gasping sigh that matched his sullen mood.

"What hope was there, really?" He sighed in turn and looked down at his bulging foot. With his finger he began to draw phrases in Darija, hoping to distract his thoughts.

"*Ana kayeen ph bhr diel Salé*," he wrote. Then he tried with Arabic lettering, from right to left: انا كين في بحر ديال صلا

"*Mohet*," he drew, looking out at the sea. مهت

"*Fin Ana? Chkoun ana?*" he carved in the buttery sands. فن انا سكون انا The dog began to howl, breaking his concentration. He picked up a stone and was about to fling it, when the animal cringed and whimpered loudly. He put the stone down again.

There were countless strays like this, worm-ridden, half-rabid, slinking through the cracked streets of Rabat. He sometimes found their carcasses tucked away in soiled alleys or picked clean on the beach, their ribs splayed open in a devilish grin. There was never anyone to mourn them. "A wounded animal always dies alone," Arès muttered to himself, and for the first time he wondered what he would do if he wasn't resettled.

Would he end up like one of these mutts? Wasn't he halfway there already? He sucked his teeth in horror and gazed out at the graveyard of the sea.

That is, unless he went home.

Home. He dug his forefinger into the sand and drew a long, winding line in the direction of the sea. Around it, he carved the contours of Africa, and at Africa's center, a wide river with a city by its side. For a moment, he regarded his handiwork. Then he swept his palm across the image, blurring it beyond recognition.

What home was there anymore? For so many years, he had been propelled ahead by his pledge to Paul and by the bright dreams of the travelers he had met on his way: the Kiwakas, the Gulis, the Buishas. To just turn around and slink back to Kinshasa with his tail between his legs? His chest constricted and his mouth felt dry. Everything within him rebelled at the idea.

He knew, though, of refugees who had gone back. Many were from the Ivory Coast, after the war's end. But there were others too, fished out of the sea on their way to Spain, unable to gain a foothold on the rocky slopes of the Maghreb, broken by the strenuous combat of exile. And whenever their resolve had faltered, the United Nations was there, peddling free passage home. For reasons that were obscure to Arès, from time to time, the HCR and its local partners quietly encouraged repatriation.

"The situation has changed, Mr. Sbigzneou," the U.N. representative had informed him during his last status update, while he stared, incensed, at the floor. "The Banyamulenge are quite safe in the DRC and you could rebuild your life there. The IOM offers free transportation by plane in addition to a stipend to help you adjust."

"I cannot get treatment in Kinshasa!" Arès had slammed the flat of his palm against the table. "This is a question for resettlement."

"The process is entirely voluntary," she had responded in a plodding, bureaucratic tone. "We understand that you are having issues integrating locally, and we want you to be aware of all your options."

He had stomped out of the HCR like a wild elephant, but now he wondered if she had been right. Would he stay on indefinitely in Rabat, growing weaker by the year, until he crawled into an alleyway to die alone?

Wouldn't life be easier among people who spoke his language and in a place where he could work? Perhaps his father's locksmithery had even survived. He dreamt of it often, its gate still rolled down and locked, with all of its tools inside, waiting for him to return. He fantasized about leaning over the counter on rue Lobo, older now, crippled, but dignified. Not an errand boy, but a professional with a trade. And who knew what girl might wander down that street and see him for the man of destiny he once was?

The thought lifted him up on a great wave of happiness. He was coasting along, imaging his triumphant return to the *marché* in Nonloso, the excited gasps of his neighbors, the head scratching of the old men. The wave crested higher and he saw himself recounting his travels to laughing, astonished friends, and even to Christelle, why not? And then another journey to his relatives in South Kivu—he still had kin after all, and who knew what surprises he might find there? The wave crested higher and higher, lofting him toward heaven, until the smell of hot sulfur flooded his nostrils and something recoiled deep in his guts. The wave evaporated beneath him.

Arès turtled his back over the sands. Minutes passed while he wheezed for breath. Gradually, he righted himself. His head was pounding and he could feel sweat sizzle down his spine. His vision slowly cleared.

No. That way was closed. It was not merely the ghosts that awaited him among the ashes in Kinshasa. It was not even the indignity of return. Over the years, an imperceptible change had taken place. He wondered if Paul had somehow infected him with his roaming intelligence, or if his brother Félix had first planted the seed. He knew only that he now belonged to this lawless, marauding world with all its barbaric beauty. He wanted to stand before the gates of Europe and behold their shining capitals. He wanted to see his father's prophecy fulfilled.

He mourned inwardly for that bright, happy boy he had been, content with his keys and the comforting dimensions of his locksmithery. Charmed by the thought of a local girl and a local life. But if all that could be restored to him, it would never be enough.

And with that realization came another. He had to get out of Rabat, foot or no foot. The HCR had led him into a labyrinth, and they would keep pulling him around by the nose until he succumbed.

The sunset burned over Salé, and Arès watched gold drip into the sea and scattered gulls whipper across a saffron sky. The first stars punctured the dark band of the horizon. Then night pressed close with its whispers of hidden dangers.

His thoughts drifted back to his first days in Dongo, so many years before. He had felt cornered then too, his right leg smashed, the villagers menacing him with death. He remembered Bugingo's eerie nocturnal visit and his dire warnings. Across so much time, the elder's words came back to him: "The fish will have to learn to swim harder."

Arès looked intently at the blackening waters. "The fish will have to swim harder," he repeated out loud.

And so it was, while the other refugees readied the engines of war, Arès decided to teach himself how to swim.

The next afternoon, he returned to the *plage de Salé*.

Clad only in a secondhand pair of FIFA shorts, he stood before the gray-blue sheen of the sea, the sky metallic with clouds. Long combers rolled gently in and even the ashen sands charmed him with their sprouts of golden ragwort. Beside him lay a small pile of tattered clothes, pitiful worn things that no one, not even the desperate, would filch.

His body shifted left onto the continental swell of his foot. Bulging around the ankle and tapering down to his swollen toes, it looked like a three-dimensional model of Africa and felt nearly as heavy.

He thought about what it would mean never to run again. Never again to dance. His hand clenched into a fist and he punched it hard against the coarse sand. His breath came sharp and heavy, and an inconsolable sadness constricted his chest.

He forced himself to calm. He had to get used to not healing. This was life. Things would never be the same. He had to move on.

Then he remembered Buisha's clever little turtle and smiled briefly. His friend was gone, and he was as slow as a turtle now. But the turtle could still come out on top. He discarded his cane and turtled into the sea.

He had no sense of how to swim. For an instant, his body floated near the surface and then it sunk. His arms slapped frantically, comically, lofting blue-gray arcs of liquid into the air. He stood up, panting. A deep breath, and he floundered down again.

The water teethed around his light frame. Children giggled on the beach as he sputtered and drowned and flopped like a wounded fish. Try as he might, he could not subdue the downward momentum of his foot. Yet a stubbornness egged him on. He gave the entire afternoon to his scupperings, and by the end felt no nearer to swimming than when he had begun.

He was depressed as he climbed out of a salmon-colored sea. But his thoughts were clearer and the heat of the day had worn down, so that he and the world found themselves in the same state of pleasant exhaustion.

He settled his wet frame onto the sands and watched the sea secrete stars into the sky. He received as given all the marvelous beauty of the world, but it struck him how indifferent, even hostile, it was; how little this beauty cared if he lived or died. Then he stretched out a hand, seeking a fluttering luminescent thing called happiness, and gave a cry.

Over the following days, he fed his body again and again into the sea. For once, he was lucky. On his fourth attempt, a young man named Kareem strolled by on the shore. Mistaking Arès' flailings for a signal of distress, he jumped in the ocean to save him.

"Are you trying to drown yourself?" Kareem asked as he hoisted the refugee out of the water.

"Let me go," Arès said. "I am fine. I am teaching myself how to swim."

"That is not swimming, *Khouya*," he exclaimed. "I have seen men without arms stay afloat better than you."

"My leg is injured, and I have no one to show me how," Arès replied indignantly.

"I will help you," Kareem said. "It is an affront to water to see how you swim." The stranger smiled brightly as he spoke, and it occurred to Arès that he meant well. The refugee smiled in return.

Kareem was a friend of the Rastas and half Berber. Arès had seen him before, playing guitar on the beach, singing lilting Gnawa songs in an uncommonly resonant voice that reminded him of his lost friend Kiwaka.

From that day onward, they met once a week on the sands of Salé. It was Kareem's idea to lasso the shipwreck of his foot to a small Styrofoam buoy.

"Now you look like a real turtle," Kareem said, when he had finished preparing the contraption.

Arès laughed heartily. If only Buisha could see me now, he thought. Then he slipped into the sea. Kareem supported the refugee with his hands, leading him through the proper mechanics of the freestyle stroke.

Over time, Arès mastered the motions: the circumflex of his arm above the ribs, the slide of his hand along his neck and over his ear, the reach for Europe, the angled push back as his torso gyrated onto its other side, and the whip up and over as his hand spurted from water to air and flung forward past his head.

When Kareem was not there, Arès trained by himself. In the water, he forgot his handicap. He could not kick as effectively as he would like, but his leg did not burden him like it did on land. He could swim for hours now, alternating between strumming sprints and the monotony of distance strokes. It felt good to have muscles sore at the end of the day; to feel the glide of tendons within his limbs; to remember something of his agile youth, of all that he had lost.

PART III

"IT'S REALLY A BAD case."

"What?" Simon asked nonchalantly. He looked up at Camille, who was sharing a cigarette with Khadija on the terrace. When she didn't immediately reply, he resumed stirring the leafy green stalks of mint in his tea, as if hoping to divine the answer.

Camille took several long drags on the cigarette, rolling serpentine curls of smoke around her tongue before exhaling. "A Congolese refugee with a lame foot the size of a melon," she finally replied. "Fatima and I conducted a status update on him this morning and I couldn't believe it. When I was interning here as a student, I took notes during an F-O visit to his domicile. Now I'm back, almost two years later, and he's still limping around on the same injured foot."

She took another heavy drag, and then snorted two impressive jets of smoke from her nostrils. Dressed in a khaki sleeveless dress and black leggings, she had shoulder-length hair, coffee-colored eyes and a gamine face that was at odds with her fuming indignation. She had assumed her post as a U.N. Volunteer a few weeks prior, but Simon hadn't realized that she was a former intern.

"Funny," he said, "I conducted a resettlement interview for a refugee with a similar foot problem. Was he from Kinshasa?"

"You conducted his resettlement interview!" she exclaimed. "Did you submit an RRF on his behalf?"

Simon straightened up self-consciously in his chair. "Well, no. Dr. Dji-deree assured me that his condition was being expertly treated by PALS."

"What?" the former intern cried. "You believed a word that came out of Dr. Djideree's mouth? PALS is a stockyard for refugees. Their idea of medicine is giving aspirin to someone who's having a heart attack!"

Simon looked at Khadija, hoping for assistance. She inhaled deeply on the cigarette and released an uncooperative cloud of smoke. "So his foot hasn't healed?" he inquired meekly.

"His foot is scheduled to heal the same day that Europe opens its borders."

"Ok. Ok. Understood." Simon felt a twinge of remorse. "What's going on with his case?"

"You tell me. You're handling it."

"I'm not the one in charge around here," he replied defensively.

"I spoke with the other people in his flat, and they all say the same thing. He's spent every day at the beach for months now, training to swim to Spain."

"What? That's insane!" Simon pushed to his feet, accidentally knocking over his glass. The sugary tea swept across the tabletop like an incoming tide. He swore and blotted at it with his napkin.

"What would you do in his place?" she demanded. "Die a cripple in the streets of Rabat? It's as mad to stay as to swim. He probably won't make it, but at least he won't finish in an unmarked grave in a dirt field somewhere." She glared at him now, half balanced on the pointed arch of her toes as if ready to lunge.

"No. He'll have all the beauty of the Mediterranean to contemplate for eternity," Simon replied, unable to keep the disgust out of his voice. "It sounds very romantic."

An image of a decaying Kinani, trammeled in seaweed at the bottom of the sea, flashed through his mind and he gritted his teeth. Ever since he had discovered his flatmate's past, he couldn't help but think of him in conjunction with the other refugees. And the refugees' myriad fates, by the crushing force of proximity, had begun to concern him as well.

"Well, we have to stop him," Simon concluded.

"Stop him!" She stomped her foot against the white terrace. "I want to give him swimming lessons."

"Camille," Khadija interjected, darting Simon a circumspect glance. "Maybe not now."

Simon ignored her. "Do you know which beach he's been swimming at?"

"So you can do what?" she sneered, her eyes full of contempt. "Denounce him to the police? Have him thrown in a Moroccan jail where he'll be lawfully beaten to death instead of inconveniently drowning at sea?"

Simon sighed. They had to stop hiring these zealots in the community services division at the HCR. "I was hoping we could walk over together and talk some sense into him. He could at least try to cross on a boat like all the other crazies out there. No reason to be exceptionally insane and swim."

"You can do whatever you want. I'm going to Kenitra to bring a former child soldier to counseling." She snubbed out the cigarette on the white table.

"Kenitra? That'll take you hours."

"To save a life is to save all of humanity." She stared at him defiantly, her body still wound like a spring.

"It's humanity who created this mess!" he shouted.

Khadija and Camille gave him apprehensive looks. "Sorry," he said, tugging at his collar. "The heat's getting to me today. Just tell me the name of the beach, and I promise you, I'll go back through his file and see if we can revive his resettlement claim in light of this compelling new evidence."

"He swims in Salé," Camille said curtly, and then bounded off the terrace. Khadija glanced at Simon with a hangdog, "I'm sorry" expression, followed by a friendly wave, before trailing her out.

Simon walked down the hall to see Hilda. Her door was propped open, so he stepped into the spacious office. A fluted vase on the stained-wood desk was crowded with white Casablanca lilies, and several flowery bouquets lay in a triangular stack on the floor. The overpowering floral fragrance tickled his nose and he sneezed.

Hilda held up a finger, a telephone pressed against her ear. "No. No! The cedar is for the railings. The railings! Yes." She paced in a tight circle and then stepped toward a window and disappeared into a blinding nimbus of light. "Two weeks!" Simon heard her cry. She hung up the phone and stepped back into sight, her hands clasped before her.

"I'm sorry, but we're adding a deck to our beach house in Skhirat and, well, these Moroccan laborers..." She exhaled expressively. "Let's just say they lack a certain Dutch efficiency."

"Sorry to bother you," Simon said, "but may I grab the Resettlement Handbook for an hour or two?"

"Please! Take anything you need. There's a whole reference library over there." She pointed to the formidable bookcase that dominated the far side of the office.

"Thank you." Simon lifted the compact manual off a nearby table. "I think this will be enough."

"Oh and take a lily. Or two! One of the ministers dropped off a hundred of them and I've been handing them out to everyone." She thrust two delicate green stalks into his hands, their bell-shaped crowns drooping toward the floor.

"Thank you," he said, gently cradling them above the blue manual. She beamed graciously at him and waved as he strode out the door.

Simon had the office to himself that day. After setting the lilies down on his desk, he leaned back in his chair and flipped open the handbook. Quickly, he scanned through the resettlement categories: Survivors of Torture, Children at Risk, Women at Risk, Family Reunification, Physical Protection, Medical Needs and Lack of Foreseeable Alternative Durable Solutions or LFADS.

"They should come up with better acronyms," he muttered. Then he opened the handbook to the chapter describing Medical Needs:

For resettlement submissions under the Medical Needs category all of the following conditions must be met:

1. Diagnosis: The health condition and/or disability is life-threatening without proper treatment; or there is a risk of irreversible loss of functions without proper treatment; or the particular situation/environment in the country of asylum is the reason for or significantly worsens the health condition.

2. Treatment: Adequate treatment is not available or is inaccessible in the country of asylum; and adequate treatment cannot be ensured through temporary medical evacuation to a third country.

3. Prognosis: The health condition and/or disability presents a significant obstacle to leading a normal life, becoming well adjusted,
and from functioning at a satisfactory level, and puts the individual
at heightened risk in the country of asylum; and there is a favorable
prognosis that treatment and/or residence in the country of resettlement
would significantly improve the health condition and/or disability or
lead to an improvement in daily functioning and quality of life.

The refugee's condition appeared to satisfy categories two and three, but he wasn't sure if it was serious enough to meet the threshold for category one. What's more, Simon had forgotten all the cautionary wording about "the complexity and difficulty in promoting the resettlement of persons with medical needs" and the requirement for an independent clinical practitioner to complete the Medical Assessment Form, which would mean Dr. Djideree.

The refugee's dossier would need a thorough review before bothering the doctor. Simon grabbed the lilies, thinking he could offer them to Lise, and hopped down the winding central staircase to the ground floor. The temperature had spiked outside and a distorting haze shimmered above the white tiles of the courtyard. After taking a deep breath, he pushed out the door.

The sun swung at Simon like a hammer. He sprinted up the smoldering steps, ignoring the friendly greetings from the Swiss intern, and practically leapt toward the front office. "Phewww," he said, as the air-conditioning lapped its cool tongue over him. Wiping his brow, he closed the door.

Lise and Nathalie appeared to have stepped out, but Ibrahim was indefatigably present. Simon tried to recall if he had ever stopped by the front office without seeing the man, dependable as a fixture, thundering into his phone. Only this time, he sat slumped in his chair. His eyes were puffy and red, and a thick finger, coarse with black hairs, was in the process of rubbing a tear off his cheek.

"What's the matter?" Simon asked.

Ibrahim looked up startled. After a moment, he spoke, his voice gravelly with emotion. "A boat went down in the Mediterranean yesterday and I just found out that two of our refugees, Michaux and Kylian, were on it."

"And you were crying because of that?" Simon asked with undisguised surprise.

"Of course I was." Ibrahim scowled at him. "I've known Michaux for years. He was a very good man and his life was finally improving. We spoke two weeks ago, and I warned him not to take the risk. I even promised to help him if he got into trouble."

Simon blushed. "I'm sorry. I really didn't mean any offense. It's just that you're always so harsh with the refugees on the phone."

Ibrahim coughed gently and dried his cheeks. "I yell at them for their own good. They have to comply with procedure, or else we can't help them. Michaux used to complain that I broke his eardrums every time he called." He smiled ruefully. "The refugees have been through so much. It's so easy for them to become apathetic. I can be confrontational, but that doesn't mean I don't care about them. Why else would I do this job? Do you think I dream of shouting myself hoarse every day?"

"No, of course not," Simon mumbled.

"This is the fifth drowning we've had this year, and summer's barely begun. It's so awful. I keep telling them it's too dangerous to cross on those little dinghies."

"I'm sorry for your loss," Simon said, gently laying the lilies on the table in front of him.

Ibrahim looked up surprised. "It's our loss. Every time a refugee dies, we are all concerned."

Simon nodded and pushed open the heavy studded door to the dossier room. This time he located the refugee's file with ease. He removed the pink folder and began spreading the documents over the top of the metal filing cabinet. Something caught on his hand, and he casually brushed off a spider's thread. He looked up to see an immense tessellation of cobwebs spanning the top right corner of the vault. An albino spider, the size of an outstretched hand, appeared to be suspended on glittering filaments of light. Simon observed it carefully for a moment, and then turned back to the dossier.

He dug through a pile of medical reports and several rejected microfinancing applications before fishing out the F-O visit from a couple years back. There were complaints of inadequate treatment and even irregularities when it came to PALS' bookkeeping, but he wasn't sure if neglect by a UNHCR partner constituted sufficient grounds for resettlement. Judging from the recent status update, also bearing Camille's name, it was clear that the refugee's condition was worsening at best.

Simon parsed through the farrago of papers. Looking at his very first resettlement interview, he cringed at his errors of judgment. Curious to see who had conducted the original RSD, he mined deeper into the past.

The induction had been handled by some intern he didn't know. The refugee status determination was conducted by... he flipped a few pages ahead... Baptiste. Baptiste! His eyes shot wide. It was Baptiste who had convinced him that the refugee's story was bunk.

He laid the folder down, his chest constricted with anger. When he looked up again, he nearly jumped out of his skin. The albino spider had silently crept off and was nowhere to be seen.

He stormed down the hall to the main office and yanked open the frosted door. No one looked up. Only three of the seven employees were present, placidly typing away at their computers. Simon leaned into the office.

"Baptiste. Can I speak to you for a moment?"

"You are speaking to me, *mon ami*," he replied with glittering eyes.

"Yes, well, how about we grab a tea on the terrace?"

"The mint upsets my stomach, but in the name of friendship, I will join you."

The two men walked up the stairs. When they drew close to the outdoor terrace, a torrid blast of air nearly stopped them in their tracks.

"I received some unpleasant news about a refugee we both know," Simon said, when they had sat down beneath the wiry shade of the olive tree.

"Do you ever receive any pleasant news about a refugee?" Baptiste asked, cracking open a can of cherry cola. "Except that one has succeeded in illegally crossing into Europe?"

"You are sounding very cynical, my friend."

"I'm just a realist."

"Do you remember my first resettlement interview? It was with a Congolese refugee, who survived the Kinshasa attacks of 1998."

"Ah, our fisherman friend. How could I forget someone so passionate about his sport that he spent six years of his life doing only that."

"Right," Simon replied, in no mood for Baptiste's clowning. "Apparently, the injury he sustained to his left foot has continued to worsen in spite of the diligent ministrations of Dr. Djideree and our local partner PALS."

Baptiste trained his gleaming eyes on Simon. "That is not news. News would suggest something surprising or new. If you had informed me that the sun had risen this morning, I could not be less surprised."

"I was reviewing his file to see if we could help him," Simon continued, "and I noticed that *you* conducted his RSD and approved his refugee status."

"Those are the facts," Baptiste replied, nonplussed. He began to lightly drum his fingers on the table.

"Then why did you convince me that his resettlement claim was defective? Or why haven't you commenced cancellation procedures if you don't believe his story?"

"What did Jesus say?" Baptiste asked, leaning calmly back in his chair. "'Go be a fisher of men.' Is that what you're about?"

"Isn't that our job here?" Simon looked at the EO in disbelief. "If his claims were sufficiently credible for refugee status, I don't see why they shouldn't be for an RRF."

"Ah, you're beginning to have regrets. That's it." Baptiste made a clucking sound with his tongue.

"I think we should focus on the refugee," Simon insisted in a hard tone.

"You did nothing wrong." Baptiste abruptly straightened his back. His eyes were spectacularly alive. "No one did. That cockamamie story of his would never have made it past a single European agency. You don't think I reviewed your report afterwards? There were too many gaps and inconsistencies to submit a resettlement request."

"But you recognized him as a refugee."

"Despite my doubts and misgivings. We can do that here. We can play fast and loose when there's a borderline case, but resettlement is a whole other game. I've had ironclad RRFs be rejected for reasons I myself cannot even fathom."

"Well, he's our problem now, and he's severely injured."

"Then he needs much closer accompaniment and advocacy here. Send all the resettlement requests you want to Europe. *Les prières du poulet n'atteignent pas le faucon.*"[71]

"So you're authorizing me to file an RRF?"

Baptiste looked at Simon incredulous. "You know I don't have the authority to do that. You need to bring that up with Maarten or Hilda."

"Oh sorry. You've been here for years, so I thought..."

"Simon, haven't you noticed something about the hierarchy here?" Baptiste leaned back in his chair again, this time with a deflated look on his face.

"What do you mean?" Simon asked, confused.

"I'm African. So is Khadija and Pacifique. Then there are the Moroccans in community services, and a few French interns who look like they just left a reggae concert. But where are all the executive officers from?"

"Well," Simon hesitated.

"Germany, Denmark, and the Netherlands," Baptiste stated definitively.

"I see."

"I am just the lonely warden of this open-air prison we call Rabat. Maybe one day when you're sitting in a glass office in Geneva, you can advocate for looser resettlement criteria so we can retire our fisherman friend in France. But the rules are not set by people dealing with the messy realities here on the ground."

"Well I'm going to bring it up with Maarten immediately," Simon said, getting to his feet.

Baptiste lifted a cautionary finger. "Be careful how you salt your dish, *mon ami.*"

"What do you mean?"

"Have you ever noticed that once you add salt to a dish there's no way to remove it?"

"Of course." Simon stepped toward the building.

"Well, then, a piece of advice. I'd be careful how you salt your dish at the UN."

"And what, pray tell, could they do to me?"

---

71   The prayers of the chicken do not influence the falcon.

"They could ask for your head on a silver platter."

"Thank you, Baptiste." Simon rolled his eyes. "Our little talks are always so helpful. Don't you have some pithy piece of African *sagesse* that can clear things up in an instant?"

Baptiste's mouth widened into its characteristic Cheshire grin. *"Celui qui transporte des oeufs, ne se bagarre pas.*[72] I believe someone still covets a post in Geneva."

"Touché." Simon gazed out over the heat-seared plains of Salé and, high above, the necropolis Chellah sitting on its rocky crag. Geneva, with its peaceful lakes, seemed very far away. "Still, we have to do something."

"Sure, but..." Baptiste paused. "I didn't want to mention this, since we're not officially allowed to consider it, but we received a credible-sounding report from another refugee that there may have been fraud in this case, and..." He paused dramatically.

"Yes?"

"That the refugee in question may belong to an exclusion category."

"That's heavy." Simon began to have a sinking feeling, as if the small ship of his good intentions had sprung a leak. "Credible-sounding, you say?"

"It's hard to tell," Baptiste replied, coolly sipping his cherry soda. "This other refugee could be lying. We've been receiving an unusual number of resettlement requests recently. From time to time, there's heightened activity among the refugee population, and whenever that happens, we tend to get a number of denunciations as well, especially against those refugees who appear most likely to be resettled."

"The fisherman sounded credible to me," Simon said. "Did you see the scars on his back?"

Baptiste shrugged. "There's a lot of ways to end up with scars. Being a soldier is one of them."

"He's training to swim to Europe," Simon blurted out.

Baptiste sucked his breath in surprise. His eyes suddenly bulged and he snorted a frondlike spray of cola out of his nose, exploding into a fit

---

72 A man carrying eggs does not get into fights.

of hacking coughs. Simon leapt toward the EO and then doubled over in laughter.

When he recovered, the EO straightened up, his eyes misty with tears. "Swimming! There's one I haven't heard before. Next thing you'll tell me that the refugees are gluing feathers to their arms." For a moment, his irrepressible grin seemed to stretch beyond the confines of his face.

Simon gave a wan smile that quickly faded. "Do we really want another drowning on our hands?"

Baptiste grabbed the dossier. "Ok. Ok. I won't make any promises, but I'll see if I can get him another resettlement interview." He shook his head as he walked off the terrace. "Swimming to Europe. *Seul un sot mesure la profondeur de l'eau avec ses deux pieds.*"[73]

---

73 Only a fool measures the depth of the water with both feet at the same time.

E VERY DAY, ARÈS TRAINED at the beach in Salé.

Upon arriving, he stretched out the way Kareem had showed him. Then he stripped down to his tattered FIFA shorts and immersed himself in the brackish sea like a sudden benediction. Stroking calmly, he swam out past the breaking waves and carved along the rolling humps of water, ignoring the sewage and the sea beds of plastic rinds. For hours on end, he drew elliptical lines before the ancient city of Rabat. As the weeks passed, he began to swim south along jagged coastal cliffs and then, even farther, to where the cliffs crumbled into sinuous yellow dunes. Gradually, he grew sinewy and strong and his stamina increased.

His training sessions over, he would often float on the sea's soft membrane, with only the luminous blue womb of the sky overhead, and imagine that he was totally free and could travel wherever he pleased. And every now and then, a gray-bottomed gull, or some gangly stork, would wing overhead and confirm his suspicion that with just a little invention he might yet find his way.

On one of those afternoons, after he exited sopping from the sea, Arès caught sight of the officer from the HCR who had interviewed him all those months before. The man held a little blue notebook clipped to a pen and wore a tidy Oxford shirt and khaki slacks, the uniform of the name-brand NGOs. He was walking toward the water, occasionally shaking his brown tasseled loafers to dislodge the sand.

Arès was in no mood to see him again. He headed the other way, but before he had made it more than a few meters, the officer hailed him with an upraised arm and strode purposefully toward him.

"Please wait. I'd like to talk to you," Simon shouted.

Arès sighed and turned to face him.

"Yes?"

"We received a report that one of the refugees was trying to swim to Europe, so they sent me down here to stop you."

Arès looked gape-jawed at the man, at a loss for what to say.

"I'm just joking," Simon said and slapped Arès hard on the back. "I'm glad to see that you're swimming. It must be good for your leg."

"Yes, it makes me feel much better."

"I love the beach as well." Simon held his arms akimbo and stared out at the pearly, rolling waves. "I live right up there." He pointed to a cluster of upmarket buildings set back a little way from the sands. "I like to walk down to the beach to watch the sunset. I've seen you swimming here quite a few times."

Arès waited expectantly for him to come to a point. Then he shivered in the waning light.

"So I thought I'd say hi. I'm Simon, by the way, in case you don't remember from your interview."

"I remember."

"Are you hungry? I have some snacks and beers in my bag over there." He gestured toward a towel, a few meters up the beach.

Arès' stomach growled. He could hardly afford to pass up a free meal. He nodded reluctantly. "Let me get my things."

"Actually, I wasn't joking before," Simon said, as he handed Arès a mouth-watering *pastilla*, stuffed with chicken and almonds and dusted with fine, floury sugar. "You can only imagine how crazy it's been in the office lately, with all these resettlement requests." He snapped a can of Flag beer free from its plastic web. "Anyway, we've been hearing rumors of a refugee who is training to swim to Spain, and I was worried it might be you."

Arès took a deep bite of the *pastilla* and his head flooded with happiness. He had forgotten the sensations that Moroccan pastries could provide.

"So is it you?" Simon asked.

Arès finished swallowing. "If you resettled me," he said, "I wouldn't have to swim to Europe." He smiled as he spoke, but there was a hard edge to his words.

"Yes, but you'll never make it," Simon insisted. "No one can swim that far."

"I'll never know until I try," Arès snapped defiantly. Who was this Mzungu, tracking him down at the beach to accuse him of insane schemes?

"As my colleague says..." Simon paused for a moment and racked his brain for a phrase. "Oh, yes, 'seul un sot mesure la profondeur de l'eau avec ses deux pieds.'" A satisfied look spread over his face.

Arès glanced at him sharply. "I am not a fool."

"I'm not calling you a fool. I get it. Life is awful for you here. But what good is drowning yourself? Things will get better, if only you can have a little patience."

"I have been advised that before."

Seething inside, he stared over the sands. A powerful set of waves crashed on the shore. Farther out, the sun hovered low on the horizon, scorching the water with quivering bands of fire. His father had tried to restrain Félix with similar words of caution and look what had come of that. Only more fire.

The air filled with a sudden rumbling and the roar of several engines throttling overhead. Both men looked up. High above, the crisscross of three twinkling jetliners, rising and descending from the air hub at Casablanca, seared incandescent contrails into the sky. They burned there briefly like six staffs of flame and then faded as gently as unwanted memories.

"It is my destiny to go to Europe," Arès declared.

Simon guffawed and quickly tried to stifle his laughter. "Your destiny? Are you serious?"

"Yes," he said, and realized that he was.

His right hand gripped the incantatory key around his neck and he peered over at the skeptical white face beside him, ghostly in the dimming light. Then he began to recount his youth in Kinshasa. He spoke of his family and of the fair, and this time he revealed what was in that prophetic box. He told the skeptical face of the countless travelers he had met and of their fates and aspirations. He even recounted his love for Christelle and

Paul's myriad kindnesses. He spoke of the demons that had driven him to Rabat and of the bright promises that carried him forward.

If he could only make one of these sauntering, self-satisfied Mzungus understand the knotty truths of his existence—how his fate was bound up, in a single glittering web, with the fates of so many others—then maybe, just maybe, there was hope for a truce. If not, the Mzungus could try all they might. There was no holding Arès and his brethren back. They were the future.

Every time he looked over, he saw the curious man scratching out notes on his small blue pad in the dark. Mzungus, he thought, extracting every bit they could. He no longer cared. He had camouflaged his past for so long—concealing it from the other refugees, adapting it to the formulas mandated by the HCR—that he felt the need to speak freely for once.

Let him write what he wants, Arès thought. The Mzungus defaced everything. He would probably end up some pink-assed baboon hooting in a primeval forest in Simon's retelling. It was better than being an anonymous number in some report.

He talked and talked. He spoke of everything that held no interest for the bureaucratic determinations of the HCR or the vengeful reckonings of the refugees, but which was all that kept him alive. The sun dipped below the horizon and night spread its purple mantle across the sky. When the heavens were at last ablaze with stars, Arès stopped speaking.

"Thank you, Arès," Simon said. "This meant a lot to me." He stood up to go. The stars twinkled gaily behind the JPO's tall frame as it rose above the refugee.

"I promise I will write something about you and show it to the people at the HCR. But please promise me something too: that you will muster a bit more patience. Give us some time so we can do our jobs."

When the refugee did not reply, he gave a stingy, embarrassed laugh. "Ok. I have to leave. Back to work in the morning, you know." He calmly walked away.

Arès sat stock-still, vacated by the effort. Slowly, a memory stirred in his mind. His lips parted and he began to sing the words to *Mokolo Nakokufa:*

Liwa ya zamba soki mpe liwa ya mboka
Liwa ya mpasi soki mpe liwa ya mayi
Oh mama uh
Mokolo nakokufa[74]

He sang the song the same way Kiwaka had sung it during their desperate march across the wastelands of Oujda. Arès' voice scaled high to the heavens, and the stars turned and hid their silvery eyes from the sight of the lone refugee, sitting on the dark beach, singing the mournful tune.

---

74 Will I die in the forest or in the city? / Painful death or will I be drowned? / Oh mama oh / The day that I will die.

SECOND RESETTLEMENT INTERVIEW
JULY 2009

I T WAS EARLY JULY.

Tourist season was in full swing, and Arès was panhandling in front of an upscale restaurant called *chez Paul*, wishing that the Cameroonian trader were really there. The wealthy Moroccans who frequented the restaurant were stingy givers, but the visiting Europeans were liberal with their dirhams. Arès was having a successful morning, much better than anything he could have earned with odd jobs in Salé. Still, it was dreary work, crouched in the dust all day, repeating *"un peu de monnaie,"* or *"ay rham lik el walideen shi dirham,"* a phrase that had taken him hours to learn by heart.

To pass the time, he twiddled the golden key around his neck and fantasized about how life would be when his foot was healed and he was living in Spain, or better yet, France.

Slightly before midday, Arès' phone chimed out an Algerian tune. It was Laurent calling to invite him to a committee meeting. The refugees were preparing another protest. Their leaders now styled themselves the *Points Focaux,* and they were losing patience with that bright white edifice on a hill. Unsurprisingly, the HCR refused to budge an inch. So both sides continued to tug with all their might, but the rope was fraying. Eventually it would break.

Arès politely demurred, but he was heartened by the news. Their small revolt was his final hope for resettlement. And if it failed? Well, maybe he could swim.

He chuckled out loud and flexed his ropy arms, admiring their astonishing definition. He could feel newborn muscles wrap his upper back and

479

drape down his shoulders like a leathery shell. Sometimes in the water he felt tireless, invincible. Still, swim to Europe? Cross a strait that swallowed ships whole? A memory of the wreck of the patera and of the deep, paralyzing cold of the sea washed over him, and he shivered despite the heat. The employees at the HCR must be mad to accuse him of such schemes.

Still… if he only could make it. He began to imagine the swim, stroke by stroke, the whipping west winds, the feathery crests of the waves, the hot splashes of sunlight as he powered ahead. He was halfway to Europe when the insistent ringing of his phone yanked him back to the present.

The HCR wanted to see him about his file. Again!

He could hardly believe it. He wondered if it had something to do with meeting that UN officer on the beach. He regretted now telling Simon about his life. In the harsh light of day, it seemed like just another clever trick by the HCR to claw more information out of him.

But it was useless to argue. He lifted himself upright and shuffled off to look for a *grand taxi*.

For a quarter of an hour, the white Mercedes tunneled beneath a gloomy stretch of low-hanging clouds. As it rolled over the steel bridge roping Rabat to Salé, the sky brightened and Arès slowly cheered. The HCR contacting him was the first bit of good news in months. Perhaps Salifou hadn't denounced him after all? Or maybe the refugees' protests were finally bearing fruit? This could be the call he had dreamt of for years.

The traffic clogged toward the end of the bridge, and the driver began weaving in and out of the oncoming lane. Suddenly, he blared the horn and jammed the taxi sideways. A few meters in front of them, two vehicles floated perpendicular on a tide of cracked glass, dented metal, and small ashen poofs. The driver cursed and wagged his fist, and it occurred to Arès that he had nearly killed a man over an error. His body sagged with the weight of the near deed.

Then it dawned on him that Simon might have interceded on his behalf. He sat up again straight. It was impossible to know anything when it came to the HCR. Dealing with them was like being lost at sea. Every time he spotted a shore to land on, it turned out to be just another mirage leading him on.

"*Il me mène en bateau*," he whispered to himself. But he was done with boats, with everything susceptible to shifting winds.

An hour later, Arès was shepherded into one of the interview rooms on the ground floor of the HCR. This time, the guard left the door a crack ajar, but it did little to alleviate the heat.

On the far side of the desk, a standing fan chugged out belabored huffs. Arès stretched out his hand. Somewhere above the middle of the desk, his fingers encountered the exact spot where the sluggish breeze expired.

His interviewer this time was a woman. Dressed in an open white blouse and office slacks, her build was of the earthy, sensible variety. Perfunctory glasses framed a wide face, backdropped by dark wavy hair.

Thank you for coming today.

Would you like a glass of water?

No.

Do you need a translator?

No.

What is your native tongue?

Lingala.

But you speak French?

Yes.

Good. You are here because we have some questions about your file.

Everything that you say here is confidential. Nothing you say here will be told to anyone, especially not the government.

We are not a government agency.

These updates are necessary from time to time in order for us to verify facts and to successfully serve the needs of our refugee population.

We appreciate your coming today.

What is your name?

You do not know my name by now? You called me to come here to talk.

We are required to retake your basic life information every time.

Please. What is your name?

I would like a glass of water.

Of course.

THE PROTECTION OFFICER ROSE AND FILLED A PLASTIC CUP WITH WATER.

I hope you are happy. Now what is your name?

Arès Sbigzenou.

What is your date of birth?

June 9, 1980.

Where were you born?

In Kinshasa.

What is your ethnicity?

Banyamulenge.

Why did you leave your country?

THE PRA TOOK A SIP OF WATER.

Can you please tell me why you left your country?

I have told this story before.

Please tell it again.

It is in my file. It is not a good story. I do not want to tell it.

We have some questions about your file. This is why we need you to tell
it again. Why did you leave your country?

Let me tell you something else. I can tell you the legend of Anansi and
the Python. Or, if you like, the story of the birth of the baobab tree.

Mr. Sbigzneou, we know that this is not pleasant, and I fully commis-
erate, but we are trying to help you.

I have told this story enough times. Is three times not enough?

We need you to tell it again.

No. I refuse. I will not tell this story again.

I see you are not feeling well. Perhaps you can come back another day and tell us what happened.

I know it is hard, but we need this story for your file.

My file? My file needs something and you respond. But three years I wait for treatment for my foot. My foot needs help. I need help. Why do you not resettle me so I can get treatment?

We are helping you. We offer you financial assistance and we pay your medical bills, which are quite expensive. Resettlement is not an option.

We urge you to try to integrate locally. We are expending extraordinary efforts to assure that all the refugees will receive residency and work permits.

PALS is monitoring your case.

PALS. When PALS treats my foot, I will tell you my story again. When you resettle me, I will tell you my story again. Until then, I will bury this story. It is a bad story. There is nothing you can learn from it.

It is because of your story that you are considered a refugee. Without the story we can do nothing for you.

Come back another day when you are feeling better.

THE PRA ROSE TO LEAVE BUT STOPPED.

HE REACHED UNDER HIS SHIRT AND THE PROTECTION OFFICER HEARD A SNAP AS ONE OF THE SECURITY GUARDS RUSHED INTO THE INTERVIEW ROOM AND GRABBED HIS ARM.

"*SHIWYA, SHWIYA,*" THE PRA SAID.

THE GUARD RELEASED THE PRA AND HE THRUST SOMETHING WITH A METALLIC CLANK
ONTO THE TABLE. THEN HE SLOWLY FOLDED HIS HAND ASIDE.

Here is my story. I have been carrying it with me for too long. I leave
it here with you. You can give it to my file.

There's nothing there.

It is yours now.

Mr. Sbigzneou, I think you should go to PALS and arrange for a psychological consultation.

THE PRA LEFT THE ROOM.

The guards ushered Arès out onto Avenue Tariq Ibn Ziad. He paused in the
sun and surveyed the vast empty bowl of the Bouregreg. To his right, the
ruined fortress of the Chellah hunkered upon a craggy bluff, and below it
intermittent flocks of birds cruised north like countless feathered crosses.
Arès felt as insubstantial as those birds, afloat on the soft, sweet drafts.

Then the ceaseless roar of traffic, the muffler pops and rattling exhausts,
brought him back to earth. He clumped downwards, past the white parapets of the HCR, toward the busy turnabout below.

About a hundred meters downhill, a tall woman in a bedazzling white
blouse strode purposefully toward him.

"Miss Federika! Miss Federika!" Arès shouted, waving his cane.

He wanted to talk to her, to make her understand that he would no
longer speak about the past. From now on, he would discuss only resettlement or treatment with the HCR. He wanted to tell her that he had cast
off the Congo just like a snake sheds unwanted skin.

Only she did not acknowledge his wave or even slow her pace. He realized suddenly that she was staring right through him as if he wasn't there.

He shouted as loud as he could, "Miss Federika! I need to talk to you!"

She continued to ignore him. His cheeks flushed, and he felt a snake braid horribly within his breast. As she strummed by him, elbows swinging for speed, he reached out forcefully to grab her, to stop her in her tracks.

His hand passed through her shoulder as if through a hallucination. He lost his balance and fell to the ground.

He sat there momentarily stunned. Then he called out her name, but she did not turn around.

CHAPTER 47

JULY 2009

S IMON SAT ON A small turquoise stool at Café Maure in les Oudayas.
Before him stretched a low wall covered with colorful Zellige tiles in
infinitely recurring diamond-shaped patterns. Above it, a wide panorama held the muddy mouth of the Bouregreg River, the frothing white
estuary of the Atlantic, and the tawny beaches and dun ramparts of Salé.

Simon looked around at the cheerful palaver, the clinking glasses of hot
mint tea, and the crinkled, smiling faces. White-aproned waiters streamed
about the terrace, carrying blue plates piled high with white *cornes de
gazelles*, pyramid-shaped almond cakes, and honeyed swirls of *chebakia*. A
refreshing breeze skimmed off the river and drew a sizable crowd through
the horseshoe-shaped entrance, with its impressive amphora and lithe tabby
kitten stretched over the top.

Ever since his encounter with Arès on the beach, Simon had begun
slipping out of the office early in the afternoon to come to Café Maure.
Georg was in Brazzaville on another mission, and either his superiors did
not notice or they did not care. Occasionally, he brought work with him,
but more often than not he ordered a glass of overpriced mint tea and
steadily scanned the shores of Salé, searching for a lone black form hobbling
over the sands.

In over two weeks, he had not once caught sight of the refugee. Still,
he kept up his vigil. From time to time, he wrote down bits and bobs of
the fisherman's story, sometimes in English, sometimes in French, but it
was a gratuitous exercise—something to do during a pointless pilgrimage
meant to alleviate his penitent thoughts.

A few days after he began frequenting the café, a rejection letter arrived from France in response to an RRF he had submitted months earlier. The request concerned an Algerian refugee with a fatal heart condition. The man had served in the French military and had commendations to that effect. Without an operation, he would likely succumb to his illness, and still the French authorities had refused resettlement. Simon doubted that he could ever justify an urgent medical need for Arès, or that Dr. Djideree would ever sign the necessary report.

There was one other avenue of appeal—Lack of Foreseeable Alternative Durable Solutions—but it belonged more to the category of miracle than to reasonable hope. There was no argument in favor of the fisherman that could not be applied to a hundred other refugees in Rabat.

Simon sipped the sugary tea and watched small ferries shuttle passengers back and forth across the Bouregreg River. He wondered whether, if even now, Arès was in the water swimming amidst the far-off waves.

He sighed. It had been imprudent to listen to the refugee's story. He should have maintained a professional distance. He peered over the kaleidoscopic wall and wondered for the thousandth time what impulse had led him to refuse his parents' wink-wink offer to facilitate a State Department career, and had whisked him first off to Rwanda and then to Rabat.

And now here he was, playing truant like some spoiled schoolboy, because he could no longer tolerate the shoddy compromise between ideals he hardly knew he had and the brutal triage imposed by the limited resources at the HCR and the needle's-eye criteria of the resettlement countries. His tenure at the refugee bureau would soon be over, and he felt only relief at the thought, even though he had no idea what came next.

He looked toward the nearby banks of Salé, with its terraced red and white architecture and its tall rectangular minaret glowing bronze in the afternoon light. Then he turned toward the vast heaving sea, and noticed for the first time how each wave, when it came close to the shore, opened like a hungry mouth.

He finished his tea and left.

* * *

By the time he stepped onto his street, it was close to sunset and the sky had taken on a rosy-pinkish color similar to that of a recent bruise. He was surprised to find Lise and Nathalie standing outside the building, shouting heatedly with the landlady. He accelerated his gait, but moments before he arrived, the landlady darted inside, leaving his flatmates exasperated in the street.

"What's going on?" he asked.

"Where were you?" Nathalie demanded.

"I was at Café Maure. Why?"

"The landlady's trying to get rid of Kinani," she wailed, throwing up her hands.

"Get rid of him? I've barely seen him in weeks."

"Well she has, and she wants him gone," Nathalie said. "She threatened to come by the apartment tomorrow to evict him herself."

Simon felt a loosening in his chest. It was a shame to see his flatmate go, but it meant a release from the tensions that had been building over the past few months.

"He makes a lot of noise with his hip-hop crew. I guess she wants a quieter building."

"No. It's because he's black," Lise replied. Her mouth was blade-thin and her eyes quivered with rage. "She says the neighbors have been complaining about all the Africans they see, and that no Africans are allowed in the building."

"What does she mean, no Africans?" Simon exclaimed. "Where the hell are we? Does she think this is Europe?"

"So now she's going to kick Kinani out!" Nathalie cried.

Simon paced back and forth in the crooked street. He wanted his flatmate out, but not on these grounds.

"Well we can't have that," he said at last. "There are principles after all." He might not be able to save one refugee, but at least he could protect another. The reasoning was leaky, but he was getting used to the tangled logic of Rabat. He considered it part of his local integration.

"So what are we going to do?" Lise asked.

"I'll deal with it."

He walked decisively to the landlady's apartment on the second floor of the building and knocked authoritatively on the door.

"*Chkoun hna?*! *Chkoun?*" a woman's voice shouted from behind the peephole.

He knocked again. She opened the door a crack and thrust out a fleshy hooked nose followed by a hooded face. A lock of black hair fell over a creased forehead and surprisingly maternal eyes.

"*Bonsoir Madame*," he began, "you were discussing an issue with my flatmates?"

"Yes. The African has to leave," she snapped. "No Africans are allowed in this building." She moved to slam the door, but Simon snuck a toe into the open crack.

"Sure. *Meshi mushkil.* We'll all move out next week."

"Good!" she replied. "Wait..." She swung open the door and stood there in her house frock and slippers. "What do you mean all of you?"

"You're kicking us out right?"

"We can't have Africans living here, but you can stay. You can't leave next week. You owe me rent." Her voice crescendoed with worry.

"Why should we pay rent if you kick us out? The rents here are really high anyway. We're happy to leave."

"No. No. You must stay!" she cried.

"Either we all stay or we all go. You can let us know what you decide."

"The African must go," she insisted, but her voice had grown smaller and even her body appeared to shrink at the edges.

"We all stay or we all go," Simon repeated firmly. "You have no right to kick us out. We have lawyers at the UN if you want to fight. Thank you for your time."

He turned around and walked away. He had to restrain himself from looking back to savor the expression on her face.

"What did she say?" Nathalie asked with expectant eyes.

"*Meshi Mushkil*," Simon replied, laughing.

CHAPTER 48
JULY 2009

———————

THE NEXT DAY, ARÈS renewed his regimen: begging, swimming, fielding small commissions for his neighbors. But he woke up panicked in the night.

He lay on the thin mattress, and to the soundtrack of his bedmates' snoring, he replayed the scene on the sidewalk ad nauseum. The ghosting of his hand through Federika's shoulder did not upset him. The doctors had warned him to stay out of the sun, and he was sure it was no more than an idle delusion brought on by the empty orange vials that littered his shelves. In any case, it was not the first time he had suffered hallucinations.

What worried him, though, was her callous manner as she pushed by him in the street. He did not know her well, but she did not seem like the sort of person to just brush him off.

What if the HCR had decided to punish him for his defiance? If that was the case, then he would never be resettled. All this for a point of dignity! He gnashed his teeth in the dark. What help was dignity when he was begging in the streets?

He decided to go back the next day and apologize. He would tell them whatever they wanted.

Afterwards he fell asleep and dozed well into the morning. By the time he arrived at the HCR, the queue of petitioners snaked twenty meters down the road. Arès could never understand it. They always gave appointments to everyone at 8:30 a.m., instead of spacing them out. It was as if they meant to ensure the longest possible wait. At least a dozen more people crouched on the far side of the avenue, slackly fanning themselves with discarded cardboard.

The heat was insufferable. The sun burned in the sky, incandescent, unreal. The petitioners canopied themselves with whatever they could find: old newspapers, garments, scraps of awning, but it was no use. The wind was blowing seawards, bearing hot blasts from the desert furnaces of Fez and Meknes. All around the air wavered strangely, as if thermal scrims, invisible and voluminous, were seesawing across the smoldering city. Each time one passed, Arès could see the Africans wilt a little more.

After only a few minutes, Arès began to feel feverish. He had halved his dosage of medication that morning, fearing another hallucination, but an hour waiting in that heat would undo him.

It would be better to go beg before one of the embassies, settled in the shade of a hibiscus tree, or more lucrative, to occupy one of the entrances to the old medina. He could probably even recoup the four dirhams that a *grand taxi* would charge him to travel that way.

He began limping toward the turnabout at the Place Abraham Lincoln, when the compound door to the HCR's garage rattled open. Arès stepped back as an engine revved and one of the U.N.'s glossy all-terrain vehicles poked out its snout. A bald man with a pugnacious bearing sat behind the steering wheel. He shouted something in Arabic, and a plump guard with a friendly face and a drooping handlebar mustache emerged in a prim powder-blue uniform.

The guard lit a cigarette and then offered the lighter to a disembodied hand. Following the hand out of the garage, a cigarette puffing contently in the corner of his mouth, was the Cameroonian EO who had conducted Arès' registration interview all those years before. He was dressed in a sharp three-piece suit, with a striped red shirt and a thin black tie.

Arès was aware of the regulations. They had told him a hundred times. All communication must be directed through the applicants' entrance. But the Eligibility Officer stood less than a meter away and he hoped that a fellow African might intercede for him when the guards began to bark.

Arès took a deep breath, while the EO laughed uproariously at something the mustached guard had said.

"*Mon frère,*" he began, "do you remember me?"

He waited for an answer from the EO, or a reprimand from the guard, but neither came. Instead, the Cameroonian turned his lips toward the refugee and engulfed him in a cloud of smoke. Arès coughed his lungs dry and looked up again, burning with shame. It was so juvenile of them. Even when he was a boy of twelve, he was too mature to play this sort of game.

"*Mon frère*," he tried again, "I am here to apologize."

The EO looked back at the guard who had lent him the lighter. "*Ah... c'était bien arrosé hier soir à Yacout.* I was shaking my hips until three in the morning."

"I don't know how you can dance in this heat," the guard replied. He mopped his face with a damp cloth and then flicked his cigarette into the road.

"It's never too hot at night, *mon gars*," the EO said, laughing.

Still chatting with the guard, he strolled back into the building. Impulsively, Arès followed him.

"I am here to apologize!" he shouted, but neither of them turned around. The all-terrain vehicle, stamped with the bright blue decal of the U.N., rolled out into Avenue Tariq Ibn Ziad and the garage door clattered shut. Arès was trapped.

He entered the building as if stepping into a mirage.

No one looked up as he penetrated into the security booth. There were three guards sitting inside, their uniforms half unbuttoned, the edges of their white underclothes showing. A guard with a large jutting belly fanned himself with a piece of cardboard while he monitored two large screens, where the feed from a dozen video cameras displayed images of the outside streets.

The Cameroonian ambled lazily in the heat and Arès had no trouble keeping pace. He followed him up the wide courtyard stairs with their miniscule risers. On a landing to the right, sheltered by a simple awning, a small man with tight blond curls and sharp blue eyes tapped away at a bulky computer.

"Your keyboard hasn't melted yet?" the EO asked, reaching out to slap him five.

The man laughed and shook his head. "Did you see Cameroon versus the Ivory Coast? I think your team melted during the match."

"Yes. The Ivory Coast is a truly weak team, but we were even weaker that day."

"Next time," the blond man said. The Cameroonian waved and pushed open the door to the front office with Arès hot on his heels.

"Are you trying to make it snow in here?" the EO asked loudly. Arès shivered at the blast of cold and sneezed loudly.

Inside, three desks were arranged in rows. In the rearmost seat, a Moroccan man of medium stature shouted into a phone. Arès recognized his booming, aggravated voice from the times he had called the HCR, but he had trouble squaring the soft face of an overtired employee with the loathsome hyena that he had pictured behind the commands barked at him over the line.

"We're making ice cream in the back. What flavor would you like?" a woman in her early twenties said from behind a computer. She had tousled hair and was wearing a flowing Indian tunic over fisherman's pants and a coral necklace. She cradled a phone against her ear, and when she repositioned her face, Arès recognized her from one of his many visits.

The EO was about to respond, but she raised a finger. "Mr. Essombe? Yes. This is the *Haut Commissariat des Nations Unies pour les réfugiés*. We are calling because you had a rendezvous today for the determination of your refugee status and you did not come."

Two other female twentysomethings exited a backroom lined with filing cabinets. One of them thumped down a mound of bulky pink dossiers. Several of the folders were tattered to the point of disintegration, and sheaves of paper sailed to the floor and were unceremoniously stuffed back in.

All three female employees were petite and casually dressed, and they reminded Arès of the bohemian white girls he often saw hanging out with the Rastas.

The woman with the pink dossiers wore a bright red tank top over yellow pants. Her brown hair was pulled back in a bun from which a single dreadlock dropped like a dangling snake. Her eyes were brown, bright and present. "Dossiers, dossiers, dossiers," she exclaimed, throwing up her arms.

"Yes. Can you come tomorrow?" the first woman said into the phone. "Ok, then you should be here tomorrow at 8:30 a.m. If you do not come, it will be the end of the process and we will terminate your applicaiton."

The Cameroonian EO opened a can of cherry cola. "What did he say?"

"He said I have a lot of problems and I am at home."

"Well why have him come tomorrow when he can always come the next day?" He grinned and took a sip of soda.

"He's lucky we didn't apply the rules right away and close his file," the woman in the red tank top said, banging another heap of dossiers against the desk for emphasis.

One of the folders clapped open, and Arès recognized a photo of Salifou, with his pronounced cheekbones and strangely cut eyes. He leaned over and surveyed the data sheet. Birth, origin, religion, ethnicity: Banyamulenge. He reached out to flip the page when the girl slammed the dossier shut and rushed out the door, her elbow gliding unhindered through Arès' forehead.

He staggered backwards. The world spun and he felt like he was going to retch. He leaned heavily on his cane and put his hand on a table to steady himself. Seeing the ruby red cola unguarded, he grabbed it and glugged it half empty.

Seconds later, he placed it back on the filing cabinet. The EO lifted it, inspected it curiously, and then shrugged. It struck Arès that he was moving among them like a ghost, and he wondered all of sudden if he were dead. What other explanation could there be?

In all likelihood, he had succumbed to hunger or fever in the past few days. That was it then, he was dead. He felt elated. No more begging, no more struggle. At this very moment, his friends were doubtless burying his corpse.

How long had he been dead? And where would he sleep that night? He was sure his roommates would quickly find someone else. Though if he were dead, he could probably sleep on the beach now without fear of being attacked.

But how would he buy food if no one could see him? He still felt hungry. He would have to steal. He smiled at the thought. All his life he had been a relatively honest man. He had to die to become a thief.

Then again, if he was dead, why was he still in Rabat? Why was he there, pleading with the HCR for resettlement? Even worse, why did his foot continue to jab with pain at every step? Would his injury plague him through eternity? Would he continue to be a refugee in death as in life? Sweat collected on his brow at the thought.

The Cameroonian stood by the door, holding it ajar. "Does anyone want coffee?" Arès instinctively raised his hand. Then, realizing he would have to fetch it himself, he followed the EO into the main building.

They traversed a number of white, high-ceilinged rooms, coming to a large multilevel hall. The EO descended a short flight of stairs that led through a frosted door into a spacious windowed office. It was wonderfully blue and cool in there, like the inside of an aquarium.

"Close the door," a woman yelled when they entered. The only sound in the office was the soft cottony whirr of the air conditioner. Six desks were spaced evenly about, each with a boxy white computer and two sizable letter racks full of dossiers.

Directly opposite the door, sipping a mug of coffee, was the Protection Officer to whom Arès had given his key. His heart beat wildly. If anyone could see him it would be her. As he entered, she looked up and her face recoiled with recognition. Then, abruptly, she rubbed her eyes.

"You look like you've just seen something horrible. Am I that badly dressed today?" the EO asked, rubbing his right hand down his stylish suit.

"Sorry, I thought there was someone behind you for a second." She looked down at her desk where a golden key glittered beside a stack of pink dossiers.

"Ah, so the mystery key was yours?"

"What key?"

"The key there on your desk." The EO pointed at the sparkle of gold. "The one that Saana found yesterday in one of the interview rooms. I hung it on the filing cabinet because we couldn't figure out whose it was."

She rubbed her eyes again and blinked, as if waking from a dream.

"Oh that. I hadn't noticed it. I think one of the refugees I interviewed for resettlement may have left it."

Arès nearly kicked the table. So that had been a resettlement interview! Why hadn't she told him?

"Ah, he wanted to help the process along with a little baksheesh?"

"No, of course not. I would never tell a refugee that he was being interviewed for resettlement. I think he left it by accident. Or I don't know. He needs psychological help. I tried to set him up with a consultation but he ran out in a huff."

"We get some crazies in here. What did he claim?"

"Nothing out of the ordinary. He was Banyamulenge and his entire family was murdered before his eyes."

"Oh," the EO said. "Because some of these people have really crazy stories. You know, like 'I am the illegitimate son of President Obiang and they're going to kill me if I go back to Equatorial Guinea,' or I remember the time I interviewed a woman who claimed that she was the wife of Mobutu. Can you believe it?"

"Well, was she?"

"Being the wife of Mobutu is a public matter, and her name was never mentioned in the press. But then she recounted everything about her life at Mobutu's palace in incredible detail. Things that were impossible to know if she hadn't been there herself."

"Maybe she was his mistress," suggested a man sitting at the desk to the left of the entrance. Black, with circular glasses and short-cropped hair, he had a mild face more befitting a monk than an officer of the HCR. Behind him, through a jalousied window, Arès could see the applicants' waiting room packed to the brim.

"I thought of that, but when she tells you that she directed the military defense against Kabila while Mobutu was ill, and that she went with the generals to sign the peace accords… These things are easily verifiable. She was nuts and she spoke for four hours without stopping."

"I've heard stranger things," the monkish man said.

"Then I got this Gabonais, who didn't breathe for two days while I interviewed him."

"What happened to him?" a short black girl in professional gray slacks and a blazer asked from another desk. She spoke with a clear West African accent. Probably from Gabon too, Arès thought.

"He was rejected for lack of credibility. Two days of interviewing and the whole time he had his lawyer next to him. He said his salary was a thousand U.S. dollars per month, which is a lot of money for Gabon, and the lawyer looks at me and says, 'You see. Why would he leave his country with such an important salary if he didn't have to.' And I reply, 'What does that prove? That doesn't mean he's a refugee.'"

The EO twisted the cap off a two-liter bottle of cherry cola and poured himself a glass.

"Or their stories are totally implausible. This guy says he survived an attack with a broken leg and that he didn't see a doctor for six months. How could he not see a doctor for six months, while he was crossing all of Africa with a broken leg? It's not very good for his credibility. And you know how he replies?"

"How?"

"He says, 'Well there are people who don't eat for years in prison. So there.' Or even better, there are these guys who make up all sorts of stuff, like they were tortured every day for weeks on end and every afternoon had electrodes put on their legs and their genitals. But then you ask them how they got around…"

"And that's when they don't know how to respond," the bespectacled woman chimed in from her desk.

"I had another guy who said he escaped from prison. And I said, how were you tortured every day and then you managed to jump a five-meter wall and escape? Or there was even one guy whose dossier I rejected for lack of credibility because he said he went to prison and one of the guards hit him one time." The EO started laughing. "So I reply, 'Prison guards don't hit you just one time. They beat you to the ground.' I figured there's no way this guy is credible." The monkish man in the corner chuckled quietly and shook his head.

"You know, when I arrived here from France I was really shocked," the woman added, her face ballooning with indignation, "because in France you don't believe anyone. You reject every dossier for the slightest inconsistency, and here you try to justify the discrepancies as much as you can."

"And even then, we only recognize around ten percent of the applicants," the EO responded.

Arès could not listen anymore. He creaked open the glass-paneled door and slipped out into the stairway, being careful not to make any noise. Then he realized the absurdity of his actions. He turned around and violently slammed the door shut. As he stalked into the multilevel hall, he heard the glass pane drum behind him like a gathering storm.

He turned right this time and found himself threading between the glass-paneled interview rooms. Inside one, he could see an old Maghreban in a baseball cap speaking heatedly with Federika.

"I am a real refugee!" he shouted. "I fled political persecution in Algeria. I am not like these Africans who just come here looking for work."

"All the refugees are the same for us," she replied. Her face looked fatigued and lines of worry snaked across her brow.

The door in front of him was locked, so Arès retraced his steps and clomped up the winding staircase at the center of the building.

The second-floor landing opened into a closet-sized office with a raised ceiling. Arès' eyes were drawn to the flicker of a lofted computer screen into which several outdoor video cameras beamed images of the street. The office was empty, so he turned left and hobbled down an open corridor that led onto a breezy outdoor terrace. Two employees chatted beside an antique table and plucked fleshy red strawberries out of a bowl. Arès marveled at the whitewashed paradise, over which an olive tree cast a latticework of shade.

When he approached, he discovered that the conversation was in a language he did not understand. On an impulse, he nicked one of the fruits and ate it with undisguised relish. If either of the employees noticed its sudden disappearance from the bowl, neither of them betrayed a sign.

To the right of the terrace was a low doorway that exhaled an array of appetizing aromas. Arès ducked in and nearly bumped into Simon.

The JPO was holding an empty glass with an expectant look in his eyes.

A moon-faced woman, in a white smock with a green kerchief wound about her head, had just finished boiling some tea. After extinguishing the flame, she scooped several strands of mint out of a watery bowl and shoved them into the pot. Then she added six white blocks of sugar, each larger than her thumb.

A second woman, undersized, with a chocolate complexion and brown glittering eyes, was stirring something on the stove. "Look there!" she suddenly cried.

They all raised their eyes to the wall, where a neon green jungle frog, with a yellow stripe running down its back, leisurely crawled.

Simon and the moon-faced woman rushed over. "How strange. Do you get frogs in here often?" he asked.

"No, never. It's the first time," the woman replied.

"Should we give him something to eat? Maybe a strawberry?"

"I think they eat insects and plants."

"Yeah, but everyone likes strawberries. I bet he's hungry." Simon rushed out, nearly slamming into Arès. A few seconds later, he bounded back in with a strawberry in his hands.

"What I don't understand is why is it here?" the smaller woman mused. "It must have come all the way from the river down there." She pointed at a minute serpentine of blue coursing through the plains below.

"Maybe it's a refugee?" Simon suggested, biting down on the strawberry.

The woman laughed. "I don't know."

"I bet it came here seeking asylum. I'll go upstairs and get a form, and we can do an interview when I get back."

"I'll make sure he stays," the woman replied.

Arès followed Simon out of the kitchen and down the hall. But instead of heading upstairs, the JPO continued along the corridor and entered a side office via a recessed door.

Sitting inside was a remarkably pallid woman with raven black hair and a charcoal-gray, crocheted shawl draped over her shoulders. Her desk was stacked high with pink dossiers, each of which held a life. Arès noticed a framed photograph of an overweight cat and next to it a brochure with the title *Refugees: Real People, Real Needs*. One of the petite employees from the front office sat inside, leafing through a dossier.

"Anna-Heintz, you wanted to see me," Simon said.

"Yes." She looked up. "I need you to respond to these resettlement requests that I've marked as unlikely to succeed. You are familiar with the form letter, of course."

"Yes. I have the template on my computer." Arès watched him collect over a dozen letters. "Why are so many refugees applying for resettlement right now?"

"I don't know," she said. "These things come in waves. We managed to resettle a significant number of refugees last November, so perhaps that has encouraged them to apply."

The JPO perused the letters. "Most of them don't even fulfill the resettlement criteria. Why are they wasting their time?"

"Desperation." She took a sip of tea from a United Nations mug. "Also, they are not very familiar with the resettlement criteria."

"How come?"

"We tend to occlude it."

"Purposefully?" His voice modulated with surprise. Arès settled onto one of the chairs.

"We cannot tell the refugees the actual criteria for resettlement, or they would invent stories to fit the criteria and increase their chances of being resettled. So we only admit to urgent medical needs and only in the rarest cases, when there is really no effective treatment in Morocco."

Her words had a peculiar delicacy to them that sent a chill down Arès' spine. He marveled at the rigidity of her facial expressions and the length and firmness of her neck. She sat perfectly erect in her chair, like a marionette pulled taught by its strings.

"But we make credibility assessments for the refugees during their registration interviews," Simon argued. "Why can't we just do that for the resettlement interviews as well?"

"There's also an enormous amount of jealousy among the refugees," Anna-Heintz said, cleanly biting off each word before passing to the next.

"We have to protect them from one another. In the past, we used to educate them about the resettlement criteria, but it was a disaster." Her eyes batted lethargically shut as if to emphasize the point.

"What happened?" Simon asked.

"First, they started denouncing each other. Refugees who had never said anything before, suddenly realized that another refugee, who happened to be a good candidate for resettlement, was in fact a member of a government killing squad or a paramilitary, or even better, was one of the people who had killed their family, or sometimes several families from several different countries at the same time." She sipped once more from her mug.

"We've had things like that here," the petite woman interjected.

"Yes, but it gets worse," Anna-Heintz continued. "We had two refugees poisoned in Cameroon because they appeared more likely to be resettled than others who were desperate to leave."

"That's awful!" Simon said.

"At the same time, there are so many refugees who seem to fit the real criteria." She leaned forward and her voice raised to an uncomfortable pitch. "For instance, the majority of our female refugees are women at risk or survivors of torture, and almost none of the sub-Saharan refugees actually manage to integrate locally. If they knew the real criteria, and they knew how many of them fulfill the prerequisites, then they would all start demanding resettlement. They will think they have a right to it, whereas it's not a right. The resettlement countries have their quotas and they pick their refugees from among the dossiers we send them."

"So we lie to keep them honest and happy."

"I would not describe it like that, but it's true." Anna-Heintz plucked a grape out of a bowl and began to peel off its skin. "We cannot reveal the entire procedure to them without destabilizing our operations."

"For instance, when we call them in for an RRF interview," Simon continued, "but we don't tell them that it's for resettlement."

The pale woman began to rock back and forth in her chair. "Yes, it gets their hopes up. The refugees do not understand how contingent the process is. So we tell them that we have further questions about their dossiers and we ask them tell their story again."

Arès kicked the desk loudly, and then froze when the woman narrowed her eyes and peered around.

"What if it's traumatic for them to retell the story?"

"An RRF interview must be much more thorough than the Refugee Status Determination. The resettlement countries are looking for any plausible excuse to say no. If there is even a minor discrepancy in their stories, the application is rejected. There's pressure on us as well. If too many of our candidates are rejected, then a receiving country can place an embargo on our submissions. We call the refugees in and they tell their story again and we see if anything has changed."

The petite woman spoke up again. "It's horrible. Normally it's the third or fourth time they've told their story and sometimes they cry every time."

"But if we tell them the truth, then they lie." Anna-Heintz laid her hands flat on the desk and stared at the two employees with an unsettling fixity.

"So when you tell them that you're going to close their dossiers if they skip appointments is that a lie too?" Simon asked.

"No. We actually do close their dossiers, but only after they miss three or four appointments. It's in their interest to come. If they fail to renew their refugee cards, then they are without protection."

"Any other white lies I should know about?"

"Not for the moment." Anna-Heintz picked up a dossier, indicating it was time for the JPO to leave.

Arès clutched his head as he reeled out of the office. *Quel arnaque!* Did they believe they would never be found out?

Infuriated, he stamped up another flight of stairs to the top floor.

Turning right, he passed by a cabin-like room lit by the glow of several technological devices. Further along were bookcase-lined walls and then a door. Arès opened it and entered a sizable hexagonal office.

A round trestle table circumferenced by chairs held several binders, a thick tome on refugee law, a manual entitled *On Resettlement,* and a book with an image of a bald black man under the banner *"les Damnés de la terre."*

Fatima was sitting beside the table, shouting angrily into the phone in Arabic. After a minute, she slammed it down on the handset.

"I would not want to be a refugee in Morocco," she exclaimed in French, and then slumped in her seat, her head in her hands.

"You cannot let yourself get so worked up, Fatima," said a woman with buttery blond hair and kindly Nordic features. She stood beside an executive L-shaped desk. An entire wing of the desk was dedicated to framed photos of a flaxen-haired boy in various poses: hanging from a tree branch; wearing cleats and holding a soccer ball; fishing on a pier, presumably with his father. The centerpiece was a large picture frame that held a portrait of the family in front of a traditional Dutch smock mill with a high thatched tower on a country canal. Nearly half of the photo was taken up by an immense meadow of red and gold tulips.

Fatima looked up. "Let me tell you, I cannot wait for a vacation. I cannot sleep at night. Oh, my head." She lay back in the chair and pressed a damp cloth against her left temple.

"Are you taking the medications the doctor prescribed?"

"Yes, but he says I need a vacation. The pills just make me sick."

"Maybe you should take a few days off."

"Who is going to take care of the refugees? There's a crisis every minute."

"The refugees can survive for a few days without you." The woman typed something into the computer and then muttered under her breath. "Damn machines."

Fatima leaned forward, her toes pressing against the ground as if she were about to take flight. "Abdoulay was ejected from his foyer again. He's completely unmanageable! I have to find him another place to stay." By the end of her sentence, she was hovering halfway out of the chair.

"Federika can do it."

"What did Sweden say about his RRF?"

"They rejected him."

"Ooah!" she moaned and flapped back into her seat. Then she sat up abruptly. *"Klaoui hada!"* Her eyes fired brightly as she cursed.

"What did you expect? No one wants a former child soldier. You know how it is with resettlement. The receiving countries never want the ones who really need it. We send them the dossiers of five handicapped minors and they always pick the cutest kid, because they figure that one will integrate best. But it's precisely the ones who won't integrate well who need to be resettled."

"I don't know what to do with him. He hasn't lasted more than a month anywhere he's lived."

"The boy was drugged for years and forced to kill people. He needs serious psychological counseling. But we don't have the resources to deal with him. The most we can get him here is food and maybe housing. I was reading his dossier yesterday. You can't even imagine the nightmares he described to the doctors at PALS."

"I can't imagine what he has been through."

"Don't try. It'll drive you crazy."

"But what can we do?"

"Take a vacation."

Arès snatched the manual on resettlement and walked through a side door into a private bathroom. A small thrill ran through him as he sat down on the porcelain bowl. It had been over a decade since he had enjoyed such a privilege.

He flipped the book open to a page near the beginning and began to read. "Resettlement may offer the only means to preserve human rights and to guarantee protection when refugees are faced with threats which seriously jeopardize their continued stay in a country of refuge."

He snorted with gusto and looked around for a faucet or pail to tidy up. When he saw the toilet paper, he smiled self-consciously. Then he paged onward.

"Resettlement should not be pursued because individual refugees have become a burden or because of their behavior or solely in response to action undertaken by refugees to draw attention to their demands—for example, violent or aggressive action toward office staff or hunger strikes. While such individuals may have concerns which need to be heard and require an appropriate response, resettlement should only be considered if the case meets the HCR's criteria."

He gave a loud grunt and looked up, worried that someone might have heard. Putting the manual aside, he hitched up his pants. He was reaching for the door when it swung open of its own accord and the blond-haired woman rushed in. He jumped aside, squeezing himself into the corner. The woman ripped off her pants, plopped onto the toilet, and began to thunderously piss.

When she bent down to extract a magazine from a rumpled pile on the floor, Arès unlatched the door and slipped out. He descended the stairs, his head on fire, physically shaken by all that he had seen.

He wanted somewhere cool to think and he gravitated toward the frigid office where he had first entered. The Moroccan employee was still inside, breathlessly shouting into the phone in his braying, antagonized voice. However, the back room, with its clutter of filing cabinets, was quiet.

Arès crept in and shut the door.

The ceiling was unusually high for the modest space, giving the room the vertiginous feel of a shaft. Indexed metal drawers crowded the walls, leaving only a narrow winding corridor to walk through.

Arès took out his refugee card, hoping to find the corresponding cabinet, but the numbers did not match up. He started sliding out drawers at random, foraging for his name amidst rows of puffy pink folders.

There were thousands and thousands of dossiers. He could not believe how many lives had been processed by the HCR. He removed an arbitrary folder and read the refugee's case file. Then he read another, and another.

For hours, he squatted in that icy den and fished out orgies of rape and massacres, men electrocuted, women imprisoned in grim dungeons, survivors adrift in forests, gobbling bark and worms; babies mauled, homes burnt, hearts pulled living from chests, a world drowning in infamies. Nowhere did he find his dossier. Instead, he chanced across dozens of men and women he knew in the refugee community, and in exhuming their sufferings, he realized that he was but a single inhabitant in a city of hopelessness.

Desperation gripped his throat.

He rose to leave. When he placed his hand on the doorknob, his eye fell upon a heap of dossiers covered in dust. And there it was, his file, like a *deus ex machina*. He opened it up and began to peruse its musty pages.

Soon he found his Resettlement Evaluation. The same elements were present as in nearly all the other files. He bowed his head and read aloud:

"**Part I: Prospects for local integration.**

Local integration in the refugee context is the end product of a multifaceted and ongoing process, of which self-reliance is only one part. Integration requires preparedness on the part of the refugees to adapt to the host society, without having to forego their own cultural identity. From the host society, it requires communities that are welcoming and responsive to refugees, and public institutions that are able to meet the needs of a diverse population.

Arès put the document down. It seemed written for another planet. He did not know whether to laugh or cry. He steeled himself and read on.

In general there are no prospects for local integration for refugees in Morocco. Refugees are without any official papers and are deprived of the right to work and/or to accede to basic services such as education or healthcare. Resettlement is considered a durable solution for refugees at risk, such as survivors of torture and violence, the disabled, and other injured or severely traumatized refugees who are in need of specialized treatment unavailable in their country of refuge. It is also appropriate for refugees without local integration prospects, for whom no other solution is available. The PRA is in need of specialized treatment unavailable in his country of refuge and is without local integration prospects. Therefore resettlement should be considered an appropriate measure in his case.

Arès flipped to the reverse side where additional typewritten comments covered half the page.

> There were nonetheless credibility problems with respect to
> the following material elements of the claim:

> 1. The PRA lacked knowledge about the number of Congolese
>   Wars and the composition of the rebel groups involved in
>   them.
> 2. It is highly improbable that a stranger discovered the
>   PRA unconscious in the street and transported him over
>   70 kilometers to his village.
> 3. The PRA cannot remember the name of the man who
>   allegedly saved his life.
> 4. The PRA digressed extensively during the interview.

> The above-mentioned credibility problems are sufficient to cast
> doubt on the applicant's claim. It is likely that any country
> to which we submit an RRF will reject the request for reasons
> of credibility.

> Therefore, I cannot recommend the PRA for Resettlement.

The document was signed Simon Bauer. Next to it was a stamp: "Resettlement claim rejected."

So it had not been Salifou at all. He stood up, his head reeling. It was time to go.

CHAPTER 49

JULY 2009

F EDERIKA STORMED OUT OF the building, juggling an armful of binders and shouting into her phone. Twenty meters up the road, a parked taxi waited.

She skirted around a cluster of applicants and whipped open the car door. Arès hurried after her, praying he would reach the vehicle before it screeched off. His biggest fear was that, unable to see him, the driver would roll forward while he was climbing in and dash him to the curb. Miraculously, though, the taxi waited for him.

"Where are you going?" the driver asked Arès as he climbed in.

The refugee nearly leapt out again in fright. The driver could see him. "I'm with her," he said in a shaky voice.

The driver spun around. "Madame? This man is riding with you?"

Federika looked up distractedly from the phone, cried "What?" once, and then repeated the address she had given him.

The driver shrugged and pumped the volume on the radio. The jaunty trumpets, drums, and synthesizers of Algerian Raï flooded the small Peugeot. Arès could make out the anguished warble of "*el harba wayn*" repeatedly intoned in a defiant voice. Then the song ended and he shut his eyes as the radio played Cheb Khaled's "Didi" for the thousandth time.

Didi didi didi di hazine di ouah
Didi ouah didi didi di hazine di didi hey yeah[75]

---

75   Take take, take take the beautiful girl away / take take, take take the beautiful girl away yeah

Federika screamed into her phone, straining her voice over the stereo and the squawk of the taxi dispatchers.

Some of her conversations were in French, and Arès eavesdropped as she frantically tried to arrange temporary housing for a group of Rwandan girls who had been forced into prostitution by their guardian. They were camped out in the street somewhere in G-5, and after several calls she landed a contact willing to lodge them for a few nights.

Then the phone rang again and she switched to a language he did not understand.

The taxi pulled to a halt in front of an unprepossessing seven-story building somewhere in Agdal. Federika tossed money up front and sprang out of the taxi, tearing the keys from her purse as she went.

Arès scrambled after her, his foot banging painfully against the pavement. Panting for breath, he managed to slide his cane into the front door before it slammed shut. He slithered in and fastened the latch.

They rode skywards in the elevator. The doors opened into a short residential hall that took only seconds to traverse. Federika inserted the key and entered her home.

Inside, the apartment was spotless and serene. A large living room, with a wooden dining table and two long sofas, adjoined an open Frankfurt kitchen. Otherwise there was little decoration. To the refugee it appeared entirely unlived in. Nothing was out of place. No one spoke. No one moved around.

Federika walked straight into her bedroom and shut the door. For a moment, Arès lingered uncomfortably in the living room. Then he began to scout out the premises.

A second bedroom branched off to the right. Inside was a queen-sized bed with thick red bolsters and a hand-woven quilt. Arès stretched out on it and exulted in the comfort.

For a moment he fluttered in and out of sleep, but the stillness unsettled him. He had never experienced such quiet. Even his nights in Nonloso had been full of cricketings, bird calls, and the creaking of joints as his brothers tossed in nearby beds. He hopped off the mattress and stamped his feet loudly as he left the bedroom.

When he reentered the living room, he noticed a narrow corridor that led past a wash closet to other quarters. At the far end, he was surprised to discover a large study with a pair of mahogany work desks and sofa chairs. So this was how the Mzungus lived! It was not as extravagant as he had sometimes imagined, but it was worlds removed from anything he had known since he fled Kinshasa.

He doubled back and opened the fridge, removing a yogurt and some refried rice. Then he drank a beer. He was feeling full and content when he pushed open the door to Federika's bedroom.

The young woman sat on a stool, backlit by the glow of a computer screen. Looking over her shoulder, Arès made out the floating torso and face of a flaxen-haired man with a high forehead and rigid cheekbones. He stood there, listening to them garble in a harsh sounding tongue until she lifted off her white blouse, revealing the trim cascade of her back.

A shock of fire raced up his belly and his feet rooted to the floor. He tried to count the years since he had last seen a woman undress. Then he shrunk into the corner, like a spider flattening against its web.

As he hung there, invisible, she giggled at something the man said. Her face crinkled and then gushed out a gay laugh. She seemed young, much younger than he ever thought possible.

The bureaucrats at the HCR looked so imposing in their official capacities. But when he thought about it, these people who held his life in their hands, were about his age if not younger. Federika had something childish about her, something in her frivolous foreplay and the almost adolescent way she held her body. Behind the diaphanous tissue of her bra, he could see the pink petals of her breasts.

She slid off her jeans, and he heard a sound of rustling cloth from the console's speakers. Federika blushed and then eyeballed the screen.

This woman had such power over him. He thought of all the times he had supplicated before her. To see her there, a carefree young girl flirting with her boyfriend, filled him with inarticulate sensations. A chill invaded his limbs and he shivered violently. Then, before he had even ceased trembling, he felt overcome by an inexpressible urge to laugh.

He doubled over in mirth, tears fountaining from his eyes. He was propped against the floor, a knee bent, hands splayed against the hardwood, when Federika's stool rolled toward him. He glanced up to see her swaying in front of the video camera to shouts of encouragement from the speakers.

Two ocular dimples waved above her buttocks, mesmerizing him, awakening the stewing lusts of so many years.

She stepped coquettishly in his direction, shearing her gossamer bra. He stared at the small cup of her crotch outlined by her panties, at the pursed paradise that was there.

Then, with a narcotic, trembling hand, he reached out to touch her naked belly.

His hand passed slowly through her, in her, and a strange miscegenation ran through his bones.

She spun around suddenly, her arm swishing into him, through him, and it was if someone had clouted him in the chest.

"Oomph!" He reeled backwards and fell wheezing to the floor. When he raised his head, winded, gasping, she was dancing in the buff.

He would have to be careful.

The computer in the corner pinged and she sat down again and began to type. He pushed himself upright. Then he stood beside her, gaping at the machine. From inside, the man—her boyfriend or husband—gazed at her intimacies: at the crescent of her seat, the fine arc of her stomach, and her small pear-shaped breasts.

He wondered what distances separated them. Incredible, these machines that could eradicate time and space. He silently prayed for the faces of his family to appear on the flickering screen, but they did not. Time, he realized, was different than space. It was irretrievable, uncrossable.

The heavy breathing of the digitized man filled the room. Federika began to touch herself and moan, and as her back arched and she opened her legs, Arès retreated shyly out the door.

Later, he watched silently while she prepared dinner and settled into bed. Then he ate something else from her fridge and laid down on the living room couch. By the time he woke in the morning, she was already gone.

CHAPTER 50

JULY 2009

———

THE ANNUAL JAZZ FESTIVAL at the Chellah was a socialite event. People dressed up in style, the men in sleek evening jackets, the women in florid dresses and chiffony summer scarves. They perched in the outdoor amphitheater like exotic birds and peered as much at each other as at the musicians on the stage.

Nadia had invited Simon to a performance by a Berber violinist she knew, followed by some jazz trio from Finland named PLOP. They arrived an hour before the show with the intention of touring the grounds. Though he worked only a few hundred meters away, Simon had yet to visit the historic site.

Just outside the thirteenth century necropolis lay the ruins of the Roman city of Sala. For a few minutes, they wandered among the modest heaps of mossy stones that had once made up the Roman forum. Then they climbed wide imperial steps that led under an arched sandstone gate with tall octagonal turrets and defensive crenellations. A verdant stepped alleyway opened before them, bordered by flowering hibiscus, tall speared papyrus shoots, and lush bougainvillaea that spilled over with pink and violet blooms.

Small tabby cats roamed about, slinking over the ruins or chasing invisible quarry into the undergrowth. Long-legged herons strutted on small hillocks, and the orange beaks of storks peeked out from a high minaret clad in colorful faïence tiles, its roof hatted by an enormous nest of wiry bramble.

"This place is phenomenal," Simon exclaimed. "Where does that path lead?" He pointed to a stone road that led up the bluff.

"There are the tombs of some famous marabouts over there," Nadia gestured toward a thick grove nestled on a hill, "and just beyond that, there's a pond full of eels which are said to increase a woman's fertility." She raised a wry eyebrow and poked him in the shoulder.

"Quick! Turn around," he cried, pushing her playfully back toward the necropolis.

"Maybe I should keep you in a pond," she said laughing. "That way you won't swim away on me."

"You can keep me wherever you like." He quickly scanned the surroundings and then discreetly grazed his hand along her thigh.

They strolled aimlessly through the pleasure garden. The Bouregreg Valley extended far below, and its green and yellow contours resembled the pattern on a tortoise shell. From time to time, the great bellow of a honking truck or a backfiring retort penetrated the shroud of stillness that hung over the funerary grounds. Otherwise, there was only the rustle of the leaves and the light tap of their footsteps.

Near the western edge of the garden, they came across the vermilion canopy of a flame tree. Beneath it stood the remains of a small arch, engraved with delicate Arabic writing, which some Merinid mason had set there a thousand years before. They sat down beside each other on the stone debris.

Nadia was wearing a royal blue tunic with white embroidery on the hem where it split at her legs. She had painted her face, plucked and plumped her brows, and farded her jade green eyes with kohl powder, so they appeared to float like precious stones on beds of black velvet. Her skin glistened in the late afternoon light like a bronze mask.

"I've never seen you so done up before," Simon said. "I feel like I'm walking beside Queen Nefertiti."

"It's the Chellah Jazz Festival," she exclaimed, as if that explained everything. "You don't like it?"

"It's just not you."

"Who said we always have to be ourselves?" She gave him a petulant glance. Then her face closed in on itself so abruptly that it seemed to be made of hard shining amber.

"Few people ever are." He looked around carefully and gently took her hands. To his surprise, they were stained with lacy filigrees of henna that wound up her wrists and lower arms.

"This is quite lovely," he said in his most cajoling voice. "Does it mean anything?"

"It's like my necklace." She extracted a delicate gold chain from beneath her tunic. A closed Fatima's hand, aimed downwards, dangled between her fingers. "The henna patterns ward off the evil eye and they also channel baraka."

"Baraka?"

"Really!" She gave him a condescending look. "Baraka is the flow of blessings from God into his creations. It connects the divine and the secular worlds. They say, for instance, that the Chellah is particularly infused with baraka."

"Do you actually have marabouts for professors at your medical school?" Simon asked with a teasing grin.

"Yes," she replied archly. "They're first-rate teachers and I've already put several spells on you."

"They seem to be working." He reached out to pull her close but a group of strangers surfaced at the edge of his vision. He quickly let go of her hand and peered innocently around at the flamboyant paradise. "I don't think I've ever seen so many civilizations together in one place," he observed in an overloud voice. "The Phoenicians, the Romans, the Arab sultans of yore..."

"The mosque and the minaret were built by Berbers," she interjected. "*Abu Yaqub Yusuf*, that one is ours." When she pronounced the mosque-builder's name, her rolling French cadence briefly squeezed into the harsh, throaty inflection of the Tamazight language. It was a translation that always startled Simon, despite its frequency, and made it seem as if she housed two very different personalities in one body.

"You seem very proud of your ruins."

"What culture isn't?"

"True," he acknowledged. Then he gestured at his watch and gently lifted Nadia to her feet. Unhurriedly, they began to circle back toward the entrance, where the concert venue was located.

"You're not going to say something about the vanity of all human effort?" she inquired with a knowing smile.

"No," he laughed, feeling a rush of warmth for Nadia. "Though it did occur to me."

They turned down a verdant alley lined by leafy fig trees and spiky rosebushes. Groups of strollers, dressed in evening finery, promenaded by in increasing numbers. A few of the cultural attachés from the Alliance Française came into sight and they exchanged friendly greetings.

"I was thinking that it's some impressively far-flung migration for a single hill by the coast," Simon said after the attachés had passed. "The Phoenicians sailed here all the way from Lebanon, the Romans from Italy, the Berbers from God knows where..."

"Probably Libya."

"Ok, Libya, but I think you've still got some sand in your hair from trekking though the desert for a thousand years." He ran a finger over the crown of her head and pretended to pluck out a few grains. "Yep, sandy hair."

"I was at the beach," she said piqued.

"And the migrants just keep coming," Simon concluded as they reached the entrance. He was about to turn toward the amphitheater when Nadia grabbed him by the arm. She pointed at a crowd of concertgoers, who were exclaiming loudly and pointing at the HCR.

Dozens of refugees had assembled in front of the bright white building on the hill. Around ten of them were moving methodically along the compound wall, gluing on signs and hooking long banners over the spiked fence. A second detachment was rolling bedding onto the sidewalk and propping lean-tos against the perimeter barriers. The usual traffic rumbled up and down Avenue Tariq Ibn Ziad, but occassionally a vehicle slowed down and honked at the refugees, whether in approval or condemnation, Simon couldn't tell.

Excited comments of "Look at that!" or "What are they doing?" tickled his ears. He squinted his eyes, trying to make out the blurry writing. "Maybe they want to be the first ones in tomorrow morning," he remarked to Nadia. "You have to admire that sort of enthusiasm."

"That's not what I'm getting from the signs."

"What do they say? I don't have my contacts in."

"Those Who Sow Refugees, Reap Fire," she read in a dramatic voice.

"Clever," he muttered.

"Oh. There's another one!" she exclaimed, after three of the refugees finished hanging a large piece of cardboard. "It says, *ASSEZ DE PRECARITÉ!*"

"What the hell are they protesting?" He peered at an enormous white banner, with meter-high letters scrawled in jagged black ink, that six of the refugees were slowly unfurling across nearly the entire length of the building.

"You really can't read that? Exactly how bad *is* your eyesight?"

"I have the eyes of a hawk," he replied with an annoyed glance. "It's just this particular hawk happens to wear glasses with thick prescription lenses."

"It says, RESETTLEMENT NOW!"

"Oh swell. That's going to go over great with the higher-ups."

The refugees began draping colorful curtains over the lean-tos, and one of them even strung some festive bunting. "It almost looks like they're setting up for a play." He narrowed his eyes again. "Only I can't tell if it's vaudeville or tragic theater."

"I guess you'll find out tomorrow," Nadia replied in a singsong voice. Behind them several storks loudly clacked their beaks like an army of paid clappers.

"Yes. Tomorrow will be interesting," Simon said with a sinking feeling.

He headed toward the edge of the bluff and sat down on a degraded stone wall. The sun began to dip beneath the horizon, and the refugees were slowly reduced to silhouettes stalked by long, angular shadows. He wondered if Arès was among them. He hoped so. He hoped that he was on solid ground and not tossing about in unpredictable waves.

For the thousandth time, he wished that he had more forcefully urged the fisherman not to throw away his life. The man had seen so much. He had travelled half the length of Africa and braved such extremes of hope and despair that Simon almost envied him. And now all of these experiences, radiant and terrible, would be consigned to the sediments of the sea, buried in a wreck of bones indistinguishable from any other.

"Do not worry about me," the refugee had said to Simon on the beach. "Like all the migrants here, I am caught like a fish in a net."

Simon had nodded, unsure how to respond.

"But this fish will find a hole," Arès had continued, staring at the JPO with steady resolve. "And when it does, it will swim all the way to Europe."

"Insha'Allah," Simon had replied.

"Not Insha'Allah. *Mektoub*," Arès had corrected him. "*Mektoub*."

Simon had pondered the distinction several times over the past few weeks. Insha'Allah essentially translated as "god willing," but *Mektoub* meant much more. It translated as "it is written," as in something prophesied in the Book of Fate.

The refugee's unshakable faith in his destiny surpassed any conviction that Simon had ever felt, and he wondered for a moment if he were not the poorer for it. He often worried that he was hollow inside, and for this reason he had drifted dangerously close to those who were truly alive—heroes, villains, or victims, it didn't matter—but those who found themselves caught up in the very maelstrom of *things*, just so he could bask in the reflective glow cast by the intense blaze of their lives and warm himself, for a few dying minutes, on the fire they left in their wake.

Nadia placed a comforting hand on his shoulder. "What are you thinking about?"

Simon leaned into the warmth of her grip and felt her soft leg rub against his arm. "People talk about the point of no return," he said, carefully monitoring the action in front of the HCR. "They think it's a point you reach by moving forward, but it's actually a point that you run from all of your life and that eventually catches up with you."

"Are you talking about us?" she half-kidded.

"No." He laughed and wrapped his fingers around her ankle. "Remember that refugee I told you about, the one who shared his life story with me and is planning to commit suicide by swimming to Spain?"

"How could I forget?" She gave his shoulder a light squeeze.

Simon plunged back into his unsettled thoughts. The sun had set, leaving behind a diffuse uncertain light that made everything seem distorted and unreal, so that even the high, steadfast walls of the HCR warbled like unruly white flames.

"Did you know that the migrants use the word '*brûler*' to refer to crossing the Mediterranean into Europe," Simon announced suddenly. "'Burn the sea,' they say. As if that were possible."

"It's part of their humor," Nadia replied. "They say that to keep their spirits up."

"Oh, I get it. But it's the sea that burns them up, and they keep piling into it like kindling. They don't seem to understand that when you pour fuel into a fire, only the fire remains."

"I don't blame them," she murmured.

"You wouldn't," he replied gruffly.

"What do you mean by that?" She stepped away from him, her body trembling slightly. He knew he should stand up and take her in his arms, but some inner disgust egged him on.

"Between your baraka and that refugee's magic prophecies, I feel like I've either stumbled into a madhouse or it's all some bloody bit of Shakespeare complete with dancing witches."

"*T'as vraiment le cœur sur la main*," she said with a sharp intake of breath.

"What do you mean by that?" He stared at her confrontationally. The rising moonlight had wrapped a halo around her head and the wavering borders of her body blurred into the somber surroundings. Two lustrous green eyes gleamed at him, mysterious, otherworldly. He turned away. "How can all this senseless death not bother you?"

"I mean that you have no heart for inexpressible things."

"What do you think is going to happen to those people in front of that building, baraka or no baraka?"

She clucked her tongue irritably. "I think that if you had to deal more directly with suffering people, you'd have a greater respect for the spiritual side of life."

One of the night guards at the HCR flipped on the outdoor floodlights and the sidewalk suddenly glowed like a brilliantly lit stage. There was an outcry among the refugees and Simon watched them relocate away from the glare.

"Perhaps," he conceded after a moment. "I'm sure it makes life easier to believe in all that junk."

"Why don't you say what's really on your mind," she responded in a sharp clinical tone that he imagined she used with her patients.

He sat up, startled. "Sure. Sometimes I worry that I'm not committed to anything. I mean, seriously committed. And until I find that *thing* I believe in, I'm basically just an impostor."

He could feel her fingers tighten around his shoulder, so that her nails began to dig into his flesh. "And how about us?" she whispered.

"What about us?"

"Exactly," she replied.

"Ouch!" He grabbed at his smarting skin and swung around. A black trail of tears had streaked down her cheeks, leaving marks like war paint below her farded eyes. She stormed off. He sat there momentarily stunned. Then he pulled himself together and dashed after her.

"Wait!" he shouted.

She waived him back. "I'm going home. Enjoy the concert."

"But I'm only here for you."

There was a *petit taxi* waiting nearby and, as a response, she hopped into it.

Bewildered, he walked back to the ancient forum and sat down again. The refugees had tossed blankets over the floodlights adjacent to the street, masking their activities once again. Somewhere nearby, someone was smoking a joint, and the heavy curls of hashish tickled Simon's nose and added to the dreamlike aura of the place.

He continued to sit, confused and despondently alone. Everything happened so fast in Rabat. He felt continually off-balance, as if he were receiving repeated, unexpected blows from numerous invisible assailants.

Soon the musicians began tuning their instruments. A lone violin lifted its melancholic voice toward the heavens and was answered by the far-off crash of thunder. Leaden clouds seeped across the sky, enveloping the necropolis in a dim shroud. When Simon looked back toward the expansive gardens, he could see a few scattered fireflies flashing their orange lights, miniscule flares of distress floating amidst a vast ocean of darkness.

He overslept again.

Lise and Nathalie had already left for work, so he washed and dressed quickly, ran downstairs, and hopped into a cab. When it arrived at the Place Abraham Lincoln, he asked the driver to stop. Then he crossed the street and crept slowly up the hill, fearful of what he might find.

From afar, it looked like a colorful flock of birds had landed in front of the HCR. As he drew nearer, the impromptu encampment came into focus, with its tattered green tarps, cardboard furnishings, and unidentifiable rags. The slums of Takadoum had settled before those immaculate white walls.

Some sixty refugees paraded before the building, shaking posters and shouting slogans. "*Assez de précarité! Assez d'insécurité!*" At least a dozen of them had wound their heads with long colorful *cheches* in the style of the desert Berbers.

Twenty meters up Avenue Tariq Ibn Ziad, the Rabati police had set up a command post in a partially camouflaged truck. An army detachment in olive fatigues stood by the vehicle, calmly smoking cigarettes.

Above the main gate, the demonstrators had taped a sign: RESETTLE-MENT IS A DURABLE SOLUTION FOR THE REFUGEES.

Simon glanced at it quickly as he hurried into the employee entrance. Inside the security shed, the guards looked strained and barely acknowledged Simon's greetings. Above them, a dozen monitors reproduced the setting he had just traversed in black-and-white pixelated video, lending a visionary quality to the scene.

The front office was empty, except for Camille. She looked up at him with her pretty, gamine face in a way that reminded him of one of those Hollywood street urchins, who later in the film always turn out to be royalty.

"What's going on?" Simon asked.

"Business as usual," she replied. "We keep our heads in the sand and ignore what's happening outside the walls."

"That's a relief," he said. "I was worried we would have to take stock or reflect deeply about our mission here and I really don't have the time." He stepped toward the main building.

"Speaking of which." Camille leapt sprightly to her feet and shoved her body between him and the door. "What happened to the refugee with the foot problem?"

Annoyed, Simon stared down at her. She had arched her back like a cobra and swayed menacingly before him. He was about to push by, but the piquant concoction of cheekiness, large dewy eyes, and pert breasts poking through her diaphanous shirt, disarmed him. He felt angry and aroused all at once.

"Who?" he asked in his most insouciant voice.

"You said you would try to get him resettled."

"Oh yes." He shrugged. "I got him another resettlement interview. Marie handled it. You should ask her."

"You don't care at all, do you?" Her voice was full of contempt. A muffled chanting rose outside, pulsing in slow insistent waves through the glass windows and half-shuttered jalousies.

"What are you talking about?" he said, dropping the act. "I even hunted him down on the beach and pleaded with him not to throw his life away."

"And?"

"And what?" His lips twisted in anger, and the vein on his right temple began to throb. "What do you want me to do? Invite him to move in with me? Buy him a plane ticket?"

"You could give a damn." Her cheeks were flushed now and her eyes burned self-righteously.

"Why? Would that feed him when he's hungry? Would that get him closer to Europe? Honestly, I don't want to feel too much for him or for any of them outside those walls."

The chanting swelled suddenly, followed by a short burst of drumming that reverberated throughout the building.

"They're no different from you and me," she insisted.

"Why does that matter?" he demanded, exasperated. "And of course they are! I'm inside and they're outside and that is as different as night and day."

"You mean black and white."

"Whatever you want to call it. They're villagers fleeing civil wars, former child soldiers, illiterate fishermen... I do my best to help them, but we're worlds apart. I'm not going to pretend that that's my cousin out there."

"Or your brother," she muttered bitterly.

"Or my brother."

"Why the hell do you even do this work?"

"That's the most outrageous question I've ever heard." He threw up his hands dramatically. "You don't need to be like someone to come to their aid. It's almost the opposite, no? It's the differences that makes working with them so compelling, and it's also those differences that protect us when everything gets botched up like usual. Otherwise, I'd spend half my time tearing out my hair."

"So you have no interest in helping the protesters?"

"There's only two things that are going to help those people out there." He pointed an accusing finger at the window. "And one of them is a boat."

"And the other?"

"Is a miracle," he snapped. "May I go now?"

She softly glided aside. "Yes, I'm sure you have more important things to do."

He stomped up to his office, slammed the door, cranked up the air conditioning, and sealed the window shut. He could still hear the protesters outside, but distant and gravelly, like the slow crunch of jackhammers biting through cement.

There were already several emails from Anna-Heintz requesting research on the Moroccan Penal Code, specifically in reference to 1) *la violence envers des agents de la force publique*, 2) *rébellion avec port d'armes*, and 3) *résidence illégal*. It wasn't stated explicitly, but he assumed this was in case things got out of hand. He spent nearly an hour sifting through conflicting versions of the Code until he found the pertinent sections.

Then Fatima phoned and informed him in an anguished voice that one of refugees from the Ivory Coast had been taken to the hospital with congestive heart failure and needed an urgent operation in Europe. After conversing with Hilda, he hurriedly drafted an Internal Resettlement Referral Form, which she hoped would bypass normal procedure under the extended mandate. Then he spent nearly an hour on the phone haranguing the cardiologist to fill out the report on his end.

It was almost noon when he finished, and his teapot was empty. Shaking the silver vessel, he headed to the kitchen to grab a bite to eat. When he stepped onto the terrace, he caught sight of several HCR employees gathered around the antique white table. They were muttering anxiously among themselves, sweat and worry staining their brows.

One of the refugees had gotten hold of a bullhorn, and he could hear a female voice inveighing against the duplicity of the HCR, and the fierce cries of applause in response. Maarten gusted onto the terrace and strode valiantly to the head of the table, his brave features staring defiantly at the invisible street below.

"Things may feel a bit rudderless right now," he shouted over the tumult, "but every ship has to weather a storm or two. We are doing all we can to right our course. Until then, please carry on with your duties."

The drums pounded hot and heavy behind him and a chanting rose that sounded hundreds strong. Overhead, the sun burned like a butane torch.

Simon shook his head and sought shelter in the kitchen with Saana and Silma. For half an hour, he drank tea and snacked on a fish tagine. The sister chefs were uncharacteristically silent that afternoon, and Simon was plunged in his own thoughts.

When he walked back out into the crucible of the day, the drumming had resumed at a feverish pitch. He wrinkled his nose. A sulfurous stench wafted through the air and made him feel like he was standing on a rumbling volcano. One of them must have set off flares, he thought. He bounded down the stairs, biting off two at a time. He wanted to check the security feed and see what was going on outside.

As he crossed the courtyard, he waived at the Swiss intern. Beneath coiling blond curls, Andrea's face was a ghostly white. It was the first time Simon had seen him shaken.

"You ok?" he asked.

"You can't hear the drumming inside, but it's driving me nuts."

A series of high-pitched ululations briefly interrupted the tireless pounding of djembes. Then they started up again, foreboding, tribal.

"Why don't you come inside?" Simon asked.

"They've struck the door several times with rocks," Andreas continued. "The security guards held them back, but we only have five guards and there's at least a hundred of them outside. They could kill us all if they break through."

"So come inside or go home for the day, if it's bothering you so much."

"I think I'll stay here," he replied weakly.

"Well, enjoy the music then." Simon spun around in disgust. Everyone was tense. He didn't have much sympathy for an intern who wanted to wallow in his misery.

He was heading toward the entrance when Camille came running outside.

"Hilda wants everyone on the terrace for an emergency meeting!" she shouted.

Simon motioned at Andreas to follow him. Then he reentered the building.

CHAPTER 51

JULY 2009

A RÈS UNDRESSED AND WASHED his clothes in Federika's bathtub. He was eating cereal at her kitchen table, wrapped only in a bright yellow towel, when his phone rang. "The sit-in has begun. You should come." Before he could reply, the speaker hung up.

He tugged his denim pants off the drying rack. They were still a bit damp and he had to shimmy his hips to get them on. He was buttoning his shirt when his brow suddenly knitted together in pain.

He walked quickly down the hall to the bathroom. His head was killing him and his pills were far away in Salé. He pulled open the medicine cabinet above the sink. Rummaging around, he found nothing the least bit palliative stashed behind the toiletries and the toothbrushes.

He strode out again and into Federika's room.

Her shelves were immensely tidy with no pharmaceuticals on display. Down on all fours, he groped under her bed, excavating keepsakes and detritus.

On the third or fourth sweep, he latched onto a circular tin box. Its top was painted with the image of a jubilant blond family riding a horse-drawn sleigh through snow-bound firs. This is what Europe looks like, he thought.

Then he opened the lid. The container brimmed with bundles of banknotes in several currencies. He pocketed nearly three thousand dirhams before replacing the nest egg.

On another sweep his fingers felt glass. Packed neatly into a turquoise fishbowl was an array of vials. The labels were indecipherable, so he indiscriminately popped a fistful of pills into his mouth, swallowing them with a sip of beer. Then he left the apartment. It was only a short walk to the HCR.

On Avenue d'Alger, he began to feel better and stopped into a café to eat. For several anxious minutes he stood uncertainly before the counter, but the waiter caught sight of him and took his order without a fuss. Shortly thereafter, he brought Arès a kefta omelet sandwich with French fries and a pot of mint tea.

The other customers in the café reacted normally to his presence and he wondered if the events of the past day had all been some elaborate hallucination.

He rubbed his knuckles hard against his forehead. Either way, he would find out at the HCR.

Yann caught sight of Arès when he arrived and clapped him hard on the shoulder. "I am glad you came. Now it is beginning. We have contacted several NGOs. They've lent us equipment and they will bring media attention. We will not leave until the HCR resettles every last one of us."

Arès nodded vigorously and tried his best to sound enthused. "This is very good," he said.

A crowd of demonstrators weaved before the HCR, chanting and waving signs to the rhythmic pounding of drums. At their center, Fofana shouted for silence and held up a bullhorn to a sizable woman with vivacious eyes. Voluminous braids covered her shoulders, and a sleeping baby bobbed off her back.

"We want the United Nations to stop lying to us!" Her amplified voice drowned out even the heavy traffic thundering up Avenue Tariq Ibn Ziad. "There are children suffering here under the sun, and you continue to lie to us!" The refugees clapped and hollered and two of them banged on metallic drums. "I am sorry for you. I am revolted by you!"

While the protesters applauded, Arès surveyed the scene. Salifou was conspicuously absent, and he breathed a sigh of relief. A Spanish NGO rolled up in a decaled van and began unloading boom mikes and professional video cameras. Soon they cordoned off an area at the southern edge of the rally and began to film.

Arès walked toward them and then kept moving downhill. At the lowest end of the building, the guards flanked an open garage door in a heavyset group of three, monitoring the demonstration.

With faltering steps, he emptied the distance between them. Their granite faces, imperturbable beneath the navy blue brims of their caps, divulged no sign of his approach. When he was only a few meters away, two of the guards brandished their truncheons and rushed toward him.

Arès' heart stitched together and he shielded himself with his cane. The guards ripped by him and launched into a group of protesters who were hassling a policeman.

Arès lowered his cane and, unscathed, entered the building.

The ground floor was strangely deserted. He wandered around, peeking into unlit offices with empty desks. It felt like he was moving through a mausoleum, and goose-bumps puckered on his skin.

The second floor was no different. But when he trailed the narrow corridor outside, he discovered the remnants of the staff gathered on the terrace, murmuring guardedly amongst themselves.

As he slunk closer, he caught snatches of conversations about an impending attack and it dawned on him that they were jumping ship. A half-concealed hook ladder led over a beige stucco wall onto the roof of the neighboring building, and from that low parapet, a drop ladder descended into a sea of pink azaleas.

The younger staff members had already evacuated, and Arès watched with infinite mirth as the old office lards heaved their disused bodies over the breach. He was the last upon the ladder, and he surveyed the scene as they weaved a jiggery path across the landscaped garden.

When no one else was left, he tossed his cane overboard and slid down the rails.

CHAPTER 52

JULY 2009

T WO DAYS LATER, HE went back to the HCR. He did not know why. Perhaps he still had hope.

The sit-in had grown larger and more organized. Brightly colored *kitenge* cloths fluttered off the security cameras and were fastened to upright poles. Children, the injured, and anyone not actively marching, sheltered themselves beneath extemporized lean-tos. The spiteful sun blistered overhead. It was only morning and already it was ninety degrees outside.

Despite the ongoing demonstration, business had resumed at the HCR and a queue of asylum demanders snaked out of the reinforced metal door on the north end of the building.

Arès stationed himself beside the applicants' entrance and waited, lost in thought. The flapping of the cloths reminded him of a morning he once spent with his brother Félix, hanging pennants for some political protest at his university. He could no longer remember the reason for the protest—he may not have even known at the time—but he did recall the gale force winds that whipped furiously across the campus, and the long tapering flags that wrestled in his hands like live crocodiles. He could still hear the two of them yelling insult after insult at each other as, one by one, the pennants escaped their grasps.

Afterwards, Arès wondered if the struggling cloths had secretly known what was in store. When a third set of pennants flew out of his hands and fishtailed toward the far-off river, the police screeched up in big ravenous vans and wrestled dozens of students inside. The two brothers barely escaped.

A lusty sea wind cracked the *kitenge* cloths together, startling him out of the past. This time, he decided, he would take no chances. When one of the HCR employees arrived, Arès slipped in behind him. Several of the protesters tried to follow, but the security guards fenced them off. The refugees were furious.

"Why can he go in and we cannot? Let us in!"

"He works here," the guard replied.

"No, he doesn't. He's a refugee from the Congo!" one of the women cried out.

"I assure you, he is German, and he's worked with us for a long time."

Arès smiled crookedly to himself.

"You are always lying to us!" The woman's voice was full of outrage.

As they pushed into the building, Arès peered into the airless waiting room. It was overcrowded with applicants and oven-hot in this weather.

He followed the German Protection Officer across the front courtyard and into the large multilevel hall, where several staff members were gathered. People were glancing around nervously and everyone seemed on edge. From outside came the chanting of the sit-in and the insistent throbbing of drums. Even more worrisome, behind that indefatigable drone, the building's occupants could sense the living static of the slum world recently erected before the immaculate white gates of the HCR.

The woman with buttery blond hair was perched on the stairs, talking down to them. Simon was there, as was the petite woman from the front office with the gamine face. Arès' eyes registered the JPO dully and slowly began to seethe. Here was the man who had blocked his resettlement request, and then, out of some astonishing perversion, had tried to dissuade him from swimming to Europe. These people were meant to help him, but their minds were as twisted as the branches of a baobab tree.

One of Paul's favorite sayings suddenly came to mind, "*le serpent se cache sous les fleurs.*"[76] That's what the HCR was. An enormous white flower with a coiled snake hidden beneath it.

"The refugees are like children," the blond-haired woman asserted loudly.

---

76   The serpent hides beneath the flowers.

"They complain and they get their result and so they complain again, and they get another meeting. I don't like to be pressured like this." Her blue eyes glistened like recently polished shields, ready for the fields of battle.

"I think they're going to be back tomorrow. It's almost certain," the Moroccan man from the front office said.

"It's such a waste of time. They know we don't have anything new to tell them. But then Maarten has to go meet with them. Why don't they protest in front of the Ministry of the Interior? It's right next door. And they can do what we can't, which is pressure the government."

"I think they called the press and alerted the prefecture and the Ministry of the Interior. They are well organized this time," the man replied. Then his phone rang, and he hurried off, braying exasperatedly into the receiver.

"Well then maybe it's good." She lifted her large expressive eyes toward the high ceiling. "The government needs to know that there is a problem. Let them do what they can. In any case, whatever happens always falls on the heads of the refugees. It won't fall on my head or Maarten's. What are they going to do? For all their complaints, they don't want to go back home or anywhere else. They know it's better here than the DRC or Central African Republic or Benin."

One of the employees laughed. "Some of them are demanding to be sent to actual refugee camps. They're claiming it would be better than living in Morocco."

"We should do that," Simon suggested, his words half-chewed by his thick American accent. "Send them to one of the UN refugee camps in Chad and see how they like it. I have a friend working there. Rebels attack twice a week and the women and children are kidnapped. Then they'd realize how other refugees live."

"Maybe we could show them movies of the camps," the petite woman suggested. "So they can understand that there are more urgent cases for resettlement…"

Arès moved on down the hallway, desperate for some sign of hope.

He made a wrong turn and then another and found himself once again in the large multilevel hall. This time he descended the short flight of stairs and opened the frosted door to the main office. A dozen employees were penned inside, shouting agitatedly, comments pinging from every corner of the room. As the refugee edged in, the saintly-looking man briefly held court. "It's unfortunate," he announced, "but it looks like another all-day sit-in."

"They'll never be satisfied by what we tell them."

"Yes, we are in a situation that is really disagreeable. It is very tough."

The French woman, who had conducted Arès' recent interview, thumped her desk. "It's really a shame, and you know, it's those refugees who are unable to listen and respond reasonably, or act reasonably." He watched the boxy glasses bounce on her nose.

"Well, we have to be prepared."

The woman from Gabon raised her hand. "Excuse me, I am working on the convocations for tomorrow. Should I still have them come?"

"Yes. If this continues, we may ask the police to send reinforcements so the applicants can enter the building without an issue. It's really a bother," the French woman replied.

"What did they demand during their meeting with Maarten yesterday?" the employee with curly blond hair asked.

"They demanded resettlement for all the refugees in Morocco." Two of the Protection Officers laughed uproariously.

"I don't understand," one of the employees from the front office said. She was wearing her red tank top again, and her hair was wrapped in a colorful tie-dyed band. To Arès' knowledge, the red tank top was all she ever wore. "Don't they know that the receiver countries give us their quotas and we send them the dossiers and they take whomever they want?"

Anna-Heintz was sitting at one of the desks on the far side of the room. She looked up suddenly from a crumpled pile of papers. "They don't listen," she said coldly, with her odd, syncopated pronunciation. As always, her back was perfectly erect and her chin sat on a horizontal plane off her long, straight neck. "We've told them this before. We told their representatives in the meeting yesterday, and we told them it again this morning."

"We even used to do a formation every Friday on how resettlement works," the saintly man added.

"Maybe they don't believe us?"

"I'm sure that we're having this protest now because we resettled cases that were too weak," the French woman asserted in a bullish voice. "The refugees look at themselves and say, 'Why that person and not me? My profile is the same.' So they think if they put pressure on us, we'll resettle them all. But with a resettlement rate of less than thirty percent, there's no way it's even possible."

"Then how do we resettle weak cases? Why do the countries take them?" the woman in the red tank top asked.

"Because the countries are not necessarily interested in our resettlement criteria," the French woman snorted. Arès had the brief impression that she was hoofing the floor beneath her chair, but when he looked under the desk her feet were quite still. "They want refugees who are young or skilled, who will pay taxes and not be a burden."

"So should we start submitting RRFs for younger refugees whom the countries are more likely to accept?"

"No, then they wouldn't meet *our* resettlement criteria." Anna-Heintz sighed. She looked fatigued and her normally pallid complexion appeared almost translucent that morning. "We only resettle people who are truly vulnerable. We focus on urgent medical need, unaccompanied minors, the handicapped, and so forth. Then we still have to leave a few spots open for high-profile cases, someone who could be assassinated by their home country or whose life is in danger in Morocco for political reasons."

"That happens?"

"Sometimes. Also, finally, and I shouldn't really say this, but we try to resettle refugees who cost us a lot." She paused and her head bobbed rapidly back and forth, like a cat suddenly faced with several running mice. Apparently satisfied, she continued. "It's a strategic choice the HCR makes. But of course, this is part of the burden sharing with other countries. If a refugee costs us a lot and will get better treatment in Europe, we definitely try to send him."

While she spoke, Arès inched closer to her chair. When he was a foot away, he crouched and peered at her with curious, incredulous eyes. A static, doll-like expression decorated her face, and, for a moment, Arès had the uncanny impression that he was looking at a perfect facsimile of a human being. He leaned over and sniffed her, but she gave off no scent and when he put his finger in front of her mouth, he detected no draw of breath.

He should have felt anger or outrage standing in front of her, but instead there was only a deep disgust. How could they give such broken people power over life and death?

He backed toward the door, shaking his head. As he laid his hand on the knob, the employee in the red tank top raised her voice. "Is a woman at risk considered an urgent case? Someone who's being beaten every day?"

"No," Anna-Heintz replied. "We only consider extreme situations to be urgent cases." Arès creaked the door half-open, then idled there, waiting to hear her full explanation. "For instance, a refugee who can't get his pacemaker replaced in Morocco and has to go to France. Or women who are victims of forced prostitution rings, or people who might be killed by organized crime. We can't even resettle every refugee who turns to prostitution, because if we do that, then word will get around, and starting next week every female refugee will suddenly be a trafficked sex worker."

He shut the door and retreated down the hall.

He felt an urgent desire to find Federika. He wanted to see her in institutional garb, see if anything had changed. He wanted to know if he could still remember her lively gay laughter, or picture her denuded on the stool.

He pivoted down the pinched corridor and urged his body up the stairs. As he neared the second story, Simon loped by, flattening him against the wall. He stopped in his tracks, his eyes ablaze. The provocation of this man was too much. Arès forgot about Federika and trailed the JPO until he skidded down a hallway and disappeared into a rectangle of light.

When Arès stepped onto the terrace, Simon was there. The hand that had signed his condemnation, locking him up forever in Rabat, was calmly scratching on a blue notepad while the Cameroonian Eligibility Officer spoke.

"This morning, a guy comes in and tells me that in 1998 his brother volunteered for the army. Then something happened, which he couldn't describe, and his parents received a phone call from someone telling them to flee. Then just like that they fled."

"And he couldn't say what happened?"

"No, he claims that his parents left him in the care of his uncle when they arrived in Brazzaville, and his uncle abandoned him in Nigeria. So I ask him, does he think that he would be arrested if he returned to the DRC and he says, 'Yes.' But on what basis? There's no reason for him to believe that. He must have been young when he left the Congo, maybe twelve or thirteen." The EO took a sip from a can of cherry cola.

"He couldn't ask his parents?"

"He says that he's had no contact with them, or his brothers or sisters, since they left him with his uncle. And then none with his uncle since he was abandoned by him. So I ask him, 'On what basis do you think you'll be arrested if you go back to the DRC?' He replies that his house has become a military post since he left. So I ask him, how does he know that if he has had no contact with anyone back home for ten years, and he replies, 'Well it was right after I left, so I know.' His story is just *mal techniquée*. That's what I find so exhausting. These interviews exhaust me."

Simon wrinkled his brow and scratched his head with the backside of his pen. "Of course, when people lie, they generally have much more coherent narratives, so he's probably telling the truth."

"Oh, I'm not saying he's lying. I never say they lie. But the story is so badly put together. It's the idiocy of it that I don't understand."

"So it's a rejection?"

"His credibility doesn't matter, because there's nothing in the story that makes it seem like he cannot go home." The EO clasped his hands together as if in prayer. "He wasn't a human rights activist or in a political group. He's a normal citizen like you or me. So there's no reason for him to fear persecution under the 1951 convention."

Drums sounded loudly from the street, and a rhythmic chanting filled the air.

"They're still there," the JPO said.

The EO harrumphed. "Yes, I find their protest very funny."

"But of course, you can understand them?"

"Oh we all understand them. There's nothing not to understand. But someone has to go out there and explain as simply as possible that there are eighty million displaced people in this world, and no country is going to take them all. They're chasing a dream."

Simon shook his head and looked distractedly at the corner of the terrace where Arès was standing. The refugee shifted uncomfortably, worried for a moment that he could be seen.

"You just reminded me," Simon said.

"Yes."

"Remember our fisherman friend from Kinshasa? He told me the most incredible story a few weeks ago."

The EO snorted. "They'll tell you anything to get you to help them. What did he want? Some money? New clothes?"

Simon laughed and began to walk off the terrace. Near the exit, he turned halfway around and shouted back to the EO, "I think he wanted a boat."

Arès felt anger spurt hot up his neck as the EO exploded with laughter. If only he could shove those words back into Simon's smug mouth. If only he could mangle that hand that had signed his death warrant and then gone off to lunch. But he was powerless in his present state. He was always powerless before these people.

The next day he returned again.

Overnight, the sit-in had grown more elaborate. There were mattresses now, sleeping bags, tents, a full bivouac crouched beside the incessant traffic of Avenue Tariq Ibn Ziad. The refugees' belongings were sandbagged around them, like levees awaiting high waters.

A large, rumpled piece of cardboard with a scrawled message had been pasted over the main entrance to the HCR: *MAARTEN, NOUS SOMMES LÀ*.

It was too dangerous for Arès to try to enter the building anymore. He could not sneak past all those bodies massed before that bright white beacon on the hill.

So he waited. He knew not why, but he waited, a ghost who sometimes flickered on the security feeds like a light interference. He stood there in the scalding sun and watched his future erode.

INTÉGRATION ZÉRO! the new banner across the building read.

Starting at around eleven in the morning, and at consistent five-minute intervals, the refugees' cellphones whistled out ringtones or pop jangles. Every time a phone rang, it was passed to an Ivorian named Didier, one of the *Points Focaux* of the demonstration. After a few of the calls, Didier grew heated and began shouting vehemently into the phone. Arès edged closer to listen.

"You can keep your fucking sexual and sexist violence for the HCR! You have secretaries there, I believe, with whom you can practice your sexual violence. We are here protesting in the sun, and we will not come to your workshop."

THE PERSON ON THE PHONE RESPONDED.

"No. We are waiting for a durable solution, and we will not leave until every refugee who is part of this group is resettled. If you take us away from Morocco, you will not see us in front of the HCR. Until you take us away, we will be here. Now for the respect of what we are doing, stop calling the refugees."

ANOTHER RESPONSE.

"You are very stubborn. Yes, stubborn. I have told you before not to call the refugees, but still you keep calling."

ANOTHER RESPONSE.

"No. It does not matter if they are in front of the building or not. Do not call ANY refugee, here or elsewhere, out of respect for our suffering. Look... I do not have to yell at you. I do not have to do you violence. But this is not a request. It is an order. If you do not stop calling the refugees, we will come down to the Fondation Oriental on Friday and there will be trouble."

ANOTHER RESPONSE.

"Take us away from Morocco. That is our demand. All of us."

A smile crept up Arès' lips. Some nub at the bureau was trying to invite the refugees to one of the monthly formations on sexual and sexist violence.

Never any respect, he thought.

CHAPTER 53
JULY 2009

BOOM! BOOM! BOOM!

*B*The heavy bass beats shook the apartment like bomb blasts. The furniture wobbled and jerked and the windows rattled like jazz cymbals. When they cracked them open, they could hear the synthetic pop sounds of Algerian Raï and the loud ululations of the celebrants. One building over, they could see the lofty white tent and at least two hundred revelers cramming a small rooftop. A perverse superfluity of speakers encircled the party, like soldiers defending battlements from attack.

Simon had been warned on several occasions. Moroccan weddings began at midnight and lasted till seven or eight in the morning, and in working-class neighborhoods like the Quartier de l'Océan, the festivities took place on roofs.

Lise and Nathalie were noticeably absent. They had gone out dancing with the Fulbrighters and, perhaps touched by a premonition, had not come home.

At two in the morning, Kinani and Simon sat in the living room, stubbornly trying to drink themselves asleep. They were failing.

"They must have at least a hundred speakers on that roof," Simon grumbled. "We should sneak over and grab a few for your next concert."

"I'm sure half of them don't work," Kinani replied with a light, mocking grin. "The Moroccans are like that. Lots of show, but most of their gear is broken."

"Really? It sounds like at least *all* of them are working right now."

As if to accentuate his point, the speakers unleashed a furious barrage of music and dozens of women screamed banshee-like at the echoing sky.

"We're going to be up late tonight," Kinani shouted over the din.

Simon nodded and stuck his fingers in his ears.

Several minutes later, the noise diminished somewhat and Kinani tapped his flatmate on the shoulder. "I heard from the girls how you helped me with the landlord. Thank you."

"Ah sure." Simon shrugged. "I just did it because I hate to be wrong."

"Well, then I'm the sucker," Kinani replied, "because I bought this bottle of Johnnie Walker to thank you. I was going to wait for a nicer occasion, but I don't think we have the choice."

He handed Simon the tall bottle, with its gold-embossed letters and debonair striding man.

"Black label. Of course."

"I would never drink anything else," Kinani said. His eyes, as always, glittered like stolen diamonds.

"You speak like someone who's always had the choice."

"I always have."

"Even in the Congo?"

Instead of answering, Kinani rose and fetched two glasses from the kitchen. "Do you prefer yours neat or on the rocks?"

"The only rocks are in your head," Simon replied, laughing. "Or are you hiding ice cubes in your pockets?"

"Here you go." Kinani handed Simon a tumbler sloshing with the amber liquid. He took a small sip, smacked his lips, and lifted his glass toward the JPO. "To friendship."

"Thank you for the gift," Simon shouted over the thudding bass that shook the apartment. They clinked their tumblers together. "To friendship," he added.

The two men reclined with their glasses, Simon on the ratty brown couch, Kinani on a nylon chaise lounge that one of the girls had salvaged from the *plage de Rabat*. Simon sipped the whiskey, feeling it burn pleasantly down his throat. Then he leaned forward and extracted two rectangular boxes from under the nearby coffee table.

"Chess or backgammon?" he asked.

Boom! Boom! Boom! resounded all around them.

"I prefer backgammon," Kinani said. "It's more true to life. It divides the world into brown and white and everything is based on chance."

"There's some skill involved," Simon objected.

"Some, but most of it is dumb luck. Like how things really are."

Simon brushed aside a lock of blond hair that had fallen over his eyes. "I prefer chess for the same reason. The better tactician prevails. Just like in life."

"Spoken like someone who was born with the winning hand," Kinani muttered, his imperturbable smile glinting in the somber room.

"Have it your way." Simon opened the backgammon set and unfolded it on the coffee table. The music stopped for a moment and the two men looked up hopefully, the tension draining from their faces.

"Do you think it's over?" Simon asked. Then a popular tune by Abdelaziz Stati exploded from the speakers, a hundred times too loud, jangling every window within a ten-block radius.

"I hate this country," Kinani exclaimed. "I can't wait to move to Europe."

"You want to move to Europe?" Simon yelled over the music. "Why? You're halfway through your master's. Your family's here. Except for the occasional wedding party, things seem to be going well."

"It might seem so," Kinani replied at normal volume, forcing Simon to bend toward him. "But then the Moroccans tried to kick me out of yet another apartment, and their children hiss *'azee!'* at me in the street. And there is something more. I am constantly reminded that I am not *chez moi*, and that is far more insidious."

"You're being a trifle dramatic, no?" Simon began laying out the back-gammon pieces. "I assume you'll play brown?"

"When I first started studying at the university here," Kinani continued, "the students used to stop me in the halls to ask for the time. All day long it was *'ch'hal essa`a? ch'hal essa`a?'*"

"So?" Simon fussed over the pieces.

"Whenever I looked at my watch to tell them, they'd give this sinister little smile. I couldn't figure out what the hell was going on, until one day, an older student from Senegal filled me in. They were asking me the time so I would look at my wrist and remember that I was black. That's why they grinned at me like that. They saw me seeing myself. But soon enough I began grinning back. Every time one of them called me a monkey or a cannibal or the son of a slave, I flashed the biggest smile I had. I said to myself, they can't rob me of that. They want to remind me that I'm black, but I'll show them that where it counts, I'm even whiter than they are."

"Sounds like pretty sophomoric humor on the part of the students," Simon observed with a light yawn. Then he tilted the tumbler into his mouth and rolled the fiery drink around on his tongue. "You know, this whiskey is quite good."

Kinani leaned back in the chaise lounge and his eyes became dim and unseeing, like two dark stones fitted into brown bezels. "A man who has never been bitten by a snake cannot understand the pain it causes."

"Why do you think Europe will be better?" Simon asked, putting down the glass.

"Spiritually who knows, but let me speak your language, l'Américain, the language of economics. There's no getting ahead here. Do you know about the Makhzen?"

Simon yawned again. "No. But if they shut down wedding parties, I'm interested."

"The Makhzen is the shadow government run by the monarchy," Kinani said in a solemn voice. "For every political, military, and bureaucratic post in Morocco, there's its double, like a reflection in the water. There's the minister and then there's the Makhzen minister. There's the general of the armed forces and the Makhzen general. There's the postman and the Makhzen postman. Everywhere there's the official elected government, and then there's the Makhzen."

"What's the matter with that?" Simon asked innocently. "Sounds like there's twice the opportunity." He laughed brightly at his joke, but Kinani bared his teeth to the gums.

"*Mon frère*, at the narrow passage, there is no brother and no friend."

"Well it must be better than the DRC."

"In some ways yes. In others no. But I admit, I would not go back there."

"See," Simon exclaimed. "You should count your lucky stars you made it here."

Kinani laughed heartily. "Oh I do. Did you know that Zaire had a space program? A real one."

"You're kidding."

"It was before I was born, but it's why I became an astrophysicist. I was tired of staring at the mess on the ground, so I decided to look up at the stars."

"The contrast must have been exceptional in the DRC."

"Yes, Gbadolite had extraordinary stars. I miss them here."

"I wasn't talking about the night sky," Simon riposted.

"Things are very straightforward for you, l'Am-é-ricain." Kinani drawled out the epithet with what Simon assumed was a fake Southern accent. It was not amusing.

"How do you mean?"

"The Congo is a mess. But it is your mess too."

"Tell me about it. Half of the refugees in Rabat are from the DRC, but you know that already." He glanced at Kinani to see if the innuendo had stuck.

"And why did they flee the Congo?" Kinani asked, unperturbed.

"Ha! Let me count the ways."

"Ok. But who was their Big Man?"

"They fled Mobutu's dictatorship and the wars that ensued. We're not talking rocket science here."

"Ah, no? Seems very clear-cut. Mobutu. A bad man. A very big man, very dangerous." Kinani swung his feet onto the floor and sat up straight. His head now rose well above Simon and he looked down at him with a scoffing, worldly smile.

"Yes. He really screwed up the country," Simon replied.

"But he was very cunning, wasn't he?"

"Well he stayed in power all those years."

"Yes, but not like the snake who slithers alone through the grass. More like the bird who sits on the back of the elephant."

"How do you mean?"

"Mobutu was weak from the start," Kinani said. "He could barely control his country. But he sat on the back of an elephant, and so no one could touch him."

The heavy bass pulsed through the living room like the aftershocks from a nearby earthquake. Simon could feel it vibrate his insides. "An elephant? You mean the army?"

"I mean you. I mean your country, l'Américain."

Simon audibly sighed. Then he smoothed back his lion's mane of hair. "I'm sorry. Just because you read a bunch of conspiracies theories on the internet doesn't mean they're true. Now are we playing this or not?" The pieces on the backgammon board waited patiently in pretty little lines. There was something tempting in the simple choices presented by the game.

"*Ah. Tant que les lions n'auront pas leurs propres historiens, les histoires de chasse continueront de glorifier le chasseur.*"[77]

"I beg your pardon."

Kinani furrowed his brows, and, for a brief moment, his smile waned. "It is a matter of public record that the CIA assassinated the Congo's first democratically elected leader, Patrice Lumumba, a virtuous man with pan-African ideas upsetting to the Americans. It is a matter of public record that Mobutu was a paid operative of the CIA, and that his coup d'état was orchestrated by your government. None of this is even controversial. There are memoirs by Belgian ambassadors and even the CIA Station Chief at the time, where they openly discuss all of these matters."

"Well that's your version of things," Simon said, looking hopelessly at the board. "But there are facts and there are stories."

Outside the speakers hammered out their percussive *Boom! Boom! Boom!*

"I disagree," Kinani said with a sly smile. "In the end, we are only the stories we tell."

"And why have I never heard these stories about American involvement?"

"Because you closed your ears at birth," Kinani remarked sharply. "You would prefer to ignore history, but here you are, almost fifty years after Lumumba's death, stuck in its web. You spend your days desperately tending to the survivors of a blaze lit by your own government. And you sit

---

77   As long as the lions do not have their own historians, the history of hunting will continue to glorify the hunter.

here, perplexed, while the survivors demonstrate in front of your building. Nathalie told me that there are death threats, and I wouldn't be surprised if violence ensues."

They heard a deafening woosh. Both men spun around to see a small rocket float indolently into the night, like a cinder wafting from a fire. Slowly, it stitched a smoldering kite trail across the sky and crossed swords with a shooting star, before erupting into a glitzy crown of gold.

Simon rushed to the window, excitedly flipping off the lights. Several more fireworks followed, and every fiery burst splashed luster across his thick flaxen hair and set sparkles in his eyes. He turned around and saw that Kinani had reclined in the chaise lounge and that a dark shadow had fallen across his face. A sulfurous whiff drifted through the window, and Kinani scrunched his fine nose and seemed to sink deeper into his thoughts.

"Well it ends tonight, anyway," Simon said.

"What do you mean?"

"HQ instructed us not to show up for work tomorrow. The Moroccan gendarmes are coming by to clear out the protesters."

"Are you people nuts?" Kinani sprang to his feet. "There are women and children there."

"It wasn't my call," Simon replied defensively. "But we can't keep working like this. There are other refugees besides them who rely on us."

"Do you think they'll just disappear like ghosts once you remove them?" Kinani strode over to the window and looked out. Another rocket burst in the sky, and his body was framed by an exploding spore of light. "These are people who have survived more than you can imagine. They're not chess pieces that you can push around on a board."

Simon thought it was finally time. "We know that you're a refugee."

"I know you know," he hissed. "I overheard the girls talking about it. Why do you think I've been avoiding the apartment?"

"I thought you had a new girl," Simon said softly.

"Anyway. It doesn't matter."

"Of course it matters!"

Kinani leaned an arm onto the window-sill. "No. It doesn't. I never even understood what it means to be a refugee."

"Well you live with three people who work at the UNCHR, so you've had plenty of opportunities to ask," Simon replied hotly.

The last fireworks exploded in the sky like glitzy supernovas. For a brief moment, night blazed like day. Then they faded with a languid, pulsating glow. Kinani stared out at heavens that appeared all the blacker for the fires that had burned there before. When he turned around his smile was gone. It had vanished just like that.

"A refugee is the name we give to an idea that frightens us," Kinani said, staring severely at Simon, "so we don't have to call it by its true name."

"Which is?" Simon stuttered, disconcerted by Kinani's sudden transformation.

"A refugee is just a person," he replied quietly. "And that's what scares us, because a person is like us. In our minds, becoming a refugee is something that happens to other people. That's why we call them refugees, or migrants, or whatever else you call them when I'm not around. We give them these names to convince ourselves that these are things that happen to someone else. That's what I thought too, until it happened to me. Then I became something that happens to someone else."

"Do you want to tell me about it?"

"It's not something I talk about."

"*Si tu ne donnes pas de nourriture à ton propre maladie, tu vas nourrir le fossoyeur,*" Simon quoted.[78]

"Ah, I see you've been spending time with Baptiste."

Simon blushed. "He has a lot of good expressions."

"Well here's another one: 'Light troubles like to be spoken of, but heavy troubles prefer silence.' That's Seneca. You should read him if you plan on spending much more time in Africa."

Simon glanced out the window. He could see the newly married couple being carried about on white cushioned podiums strewn with pink flowers. The guests danced around them, holding bright sparklers that glimmered like magic wands. The high fluctuating flutes and jangling cymbals of traditional châabi wedding music crashed through the neighborhood, so

---

78   If you don't give food to your illness, you will just nourish the gravedigger.

that even the far-off ocean liners, twinkling on the high seas, seemed to rock to the melody.

"Well you're not going to get much silence here."

"I know," Kinani said resignedly. He sat back down and finished another tumbler of whiskey.

"How about that backgammon game?" Simon suggested, switching on the lights.

"I've lost my appetite for it. I'm tired of all these battles. No matter how far the refugees run, violence stalks them. It reminds me of one of the Greek tragedies; the *Oresteia*, perhaps. They can flee all they want, but it is like fleeing from one's own shadow."

Simon gave Kinani an admiring look. "You never cease to surprise me."

"If you lived through what I lived through, you would find the Greeks very instructive."

The married couple dismounted from their thrones and the guests began milling about on the rooftop. There was a moment of silence, while the DJ made whatever mysterious adjustments DJs make, and then one hundred speakers began boisterously blaring "Ya Rayah" by Dahmane El Harrachi.

"Always this song!" Simon shouted, splashing whiskey into his empty glass. "I think I've heard it at least a thousand times since I moved here."

"It's a Moroccan favorite," Kinani replied. "The song is called 'The Emigrant' and it captures everything perverse about my situation. For the Moroccans are migrants as well. They too carry the heavy cross of exile and are greeted with harsh words of hate and have sharp stones cast at them in the street. Yet this does not prevent them from doing the same *chez eux*."

"What's it about?"

"It's the ballad of the exiled. It tells of the trials of emigration, of what we have lost and what we lose on the way. Of the crowded and desolate territories we cross. Of how we travel on with no clear destination in sight."

Chhal cheft al bouldan laamrine wa lber al khali
Chhal dhiyaat wqat chhal tzid mazal ou t'khali
Ya lghayeb fi bled ennas chhal taaya ma tadjri
Tzid waad el qoudra wala zmane wenta ma tedri

Aalach qalbek hzine waalach hakdha ki zawali
Matdoum achadda wila tzid taalem ou tabni[79]

Simon threw open a window and the music suffused the apartment. He could not understand the words, but he felt strangely moved by the elegiac melody, and his heart lifted again and again with the violin's jaunty refrain. Moist breaths of ocean air filtered in, so that even the night sky seemed to be shedding tears. Simon instinctively flicked off the lights, and the two men wiled in darkness for the duration of the song.

Then, out of that darkness, Kinani began to speak.

"My father was trained as a diplomat. He was not Congolese, and neither is anyone in our family. We are from Gisenyi in the northwest of Rwanda, though my ancestors came from the south. My father represented Rwanda first in Ethiopia and later in Switzerland, but President Juvenal Habyarimana called him home to act as a personal advisor. This is where I get my name. Kinani was Juvenal's nickname. In Kinyarwanda it means 'invincible.'"

"Very modest of your parents."

"I believe they guessed well," Kinani said with a light chuckle. "While he was working for Habyarimana, my father met Mobutu and the two of them grew close. When the situation began to deteriorate in Rwanda, my father reached out to the Maréchal. He was offered a similar post in Zaire. Then Habyarimana's plane was shot down, and the Rwandan Patriotic Front launched its invasion from the north. Three days later, we boarded one of Mobutu's private planes in Kigali and flew with Habyarimana's remains to Gbadolite."

"Gbadolite? Why did you go there?"

---

79   How many overcrowded and empty lands have you seen? / How much time have you lost? / How much do you have still to lose? / Oh emigrant in other people's lands / Do you even know what is happening? / Destiny and time follow their course, but you know nothing of them / Why is your heart so sad?

Kinani swilled a heavy draught of whiskey and shook his head scornfully. "It is stunning to me that after more than a year working with Zairian refugees, you still do not know of the Versailles of the Congo."

"Well that's the problem." Simon plopped back down onto the couch. "Most of our refugees did not belong to the Congolese aristocracy."

"Ah, but you didn't have to belong to anything to be there. Gbadolite was Mobutu's ancestral village. Before he became president, it was a scattering of mud huts beside a river. By the time my family arrived, Mobutu had carved a city out of the jungle, with five-star hotels, a runway long enough for the Concorde, and three palaces for his family and staff."

"Sounds like the sort of kleptocratic madness that would cripple an entire country."

"You cannot imagine the opulence of that place," Kinani continued. "My brother and I were enrolled at the presidential school in town, but sometimes we would visit my father at Mobutu's palace in Kawelel. The Maréchal had a fleet of Mercedes and one of his chauffeurs would bring us there. It was ten kilometers through pure rainforest and, all of sudden, you pulled up in front of two illuminated fountains that played classical music. When you walked inside, it was like entering an enchanted castle. The corridors were lined with Renaissance paintings and Roman sculptures. The rooms were decorated in Louis XIV and the floors were finished with rare Italian marble. White-gloved butlers wandered the halls. Sometimes they carried champagne, sometimes roast quail, or lobsters, or Norwegian salmon, anything you could imagine. The walls were covered in damask or tapestries, and outside were swimming pools surrounded by oriental vases and statues of lions sculpted from gold.

"And we were *chez nous*! Our father was a good friend of Papa Maréchal and we were like his adopted children. The palace was our playground. We'd run around for hours and then go find our father on the veranda. He was always there, drinking gin and tonics with a group of diplomats, waiting for the sun to set." Kinani sipped his whiskey. "Then the sun finally set. It was a dream of paradise and it couldn't last." He sighed.

"And a nightmare for everyone else in the country," Simon said, aghast. "Nothing else was left for them."

Kinani grinned. "Yes, there was a popular saying in Zaire that the public servants would pretend to work and the government would pretend to pay them."

"Didn't that bother you?"

Kinani straightened up in the chaise lounge. He lifted his dignified face and regarded Simon calmly with brilliant, bejeweled eyes. "For three years of my life I was part of an aristocracy. How do you think the peasants lived under the French kings? Or the British throne? All monarchy is theft. The Moroccan royal family is one of the richest in the world because they have impoverished their countrymen."

"But you were part of that system. Your family participated in the rape of the Congo."

Boom! Boom! Boom! The DJ had rebooted his collection of Algerian Raï, and the heavy percussive bass thudded through the apartment like far-off explosions.

"And you think you did not?" Kinani shouted over the noise. "I have seen your expensive laptop. Where do you think the metal comes from in those machines? My father helped Mobutu broker deals with your government. Patronage and protection in exchange for Zaire's resources. There were several uprisings against the Maréchal in the 1970s, and each time the Americans and the French sent in their troops and quashed the opposition."

"It was the Cold War," Simon retorted.

"You beggared the largest nation in Africa as part of a game of three-dimensional chess with the Soviets. And now you want to keep prices down in the West for your electronic toys, so you support Kabila just like you once did with Mobutu. Your country may crow about democracy, but when it comes to market economics, dictators will do."

"Sure," Simon said, glaring at his flatmate, "but I'm a passive consumer of products whose supply chain is tainted by human rights abuses. Your father was providing strategic advice to one of the worst kleptocrats in history."

Kinani calmly got to his feet, his regal features on proud display. "My father was a political advisor to presidents. First Habyarimana, then Mobutu. You cannot choose where you are born or what possibilities life will present to you. To rise in the ranks, to fulfill his political destiny, he had to serve the leaders where he was from."

"Did he never think of giving it up?" Simon asked in a subdued tone.

Kinani gazed down at his flatmate with burning eyes. Then a shadow passed over his face and the flames extinguished. "He complained about it often, but my father was a pragmatic man as well. Look at the misery of the refugee population and you will get but a taste of the misery in the Congo. It is not a place where you toy with failure or with ideals. We did not have that luxury."

"So what happened?"

"What do you mean?"

"How did you end up here?"

Kinani collapsed back into his chair. Then he held out his empty glass. Simon poured it full of whiskey.

"Like every fiefdom, Gbadolite was also an army base. Mobutu had a private Presidential Guard of about five thousand soldiers. They were, I believe, the only regularly paid government employees in all of Zaire's history." He chuckled again and took another sip. "The presidential school was adjacent to the garrison where they stored their weapons. When Kabila's army began its march across Zaire, we knew they would eventually come to us. The symbolic pull of Gbadolite was too strong."

Kinani fell silent. The two men quietly imbibed their drinks. The music had died down a bit, and it sounded now like the continuous crashing of waves on the shore. Simon's head was spinning gently, and he felt like he was floating on those waves.

"It was the eleventh of May," Kinani began again. "We heard that Kisangani had fallen a few days before. We even packed our bags to leave, but the latest reports said that Kabila's army was over a hundred kilometers away. So the next morning, we went to school like usual."

"That doesn't seem very far," Simon commented.

Kinani looked at him, surprised. "There were no serviceable roads outside of Gbadolite. Zaire was a country without infrastructure. Travelling a hundred kilometers with an army could take days or even weeks, depending on the conditions."

"But it didn't?"

"We had just been let out of third period when the shooting began. The first thing I heard was a mortar blast. Then *Pock! Pock! Pock!* The teachers gathered all the students inside the gymnasium. I thought they were going to send us home, but instead they cried, *"Enfants. Defendez-vous!"* and began handing out weapons.

"I couldn't believe it. I had never held a rifle in my life. We crept outside on our bellies and crouched behind a low wall that ran around the school. We could see Kabila's army assaulting the garrison nearby and the Presidential Guard returning fire. Some of the students began shooting at the soldiers, and they turned and fired back at us. There were bullets flying everywhere. One hit the wall directly above my head and showered me with dust. I was with my older brother, and he grabbed me by the shoulder and pulled me down below the wall. 'This is crazy!' he shouted. So we threw down our guns and began to run."

"Shit," Simon said.

"It took us nearly an hour to get home. Our parents were sick with worry. My mother burst into tears when she saw us, but my father just picked us up. I am not exaggerating. He lifted my mother, myself, and my brother off the ground and tossed us like luggage into a waiting car. My little sister was inside, crying. We drove to the airport, but the car didn't stop in front like usual. It continued straight onto the tarmac where an enormous cargo plane was waiting with the hatch open."

"Hundreds of servants from the palace were piling gold, paintings, jewels, all the stolen wealth of the Congo, into that plane. We had no seats. Two soldiers from the Presidential Guard led us into the hold and sat me beside my brother on a pile of Persian rugs. My father sat on a crate of rare French wines. The servants wrapped my mother and sister in furs and jewelry and placed them next to us."

Kinani stopped abruptly. He had been speaking breathlessly for minutes and he was trembling with the effort. Simon saw him steady himself on the rickety chaise lounge and gulp down a full tumbler of whiskey. He could hear Kinani's belabored breathing.

"You ok?" Simon asked, concerned.

Kinani nodded. He refilled his glass and took another quick swig. Then he began speaking again.

"Worst of all, several of my classmates were there. They stood with their families on the tarmac, begging to be allowed onto the plane. I could hear the mortar explosions drawing nearer and I could see great clouds of smoke rising over the jungle. There was a moment of total panic, and a large crowd of people rushed the soldiers. I saw friends of mine whipped and smacked with rifle butts. I thought I was going to be sick, and I grabbed onto an ivory statue of Nefertiti like I was about to drown. There were even rare cats in the plane. They saved a lion instead of my friends." He gave a brief sob and swallowed half his whiskey.

"After they subdued the crowd, a funeral procession arrived. Twelve men, dressed in black suits with white gloves, carried the remains of Habyarimana. People were screaming and wailing like in a real funeral, and the gunfire was so close that some of the soldiers fanned out and began returning fire and there were stray bullets bouncing off the fuselage. But those men marched calmly ahead, as if nothing was wrong, and it was like a funeral for Zaire and for Rwanda as well.

"They placed the coffin in the plane, just a few meters from my family, and the door shut like a mouth. Again we flew with Habyarimana's body, this time to Kinshasa. Our exit visa from Zaire was the last one personally signed by Mobutu as president."

While Kinani told his tale, the sky spun languorously overhead, carrying within it countless constellations. Gradually, it began to lighten. The boisterous wedding party died down. Its guests departed and a daybreak breeze blew in from the sea. Then the sun rose over the city like an immense crown of gold. Kinani turned his face toward the burgeoning light, and to Simon his profile looked like it had been struck in bronze.

"Did Habyarimana come with you to Morocco as well?" Simon asked, a shiver running down his spine.

Kinani snorted and bent forward, resting his elbows on his knees. "No. His body sat on the tarmac in Kinshasa for almost a week and was hastily buried the day before Mobutu fled. He was a devout Roman Catholic, but I heard they had a Hindu oversee the ceremony. Good riddance." He took a long sip of whisky and then held his empty tumbler up to the sunlight, so that it briefly appeared to sprout a flame. "But Mobutu came here, so in the end, we merely exchanged one dead despot for another."

"Is that why your family ended up in Morocco?"

"We went to Switzerland first on a transit visa, and then to Ethiopia. But yes, I suppose we're here because the Maréchal is here, dead or alive. He was great friends with Hassan II. Like I told you, monarchs stick together. Hassan II offered sanctuary to all of Mobutu's retinue. His children are here, his wives, his consorts, old advisors and ministers and their families. They often meet at his grave on Sundays and lay down fresh flowers. Even my parents go sometimes."

"And you?"

"What do I have to do with all of that? The Maréchal brought destruction down on his head. He should have been guillotined. Did you know that his first wife was named Marie-Antoinette?"

Simon smiled. "History has a sense of humor."

"Yes, or maybe his destiny was clear to him from the start. Perhaps that's why he lived so extravagantly, while it lasted." Kinani settled back into the chaise lounge and stretched out his feet. "My father used to say that we live our lives beside the sleeping elephant."

"How so?" Simon asked, yawning.

"So long as the elephant is asleep, you can do whatever you want. You can build a house, raise a family, win glory. But when the elephant wakes up, it tramples everything."

Then, just like that, Kinani fell asleep and began snoring.

Simon staggered to his feet. He looked down at his flatmate with a mixture of envy and awe. Then he peered around at the seedy apartment where they had discussed the fate of fallen empires, and at the exiled prince passed out on a shoddy blue beach chair with festive white stripes.

His head was still spinning from the alcohol and he was worried that if he lay down he might throw up. So he gently opened the front door and climbed the stairs to the roof.

The wedding party had fully disbanded and the normal sounds of the neighborhood had resumed. Simon strode to the edge of the roof and the vast expanse of the Atlantic opened up before his eyes. The wind was unusually fierce that morning and soft chevrons of foam curled over the tops of the chopping waves. He could see the black silhouettes of birds hunkered down on the water, unable to fly. But everywhere streamed coppers and golds and crimsons, as if someone were pouring a precious elixir over the horizon into the empty bowl of the sky.

Simon rubbed his bleary eyes. He suddenly realized that he was shivering, and he wrapped his arms around his body and sat down on the edge of the roof, his feet dangling below. He idled there until the sun stood firmly above the city and its hot rays pooled on his face, warming him awake.

With growing astonishment, he began to parse through everything Kinani had said. It seemed like the stuff of history books. His father a Rwandan diplomat and then a personal advisor to Mobutu. And now a refugee! Simon's old man had worked at the U.S. Embassy in Tanzania in the early 1990s, and he wondered, in passing, if Kinani's father had crossed paths with his own. Then, with a light shock of recognition, it dawned on him: Kinani was just like him, a diplomat's son.

Un serpent sur le rocher, tu le frappes avec la hachette; tu tues le serpent, mais tu casses aussi la hachette. —Paul

ARÈS WAS MATTED AGAINST the bedsheets, his body coated with rivulets of sweat. The phone rang. It was Yann.

"The Moroccan gendarmerie came last night and attacked the sit-in. They loaded everyone into fourgons and trucked them off to Parc Tejlit."

"Even the women and children?" Arès asked, horrified.

"Yes. They used truncheons on anyone who resisted."

"What are we going to do?"

"The *Points Focaux* have organized a meeting with the director of the HCR in three days. They're supposed to discuss the incident and decide when they will finally resettle us, but the rest of us are coming armed. We will be outside and if they refuse our demands, this time we will make them regret it. We expect you to be there with us."

"You know, I will not be very useful in an attack."

"You should come to show your solidarity. There have been rumors going around that you are working with the HCR. Some of the refugees claim they saw you enter the building several times during the sit-in. I am your friend, but I will not be able to protect you if there is a clash."

"I do not know," Arès replied. "What will happen if the police attack and I cannot run away?"

"I am telling you this for your own good. There could be serious repercussions from the refugee community. I would worry less about the police."

Arès reflected in the dark. Once again, he found himself trapped between battling elephants. At least no one at the HCR could see him. He hoped the same held true for the gendarmerie. "I will be there with you."

"Good," Yann said. "We are meeting this Thursday in front of the HCR. Bring rocks with you. Lots of them."

Then he hung up.

On July 23, 2009, a sizable faction of sub-Saharan refugees marshaled before the shining white parapets of the HCR.

The meeting was set for noon, and the dozen *Points Focaux* filed between a gauntlet of powder-blue guards over burning sidewalks beneath a blight of a sun. Another fifty men, and a handful of women, paraded before a rail of olive-garbed Moroccan police, standing stiffly as pawns in the blasted light.

Only the women carried signboards. On them were scrawled slogans like *DIGNITÉ POUR LES RÉFUGIÉS!* or *RÉINSTALLATION TOUT DE SUITE!* in heavy felt pen. Two of the women had crying babies bundled onto their backs.

The men had draped themselves in red foulards and had looped bulky gunnysacks over their shoulders. Dipping slightly above their sacrums, the sacks sagged with invisible ballast.

Three boxy fourgons stood ready, their windows grilled with wire mesh. Inside, empty jitney benches waited beneath iron bolts. On either end of the wagons, officers plated in thick riot gear stood locked in rigid columns.

When Arès arrived, he was relieved to find the protesters relatively restrained. He caught sight of Yann conferring with a tight group of men in front of the main gate, and he headed toward them. All of a sudden, they disbanded. Arès' heart skipped a beat as Salifou leaned casually back against the gate and grinned at him.

Yann rushed up to Arès. "I am very glad you came."

"Yes, how could I not..." His voice died out, but Yann had already hurried off to greet another arrival.

Arès was alarmed. Salifou's presence at this protest was as inexplicable as his absence from all the others. It seemed a bad omen that he had finally resurfaced. For a moment, Arès considered leaving, but some secret voice commanded him to stay.

Slightly downhill, the goatherder idled nonchalantly before the HCR. He wore his foulard loose atop his head, like one might a wig, and from beneath its shadowy tent the odd slit of his eyes surveyed the grounds. Unlike the other men, he had opted for a distinctive dark red color that reminded Arès of an open wound.

Dismayed, Arès forced himself to look away. His foot was beginning to ache and he sought around for somewhere to sit. The shantytown that had accompanied the sit-in was gone, so he snaked along the line of bollards and settled onto the ground near the applicants' entrance. There was no shade anywhere to be found.

For hours, the protesters milled about in the crucible of the day. The sidewalk simmered. Before them, the white building lorded silent, indifferent.

Then the feverish morning burned into a white-hot afternoon and temperatures rose within as well as without. One of the Congolese refugees that Arès recognized, a woman by the name of Emilie, marched up to a burly police officer. The baby on her back wailed as she jabbed an accusing finger at his chest and shouted, "Why are you here? Go Home! Stop abusing the refugees!"

The man's mustache twitched, but otherwise his face remained steely, impassive above an overstarched collar. The veins popped along his forearm as his hand hardened over a truncheon.

A pale, portly man in a black turtleneck, slacks, and a garrison cap on his head, marched authoritatively up the sidewalk. A gilded badge glittered as he moved, and the officers firmed their ranks in tempo with his approach.

His hand landed on the woman's shoulder, and a surprising boom of a voice issued from that modest height, "*Madame, maîtrisez-vous!*"

She turned and spat at him. "Why are you touching me?"

The man daubed at his face with a light-blue handkerchief. Suddenly a trio of Congolese men pushed into him. He pitched forward, inadvertently jostling the woman into the officer beside her. For an instant, the officer lost his balance. Then a tidal flow of policemen rammed him upright and pushed the refugees back.

A rush of guards precipitated out of the HCR and two gendarmes moved in, truncheons drawn.

More refugees arrived, their hackles raised. Yann and Fofana were among them, and Arès watched them scramble their bodies against two of the turtle-plated officers.

All three groups—the red-sashed refugees, the olive-green gendarmes, and the powder-blue guards—shoved and yanked, and the colorful mish-mash tore wildly to and fro like a punch-drunk dance.

Then, abruptly, the dancers uncoupled, and the three parties panted in the glare, eyeing each other warily.

"*Calmez-vous! Calmez-vous!*" the guards shouted now that the scuffle was over. Still firing off recriminations, all three parties reverted to their initial staging. The guards sentinelled the entrance, the gendarmes railed the sidewalk, and the refugees stewed in the street.

Arès hobbled over to Yann. "Why are you provoking the police? They will beat us for real next time."

"Good. Let them attack. Then the whole world will see what is happening here in Morocco. How its refugees are treated." He spoke agitatedly, still juiced up from the altercation.

"My friend, you do not want to end up spending your life like me." Arès pointed at his bloated foot. Its skin had cracked in the heat, and around it swelled a pulp that gave it the size and consistency of a putrefying melon.

"Do you not get it?" Yann shouted. "We all look like you! We are all perishing of injuries that cannot be healed. This foot," he tapped it with his toe, "is our life here. The only cure is to leave. But the world never notices the misery of a single foot. It wants casualties before it will pay attention to suffering."

Arès shook his head. "Even if we all die here, the world will never care. You are doing exactly what the Moroccans want. You will just give them an excuse to take even more of our rights."

Their animated gestures had caught the crowd's attention, and Arès sensed Salifou slinking close.

"What rights?" Yann shouted. "We do not even exist here! Our presence is illegal. When we eat, it is a crime. When we piss, we go to jail. Every breath we take is an offense against the Kingdom of Morocco."

Salifou leaned in and placed the wide rakes of his hands upon the two men's shoulders. "We are criminals already," he whispered. "I think it is time we began to act like it."

Arès shivered at his touch. "Do what you like," he replied coldly. "But I want no part."

"We are all being held prisoners here. Do you not see it?" Yann clasped his fingers over Arès' wrist. "They fool us by promising a way out, but they are demanding a ransom that none of us can pay."

"Are you not tired of running?" Salifou asked, his eyes lit with a red-hot gleam. "You see that man." He pointed at the golden badge in the turtleneck. "That is the Chief of Police of Rabat. If we are not resettled, he is the first one I will get."

Arès looked at him. "Fire, my old friend, leaves only ashes behind."

He turned and left. As he hobbled downhill toward the roundabout, Salifou cried after him. "The lion may roar all he likes, but the teeth are cracked in his mouth. *Ce qui est plus fort que le lion, c'est la brousse.*"

Some five meters downhill from the HCR, a grass alley led to upleading steps and a trellised arbor with pink and violet flowers. A faucet protruded out of the wall, and Arès twisted the handle and released a blue meteor of water onto his overheated skull.

Seconds later he was dry. Everything evaporated in this heat. He thought about climbing the stairs and heading home, but he could not bring himself to leave. Instead, he stationed himself at the mouth of the alley, halfway between the ramparts of the HCR and the American Embassy's reef of cement barriers.

An hour later the *Points Focaux* tempested out of the building, yelling "The same lies! The same lies!"

The protesters' eyes seethed. Cries of disbelief cut the air. Drums pounded. Men and women whipsawed wildly, chanting, whooping, riotous with outrage. They seemed not the least bit tired, as if the day's fiery heat had only kindled their fury.

Fofana snatched the bullhorn, his face contorted with indignation. "*Lies!*

Lies! Lies!" he cried. *"Justice pour les réfugiés! Justice et dignité! Justice! Justice! Justice et dignité!"*

The maddened crowd shouted beside him. *"Justice! Justice! Justice!"*

Every time a group of gendarmes tried to contain the demonstrators, a liquid surge of barking men knocked them back. The refugees spit in their faces, taunted them, incited them.

Then, from the roundabout below, the snarl of hulking diesel engines and massive tire treads sounded above the tumult. Arès spun to see a heavy convoy of military vehicles rumble up Avenue Tariq Ibn Ziad.

Two truckloads of infantrymen in tan fatigues dismounted, followed by a pair of jalopies.

To hostile cries, the regiment spun a fast perimeter around the protesters, rifles jackknifed before them. Then they stood calmly, their eyes boring into the Africans with an empty narcotic gleam.

Arès shrunk back despite himself, cowed by the display of power. But the refugees protested ever more violently: their frenzied feet slammed the ground; their chants grew louder, more enraged. *"Justice et dignité! Justice pour les réfugiés!"*

Waving his red scarf aloft, Salifou gave a chittering war cry that snapped at Arès across the gulf of a decade. He watched with burning eyes as the man from his village scudded with spectacular acceleration toward the doubly reinforced main door of the HCR. Salifou bashed down with his upraised workboot as if swiping with a claw. The detonation was earsplitting.

For an instant the raucous theatre silenced, and all the everyday sounds— the rumble of traffic, the singing of birds, the irritated honks from the roundabout—reasserted themselves over the contested space.

Then the metal door clanged like a snare drum as a group of four refugees catapulted themselves against its obdurate frame. To the tempo of these batterings, the women calved off from the demonstration till all but one clustered in the nearby alley, shouting out encouragement.

Another martial cry and a tumbling rock traced a parabola upon an unblemished plane of blue and wrecked down into a second-story window of the HCR, pulverizing against an oak desk jumbled high with pink dossiers.

Cheers discharged all along the building. Arès took an eager step forward and then checked himself.

The crash of that rock had unleashed something in the refugees, and he felt it too. It was as if they had just desecrated a temple. His entire body was aquiver with spiteful joy. At last, he thought. There it is.

Gunnysacks twirled down to the ground, and paroxysms of stones pelted the facade of the United Nations. Up they rocketed, over the jutting white spears of the fence, over the beige tiles of the courtyard, pounding the windows and powdering the walls. Arès felt a small jubilation as a razor-toothed rock chewed a rent through the fluttering UN flag and dented its mastpole.

Inside, the employees shouted for help, but the commanders growled orders from their jalopied posts and the soldiers and gendarmes stood stock-still. Not a single rifle listed even the slightest, though Arès swore he saw some of the hardened faces wrinkle with half-suppressed grins.

One of the refugees spidered onto the spiked fence, and with a serrated chunk of cement bashed at the arm of a security camera. The powder-blue guards tried to dislodge his feet, but on the seventh or eighth clout, he beheaded the device.

It hit the ground with a gray rattle and a splash of metal, and seconds later was in the refugee's hands. Lifting the box above his head, he ululated wildly and then double leapt and launched the machine high over the prickly gates. It shafted between a lowered iron grate and cleaved a sizable hole into the large picture window that fronted the building.

Soon three other video cameras winged off the building's frontage had been smashed to the ground and catapulted onto the tiled courtyard, where they landed in frazzled heaps.

"*Fais du bien à un chien, il te chie dans la main*," a soldier exclaimed loudly. Flamboyant laughs erupted up and down the line of infantrymen.

Fofana heard him and jumped forward, spitting in his face. "You are calling us dogs?" The fan of his fingers swung into a tight fist and met the soldier's shoulder with a hard clap.

For one clabbered moment, time trembled. Then all bedlam broke loose.

The soldiers raged into them. Blows flurried and blurred, formed bright webs of flickering wood, punching down with a pugilist's precision. The refugees fought back, defending themselves with jagged rocks and broken metal.

Arès watched black welts surface on men's arms, like dark puddles gathering in the rain. Then a dirge of cracked jaws and gnashing grunts, spasmed insults and spouts of blood filled the air. High above them seabirds cawed and wheeled and the balefire sun seesawed through the sky as if intoxicated by their quarrel.

The Chief of Police, armed with a baton, rushed between the battling hordes and shouted for an end.

Arès cried out as Salifou lunged forward, his palms heavy with a crag of cement. The Chief of Police spun and his garrison cap tipped to the ground as he shielded himself with an upraised hand. The refugee hatcheted down, mauling the man's brittle forearm into bony ruins.

From below, the impossibly frail physique of Doumba galloped uphill into the fray. "Stop! Stop!" he shouted.

No one listened.

A grinning cadet shoved Doumba aside and raised a truncheon to strike a refugee named Yendi, whom Arès knew from his masonry days. Doumba launched himself between the two combatants, "Stop this madness! This is madness!"

The cadet paused ungainly, but another soldier, with drooping eyelids and a thick faucet nose, stepped forward and swiped his baton at the interloper. Doumba's arm snapped like a twig beneath the blow, and he collapsed to the ground, yelping in pain.

The same soldier jabbed Yendi with a butt of wood, and then stepped high and crunched down his boot, pinning Doumba's good hand. As the refugee lay helpless on the cement, the soldier leaned in and hammered the exposed limb with his white baton. Doumba's forearm shattered, and ivory shards of bone erupted from their envelope.

Someone hissed, and the soldier's eyelids flapped up like blinds as Salifou smashed a blood-splattered rock against his forest-green helmet. Another crack and a maze of fissures spread along the man's plexiglass visor, and his nose discharged a web of gore. Yendi swept out the soldier's feet, and Salifou pounced on him, hammering him hysterically. With every granite blow the man diminished in size, as if being pounded like a stake into the earth.

Then a mêlée of men carried Salifou off and there was the retort of fracturing bones and a howl of pain. Doumba lay on the ground, his arms hanging pitifully askew.

Arès moved toward the fray till he stood at its volatile perimeter. There he paused, unsure what to do. Everything wavered before him in a nonsense of fratricide.

A group of combatants swung his way, and among them he saw Laurent. When a soldier raised a truncheon to brain the soft-spoken man, Arès axed up his cane and felt the sharp glance of an impact as the plunging wood sheared off into a vacuum of air. Another soldier stepped forward and swiped at Arès, but his baton passed through the refugee's chest in a phantasmagoric slide.

A high keening wail cut through the disorder and the protesters broke ranks and fled toward the roundabout below. Nearly a dozen refugees, and half as many Moroccans, lay felled in the floodlights of the sun before the lily-white shining doors of the HCR.

When they reached the American Embassy, those who could hopped the cement barriers and began lifting the injured over, while the embassy guards shouted at them to stop. Arès caned downhill as fast as he could. Bypassing the cement obstructions, he slipped under a drawbar and clomped after the others.

A few meters ahead, six rock-armed refugees had spun a defensive ring and were fending off an assault by almost ten embassy guards. Behind them, the rest of the escapees hauled the wounded across American grounds to the safety of the public thoroughfares. Arès strained up the hill. As he neared the top, two of the refugees took sharp raps and their foreheads c left open.

Then, once again, they passed into Moroccan territory. The embassy guards held to their cement-barrier domain, and when the last of the Africans reached the road, they fell back yelling insults.

The scraggly party staggered ahead. There were about thirty of them, faces bruised and swollen, chests matted with blood. Four refugees who could not walk were trussed over bent backs, and one of them wore a wig of gore.

They advanced about two hundred meters and then the entire host ground to a halt. Bustling up the street were eight employees of the HCR. The small white girls from the front office; the French and Senegalese Protection Officers; the pony-tailed Moroccan woman from community services; one of the green-smocked cooks from the kitchen; the diminutive intern with his scrunched blond hair; and tall, clean-shaven Simon in his Oxford shirt and office slacks.

The other group skidded to a stop as well, and Arès could see Simon tense, as if bracing for impact. Expressions of fright and panic crawled over the pale faces of the interns, and the cook from the kitchen appeared to shrink into her smock.

"Finally!" Arès rejoiced. "Justice." He trained his eyes on the JPO, like someone lining up a hammer with a nail.

Then, for several infinitely long seconds, nothing happened in that quiet street.

CHAPTER 55

JULY 2009

A T FIRST HE THOUGHT it was a volleyball, the twirling white thing, perhaps tossed by one of the Sudanese refugees from the poster downstairs.

The projectile rose in a graceful arc, easily cleared the high spiked fence, and touched the apex of its flight around eye-level with Simon. It was then he recognized the security camera that normally hung in a tight elbow above the main gate. He blinked in surprise while it blurred earthwards and fisted through one of the picture windows on the ground floor.

Simon cautiously stuck his head out of the office window. Stone after stone poured down on the HCR, shattering glass panes and pummeling the walls. One of the missiles came hissing directly at him and he instinctively ducked. Then he heard a window collapse like a crash of cymbals on the floor below.

"There goes another one," he said to no one in particular.

The sky emptied of stones and the refugees began bashing at the front gate with some heavy object. The guard with the jutting belly thrust his full weight against the metal barrier, so that he appeared to be holding it up. Two other guards dangled off the lip of the gate, as if trying to climb out and escape.

The mayhem was extraordinary, like nothing Simon had ever seen. Intellectually he understood the danger, but there was something in it that bordered on the sublime, and he watched enraptured like a spectator at a sporting event.

There was a sharp rap at the door. Baptiste leaned in, an urgent look on his face. "What the hell are you still doing here?"

"What do you mean? I'm watching the show."

"Let's get out of here. This is no time to play." The EO looked frightened.

"What? You're not going to stay? Didn't you see that guy behead the security camera? It was magnificent."

"Yes, and we might be next."

The deafening rumble of an approaching military convoy reverberated up Avenue Tariq Ibn Ziad.

"The army is moving in!" Simon cried exuberantly, pointing to the street below. He felt tipsy, intoxicated by the pandemonium around him. He wondered if Kinani had felt similar emotions, even as death pressed in on all sides.

"Those are people down there," Baptiste said gravely.

Simon looked up startled. It felt like the EO had splashed cold water against his face. "Right," he replied, chastened. "Let's go."

They took the same escape route as before. Traversing the terrace, they dropped onto the neighboring building via a concealed hook ladder, and descended three stories of metal rungs to alight in a walled pleasure garden behind an elegant colonial mansion.

The executive command of the HCR had long since absconded, but more than a dozen colleagues remained, looking shell-shocked and disoriented, while flowers soughed in the breeze.

"Quickly," Baptiste shouted, clapping his hands. "This is no time to smell the roses."

He speedily divided the remaining staff into two teams. "Simon, take your group down Avenue Mohammed V toward the medina, and I'll head with mine to Agdal. We'll call each other if there's trouble."

"Are you sure it's safe?" Simon asked.

"If we hurry. They're busy out front, but who knows for how long."

"Why don't we just stay in the garden?" Nathalie demanded.

"If they break into the building, they'll tear us to pieces," Marie objected.

"She's right," Ibrahim agreed, his voice uncharacteristically subdued.

"You ready?" Baptiste asked.

Simon nodded.

They steeled themselves and cracked open the gate.

"All clear!" Baptiste shouted.

The two teams rushed out. Simon swung to the right, followed by seven other staff members. After twisting down several side streets, they turned onto a broad boulevard lined with stately residences and landscaped gardens.

The boulevard's sidewalks were arcaded by lofty trees, but the HCR employees kept to the sun-cooked center of the road and scurried ahead like hunted animals. Several of them were in soft office shoes, and the burning blacktop pricked at their feet like small knives. None of them were used to this sort of exertion, and Simon could hear the belabored breaths of his colleagues straining beside him.

After a few more minutes of reckless flight, the fugitive party collapsed beneath the flared canopy of a cork tree.

"Where are we going?" Nathalie cried out in an anguished voice.

"The medina," Simon replied, panting.

"Don't you think that's a bit far?" Marie asked, anxiously wiping her brow. Her blouse was drenched in sweat.

A dozen jittery eyes scanned the tranquil streets. A gardener idled nearby with a rubber hose and a uniformed maid calmly strolled a dog on a leash. From the trees came the rhythmic chirping of birds.

"It's not a good idea," Fatima said. "The refugees will go there too and we may have trouble."

"Do you really think they would harm us?" Khadija asked. With her plump, cherubic face, she seemed even more than usual a child thrown among adults.

"I don't think even *they* know what they're going to do," Fatima replied.

Simon stared at the Community Services Officer, searching her ink-black eyes for intelligence of what she knew. She felt his gaze and turned away. He was surprised by her graceful, tapering profile, like that of a doe. She must have been a beautiful woman once, he thought, and then quickly banished that line of reflection.

"I know someone at the American Bar Association," he announced. "It's just around the corner."

Without waiting for a response, he turned decisively into a nearby street and the group trailed behind him. A few minutes later, he paused like a hound uncertain of the scent. Then he recognized a canary-yellow building and led his colleagues down a narrow lane. A hundred meters further on, they stopped before two white curving walls that spread like a seagull's wings. A trellised pathway led to a beige, three-story building.

Simon walked up to the heavy wooden door and rang the bell. No response. He jabbed the brass nub frantically, but no lights switched on and no one came to the entrance. When he took out his phone to ring his contact at the ABA, the call went straight to voicemail.

He turned around and gazed abashed at the seven people he had towed in his wake. They leaned wearily against the pebble-dashed wall, or slumped on the steps, looking for all purposes like a tattered group of IDPs, freshly escaped from a raid on their village. And here they were, pounding on the doors of power, pleading for refuge, and no one answered.

How quickly fortunes change, Simon mused. He couldn't help but think of Kinani's family and he wondered if a similar fate could ever befall his own.

"Simon!" Nathalie shouted at him. "What *are* you doing over there?"

"Sorry." He needed to concentrate. There were outcomes far worse than mere exile. He began dialing in the number for his contact again, but his phone vibrated with an incoming call. He picked up. It was Anna-Heintz.

"It's over," she said.

"What's over?"

"The army has resolved the situation. The refugees are gone. You should come back to the HCR."

"We're at the American Bar Association, and it's safe here. Shouldn't we stay out of harm's way?"

"Consider this an order. Return to the HCR. Immediately."

"Ok," Simon grumbled.

"Who was that?" Fatima asked.

"It was Anna-Heintz on the phone. They're ordering us back to the HCR."

"What?" several of them cried at once.

"*C'est n'importe quoi!*" Nathalie exclaimed.

"They say that the refugees have left and it's safe to go back," Simon related wearily. It was total nonsense. The command at the HCR had run their ship straight into the rocks, and here they were, ordering the survivors back to a sinking wreck. It was a form of institutional madness, part of the illusion of control that had spawned this entire mess. He glanced rapidly at the street and was comforted to see Andreas positioned there as a lookout.

"See anything out there?" he shouted at Andreas. The intern tipped out, like a sailor peering off a crow's nest, and shook his head.

"So what the hell do we do?" Marie exclaimed. "Of all the bloody, stupid gambles."

"We have to go back," Fatima asserted calmly. "We have no choice."

From far off, they could hear the soaring voice of a muezzin calling the faithful to the *Asr* prayers. Moving to the cadence of those hymns, they assembled into a tight phalanx and ventured out.

Cautiously, they crept up the narrow lane, listening for any hints of approaching danger. Soon they had stepped back onto the broad boulevard, but this time not a soul was in sight. The forbidding gated residences and the hushed, empty streets increased their terror tenfold. Then a breeze kicked up, and the leaves began to murmur in the trees overhead like the sound of whispering voices.

Harried by unseen pursuers, they raced wildly ahead. Soon their panicked feet led them astray. When they realized they were treading downhill toward the medina, they spun around and fled back the way they had come with heedless, hunted steps. The pitiless sun stalked them overhead, and the day's heat billowed around, stealing their breath. The world wavered before Simon's eyes and took on dreamlike sensations.

"I'm a bit turned around," Simon confessed.

"Don't worry," Fatima said. "Follow me."

They flew down one twisting lane and then another. A serpentine street deposited them in a tree-lined avenue with imposing mansions and daggered fences. Then Nathalie spotted the flag of the American Embassy cresting above a nearby hill, and they redoubled their pace at the prospect of safety. They were charting a course around a bend, rejoicing at the end of their ordeal, when Fatima ground to a halt.

"*Merde*," Simon heard Marie mutter under her breath.

Scrambling precipitously down the very street they were climbing, came thirty of the refugees who had attacked the HCR. Some of them hauled wounded friends on their backs. Others held half-filled gunnysacks and cruel, makeshift weapons, several of which spun to the ground, ready for use.

Simon's heart bashed wildly in his chest. He could hear Saana mewling with fear and Pacifique muttering prayers and Marie cursing fiercely.

I'm going to die here, he thought. They're going to kill us and I'm going to die.

Then flickering in that crowd he saw Arès, the man he had condemned to this madness, and he thought it fitting that he should be there to exact his revenge.

Simon threw himself instinctively in front of Lise and Nathalie, shielding them with his body and preparing for the assault. His muscles bunched, and he felt astonishingly present, as if all the will he had accumulated in his life had condensed into that burning pinprick of an instant, like the nucleus of a star.

Several of the refugees gave hostile shouts and Fofana stepped forward, his face horrible with injury. A large gash smiled wickedly on his left cheek, and a black amoebic sack had swelled his right eye shut. His shirt hung in shreds and his right arm was fissured and bleeding.

"*Passez. Passez.*" He could barely chew out the words, and he waived them on with the contused claw that was left of his hand.

"*Merci!*" they cried and hurried off, disappearing up a hill behind the drooping bowers of a magnolia tree.

CHAPTER 56
JULY 2009

THE DEFEATED HORDE MOVED on, turning down the very street the HCR employees had just climbed.

Arès trailed briefly behind them and then stopped. The scalding afternoon air blanketed his face and he had the sudden sensation that he could not breathe. He staggered to the sidewalk and settled beneath a wiry cork tree, snorting and gasping for air.

Slowly, he caught his breath. Below him, the refugees vanished into a tangle of azaleas on a road that would carry them past royal gardens and foreign ministries and finally surrender them to the blood-red walls of the medina and the wretched streets of Rabat. Arès lingered in the cool shade. When the last of the refugees had skirted around a bend, he turned purposefully uphill.

Salifou had not been among those who escaped via the American Embassy, and his disappearance worried Arès. It reminded him too much of the race they had run so long ago, when Salifou had been swept downstream only later to reappear. Once again, the murderer had wreathed into the air like a puff of smoke. This time, though, Arès would not let him escape so easily. Hoping at last to put things to rest, he made his way back to the HCR.

It was too dangerous to take the route he knew, so he turned up an unfamiliar road past dozens of gardened villas, until gradually it looped around on itself. Confused, he backtracked and took a right on a side street but came to a dead end. Again, he retraced his steps and forked left instead of right, but the streets in that part of town curved unpredictably and sent him back to the same flower-choked intersection so many times that he threw down his cane in disgust.

By the time he finally arrived at the HCR, the army had already decamped, save for a modest detachment that continued to survey the area from a blue jeep.

All of the wounded were gone as well.

Only a few shards of metal strewn about, some rust-colored stains on the cement, and the disfigured facade of the HCR, gave any evidence that there had been a battle.

Salifou was nowhere to be seen. He had left no trace of his passing. Like one of those evil spirits of legend, he had been sucked back into the maelstrom of violence that he had helped inflame.

Arès combed the sidewalk in front of the bureau, but there was nothing to be found. He began to doubt himself again, doubt everything he had seen. Salifou's reappearance after all these years, his own ghostlike powers, this improbable community of exiles and their hopeless struggle against these alien, hostile lands.

He planted himself beneath the hot glove of the sky and prayed he would suddenly awake in his bed in Kinshasa, his mother stroking his feverish brow. Minutes and minutes passed.

Before him, the white building bided indifferently. His forehead began to burn in the sun and he knew that he was there, irrevocably, permanently. Seeking shade, he strode through the open front gate, pausing for a moment to admire the shoveled dents the refugees had pounded into the white metal. Abruptly, his eyes widened with recognition.

There, snagged on the inside of one of the gate's grills, a shred of dark red foulard hung limply like a flag of defeat. The white metal was twisted into a sharp fishhook, and Arès carefully rubbed off the rag with the same thumb motion he had once used to remove a piece of spoiled bait.

For nearly a minute, he wove the cloth between his fingers. Then inspiration leapt hot into his head and he scooped the rag into his pocket. Carefully stepping around the gray shards of metal and broken glass, he caned into the building and rapidly thudded up the winding stairs.

As he had anticipated, the HCR executives were frantically removing funds from a combination safe. He flurried his hand into the steel box and thieved a bundle of dirhams for a train ticket to Tangier. He considered it his due.

When the order went out to evacuate the building, he hurried downstairs with the rest of the staff.

Then, for the first time upon exiting the HCR, he turned uphill.

Resolutely, he ascended the dusty avenue. He had no intention of looking back, but at the summit of the hill, something inexpressible arrested his climb. Beside a stiff quorum of soldiers, Arès paused, started again, and then brought his feet and cane to a decisive halt.

He swiveled about and, shielding his eyes with his right hand, took a final survey of the place.

The hated building, barren, empty, towered above the fertile plains of Salé over which white egrets flew. The afternoon was uncommonly calm. Even the ceaseless din of traffic seemed muted as it counter-streamed along Avenue Tariq Ibn Ziad. Against a quiltwork of clouds, the flag of the United Nations whipped raggedly, a hole rent through its white gridded world.

Yet nothing had changed. The flag would be mended; the rust-colored splotches would be scoured off the sidewalk; the security cameras would be replaced and the facade repaired. The same dramatic play would go on and on with no end in sight.

Arès turned again to go. Behind him, in the distance, a twinkling jetliner fired across the sky like the last spark from an immense conflagration.

CHAPTER 57
JULY 2009

———

"IT'S OVER," SIMON SAID.

Baptiste looked out at the street. "You think that once you've swept out the dust, it won't come back?"

"Let's hope not anytime soon." Simon peered around at the severed arms of the security cameras, the chipped and bloodied facade of the HCR, and the shattered windows that hung open like mouths gaping in surprise. They walked into the front courtyard through a cratered gate and listened to their feet crunch over shards of glass.

"I still can't believe this happened," he said.

"What is a wise man?" the EO asked, as they stepped into the multilevel hall through one of the missing picture windows.

"Tell me."

"Someone who foresees the consequences."

"Perhaps," Simon replied. He felt jumpy and weak and couldn't keep up with Baptiste's allusive patter. Anna-Heintz had instructed all personnel to clean out their desks and go home. They were on leave until further notice. "Hopefully they'll learn something from this," he added, following the EO into his office.

Baptiste snorted. "This isn't the first time this has happened and it won't be the last." He waved goodbye to Pacifique and Khadija, who were carrying their belongings out the door. "Give a foolish person all the lessons in the world, it's the same as pouring water into sand."

"At least we're on vacation," Simon said. The idea of returning the next day to the HCR was unbearable. "Should we meet at the beach tomorrow? We can lay out on the sands of foolishness."

"As long as we are laying above the ground and not below it, I am content," Baptiste replied with a wink.

Simon shuddered. "I thought I was going to die there. That several of us were."

"I know, *mon ami*. It was poorly handled." Baptiste shook his head. "I am glad that you are safe. I am truly happy. But I am also glad that you have had a taste of the fear that is the daily bread of the refugees. They were not as lucky as you. There are several in the hospital, and two may not live through the night."

"I hardly know what to take away from an experience like that."

"Maybe you will understand them better, or even yourself. They were far more merciful to us than we were to them. But for now, enjoy your brief exile from the HCR."

"Yes. until we're resettled."

"I, my friend, am going to go resettle myself in a bar. There are several waitresses who must be worried sick about me. Would you like to come?"

"Thank you," Simon said, rubbing his neck, "but I have some injuries that need to be looked at by a certain doctor."

Baptiste cracked his irrepressible Cheshire grin. "That sounds like a responsible choice."

Simon said goodbye and bounded upstairs to clean out his desk. He had a sour taste in his mouth and went to pour himself a glass of mint tea. To his astonishment, the silver pot was still warm. He looked at the time. Barely an hour had elapsed since the attack had begun.

The next morning, he received a message: the UNHCR was off-limits to all non-essential staff for the next two weeks.

The closure coincided with the end of Simon's JPO mission and he realized, with mixed feelings, that he would never set foot back inside the bureau as an employee. On the bright side, Nadia had finished her exams and that meant they were both on vacation.

They hastily put together an application for a Schengen visa—a letter from the hospital where she interned, another from her university, and a somewhat aspirational bank statement that they hoped no one would double-check. It was impossible to use her parents as references, so Simon drafted an official-looking communication on UNHCR letterhead guaranteeing Nadia Agdid's return. He hoped it would pass muster.

A few days later, they stood in front of the Spanish consulate. "I have to go in alone," she said. "Will you wait for me outside?"

"*Meshi Mushkil*," Simon replied. He leaned in for a kiss, but quickly yanked back when her eyes blew white with fear.

An hour later, Nadia exited the consulate, a cloud hanging over her face. "They rejected the visa."

"Oh no," he exclaimed. "Why?"

"They didn't say." She stamped her foot against the sidewalk. Then she looked up at Simon with an apologetic smile. "How does it feel to be trapped in Africa?"

"Probably serves me right," he replied with a resigned shake of the head.

They were turning to leave when Simon caught sight of Diego, one of the consular officers from the riad parties, smoking beside the staff entrance. He shouted ecstatically and a pair of geometric glasses spun his way. Then Diego stepped toward them and his lenses caught and released a ray of sunlight, giving off a stroboscopic flash not unlike an SOS at sea.

The two lovers raced home to pack, overjoyed at the stroke of good luck.

Kinani was sitting in the living room, practicing guitar, when Simon entered the apartment.

"We got the visa!" he shouted as he slammed the front door behind him. Fifteen minutes later, he exited his bedroom, lugging a suitcase.

"Safe travels," Kinani said, followed by a fist pound and a quick embrace. For a moment, he looked at Simon as if he were about to say something more. Neither of them had spoken of the night of the wedding, nor of all that Kinani had revealed. Afterwards, they fell back into their usual bantering demeanor and treated the incident like a forgotten dream.

Still, there had been some change. Kinani no longer smiled oppressively in Simon's presence. He regarded him with a neutral face, which Simon took as a mark of friendship. His eyes, though, had preserved their dazzling luster. To Simon, it seemed that all the stolen riches of the Congo were stashed behind those two shining jewels.

"Don't show her too nice a time over there," Kinani finally added. "I'd like her to come back."

"First you worry about me running off without her, and now you don't want me to run away with her?"

"You can never trust a Mzungu," Kinani countered with a big man laugh and a friendly punch to the shoulder. "Just make sure you bring her back."

"Same to you. Don't go anywhere." Simon deposited his bags outside the door. "I worked hard to keep you in this apartment."

"Where could I possibly go?" Kinani replied. Then his perennial smile settled once more over his face.

Simon picked up Nadia and a boxy green Fiat at a nearby rental agency. They made quick time up the coast to Tangier, where ferries left almost every hour for Algeciras, Spain.

When the glittering blue Mediterranean rose into sight, Simon suggested they find a nice hotel and explore that famous city of the senses. Nadia rejected the idea out of hand. She wanted to spend their first night together in the same suite, not furtively shuttling between two separate rooms.

An hour later, they stood on the upper deck of the ferry and watched the port dissolve into a hazy outline on the horizon, capped by the cloud-ringed peak of Jebel Musa. How simple it was to board a ferry for a two-hour jaunt and find yourself in Europe, Simon thought. How simple and how impossible.

He began humming the melody to *Mokolo Nakokufa*, with the same mournful, starlit inflections that Arès had given it on the beach.

"What's that tune?" Nadia asked.

"I don't know. I heard that fisherman refugee singing it, and it's stuck with me ever since."

"Keep singing," she said and drew close to him. Soon she began humming along, and the two of them duetted while the boat plowed ahead over light-strewn waves toward the promised land of so many refugees' dreams.

When they were done, Simon looked back at the charging white wake of the ferry, and behind it, the far-off shimmer of Africa. For the past few months, his life had been like those frothing waters. It was only now, thanks to some distance, that he could perceive the gleaming surfaces that lay beyond them.

Hundreds of seabirds circled above the bouncing waves and he thought of the migrants in Takadoum with their pitiful dinghies, and of Arès, who could be swimming through those currents even now. The rumble of the ship's engine sounded like the pounding of drums before the white walls of the HCR, and once again Simon could hear the refugees' frenzied chants and their impassioned cries for dignity to the festive crash of shattering glass. He wondered what their uprising would bring.

He had no good answer. Only the bright wheeling sun and the bracing sea air, so he breathed it all in deeply, filling his lungs with a sky of piercing blue.

All that was behind him now. He felt free out there on the water, floating in a limbo between two continents, away from all the agendas and shoddy moral compromises of the past months. He sympathized with the refugees, but he was a realist. To outsiders, their revolt would merely seem another chapter in the bitter history of conquest and retribution that had blackened that part of the world for well over a thousand years.

Then he looked down at the desert bird nestled in his arms and felt his heart swell with hope. She had cozied up against him because they were in international waters and, finally, she could.

"Do you think you'll keep working at the United Nations?" Nadia suddenly asked.

Simon stayed silent for a long time before he answered. The deck rocked softly beneath his feet and his eyes strained toward the horizon. A vision rose before him of his father sitting on the veranda of Mobutu's jungle palace, clinking glasses with Kinani's father, while everything around them burned.

"No. I think I'll do something else," he said at last, and felt dangerously adrift. He hugged Nadia tight to his chest. "That reminds me. I have something for you." He handed her a metal necklace from which dangled a golden key.

"It's a key," she said with surprise. She held it up and the key gathered in the turquoise complexion of the sea and gave off small coruscations of light as it twirled in the fresh breeze.

"The key to my heart." He grinned and slipped it over her neck. "So make sure you take good care of it."

She kissed him bravely on the lips and caressed his lion's mane of hair. "And what if I misplace it?" she asked with a playful smile.

"Then I'll never be able to love anyone else."

"Thank you." She kissed him again. "I promise to be exceedingly careless with it."

He laughed out loud and they held each other close as the green hills of Spain drew near.

And there it was! The Rock of Gibraltar rose into view like an immense shark's fin over the land, as if Europe were a prehistoric fish ready to swallow the ferry whole. Its inland side was dotted with trees, and on that flank stood a Moorish castle, whose foundations were laid shortly after Tariq Ibn Ziad's victory in 711 A.D.

Gibraltar, named by the Moors but governed by Great Britain, much as slivers of Morocco had been seized by Spain. So many contested spaces: England clawing into Spain, Spain nibbling at Morocco—a patchwork world in every which way, except for the fertile sea that they shared and the same cloud-spotted sky that stretched overhead.

"*Jabal Tariq*," Nadia pronounced with a throaty Tamazight squawk that made Simon jump. "The mountain of Tariq. Did you know that when Tariq Ibn Ziad landed at the Rock of Gibraltar, he burned his entire fleet of ships?"

"Why would he do that?"

"No possibility of retreat," she said with a high-wattage smile and a nuzzling cheek. "Should we do that too? Then we could never go back."

"Kinani would kill me," he replied with a laugh.

"He can't reach us here," she murmured, and bit at his mouth like it was territory to be conquered.

"He burned his entire fleet," Simon repeated, astonished by the enormity of the act.

A balmy sirocco wind rose at their back, and they sailed like Tariq Ibn Ziad toward Andalusia. And behind them diminished, minute by minute, the stupendous coast of Africa.

RESETTLEMENT

JULY 2009

———————

THE NEXT MORNING AROUND 6 a.m., Arès gently shut the door to his flat and slid the key under the mat.

He exited the building and shuffled through several shadowy arcades, dyed cinnamon by the morning light. In a few minutes, he came to the market street, where he hailed a *petit taxi*.

"*Salaam Aleikoum*," he said as he climbed in.

"*Wa Aleikhoum Salaam*."

"*Gare de Rabat*," he instructed. The taxi sped off.

He leaned back against the plush seat and watched the inhospitable city fade into memory. Its sour avenues, with their conspiracies of dust and detritus, evoked only nausea. He was happy to be leaving them behind.

The taxi crossed the bridge over the Bouregreg River and sped down toward the medina. When it shuttled by the *marché central*, Arès caught sight of Doumba slumped in the shade. His arms were pitifully bound in makeshift slings and his face caved into two stagnant pools of suffering. Then the refugee vanished into the past as the taxi drove on.

Arès cranked open the window and peered out at the parade of the Place Bab el Had, the last merriments of the sunrise Rastas, and the floods of the faithful pooling before the mosque.

The taxi swerved up Avenue Mohammed V and slowed to a crawl before the Hotel Balima. Beneath the leafy bowers of its terrace café, several employees of the HCR sipped morning tea and chatted. But they too melted away as the tires spun against pavement and minutes later wheeled to a halt in front of the *Gare Rabat Ville*.

The cake-shaped station, with its gargantuan marquee that jutted out like an immense jeering tongue, was under construction. Pushed along by the rush-hour crowds, Arès circled the building and entered through the swinging doors situated on its side.

He looked up at the Solari board and saw that there was a train leaving for Tangier almost immediately. With his faded knapsack hoisted on his right shoulder, he purchased a ticket and hurried to the first-class compartment.

Serious-looking men in spectacles and tailored suits, probably off to business meetings up north, muttered among themselves as he settled his bedraggled self into a palatial armchair. One of the conductors beelined his way and checked his ticket twice, before allowing him to keep his improbable place among Morocco's managerial caste.

The whistle blew, somewhere a dog howled, and the train sputtered ahead.

Arès had taken leave of no one. He thought it better to vanish completely, like a cloud dissolving into the sky.

For six hours, the train muddled along the Moroccan coast. Kenitra, Oulad Mahdi, Diasra, Larache, Asilah. He said the names out loud as the engine chugged north. A direct bus ran from the *gare routière* at Kenitra to downtown Tangier in a little under three hours, but a quiet voice had told Arès to draw out this trip. He sensed that either way, it would be his last journey in the Maghreb.

He knew that he could have lived better now, filching bundles of banknotes from the employees of the HCR, but the other refugees were right. They were all dying the slow death of exile in that place.

As the locomotive scaled up the horn of Africa, Spanish locutions began to pepper the speech of the newly embarked passengers. The landscape altered as well. Flat dunes and plains gradually flexed out hills and ramped into mountains. Arès dozed off. When he woke up, the train had arrived.

He dismounted at the *Gare Ferroviaire Tanger Ville* and marched out of the monumental station with its mosque-like exterior. Behind him loomed two flat-brimmed towers with cerulean inlay and gilded arabesques. The whitewashed dazzlement stung his eyes and he shaded them with his right hand as he hobbled ahead.

The *petits taxis* in Tangier were cardinal red, and he whistled at a few of them before one jauntily pulled to a halt. The driver asked him a few things in Spanish, but he shook his head and requested the *gare routière*.

The Peugeot throbbed along rue Abi Jari Tabari on a quaking chassis for what seemed a blink of an eye. Within half an hour, Arès was on a bus heading for the small fishing village of Ksar es Seghir, located about fifteen kilometers from Tangier-Med, the largest port in Africa.

The bus wound along the N16, rolling high over ridges and up cusped mountain crowns. The slopes flared a bright emerald green wherever shafts of sunlight poked between the peaks and energized the countryside's native verdancies.

After about an hour, Arès asked the driver to stop along a deserted stretch of highway somewhere north of Talaa Cherif. When he balked, Arès clipped fifty dirhams to the dashboard.

The bus shuddered to a halt on an empty mountain slope. The refugee dismounted, and the rectangular machine bellowed off again.

Below him, a spit of land dug into the sea off Africa's great skirt of a coast. His small knapsack balanced on the same shoulder as his cane, Arès descended an uneven footpath in the waning afternoon light.

He crossed a brief dunespace, with bright yellow ragwort, and stepped onto a deserted shore. There was very little noise, only some insect stridulations and the occasional calls of birds.

Two sea-scoured logs cast long shadows over the flaxen sands, and an ashen boulder, cockled with barnacles, rose above the foam at the water's edge. As he walked, Arès listened to small ginger-colored pebbles grind beneath his boots.

Then he unshod his feet and dug his toes into the sand. The beach here was soft and clean, unlike in Rabat, and strings of sea-smoothed stones, deposited along the water's edge, made it appear as if the shoreline were encrusted with precious jewels.

He held a glossy pebble in the cup of his hand and wondered how long it had migrated alone across ocean floors. Then he lifted it up to the goldening sky and wondered if ever it had been jagged or rough.

His other hand uncurled and there, upon the lifeline of his palm, wound the wine-dark shred of Salifou's foulard. His eyes smoked with an unseen thought and the wing of his arm flapped open and flung the red rag onto the water's rim. It floated gently for a moment and then dissolved away like a splotch of blood.

Something small and soft broke inside of him. He knelt in the wet sand and wept. He wept for the faces of his family, for the irretrievable certainties of his locksmith's dreams, and for the terrible things he had seen and endured and still carried. And Félix's brash, knowing laugh echoed in the air, and behind it, like a counterargument, sounded the steady contours of his father's voice. He hoped his father was right. He had had enough of the Salifous of the world trying to set everything ablaze. It was time to leave them behind. So here he stood, before a body of water so immense that it could quench all the fires ever lit by men.

The sun began to cave below the horizon, and in the gelatinous light of dusk, a crimsonness leached across the landscape. Arès looked up, and the sea rustled before him like a golden field of ripened grain.

He stripped off his clothes and folded them neatly into a watertight bag he had purchased for this purpose. The money he tucked inside as well, but his decrepit shoes and the wreck of his cane he left behind. He wanted to be as buoyant as possible for the swim.

He cinched the bag onto a flotation device and tossed it onto the water, where it drifted silvery like a lost balloon.

Depending on the geometry of his swim, it might be short or long, and after daybreak he would be wildly conspicuous.

Unless, of course, if they couldn't see him.

Arès stood at the lip of this mighty jug of a continent. It was a jug that held so many keys inside, so few of which opened the right door. He fingered the empty space above his chest and hoped that at last he had selected the right one.

Then he thought of Paul and wondered where, in all of Africa, that laughing marauder could be.

Upon that sandy, desolate beach, he murmured what might be his last terrestrial prayers. Then he bent his head and curled his back. The sea puckered like a woman's lips as he turtled into the water. The surf was warm, and Arès stroked out placidly on placid tides. He felt long and loose and blithely unaware of the gravity of his act.

The last flickers of twilight faded to darkness, and the moon, which had long since risen, surfaced upon the dark empyrean of the sky. All around it, suffusing the night with brilliance, blazed a bright web of stars.

Arès continued to swim. He was far out now, farther out than he had ever dared to go. In the distance, he could hear the mournful foghorns of mountainous ships ferrying their vastness to and from the tremendous port at Tangier-Med.

He breached the horizon, and as the shores of Africa faded from sight, he began to pray. He swam and prayed and measured his strokes on the cadence of his prayers. So far out, and yet still so strong. His breath came even and clear and he began to lose himself to the hypnotic rolling motion of the distance swim and sense that long-lasting second wind that can carry a swimmer forever. And there it was.

His body suffused with warmth and ease and small ecstasies, and he had the sudden electrifying sensation that his dead family was there, swimming beside him. When he next lifted his head to breathe, he clicked open his eyes and he could see their silvery souls rippling through the watery crests, and then his arm reached for Europe and he smiled toward the abyss.

And each time he breathed, he peered out to make sure they were still there, but soon it was not they alone he saw, but so many more. He saw and he prowed his chest high out of the water to drink in the sight.

The whole sea, from horizon to horizon, was seeded with silvery swimmers stroking by his side. Thousands of African souls stroking through those hostile waters, so many that they submerged the waters beneath a vast silvery stream flooding north toward deliverance.

They ghosted with him for an unknowable distance and then the visions subsided. Arès swam alone in the creamy sidereal light and beneath him swept nations of innominate things.

And onwards and onwards he swam.

SPENCER WOLFF is an award-winning documentary filmmaker and journalist based in Paris, France. His work focuses primarily on diaspora, migration, and racial justice, and has previously appeared in *The Guardian*, *The New York Times,* and *Time*, among others. An adjunct faculty member at the École normale supérieure (Paris), he is a graduate of Harvard College, Yale University, and Columbia Law School. In 2009, he worked at the UN Refugee Bureau (UNHCR) in Rabat, Morocco. *The Fire in his Wake* is his first novel.